James Mitchell was born in South Shields in 1926 and was educated at South Shields Grammar School and Saint Edmund Hall, Oxford. After a brief spell at local repertory theatres he took up writing as a career. He now lives in London.

James Mitchell is well known as the creator of *Callan* and *When The Boat Comes In*, both extremely successful television series. *An Impossible Woman* is the second novel in a trilogy which began with *A Woman To Be Loved*, also available from Headline.

'Terrific story, a guaranteed page-turner . . . should be his biggest best seller' *Daily Mail*

'A novel of stature and honesty, and immensely enjoyable' *Sunday Telegraph*

D1375573

# An Impossible Woman

James Mitchell

HEADLINE

First published in 1992
by Sinclair-Stevenson Ltd

First published in paperback in 1992
by HEADLINE BOOK PUBLISHING PLC

10  9 8 7 6 5 4 3 2

ISBN 0 7472 3919 3

Printed and bound in Great Britain by
HarperCollins Manufacturing, Glasgow

HEADLINE BOOK PUBLISHING PLC
Headline House
79 Great Titchfield Street
London W1P 7FN

For Mina

# 1

IT WAS FAR too hot. True, they were in Delhi just before the monsoons broke, but it was really *terribly* hot, even in the shade of the pavilion specially put up for the people like Mummy and Daddy and herself and her brothers so that they could watch the Great Durbar, in the year 1903, when Lord Curzon became Viceroy of India. Jane's underwear was beginning to irritate her skin because of the heat, but she daren't scratch, not when Mummy was sitting so near, and with that bump on her tummy Ayah said meant that she would have another brother or sister soon. It would be nice to have a sister, tiny, like her dolls; but two brothers were quite enough.

Daddy said Lord Curzon was a very clever man, and Daddy hardly ever said that about anybody except himself, which made him sound very vain, which he was, Jane supposed, but only in a clever way that made her laugh. But if Lord Curzon was so jolly clever why did he have to hold his Durbar just before the rains? I shall melt in a minute, she thought, and the elastic of my solar topee is chafing my chin and it's utterly beastly agony.

Then the next lot of soldiers went by. Highlanders first, and she liked the Highlanders, pipers squealing away and drums rattling, the kilts all swaying in a kind of rhythmic swagger. My goodness, she thought, how hot *they* must be with no shade at all. . . . And after the Highlanders for some reason there were elephants: the elephants of the maharajahs who were all swanking like mad, each one trying to outdo the other, and the sun hitting all that gold and glass and jewellery like a blow, so that her eyes hurt just to look, and then one of the elephants started to trumpet, and another and another, and it sounded as if the elephants were making game of the Highlanders, and she forgot all about the ache in her eyes in her efforts not to giggle, because she couldn't possibly giggle, not with Mummy so close. . . .

After the elephants came the Gurkhas, and they too were led by a pipe band squealing away like mad, so that it sounded as if the Gurkhas were making game of the elephants, and she had to look away, simply had to, and steal a glance at her two brothers. Solemnly Guy and David winked at her, which meant they knew what she was thinking, and she had to look away again or else the giggles would really come. Vaguely she wondered what her brothers were doing there. They were supposed to be in England, at school. But there was nobody she could ask, not in the middle of Lord Curzon's Durbar. All a nine-year-old could do was watch, even if her underwear did scratch. She risked a glance the other way, where her Uncle Walter and Aunt Penelope were sitting. Uncle Walter was a box wallah, in trade, and had pots and pots of money, but even so it was Daddy who'd got them the seats in the pavilion, because Daddy was a collector in the Indian Civil Service, which Ayah said was like a rajah, or even a maharajah.

Mummy's hand touched her shoulder, which meant she was fidgeting too much, so she folded her hands meekly and watched the procession once more. Bengal Lancers this time, with beautifully draped turbans and gorgeous horses, and lance points flashing like diamonds in the sun, and after them a single rider, an infantry officer in khaki, mounted on a bay mare called Bridget. The officer was called John Patterson. She had met him in France in 1917, when she had driven an ambulance Uncle Walter had paid for. They had become lovers, and had planned to marry after the war, but he was killed on the 10th November, 1918. He'd survived for three years, which was longer than most, for an infantry officer, but he had no business at Lord Curzon's Durbar.

Jane said aloud, 'This is ridiculous. It can't possibly be happening,' and of course it wasn't, because then she woke up. She thought: Every single one of them is dead, except me, and Mummy and the baby she was carrying: my brother Francis.

It had been so real: the sound and splendour and the brilliant colours, and then John Patterson at the end, to show them all what war was really like.

And she wasn't in India, either. She was in South Terrace in Knightsbridge, and she wasn't nine, she was thirty-five, and it was New Year's Day, 1929, so why was she so *hot*?

She sat up in bed and struggled against a mound of blankets and an eiderdown. Her housemaid seemed obsessed with the fear that she would catch pneumonia. Central heating full on, too, she thought, and no window open – and she'd had rather too much champagne to be bothered to check. . . .

It had been after the Durbar that she'd met the saddhu, she remembered. Mummy and Papa had gone to some reception or other, and Guy and David had gone off on their own, and her ayah had taken her back to the bungalow they shared with Aunt Pen and Uncle Walter. Uncle Walter had paid for the bungalow, and Papa had made it sound like a privilege. She'd listened on the verandah when he'd said it, and Mummy for once had seemed upset.

Her ayah had been cross because she had wanted to stay and gossip with the other ayahs, and then they had met the saddhu, the holy man. He sat in the shade of a banyan tree and called out to them, and Ayah went to him at once, put her hands together, finger-tips touching, and bowed in the namaskah, the gesture of greeting. Jane didn't know how to do that, so she curtsied instead, the way she had been taught in dancing class. The saddhu spoke in Urdu, and Jane, like any other child of her generation in India, understood every word.

'This child is a special one,' the saddhu said. 'She will find great happiness and great sorrow, and she will do brave things, dangerous things. And later there will be a kind of greatness, and then more courage.'

Her ayah had given the holy man ten annas, she remembered, largesse indeed, but there'd been no sign of greatness since then. Happiness and sorrow, yes. That was John, and her breakdown. And brave things? To go through Passchendaele you had to be brave, and maybe a little demented too, even before they packed you off to the loony doctor. But destined for greatness? Not yet. Not ever. Her destiny was wealth, affaires, and occasional journalism.

Jane got out of bed, and at once her Scotch terrier, Foch,

asleep on his cushion, woke up and came over to her, grumbling because he wasn't as young as he once was.

'I'm surprised you weren't at the Durbar too,' said Jane, and lit a cigarette from the box at the bedside table. Foch snorted, then walked with her to the window. She drew the curtains, and pulled one window down from the top. It was still dark, and there had been snow, silvered now by the lamplight, and the air was pure and cold. One might have been in Switzerland.

Too much champagne, she thought again. There had to be a reason for that, and of course there was. The New Year's Eve party at the Savoy had been given by Jay Bower. His had been a big table – far too big for intimate chat – but then Jay hadn't given the party for intimate chat. That night of all nights he had decided to announce his engagement, and as soon after midnight as he could manage it, once the squeaker blowing and streamer throwing, the kissing and the singing of 'Auld Lang Syne' were over. . . . Engaged to Lady Catherine Hilyard, half his age, much less than half of his devious cunning, and wildly unsuitable, and yet a nice child all the same, and if she didn't exactly love Jay, she seemed tremendously impressed by him, which suited Jay just as well.

His guests had been those of Bower's friends and acquaintances he'd most needed to impress – for Catherine was a catch, there was no doubt of that: a dark, slender beauty, daughter of an Irish earl whose father had married a Midlands fortune. Definitely a catch: and so Jay had invited his friend the cabinet minister and his friend the merchant banker and his friend the popular novelist, and half a dozen more like them, all the ones who would be of use to his newspaper – and their ladies. And Jane Whitcomb.

And that was a funny one if you like, thought Jane. I'd been his mistress for absolute ages, and very nice it was too, and we didn't part in anger, far from it. More like relief really. And I knew already that he'd begun to be interested in Catherine. But why ask me to his engagement party? After all, she could hardly refuse, could she? And when she'd asked who would be her partner he'd just said anyone she liked and hung up.

So of course she'd asked Charles Lovell because he and she made up a pair now and again, and he'd turned her down flat which was another mystery, saying he already had a New Year's

Eve party to go to, when she knew damn well he hadn't. And even if he had, why didn't he ask her to it? They'd met at a New Year's Eve party, after all. . . . So in the end it had to be her old reliable, darling Lionel, as queer as a coot but the best dancer in the ballroom. And Jay hadn't liked her bringing Lionel one bit; she could tell as soon as they walked up to him. Could it be, she wondered, that being engaged was bringing out the prig in him? She had never thought there'd be enough prig to bring out.

The cold air reached out to penetrate the thin silk of her nightdress, and she got back into bed. Foch sighed, and went back to his cushion and his own dreams – nearly always rabbits, Jane was certain – but she sat up, huddled in the eiderdown, and continued to smoke and think. What had been wrong with bringing Lionel? He'd escorted her dozens of times, and often when Bower was there. She'd determined to ask him, but he'd only danced with her once and it was impossible to examine such serious matters while the band played 'Horsey Keep Your Tail Up', with cow-bells and sirens and God knew what else as they jogged up and down. And anyway, all he'd wanted to talk about was how lovely Catherine looked, then tried to hide his relief when she agreed with him.

Lionel had spotted that he wasn't wanted, *of course* – Lionel always spotted everything – and being Lionel took Catherine Hilyard off to dance the first chance he had, and danced far, far better than Jay Bower. When he came back to Jane he drank a great gulp of his wine then sighed like a man who had got the serious business of the evening over.

Jane grinned at him. 'Honour satisfied?' she asked.

Lionel put out his tongue at her, quick as a lizard, then grinned back. 'She's a pretty child,' he said, 'but she can't dance. Not like you. And Chanel didn't make her dress. Again not like you.'

It had been rather that sort of evening, hence the champagne. Jane put out her cigarette and switched off the light. It wouldn't do to have a head in the morning. She was lunching with Mummy.

Her mother continued to live in Kensington, though not in the same house. After Sir Guy's death she had told Jane that Offley Villas contained memories of India that made it insupportable.

'As if your father had tried to cram the entire United Provinces into a terrace house,' she had said, and so she had married Major Routledge, racing correspondent of the *Daily World*, and moved into Minton Gardens, three streets away, and Major Routledge had proceeded to cram *his* terraced house with every possible aspect of British racing, flat, hurdles or jumps, and Mummy, to Jane's astonishment, hadn't minded a bit: but then it seemed that Mummy was rather fond of racing, and accompanied her husband to lots of meetings. She greeted her daughter in a hall-way lined with Stubbs prints, kissed her and took her into the drawing room (more Stubbs, a statuette of 'Eclipse' and on the piano signed photographs of various notables, leading in their Derby winners). Mummy wore a tweed suit and had experimented, successfully, with a new hair style, and seemed in formidably good health. She went to an ice bucket on the sideboard.

'I cannot get used to cocktails,' she said, 'though I did try. And sherry seemed much too ordinary a drink for New Year's Day, so I thought we would have champagne.'

When married to her father, Jane remembered, Mummy had drunk almost no alcohol, could indeed make even mineral water seem like a shocking over-indulgence. . . . And then she noticed the label. Mumm . . . The major must have had a good spell lately.

'Extravagant, you may feel, but George has been doing rather well lately,' said her mother, and Jane remembered for the ten thousandth time how sensitive her mother's antennae were. Mrs Routledge extracted the cork and poured.

'Where is the major?' asked Jane, accepting a glass.

'At his club,' said her mother. 'He has been obliged to concentrate rather hard recently, which is a strain to which I fear he is not equal. It seemed only fair to allow him a little outing. He sends his good wishes, of course.'

Her mother's attitude to her second husband was that of a huntsman to a hound which, though utterly deficient in every other respect, yet had a remarkable nose for a scent. The trip to his club was the equivalent of an extra bone tossed at feeding time, a bone with rather a lot of meat on it. And yet they were happy together, could even be said to love each other. But then, thought Jane, the major was proud of Mummy's cleverness, relied on it even, unlike Sir Guy, who had found it a subject for mild wonder at best.

'Gwendolyn Gwatkin telephoned me before you arrived,' Jane's mother said.

'Oh yes?' Miss Gwatkin was an old friend and enemy of her mother's, who never telephoned unless there was the possibility of gossip, preferably scurrilous. 'How is Miss Gwatkin?'

'Bigger than ever,' said her mother, not without satisfaction. 'Quite enormous. She would appear to be devoting the rest of her life entirely to food. She dined at the Savoy last night, and no doubt took lunch at the Ritz and tea at the Dorchester. She had observed you arriving for the dance there.'

'I didn't observe her,' said Jane.

'Now that I would under normal circumstances find extraordinary,' said her mother, 'particularly as she informed me that she wore her mauve, together with a garnet parure left her by her mother.'

'Golly,' said Jane. 'How could I have missed that?'

'She was behind you,' her mother said. 'You did not look round. You were, she said, escorted by a man she considered effeminate.'

'Lionel Warley,' said Jane.

'So I assumed,' said her mother. 'I told her that Lionel was a Royal Flying Corps officer of considerable distinction who has a DSO.'

Lionel was a favourite of Mummy's, but then he was a favourite of so many women. And there's another thing, thought Jane. Since the major I've told Mummy so much of my life. She even knew about Charles Lovell in a vague sort of way, and at least suspects about Jay Bower.

'What was so earth shattering about seeing me at the Savoy?' Jane asked.

'You were not escorted by your usual man,' said her mother.

'Did she mean Charles?'

'Presumably.'

'But how extraordinary,' said Jane. 'Has she turned private detective? And even if she has, what's the point of following me about?'

Mrs Routledge sipped her champagne.

'Not a private detective,' she said judiciously. 'At least not the kind that follows one about inconspicuously. As well be followed about by a dirigible. She belongs to a group of gossips who spend their time observing the gossip-worthy in London – and you *are* rather gossip-worthy you know. And then they meet from time to time, and pool what they've got.'

'But why?' Jane asked.

'That kind of gossip is power,' said Mrs Routledge. 'It can also be extremely hurtful.'

'But why?' Jane asked again.

Her mother snorted. 'Just compare the way you live with the way she lives,' she said.

'I don't think there's all that much difference,' said Jane, 'except that I don't wear mauve.'

'Charles Lovell?'

'It isn't working, Mummy. I had high hopes, but it isn't. Not that *that's* the end of the world. I mean if I want to go dancing, there's always Lionel. Now there's an odd thing.'

Her mother waited.

'Jay Bower was absolutely beastly to poor Lionel last night – for no possible reason that I could see.'

'I wonder,' her mother said.

'I assure you he was, Mummy.'

'No no,' said Mrs Routledge. 'I accept what you say – but was he resenting Lionel's presence – or Charles Lovell's absence?'

'I have no wish to indulge in the kind of antics Gwendolyn Gwatkin finds so satisfying,' she continued, pouring more champagne, 'but George cannot help hearing things, though he is usually at a loss to interpret them.' The smile with which she said this was totally devoid of malice. 'It is possible, perhaps even likely, that Mr Bower may find himself rather short of what is called ready money, just at the moment, and Mr Lovell is rich, one gathers?'

'Extremely,' said Jane.

'Richer than you?'

Her mother, thought Jane, had none of the usual English inhibitions about asking such questions, and indeed, Aunt Penelope had left her Uncle Walter's all.

'Compared with Charles Lovell, I can claim no more than modest affluence,' said Jane.

'Then it is entirely possible that Bower hoped to meet Lovell with you in order to arrange a further meeting.'

'But he didn't know I'd bring Lionel,' said Jane. 'He told me to ask whoever I liked.'

'And who did you ask?'

Jane giggled. Really this champagne drinking would have to stop. 'You know, Mummy, in the old days they'd have burned you as a witch,' she said.

'They'd have had to catch me first,' said her mother.

The parlourmaid announced luncheon.

It was rather good: potage St Germain, hot lobster and a chantilly cream. Over it they talked about her dream and thus of Lord Curzon's Durbar, which had not been held just before the rains, nor had Giles and David been there.

'But you were right about Francis,' her mother said. 'I was carrying him.' The parlourmaid left the room. 'He kicked rather a lot, I remember. No doubt it was the Highlanders.'

'Or the elephants,' said Jane. 'How is Francis?'

'I take it you mean *where* is Francis? He was nowhere to be seen at Christmas, as you know. He spends rather a lot of time in his vacations visiting Berlin with a rather disreputable friend. Perhaps he went there.'

'Burrowes?' Jane asked.

'I believe so. . . . Francis told me the last time we met that he must be allowed to lead his own life. I replied that no one else could possibly do it for him.'

'And yet he clings to this Burrowes.'

'Clings?' said her mother, but took the matter no further. Age, breeding and background forbade it, especially with her daughter.

'He is doing extremely well at Cambridge,' she said, as the parlourmaid returned. 'He is a senior fellow now, and his new book was well reviewed, though not, I should imagine, as widely read as yours. It is a pity your father did not live to read it. He would have enjoyed it enormously.' Considering how much her mother had detested her first husband this was handsome indeed.

They took coffee in the drawing room, and once the parlourmaid had left them, Mrs Routledge returned at once to personal matters. 'Your book came out eighteen months ago,' she said. 'What on earth have you been doing with yourself since then?'

A good question to ask, thought Jane, and an all too easy one to answer. Her book, *Striking for Beginners*, had been a series of essays about the General Strike of 1926, many of them first published in Bower's newspaper, the *Daily World*. She had written because of Felston, the town where her dead fiancé had been born, a town slowly but inevitably dying of unemployment, poverty and hunger. But even Felston it seemed no longer needed her.

'Well, Jane?' said her mother, as if to a much younger Jane.

'What have I been doing?' said Jane. 'Nothing, Mummy.'

'That simply will not do,' said Mrs Routledge. 'Your Aunt Penelope could do nothing quite beautifully, day after day – it was why her husband married her after all – but you cannot. And I do not believe that Penelope Nettles left you her fortune so that you should emulate her idleness. She loved you too much.'

'I don't want to be idle,' said Jane. 'It's the last thing I want to be, but the clinic at Felston needs me only as a fund raiser. I don't mind that. I cadge for them and they get all the royalties from my book, but what I really liked was organising things for them, and driving the ambulance. Unfortunately they don't hold with females up there. Not really.'

'Gratitude should never be expected,' said her mother. 'Merely appreciated, as and when it occurs. . . . But you could write something else, could you not?'

'Bower hasn't asked me.'

'It would be unwise for him to approach you too closely while his engagement lasts, but there are other newspapers.'

Jane said lamely, 'It wouldn't be the same,' and knew that she was blushing. At once her mother changed the subject.

'That's rather a pretty dress,' she said.

'Hartnell,' said Jane at once. 'One can't keep popping across to Paris for fittings all the time.'

Her mother nodded and smiled as if Jane had just murdered a lazy serve at tennis.

'But you must *do* something,' she said. 'You're not yourself when you're idle.' Which was as good a way as any, thought Jane, of telling her that she had once had a nervous breakdown brought on by the horrors of the war, and the savage irony that John should die just one day before it ended, and that life had been hell for the entire family while it lasted, and hell's innermost circle for herself.

'I'll see if I can find some more good works,' she said.

As she walked towards her car, later in the afternoon, a taxi passed her and pulled up outside Mummy's house, and the major got out. He was obviously a little drunk, and yet he walked up the steps of the house without the least sign of fear. Goodness how Mummy had changed.

# 2

GOOD WORKS MEANT her friend Harriet, never to be addressed as Dr Watson, who ran what she called a panel surgery in a decaying area of Hammersmith. So far as Jane could see, 'panel' really meant 'charity', and yet Harriet treated her patients as if they were worth five guineas a visit.

'I don't know if there's an awful lot you *can* do,' she said. 'Not unless you want to spend the next five years reading medicine.'

'I can drive,' said Jane, 'and answer the phone.'

'So can I,' said Harriet. 'There isn't really any *room* for you here. Surely you can see that?'

'Harriet darling,' said Jane. 'Please tell me the truth.'

Harriet Watson looked round her little surgery with its dark lincrusta walls. Outside, a dispirited lime tree did its best to stay alive. Then she looked back at Jane. Paris hat, Russian sables, cigarette in a long jade holder.

'You're too gorgeous, my love,' she said. 'All I ever get here are Cockney sparrows – well, Hammersmith sparrows – and the women wouldn't like you at all.'

'But why not?'

'Why should a sparrow like a bird of paradise? The mums I get are either worn out by too many kids, or anaemic, or suffering from malnutrition. Sometimes they're all three. Seeing you wouldn't help them.'

'I did my best for them in the General Strike,' said Jane.

'*Striking for Beginners* was a good book,' said Harriet. 'Witty, honest, compassionate. But that isn't the point.'

'What is the point then?'

'The strikers lost.'

Jane nodded, and extracted her cigarette from its holder and stubbed it out. 'Do you think,' she asked, 'that that's the reason they got rid of me at Felston Clinic? Because of my bird-of-paradise tendencies?'

'Probably,' said Harriet.

'Bird of paradise,' said Jane. 'My God, I sound as if I should be standing alongside Josephine Baker, prancing at the Casino de Paris and shedding my clothes.'

'You'd do it rather well,' Harriet said.

'Thank you very much,' said Jane, 'but that's not precisely the kind of work I'm after.'

Her mind switched to the two men who ran the Felston Clinic: Canon Messeter, the Anglican parson. He wouldn't have given a damn if she had pranced about starkers, as long as she raised money and drove that vast Lanchester that they'd used as an ambulance. But Dr Stobbs probably would. He believed that the time was not yet right for birds of paradise: that it never would be, until all the sick were healed. Only a very clever man could be so stupid, thought Jane, but then Stobbs *was* very clever. He was also the MO, which made him the boss.

'Let's change the metaphor,' said Jane. 'I'm sick of those damn birds. Some grasshoppers can do ants' work you know.'

'Of course I know,' said Harriet. 'I helped you drive an ambulance. But this is different, my love. Really it is. . . . Why the frantic urge for employment anyway?'

'Mummy thinks being idle is bad for me.'

'And your mother is right, as usual.' Harriet watched as Jane fitted another cigarette into the holder, and lit it with a little gold lighter. 'You're smoking too much,' she said.

'It's because I'm bored, and that for some reason makes me nervous.'

'You're afraid you may have another breakdown?'

'I'll always be afraid of that,' said Jane.

'You won't,' said Harriet. 'Believe me you won't. But your mother is right, even so. You'll be better off with something to do.'

'I'll buy a few feathers and pop over to the Casino de Paris,' said Jane.

When Jane had gone Harriet sat back for a few minutes and thought about her. The waiting room was full, but she owed Jane that much. Rich, attractive, amusing, with a disastrous penchant for the wrong sort of man: one who was going to marry somebody else, and one who had a mad wife raving in a Swiss sanatorium: a sort of pompous Rochester. And all she really wanted to do was be useful. Dr Watson sighed, and pressed the buzzer on her desk. Time for Mrs Truscott and her bunions.

So it was back to raising money for Felston, to begging and cajoling and giving little talks at the end of which a hat was passed, and her powers of persuasion could be measured in half-crowns and florins, but far more often in shillings and six-pences, and even threepenny bits.

Writing didn't happen, because Bower didn't ask her for any, and, as she'd told her mother, she still couldn't find it in herself to write for anybody else, and what, she wondered, would Sigmund Freud make of *that*? But at least she was working, and working hard, because all work is hard when you don't enjoy it, and trying to gouge money out of suburban matrons who came to listen just so that they could gawk at her clothes was very hard work indeed. Once she took Harriet's advice and tried dressing down: grey tailor-made suit, nondescript hat, service-able brogues, and got the worst collection she had ever achieved. Nobody, it seemed, loved a drab bird of paradise. So she per-severed, and each month sent a cheque to Canon Messeter, who each month wrote to her in reply, though whether Dr Stobbs wished her well, Canon Messeter did not say, which probably meant he didn't, she thought.

Charles Lovell seemed to disappear after New Year's Eve. There were gossiping reports of him in Switzerland (his wife?), New York (almost certainly business) and California. (More busi-ness with a generous dollop of pleasure.) For her mother and the major there was racing again, the jumping season that culmi-nated in the Cheltenham Gold Cup and the Grand National, and the major's forecasts that continued to be quite astonishingly accurate, as the *Daily World* never tired of telling its readers. But for Jane life continued to be 'little talks', and row after row of women assessing the value of each article of clothing she wore.

But Harriet was right about that. She had never felt more sane. Or more bored.

And then one day Charles Lovell came back and telephoned her. Could they dine? he asked, and she said Well of course. At least she could wear the kind of clothes they both liked without having their value assessed. So they met at the Brompton Grill, just after Easter, and she wore a bunch of violets pinned to her coat that was Persian Lamb with a chinchilla collar, for the nights were still cold. Charles Lovell was tall and elegant, but with the sort of English-gentry good looks that belonged more with tweeds and country houses than a London restaurant. He looked tired and yet triumphant, she thought, like a cabinet minister who had steered his bill through the House at three in the morning, in the teeth of ferocious opposition. The maître led her to him, and he kissed her cheek as he always did, and asked her what she would like to drink.

'I've been neglecting you,' he said.

'A bit.'

'A great deal. And by an act of choice, too.'

'Goodness how brutal,' she said, and then: 'I do so adore masterful men.'

The wine waiter brought their drinks; a martini for her, and Scotch for him.

As he left Lovell said: 'I'm serious, Jane.' At once her face assumed a look of such seraphic concentration that he laughed aloud. 'God how I've missed all that,' he said. 'But I had to.'

'May I know why?'

'I've been making my fortune,' said Lovell.

'But you've got a fortune.'

'Well now I'm busy making it bigger.'

'Turning Ben Nevis into Mont Blanc?'

'That just about expresses it so far,' he said. 'I think we can say I've reached Mont Blanc.'

'So far?' said Jane. 'But what on earth is there left?'

'The Himalayas,' said Lovell.

'*Everest?*'

'No,' said Lovell. 'I started too late for that. But twenty thousand feet certainly. Maybe even a bit higher.'

'No wonder you're tired,' she said.

'Does it show?'

'And the satisfaction,' she said. 'That shows too. The cat with all the cream.'

He smiled then, and just for a second she saw how ruthless he could be, and then the smile vanished, and the Home Counties charm came back.

'You know I lied to you about New Year's Eve?' he said.

'Of course.'

'Of course you do. How could New Year be the same if you weren't there? But as it happened I didn't go to a party at all. I went to one of the most boring business meetings of my life – and certainly the most lucrative.'

'Whereas I went dancing at the Savoy,' said Jane, 'and I've no doubt that would have been boring too – except for darling Lionel.'

'Jay Bower's party?' said Lovell.

'That's right.' And you jolly well know it's right, she thought.

'Don't let's talk about other people,' said Lovell. 'It's so marvellous to be with you again.'

But what he meant was: Don't let's talk about Jay Bower.

'Tell me what *you've* been up to,' he said.

'Raising money for Felston.'

'And?'

'That's it.'

'Oh,' he said. 'Not exactly frantic excitement, I take it?'

'Not exactly.'

'No more articles?' he asked. 'No new book on the way?'

No new man either, she thought, though I have had offers. Aloud she said, 'I only seem able to write about uproar, and at the moment there isn't any.' She waited while the waiter served their soup, then said, 'Where have you been?'

'All over the place,' said Lovell. 'America mostly. New York and Chicago and Detroit and California. What they call the Coast.'

'Sounds exciting.'

'They're all raving mad over there – but really rather amiable lunatics. Total prohibition and everyone drunk as owls – and as for this boom of theirs, they behave as if money had only just been invented, and they were the ones who did it.'

'Did you meet Al Capone when you were in Chicago?'

'As a matter of fact I did,' said Lovell. 'At least he and I were at the same banquet – along with several hundred other people.'

'And it didn't occur to you to write to me and tell me all about it?'

'It occurred to me,' he said. 'It occurred to me in all kinds of places. The thing is – I was trying to give you up.'

'I sort of gathered that,' she said.

'It wasn't working as it should,' said Lovell. 'You know it wasn't. The trouble is I want to marry you – have done since I met you at Harriet's New Year party – but how can I without being arrested for bigamy? Even supposing it's what you want – and I really don't think it is. You've been looking over your shoulder ever since you met me.'

'Have I?' said Jane. 'At what?'

'At whom, you mean,' said Lovell. 'At Jay Bower of course.'

'Even supposing it's true,' said Jane, 'and I don't admit it for a moment, there'd be no point in looking now, would there?'

'Not while he's engaged,' said Lovell. 'But once he's married, once the boredom starts –'

'You don't have much of an opinion of Jay, do you?' she said. 'Nor of me for that matter.'

The waiter cleared their soup plates, and replaced them with grilled sole, and Lovell sipped and nodded approval of the Meursault. Interesting that Charles too thought that Jay would soon be bored.

When they were alone, Lovell said: 'I didn't mean that you would go back to Bower, honestly I didn't. I just meant he'd come and ask you.'

'He would do that whether we were married or not – if he wanted to,' she said.

He threw back his head and laughed aloud then, and she began to remember why she had liked him so much.

'That's absolutely right,' he said. 'Clever Jane.' And then, 'Would you marry me, if it were possible?'

She said, 'That's an impossible question to answer, since I know I can't.'

'Kind Jane too,' he said. 'You realise I'm telling you I love you?'

'Yes.' There was a silence she began to find unbearable. 'What do you plan to do after dinner?' she said at last.

'Rather up to you,' said Lovell. 'Go and dance somewhere if

you'd like that –' he looked at his plate, '– or my flat in Jermyn Street if we're still on those sort of terms.'

'Jermyn Street please,' she said.

'Very kind Jane.'

Over coffee he fished in his dinner-jacket pocket, and gave her a jeweller's box in Russian leather. She opened it and gasped. Inside it was a necklace of sapphires, the purest and most beautiful she had ever seen.

'I bought it off a feller in New York,' he said. 'He kept telling everybody he was a Russian count and we did a check on him and he was. He'd had the necklace made for his wife by that chap Fabergé – the one who did those incredible jewelled Easter eggs for the Tsar.'

'It must have cost a fortune,' she said.

'Beggars can't be choosers,' said Lovell. 'And neither can Russian counts these days, and this poor devil was both – but I paid him a fair price. I really can afford it, you know. Please keep it.'

'Just for now,' said Jane. 'Then we'll see.' Really, she thought, I'm talking as Mummy talked to me when I was seven.

Lovell grinned at her. 'Better than a postcard from Detroit,' he said.

She thought he had learned a few things since last they had gone to bed together, and she could hardly blame him for that. He was healthy, comparatively young, and extremely rich after all. That he should come back to her was in itself a compliment, as was his love-making. He was as considerate as he was vigorous, and she did her best to pay him back in kind. When they had done, she went to the bathroom, then to the dressing-table mirror.

'What on earth are you doing?' he asked.

'Getting dressed.'

She came back to him. All she wore was the necklace, and he chuckled appreciatively. She had done it before, she remembered, one Christmas years ago when Bower had given her a pair of ruby ear-rings. Really she was like a poule-de-luxe of the Nineties, la belle Otéro or somebody, lying there like Danaë while Grand Dukes showered her with gold. And all for doing what she enjoyed anyway. Perhaps love made him intuitive. Certainly he echoed her thought.

'That necklace,' he said. 'It wasn't –' he hesitated – 'it wasn't a bribe, you know.'

'You mean a fee,' said Jane. 'I know that, silly. Don't spoil it.'

'It was just,' said Lovell, 'that the whole thing seemed right. The Russian count, and the necklace, and Fabergé, it all seemed absolutely you.'

And what more could a girl, no – not girl – woman reluctantly approaching middle age, ask for, she wondered.

'What are you going to do next?' she asked. 'Stay in London for a while?'

'I have to go to your adopted country,' he said.

'Felston?'

Impossible, quite impossible, to see Charles Lovell among the pit heaps and the shipyards and the colliery rows.

'Near, anyway,' he said. 'In Northumberland. I may be going to buy a house there.'

But not in a colliery row. 'Something vast, no doubt?'

'Biggish.' Lovell stretched out a hand to touch her, and she almost purred like a cat. Sex really was delicious, even in near middle age. 'Blagdon Hall,' he said. 'The Earl of Blagdon's place.'

She knew all about Blagdon Hall, and Lord Blagdon. Felston had told her. It was Felston, after all, that had paid for both.

'But they tell me that Blagdon Hall is magnificent,' she said.

'They tell you no less than the truth.'

'Then why is he selling?'

'Because he can't afford it,' said Lovell. John's brother Andy, and the rest of Felston, would be delighted when they knew.

'But why on earth should you buy it?' she said. 'You've *got* a house in the country.'

'A modest manor in Berkshire,' Lovell said. 'This one is to impress the American millionaires.'

'So now they're coming to you?'

'Not yet,' he said. 'But soon. After my next visit to them.'

'And when is that?'

'Next week.'

His hand became more pleasing still, and now it was her turn. 'Be a darling,' she said, 'and help me to take my clothes off.'

She was back in South Terrace by two. Never stay the night, her friend Georgie had told her. It's the hardest habit of all to break, especially if it was scrumptious. And scrumptious it had been.

The servants were in bed because she never allowed them to wait up for her, but she was sure that at least one of them would hear the slam of the taxi door, the click of her heels on the parquet floor, and take a look at the gossip columns next day. Foch of course heard both, and came to greet her, yawning.

'You're looking very Scottish and Presbyterian tonight,' she said, 'and if you disapprove I can't say I blame you, but oh darling Foch it was fun.'

They were half way up the stairs when the phone rang. At that time of night it could only be one of the two living men who had loved her, and almost certainly Bower. She went downstairs again and picked up the phone, and found that she was wrong. There was the crash of coins as button 'A' was pressed.

'Jane?' Andy Patterson said. His voice sounded strained, wary, as it always did when he talked to her, but this time there was more than that.

'Yes, Andy?'

'This is a terrible time of night to bother you,' said Andy. 'Though I did try twice before.'

'I gather it's important.'

'I think so. It's Da.'

'Your father's ill?' Jane asked.

'He's dying.' There could be no doubting the certainty in Andy's voice. 'Heart, Dr Stobbs says. He's got mebbe three or four days. He wants to see you –'

'I'll come up, of course.'

'– Only he doesn't know I've come to ask you.'

'Whyever not?' she asked.

'He doesn't want to spoil your plans,' he said.

And there in a nutshell was Stan Patterson, she thought. He didn't want the fact of his death to spoil a cocktail party at Lionel's, followed by dinner at the Savoy and dancing at the Embassy.

'Then don't tell him,' she said. 'I'll get the first train I can.'

She put the phone down, went into the kitchen and made coffee. Cook wouldn't like it but Cook would have to lump it. Stan's imminent death deserved at least the dignity of contemplation, and if Dr Stobbs said it was imminent then she had no doubt it was. Whatever else he might be, Stobbs was a first-rate doctor.

She took her coffee into the drawing room and Foch, timing her mood brilliantly, jumped up beside her. This was one time, he knew, when she would let him stay. Her hand reached out to stroke him and he shivered in silent ecstasy. . . .

Stan was a Christian Socialist of a kind almost extinct, she remembered, the kind that believed the origins of Socialism began not with Marx or Engels, but with the early Christians living and sharing everything together: the kind who worshipped Jesus not just because He was God, but because He was a good carpenter also.

He had always lacked the fire that warmed his sons, and sometimes inflamed them. Even John, who had always shown something of his father's gentleness in his dealings with her, had also won a DSO and and MC, which meant he had killed not only with determination and courage, but with a kind of dedication that she found hard to consider. Andy also had a reckless and combative courage – she had seen it in action when he had harangued the strikers at the Elephant and Castle – that contained in it also the need for violence. And Bob, too. What she remembered most vividly about Bob was the deliberately foul kick he had aimed at the Cambridge don – ex-amateur heavyweight champion and far too big for Bob, if Bob fought fair. What *was* his name? He had tried to seduce her once, in fact more than once, and still she couldn't remember. Getting old, Jane old girl, she thought, and letting your mind wander. Pardoe! that was it. . . . Oh for heaven's sake, get back to Stan.

Stan also had courage but, unlike his sons', it was the stubborn and enduring kind that had seen him into his sixties in a town where the average lifespan was fifty. And how old did that make Grandma, who possessed the same fiery courage as her grandsons? Eighty at least, and how must she be feeling? And his daughter, Bet, of all his children the one most like him. Stern in judgement, self-denying, stubborn in survival. Bet was married, having got herself pregnant by a widower. She was happy, but Stan had found it hard to accept. Pregnancy outside wedlock he found bad enough, but that the man responsible should be a widower somehow made it even more appalling. Bob had said that his father firmly believed that one partner was your ration, and when it was finished you just had to manage without, and maybe that was it. Stan hadn't been all that impressed with sex, she thought. Probably considered it an over-rated pastime. Of them all he was probably the only one who didn't realise that she and John had slept together.

What Stan had been impressed by was God. He knew his Bible as well as any theologian, and could argue the tenets of his faith with the tenacity of a first-rate counsel. But these were what he would regard as the aesthetic and intellectual pleasures of his faith: its foundation, only true reality, was prayer. In prayer Stan Patterson was transformed. She had seen it happen. 'I know that my Redeemer liveth.' It had taken no music of Handel, no soaring soprano voice, to convey that message. He had simply spoken the words, a statement of obvious fact, as a prelude to invoking his God, as one might begin a letter with the words 'Dear Sir'. Bigoted but steadfast, censorious but kind, and he had said he would like to see her.

The telephone rang again, and Foch snorted his disgust. The time for silent ecstasy was over. Jane went to the phone and looked into the mirror above it as she did so, seeing the necklace glow against her skin. It was much, much more than three hundred miles from Felston to Knightsbridge. She picked up the handset. 'Jane Whitcomb,' she said.

'And about time too,' said Jay Bower. 'Do you realise how many times I've called you tonight? Where the hell have you been?'

This one has even less time for Christian Socialism than Bob, she thought, and said aloud, 'You'll either speak to me politely or I'll hang up.'

'Oh God,' said Bower, 'was I being rude? It's been the hell of a day. . . . I'm still in Fleet Street.'

'Something juicy?'

'Somebody's gone and got themselves murdered in Brighton,' said Bower. 'They've found the bits in a laundry basket.'

'Quite adequately juicy, I'd have thought,' said Jane.

'It'll sell a lot of papers,' said Bower. 'But that isn't why I called.'

'Why then? Do get on with it, Jay. It's –' She looked at the clock. 'My God! It's ten past three in the morning.'

'I heard Charles Lovell's in town,' said Bower. Jane stayed

silent. 'I heard you dined with him tonight.' Still she didn't speak. 'I want to know where I can reach him.'

This was a tricky one, but she couldn't just stand there, earpiece in one hand, mouthpiece in the other, and admire her new necklace.

'I don't think I can do that,' she said. 'Charles values his privacy.'

'Please Jane, it's important,' said Bower.

'Please' from Jay Bower? It must be important.

'I can tell you this,' she said. 'He's going up to Northumberland tomorrow. A place called Blagdon Hall. You could try there.'

'Thanks,' said Bower. 'Can you lunch with me tomorrow?'

'No,' said Jane. 'I'm going North too.'

'With Lovell?'

'None of your damn business,' she said equably. 'You remember Bob Patterson – from Felston? He worked for you a couple of years ago.'

'I remember. Bright lad.'

'His father's dying. He wants to see me before he dies.'

'And you're going?' said Bower, incredulous.

This time she did hang up.

# 3

T HEN OF COURSE she had to phone Lovell, and wake him, which was rather a pleasure as she hadn't yet been to sleep, and tell him what had happened. He thanked her for the way she'd handled it and claimed to have no idea what it was about. That he lied, she was quite certain. There was no mystification in his voice; only a kind of satisfied amusement. When he heard that she was going North too he offered her a lift, but she declined. On the train she could sleep.

Six hours in a Pullman at least helped her to recover from some of the effects of the night before, and at the end of it all the garage in Newcastle had supplied a Daimler, just as she had requested by telephone, and she was able to drive to Felston in her own time, and leave her luggage at the Eldon Arms, as she had done so many times before. But always in the past she had gone to Felston if not with hope, at least with the satisfaction of combat. This time there could be nothing except the acceptance of the inevitability of death: just as John had died, and Aunt Pen, and her father. 'For inasmuch as all shall die, so shall all be born again' it said in the prayer book, but it wasn't always the consolation it was supposed to be, not to the ones who were left behind. . . .

She drank a cup of tea in her room at the Eldon Arms, then examined herself in the mirror: no make-up, nails untinted, and the sad little grey suit she had bought in Felston's biggest store years ago, to exorcise frivolity. Nothing about her to mock the seriousness of death, she thought. If it had been Lionel Warley on his deathbed he would have demanded Chanel and the sables at least, but death had no constrictions: its victims made their own rules, and so she took off her ear-rings and put them in her handbag.

The drive from her hotel to John Bright Street held no surprises, except that Felston had if anything become even more itself: the poverty had intensified. The groups of men squatting or lounging at street corners, the children playing so listlessly that play itself became a chore: there seemed even more of them, and this time their attitude seemed not so much of defeat as of surrender.

She arrived at John Bright Street, and pulled up outside Number 36. There was no swarm of children to greet her, even though in John Bright Street any car was a delight, and a Daimler a sensation. The older ones would remember the woman with a posh car, she was sure, but the younger ones it seemed were simply too tired, too exhausted. She rapped the knocker, and almost at once Andy was there, poor Andy, sad and tired and bewildered by the confrontation with an enemy that no one can defeat.

'Good of you to come so quick,' he said.

'The least I could do,' said Jane. 'You know how much I like your father.'

'Come on up.'

He led the way up the stairs of the upstairs flat, and as she followed she asked, 'Who else is here?'

'Grandma,' he said, 'and Bet. His minister's with him now, and Dr Stobbs'll be along when the clinic shuts.'

'And Bob?'

At the top of the stairs Andy turned to face her.

'I've been phoning London all day,' he said, 'but he's never there when I try.' His face twisted, but whatever his thoughts were he kept them to himself. 'All I can do is keep on trying. We both owe Da that much.' He motioned her to go into the kitchen. 'Grandma's in there with Bet,' he said. 'I'll just tell Da you're here.'

Jane went into the kitchen and at once Grandma came over to embrace her. Eighty something or not her embrace was fierce, her movements quick. Her body was as thin as a stick, but it was a stick not yet ready to break.

'Well me bairn,' she said, and looked up into Jane's face. 'It's been a long time.'

'Too long,' said Jane.

'And whose fault is that may I ask?'

'Not mine,' said Jane.

Grandma took her time to think about it. 'No,' she said. 'You aren't one to go where you're not wanted – and there was some went out of their way to show you weren't wanted here.'

She was remembering the scandal stirred up when she had gone to the Quart' Arts Ball in Paris as Cleopatra, Jane thought. Bower had managed to smother it but Francis's awful friend Burrowes had done his best to turn her into a cross between Theda Bara and Mata Hari, and all because of some devious machinations of Far-Left politics that still didn't make sense to her. Andy had been mixed up in it too, but then though Andy was an atheist he was also a puritan.

'Grandma, I've told Jane I was sorry,' said Bet, and came over to them, her hand held out warily.

Of course, Jane remembered. Bet had been mixed up in it too, turned her back on her, refused to speak. Cut her dead in fact. But what a foolish virgin she'd been, to go and get pregnant so soon afterwards. Jane took her hand, then kissed her on the cheek.

'How's the baby?' she asked.

'Oh he's fine,' said Bet. 'Frank's got him for now. We called him Frank John after his da and our John.'

'You must let me give you something for him,' said Jane, and opened her purse and handed over a five-pound note, the first that Bet had ever held.

'Oh I couldn't,' said Bet. 'It wouldn't be right.'

'Please take it,' said Jane. 'I'm always being told how quickly babies grow out of things.'

'And that's true enough, girl,' said Grandma. 'Take it and be thankful.'

'Oh I am,' Bet said, and looked at it once more, at the white gleam of the crackling paper and its soot-black lettering, before folding it carefully once, then again, and putting it in her purse. As she did so Andy came in, caught one glimpse of that wonderful piece of paper.

'Jane gave it to me – for the bairn,' said Bet. 'It'll come in that handy.' She went back to Jane and kissed her again. 'Thanks, pet,' she said. 'You're quite right. Bairns eat money, and don't I know it.' And then to Andy once more, 'Wasn't it good of her, Andy?'

'Very nice,' said Andy, and left it at that.

'Well there's no need to start singing and dancing just because you appreciate a kind deed,' said Grandma.

But for once Andy was able to ignore the old lady. He had the perfect excuse after all. 'Da wants to see you,' he said to Jane.

'The minister's with him,' said Grandma.

'Da wants him to bide for a while,' said Andy, 'but he wants to see Jane for now. He says has she had any tea.'

'Good heavens,' said Grandma, 'she's only just got in the house,' but she placed the kettle on its stand over the fire, even so, as Jane followed Andy across the passage to the door of the front bedroom.

Stan lay in the centre of the double bed. Illness seemed to have shrunk him: he looked no bigger than Grandma. The man in the chair beside him seemed about three times his size, a squat man, running to fat, with a clean-shaven face and guileless blue eyes. Like almost every other man in Felston when he wasn't at work, the minister wore a blue-serge suit, but he wore a tie instead of the universal white muffler, and his headgear was a bowler, not a cap. But then the minister *was* working. He got up as Jane came in.

'Mr Coombs, this is Jane Whitcomb,' said Stan. 'Mr Coombs is our minister at the chapel.' His voice was a whisper as wasted as the rest of him.

'Very pleased to meet you,' said Mr Coombs.

His voice was strong, pleasant and effortless. A tool of his trade.

'Jane was engaged to our John over in France,' Stan whispered. 'Maybe you've heard about her?'

'I should think all Felston's heard of her,' said Mr Coombs. Jane looked at him sharply, but the blue eyes stayed guileless. 'What you did for this town was an act of pure Christian charity,' said Coombs. 'If it hadn't been for you Felston would have lost its clinic, and we're grateful to you.'

'Why, thank you,' said Jane. 'I did what I could, but it's Stan I've come to see this time.'

She moved closer to the bed, and Coombs brought up the room's other chair. 'Well Stan?' she said, and offered her hand. He took it at once. His hand was as rough and hard as the paw of an animal, and much too cold.

'Well, I'm not,' said Stan. 'I'm dying.'

Jane waited for Mr Coombs to contest this, but he merely nodded as one conceding an important but quite obvious fact.

'Is that what Dr Stobbs says?'

'It took a lot of hard work to get it out of him, but I beat him in the end. He admitted it.' She smiled. 'It isn't everyone gets the better of Dr Stobbs.' Then his grip on her hand tightened. 'This is no place for you,' he said. 'Andy shouldn't have told you. Bringing you all that way to a deathbed. A fine lady like you.'

'From what I hear,' said Mr Coombs, 'it wouldn't be the first one she's attended.' He looked at Jane. 'Drove an ambulance during the war, didn't you, Miss Whitcomb?' Jane nodded. 'There you are then,' said Coombs to Stan Patterson. 'You'll be a treat compared with some of the ones she'll have met with.' Once again he looked at Jane. 'I was a stretcher-bearer myself. RAMC. I know what I'm talking about. Stan here's got it into his head that you're sensitive – being rich – but I keep telling him you weren't all that sensitive when you drove Canon Messeter's car round Felston picking up bairns with rickets and head lice and women with tuberculosis. You were a Christian woman offering her talents to the greater glory of God, and that beats being a fine lady any day.'

'Amen to that,' said Stan, and then, 'I'm glad you came, me bairn. I never got the chance to tell you, but our John chose well. If he'd lived he'd have been the luckiest beggar alive – and I bet he knew it. He was a fine lad, our John. The pick of the basket.' His head shifted slightly to where Mr Coombs sat. 'Maybe not in God's sight,' said Stan, 'but he was in mine, and I've missed him every day since he died. Nigh on eleven year. It'll be grand to see him again.'

'You'll have a lot to talk about,' said Mr Coombs, matter of factly, and all of this, thought Jane, as if Stan were setting off for Australia rather than the possibility of a Heaven. But then for Stan there was no question of possibilities: Heaven was as real as Newcastle, and infinitely more welcoming.

'It's been a long road,' Stan said.

'Long enough,' said Mr Coombs.

'Aye,' said the whispering voice. 'I'll be glad when I get there. Felston isn't the best place to set off from.'

'Don't you be too sure,' said Mr Coombs. 'It's a lot easier to leave than most places.'

Stan chuckled then. Even his chuckle was a whisper. Mr Coombs looked at his watch.

'Time I was shaping,' he said. 'Mrs Henry in Gladstone Street – she's about ready for the journey an' all.'

'Give her my regards,' Stan whispered. 'I'd appreciate a bit of a prayer if you've got time.'

'There's always time for a prayer,' said Mr Coombs, and went on his knees as sleekly and easily as a dolphin dives. Jane followed hastily, clasped her hands and lowered her head, eyes closed, but Mr Coombs knelt erect, eyes open, talking to his Redeemer man to man.

'Oh God we thank You for the presence among us of Thy servant Stan Patterson,' he said. 'He has been a good servant, a fine husband and father, a skilled craftsman and a loyal trade unionist. In this Vale of Tears he has struggled to stay upright and honest as a man should, and tried always to love You and honour his fellows.

'Life has not been easy for him, Father. His wife died when he was still a young man, and his eldest lad was killed in the war to end wars. But he's had his blessings, too. A loving mother and three surviving children, and a gift for prayer that has caused me often to commit the sin of envy.'

And that, thought Jane, is the deftest compliment I've heard for long enough, – and what nicer thing to say to a dying man?

'Prepare Stan's soul now for his departure,' Mr Coombs was saying, 'and receive him into Your kingdom when his time shall come. Remind him of the words of King David, Father. "Yea though I walk through the valley of the shadow of Death the Lord is with me. Thy rod and Thy staff they comfort me." Help him to understand, Father, that Death's valley is but a shadow, and remind him of what is waiting beyond it in the light.

'"Thou hast prepared a table before me in the presence of mine enemies. Thou hast anointed my head with oil, and my cup shall be full."

'It is good to know that a feast awaits him on the other side, dear Father. He had short commons often enough in this Vale of Tears. . . .

'"We shall mourn for his family when he is gone, but we shall rejoice also to know that You have him in Your keeping. The Lord giveth, and the Lord taketh away. Blessed be the name of the Lord."'

For the one and only time, Stan's voice was as strong as Mr Coombs's as he said 'Amen', and once more Mr Coombs nodded as though a point had been made, then rose from his knees and shook hands, gently with Stan, firmly with Jane.

'I'll look in tomorrow,' he said.

'I wouldn't leave it too late,' said Stan. 'Not if you're going to envy me prayers,' and smiled. Coombs looked at him.

'You've got a feeling?' he asked.

'I have,' said Stan. 'I'm just trying to hang on till our Bob gets here.'

Mr Coombs nodded. 'I'll do my best,' he said. 'You know that, Stan. But this is a bad time. . . . So many.'

'I know that too,' said Stan. 'But come by if you can. I promise I won't stray far.' As he left the room Mr Coombs laughed aloud. 'I meant what I said,' Stan whispered, 'about hanging on to see our Bob.'

'Of course you did,' said Jane. 'And I know Andy's doing his best to reach him.'

'John would have been here by now,' said Stan. 'He was never a one for putting things off.'

'Nor is Bob,' said Jane. 'But he may have been called away on business.'

'Business,' said Stan. 'What in the world's he want to get mixed up in *business* for? Our Bob's a printer.'

He speaks the word 'business' as if it meant corruption, thought Jane, then bent to hear Stan's next whispered words.

'I hope our bit prayer didn't upset you.'

'Well of course not,' she said. 'I'm a Christian too.'

'Are you?' He sounded surprised. 'Good lass.'

'Well I try to be,' said Jane.

'That's all we *can* do,' said Stan. 'Try. . . . But I don't expect your prayers are the same as what you heard here.'

'No,' said Jane. 'But it's all prayer, after all.'

'We try to speak to God direct, you see,' said Stan. 'Tell him what we really mean. Must have seemed a bit strange to you.'

As strange, she thought, as if I'd joined a group of Roundheads praying before the Battle of Naseby.

Suddenly Stan's eyes closed, and her hand reached out for his pulse. It was still there, the tiniest thread of life, holding on, waiting for Bob.

Jane tucked the blankets around him and went back to the kitchen.

Grandma had made tea, and there were sandwiches, and a piece of plum cake. Jane declined the sandwiches, but took a piece of cake. It was a ritual, after all.

'How did you find him?' Grandma asked.

There was no sense in lying, not to this woman of all women. Gently she said, 'He's dying, Grandma.'

Bet cried out, then stifled the cry as the old woman glared at her. 'Aye,' she said. 'First Dr Stobbs. Then you. You'd know, all right.'

'He knows it too,' said Jane. 'He told Mr Coombs so. The only thing that's keeping him here is that he's waiting for Bob.'

'He would,' said Grandma. The thought seemed pleasing to her.

'Our Bob never could think of anybody but himself,' said Bet.

Jane said patiently, 'He doesn't know. It can't be his fault,' and then turned back to Grandma.

'I felt his pulse just now,' she said. 'It's very weak. I hope Andy gets through to Bob soon.'

'I'd better go and sit with him for a bit,' said Bet, and hurried from the kitchen. By the time she reaches that bedroom she'll be crying, thought Jane, and much good that will do Stan.

'She's taking it hard,' Grandma said.

'Tears won't help,' said Jane, and the old woman, eyesight sharp again after her cataract operation, looked up at once.

'You didn't cry when your father died?' she asked.

'Afterwards I did,' said Jane. 'But not when he could see me. *He* was the one who needed *me*. I wasn't there when he died, but afterwards I wept for him.'

An arrogant, immoral and utterly selfish man, she thought. Not like Stan at all. But with the gift of making you love him and weep for him.

'You're a lot harder than Bet,' said Grandma, 'and anyway Stan'll enjoy comforting her. He's done it all her life, after all.'

They sat on in easy silence until there was a tap at the front door. Jane went to the head of the stairs and pulled the end of the cord looped round the banister rails and knotted to the door latch. The door opened. She was looking at Dr Stobbs.

'Hello. You back?' he said, and at once climbed the stairs, moved past her, and went into the sick room.

The rudest man in Felston, she thought, and probably the most overworked and most dedicated as well, unless he dead heats with Canon Messeter.

Stobbs came into the kitchen quite soon, poured water from the kettle into the sink, and washed his hands with the coarse carbolic soap that lay beside it, and at once that pungent, utterly clean smell took Jane back to the hospitals of France.

'How is he, Doctor?' Grandma asked.

The poor use that word doctor with the same intonation that a peasant would use when calling a Cardinal 'Your Eminence'. And why not? They're both medicine men when you need them.

Stobbs was drying his hands on a strip of cloth with the texture of well-washed sacking.

'I won't lie to you,' he said, and Grandma's fists clenched; Jane went to stand beside her, put her hand on her shoulder. 'He hasn't got long.'

'I'd better go to him then,' Grandma said.

'In a minute.'

Stobbs moved closer to her, projecting a will as strong as Grandma's own. The doctor was as thick-set and solid as the minister, but with none of Mr Coombs's sweetness.

'There's one comfort I can offer you,' he said. 'He's in no pain. I promise you that. And there's maybe another as well. The reason he hasn't got long is he doesn't want long. He's impatient to be off, like a young man who can't wait to get to a dance.'

'It'll be better than a dance where he's going.'

Agnostic Stobbs had no answer to that, and ignored it.

'All that's keeping him's your Bob.'

'Andy's doing his best to fetch him,' Grandma said, and got up and left them. Her steps were slower, but her back was still straight.

Stobbs said, 'Do you mind if I sit down a minute?'

Jane gestured to Grandma's rocker, but he chose a wooden kitchen chair, stretched out his legs, then rubbed his eyes.

'You'll have to forgive me,' he said, 'but I was up with a cross birth at six.'

'Would you like a cup of tea?' Jane asked.

'No thanks. Just a word.' She waited as Stobbs fumbled in his pockets and at last found his pipe.

'You're still sending money for the clinic,' he said, and she made no answer, because there was nothing to say.

Stobbs sighed. 'What I'm getting at,' he said, 'is that I virtually gave you the sack – when you were doing good work here – and yet you go on helping us. Is that what Messeter calls turning the other cheek – or do you just want to make me feel bad?'

Jane said pleasantly, 'What an egoist you are. It has nothing to do with you.'

'What has it to do with then?' Stobbs asked.

'Felston.'

'Touché,' said Stobbs, and found his matches, began to light his pipe. 'Would it help if I told you why I got rid of you?' he asked.

'Not in the least.'

'It would help me, damn it.' The words came out like a snarl.

'You'd got another ambulance,' said Jane. 'Extra drivers. *Men* drivers. It was time for the little woman to go.'

'Nonsense,' said Stobbs. 'You were better than any of them and I bet you know it. It was gossip made me get rid of you. Muck raking. Felston morality.'

'Go on,' said Jane.

'Those biddies who work for me didn't mind you being rich,' said Stobbs. 'Well they did as a matter of fact, but they could put up with it. What they couldn't stand was that you were obviously having such a good time when you scooted back to London.'

'On leave,' said Jane. 'One always tried to have a good time on leave.'

'Felston doesn't believe in that sort of good time,' said Stobbs.

'What you're saying is that in Felston sex is more duty than pleasure.'

Stobbs flushed brick red. 'Something like that,' he said. 'And it wasn't just the rumours that were flying. It was you, as well.

There were times when you were just back from London – if you'd been a cat you would have been purring. You didn't even *try* to hide it.'

'Why should I? I was happy.'

'Felston wasn't. Not the women anyway. And the men had never seen anything like you before – or those other three you brought up for the charity concert.' – Catherine and Sarah and Georgie, she remembered, and all at their most devastating. 'The four of you did more damage than an air-raid.'

Jane chuckled then.

'All very funny, no doubt,' said Stobbs, 'but I'd have lost every helper I had, and *that's* why I fired you.'

'And quite right too,' said Jane.

Stobbs blinked at that. 'I call that handsome. I really do,' he said.

'Never mind that,' said Jane. 'Tell me about the rumours.'

'A chap called Burrowes did a lot of it,' said Stobbs. 'Cambridge man. Quite the nastiest homosexual I've ever come across.'

'I've met Mr Burrowes,' said Jane. 'Go on.' Stobbs hesitated. 'You won't like this,' he said at last.

'I'm quite sure I'll hate it, but I need to know.'

'Andy Patterson,' said Stobbs. 'I don't think he enjoyed it though I can't be sure. – There's enough primeval slime in all of us. Whatever his reasons, Andy did his share.'

And as he spoke the door opened and Andy came in.

'You know a cue when you hear one,' said Stobbs affably, but Andy was scarcely aware that Stobbs was there. He spoke only to Jane.

'I got to him,' he said. 'At last. It's cost me a fortune in phone calls.' He flinched as he heard his own words. 'I don't grudge it, not for Da – of course I don't – but why couldn't he be in just once? Twenty-four hours I've been after him.'

Jane could think of reasons, but now was not the time.

'So finally he deigns to answer and I told him, and do you know what he said? I'll come up on the sleeper, he said.'

'Very sensible,' said Jane.

'Where the hell would our Bob get the money for sleepers? He's a working man,' said Andy.

Oh no he's not, thought Jane. It's what you'd like him to be, but it isn't what he is. No more boots and cloth cap and muffler, not for Bob, any more than John.

'He might be in time then,' said Stobbs, and at last Andy became aware of his existence.

'That bad, is it?' said Andy, and Stobbs nodded.

'Can I go in to him?' Andy asked.

'No reason why not,' said Stobbs. 'But don't excite him. He's earned his peace.'

'I just want to be there,' Andy said.

'No harm in that,' said Stobbs, and Andy left them. Jane gathered up her handbag.

'You off?' Stobbs asked.

'He has his family with him,' said Jane. 'He won't want me.'

'That's where you're wrong,' Stobbs said. 'I'm not saying you should stay the rest of the night, but he wants another look at you while he still knows who you are. He told me himself.'

'And did he tell you why?'

'Because of his son who died,' said Stobbs. 'You were exactly the woman he wanted for him – and you came back even when his son was dead. He loves you for that.' Stobbs paused for a moment then added surprisingly: 'And so he should.'

'What do you want me to do then?'

'Go in to him. Smile at him. Be the woman you are, then go to your hotel, and come back in the morning. It may all be over by then, but even if it isn't, he won't know who you are.'

'Shouldn't I stay now?'

'The house is full,' he said. 'Bursting at the seams. The Pattersons know all about this kind of death. Let them get on with it.'

She went into Stan's bedroom. Bet and Grandma were on their knees by the bed, and Andy stood in the shadows. Jane went up close to Stan's side.

'Come to say goodbye, have you?' he whispered.

'Ta-ra more like,' she said, doing her best to imitate his accent. 'You won't get away from me that easily.'

The smile he gave her was delighted, spontaneous, and somehow made him look about half his age, and Jane knew more than ever how close he was to death. She knelt beside him and kissed his forehead. 'Ta-ra, Stan,' she said.

'Ta-ra, lass,' Stan whispered. 'I'll be seeing you.'

'You'd better,' she said, and once again the smile came, and somehow she found her way to the door and Grandma followed.

'Thanks, pet,' she said, and hugged her.

'Dr Stobbs thinks there are too many people here as it is,' Jane said, 'so I'm going back to the hotel before Bob gets here. If I'm wanted – for any reason – get one of them to telephone.'

'He's seen you,' said Grandma, 'and he's happy. Get yourself a good night's rest. We'll see you tomorrow?'

'Of course,' said Jane, and kissed her cheek.

# 4

OUTSIDE SHE SAW that the moon was up, but not even moon-light could do anything for Felston, any more than it could for the Somme. The town was as ravaged and spent as an old battlefield. Jane got into the Daimler and drove to the hotel, and as she drove she wept.

The manager of her hotel greeted her with the news that she'd had a phone call from a Mr Lovell, who was staying at Blagdon Hall. He seemed far more excited about it than Jane was, so much so that he almost forgot to tell her that Mr Lovell would call again. Jane went to her room to repair the damage that tears had done to her face, then ordered coffee and sandwiches in the hotel lounge and waited for Charles's call. How easily Stan had accepted death. Her mother had told her that her father had fought it all the way. Aunt Pen, like Stan, had welcomed death as friend, but Aunt Pen had died of a particularly agonising form of cancer. Stan was in no pain, Stobbs had said, except perhaps the aching burden of a life too heavy to carry.

She had forgotten how terrible the coffee at the Eldon Arms was, and after one sip she sent it back and ordered a whisky and soda instead. The waitress who served her gawked in astonishment, and perhaps it was worth it just for that. It had stopped her thinking about death, anyway, and setting out a list in her mind of dear departeds. Far too early in her life for her to begin on *that*, and if you counted in the war dead it would be a very long list indeed. . . . The hall porter appeared beside her. Mr Lovell was on the phone, he said. From *Blagdon Hall*, and he too seemed to pronounce the name of the place in block capitals. She went to the phone booth and picked up the receiver.

'Charles?' she said.

'One moment, madam,' said a voice that could only be a butler's. 'I will connect you to Mr Lovell.'

A click, and then Charles's voice. 'Hello? . . . Jane?'

'Goodness,' said Jane. 'How grand you are. You didn't warn me there'd be ordeal by butler.'

'Well it is very grand,' said Lovell.

'Have you bought it yet?'

'Still thinking. Would you like to come and see it and advise me?'

'When?'

'Tomorrow?'

'Tomorrow may be a bit tricky,' said Jane.

'The next day?'

'I may have to go to a funeral, but if not I'll come. How long are you staying?'

'Till I make up my mind. Believe me, nobody's in a hurry to toss me out.'

'I should think not. They want your money. . . . I'd like to come, Charles. I will if I can. It's all very sad here.'

'Poor darling. I'll warn Proudfoot to expect you.'

'Proudfoot?'

'The butler.' Somehow she knew that Charles was smiling.

'Charles, he can't possibly be called Proudfoot.'

'It's what he answers to,' said Lovell. 'But then Blagdon does have a rather weird sense of humour.'

The Earl of Blagdon, Jane remembered, was the house's impoverished owner.

'I'll let him know as soon as I can,' she said. 'Goodbye, Charles.'

'I love you,' Charles Lovell said, but she was already hanging up, too exhausted to do more than go upstairs, take a long, hot bath, then go to bed and sleep. She dreamed she was driving the ambulance in winter, taking a load of wounded from the field dressing station to Arras on an icy, shell-pocked road. It was a hard and menacing dream.

At breakfast next morning she could still recall the dream: the strain of making sure that the ambulance didn't skid and make the agony of the men behind her even less bearable: the wrecked vehicles and smashed gun-limbers pushed from the road into the empty fields where the snow lay heavy, smoothing out the shell craters. But there had been no horses, and for that at least she was grateful. When she had had her breakdown, her dreams had always been of horses, mutilated by gunfire, legs missing, or jaws, the dead ones ripped open so that their guts spilled out. And they were all horses that she had seen in France, which was why she had had the breakdown. That and John's death. But this time, no horses. She hoped that meant she wasn't about to go mad again just yet.

After breakfast she drove back to John Bright Street. She had promised Grandma, and it was what she had come for after all. This time it was Bet who pulled on the cord that opened the door, and motioned her into the kitchen. Grandma was there, dressed in the same clothes as the day before. Perhaps she hadn't gone to bed.

'The doctor's with him,' said Grandma. 'Stan hasn't much time left, he says.'

'And Bob?'

'Not here yet. Andy's down at the station to fetch him.' She stirred in her chair by the fire.

'I'll miss our Stan,' she said. 'He often got the rough edge of me tongue, but that was because he was so gentle and forgiving, and we can't go about being gentle and forgiving all the time – leastways I can't.' She was quiet for a moment. 'Where was I?' she said at last.

'You'll miss Stan,' said Jane.

'Well I will,' said Grandma. 'There's no one can offer a prayer like our Stan.'

Her eyes closed then, and her head began to nod. So she hasn't been to bed, thought Jane, but now was not the time to mention it. Grandma would wait to the end.

The door opened and Stobbs came in, but it wasn't his usual, bustling walk; the urgent rush to examine and heal. This time his walk said there was no point in rushing.

'You'd better go to him,' he said, and Jane touched Grandma on the shoulder. Her eyes opened at once, wary, afraid.

'It's time you went to him, Mrs Patterson,' said Stobbs.

Grandma's chin trembled, but only for a moment, then her

head came up and the fear vanished. Fear was not what Stan needed now.

Gently Jane and Bet took Grandma's arms, and guided her to the best bedroom, where Stan lay motionless, eyes open but unseeing, his face already sharpened by the onset of death, his breathing the tiniest whisper.

Grandma moved to the side of the bed, and the two young women helped her to kneel, then knelt on either side of her. Grandma prepared for prayer the way Jane had been taught as a child: 'hands together; eyes closed', and Jane and Bet did likewise.

'Our Father,' said Grandma, 'which art in Heaven, hallowed be Thy name.' They said the Lord's prayer to the end: 'For Thine is the kingdom, the power and the glory, for ever and ever, Amen.' The three female voices said 'Amen', and for the first and last time, Stan did not join them. Jane opened her eyes. It seemed that she heard Stan sigh, the kind that comes from sheer content, and after that she could no longer hear even the tiniest whisper of his breath. And then there came the rattle of a taxi outside, the slam of its door, and the clatter of feet racing up the stairs. The door burst open and they came in, first Bob, then Andy.

Bob stood in the doorway, looking at the three kneeling women. 'Is he –?' he said.

'Go to him,' said his grandmother. 'Quick.'

The two men moved, one to each side of the bed, and each one clasped his father by the hand.

'He's cold,' Andy said.

'Well, of course,' said his grandmother. 'Nothing can warm him now. But you could try kneeling down and saying a prayer.' Bob knelt at once.

'I can't do that,' said Andy. 'You know I can't.'

'Just kneel then,' said his grandmother, and Andy knelt.

'Help us up,' Grandma said, and Bet and Jane lifted her. She seemed no weight at all. Then she turned to Jane. 'Get the doctor, pet,' she said, and Jane went to the kitchen, where Stobbs was boiling the kettle to make tea.

'That clatter was Bob coming, I take it?' Jane nodded. 'So he was in time?'

'Perhaps,' said Jane, 'though I doubt it.'

Stobbs looked up at her. 'You know about death, do you?' he said, and then: 'But of course you do.'

'I think he was two minutes too late,' said Jane. 'But there's no point in telling him that.'

'None whatsoever,' said Stobbs. 'But why tell me?'

'Because you would have asked me, like any other doctor.'

Stobbs nodded. 'Quite right,' he said, and poured the boiling water into the teapot. 'Now let's go and see them, and do a bit of play acting.'

Once more Jane went into the best bedroom, and Stobbs followed, again with his bustling walk, because Stan Patterson was now beyond his aid and there were a hundred others waiting. He picked his way past the mourners and took out his stethoscope, bent over Stan's body. After a long pause he said: 'I'm afraid he's gone.'

Bob said, 'I was in time then?'

'Just about,' said Stobbs.

'Not that he recognised you,' said Andy.

'At least I was here.'

'But he didn't know that,' Andy said.

'That's what you think,' said Grandma. 'It just so happens that I think different. Now we'll say our goodbyes to him, and I'll send for Bella Proctor to lay him out.'

She bent to kiss Stan's forehead, looked at him, then walked to the door. 'You next, Bet,' she said. 'You're the one'll have to run over to Mrs Proctor's.' Then she left the bedroom without looking back. Bet kissed her father in her turn, then Andy gestured to Jane to do the same, and Jane bent to touch her lips to the hard, dry flesh. No sense of being gracious, she thought. No sense of doing it because it was what the others wanted. Just a ritual observed. She straightened up and went into the kitchen, and took Grandma in her arms, and at last the old woman began to cry with hard, heart-wrenching sobs that made her whole body shudder. Jane could do nothing but hold her.

At last the old woman said, 'There. I've done.'

'You're sure?' Jane asked, and the old, proud head nodded. Jane opened her bag and handed over her handkerchief. Grandma wiped her eyes.

'It should have been me,' she said.

'Now Grandma.'

'Well it would have been if I'd had my choice,' Grandma said. 'Why take him when there's a useless old woman like me going begging?'

'You've never been useless in your life,' said Jane. 'And anyway it isn't your choice.'

'God's will be done I suppose,' said Grandma.

'That's the way your son saw it,' said Jane.

'Always got an answer, haven't you?' said Grandma. 'Clever as a box of monkeys, aren't you, Jane Whitcomb?' And then, 'Aye . . . you're right. But like I say, I'll miss him.'

She looked at the teapot ready on the table, and the cups, sugar and milk beside it.

'That Dr Stobbs,' she said. 'Working overtime to show how hard and unfeeling he is, and then he goes and has the tea ready on the sly, just when he knows we'll need it. Pour us a cup then, pet.'

Jane poured Grandma her tea just as she liked it, with three spoons of sugar, and then the men came in, Stobbs leading. He took Grandma's hand and leaned over her, but seemed reassured by what he saw. 'I've had a word with Bob and Andy,' he said. 'About all the business matters. Death certificates and so on. They'll take care of all that.'

'Thanks, Doctor,' said Grandma.

'No need to worry about post-mortems or anything of that sort,' said Stobbs. 'The illness was of long standing. You can bury him as soon as the formalities are taken care of.' And then, belatedly, 'I'm very sorry. . . . I should have said that before, shouldn't I?'

Grandma smiled. 'That's all right, Doctor,' she said. 'You go and take care of the living. You did your best for my Stan and I've no doubt he's grateful. I know I am.'

Stobbs smiled back at her very quickly, as if he had only a limited supply of smiles, then left, the bustling walk more obvious than ever, and Bob came in. At once Grandma poured him a cup of tea.

'Have you eaten?' she asked.

He looked at her as if her words were meaningless, then said at last: 'I'm not hungry.'

Jane thought, it hasn't come home to him yet. He still doesn't understand.

'What in the world kept you so long?' Grandma asked.

'Don't you start,' said Bob. 'I've had enough of that from Andy.'

'Well, what did?' said Grandma. 'Surely I've a right to ask?'

'Aye,' said Bob, 'you have.' He sat at the table, began to sip his tea. Jane noticed then the cut of his suit, and that he wore shoes, not boots: expensive shoes, and his tie was made of silk.

'I was working,' he said.

'I thought you'd left that job on the paper,' said Grandma.

'The *Daily World*? So I had. This is a bit better than typesetting.'

'Doing what?'

'Selling wireless sets. – And renting them.'

There was a snort from behind them. Andy stood in the doorway.

'So you're a tally man now, are you?' Andy said. 'On the knocker?'

Bob turned to face him: easy, unhurried.

'Eavesdropping as usual,' he said, 'and getting it wrong as usual an' all.' He turned back to Jane and Grandma.

'I'm what my brother would call a bloated capitalist,' he said. 'I own the sets I deal in.'

'But how could you rent a wireless?' said Grandma. 'Renting's houses.'

'Renting's money,' said Bob. 'There's a lot of folk would like a wireless that can't afford one, but they can manage a few bob a week to borrow one – and I'll maintain it for them.'

'And where did you get the money to become a capitalist?' Andy asked.

'There was a canny few bonuses going around when I worked for Jay Bower,' said Bob. And there were indeed, Jane remembered. Bob had a remarkable talent for ferreting out information, and had progressed from typographer to sniffer-out of secrets, a cross between a private detective and a spy. But it seemed he hadn't told Grandma so.

'Not that I had nearly enough,' said Bob. 'I had to borrow most of it.'

'Where from?' said Grandma suspiciously. She hated borrowing. To her it meant only the last extremes of poverty and humiliation.

'The bank,' said Bob.

'Well I'm blowed,' said Andy. 'You got money out of a bank?' He sounded more admiring than condemnatory.

'Why didn't you come to me?' Jane asked.

'How could I?' said Bob. 'This was business, not family. I might have failed, and if I had, I couldn't pay you back.' He was utterly serious, Jane knew. His system of morality might be eccentric, but it was as rigid as Stan's had been.

'But you didn't worry about not paying the bank back?' Andy asked.

'Course not,' said Bob. 'They'd have put me out of business, made me bankrupt. Jane would never do that. And anyway, it's not going to happen. I'm coining money.'

'So long as it's honest,' said Grandma.

'Why steal when there's the BBC?' said Bob, and then his smile faded. 'And that's why I was late,' he said. 'It's hard work, coining money. Still – at least I was in time.'

'Just,' said Andy, but Bob didn't hear him. He turned to Jane. 'I was in time, wasn't I?' he asked.

'Oh yes,' said Jane. 'He was alive when you and Andy touched him.'

'Aye,' said Bob. 'You would know all right.'

'And what's that supposed to mean?' said Grandma.

Jane said gently: 'I drove an ambulance, remember? I saw a lot of dead soldiers then.'

'I was forgetting,' Grandma said. 'It's hard to see you with all those dead bodies – a lady like you.'

Andy said, 'But Da didn't know it was us, did he? If you could have dragged yourself away from your money bags a bit sooner he would have seen we were there.'

Jane said gently, 'Grandma said it before. We can't possibly know whether he knew or not. He may well have known your voices, felt your touch.'

'Thanks pet,' said Bob. 'I hope you're right.'

Bet came in then, with Bella Proctor, stout, placid, middle aged, with a calm certainty of movement that was very reassuring, thought Jane, considering what she was about to do.

'I'm sorry to hear about your trouble, Mrs Patterson,' she said. 'I came over as soon as I changed me pinny.'

'Very good of you, Mrs Proctor,' said Grandma. 'Would you like a cup of tea before you start?'

'After if you don't mind,' Mrs Proctor said. 'It's best to get these things over and done with.'

'Tell us what you'll need then,' said Grandma.

'Just the things you want on him,' Mrs Proctor said, 'and soap and water and a towel. Oh – and his comb.'

Bet moved at once, but Grandma motioned her to stay.

'You bide where you are,' she said. 'I'll get his things. You put a pan of water on to boil.'

She got up then, and led Mrs Proctor from the room.

Bob said, 'It's hard to believe, isn't it? Da's really dead.'

'Well of course he is,' said Bet. 'You were there. We all were.'

'I don't mean that,' said Bob. 'What I'm saying I *knew* he was dead but somehow I couldn't believe it. Not till Bella Proctor walked in.' Suddenly he put his hands to his face. 'I'm sorry,' he said. 'I'll have to go out for a minute.' He went into the front room that was only used on state occasions: births and marriages and deaths.

'Soft,' said Andy. 'Soft as muck.'

'No fears of you crying,' said Bet.

'I'm not crying because there's no sense in crying, but it doesn't mean I'm not feeling,' Andy said.

And indeed the pain was there in his face.

'But crying won't bring him back,' said Andy. 'Nothing will.'

'He's with God now,' said Bet, and Andy opened his mouth then shut it again and stayed silent. This was not the time to tell his sister that God did not exist.

'What about the funeral?' Jane asked.

'What about it?' said Andy.

'When will it be?'

'Friday, likely. We'll have to warn people.' Friday was two days away.

There was no way to be polite about it. 'Will there be enough money for the funeral?' she asked.

'Da had an insurance,' said Andy. 'But thanks, anyway.'

'That's all right then,' said Jane, and waited till Grandma came back. She wasn't long. Even Grandma's iron control couldn't cope with Mrs Proctor's task.

'Would you like to go for a drive?' Jane asked her. Being driven in the Daimler ranked high on Grandma's list of treats.

'Not today, pet,' Grandma said. 'It's a bit soon. Maybe after the funeral –'

'Of course,' said Jane, and then: 'Would you mind very much if I went off tomorrow – to see a friend of mine? I'll be back for the funeral of course.'

'Why certainly,' Grandma said. 'Why wouldn't you? Does your friend live far?'

'He's staying at Blagdon Hall.'

'Well I never,' Grandma said. 'He must be one of the nobs.'

'Yes,' said Jane. 'I suppose he must.'

'It makes you think,' said Grandma. 'One day you're in John Bright Street, and the next day it's a palace. Leastways it seemed like a palace to me.'

'You know it?'

'I worked there,' said Grandma. 'Sixty odd years ago, when I started. I was a kitchen maid. Going to be a cook. Then I met Stan's father instead. He worked in one of Lord Blagdon's pits. . . . Then they moved him to Felston to another one, and we married.'

In the eighteen sixties, thought Jane. Queen Victoria on the throne, sulking out her widowhood in Balmoral or the Isle of Wight, and who would be Prime Minister? Palmerston? And the Indian Mutiny a very recent memory.

'We had four children,' said Grandma. 'Two boys, two girls. Stan was the last. I lost the other three before they reached their teens. A diphtheria epidemic that was, and only Stan was spared. Proper little titch, our Stan, but he was tougher than he looked.'

'And when did you lose your husband?'

'Nineteen hundred and three,' said Grandma. 'Idolised our John. Idolised him. And Andy and Bob too, of course.'

'No need for tact, Grandma,' said Andy. 'Our John was always his favourite.' But his voice was kind.

'It was his lungs killed him,' said Grandma. 'All that muck they breathe down-by in the pits. It's killed a lot of miners round here.'

'No better than murder,' Andy said. 'It shouldn't be allowed.'

'And if they stopped the pitmen going to work,' said Grandma, 'who would feed their bairns?'

It was Bob's return that saved them from a lecture on Marxist economics. One look told her that he had been weeping. Grandma spoke up at once.

'We'd better have a think about the funeral,' she said. 'Who's to go to the chapel and who comes back here. Get a pencil and paper one of you and we'll make a list.'

'We'll have to have a tea,' said Bob. 'Cake and sandwiches, and sherry and whisky.'

'And champagne an' all, I suppose,' said Andy. 'Talk sense. Da's burial club only pays the funeral. Who's going to pay for whisky and sherry these days?'

'Me,' said Bob. 'We'll have the thing done right.'

'Us,' said Jane.

Bob looked at her angrily, then remembered her kneeling by his father's bed. 'Aye,' he said. 'Us.'

'I can't contribute,' Andy said. 'I suppose you realise that?'

Grandma said, 'They're not asking you to, pet. They know you would if you were flush. And it's my son they were thinking of after all.' She turned to Jane.

'Our Stan was TT all his life,' she said.

'TT?' Jane asked.

'Teetotal. Signed the pledge when he was a bairn and never once fell by the wayside. But he never once grudged a drink to them that wasn't, either. Weddings. Christmas. Funerals. . . .' Her voice wavered, then grew strong again. 'We'll do it properly,' she said. 'Our Stan deserves a good send off.'

## 5

NEXT DAY JANE set off for Blagdon Hall. It was like driving from Hell to Paradise, or even the outskirts of Heaven. Hell was the road from Felston to Newcastle, a road that was an unending sequence of grimy streets, coal mines, and shipyards that were idle and rusting. The inhabitants of Hell were mostly men in the uniform cloth cap and muffler, hands thrust deep in the pockets of ragged trousers. Most of the women she saw wore a sort of headscarf, though some of the older ones wore shawls. Old and young alike scuttled quickly about their business as if they had no right to be outside where the men were loafing, standing and staring for the most part, the lucky ones sharing a cigarette. They hardly spoke, but then, thought Jane, what would they speak about? No job and no chance of a job: not then, not ever. Even the sight of a Daimler passing by was enough to make them stare; a tiny break in the day's monotony. She was glad to get out of Hell.

Paradise began on the road to the coast that headed north to the Scottish border. First there were farmhouses, sturdy and enduring, built of local stone, with flowers and hedgerows, sheep and cattle, and once a horse galloping for the sheer joy of it, running parallel with the car across an empty field. And then the moorland began, vast and empty except for herself and the sheep and seagulls: first grass, then bracken and heather. And last of all the sea on her right as she drove: a bottle-green sea, heaving gently, but the waves still massive, the white spume catching the sun like showers of diamonds. And at the edge of the sea, mile after mile of pale and empty sand, interspersed with the ruins of castles, for this had once been the target for Scottish raiders. Even in ruin, the castles were majestic, with the calm of aristocrats who can no longer afford to keep up appearances. Like Lord Blagdon, she thought, and put her foot down. She mustn't keep Proudfoot waiting.

Jane turned off the coast road at Alnwick, and headed west, back into farmland, mixed for the most part: arable and cattle, and sheep on the high fells. Then at last the first sign: 'Blagdon Hall 7 miles'. 'Look for a village called Calbeck,' Lovell had told her, and there it was, a picture-postcard place, built for the most part of stones quarried by the Romans nineteen centuries ago, to make their wall. Away to the south, like a vast snake slithering across the moors, was the Roman Wall itself, but Jane told herself firmly that this was no time for walls. Today was Proudfoot Day.

Another sign, that pointed to a secondary road. Jane bumped down it to a gate lodge rather in need of repair, and two lodge gates of massive ornamental iron work in need of paint. A man came out to open the gates and touch his cap as he passed, but he didn't hurry.

The Daimler seemed more at ease bowling down a carriage drive than in John Bright Street, she thought. All the usual country house ornamentation was there, parterres and topiary and grass, and even a folly. She followed the bend in the drive and found that she was looking at a lake, and behind it the house, with precisely arranged woodland beyond.

Dear God it's beautiful, she thought. A central block of dove-grey stone, with two great wings like arms outstretched, and a massive dome that yet seemed perfectly proportioned, so vast was the house. And no doubt stables beyond the house and a kitchen garden beyond the stables. And the farms and woods would all be the earl's too. Blagdon Hall might well generate more work than the whole of Felston, and still his lordship couldn't afford it. Jane parked the Daimler at the foot of the steps that led to the main door, and got out of the car, relieved that the one good suit she had brought was made by Chanel.

As she reached the top of the stairs the door opened and Proudfoot appeared. He really was magnificent, thought Jane: massive in stature, like the house, and well over six foot in height. Was there a minimum height qualification for butlers, she wondered, like the Guards or the police? Rather a splendid profile too, like one of the more preachifying Roman emperors. Antoninus Pius, perhaps. She would have to ask Lionel.

'Miss Whitcomb,' she said. 'For Mr Lovell.'

Proudfoot bowed. 'Mr Lovell is in the little day room, miss,' he said. 'I shall take you to him.'

The voice was like her father's description of Beerbohm Tree's.

Proudfoot set off and Jane followed, down a vast corridor lined with statues circling the base of a marble staircase and on to another corridor, panelled in mahogany, with pictures on the walls very much in need of cleaning, but one was a Canaletto and another a Rubens. Proudfoot sailed majestically on, and Jane followed as if taking part in a procession, until they arrived at another mahogany door. Proudfoot tapped on it and went inside.

'Miss Whitcomb, Mr Lovell,' he said, and Jane followed. The room, she saw at once, was one that received frequent use, the furniture for the most part Edwardian: leather chairs and sofa of heroic proportions, a revolving bookcase and a desk that would dominate any room she owned, yet here seemed almost unobtrusive. The little day room, she observed, could house a dozen people at least.

Lovell was busy at the desk, and got up as soon as she entered, came up to her and took her in his arms. She struggled furiously. What would Proudfoot think? She looked over her shoulder. The door was closed, Proudfoot had gone, like a genie returned to his bottle. . . . Her arms came round his neck and she kissed him.

'What on earth was all that about?' said Lovell.

'Proudfoot.'

He smiled. 'He really is quite something, isn't he?'

'Are you going to buy him, too?'

Lovell laughed aloud. 'The place wouldn't be the same without him,' he said. 'Sort of a zeitgeist wouldn't you say? . . . But how are you?'

'Miserable,' she said. 'Mr Patterson died. It was all very miserable.'

'Do you good to get away.'

The Pattersons can never get away, she thought, but that was wrong. All three brothers had escaped: John into business and the army, Bob to London: even Andy went off to study courses in Cambridge. Only the Patterson women were trapped, as the rest of Felston was trapped.

'I'm glad I came,' she said. 'This place is fantastic.' It was the easiest thing to say. It was also the truth.

'It should give the Americans something to think about,' he said. 'There's a grouse-shoot too, you know, *and* a salmon stream. Blagdon will show us over the place later. What did you make of him, by the way?'

'I've never met him,' Jane said, then remembered what Lovell had said about the earl's weird sense of humour.

'Proudfoot?' she said. 'Proudfoot is *Blagdon*?'

'Not just a pretty face, are you?' said Lovell. 'Got it in one. . . . What made you think of it?'

'He was too much like a butler,' said Jane. 'More like an actor on a stage than any butler I ever saw. Just – it's hard to explain – just this side of caricature. But why on earth does he do it?'

'God knows,' said Lovell. 'He enjoys it. That's obvious. Perhaps he wishes he could have been an actor. Perhaps it's just a way of escaping reality. He doesn't just do butlers, either. He's been a general, a maharajah, and all kinds of clergymen. He once preached a sermon in York Minster.'

'But he can't save his house,' said Jane.

'No,' said Lovell. 'Only I can do that – or someone like me. And it'll be a hell of a lot of work.' He gestured at the pile of papers on his desk. 'And even if I do it – it won't be his any more.'

'And where will he live?'

'He's got a place in Hampshire,' said Lovell. 'Twenty rooms. Five hundred acres.'

'Sort of a cottage,' said Jane.

'Sort of.'

'You keep saying *if* you buy. Is there a problem?'

'Not a problem exactly,' Lovell said. 'But I want you to look at it first before I make up my mind.'

Jay Bower had shown her his house once: a slender and elegant Queen Anne mansion, as exquisitely feminine as this was masculine, and almost impossibly so by moonlight.

'You can hardly expect me to make that sort of decision,' she said.

'Not decide for me, of course not,' he said. 'Just tell me what you think.'

He went to shovel his papers into his briefcase, and there was another tap at the door and Lord Blagdon came in. He wore a Lovat tweed suit, and looked much slimmer than Proudfoot, and at least five years younger.

'Sorry I'm so late to welcome you,' he said, 'but I gather Proudfoot took care of you. I've given him the rest of the day off, by the way. He's got a horse running in the three thirty at Newcastle and rather wanted to be there. Blagdon Bolter. Seven to one. Not a bad bet. If you're interested I can telephone my bookmaker.'

If I were interested, thought Jane, I would telephone my step-father, but I'm not.

'Charles says the two of you would like to look over this mouldering pile,' said the earl. 'My pleasure of course, but Charles seems to be making rather a hobby of it. He's already been over it twice.'

Blagdon spoke with a kind of barely subdued ferocity that seemed very close to breakdown, and yet he seemed calm enough. Only his hands betrayed his tension, moving restlessly from pockets to lapels to his face.

'Maybe it'll be third time lucky,' said Lovell, and Blagdon made a face. Whatever Lovell's decision it would not be the right one.

'Before lunch suit you?' Blagdon asked. 'We can take sherry in the drawing room and start the tour at the same time.'

He moved off at once, leaving Jane and Charles to follow. I don't suppose he's really rude, thought Jane. He's been so rich for so long that he doesn't know there's any other way to behave, even though he isn't rich any more. . . .

Back to the marble corridor, to double doors painted in white and gold, and a couple of footmen to open them, and then into a room rather larger than Jane's house in South Terrace, and distinctly chillier, she thought, even though the month was May. No sign of central heating, no sign at all, but a fire burned in the massive marble fireplace, almost certainly by Adam. A fire of apple logs, that gave off a scent like Bramleys roasting, but didn't give off enough heat.

A far less impressive butler than Proudfoot came in with decanters and glasses on a tray, and Blagdon waited impatiently as the sherry was poured and the butler left, then went at once into his second characterisation. This time he was a don, nervous of an audience, yet secured against his nervousness by the weight of his learning.

'The house was built pretty well as you see it now – all of a piece, as it were – by the fifth earl. The foundations were dug in 1783, and the final decoration completed in 1794. There were later internal decorations by the Adam brothers, but they were for embellishment only. The house itself is a unity.'

His voice had become that of a much older man, several tones higher than Proudfoot's, and with the expert's rapidity in dealing with a subject long since mastered.

'The silk draperies and the furniture you see were ordered in Paris in 1787, and delivered in the nick of time, the *very* nick of time, two months before the fall of the Bastille in fact. The Graeco-Roman statue was a gift from the Sultan of Turkey to the sixth earl when he was ambassador to the Ottoman Empire, and the painting above the fireplace is a Velasquez, the Duke of Nerja at the Spanish court.'

Blagdon broke off then to indulge in a fit of coughing that was exactly in character with the don he was playing, ending with a nose-blow like the blast of trumpets, and continued exactly where he'd left off.

It was another virtuoso performance, thought Jane, but it was boring, and the reason it was boring was that it wasn't a lecture at all. It was more like a catalogue in which every item must have its provenance declared, its authenticity proved beyond doubt. And there was an awful lot to display, from Persian carpets to Chinese urns of the Tang period. Jane had long finished her sherry. Lovell took her glass from her, went to the drinks tray and refilled it, and still Blagdon went on listing his treasures in a kind of furious gabble.

The place was like a museum, she thought, a very nice museum, with so much space that even all those objects stored inside it didn't make it look crammed, but a museum none the less. She began to think about lunch. It had been a long time since the one piece of toast and marmalade she had eaten for breakfast. Determinedly she looked at her host, trying to look like a student, earnest and eager, but all she could think about was food.

Blagdon stopped talking at last, and she tried not to look relieved, and just as well, she thought bitterly. It had only been a pause to rest his voice before he started off again.

'That gives you a rough idea of the place,' he said, in his rôle of professor recapitulating the essential points of an introductory lecture. 'Now . . . where shall we begin our exploration of the house in detail? Seek out the minutiae, as it were?'

'The dining room,' said Lovell firmly.

'But the state dining room is being restored,' said Blagdon. 'All the best stuff is in storage.'

'The dining room,' said Lovell, 'where we are going to eat lunch.'

Lord Blagdon got to his feet, suddenly and angrily. He really is a big man, thought Jane, and an angry one. Charles shouldn't tease him so. And yet Charles continued to sit, benignly smiling the smile of a man who has produced the only possible solution to an otherwise impossible problem.

'Lunch?' said Blagdon vaguely, and then: 'Oh . . . lunch. Yes of course.' He went to an electric bell button by the mantelshelf, and pushed it as if he were firing torpedoes.

'The butler will take you in,' he said. 'Unfortunately I can't join you. I remembered I promised Proudfoot I'd go to Newcastle and watch his horse run. Proudfoot gets very nervous when he has a horse running.'

'What about the tour of the house?' Lovell asked.

'You do it,' said Blagdon, with a smile like a howl of rage. 'After all, you've been round it often enough.'

'You're very kind,' said Lovell.

'No I'm not,' Lord Blagdon said. 'I'm bloody stupid, that's what I am – but I'm not going to give you this house on a platter.'

'Why should you?' said Lovell. 'If you don't like my price you can always go to someone else.'

Blagdon left them, and the only reason he didn't slam the door was that it was too big to slam, even for a man of his size, and almost immediately afterwards the butler came in and announced lunch, and a very stately lunch it was too, thought

Jane, in the little dining room that could never possibly have accommodated more than twenty people. . . . Local lobsters, local lamb, and grapes from the greenhouse with the local cheese. And always with a butler and two footmen in attendance, which meant that the weather was the only possible topic for discussion.

But coffee was served in the little day room, and there at last they could talk.

'At least we were spared Proudfoot,' said Lovell.

'Goodness how pompous it all was,' said Jane. 'Will you live like that if you buy?'

'Only when I'm entertaining Americans.'

'I hope for your sake it doesn't happen too often,' said Jane.

'How one suffers to be rich,' said Lovell, then: 'Shall I buy it?'

'Let's have another look round first.'

Together they went from room to room, for another look at the Canaletto and the Rubens, and then the Vermeer and the Velasquez, the Cellini salt-cellar and the Gutenberg Bible, and so much more. The earls of Blagdon had collected like magpies, and hoarded everything they possessed.

At last Jane asked, 'What's he asking for it all?'

Lovell's was a financier's reply. 'I can get it for fifty,' he said.

'Fifty thousand pounds? For all this?'

'Then there'll be repair bills,' said Lovell, 'and loans to repay and debts to settle. It'll be nearer a hundred.'

'All the same,' Jane said, 'it still seems a bargain – to me at any rate. And it would be wonderful if one were to remove the pomposity.'

'Do *you* want to buy it?'

She looked at him warily, but he seemed quite serious.

'Certainly not,' she said. 'The dower house is the place for single ladies.'

'Would you come here if I did?'

She said firmly: 'As a member of a house-party, yes. But not otherwise.' And then for some reason she added: 'I could buy it if I wanted to. My aunt left me rather a lot of money.'

'Blagdon would probably swop it for the contents of your jewel box,' said Lovell. 'It isn't lack of funds that puts you off. I know that. So why wouldn't you buy?'

'It's so damn big,' she said. 'I'd rattle around like the last remaining pea in an enormous pod. And I have absolutely no dynastic ambitions.'

'Pity,' said Lovell. 'Then house-parties it must be.'

'But not the pompous ones,' she said. 'Not the ones where the rich Americans are impressed.'

'Certainly not,' said Lovell. 'I shan't let you go near rich Americans. Some of them are very attractive.' He was thinking about Bower, she thought, but there was no point in pressing him. Lovell always maintained his own pace.

They looked at Chinese jade and Japanese porcelain, Hepplewhite furniture and Shiraz carpets that could have covered a cricket field.

'So you're definitely buying?' she asked, and he nodded.

'I won't get anything better, not at the price,' he said. 'It's a bit far from town, but the Yanks like motoring. . . . I'll tell Blagdon before dinner – if he's back in time. Not that he'll be overjoyed, whatever I tell him. I just hope he decides to be himself for a change. . . . Care to walk off some of that lunch?'

She changed her shoes for the pair she used in the car, and put on her coat. It was early May, but the north-east wind still had bite. Together she and Lovell looked at the lawns and flower-beds that were in urgent need of gardeners, the ornamental lake now half silted up. Even the pretty bridge they crossed needed repair.

'I see what you mean about having to spend money,' she said. 'But all the same – what a view you're buying.'

They looked from the bridge to an elegant and artfully contrived stream that tumbled down to the lake as a colt might frisk. Beyond it was woodland: oak and chestnut and copper beech, the position of each tree worked out by an expert a century and a half ago. And in the grass that fronted the trees, red deer grazed.

'There's a fountain, too,' said Lovell. 'Copy of the Trevi fountain in Rome, only it doesn't work of course. And there's a folly in the woods.'

'Stables?'

'They're still standing. Just. . . . But I wouldn't advise sneezing if we visit them. . . . No point anyway. The only horse he's got now is Blagdon Bolter.'

'I hope he wins,' said Jane.

'Dear God, so do I,' said Lovell. 'It might put a curb on the amateur dramatics.' He hesitated, then said at last: 'Bower came to see me. He flew here, as a matter of fact.'

'He quite often does,' said Jane. 'Fly, I mean.' Was that all? she wondered, but at last Lovell continued.

'He wants me to invest in something of his,' he said.

'And will you?'

'No,' said Lovell, and that, it seemed, *was* all. He hesitated once more, then said, 'You're next door to me. Your bedroom I mean. There's just a bathroom between us.'

'What a lubricious mind your friend Blagdon has,' said Jane, and then: 'I've always wanted to use that word, but he's the first one it fits. Filthy *and* oily. . . . Bathrooms indeed. What does he expect of us? A Roman orgy?'

'I doubt it,' said Lovell. 'The thing is, ours is the only bathroom that works. All the same, it's an idea.'

'Rather a good idea,' said Jane, 'so long as we get it over with before your friend Blagdon gets back. Not to mention Proudfoot. . . . And what about the other butler and his minions?'

'If we don't bother them,' said Lovell, 'they certainly won't bother us. . . . Shall we go?'

It was death, she thought, that made her feel so randy. John had often said that, and it was true. It was a sentiment that would have horrified his father, but then Stan had never been shot at, shelled, machine gunned, and for three years that had been John's life, that and herself, Jane Whitcomb. And death had made her randy too. She'd seen her share. . . . The act of love, she thought. Life's only reply to death. . . .

'It seemed as if you needed that,' said Lovell.

'I'd like to think we both did.'

'Well of course,' said Lovell. 'I'll always need you. But this time –'

And so she told him, and he listened gravely, attentively, until she had done.

'November?' he said.

'November 10th, 1918,' she said. 'Just one more day to go.'

'You poor darling,' he said, and kissed her. They were naked, yet he kissed her as he might kiss a weeping child.

'It was dreadful,' she said. 'I went mad. I mean quite literally – but I expect you were told?'

'I heard stories,' he said.

'I've no doubt they were true. But I'm not mad now. John's just as dead, but I've learned to accept it.' She turned to him. 'Please let's do it again before Proudfoot gets back.'

But it wasn't Proudfoot who returned from Gosforth Races. This time when Blagdon appeared he wore tweeds so loud as to be deafening, thought Jane, brown boots, and what she rather thought was a billycock hat, also brown; headgear so rare that it must have been specially made for what she thought of as his cast of characters. This time, she thought, he was playing the sort of bookie that her stepfather automatically avoided. 'Honest Joe, the Safe Man', perhaps. He even carried a satchel. What he didn't have was the look of a bookie who had had a good day. Gloom came from him in almost tangible waves.

'Horses are hell,' he said.

'Blagdon Bolter?' said Lovell.

'Fifth,' said the earl. 'In a field of seven.'

'Oh dear,' said Jane.

It was a banal thing to say, and she knew it, but the earl structured his little playlets so that he had the only speakable lines. Very well. Banality it must be. She rose to her feet.

'I'll leave you men to your talk,' she said.

# 6

SHE BATHED IN a copper bath, cowering beneath a vast boiler that loomed above her, the sort of thing that should have provided the steam for a battle cruiser, but in fact yielded only a couple of inches of tepid water. She put on the one evening dress she had brought from London: a glistening affair in blue silk, made by Poiret: a dress she had always thought to be rather pompous, but then this was a pompous house, and anyway it meant that she could wear the sapphires. She needed something to help her through what looked like being an eccentric evening at least – and not just sapphires, she thought: and went downstairs to find the room with the double doors and the hope of a glass of sherry.

Lovell was already there, drinking whisky and water. Even better.

'Get me some of that,' she said, 'before Honest Joe gets here.'

Lovell got up at once, and poured her a drink.

'I don't think he's coming down to dinner,' he said.

'What's he doing?'

'Praying.'

'Oh,' said Jane. Damn the man. Even in his absence he could stop a conversation dead in its tracks.

'He began with what you quite rightly describe as his "Honest Joe" turn,' said Lovell, 'and for once he'd miscast himself. Bookies are never losers. Blagdon was designed by Nature to be a punter, and nothing more.'

'He lost a lot?'

'Pretty well all that was left.'

'All on Blagdon Bolter?'

'So he told me. He seemed to find it difficult to believe it had lost.'

'It wasn't in his script,' she said. 'In the one he wrote Blagdon Bolter romped home at seven to one and he came back here and sent you packing.'

'But that's crazy,' said Lovell.

'Certainly.'

'You think he's mad? I mean really mad?'

'Not exactly raving,' said Jane, 'but I've seen one or two rather better than him at Lockhart's place. The doctor who cured me. – And it takes one to know one, so they say.'

'Don't talk like that.' The words were snapped at her. 'Don't ever compare yourself with him.'

'But I was worse,' she said. 'Much worse.'

'And now you're better. But Blagdon –'

'Does he want to sell?'

'He said he'd have to – unless there was a miracle – and then that set him off again. "That's it," he said. "That's precisely it. Miracles happen. The New Testament's stuffed with them. It's all a question of technique."'

'Technique?' said Jane, fascinated.

'He said it was all in the Bible,' said Lovell. '"These things come not but by prayer and fasting," he said.'

'Which explains no dinner,' said Jane.

'And the praying,' said Lovell. 'Damn it you're right. He must be mad.'

'If he is, he can't sell his house. Or can he?'

'One for the lawyers,' said Lovell. 'But I doubt it. Another drink?' She shook her head, and he poured one for himself.

'You're looking very grand tonight,' he said, 'and me only in a dinner jacket.'

'The only dress I brought,' she said.

'Because it shows off the sapphires?'

'Because it's pompous,' she said, and then the butler came in and announced dinner.

Once again they ate a meal without their host, but this time it was in the state dining room. The butler led the way, and when they went in Jane gasped aloud. 'Being refurbished', Blagdon had said, but that hardly began to explain what they saw. About a quarter of the painted ceiling had been cleaned and the rest remained dimmed with candle smoke, presumably because the money had run out, which no doubt explained why only two and a bit of the nine muses were visible. No doubt it also explained why only one of its six walls had been repainted and gilded. Furniture in storage, thought Jane, would explain why there were only two chairs, one at either end of a table which could accommodate fifty. Firmly the butler led Jane to the foot of the table, then left them briefly.

'He might have given us a couple of telephones,' said Jane, and then: 'Your chum may be crackers, but he knows how to get his own back.'

'This is ridiculous,' said Lovell. 'Get up.' He walked down to her, took her chair, and carried it to the right of his, as the butler came in with the soup, checked for a moment when he saw them, then put down the tureen and rearranged Jane's place setting, served their soup, and left them.

'He may not be so impressive,' said Jane, 'but this one's a jolly sight more matey than Proudfoot. What's his name?'

'Brown,' said Lovell.

'I should have known,' said Jane. 'Your chum's not one for competition.'

Course followed course. There were nine in all, some of them served by the footmen as well as the butler, and all well cooked.

'I should hang on to the kitchen staff,' said Jane.

'I'd be a fool not to.' Lovell ate the last of his devils on horseback, sat back in his chair, and didn't quite groan as Brown came in with a decanter of port.

'There is coffee in the little sitting room, madam,' he said.

'No doubt,' said Jane. 'But there is port here. I'll have some.'

Brown bowed. If not appalled he was deeply shaken, but he brought another glass.

'No problems about passing the decanter,' said Lovell. Together they sipped. 'Good God,' said Lovell. 'It's as old as me. . . . At least. . . . Nectar!'

'What's he up to?' said Jane.

'Blagdon? Telling me I'm the master now, perhaps,' said Lovell. 'He starves and prays, and my fancy woman and I –'

'Your what?'

'My concubine, mistress, chère amie, bit of fluff – whatever phrase excites him – we sit here and dine in splendour.'

'More decaying grandeur, I would have said.'

'At least we dine. All he can do is starve and pray for miracles.'

'Poor Blagdon.'

'Do you really mean that?' Lovell asked.

'No,' said Jane. 'Stupid remark. The people I'm sorry for don't go to live in Hampshire manor houses because they're hard up.'

Lovell grinned. 'I would like to buy this place,' he said.

'I hope you do,' said Jane, and looked up at the ceiling. 'At least you would finish the spring cleaning.'

Together they took coffee in the little sitting room, and yawned over the illustrated papers.

Lovell said at last, 'I shall be going to the States again soon.'

'I shall miss you.'

'My God I should hope so,' he said. 'But maybe you'll come out, too.'

'Maybe,' she said, and then: 'I've got to settle things in Felston before anything else.'

'That's so important to you?'

'Top priority.'

'Lucky Felston,' said Lovell, and added, 'I wish we could have married.'

'What we've got is nice,' she said.

'It isn't enough,' said Lovell, 'but it's all I'm going to get, I know. So I'll take it and say thank you.'

She didn't see Lord Blagdon again. Next morning Brown told her he was still engaged in prayer, and she knew it was true. She could hear him from the hall.

'Let it not pass from me, Lord,' the great voice boomed. 'Thou knowest how intensely I dislike him, but surely he is preferable to a minion of Mammon.'

Lovell joined her in the hallway, just in time to hear himself described, and grinned.

'He knows how to put on a show,' he said.

'Who is it he dislikes so much?'

'The heir,' said Lovell. 'His nephew. Son of his younger brother who was killed at Gallipoli.'

They walked outside.

'A distinguished family despoiled of its heritage,' boomed

Blagdon. 'Unto him that hath shall be given, and from he that hath not shall be taken away, even that which he hath. But do not let him deprive me of my home, oh Lord. Let him not take my dwelling place.'

They moved out to the flight of steps and down to the Daimler, and the voice faded into silence. Jane looked back at the vastness of the house.

'Home?' she said. 'Dwelling place? Really!' and then she asked: 'Were his family so distinguished?'

Lovell snorted. 'Certainly not. One general, two diplomats and a bishop. Not much of a haul for three hundred years.'

'How on earth do you know?' she asked.

'Blagdon told me himself. . . . Do you still think he'll sell?'

'I think he'll have to,' said Jane. 'God won't be very impressed with prayers like that.'

'I'll be in London at the weekend,' Lovell said. 'Telephone me as soon as you're back.'

'Of course.'

They couldn't kiss, not with the butler hovering, resolutely trying not to look like a man who could hear his lordship at prayer. She was sorry they couldn't kiss.

On the way back she thought about Blagdon and his prayers. Stan Patterson would have told him that prayers to God are always answered, but not always in the way one might expect, or even like. He might well have added that to tell vainglorious lies to God about one's ancestry was a daft thing to do.

She made the journey back to Hell from Heaven. The high fells, empty and vast, the grimly surviving castles and the glittering sea, and then the factories, the shipyards, the pits, and their tattered, hungry victims, on the road that led to Felston.

The Eldon Arms first, she thought, and a cup of tea and a sandwich before John Bright Street. When she came into the hotel lounge, there was only one other person in it. It was Bob Patterson. He rose to his feet as she came in.

'There's nothing wrong, is there?' she asked.

'Wrong?'

'I mean you weren't waiting for me?'

'No no,' said Bob. 'Cup of tea's what I'm waiting for. I'm staying here.'

'I see,' she said.

'Well there's not much room at home,' he said, 'and our Bet took the spare bed when she moved in with Frank.' He sounded somehow defensive.

'Very sensible of you,' said Jane, and then, because she couldn't help it: 'What did Andy say?'

'He said the hell of a lot,' said Bob. 'Like if the spare bed was at our Bet's I should move in there and not go lording it with the toffs here.'

'Is that what you're doing?' she said. 'Lording it with the toffs?'

'More than you're doing,' said Bob. 'You're a toff yourself.'

'Of course,' she said. 'Silly of me. How soon one forgets.'

Bob chuckled. 'Catch me moving in with Bet,' said Bob. 'She's a rotten cook and the bairn's always yelling. "They're your own kind," says Andy. "Not any more," I told him. "I'm a capitalist meself now." I thought he would hit us.'

'Would you have let him?'

Bob chuckled again. 'You've got us off by heart,' he said.

'That's not an answer.'

'Best I can do,' he said. 'There's times I never know what I'll do till I've done it – and there's Irish for you.' The tea arrived.

'We'll have to go to John Bright Street after we've finished this,' she said.

'Aye. We will.' He sipped his tea then looked at her, rather warily she thought. 'What d'you think of mourning?' he asked.

'I brought a black coat and skirt,' she said. 'Naturally.'

'I didn't mean that. Will you cry at the grave?'

'Probably. I liked your father.'

'Me an' all. I don't have to be the same as him to do that.'

'Of course not,' she said. 'But what on earth are you leading up to?'

'There's a place on the Newcastle road,' said Bob, 'where we can get a meal and a drink. What they call a roadhouse. There's dancing an' all – but you wouldn't fancy that.'

'Of course not. Your father would have hated it.'

'Da would have hated the whole place,' said Bob. 'I said we were different. – I loved him, like I say. I did, honestly. But I like to enjoy meself sometimes.' He looked at her earnestly: a small boy working hard for his treat. 'If being miserable could bring him back I'd do it,' he said. 'But it won't. Nothing will.'

'I haven't brought the kind of dress one would wear at a roadhouse.' It was a weak reply and she knew it, and in any case what did one wear at a roadhouse?

'Day clothes is fine,' said Bob. 'I asked.'

She said firmly, 'Supper then. Not dinner. We can't leave Grandma till she's ready for bed. And no dancing.'

'Suits me,' he said. 'My heart wouldn't be in it. Not tonight. But I could bear to hear the music.'

'Do you want to tell the others where we're going?'

'No,' said Bob. 'If I did, Andy and me would really have a fight.'

When they got to John Bright Street only Grandma was there, and Canon Messeter. They knelt on the kitchen floor, praying together. Jane and Bob clasped their hands as the canon continued, unhurried: his voice contained a sort of gentle strength that in itself comforted the old woman kneeling on the mat Stan had helped her make out of rags, twenty years before.

'We give Thee hearty thanks,' the canon said, 'for that it hath pleased Thee to deliver this our brother out of the miseries of this sinful world.' And that was the point, thought Jane. Not only did Stan believe he was free of a world that held little but misery, Grandma believed it too. Her face was alight with the knowledge. Tomorrow she will cry again, but the knowledge will stay.

'. . . that we, with all those that are departed in the true faith of Thy holy name,' said the canon, 'may have our perfect consummation and bliss, both in body and soul, to Thy eternal and everlasting glory: through Jesus Christ our Lord. Amen.'

Slowly Grandma straightened her back, and Jane and Bob helped her to her feet.

'I'm glad I heard that one,' she said. 'I doubt Mr Coombs'll use it tomorrow and it always helps me. Thank you, Mr Messeter.'

'You can read it in your prayer book,' Messeter said.

She shook her head. 'It wouldn't be like this,' she said. 'You say it lovely.'

'You're very kind,' Canon Messeter said, and then, 'I must leave you now I'm afraid.' He smiled. 'It's quite safe for Andy to return. There won't be a priest in the place.'

'Meetings,' said Grandma. 'Always meetings. You'd think he

could miss just one – this night of all nights.'

'He wants to save the world,' said Bob. 'You've got to graft to do that.'

'The world has already been saved,' said Messeter, 'but Andy has great compassion, and shows it. It's a rare quality.' He turned to Jane. 'It's nice to see you again,' he said. And he means it, thought Jane. 'Will you be at the funeral?' she asked.

'Certainly,' said Messeter.

'But Da was a Methodist,' said Bob. 'Primitive.'

'It always pays to keep an eye on the competition,' said Messeter. 'You're a business man, I'm told. Surely you know that?' And then he was gone, moving lightly down the stairs. How thin he is now, thought Jane. Attenuated as an El Greco saint. But it isn't because he's starving himself to mortify the flesh, it's because he forgets to eat – or gives his food away.

'What beats me,' said Bob, 'is what that chap was doing here at all.'

'Why shouldn't he?' said Grandma.

'Well you're a Primitive an' all.'

'You haven't been near church or chapel for years,' Grandma said. 'Any more than Andy has. How would you know what I am?'

Bob looked bewildered.

'I changed,' said Grandma. 'I go to the canon's church instead.'

'But why?' Bob asked.

'Because it's beautiful. The words and the vestments and the music. . . . The canon took us on a trip to Durham once. To the cathedral. And if Heaven's as good as that your father's in for a treat.'

She sat down suddenly, and Jane waited, but the old woman was still not ready for tears.

'There's something you should know about religion,' she said. 'My Stan was right, and Mr Coombs is right. But the canon and me, we're right an' all.'

'Like they say at the fairground, every time a prize,' said Bob, but he said it gently, and Grandma chuckled.

'That's right,' she said, and then: 'I'm tired. My Lord I'm tired.' She turned to Jane. 'If you want feeding, the pair of you, I'll have to ask you to get it yourselves.'

'We're all right,' said Jane. 'We've just had a sandwich.'

'You're comfortable in that grand hotel of yours?'

Jane thought of the Savoy in London, the Crillon in Paris, the Arabian Nights splendour of the Garden of Allah in Hollywood.

'Very nice,' she said, and Grandma answered at once.

'Not all that grand, you mean?'

Still shrewd, thought Jane. Old, exhausted, and shrewd.

'Good enough for Felston, I suppose,' Grandma said. 'If my Stan's in a place like that this minute he'll be wishing they'd sent him somewhere he could take his boots off.' She rose to her feet and added cryptically, 'Many mansions,' then went to Bob and kissed him. 'Now you behave yourself tomorrow,' she said, 'and tell Andy I said the same. I'm off to me bed.'

She went to Jane, who put her arms about her and hugged her.

'Good night me bairn,' she said and kissed Jane's cheek.

'Good night, darling,' said Jane.

'Darling,' the old woman said. 'Well now. Nobody ever called me that before in my whole life. I thought it only happened in books.' She went off to her room.

'Many mansions,' said Bob. 'What's all that about?'

'In my Father's house are many mansions,' said Jane. 'Christ said that. Grandma's saying it means that in Heaven there's a choice of accommodation.'

'If there is our Andy'll ask for the Public Library reading room,' said Bob. 'Or a Cambridge college mebbe.'

'And you?'

But before he could answer, Andy came in. He looked them up and down as if assessing the value of what they wore, and Jane was aware of how good Bob's clothes were when compared with his brother's.

'So,' said Andy, 'you're honouring us with your presence.'

'No,' said Bob.

'What do you mean, no?'

'This isn't your house we're honouring,' said Bob, 'any more than it's mine. It was Grandma we came to see, and we've seen her.'

Andy flinched. 'And now you're off?' he said.

'Now we're off.'

'Gallivanting?'

'If that means what I think it means,' said Jane, 'I can only say I'm not surprised. You've always had a penchant for sexual innuendo about me.'

'I didn't mean you,' said Andy.

'Then I'll bid you good night.' She went to the door and turned back. Far better that Grandma's message should come from her.

'Your grandmother left a message for you,' she said.

'What was it?'

'You're to behave yourself tomorrow.'

'And what did she mean by that?'

'I think first of all she wanted to be sure that you would go to the funeral.'

'Of course I'll go.'

'And that once you were there, if you couldn't behave like a Christian, you would at least try to be neutral.'

She went downstairs and sat in the Daimler. It didn't take Bob long to join her.

'You sharp put him in his place,' he said.

'So did you,' said Jane. 'Not his house indeed.'

'Well it isn't,' said Bob. 'Like I said. Any more than it's mine.'

'Then whose is it?'

'Henry Potts,' said Bob. 'The feller who owns it.' And then: 'Oh, I see. You thought it was Da's house?'

'Well of course,' said Jane.

'Only capitalists own houses,' said Bob. 'Ask Andy if you don't believe me. And Da was never a capitalist. Except in Heaven maybe. He might have one of those mansions you were on about. God knows he deserves it.'

# 7

THE HOLLYWOOD INN was on the Hexham road, and pretty well what she'd expected. Rather like the place that dear, drunken Cambridge don had taken her to years ago, the night he'd asked her to marry him. A little larger perhaps, a few more pretensions to grandeur, but like its predecessor creating the impression that the paint had only just dried, that the building itself was no more than a converted barn. And perhaps it was, thought Jane. Our ancestors built barns to last.

But the food and wine were more than passable, and the music – Johnnie Trubshaw's Dixielanders – far better than their name had promised. She settled down to listen: 'Sweet Georgia Brown', 'But Not For Me', 'Our Love Is Here To Stay'. On and on they flowed, and the cornet player knew his business, and so did the clarinettist. At last the music ended, the dance floor cleared, and she was aware that Bob had been speaking to her.

'I beg your pardon,' she said.

'That's all right,' said Bob. 'We're here to enjoy ourselves. That's what I was saying. I'd no idea you liked this kind of music.'

'I told you once,' said Jane. 'Don't you remember?'

And suddenly he did. 'That's right,' he said. 'I'd made a crystal set and tuned in to 2LO. Music at the Savoy Hotel – and you were there that same night. I remember you saying.'

'I heard it in New York too,' she said. 'A man called Beider-becke. At a party.'

'What sort of a party?'

'It was given by a bootlegger,' said Jane.

Bob was delighted, but not in the least surprised. It seemed almost as if he expected it of her: 2LO and the Savoy, Cleopatra in Paris, Beiderbecke and bootleg gin.

'You get about all right,' he said.

'But not in Felston. Not any more.'

'It beats me why you should want to,' said Bob.

'Because this is the only place where I've ever been of the slightest use to anybody since the war. I worked hard here –'

'You did that,' said Bob.

'And I felt good about it. Those bitches have locked me out.'

'To them you're a blackleg,' said Bob.

'How could I be?'

'You're always having a good time, and it shows. Being happy's not a woman's business. Not in Felston.'

She shrugged. There was no point in moaning. She was out and that was that. 'What's all this about Andy and Cambridge colleges?' she asked.

'He goes there sometimes. – To study economics, he says. He learned some an' all. Tapped me for the price of the fare before he even went.'

'Which college?' asked Jane.

'Clare would it be?'

'My brother's a don there now,' said Jane.

'Don?' said Bob. 'Sort of like a teacher?'

'Sort of. He teaches economics.'

'Maybe Andy knows him then.'

Maybe he does, she thought, but Andy wouldn't be nearly pretty enough for Francis. 'How does he live?' she asked.

'Andy? Best way he can,' said Bob. 'Dole, mostly. And the toffs at Cambridge help him from some sort of fund or other.'

'But what does he want to be?' she asked.

'The boss,' said Bob.

'*Andy?*' There could be no hiding her astonishment; her disbelief.

'Oh not a capitalist boss like me,' said Bob. 'A government boss. The feller that bosses everybody.'

She knew at once that Bob was right. 'And will he?' she asked.

'He might. He works at it hard enough. When the revolution comes –'

'And will it?'

She had expected a scornful denial, but it didn't come.

'It's possible,' Bob said. 'Mostly it'll depend on the likes of me – the new fellers from nowhere that believe in getting on. Your lot –'

'The old fellers from somewhere,' she suggested, and he grinned.

'The very same,' he said. 'They've all gone lazy and soft. They couldn't even be bothered to save their own skins.'

'I'm not like that,' she said.

'There's always exceptions,' said Bob. 'And that's another reason Andy's against you. If he started on you and yours you'd go straight for his throat.'

What an Amazon he makes me, she thought, and yet his look was admiring.

'You'd have to go,' he said.

'And you?'

'He'd shoot me,' said Bob. 'He knows I'm – what's the word?'

'Incorrigible?'

'That's the one. So I'd have to go. He'd be sorry, mind. Me being family. Probably give me a little talk about the greatest good of the greatest number before he pulled the trigger. – Unless I shot him first, of course.'

'Could you do that?'

'If Grandma would let me I could,' said Bob, and she laughed aloud. Suddenly by the exit doors, a man's laughter echoed hers, a laughter that seemed familiar, but when she looked, whoever it was had gone.

Regretfully Bob finished the last of the claret in his glass, and the obvious pleasure he took in its taste reminded her of Bower. Here was another of the ones for whom money meant pleasure as well as power. Perhaps it was working for Bower that had taught him.

'We'd better be going,' said Bob, and beckoned to the head waiter for the bill.

'I suppose so,' she said. 'Tomorrow will be a long, hard day. You were right to suggest we come here. I've enjoyed myself enormously. Thank you.'

'Aye,' said Bob. 'Tomorrow will be hard all right. It was good of you to come.'

# 8

THE WORK HAD all been done while she was at Blagdon Hall: the coffin and the refreshments, and the flowers, all except her own, which she bought that morning. A dozen roses in a sheaf, she thought, but Bob wouldn't hear of it. It had to be a wreath, he said, and as big as they could make it. Everyone would know who had sent it, and anything less would make her seem mean as well as uncaring. And so the florist produced a vast, uneasy structure of roses and lilies, gladioli and carnations, in memory of a man who had told her once that roses were his favourite flower, because they were so simple.

The cortege that Bob had paid for was as elaborate as her flowers: a hearse with its coffin drawn by four black horses with plumes, two black horses to each attendant carriage, and the undertaker walking in front like a drum-major before a band.

I shall never see anything like this ever again, she thought, as she got into the second carriage with a group of people she had never seen, behind Grandma and Andy and Bob, and Bet and her husband. The undertaker checked his list and was satisfied, raised his top hat by way of a signal, and moved off, and the horse-drawn vehicles followed. The sound of hooves on cobblestones, the soft clatter of tyres, seemed to Jane to evoke a melancholy that was almost unbearable, and then she realised why. It was the sound that the artillery had made, going up to the Front, each gun and limber drawn by just such patient, plodding beasts as these, and many of them doomed to be shattered, smashed, along with the guns they pulled.

Ten years ago such knowledge would have reduced her to hysterical screaming, but now all she knew was sadness. Stan was gone. The oak coffin they'd put him in, as in a bed, the great sheets and quilts of flowers, bore no relation to that patient, forgiving man whose greatest joy was simplicity. This elaborate and pompous ceremonial was not for him, but then it wasn't meant to be. This was for Grandma and Andy and Bob and Bet, to show Felston that they had loved their son, their father, and that one of them at least had got on well enough to pay for it.

They stopped first at the chapel, and a form of service entirely strange to Jane. There were hymns, a great many, most of them unfamiliar, and for the rest it was mostly Mr Coombs at prayer or in the pulpit, reminding God almost chattily, as he might a kindly neighbour, what a good, believing chap Stan Patterson had been. Then they went back to the carriages and clattered on to the cemetery, which was large and tree lined and covered in grass. Trees and grass alike were black with soot, as were the graves. So many graves, from tiny headstones to elaborate compositions of angels, crucifixes, broken columns, even a chair carved in marble, which looked startlingly like one of a set of six Louis Quinze in her house in South Terrace. From hovel to villa she thought. Many mansions.

Mr Coombs moved majestically to an awaiting grave, and the mourners followed, in stumbling groups, to where the grave-diggers waited, and Mr Coombs launched himself once more into extempore prayer. Jane glanced swiftly at Canon Messeter at the edge of the crowd, and then away. The poor man was doing his best to hide his bewilderment, and failing utterly. Dr Stobbs beside him had the look of one who knew beyond doubt that he would be late for surgery.

Then suddenly Mr Coombs's speech rhythms altered, the very timbre of his voice was changed, and he spoke the words concerning death Jane knew; words last heard at her father's funeral.

'Man that is born of woman hath but a short time to live and is full of misery,' said Mr Coombs, and later: 'In the midst of life we are in death'; and then at last, as the grave-diggers lowered the coffin into the grave: 'We therefore commit his body to the ground; earth to earth, ashes to ashes, dust to dust, in sure and certain hope of the Resurrection to eternal life.' One by one the family moved forward to drop clods of earth on to the coffin: first Grandma, then Andy, then Bob, then Bet and her husband, and then Grandma beckoned to Jane to do the same, and she picked up a lump of soil, heard its dull thump on the coffin lid, and turned away. Behind her she could already hear the scrape of shovels as the grave-diggers began their last task, and still it had nothing to do with Stan Patterson. Nothing at all.

Grandma beckoned once more and she went to walk with her back to the carriages, Bob and Andy on either side of her. There had been cloud all day, and the threat of rain, but no rain had fallen, and now, incredibly, the sun came through the clouds. Jane looked back at the grave. The flowers piled around it glowed like jewels.

'Well at least it stayed fine for him,' Andy said.

Grandma glared at him, suspecting insult, but there was none; merely a statement of fact.

'Your father did a bit better than that,' she said. 'The sun shines on the righteous, they say. Well it's shining on him.'

Then her lower lip quivered, and Jane thought: Now is the time. Now the tears will come, but the old woman straightened her back and clenched her fists, and bade the tears wait their turn. She would not cry among strangers.

They crunched their way down the gravel-strewn path to where the carriages waited to take them back to John Bright Street, and the refreshments that custom demanded: sandwiches and seed cake, and tea for the total abstainers, and sherry and whisky for the rest. Past the Village they went, and the only expensive houses that Felston possessed, then on to Percy Street and the crossroads by the Town Hall, and that was where it happened. The undertaker still strode on, majestic, then suddenly he halted, and swivelled to face them, arm upraised. Jane's coachman, like all the rest, reined in, and she looked out of the window to see what had happened. Faintly on the wind she could hear the sound of music: the rattle of kettle drums to the tune she had heard in Felston many times: 'Blaydon Races', a jaunty marching song she had first heard in France in 1917, when a battalion of the Tyneside Irish had passed her, and their band had thundered. But there was no thunder in what she heard then: the music was thin, wavering, uncertain.

'Well I'm blest,' said the Primitive Methodist beside her. 'I'd clean forgotten it was today.'

'Me an' all,' said Stan's Branch Secretary. 'Let's have a look.'

The two of them left the carriage, and Jane followed. The road to the Town Hall sloped downwards, so that she had a clear view of what happened below, even when people came out of houses and shops, responding to the music's summons.

At first she could see only a crowd of people round the Town Hall, watching, craning as the music grew louder, but shrill and uncertain still, and then they appeared. Children. Children dressed like toy soldiers of the kind her brothers had once played with: blue trousers, red jackets, pill-box hats. At their head was a banner on two poles and ropes painted to look like gold, and on it the words 'Saint Oswald's Lodge Children's Section', and the picture of a winding engine flanked by two miners with pick and shovel, and then more words: 'Unity Is Strength'. The banner moved forward in splendour, and behind it came a girl. Twelve? Jane wondered. Thirteen? Certainly no more. She too was in uniform, with a sergeant's stripes, and a drum-major's baton that in her hands became a magic wand. It spun, rotated, shot up and over and into the air, and the child never missed a beat, never ceased to emphasise the majestic swagger of her marching step. The crowd roared its pleasure.

Behind her came the band, boys and girls all dressed like their drum-major, and playing on instruments that looked like bugles but were in fact things called kazoos, said the Branch Secretary: hardly musical instruments at all, inasmuch as you had to hum into them to get a sound out of them, but they did a good job with the 'Blaydon Races': tots of six or seven in the front, grading up to eleven-year-olds in the last rank. Behind the kazoo players came the drummers, a little older for the most part, rattling out the beat for the music's tale of jaunty disaster, and then, in the rear, a lad of fifteen or so, just and only just big enough to cope with the bass drum he carried.

The band marched on, proud parents in street clothes walking on either side, and then a lorry appeared, grinding along in bottom gear, its cab decorated with ribbons and streamers, and mounted on it a set-piece, made no doubt at the Felston Hall for the Unemployed. Neptune's Grotto it was called, and there he was, a giant sea-shell for a throne, waves curling over his head where a battleship floated with a vast Union Jack. Mermaids surrounded the sea-god, but what decorous mermaids they were, thought Jane. They'd never have done for the Quart' Arts Ball. Still, she admitted fairmindedly, the North East was a chilly place, even in May.

The lorry rattled on, and a bass drum boomed like a gun shot as another band came into sight. These were dressed like miniature guardsmen, and the banner that preceded them said: 'Bethesda Sunday School'. Jane watched as another drum-major gave the beat, keeping her staff close to her side, as the band marched in silence till the bass drum boomed once more, and stiffly, in unison, the kazoo players raised their instruments, the drummers raised their sticks. One more beat from the drum and 'Pack Up Your Troubles' blared, and the drum-major twirled her staff with the same magic as the one before: or perhaps with even more: for this one would on occasion turn back to face her band, the staff still twirling. And again all along the street by the Town Hall, people called out their pleasure.

Then another lorry, this time with a tableau from *Alice in Wonderland*, the Mad Hatter's Tea Party, grinding slowly past. A pretty Alice, thought Jane, and the Mad Hatter was the sharp ex-corporal who had first introduced her to Dr Stobbs. Then the crowd roared again as he and the March Hare lifted the Dormouse into a gigantic teapot.

On and on it went, band after band. Highlanders, Marines, Foreign Legionnaires, and what appeared to be the band of a Roman Legion, too, each interspersed with lorries and tableaux: 'Our Glorious Empire', black, brown and yellow persons looking up devotedly at a Union Jack-bearing Britannia; *The Wind in the Willows* – Ratty, Mole and Badger fighting the weasels and stoats, and at last heartrendingly, 'Felston For Ever', a miner, two shipyard workers and a sailor, all dressed for work *and working*, the miner cutting coal, the riveter and his mate putting in rivets, the sailor on the deck of his ship. This too the crowd applauded, Jane noticed, but there were no yells of delight. This was applause for a point well made. . . . And still it wasn't finished, for after the bands and the tableaux came the fancy-dress parade: the Bo Peeps and the Lillian Gishes and Theda Baras, the Tarzans and Charlie Chaplins and Laurel and Hardys. There was even, Jane saw in astonishment, a Lady Godiva, but with enough blonde hair to swathe most of the horse as well as herself and, Jane was sure, at least three petticoats under that. All the same Jane noted with satifaction that Lady Godiva's feet were blue with cold. In the Cleopatra affair she had been one of Jane's severest critics.

The last of the fancy-dress parade moved on, to be followed by a straggle of small boys, and the crowd by the Town Hall began to break up. Soon it would be possible to move on.

'As good as I've seen,' said the Branch Secretary.

'Good enough,' said the Primitive Methodist, 'but there was no call to exhibit a naked woman.'

'Don't talk daft,' the Branch Secretary said. 'She was about as naked as you are.'

The Primitive Methodist walked away without a word, and the Branch Secretary turned to Jane.

'Touchy feller,' he said. 'Some Primitives are like that. I reckon it must be this repression you read about.'

But Jane had long turned her back on analysis.

'Would you mind telling me what we've just been watching?' she said.

'Carnival,' said the Branch Secretary, and smiled at her astonishment. 'Up here that's nowt to do with Lent. Too cold then. Even with a Lady Godiva wearing two of everything. We hold it in the fine weather. At least we hope it'll be fine.'

'But why?' asked Jane, and it was the Branch Secretary's turn to be astonished.

'Something to do,' he said at last. 'Something to aim at. Bit of competition.'

'Prizes?' Jane asked.

'Nowt special,' he said. 'Tea set maybe, or a biscuit barrel. It's the doing it, you see. The bairns get a day off school, and folks comes miles to watch. It takes their minds off –' He hesitated.

'Off what?'

'Being stuck here in Felston,' the Branch Secretary said.

The funeral tea, everyone agreed, was a great success. Bob had done them proud: four kinds of sandwiches, three kinds of cake, tea by the gallon, sherry, whisky and beer. A real old-fashioned do, was the verdict. Jane took a glass of sherry and went over to Grandma, who sat erect in the best chair in the front room, as she had when Jane first met her, but this time she was flanked by her grandchildren. Jane kissed her.

'Have you eaten today?' she asked.

'I will,' the old woman said. 'But not yet. Don't press us.' For once her voice was almost pleading.

'Then drink some of this,' said Jane, and offered the sherry. The old woman sighed.

'All right,' she said, 'but just a sip mind,' and put the glass to her lips.

'That's more than you'd do for me,' said Bob.

'This one would give us no peace till I did,' Grandma said, and her voice was admiring. Still there was no sign of tears.

'The Carnival didn't upset you?'

'No,' Grandma said. 'Stan was always a great one for the Carnival. I'm glad it was today.'

'Did you spot Lady Godiva?' said Bob.

'She was impossible to miss, surely?' said Jane.

'Covered up from neck to ankles,' said Bob. 'The only thing bare was her feet. Lord Godiva saw to that.'

'Who?' asked Bet.

'Her husband,' said Bob.

'What a daft-looking ha'porth she was,' Grandma said.

'Daft as a brush,' said Bob.

'She can't help the way she is,' said Bet. 'None of us can.'

Grandma turned to her. 'If I'd believed that I'd be where your father is,' she said. 'And you know it's not true anyway. Look at you – with a husband and a bairn.'

Frank, Bet's husband, said, 'She didn't mean it, Grandma. She's upset, that's all.'

'It's a day for upsets,' said Grandma, and turned back to Jane. 'I'll trouble you for another sip of sherry. It's time the wake was started.' She drank again, and the faintest tinge of pink appeared in her face that until that moment had seemed made of ivory. 'What did you make of the Carnival, me bairn?' she asked.

'Incredible,' said Jane. 'Quite incredible.'

'Will you write it up in your paper?' Bet asked.

Now there was an idea, if Bower would wear it.

'If they'll let me,' she said.

Frank took a pull at his beer. 'What's so incredible about it?'

'Why the costumes,' she said. 'The preparation. Work.

Rehearsal. It must have taken for ever. And the cost. The uniforms alone –'

'All hand made,' said Grandma. 'Every one. Needle and thread and a Singer sewing machine for the lucky ones. And the cloth all scraps. What they call remnants. Taken up or let out when the new bairns join the band.'

'But Lady Godiva's hair – surely wigs are terribly expensive.'

Andy chuckled. 'Wig?' he said. 'That wasn't hair.'

'What was it then?'

'New rope,' said Andy. 'Teased out fine. Enough to outfit a ship's lifeboat.' The smile faded. 'What did you make of the tableaux?'

'Very ingenious,' said Jane.

'I was thinking of the last one,' said Andy. '"Felston For Ever".'

'I thought you might be.'

'That was ingenious too?' Andy asked, and his voice hardened.

'Andy man,' said Bob, but Grandma motioned him to silence, her gaze flicking from Jane to Andy like a spectator at a tennis match.

'They were all ingenious,' said Jane. 'They had to be. There was no money. Without ingenuity there would have been no tableaux. But "Felston For Ever" was something else. It was brave.'

'Brave?' said Bet, and Andy flicked a glance at her, amused, then turned back to Jane.

'Tell us why,' he said.

'It's message was obvious,' she said.

'Was it?'

'To me it was. And to the crowd. You could tell by their reaction to it. They didn't laugh. They didn't see it as ironic. But they did applaud, because they'd read the message and believed it. Felston isn't quite ready to die, not yet. Felston can still be saved. The only medicine it needs is a massive dose of work.'

'Right as usual,' said Grandma. 'Clever bairns is a terrible strain at my age.' The pride in her voice was more obvious than ever.

'I agree with you,' said Andy. 'That was the message and I'm proud of it. No dole. No hand-outs. Just wages paid for a job done. But suppose there isn't any work? Any medicine as you call it.'

'You know as well as I do,' said Jane.

'The town will die?'

'We all have to die when our time comes,' Grandma said. 'That's why we're here in this room this minute.'

'When our time comes,' said Andy, 'but not before.' He turned to Jane. 'Am I right?'

'Of course you're right,' said Jane.

'This is all getting too serious for me,' said Bet, and blushed crimson. 'Oh Grandma I didn't mean –'

'I know what you mean. This isn't the time and place for politics. Well it's not. This is the time and place for a bite and a drink, so go and hand round the sandwiches.'

Bet hurried to the fish paste and the potted meat, and her husband followed.

'All the same,' said Andy, 'you got it right, and so far as there is hope, that's where it is. Clever of you to see it.'

'Kind an' all,' said his grandmother. 'There's plenty wouldn't even have bothered their brains to think about it.'

Andy went off to help his sister by offering the tongue and the egg and cress. His grandmother watched him as he moved through the guests. In her best black, with her jet brooch and hair scraped back in a bun, she looked like a picture by Goya, thought Jane. Only the fan was missing.

'I was wrong to say what I did,' she said. 'Any time and place is the right one for politics for our Andy – just like for his father any time and place was right for a prayer.' For the first time her voice shook. 'Oh dear God,' she said. 'Why did he have to go before a silly old woman like me?' And then the tears came at last. Instinctively, without thinking, Jane reached out to hold the slight and shaking body. Still as thin as a stick, but a stick much more ready to break than it had been a few days before.

Grandma cried almost daintily, with no more noise than a few shuddering sighs, while Jane whispered the endearments and consolations she might have offered to a child. Around her the mourners watched, and ate their sandwiches, and approved. It was what death was about, after all. Stan Patterson had been a real nice feller. It was right his mother should weep for him. At last Grandma eased herself from Jane's arms.

'I've done,' she said. 'For now anyway.'

She dabbed at her eyes with the back of her hand, and Bob offered his handkerchief.

'Thanks,' she said, and dried her eyes, then stood a moment with her hands clasped together. As she watched, Jane could see the old woman's courage come back into her, as her shoulders squared, her chin came up. 'There's a few'll expect a word with me before I go to bed,' she said. 'I'll not disappoint them. I'd best start with Mr Coombs. He won't hold it against me that he's chapel and I'm church. Not this once.' She moved off into the crowd.

Bob said, 'They'll never find the pair to my Grandma,' and Jane agreed. They never would.

When she left John Bright Street the – party should she call it? Ceremony? Wake? – was still going on. It wouldn't end, Bob told her, until all the food and drink had gone. But Jane had had enough. Bet had taken Grandma off to bed, and Bob and Andy were more than adequate hosts. Once again Felston had no need of her. Surplus to requirement, as the army said. And there's self-pity if you like, she thought. After just a glass and a half of sweet sherry, too. She moved off to the car, and suddenly a figure on a bicycle appeared. It was Canon Messeter, not quite master of his machine, the skirts of his cassock an additional hazard. He wobbled over to her and managed to dismount before the bicycle threw him. With him up, it took on the characteristics of a horse, and a restive one at that.

'Miss Whitcomb,' said the canon. 'I wonder if I might have a word.'

'Certainly.'

'I was coming back to the Pattersons' house in the hope I might find you. I wonder – there's a little church round the corner. St Oswald's. Do you remember it? We talked there once before. May we go there?'

Jane remembered very well. It had been after Dr Stobbs had told her she could no longer help in the clinic. The canon had pleaded with her not to give up fund raising, and she had agreed. It had not been a difficult decision. The prudes who detested her were one thing: the all-too-visible suffering quite another.

'Of course,' she said, and they walked to the church. Even

when he pushed it, Messeter's bicycle seemed as nervous as a colt, but once inside the church he was a creature restored to its own element, moving down to the chancel steps and dropping to his knees in prayer.

Jane stayed back in the nave, and knelt to say the Lord's Prayer. Faith? she wondered. Good manners? And hoped it was both. When she had done, she looked about her. The same shabby ranks of deal chairs, ageing hassocks, time-worn hymn books. The same green paint, and a green cloth on the altar, covered by another in cheap lace, and on that a brass cross, polished till it gleamed like gold, and flanked on either side by vases of carnations that would soon need renewing.

High above the altar was a crucifix, rather a fine one, in dark wood and what seemed like ivory, and a little chapel on her left was dominated by a framed print of Leonardo da Vinci's 'Madonna of the Rocks' and a Mothers' Union banner. Jane thought that Canon Messeter must be high, use vestments; perhaps even incense not unknown. And then she remembered what Grandma had told her. This must be the church where beauty had seduced her from Primitive Methodism.

At last the canon rose, crossed himself, and came to sit beside her. 'First of all I want to thank you for coming here,' he said. 'Mrs Patterson has told me how much it means to her.'

'It wasn't an obligation,' said Jane. 'Not even a nuisance. I like Grandma. I liked her son.'

He nodded. 'I remember now. You dislike being thanked,' he said. 'Nevertheless what you did is a work of Christian charity. It's as well you should know it. – Like your work for Felston. Your cheques are always most welcome.'

'Now that *is* an obligation *and* a nuisance,' said Jane. 'All the same I do it.'

'With no thought of reward?' the canon asked.

'Driving an ambulance?' He nodded.

'I was useful,' said Jane. 'That's a rare experience for one of the idle rich. I enjoyed it. But I never made it a pre-condition, now did I?'

'You behaved like a lady, and I'm grateful,' said the canon. 'I'm glad to hear that you intend to continue.'

'Things are that bad?'

'No,' said Messeter. 'We continue to ride along quite

adequately at the clinic, which for us is the equivalent of a succès fou. But I still have friends beyond Felston. Some of them are good enough to write to me from time to time, and send me money.'

Another saddhu, she thought. Another holy man. Not a penny in the world, but a dab hand at extracting cash from others.

'Some of them are in the world of finance,' said Messeter. 'And some of *them*, the clever ones, are by no means sure the present state of affairs will continue.'

'Things will get better?'

'Things will get worse,' Messeter said.

'Oh dear God,' said Jane.

Before she could apologise Messeter said to her, 'You do right to call upon Him, Miss Whitcomb. But you see now why we need your money. – And everybody else's.'

'For a rainy day?'

'I rather fear that it will be a downpour.' He hesitated for a moment. 'I understand that you are acquainted with Charles Lovell?'

Really, thought Jane, there was nowhere, nowhere in the world, to touch Felston for gossip.

'Who gave you to understand that?' she asked.

'Mrs Patterson told me of your visit to Blagdon Hall. I found it strange that you should call upon that oaf Blagdon, then I recalled that one of my correspondents told me that Lovell was visiting there, even contemplating buying the place.'

'Amazing, my dear canon,' said Jane, and Messeter smiled.

'Elementary, my dear Miss Whitcomb,' he said. 'But my point is this. If Charles Lovell was or is contemplating the purchase of Blagdon Hall then he must be remarkably rich. We served together in the Rifle Brigade in the war, and I knew him for a reasonably successful banker even then, but to contemplate the purchase of Blagdon Hall argues enormous wealth.'

'And you want me to ask him to give some of that wealth to Felston Clinic?'

'I do indeed.'

'Then I will,' said Jane, 'if you'll answer me one question.'

'I shall do my best.'

'Why did you call Blagdon "that oaf"?'

'He was my fag at school,' said Messeter. 'A loud-voiced, self-opinionated boy with a totally unwarranted faith in his abilities as an actor.'

'Then he hasn't changed much,' said Jane. 'Except that he now seems slightly demented, too.'

'Charles had better look into that before he buys the house,' said Messeter, and then: 'Shall we pray together before we leave?'

And there you had him, thought Jane. Worldly wisdom, financial shrewdness and a kind of sanctity, all combined in that thin ascetic's body. She was on the train heading South, and it was the view of Durham Cathedral from the train that made her think of him. Grandma had thought it a foretaste of Heaven, and so it was, a Heaven that had regard for strength as well as beauty. As the train steamed past, the sun lit up the incredible splendour of that blackened stone. She watched until she could no longer see it, then lay back in her seat to think about the canon. That he thought her to be Charles's mistress was obvious. It was equally obvious that he didn't give a damn. What he cared about was Felston Clinic, and any trick, any device, was justified to achieve that end. Love God, help your neighbour, and live and let live. No wonder he and Grandma got on so well. They were two of a kind.

# 9

GRANDMA HAD CRIED when she had left, but not bitterly, and not for long, drying her eyes briskly to mark the end of self-indulgence, and telling Jane not to leave it so long till next time, then turned back to her potatoes on the fire. The strength was coming back into her, would stay till she died, but that surely could not be so very long now. It was a thought she did not want to face, and so she thought of London instead. She would be seeing Lovell soon, and get money for Felston by playing la grande horizontale. She had to see Bower too, and coax him into taking an article about the Carnival, and she had to buy a wedding present for him and Catherine, and what did one buy the man who has everything?

Then she had to see Lionel Warley. It was high time that he took her out to dinner again, or a party. The best dancer in London had no business neglecting her. Maybe she would coax him over to Paris to help her choose some new frocks. . . . Suddenly she found herself thinking about Bob. He must be making lots of money, she thought. The casual way he spent it showed that, and his clothes, and the way he'd behaved in that roadhouse place. He and Andy really were like the two faces of the same coin: both shrewd, both in their own way ambitious, though Bob hid it better. And Andy had got to Cambridge. Would the fund, whatever it was, help him into a college, take a degree? With Andy anything was possible, but she doubted whether he'd shut himself up for three years when there was so much to be done. The steward called, and she went to the restaurant car for lunch.

## 10

I T SEEMED THAT the servants were pleased to see her back in South Terrace. Even Foch, in his austere way, allowed her to assume that he was pleased. Quite a lot of people had written or called, including Bower (two telephone calls and a note), which under the circumstances was gratifying. A note from Lionel too (Darling I must see you *soonest!*), and two calls from her brother Francis. What on earth can he possibly want? she wondered. That he wanted something was obvious, otherwise why spend money on long-distance calls? She telephoned Lionel and invited him to dine with her, and perhaps go on to the Gargoyle or somewhere and dance. He accepted at once.

'Such goings on since you've been away,' he said. 'Really you shouldn't leave me on my own so much. You know how unreliable I am.' But more he would not say till they met, and so she went upstairs to dress. The Molyneux in blue and white, she thought, but *not* the new necklace. That was far too grand for the Gargoyle, and anyway, Lionel would be bound to be nosy. She opened her jewel case and took out the diamonds Aunt Pen had given her, and beside them was the little Cartier leopardess, gold, diamonds and rubies, another gift of Aunt Pen's. 'This is you,' Aunt Pen had said. 'That's why I had to buy it for you. It couldn't belong to anyone else.' She touched it lightly with one finger, then became aware that Foch was looking at her.

He must think I'm demented, she thought, standing here in my knickers, stroking one gew-gaw and fondling another.

'Allow me to inform you,' she told Foch severely, 'that there are quite a lot of gentlemen who would pay a great deal to see me like this.'

Foch snorted. No doubt he knows that a couple of them already have, she thought, and reached for the Molyneux dress.

Her mother telephoned as she came downstairs and paused for one last look in the hall mirror. Lionel was her severest critic.

'Hello, Mummy,' she said. 'You're well, I hope?'

'Extremely,' said her mother. 'George too, I'm happy to say. The flat season continues to do well by him.'

As if it were the flat season's obligation, thought Jane.

'And you?' her mother continued. 'How was the funeral?'

'Sad, of course,' Jane said, 'but not excessively so. I've a lot to tell you, Mummy.'

'Then we must meet,' said her mother, 'but not before Ascot I fear. The flat season is extremely demanding.'

She has never been happier, thought Jane, delighted for her.

'It was because of Francis that I called,' her mother said.

'He's phoned me twice,' said Jane. 'What on earth does he want?'

'It seems that your brother has developed social ambitions,' said her mother. 'Doubtless professional ambitions are involved also. However that may be he is desirous of getting up a party for the May Ball at his college. May Balls, as you know, are held in June. – How tiresomely whimsical the older universities can be. – Francis is finding some difficulty in putting together the right sort of party. He even suggested that George and I might attend, but I was obliged to decline. The flat season will be at its height.'

'And now he's after me, faute de mieux?'

'There isn't any faute de mieux about it,' her mother said. 'He'll be lucky to get you, and so I told him.' There was a pause. 'Will you go?'

'Probably,' said Jane. 'If he asks me nicely. But it's all rather tricky, isn't it? I mean the last time he took me to a dance was a disaster.'

Rather more than that, if Mummy did but know it. She had ended up tight on champagne, and without the help of Hawkins, Mummy's housemaid, God alone knew what her punishment would have been.

'My fault, I have no doubt,' her mother said, and Jane knew she meant it. 'But then neither one of us understood the other in those days. Now I think you'll agree it's different. All I'm asking is that you do your brother a favour.' There was a pause, then: 'I take it you do know why your brother has a problem in asking females to dances?'

'Yes, Mummy.'

'Of course you do.' Once again Jane was quite sure there was no, or at the most very little, intention to wound.

'I went to a party he gave at Cambridge once,' said Jane. 'He didn't seem exactly overjoyed.'

'I don't suppose he was,' her mother said. 'I have no doubt that you were a raging success. Not exactly what's expected of a sister at her brother's party. But this time I gather he *wants* a raging success. Do give him one, won't you?'

'If he asks me nicely,' said Jane once more, and there they left it.

She put the phone down, and went to check the ingredients for the dry martinis – Lionel made an awful fuss about dry martinis – and as she did so the telephone rang again. This time it was Bower.

'Do you spend your entire life on the goddam phone?' he said.

'Such language,' said Jane. 'I was talking to my mother.'

'Oh,' said Bower, then added surprisingly: 'I like your mother.'

'What you mean is you like my stepfather because he's good for your paper.'

'Isn't he just,' said Bower, 'and doesn't your mother make me pay for it? All the same I like her. How would you like to go to New York?'

'Any particular reason?'

'To write some pieces for me, idiot.'

'Goodness,' she said. 'How persuasive you are. When?'

'Before my wedding. September say. You could weekend in New England. It's lovely then.'

'I remember,' she said.

'Hey, that's right,' said Bower. 'That's when you stayed at my father's place. Not that you have to stay there this time.'

'Just as well,' she said.

'OK,' said Bower. 'It didn't work. But we had fun together.'

'Frequently.'

'*Will you go?*' Bower's voice was a howl.

'Yes,' she said. 'I'll go. But I've got an idea for another piece before then.'

'Let's have it.'

She told him about the Carnival at Felston.

'That sounds just great,' he said, 'and it's just the right slant for the *Daily World*. I'll take it as soon as you've done it. OK?'

As he spoke the doorbell rang, and Truett, the parlourmaid, sailed past to admit Lionel Warley, who went at once to Jane and kissed her cheek.

'I said OK?' said Bower.

'I heard you,' said Jane. 'Of course OK. I was being kissed by a strange man.'

'A very strange man,' said Lionel.

'Give Warley my regards,' said Bower, 'and don't forget – New York in the fall. That's definite.'

How odd, she thought, for Bower to make an offer twice, especially when he's paying.

She went into the drawing room where Lionel was already mixing dry martinis, exact as a chemist, grave as a priest. At last he poured, and handed her a glass.

'How could one exist without them?' he asked.

'Mortify the flesh, I suppose,' said Jane.

'My flesh has been mortified quite enough, thank you,' said Lionel.

'Oh darling,' said Jane. 'You're not in love again?'

'Not any more,' said Lionel. He sipped his martini, approved its contents and continued: 'The most divine ship's purser. Young and blond and Scandinavian. He worked on a liner of something called the Fred Olsen Line. The way he said it even that sounded erotic. I was going to take a cruise with him. Fjords and mountains, and long, long sunsets.'

'But why didn't you?'

'He left me,' said Lionel. 'For another. Not, I hasten to say, another old queen like me. For a woman.'

'Oh you poor poor thing,' said Jane.

'A Norwegian woman,' said Lionel. 'A widow, who had inherited a million kroner or whatever they are. He wrote to tell me they were married last week, but he said we could still be friends. I could have killed him.' He finished his martini and poured another. 'And you?' he said. 'Are you well?'

'Well enough,' said Jane. 'The funeral was sad of course, but the most extraordinary thing happened after it. I'm to write an article about it for the *Daily World*.'

'Tell me when it appears and I'll buy a copy.'

Jane sipped her martini. 'Mm,' she said. 'It is good to have you back.'

'Any more news?' said Lionel.

'Bower wants me to go to New York to write articles in what he calls the fall.'

'Does he indeed?' said Lionel.

'And I've been asked to a ball at Cambridge.'

'Cambridge?' Lionel spoke the word as if it must have a meaning of some sort, but that for the moment it escaped him. Lionel had attended Magdalen College, Oxford.

'It's to help my brother Francis,' she said. 'He wants to cut a dash at what they call a May Ball.'

'What we call a Commem,' said Lionel. 'I wish you joy, my dear.'

'Would you like to come?'

'If you want me to,' said Lionel, 'but three ladies together might look rather odd, wouldn't you say?'

'I gather he wants to get up a party.'

'Then of course I'll come.'

'How sweet you are,' said Jane. 'Just for that you can take me to Paris and help me try on some new frocks. But no more sailors. Not till after Cambridge. We can't have you attending a May Ball in floods of tears.'

Mrs Barrow, Jane's cook, was devoted to Lionel, who praised her best efforts in a knowledgeable, discriminating way. She was also glad to see Jane back, with the result that dinner was sumptuous in the extreme, and Lionel ate far too much and drank rather a lot of burgundy, an exercise he described as drowning the purser.

'Do we have to go to the Gargoyle?' he asked as they took coffee.

She looked at his white tie: 'We're a little overdressed for rolling back the carpet and dancing to the gramophone,' she said.

'It's just that there's a rather smart party we could go to,' Lionel said. 'Soho's such a journey at this time of night.'

'Whose smart party?'

'Cynthia Townsend. She's in Knightsbridge. Just round the corner, really. A vague sort of cousin of mine. Married to a man who makes agricultural machinery.'

'And money, no doubt.'

'In fair quantity. . . . We could just as easily dance there.'

'Are you sure we won't seem overdressed?'

'If I know Cynthia,' said Lionel, 'we'll look like poor relations.'

The party was being held at a big, ugly house near the barracks, and Mr Townsend must be doing well, thought Jane. He owned all of it. Mrs Townsend greeted her vague sort of cousin with enthusiasm, kissing lavishly and screeching like a macaw, until Lionel made her put him down and introduced Jane as 'Jane Whitcomb, the celebrated writer and sociologist'. Mrs Townsend assessed the value of Jane's diamonds, and allowed her into her drawing room.

'That was a rather rotten thing to say,' said Jane. 'Writer and sociologist indeed.'

'*Celebrated* writer,' said Lionel. 'Cynthia enjoys celebrities. Tomorrow she'll tell her secretary to find out what you've written, then she'll boast about you for weeks.'

The drawing room had been cleared for dancing: Lionel's foxtrot was as perfect as his martinis. He really is a darling, thought Jane. Every girl should have one. . . .

Around her was more evidence of the Townsend wealth. Pictures that were fashionable and expensive, furniture hardly less so, hired waiters and champagne. And a trio, piano, tenor saxophone and drums, that played very well indeed. The pianist in particular was enjoying the rare treat of the Townsend Bechstein. She had never heard 'But Not For Me' played better.

For the most part their fellow guests seemed merely rich and smart, with a tendency among the women to wear far too many jewels, as Lionel had hinted. But then she saw two dancers who weren't like that at all.

'Two more celebrities present,' said Jane.

'Do I know them?'

'Michael Browne,' said Jane. 'The painter. He was at the party where I first met you.'

'I remember,' said Lionel. 'He was very drunk.'

'He's dancing with Sarah Vane.'

'The actress?' Jane nodded. 'Well well,' said Lionel. 'Cynthia's little heart will be all aglow. Do you know Miss Vane?'

'We used to drive ambulances together in the war.'

'Well well *well*,' said Lionel. 'A night for the annals.'

The dance ended, a waiter brought champagne, and soon a determined creature in pink, and diamonds that needed cleaning, hinted and cajoled until Lionel asked her to dance. Fair-mindedly Jane admitted that it would be wrong, even impossible, for her to monopolise such a partner at a party – but not that pink, not with dirty diamonds as well. Then Michael Browne came over to her. He was one of the few men there in a dinner-jacket, but he was an artist and a name. No doubt Mrs Townsend would have accepted him in plus-fours and a fisherman's jersey. Firmly Jane told herself not to be bitchy, but she knew from experience that Michael Browne was a rotten dancer.

'It's been a long time,' he said.

'It has indeed.'

'Not since that ghastly flat in Fulham where I lived with Georgie.'

'The day your wife turned up and tried to slash that picture of Georgie with the carving knife.'

Best to get that one out of the way at once. Jane and Georgina Payne had been friends, good friends, and the picture she had mentioned was a nude, perhaps the most lush and exotic thing Browne had ever done. That was when Jane and Jay Bower had been lovers, until the day she had discovered Georgie's picture in Bower's flat at the top of the *Daily World* building in Fleet Street. She was quite sure that Georgie had no idea that they were sharing Jay, but even so it had been time to move on.

'My God I'd forgotten you were there that day,' said Browne. 'Talk about la vie de Bohème. Do you ever get any word of Georgie?'

'Last seen in Hollywood,' said Jane. 'We were both being very grand at the Garden of Allah Hotel.'

'She still is being very grand there,' said Browne. 'Would you like to dance?'

Of course she had to lie and say yes, but then, she thought,

– 93 –

he probably didn't want to dance anyway. He must be perfectly well aware how bad he is. Deftly she managed to steer him without making it too obvious that she was doing so.

'I miss her dreadfully,' said Browne.

'Georgie?'

'Who else?' he said, but he was sad, not angry.

'Georgie said you'd found another lady.'

'Well so I did,' said Browne. 'I found several. But they were none of them any good. When you've been used to caviar you've no taste for cod's roe.'

Thank you on behalf of fifty per cent of the human race minus one, she thought, but still she couldn't be angry. He meant every word, even if he was probably living with some girl or other even now. 'Nevertheless, Michael darling,' she said, 'do you think you could bear to concentrate just a little? "Look For The Silver Lining" is not a waltz.'

Michael Browne begged pardon and concentrated till the end of the dance, and then: 'Do you think Georgie would have me back?' he asked.

Before she could answer – and what could she answer? – Cynthia Townsend came up and led Jane away. Celebrities were there to be shared, Jane gathered, passed round like the Bollinger. She found herself dancing with a fat man who talked about racing, and reminded her of Lord Blagdon.

Fat men, thin men, tall men, short men, and only two more dances with Lionel, but she did insist that he took her into supper. Once she saw Sarah Vane and waved, and Sarah headed towards her, but Cynthia Townsend was too quick for them, and herded her into the arms of the fat man to be told about racing. Supper was lobster salad and Chablis, and very nice too, but she wished very much that they had gone to the Gargoyle, and said so.

'Me too,' said Lionel. 'Serves me right for being so lazy.'

'It doesn't serve me right.'

'But you owe me a good deed,' said Lionel. 'I said I'd go to Cambridge.'

'I don't see why you wanted to come here anyway.'

'Because Agricultural Machinery owns a house at Cap d'Antibes,' said Lionel. 'If I'm specially sweet they'll invite me.'

'Oh well,' said Jane. 'Anything to help a friend. By the way, who is Agricultural Machinery?'

He turned out to be the fat man who talked about racing.

As she finished her lobster salad Sarah Vane came by. Jane turned, but Sarah put a hand on her shoulder. 'Don't get up,' she said. 'The Townsend cow's got eyes in the back of her head. Come and powder your nose in five minutes.' She went away before Mrs Townsend could intervene.

'What was all that about?' said Lionel.

'Celebrities aren't allowed to talk to each other. House rules.' She finished her Chablis and rose. 'Why don't you go and ask Agricultural Machinery for a dance?' she said. 'He knows the devil of a lot about Uttoxeter. *And* Chepstow.' Then she went upstairs to what she had heard called the ladies' retiring room, which was in fact a bedroom en suite, where Sarah Vane stared darkly into a mirror as if she disliked what she saw. Which was ridiculous, thought Jane. Sarah had never looked more beautiful.

Both women said 'Darling', and kissed, a ritual as formal as the steps of a minuet, but to some degree both women meant what they said.

'That *cow*,' said Sarah. 'To think we have to hide in the lavatory just to say hello.'

'We're celebrities,' said Jane.

'Well yes,' said Sarah. 'I suppose we are.'

She started to giggle, and in a few seconds Jane did, too, then suddenly the two women embraced warmly and honestly, the memory of wounded men, ambulances, field hospitals, in their touch.

'How are you darling?' Sarah asked.

'Very well.'

'I must say you look well. And such a dress.'

'And you?' said Jane. 'And Mr Beddoes?'

'Mr Beddoes,' said Sarah. 'Don't you ever read the papers?'

'Oh darling,' said Jane. 'Not again?'

But this time, it seemed, Mr Beddoes had left Sarah and had gone to the South of France with a chorus girl.

'Not even the legitimate theatre,' said Sarah. 'I must have been mad to marry him.'

'And now you're divorcing him?'

'Oh yes,' said Sarah. 'He's still quite rich you know. – And talking of being rich, have you come across Bob Patterson lately?'

'I was at his father's funeral two days ago,' said Jane. 'But I didn't know you knew him.'

'Don't you remember,' said Sarah, 'we all went up there for that Charity Concert? Georgie Payne, and that debby girl who's going to marry Jay Bower –'

'Catherine Hilyard,' said Jane.

'That's the one. And you and me. You wrote a sketch for me. – People still ask for it. It's lovely. – And that village Romeo of yours danced with us all, one after the other.'

'Of course I remember,' said Jane. 'But that's not to say you knew him.'

'Well I do now.' Sarah looked at her. 'It's all a bit personal,' she said. 'If you don't want to hear –'

'Of course I want to hear.'

'I went to a party some BBC people gave,' Sarah said. 'Mostly writers and producers and madly highbrow, and then somebody must have remembered that if you're going to listen in you have to have a set, and so they invited Bob. He runs that radio business, you know. PWR. Patterson's Wireless Rentals. Surely he told you?'

'He did say something,' said Jane. 'But I'd no idea it was such a success.'

'My dear it's a runaway,' said Sarah. 'All the intellectuals hated him at first.'

'But why on earth should they?'

'Because he never went to Oxford. Or even Cambridge.'

'Was he upset?'

'Not in the least,' said Sarah. 'He just stood there all shining clean in his brand new Savile Row suit, and answered all their barbed witticisms in that incredible accent of his – and of course they melted.'

'Did they?'

'Well of course they did. His very voice told them what cads they were, making elegant fun of a poor working-class boy who'd never been to public school. Poor indeed. He could have bought and sold the lot of them. My dear they simply surrendered. It was bliss.'

The door to the bedroom began to open, and Sarah continued to speak, her voice trembling on the edge of hysteria: 'But of course these attacks don't last very long, though I do scream rather a lot. And if a stranger comes in unexpectedly I can't be answerable for the consequences. I'm much stronger than I look.' The bedroom door closed.

'Did you tell him so?' asked Jane. 'That it was bliss?'

Sarah looked up sharply. 'As Bob would say,' she said, 'you're so sharp you'll cut yourself. I fell in love with him.'

'There and then?'

'There and then. Especially after he told me he'd only come to the party because he'd been told I was there. Of course I knew it was a lie, but what a sweet thing to say. We had the most gorgeous time.'

'For long?'

'Three – four weeks,' said Sarah. 'Of course you might think he was a little young for me –'

'Not at all,' said Jane.

'My sentiments exactly. And my dear there's a lot to be said in favour of the younger man, I assure you. But then Beddoes decided there was a lot to be said in favour of the younger woman, too, and found himself this tart in the chorus, and of course I had to kiss poor Bob goodbye.'

'But why?'

'My dear,' said Sarah, 'I realised at once that this time I really must divorce the old bugger, and having Bob in tow was hardly likely to help my case, now was it? So it was: Since there's no help, Come, let us kiss and part. Which we did. Then a part came up in the new Lonsdale play, and my lawyers put the wind up the old bugger so effectively he's allowing me to divorce him. Undefended suit and oodles of alimony. So all's well that ends well.'

She looked once more into the mirror, and smiled. 'Funny thing though.'

'What?'

'As he was leaving, Bob asked me if I ever heard from Georgina Payne these days.'

'Most odd,' said Jane. 'Michael Browne was asking me the same thing half an hour ago.'

'Popular girl, dear Georgie,' said Sarah, and sighed. 'Of course one sees why.'

'One does indeed.'

'A film star,' said Sarah, sighing again, 'with a *huge* salary. I keep telling myself she'll never play Lady Macbeth, but somehow it is *no* consolation.' She examined her face in the mirror. 'Back to the merry throng, I suppose. When I accepted an invitation to this party I had no idea I'd be passed round like a packet of wine gums, and I bet you didn't either.'

The two went downstairs together, and Mrs Townsend pounced at once.

# 11

NEXT DAY SHE began work on the Felston Carnival piece, and had begun the third sencence when Francis telephoned.

'Where on earth have you been?' he said.

'To a funeral,' said Jane. 'In Felston.'

'Oh.'

Francis did not approve of Jane's visits to Felston. She went because she was sorry for the people who lived there, to help them, and cared not one jot for correct Marxist attitudes or the dialectical approach, even though she had quite a decent brain.

'Have you talked to Mummy?' he asked.

'Last night.'

'Did she tell you to come to our May Ball?'

'Of course not,' said Jane. 'Mummy and I aren't like that any more, and I bet Mummy and you aren't the way you were either. – I beg your pardon?'

'I didn't speak,' said her brother, but he had. He had said 'Bloody Routledge' and said it as if he meant it, what's more.

'I told her I'd come if I was asked and if I had nothing better to do.'

'Don't put yourself out, will you?' said Francis.

'Not to go to a May Ball and dance with my brother.'

'It's frightfully important, Jane,' he said. 'I mean it's not just the dance – I couldn't care less about dancing, as you know. But if I want to get on academically it's been hinted I should be a bit more social. So if you wouldn't mind. – It's on the ninth of June.'

'I'll look in my book.' She reached for her diary and thought,

This is ridiculous. No one gets a professorship by going to the right cocktail parties. He must have a new boyfriend.

'The ninth's free,' she said. 'Book me in at that hotel. The nice one.'

'The Baron of Beef,' said Francis. 'Thanks, Jane. You – you couldn't persuade any more people to come?'

'What sort of people?'

'Your sort. You know.'

'Smart?' She had to force him to say it. Even when he cajoled he was grudging.

'Yes. That sort,' Francis said. 'It would make all the difference, Jane.'

'Mummy sort of hinted you might ask,' said Jane. 'She turned you down, I gather.'

'The major has to go to the races,' said Francis bitterly.

'It's what they pay him for. How many of us smarts do you want?'

'Six would be perfect,' said Francis. 'I really must go. These long-distance calls cost the earth.'

He didn't add, 'And Aunt Pen didn't leave me any money,' thought Jane, though he might just as well have done. He hung up instead.

Who to invite? She had already booked Lionel for herself to dance with. Francis would detest him, but that was not the point. Lionel was very smart indeed, and that was the object of the exercise. . . . The object of the exercise. . . . John had learned that phrase in the army, when he'd been sent on the officers' course, and for some reason it had fascinated him. It had even become part of their love talk. 'The object of the exercise is to achieve matrimony, and make all this hand-to-hand combat respectable.' Suddenly she could see John clearly, hear his voice. She couldn't, always, not after all these years. . . .

Who to invite? Who else was smart? Not Harriet Watson or her husband Alistair, and anyway they'd be far too busy to go. Catherine Hilyard was smart, and really rather beautiful. She also liked Jane, which would be a help, but then if she went, Bower would have to go, too. It would be a triumph if she could persuade Bower to go. And two more. No, three. Because Francis's maths were all wrong, or more likely his knowledge of dances. Six plus Francis equalled seven. Another couple was needed, and a spare female. Bob Patterson! He was not smart in the Lionel sense of the word, but he danced well and talked amusingly, and his brother seemed to be the pet of the place. She'd have to find a girl for him, or, more likely, he'd insist on bringing his own. She'd have to risk that. Bob at Cambridge would be a sight worth seeing, especially if Andy were there too. One more female. Sarah would have been nice, but not with Bob there, and anyway she was rehearsing. If only Georgie were still about. It will have to be Brenda Coupland, she thought. Brenda was pretty, rich, and far too fond of recounting the number of times she'd danced with the Prince of Wales, but she was undoubtedly smart. Every gossip column in London testified to the fact.

She realised that she hadn't even considered Lovell, but that was not surprising. They never formed part of a crowd in London if they could avoid it, but went to quiet restaurants and clubs where they were not known. Both of them preferred it that way. She must telephone Lovell soon, but first she must talk to Bower, before her courage failed her.

Lovell took her to lunch at l'Apéritif. Champagne cocktails first, then early asparagus, Dover sole, and a wickedly fattening Chantilly cream. And hock. All quite scrumptious.

'You do know how to make a girl feel wanted,' she said.

'You are wanted,' said Lovell. 'At least –' She waited. 'At least I want you as much as you'll let me.'

It was gracefully done, but it was not what he had started out to say.

'Tell me about Blagdon Hall,' she said, and took out her cigarettes and holder.

'Not much to tell,' said Lovell. 'Blagdon stopped praying eventually and must have come to the conclusion that God was on my side, because he agreed my price. It's with the lawyers now.'

'So you don't think he's really potty?'

'As a matter of fact I do,' said Lovell, 'but I got a couple of mental specialists to have a look at him. Couldn't risk a contract like that on a maniac. They say he's sane – for now anyway.'

This was a ruthless side of Charles Lovell she had never encountered before. He had meant every word.

'Was one of them Jabber Lockhart?'

'Yes,' said Lovell. 'It was.'

'If Jabber says Blagdon's sane then he is. After all Jabber told me I was sane – after a bit – and it was true.' Not like your wife, she thought. Your wife will stay mad till she dies.

'Go on about Blagdon,' she said.

'Nothing left to tell. He changed into that terrible bookmaker's suit of his, borrowed twenty quid from me and went off for a night on the tiles in Newcastle. I didn't know they had those sort of tiles in Newcastle.'

'That's just your London–Paris–New York grandeur,' said Jane. 'They have all sorts of tiles in Newcastle, and outside it too. There's a roadhouse called the Hollywood Inn, for instance.'

'Indeed there is,' Lovell said. 'He went there.'

'So did I,' said Jane. 'With Bob Patterson. It was the night before the funeral. We both felt utterly miserable and went to this haunt of Tyneside's jeunesse dorée. We didn't dance of course, but the food was decent.'

'I know you were there,' said Lovell. 'Blagdon told me.'

'I thought I heard a laugh I remembered,' said Jane. 'It must have been his. But when I looked round he'd gone.'

'Blagdon said you seemed very intense. Very close.' His face told her nothing, but she was aware of what drove him on to speak as he did.

'So we were,' she said. 'Next day we were going to bury a man we both cared for dearly, and the man's mother would be there too, an old woman who is infinitely precious to both of us. We certainly were intense. And sharing a love for someone is a bond that ties you closely. But I only sleep with one man at a time, Charles, and you can tell Lord Blagdon I said so.'

'He was out for revenge,' said Lovell, 'and he took it. I didn't say I believed what he was hinting at.'

'Do you?'

'No.' The one word was enough. She knew he meant it.

'That's all right then. Pompous old sod.'

'Me?' Lovell was bewildered. She had never spoken like that before.

'Blagdon, you ass. – Are you working this afternoon?'

'Only if I have to,' Lovell said.

'I want you to work,' said Jane. 'I want you to work jolly hard.'

'We're going back to Jermyn Street?'

'Yes we are,' said Jane. 'We'll show old Blagdon where he gets off.'

Messeter had known Blagdon. 'That oaf Blagdon', he had called him. Charles would be amused when she told him. But that would be after all his hard work, when he was lazy and relaxed and acquiescent, when she'd put him in the mood to spare a copper for Felston Clinic.

She got it too. A handsome cheque, *very* handsome, which wasn't bad considering the delight they had shared. A good time was had by all, in fact, but the best time would be had by Felston, which was as it should be, and all because of that old whoremonger Messeter. Well, she thought, even if that extraordinary parson has no more illusions, neither have I.

Lovell said, 'You're looking very thoughtful.'

'And so I should,' she said. 'I'm off to Cambridge.'

'Good Lord, why?'

Another Oxford man, she thought, and then: well of course he is. Winchester and Christ Church. She'd looked him up in *Who's Who.*

'We weren't born into the world for pleasure alone,' she said, and told him about the May Ball.

'Who's going?' he asked.

'My young friend Bob,' she said, 'and his friend, who is something called a speciality dancer. I gather that the speciality is being able to dance with very little clothes on. I trust she won't feel obliged to do that at Cambridge. And Lionel, whom you know, and Brenda Coupland, whom you must have read about. And that's it, really. I tried to get Bower and his fiancée, but he declined.'

'Why?'

'Pressure of work,' she said. 'Surely you know all about pressure of work?'

'I did a little while ago,' he said. 'Why Bower?'

'Something of a triumph,' she said. 'Just as Catherine Hilyard would have been.'

'Mm,' he said. 'I see what you mean. Now you'll have to make do with somebody a little less glamorous?'

She pulled on a stocking.

'If I can find them,' she said. 'It's awfully short notice. Oh by the way, I'm going to New York quite soon. What I mean is I'd have gone there anyway, but it's nice to have a reason. I'm going to do some pieces for the *Daily World*.'

'So we'll see each other.'

'You'll have no choice,' she said, and kissed him. 'You really are awfully nice.'

'Felston's worth every penny,' he said, which only went to show, she thought, that he isn't just awfully nice. He's awfully clever, too.

She and Lionel flew to Paris. They had very little time, and anyway Lionel still adored flying. He had been a pilot in the Royal Flying Corps during the war and the contrast with civilian aircraft delighted him. 'Like a semi in Penge with wings,' he said. Paris was mostly Chanel, that time, because Worth and Poiret still could not rid themselves of the idea that unrestricted movement was not for the woman of fashion. 'Cribbed, cabined and confined,' said Lionel. 'Not for you, my dear. Indeed not.' So they spent their time in the rue Cambon. Coco Chanel was a bully of course: (she was not only French and a genius, but female as well, as Lionel explained) but Lionel also could be quite waspishly aggressive – after all, he'd won a DSC for being just that – so that in the end Jane bought nothing that she did not want, and included among her triumphs a black evening gown with a mid-calf, swirling skirt and bare back. Far too good for Cambridge, as Lionel said, but at least it would give them something to think about. He'd been told that Cambridge was rather keen on thinking.

For the rest Lionel decided that it was time to seek a little culture, which was delightful when it meant going to the Ballets Russes, but a little wearing when it meant soirée after soirée with Gertrude Stein, or the Princesse de Pelignac, or Natalie Barney. Poetry, music and painting, little of which she admired, and much she found boring, and egos that became impatient if her admiration faltered for a second, even in English.

'Are all the arts patrons lesbians?' she asked at last.

'Every single one,' he said proudly. 'Isn't it splendid?'

'No, it's not,' she said. 'It's a bit late in the day for me to have to fight for my honour.'

'Oh you poor thing,' said Lionel, and took her at once to La

Coupole, to look at the Russian emigrés there.

It was a big café in Montparnasse, and a lot of its character was derived from its customers. Before the war they had been political exiles like Trotsky brooding over coffee and newspapers, planning the great things they would achieve when the dawn came. When it did come (nobody perhaps more surprised than La Coupole's habitués) they moved eastwards en masse, to be replaced almost at once by another tide of refugees, the nobility and gentry of what had once been Imperial Russia. They had plunged from enormous wealth to destitution in a matter of days, but being Russian, most of them bobbed up like corks. Ladies in waiting to the Czarina became companions to the wives of industrialists, princesses became governesses, colonels became doormen, and all over Paris exiled Russian noblemen drove taxis. And on their nights off they all went to La Coupole, and the men kissed the hands of their ladies, the ladies graciously inclined their heads, as if they were still in St Petersburg and the Czar was still on his throne. Jane found that she enjoyed it far more than George Antheil assaulting a piano, apparently with his fists.

Then to make it even better she saw Peggy Hawkins, once Mummy's housemaid, and now Miss Margaret Hawkins, MA (Lond.), holder of the first of the scholarships Jane had founded in memory of her father. She was with a tall and rather elegant Frenchman, and waved at once when she saw that Jane was looking at her. The pert housemaid prettiness had given way to much more elegant good looks, and far more elegant clothes, but even so she eyed Jane a little nervously, fearful of pushing too hard as she came over to them. Jane was having none of that. She got up at once and kissed the other woman's cheek.

'Margaret,' she said. 'How wonderful to see you.'

'It is indeed,' said Lionel, rising in his turn. He had coached Margaret Hawkins for her university entrance examinations.

'How well you both look,' Margaret said.

'And you,' said Jane. 'You look marvellous. Are you living in Paris?'

'Geneva,' said Margaret. 'I'm working as a translator at the League of Nations.'

'Do you like it?'

'It keeps one on one's toes but the pay's rather good,' said

Margaret, 'which is why I'm spending some of my leave in Paris.'

And this from the woman whose conversation had once gone little further than, 'Thanks ever so, miss' or 'Oo miss you look lovely.'

At least, thought Jane, I've done some good in the world, and had no doubt that her father would have felt the same, especially as Margaret was pretty. Her father had been as lecherous as he was learned.

'Buying clothes?' she said.

Margaret Hawkins nodded. 'A habit I got from watching you,' she said. 'It's sinful, the price one pays.'

'But so satisfying.'

'Of course. Immensely.' Margaret looked over to where her tall young man sat, and said: 'I wonder if you'd care to join us for a little while. My friend is Olivier Lefèvre. I know he'd be delighted to meet you.'

'He knows about us? – The scholarship? All that?'

'No,' said Margaret. 'Not yet anyway. If you don't mind.'

'Not in the least,' said Jane. 'We'll just be old friends. And why not? You looked after me often enough in the past.'

They went to join the tall young man, who rose in his turn, and shook hands, and was instantly charming.

He was a banker, which was good, thought Jane, because she could ask Lovell about him, and if Lovell didn't know she was quite sure he could find out. Lefèvre had met Margaret in Geneva. He had gone there from Paris to advise some League of Nations committee or other on the problems of financing famine relief. That he was in love with Margaret was obvious: not so obvious what form his love would take. How wise of Margaret to say 'Not yet', thought Jane. In the meantime Lefèvre continued to charm.

'Have you dined?' he asked.

'No,' Lionel said.

'Then why not join us? We're going to Le Boeuf sur les Toits.'

'Oh yes do,' said Margaret. 'The food's not bad, and the jazz is good, if you like jazz.'

'We both do,' Lionel said.

'Sometimes the oddest people play there. Really quite serious composers like Satie and Poulenc. But even their jazz is good.'

'It is because of Jean Cocteau,' said Lefèvre. 'He can make anybody do anything. He even made my father lend money to Diaghilev.'

'You can watch the Dadaistes too, trying to shock the bourgeois.'

'They work so hard at it, poor things,' said Lefèvre.

'Aren't they the ones who wanted to reduce all the buildings in Venice to rubble and use it to fill up all the canals?' Lionel asked.

'The very same,' said Margaret.

'They should have called in the German Army,' said Jane. 'They'd have done it in no time.'

They went in two taxis, and Jane's was driven by a Russian count: at least he said he was a count; he was certainly Russian, she thought.

'Of course he is,' said Lionel. 'He drives as if we were being pursued by wolves.'

They arrived at the rue Boissy d'Antan long before the others. No Dadaistes. That was the only disappointment, but as Lefèvre pointed out they were rather old-fashioned these days. Something new was bound to happen soon. In the meantime there were Dadaiste pictures on the walls and behind the bar, where Moysès, the head barman, produced a dry martini that moved Lionel almost to tears at its perfection. The dinner, by English nightclub standards, was superb, and while they ate and drank they watched the great ones come and go: the Grand Duke Dimitri, King Ferdinand of Roumania, Cocteau himself with Diaghilev and his latest boy, and last of all, very late, Josephine Baker with a group of black musicians who promptly sat in with the band and began a jam session, the man on drums sitting next to Georges Auric, the classical composer, who was playing bass. Jane took out a little note book and pencil from her bag and made notes. She was still a little piqued by Bower, but this was newspaper business after all: just the thing for the *World*'s gossip page, 'This Wicked World'.

It would have been fun to have taken Margaret to Cambridge, Jane thought, because Margaret had become very smart, but it was not to be. She had to go back to Geneva. So they parted at last with many kisses and promises to keep in touch which neither woman believed would be kept.

'Well,' said Lionel as they drove back to the Crillon. 'Our Hawkins. Whoever would have believed it?'

'I know,' said Jane. 'Isn't it wonderful?'

'And to think I had a hand in it too,' said Lionel. 'The only useful thing I've ever done.'

'Nonsense,' said Jane. 'You took me in hand when I needed it. If it wasn't for you I couldn't even dance the Charleston.'

'Almost you persuade me that mine has been a full and useful life devoted to good works.'

'Well so it has,' said Jane. 'Margaret and I aren't the only ones.'

'I wish it had been.' Lionel wasn't teasing any more. He was serious.

'Darling, what's wrong?' said Jane.

'Getting old,' Lionel said. 'Or maybe it's what the Germans call Schadenfreude, or is it Weltanschauung? I looked at that crowd in the nightclub tonight and I felt older than God. I hope it didn't show.'

'Not for a minute,' said Jane. 'Do you want to go home tomorrow?'

'If you wouldn't mind, darling.'

'Not at all,' said Jane. 'I've spent quite enough money already.'

She rang Bower as soon as she got back. He thought it was about her Felston Carnival piece.

'I told you it was good,' he said. 'Stop bothering me all the time.'

'Coming from you that's bitter,' she said. 'Every other call I get is you being foul mouthed. And if it's so good, tell your accounts department to pay me for it. But I didn't call about that.' She told him about Le Boeuf sur les Toits.

'Might be something in it,' he said. 'Any famous English people there?'

'Not famous,' she said. 'No.'

'It'll have to be you then. Put yourself in. And Lionel. Much-decorated hero of the Royal Flying Corps. All that.'

'But why on earth should I?'

Bower sighed his God-give-me-patience sigh.

'Because I produce an English newspaper to be read by English people,' he said, 'and English people don't believe that any-place is any good unless other English people go there.'

'Sorry,' said Jane. 'I'll put us both in.'

The apology surprised him, but it soothed him too.

'I'll take four paragraphs,' he said. 'Usual rates.'

More for Felston. Jane waited for the phone to be slammed down, but there was a pause instead.

'Something else,' said Bower. 'What was it? Oh yes. There's been a change of schedule. Catherine and I will be OK for Cambridge.'

*Then* the phone slammed down. He doesn't seem very happy about it, thought Jane.

So they went. Lionel appointed himself OC transport. Smart people, he ruled, did not travel in Rolls Royces, so they went in Bower's Bentley (Catherine and Bower) and a Hispano-Suiza which Lionel had somehow contrived to borrow and which Jane drove. (Jane and Lionel, and Bob and his girl, known professionally as Tiger Lily, but for the Cambridge jaunt, Jane said firmly, to be known by her real name, Lilian Dunn. She looked quite exotic enough without advertising the fact.) Brenda Coupland had been staying with friends in Suffolk, and would make her way to Cambridge on her own.

The men were all booked into the University Arms. This was at Catherine's grandmother's suggestion. Lady Mangan held strong views about engaged couples staying at the same hotel, but it was Bob who reacted most violently, though no doubt love would find a way, thought Jane. Or Bob would.

They drove there in weather that was tentative at best, though when they arrived the sun did at last come out, strongly enough to do the Hispano-Suiza justice. One group of undergraduates on bicycles even applauded. Jane drove Lionel and Bob to their hotel, then went on to the Baron of Beef, where Catherine waited for them. Miss Dunn at once disappeared.

'I say,' said Catherine. 'This Tiger Lily –'

'Lilian Dunn,' said Jane firmly.

'Yes I know,' said Catherine. 'But this speciality dancing – does that mean in the altogether?'

'As near as she can get away with.'

'Golly,' said Catherine, and then: 'Could you do that?'

'Not with a lot of strange men watching.'

'No more could I. Is she – all right?'

'Looks sane enough,' said Jane.

'No no, I mean – does she talk properly? Say the right things?'

'From what I saw of her she hardly talks at all, but when she does she sounds well enough.'

'What does she do then?'

'Eats,' said Jane, and it was true. Miss Dunn had been blessed with not only a gorgeous figure but an enormous appetite. When they called on her in her room she was half way through a large bowl of strawberries and cream.

Jane bathed, and changed quickly into the Chanel dress. With it she wore Lovell's sapphires and nothing more. The sapphires were quite enough. Then it was time to call on Catherine. Lady Mangan had made it quite clear that she regarded Jane as a chaperon, and Lady Mangan was very good at making things quite clear.

Catherine was wearing a translucent dress of pale blue over a white slip, and looking quite adorable, but her thoughts were all on Jane.

'Black and sapphires,' she said. 'And such sapphires. How do you get away with it?'

'Perhaps because there's not an awful lot of black,' said Jane. 'Chanel isn't exactly liberal with her material. What jewels are you wearing?'

'Pearls,' said Catherine dismally. 'Grandmother insisted.'

'Show me.'

The pearls were large and real and there were a lot of them, but they were still pearls.

'So debby,' Catherine sighed. She had been 'out' for three whole years.

Jane went back to her room, and came back with a series of thin gold bracelets.

'Indian,' she said. 'My Aunt Pen gave them to me. Put them on.'

'But I can't,' said Catherine.

'Of course you can. They aren't jewellery. They're gold.'

Catherine slipped them on, one after the other, and they glowed like honey against the creamy whiteness of her skin.

'Bless you darling,' she said. 'Now I look grown up.'

'The way an engaged lady should look,' said Jane. 'Let's see your ring.'

Catherine held out her hand. A solitaire diamond of vast proportions . . . a real Bower ring. No wonder it was rumoured he had cash problems.

'Gorgeous,' she said.

'He does rather spoil one,' said Catherine, and Jane remembered how true that was, but was in no position to say so. Instead she went to call on Miss Dunn.

The speciality dancer said at once, 'You never got that dress in England.'

'Paris,' said Jane. 'Chanel.'

'You know what's what, Miss Whitcomb.'

'Please call me Jane.'

'Glad to. I like the way you call me Lilian. Got a bit of class to it.'

Casually the girl got up and took off her kimono, and Jane gasped aloud. The girl's body was incredible: firm and rounded and oozing sex, as a ripe peach oozes juice.

'What's wrong?' said Lilian Dunn.

'Why nothing,' said Jane. 'Nothing at all. I just hadn't realised just how much of a speciality you were.'

'You mean the body,' said Lilian Dunn. 'I reckon it'll last me another five years if I can cut out the puddings. Still – I ought to be married by then.'

'You should indeed,' said Jane. 'If only for the sake of the rest of the female sex.'

'You're good with compliments,' said Lilian Dunn, and then: 'Here – you're not one of those what's names are you?'

'No, I'm not,' said Jane. 'I had quite enough trouble with them in Paris, thank you very much.'

'Yeah,' said Lilian Dunn. 'I reckon you would.' Jane decided that that too was a compliment.

'Want to see my dress?' the other girl asked.

'Love to,' said Jane, and here it was, the moment of truth. But Lilian Dunn had chosen a dress of pale rose silk that even a deb's mama would have approved, though no deb could have filled it as Lilian Dunn did. Gold and diamond bracelet, gold and diamond necklace, the gold echoing almost exactly the colour of her hair. Or was it the other way round? Jane wondered.

'Will I do?'

'Perfectly,' said Jane. 'Your jewellery's nice.'

'Bob gave it to me.'

'Are you going to marry Bob?'

'Me?' said Lilian Dunn. 'Of course not. I mean Bob's sweet – well I wouldn't be here with him if he wasn't – but he's not the sort you'd marry, now is he?'

'I nearly married his brother,' said Jane.

'You never did.'

'Didn't Bob tell you?'

'Not a word,' said Lilian Dunn. 'What happened?'

'He was killed,' said Jane.

'An accident?'

'The war.'

'Oh, the war,' Lilian Dunn said.

She'd have still been at school even when it ended, thought Jane: starved of sugar and butter and all the other good things that go with puddings. For Lilian Dunn the war was only just a memory. Lionel, she thought, was right to feel old.

# 12

BRENDA COUPLAND HAD arrived, it seemed, and dashed upstairs to bathe and change, as the other women drifted downstairs to the hotel lounge to await their escorts. All the rest of the lounge's guests were men, Jane noticed, dons and clergymen for the most part, dressed with the kind of rusty shabbiness that only years of intellectual effort can achieve. When the three young women entered they looked up, startled as starlings menaced by kingfishers. Several of them left the room.

'Cambridge isn't the sort of town that cherishes its women,' said Jane.

'Just like Oxford,' Catherine said.

They sat and gossiped. Lilian Dunn told some hair-raising stories about the risks involved in speciality dancing, and Catherine listened open mouthed. Jane wondered if there might not be a piece in it for the *Daily World*, until at last Brenda Coupland appeared, and another don said, 'Oh my God', quite audibly, and left. But Brenda had earned the tribute. A gown of green that suited her dark good looks, and emeralds. Jane went to her.

'Darling, how well you're looking,' said Jane.

Brenda Coupland looked from Catherine Hilyard to Lilian Dunn then back to Jane.

'Just as well,' she said.

And then the gentlemen arrived, all except their host, Jane thought bitterly. Has he forgotten we're all coming?

Bower went at once to Jane to question the origin of the Indian bracelets. Evening dress didn't change him in the least. He looked just as menacing in a tail-coat as in a country suit, and just as attractive too, thought Jane. Darling Lionel now, he looked absolutely marvellous in evening dress, as if it had been designed for the sole purpose of making him look even more elegant than usual. As for Bob, he merely contrived to look as if he'd worn evening dress on occasions like this all his adult life, which was the greatest achievement of the lot. His Tyneside accent, too, was much less broad than it had been at Felston. Jane went across to Catherine and Bower. He was still being pugnacious about those bracelets.

'Oh for heaven's sake,' said Jane. 'Stop nagging. You're not married yet. And anyway they look lovely on her.'

'Well of course they do,' said Bower. 'That's just the point. If she wants Indian bracelets she should tell me and I'll get her some.'

'I doubt if Catherine knew they existed,' said Jane.

'I didn't,' Catherine said. 'And a little less of this "she" business, Mr Bower. Jane can remember my name is Catherine, so I don't see why you shouldn't.'

Bower began to apologise, as near to abject as Jane had ever seen him. That he was deeply in love was obvious. But with what? A clever, pretty, captivating girl, or the daughter of an earl? Please God let it be both, she prayed, and began to tell him about Lilian Dunn.

'She told both of you all this?' said Bower. Fear of what Lady Mangan might say was at once apparent.

'Now don't be pompous, Jaybird,' said Catherine. 'It doesn't suit you. I was just thinking what a marvellous piece it would make for the *World*.'

'So was I,' said Jane, 'but if you're going to behave like a prude –'

'A prude?' said Bower. 'Me? No no. The *World*'s not afraid to tackle life as it is. Not like those nervous Nellies down the Street.'

'What nervous Nellies?' Catherine asked.

'The *Daily Wail* is it? The *Daily Depress*?'

It was every bit as good as Lionel trying to remember precisely what one *did* at Cambridge.

Then at last Francis showed up. His tie was askew and his coat didn't quite fit, and he wore a wrist watch, but at least he was there. And it's no good accusing me of snobbery, Jane told her conscience. He's the one who wants to get on in Society. And he does look handsome, in a frail sort of way.

'Francis darling,' she said, and kissed his cheek. 'How good of you to come.'

Beside her, Bower chuckled. He had the air of a man who thinks it may turn out to be a pretty decent evening after all.

Francis looked at them rather wildly, as if he knew in his bones it would be impossible to cope with all this smartness, with Chanel and Molyneux and Savile Row, and a Bentley parked outside.

'I had a meeting,' he said. 'I couldn't get away.' He paused and added: 'Honestly,' saying it as if he were twelve years old.

'Of course not,' said Jane. 'Do come and meet your guests.'

One by one she introduced them, and Francis mumbled his joy that they could come. Lionel, always the softy, went to fetch Francis the drink he so badly needed, even though, Jane knew, Francis disliked Lionel, who was not at all his type of pansy, making no attempt to hide that that was what he was, and yet staying on equal terms with men like Bower, being positively courted by Brenda Coupland, who wanted as many dances with him as possible.

They dined in Francis's rooms, walking to the college through streets already beginning to throng with other ball guests, undergraduates and debs for the most part, the debs back on the first possible train to town next morning, and with an elaborate system of roll call devised by their mothers. It felt a little odd to walk about in evening dress and jewellery in daylight, but at least the sun was shining, and the Backs looked beautiful: sunlight glittering on the tree-lined river, and laughter echoing across the water. . . .

The dinner, astonishingly, was a success. This was because Francis had put the whole affair into the hands of his gyp, who had arranged everything from the flowers to the dinner menu, and consulted the college butler about the wine. Consommé, cold salmon, cutlets reform, bombe surprise, Moselle and claret, and champagne flowing like a fountain. The gyp and his assistants worked like beavers. They had never ever expected Mr Whitcomb to give a party like this. At the end of dinner Francis even made a little speech, and thanked them once again for coming. *What is he up to?* Jane wondered. It was time for dancing.

A marquee had been erected over the college's front court, and in it the first band was already playing, couples were already dancing or seated at the tables around the edge of the marquee. Outside, a shred of moon shone silver on the gardens, but the marquee glowed with soft electric light, and the air was filled with the scent of cut flowers, cigars, the powder and perfume of women: the old familiar battleground in fact, that until now had always brought at least a hint of exciting possibilities: but this time – here I am about to dance with my own brother, Jane thought, and when that gets too much for me I'll have the best dancer in the room instead, and he's as queer as a coot, bless him. Just like my brother. She took hold of Francis and steered him in the right direction.

'I meant it you know,' Francis said. 'I am grateful you came. Grateful to you, especially.'

'Francis,' said Jane, 'are you really telling me that trundling your sister round a portable dance floor will help you to get on?'

'Not here,' said Francis. 'This college isn't like that. But I'm after a senior fellowship at King's, and King's is a very smart college indeed.'

Even Jane knew that. Eton and King's were the sort of inevitable progression that only the wealthiest and most powerful could aspire to, so that either her brother was telling the truth or he had devised a most convincing lie.

'I wish you luck,' she said.

'I'm not telling anybody just for the moment,' he said. 'About trying for the King's fellowship. I'd rather you didn't tell anybody either.'

'Very well.'

'Promise me,' said Francis, and she knew then that he was lying, but before she could answer he backed her into the man behind her. Jane turned to apologise, and found that she was looking at Tom Robins, the don who had got so disastrously drunk the night he had asked her to marry him. Robins was clutching a small, dark woman, lady don written all over her, who was not at all pleased by the way Robins was smiling at Jane.

'I really am most awfully sorry,' said Jane.

'Not at all, not at all,' Robins said. 'It's delightful bumping into each other like this.'

Francis winced and Robins turned to him.

'I say, Whitcomb,' Robins said reproachfully. 'You didn't tell me your sister was coming.' The small, dark woman scowled, and Robins said vaguely: 'This is Dr Bender by the way.'

'Rather a last-minute arrangement,' said Francis. 'We got up a party as a matter of fact.'

'Not like you,' said Robins. 'Not like you at all.' The band stopped playing, and Dr Bender's scowl deepened. 'Left-Wing asceticism. That's your line, surely?' He seemed upset that Francis had departed from his norm. 'Anyway, now you're venturing into grandeur, come and have a glass of champagne.'

He took Jane and Dr Bender by the arm and led them to a large table shielded by potted palms, and Francis tagged along behind. He had no objection to drinking Robins's champagne. Perhaps a dozen people were seated at the table: debs, undergraduates, a few obvious Londoners, and Robins sprayed out names as he poured. Jane made no effort to remember any of them. Besides, there was somebody there she knew.

'Piers,' she said. 'My dear. How lovely to see you.'

Piers Hilyard rose and kissed her cheek, and it was Robins's turn to scowl.

'Do you know your sister's here?' Jane asked.

'Didn't know I was coming myself until this afternoon,' he said. 'Chum of mine had to drop out and I took his place.' He smiled at the tall, fair debutante beside him. 'Bit of luck for me.' The debutante blushed. 'How are Bridget and Bridie?'

'Both breeding,' said Jane. 'I don't know how the old girl does it at her age.'

'Oh I say,' said the debutante.

'Horses,' said Piers hastily. 'Mother and daughter. The daughter's won quite a few point to points.'

'And now there's a grand-daughter who'll be even better,' said Jane. 'Do come and have a word with Catherine.'

'Bower with her?'

'Of course,' said Jane. The band began to play.

'Then I'd better come.' He rose, and excused himself to the debutante. 'Back soon,' he said. 'Save me the next one.'

'And I hope you'll do the same for me,' said Robins.

'Delighted,' said Jane, and nodded to Dr Bender.

'So nice to have met you,' Dr Bender said.

Piers and Catherine were identical twins blessed with the kind of austere good looks that appeared well in either sex. They greeted each other happily enough, but without any great outward show of affection, and yet it was apparent as soon as they sat next to each other that they were linked in a way that Catherine and Bower could never be, and Bower knew it too.

'I thought it was about time I saw you again. What have you been up to?' Catherine said.

'Spot of leave,' said Piers. 'Went over to Ireland.'

'At this time of year?'

'I got word of a horse,' said Piers. 'Rather a good one. Rather a good price, too, so I had to see Granny.'

'I might have known. . . . Is the horse really good?'

'Absolute stunner. Jumps off his hocks.'

Francis was looking at them as if they were creatures from another planet.

Bower said, 'I hope Lady Mangan is well?'

'Top hole,' said Piers. 'A bit lighter in the cheque book than before I came, but she never minds that if the horse is a good one. Have you set a date yet, the pair of you?'

'October,' said Bower. 'We thought perhaps the twenty-second. You won't forget, will you? You're down as best man.'

'Of course I won't forget,' said Piers. 'Nothing I'd like better. Trouble is I'll be in India.'

'Surely you could get leave for my wedding?' said Catherine.

Piers looked at Brenda Coupland. 'Do my best,' he said, then his voice faded, and for a moment that self-possessed young man stood with his mouth open, gawping like a yokel. Jane looked behind her, not at all surprised to see Bob leading Lilian Dunn back to the table. The girl was as effective as a hammer blow, thought Jane, but Piers made a quick recovery, gracefully acknowledging Jane's introduction. That Bob had seen what happened Jane was quite sure. He looked so pleased with himself.

'I remember you, surely,' Piers said to Bob. 'Didn't we meet during the General Strike?'

'The East End,' said Bob. 'You were driving a lorry that got ambushed. There was a bit of a barney.'

'A fat lout was giving me a hiding,' said Piers. 'Then you came along and kicked him in the – er –'

'Nick of time,' said Bob. 'I remember.'

The fat lout in question, thought Jane, was Cuthbert Pardoe, a fellow of Clare College. Would he too come to the ball, Jane wondered, and would there be a return bout?

'You taught me a lesson,' said Piers. 'Straight lefts aren't much help if you're giving away three stone. You have to learn to make alternative arrangements.'

'You could try staying out of fights,' said his sister.

'Hardly,' said Piers. 'I'm a soldier.' Then Robins came over to claim his dance.

'Who is our gallant young friend?' he asked.

'Piers? He's one of your table, surely,' said Jane.

'Certainly. But I've never met him. You obviously have.'

Nice to be wanted, she thought, and by such a nice man. He's dancing better, too. Perhaps he's been taking lessons, or maybe it's just because he's sober.

'He's Lord Mangan's son and heir. His sister's engaged to Jay Bower.'

'The newspaper magnate?'

'He has been so described.'

'And Piers is in the Rifle Brigade?'

'Subaltern,' said Jane. 'Did well at Sandhurst. Did well at Oxford come to that.'

'I thought I recognised the manner,' said Robins. 'Not surprised he did well, either. He looks the type who would. I say.' Here it comes, thought Jane.

'Who was that absolute stunner with the other young chap?'

'Lilian Dunn,' said Jane. 'She's a dancer.

'Ballet?' He sounded incredulous, and rightly.

'Something more experimental than that,' said Jane. 'Free form or something I believe it's called. How's your work these days?'

'Still working on the atom,' said Robins. 'Still inspiring chaps like Bower to accuse us of plotting to blow up the world.'

'And are you? Plotting to blow up the world I mean.'

'No,' said Robins. 'We're trying to understand it. That's what science is for. That other girl at your table's a stunner too.' She had forgotten what a single-minded person Robins was. 'What does she do?'

'Brenda Coupland? Dances with the Prince of Wales, gets her name in the illustrated weeklies, adds tone.'

'And then there's you. Your chaps have monopolised the best-looking women in the room – and one of them's your brother. It simply isn't fair.'

'Tell me about Dr Bender,' she said, and Robins chuckled.

'That's not fair either,' he said. 'Dr Bender is a Fellow of Newnham.'

'Another world-blower-upper?'

'A classical historian,' said Robins, 'who likes to dance, as I do. And that's about all we have in common.'

That's what you think, thought Jane, but had been too well brought up to say so.

'Do you remember the night I proposed to you?' Robins asked.

'Do you?'

'Yes,' said Robins. 'I was pretty well plastered, wasn't I? You had to drive me home.'

'You'd forgotten to eat for absolute ages,' said Jane. 'Too busy with your bangs and stinks.'

'All the same I remember proposing to you,' said Robins.

'It seems to be a custom at Clare,' said Jane. 'That chum of my brother's decided he was smitten, too, once upon a time.'

'Pardoe asked you to marry him?'

'I didn't allow it to get to that,' said Jane mendaciously. Pardoe had assured her it would never get to that because he was far too busy to take a wife, but he was very good in bed.

'Well I'm blessed,' said Robins. 'Who will it be next? The Dean? It can't be the Master. He's already married.'

'We'll just have to see what the night brings,' she said, and added firmly: 'Everybody is allowed one try.'

'Like Portia and the caskets,' said Robins. 'Point taken.'

'Nobody knows about Pardoe,' she said. 'Please keep it a secret. I can't think why I told you.'

'To stop me trying again. Obviously,' said Robins, and Jane reminded herself that nice, jolly men too can be clever.

'Of course I won't say anything,' he continued, 'but you can tell anybody you like that I proposed. If I ever get into *Who's Who* I'll put it there in print.' They danced on till the music stopped, and he took her back to her table, then went to do his duty by Dr Bender.

The night moved on to its prescribed pattern: the second band, then supper, and then more dancing: several young men drunk, two young men helped away to be sick, Brenda Coupland gossiping with Lionel.

'The little man,' she kept saying. The little man. The little man. At the Embassy. At a point to point. At Badminton with Fruity Metcalf. She was still talking about the Prince of Wales. Then Bob went to ask her to dance, and still she talked on, and no doubt the topic would be the same. Jane wondered if Bob would ask her whether the Prince of Wales's aide was any relation to his brother-in-law, Frank Metcalf, who had married his sister and lived in Dock Street, Felston. He was perfectly capable of it.

Lionel asked Lilian Dunn to dance, and she got up at once. She was really a jolly good dancer, thought Jane, speciality or no speciality; then Francis nerved himself to do his duty again.

'You really should ask one of the others,' said Jane as they rose.

'How can I?' said Francis. 'They terrify me.'

'I bet they don't dance with their sisters at King's,' said Jane.

When duty was done Francis went off to talk to some don or other about yet another committee, and Jane lit a cigarette and sat on her own and glad to be so. Soon it would be dawn and time for the obligatory punt trip before driving to breakfast at Grantchester. Thank God she had remembered to bring shawls. English rivers were beastly cold at dawn, even in June. . . . She had almost nodded off when Lionel came to sit beside her.

'I really am getting too old for this,' he said.

Jane struggled awake. 'I rather think that I am too,' she said.

'Exactly.' It was obvious that Lionel hadn't understood a word she had said.

'That girl,' he said.

'Miss Dunn?'

'Of course Miss Dunn. I've never experienced anything like it. . . . Thank the Lord I'm as queer as I am.'

'Otherwise?'

'She might have made me untrue to my nature.'

'Oh Lionel,' said Jane, 'you couldn't possibly be unfaithful to the Merchant Navy. Not you.'

Lionel smiled. 'All very well to laugh,' he said. 'But the thing is she knows the way I am. I mean I don't try to hide it, do I?'

'Not a bit.'

'And so she set out to show me what I was missing. Not a word said, mind you. She just moved in very close and sort of massaged me. It was like being buffed by a sack of grapefruit. I tell you for a moment, I –'

'Not you,' said Jane. 'I don't believe it.'

'Touch and go,' said Lionel. 'I promise you. That Yank – what's his name – Eliot! That's it. He had exactly the word for it. Poem called "The Waste Land". Promise of pneumatic bliss. . . . Touch and go,' he said again, and mopped his forehead. 'And all the time she never said a word. Not till we'd finished, and then: "Thank you very much," she said. "I did enjoy that." I tell you, Jane, I didn't know where to look.'

It was the only time in their friendship that she had seen Lionel disconcerted.

'There there,' she said. 'It's over now. I just wish she'd try it on Francis.'

Lionel giggled. 'I'd pay money,' he said, 'I'd pay vast sums, to be there when she did.'

Then Catherine came over to join them. Bower, it seemed, was telephoning the *Daily World*, which surprised no one. Somehow they found themselves talking about Paris, and Lionel was remembering the time – in the spring of 1913 – when he'd gone there to find out if he could ever be a painter, or was doomed to be a dilettante for ever.

'I can do the pretty stuff,' he said. 'Can't I, Jane?' Jane nodded. 'But that's all it is. Pretty stuff. So off I went to see if I could do the good stuff as well. All the talented ones were hard up. Even Picasso. He lived in a studio that was so cold in winter his tea froze overnight in the pot. He used to thaw it out next morning for breakfast.'

Piers came up with his debutante to sit beside his sister. Then Bob and Lilian Dunn appeared. Lionel went on talking. 'He soon began to make money of course, but rich or poor he had no time to talk to me. I went to a place on the rue Dantzig near the abattoir. Place called La Ruche.'

'The hive,' said the debutante, then blushed once more. 'Oh I'm sorry I –'

'Quite right, my dear,' said Lionel, 'because that's what it was. I wore the oldest clothes I had when I went there, and next to the others I was Beau Brummell. It *was* a hive. Little stone studios the artists called the coffins because they were so small. No heating. No chimneys. One tap to each building. A man called Boucher ran it. Quite appropriate considering we were so close to the slaughterhouse.'

'He must have been a monster to treat people like that,' said the debutante.

'Well no,' said Lionel. 'He was an artist himself, you see. A sculptor. Not a very good one and he knew it, but he'd made a bit of money and built the place to house artists with real talent who didn't mind roughing it à la vie de Bohème. He was supposed to charge a nominal rent – a hundred and fifty francs a year or something – but when I paid him mine he thought I must be weak in the head. He used to wander about the place talking to the artists, discussing their work. He had a pet donkey that used to follow him about like a dog.

'In that place I saw men work as if their lives depended on it, and in a way I suppose they did. I'm not saying that if they'd given up painting or sculpting they'd have died, but they'd have ceased to be the men they were, and so they hung on, living on two bob a week, and what should have gone on food went on canvas and paint and stone.'

'And were they good?' the debutante asked.

'Not all,' said Lionel. 'By no means all. But some had great talent, and some, a few, had genius. Chagall was there, and Brancusi. There was a great deal of talent, but none of it was mine, and even if it had been, I had neither the dedication nor the stamina. The best I could manage was the pretty stuff, but after all, a lot of people can't even manage that.'

'So what did you do?' Bob asked.

'I gave a party,' said Lionel. 'For about eighty people. It lasted three days and cost me twenty quid. The best party they ever had, they told me.'

'A party in those tiny coffins?' said the debutante.

'No no,' said Lionel. 'There was what had once been a garden near by. They held it there. On the third day there was the most colossal thunderstorm, I remember, but we just took our clothes off and went on drinking. The garden was just a sea of mud by then, and for some reason those of us who could still stand began a sort of mass wrestling match, stark naked, in the mud.' He smiled. 'I suppose an unkind person might say that I had my twenty quid's worth, but whatever one says it was a memorable way to celebrate the fact that I had no talent.'

A voice behind them said, 'A more drivelling story I have never heard.'

Jane took her time in turning round. She knew at once who it was.

Lionel said wearily, 'Oh it's you, Burrowes. Naturally you would think that.'

So they know each other, thought Jane, and then: well of course they do. Each of them knows everybody. The band began to play 'Goodnight, Sweetheart'. Soon it would be the national anthem. Already some of the dancers were leaving, on their way to the Backs where the punts lay waiting.

Burrowes was wearing a dinner-jacket, and for once looked clean and not too drunk. Beside him was Francis, in what Lionel had once called his Martin Luther stance: 'Here I stand, I can no other.'

'Contemptible bourgeois drivel,' said Burrowes. 'I'm surprised you didn't throw in a few chapters of *Trilby* while you were at it. Real people are beyond you.'

Lionel lounged back in his chair, took a sip of champagne.

'Real, dear boy?' he said. 'Are you going to define "real" for us?'

'And don't think you're going to start any damn Socratic symposiums with me,' said Burrowes. 'You're a bourgeois to the tips of your fingers, you old queen. No wonder you talk about prettiness.' He is not nearly so sober as he looks, thought Jane.

'And what do you talk about, Burrowes, my pet?'

'I'll have some of that for a start,' said Burrowes, reached out for the champagne bottle, and poured some into a glass already half full.

'Art,' he said, 'is about Socialism, about the needs and aspirations of the workers to achieve a free and just society. We don't need any of this fucking nonsense about geniuses in coffins.'

Drums rolled; the surviving guests began to stand up.

'That's all over,' said Burrowes. 'Finished.' He was obviously about to talk his way through 'God Save The King'.

Jane got to her feet as Piers moved past her and murmured, 'Excuse me,' while Bob moved round the table from the other direction. They stood on either side of Burrowes and yanked him to his feet.

'If you don't shut up, bonny lad,' Bob whispered, 'I'll break your jaw.'

Burrowes shut up. To the other people there they must have looked like two friends supporting a drunk.

Slowly, interminably almost, the national anthem moved to its close, and Jane found herself repeating the closing words in her mind:

> May he defend our laws,
> And ever give us cause,
> To sing with heart and voice
> Go-od – save – the – King.

Then the band disappeared with the speed that only musicians can achieve, and Burrowes opened his mouth.

'I haven't finished yet,' said Bob. 'Shut your gob.'

His accent is broader and cruder than it's been all night, thought Jane. He's enjoying what he's doing.

'Tell these ladies you're sorry for the language you used,' he said.

'But I'm not,' said Burrowes. 'I wasn't talking the language of ladies and gentlemen. This was the language of the proletariat. I used the words "fucking nonsense" instead of ridiculous nonsense because to my mind "fucking" seemed the more appropriate.'

Bob's grip on Burrowes's arm tightened, and Burrowes gasped.

'That's three you've managed,' said Bob. 'We won't have a fourth one. Now – tell these ladies you're sorry.'

'I'm afraid I can't,' said Burrowes. 'It's a matter of principle.'

'Oh please,' said the debutante. 'It doesn't matter. Honestly.'

'Shut your face,' said Lilian Dunn.

Brenda Coupland leaned forward in her seat, observant yet relaxed, as if she were in a stalls seat at a very good matinée with an enormous box of chocolates on her lap.

Bob said, 'We can't do it here,' and the debutante gasped aloud.

'Wouldn't do at all,' said Piers. 'Better take him outside. There are gardens and things.' He looked relaxed yet utterly determined, and happier than he'd been all evening.

'Not too rough,' said his sister, with the air of a nanny talking to a three-year-old.

'Certainly not,' said Piers. 'A just rebuke, no more.' He looked about him. Near them there was a side exit which the waiters had used to bring in fresh supplies.

'That way I think.' Bob and Piers moved forward.

Burrowes said, 'I'm sorry.'

'Louder,' said Bob. 'Let's hear it.'

'I'm sorry,' Burrowes said again. 'I apologise for my use of bad language in front of these ladies.' He paused for a moment, then continued: 'But it isn't because I was afraid of you. I just don't want a scene. . . . It isn't as if I believe your stupid threats either, though there are two of you after all.'

He sounds about fourteen, thought Jane.

Bob said, 'You brought a mate along an' all.'

Burrowes pushed past them, and out of the marquee. Already he was weeping.

Francis said, 'That was disgraceful. I fully intend to report it.'

'My dear chap,' said Piers, 'who would believe *you*? My father's a lord.'

Francis hurried out after Burrowes.

The debutante stood open mouthed at Piers.

'Would you have done it?' she asked.

Piers shrugged. 'I've no idea,' he said. He lied.

The debutante turned to Bob. 'Would you?'

Bob had been brought up in a different tradition. 'Well of course,' he said.

When Bower came back from his telephoning, Piers had the debutante on one arm and Brenda Coupland on the other. Bob and Lilian Dunn had gone.

'What a dramatic little group you look,' he said, 'and I've just seen that guy Burrowes in the gardens sobbing his heart out. Have I missed a story?'

'Yes,' said Jane, 'but it's not for publication.'

'Then I guess we'd better go,' said Bower. 'There's no one else here anyway. How about the river?'

The debutante couldn't: she'd promised Mummy, but Brenda Coupland could and did.

Jane went to the cloakroom to fetch the shawls.

'You will observe,' said Lionel, 'that I'm punting from the wrong end. That's because I went to Oxford, where this is called the right end. . . . I trust you had a good time?'

'Fascinating,' said Jane. 'But I didn't dance with you nearly enough.'

'Indeed you didn't,' said Lionel, and then: 'How odd your brother is, if I may say so.'

'Indeed you may,' said Jane, 'but do you mean because he asked me to get up this party?'

'Oh that,' said Lionel.

The punt moved past a clump of willows to show them St John's College gardens moving in great steps to the water: above the gardens, the college buildings glowed in the early sunlight. It was part of a dream world: reality could never be so perfect.

'My sweet,' said Jane, 'you can't just say "Oh that". There has to be more and I want it. He's my brother.'

'In confidence,' said Lionel. 'In the very strictest confidence.'

'Of course.'

'Your brother's a Communist,' said Lionel.

'I know that,' said Jane.

'He'd be hopeless on a soap box and God knows what he'd manage to do with a machine gun. But he's good at collecting facts and he can think. So naturally King Street has a use for him.'

'King Street?'

'Communist Party Headquarters.'

'Lionel,' said Jane, 'you're not some sort of secret agent, by any chance?'

'No darling,' said Lionel, 'I'm an ageing queen who's rather good at dancing, as well you know, but after Knut left me for the joys of matrimony, if such there be, I sought consolation with such a dear little sweetie in what is called public affairs, and who is rather a chatter-box. Your brother's name came up. King Street want him to change his image. It seems that Cambridge is stuffed to the bung with earnest, hard-working Left-Wing homosexuals. A lighter touch is required. Our merry band was the lighter touch.'

'And poor Francis went and muffed it.'

'But did he?' said Lionel.

'Well of course,' said Jane. 'Burrowes thumping his tub and Piers and Bob yelling for the thumbscrews and red-hot pincers.'

'That won't get into the papers,' said Lionel. 'You said so yourself. What the gossip columns will say is that Francis was the charming and popular host of a select party at the Clare May Ball. There'll probably be photographs too. The flash bulbs were popping all night.'

'So he's got away with it?' Lionel nodded. 'But I don't understand why he does it all. He hates social life. It's agony for him.'

'He wants to change the world,' said Lionel. 'All Left-Wingers do. From what you tell me, Bob's brother is the same. And to change the world he must do as he's told, so he does.' He poled on for a moment in silence. 'I'm very upset,' he said.

'Those two bashi bazouks?'

'No no,' said Lionel. 'In their place I'd have done the same. At least I hope so. But it was such a jolly evening, and Burrowes ruined it in three minutes. . . . Can I take you back now, my dear? If I don't get breakfast soon I shall burst into tears.'

Breakfast at Grantchester was good, which was just as well, thought Jane. Poor Lionel deserved a good breakfast. Catherine and Bower joined them, both yawning hugely, and Piers came in with Brenda Coupland. Piers seemed almost asleep where he sat, but Brenda was alert and eager to be amused, though not once did she mention the Prince of Wales. Of Bob and Lilian there was no sign, which did not surprise Jane in the least. After breakfast Jane drove back to Cambridge and up to her room, where she fell asleep at once. No remembered dreams, only oblivion. Bliss.

# 13

B LISS ENDED WHEN Brenda shook her awake and said that she was frightfully sorry but it was after three o'clock and she simply must get back to town, and Jane acknowledged that she had a point. Slowly, feeling very old indeed, she bathed, dressed and made the telephone calls that would set their caravan in motion, then packed and went downstairs. Bob and Lilian were already there. Jane doubted whether Bob had been inside his own hotel since they first arrived, except to change his suit.

'You look rested,' she said, and it was true.

'Nothing like a good night's sleep to set you up,' said Bob.

'Nothing at all,' said Lilian Dunn.

Jane said hastily, 'Shall I run you over to the University Arms to collect your stuff?'

'No need,' said Bob. 'I brought it over earlier – to save trouble.'

Lilian Dunn snorted.

Jane said, 'Did you enjoy the ball?'

'Lovely,' said Lilian. 'Never a dull moment.' Then: 'I like your Lionel.'

'Everybody does,' said Jane, and thought, But he isn't mine, poor darling. He isn't anybody's. That's his trouble.

Then the lounge door opened and two men came in. Oh dear, thought Jane. Andy and Cuthbert Pardoe. Dimly she remembered that Bob had said that Andy might call on them, but nothing had been said about Pardoe.

Pardoe looked first at Lilian Dunn, which was perfectly understandable. Any normal man would. Then his gaze went to Jane, and then to Bob. 'Good God!' he said, and Jane was aware at once that he knew about Burrowes.

She rose to her feet, fluttered like a cygnet in *Swan Lake* to where he stood, placed a hand on one massive shoulder and kissed him on the cheek. He is getting fat, she thought, delighted.

'Cuthbert, my *dear*,' she said. 'How lovely to see you. How is darling Marigold?'

This was a low blow indeed. Pardoe's interest in Marigold Ledbitter had been purely carnal, a fact he had done little to hide, and she was making it seem that they were engaged, perhaps even married: but this was no time for the Marquis of Queensberry's rules.

'Well enough so far as I know,' said Pardoe, flustered. 'I see very little of her these days.'

'Oh what a pity,' said Jane. 'Don't tell me you've quarrelled. You always looked so right together.'

'There was never the possibility of any sort of understanding,' said Pardoe. 'I thought I once made that clear to you.'

Jane's face bore an expression of compassionate sadness, and Pardoe stopped. He knows what I'm up to, thought Jane. How cunning they all are at Cambridge.

'I have no wish to discuss Marigold Ledbitter,' Pardoe said.

'Oh very well,' said Jane. 'Then how are *you*? Tell me all about yourself. What have you been up to?'

'That's a question I'd prefer to put to you,' said Pardoe. 'That disgraceful business at the May Ball last night –'

'But where are my manners?' said Jane. 'I haven't introduced you. Miss Lilian Dunn – Mr Cuthbert Pardoe.'

'Dr Pardoe. I thought at least Francis might have told you,' Pardoe said.

'Dr Pardoe. Congratulations. And this is Miss Dunn's friend and Andy's brother, Bob Patterson.'

Bob and Lilian said, 'How d'you do?' Pardoe grunted.

'Disgraceful,' he said. 'And from what I have been told, totally unjustified.' He turned to Andy. 'Am I right, Patterson?'

Andy said firmly, 'I'm out of this.'

'That is one attitude to the whole revolting business. Not a particularly constructive one, I'm afraid. Still, one allows for the fact that a relative of yours was involved.'

'What *are* you talking about?' said Jane.

'About the fact that some aristocratic bully-boy or other and this man here threatened violence against the person of a distinguished member of this university, simply because he refused to kow-tow to that wretched little tune that expresses nothing but an outmoded jingoism.'

'God Save The King,' Jane explained to Lilian, and then: '*Burrowes? Distinguished?*' Even Pardoe didn't wait to argue that.

'A gross piece of bullying,' he said. 'A scholar of his college manhandled.' He looked more closely at Bob. 'Haven't we met before somewhere?'

'Never mind that,' said Bob. 'You're talking about me and Piers Hilyard, am I right?'

'I believe that's his name. – Some lordling or other.'

'And is this Burrowes going to press charges? Because if he's not I'll have you up for libel.'

Beside him Lilian Dunn murmured, 'Go get him, tiger.'

'It just so happens – luckily for you –' said Pardoe, 'that Burrowes has decided to let the matter drop.'

'Then you'd better do the same,' said Bob.

'I have no choice,' said Pardoe, 'but I feel bound to say that the whole incident seems to me typical of the way in which a high-handed and reactionary class can impose its slightest whim on any innocent victim who stands up for his rights. I can understand a militarist thug acting as he did, but you – Andy Patterson's brother – why on earth did you do it?'

'Do what?' said Bob, and Pardoe sighed.

'Very well,' he said. 'Do you know what a hypothetical question is?'

'I used to be a printer,' said Bob. 'Printers pick up a lot of words – and if I'm stuck I can always ask our Andy.'

'I take it that means yes,' said Pardoe. 'Now if the incident I described had happened, and if you and this – Hilyard is it? – had threatened to assault Burrowes – why you? I mean I can understand the other fellow – typical of that class – effete and aggressive at once – but why *you*? Why should you be a lackey of the capitalists?'

'I'm not a lackey of the capitalists,' said Bob.

'Then what the devil are you?' Pardoe asked.

'I'm a capitalist.'

Pardoe threw up his hands and stamped to the other end of the lounge. From the door Brenda Coupland said, 'Oh dear, I hope we didn't miss another one.' She and Catherine stood there side by side. Both of them looked enchanting, but Pardoe didn't seem to think so.

'Not really,' said Bob. 'More like shadow boxing.' Pardoe snorted.

'How're you keeping, Bob?' Andy asked.

'Canny,' said Bob. 'And you?'

'All right.'

'I'm not much of a hand at writing,' said Bob, 'so I told Grandma I'd put a phone in and pay for it. She wouldn't hear of it. Did she tell you?'

'Aye,' said Andy. 'She can't stand the phone. She thinks it's like the wireless. It can hear everything you say *and* pass it on.'

Jane said, 'I think the rest of us will organise the luggage. We'll leave you two to your chat.' She waited for Pardoe, who appeared fascinated by a twenty-year-old edition of *Encyclopaedia Britannica* in a bookcase against the wall. The four women left, but Brenda Coupland's voice came back into the room.

'You do know the most enthralling people,' she said. 'Who was the sad man in the dreadful suit?'

'Typical of that class,' Pardoe told the *Encyclopaedia Britannica*. 'Typical.'

'Is that what I am?' said Andy. 'A sad man in a dreadful suit?'

'You're my brother,' said Bob. 'It's hard to be – what's the word? – about you.'

'Objective?'

'Objective. Aye. You're a clever chap and you're a bloody fool and that seems to me the right combination to do well in this place.'

This time Pardoe yelped. His inability to join the debate hurt him like a physical pain. He couldn't see that Bob was smiling at his brother, and that Andy was smiling back.

'And three years ago you made one of the best fighting speeches I ever heard. . . . Outside the Elephant and Castle, you remember?' Andy nodded. 'Then you went and got yourself clobbered by that copper on horseback. Truncheon like a tree trunk.'

'Those were the days all right,' Andy said.

'By God!' said Pardoe, and abandoned the *Encyclopaedia Britannica*, strode up to Bob. 'I remember you.'

'We're having a private conversation,' said Bob. 'I thought that's why you went to look at the books. You should have gone with the girls, man. Better than books any day.'

'I stayed here,' said Pardoe, 'in case my friend Andy should need my help.'

'You thought we were going to fight?' said Bob. 'Jacob and Esau stuff?'

'I thought you might try to tempt him away from us.'

'Fat chance,' said Bob.

'But that isn't the point,' Pardoe said impatiently. 'You were referring to the General Strike. Don't deny it.'

'Who says I'm denying it?' said Bob. 'Andy here was a star turn.'

'How dare you say that?' said Pardoe. 'You were on the side of the Fascists. The strike-breakers.'

'I was working for the *Daily World* at the time,' said Bob. 'We were trying to see all sides.'

'You assaulted me in that fight by the lorry those strike-breakers drove,' said Pardoe. 'You deliberately kicked me. – A foul, unfair and disgusting blow, that caused me months of anguish.'

'As I remember,' said Bob, 'you were knocking seven bells out of another chap at the time, a chap about half your size. And by the look of you, you were a trained boxer, and by the look of him, he wasn't. So I did what you did. I took an unfair advantage.' He turned to Andy. 'I'll have to be off, kidder,' he began.

'Oh no,' said Pardoe. 'This thing is not yet over between us. We'll go outside to somewhere quiet and settle our difference.'

'No, Cuthbert,' Andy said.

'How can you say no?' said Pardoe. 'I told you myself. Your brother's a Fascist. He's beyond the pale, and what is more he owes me this. I promise you that if our positions were reversed and it was my brother involved I should feel exactly the same.' He turned back to Bob. 'Well?' he said. 'Do you accept my challenge? Or are you too afraid?'

Andy said, 'Of course he's not afraid. But show some sense, Cuthbert man. He'll go off with you somewhere quiet, you'll put your fists up and he'll land you another foul.'

'Not this time,' said Pardoe. 'This time I'll be ready for him.'

'You're still talking daft,' said Andy. 'Do you think one dirty trick's all he knows? He's got a barrow-load of them.'

Pardoe looked at Bob in horror, then went back to the bookcase.

'I'll have to go,' Bob said softly.

'Aye,' said Andy. 'Good dance was it?' Bob nodded. 'They tell me you had a real bonny lass on your arm.'

'They told you right,' said Bob. 'She was the one next to Jane when you came in.'

'Well I'm blessed,' said Andy.

More softly still, Bob murmured, 'How are you fixed for money, kidder? I can let you have some. No trouble.'

Pardoe said to the bookcase: 'I utterly forbid that. The Left looks after its own.'

Unperturbed Andy said, 'I'm all right for now. Honest. If things get bad –'

'You know where to come,' said Bob, 'so long as I've got it.' He tapped Andy lightly on the shoulder. 'You know,' he said, 'it's all very fine Grandma worrying about what the telephones is up to. But if she had your friend Cuthbert in the same room she wouldn't have time to worry about phones.'

Outside the hotel, the hall porter and his minions loaded luggage into the Hispano-Suiza and the newly arrived Bentley, as Jane tugged on her driving gloves. Bower strode over to her, a cigar between his teeth.

'It looks like I'll have to push on a bit,' he said. 'Your friend Brenda wants to go home and rest. She has a date at the Embassy tonight.'

'HRH?'

Bower sighed. 'I wonder she doesn't just get a "By Appointment" sign and have done with it.'

Jane giggled. 'I'll try to keep up with you,' she said.

'You could pass me any day you wanted,' he said. 'You drive the way Dempsey punches. I know. And speaking of punches – she was saying it looked as if there might be a fight in the hotel lounge, only there wasn't. She *was* disappointed.'

'Something to do with a pompous fat man, Cuthbert Pardoe,' said Jane. 'Do you know him?'

Bower thought hard. 'One of the best physicists in the

country,' he said at last. 'We did a piece about him and his pals once. "Atoms. Does This Mean The End Of The World?"'

'My friend Robins says it means no such thing,' she said, 'but is Pardoe so marvellous?'

'At his own thing he's one of the best,' said Bower. 'But outside it he's a pest. A cross between school bully and Marxist know-all.'

Jane said: 'He always seemed to me rather a stupid man.'

'Outside his own field – where he's something approaching a genius – Pardoe *is* stupid,' said Bower.

'Poor Andy,' said Jane.

'Bob's brother? He said he came here sometimes. Don't worry about Andy. As I told you, Pardoe's a physicist. Andy'll be with the economists and historians. My guess is that Pardoe came with him today as his bodyguard.'

'But why on earth should Andy need a bodyguard?'

'To see that wicked capitalists like us didn't entice him back to the haunts of Mammon.'

Not all the sharp minds were in Cambridge, she thought, then Bob hurried out of the hotel and it was time to go.

Jane said to Bower, 'I don't mind cracking on a bit, but you will be careful, won't you? After all, your fiancée will be sitting beside you, and we can't have HRH dining on his own.'

'You're the most beautiful mother hen in the world,' said Bower, and they went to their cars.

On the way to Town Bob told them about his brush with Pardoe.

'Good heavens,' said Lionel, delighted. 'He challenged you to a duel. It's positively Baroness Orczy.'

'Well I suppose he did in a way,' said Bob, 'but there wasn't going to be any swords or pistols.'

'What then?' said Lilian Dunn.

Bob held up his fists. 'These,' he said. 'Leastways *he* thought it would be just fists.'

'Then why didn't you fight?' said Lilian. Like Brenda Coupland, she found the absence of fighting irritating.

'Look pet,' said Bob, 'our Andy took it for granted I'd –'

'Accept the challenge,' said Lionel.

'Right. He thought I'd step outside and kick him in the you know whats again, only I wasn't so sure.'

'Whyever not?' said Lilian.

'Because I only fight when I have to,' said Bob. 'My name's not Sir Percy Blakeney.'

'What a well-read chap you are,' said Jane.

'Printers'll read anything,' said Bob. 'They have to.' The Hispano-Suiza moved on to open road, and took off after the Bentley.

'Hey, this thing can shift, can't it?' said Bob. 'One of these days I'll have to get one of these.'

There was no doubt about it, Jane thought, Bob and Andy were like two separate halves of John.

They reached home without accident, and she hung on close enough to see that Bower did too, then dropped Lilian and Bob at a service flat in South Molton Street, and Lionel at his flat, before ending up at last in South Terrace. A chauffeur would come next day to collect the Hispano-Suiza said Lionel, and she felt no pangs at losing it. She much preferred the Bentley.

# 14

Truett told her that there were three letters and one telephone call: a Mr Lovell. The first two letters were not exciting: an invitation to view the Molyneux autumn collection, and a telephone bill, but the third envelope bore American stamps. She opened it quickly. There was an awful lot of it, and each page bore at the top a printed address in Teutonic writing she found hard to decipher. She turned to the last page and looked at the signature. 'Believe me,' she read, 'yours in the struggle for the advancement of all people everywhere, Erika Bauer' . . . Jay Bower's sister, she remembered. The American branch of the family still spelt their name in the old way. But why write to her? They had all, without exception, detested her. She went back to the beginning.

Dear Jane Whitcomb [she read],

This is not an easy letter to write, nor should I expect it to be. There is no reason why you should even bother to read this, but please oh please do so. I am not the person who behaved so disgracefully to you years ago.

It is said by the mind doctors that people do not change: that they cannot change, that they can only become more themselves: but that is wrong. I am living proof that it is wrong. Wrong. Wrong. WRONG. For I have changed. I am no longer the grubby little capitalist lackey who was so rude to you –

Oh my God, thought Jane. Not another one. Why do they always pick on me?

    – I have learned to think about such matters as poverty and wealth and social justice, and to realise that ours is an unjust society, full of iniquity and inequality, and the person who first taught me to realise these truths is you, and I humbly thank you for it.

Oh no, thought Jane. You can't put it all on me. But she read on.

    I do not mean that you taught me these truths, because you never did, except by your example, your approach to life. What you taught me was something even more precious: how to be one's own person, captain of one's soul, and I thank you for that even more.

Nothing to be ashamed of in that, thought Jane. If I taught anybody at all to think for themselves I should be proud of the fact. But how on earth did I do it?

    Once when you were here, [she read] I discussed with my brother Joachim the things you did and wrote, your participation in the great struggle for justice in that tragic little town in the North of England, and Joachim has sent me copies of the articles you wrote then and since, and in particular the book you wrote about that glorious strike which so nearly succeeded: which might have changed the destiny not only of England but of Europe had you won: perhaps even of the United States itself. I honour you for that.

Jane thought, But it wasn't like that. It wasn't like that. Not for me. Honestly it wasn't. For me it was like the war. I had no thought of stopping it because I knew it couldn't be stopped. What I could do, what I did, was pick up casualties whenever I found them, and rush them off to where they could be helped. – And I wish she wouldn't keep calling Jay Joachim. It makes him sound like somebody I never even met. Besides, he hates it.

Thanks to you [Erika wrote], I realise now that the whole rotten system as we know it is wrong.

(Oh dear, oh dear, thought Jane.) She read on, flicking through the pages. Quotations from Marx, from Lenin, from the *New Republic*, and quite a lot which must have been pure Erika Bauer: honest, compassionate, earnest, and very German. The best kind of German, she thought: the kind that not only thinks good thoughts but believes that something can be done about them. Which is more than I do. I run about with bandages while Erika is trying to build a whole new body: a sort of saintly Frankenstein trying to create a race of benign monsters.

I'll tell you a secret [Erika wrote at the end]. You can discuss it with Joachim if you like, but please nobody else. A little while ago an aunt of mine, who is also my godmother, died, and left me some money. No more than a hundred thousand dollars, but for me that is enough with care to live on my own with freedom, among the workers and intellectuals on whom the future of the world depends.

A hundred thousand dollars, thought Jane. Twenty thousand pounds. Anyone in Felston would call it the riches of Rockefeller, but not Jane Whitcomb, and not Erika Bauer either.

I shall escape from this stifling bourgeois world [Erika wrote], and dedicate myself to helping to build the wonderful classless society of the future, and for helping me to see this as my duty, once again I thank you. Believe me, yours in the struggle for the advancement of all people everywhere,
Erika Bauer.

Beneath the signature was a PS. 'Please don't bother to reply to this,' Jane read. 'It is only a belated, but most sincere thank you.'

Why pick on me? thought Jane once more. She might as well thank me for handing her a live grenade. And yet she means it and is sweet about it. No reason to be angry, and yet I am angry. Perhaps it's because as I understand it she wants to live with the likes of Burrowes and Pardoe and my brother Francis. . . . If it were Andy, now . . . she'd be safe with Andy. . . . In the meantime, what the hell was she supposed to do? She locked the sheets in her desk drawer, and asked the operator for Lovell's number at his service flat in Jermyn Street.

'How was Cambridge?' he asked.

'Quite fantastic.'

'Really?' He sounded surprised, but then Lovell had gone to Oxford. 'Want to come over here and tell me about it? I'm camping out here overnight with a hamper from Fortnum's. There's more than enough for two.'

'Sounds like fun,' said Jane, and looked at her watch. Almost seven o'clock. 'But darling you won't be cross if I leave early, will you? I'm half asleep as it is.'

'Not at all,' said Lovell. 'I remember those Commem Balls. Get yourself over here and I'll look for the tin opener. I know where the corkscrew is.'

They made love as soon as she got there, and it woke her up for once. It also made her feel hungry, and really Charles's hamper was sumptuous. But she would not eat in the nude. Those globules of caviar got everywhere. She searched in the kitchen and found an apron that had belonged to a long-departed parlourmaid, and darling Charles started to get excited all over again. Really men could be the oddest creatures.

'Not until after we've eaten,' she said. Charles took out asparagus, a jar of caviar, and foie gras from the hamper, and Jane wondered what Erika Bauer would say if she knew, but now was not the time.

'Tell me about Cambridge,' said Charles, and she told him. Not all, of course. She found that she wanted to tell him nothing about Francis, except that he was there. There wasn't much more than she could tell him about Jay, either, though Lovell asked a lot of questions. Bower was there, had been agreeable, done all his duty dances and made a lot of telephone calls. The rest of the time he had spent with Catherine, as was right and proper.

Her big story was of course Burrowes, and Bob and Piers. Lovell enjoyed it enormously.

'The boy's in the Rifle Brigade?' he said.

'Just like you.'

Though I would hardly have called him a boy, she thought, and I doubt if Brenda Coupland would either.

'Yes.' There was no doubt that the thought was pleasing to him. 'Shocking language to use in front of ladies.'

'Burrowes regards that as his mission in life – shocking people.'

'Only this time he was shocked instead. Do him good, don't you think?'

Nothing would do Burrowes any good – he'd go to great lengths to see that it didn't, but there was no point in arguing.

'What would you have done?' she asked.

'What Hilyard did. At least I hope I would. Two things that just weren't on – that language in front of women, and then insulting the King. I'd have had to do something. Hilyard behaved very well.'

Jane thought: He means it, bless him. He means every word. And then: But why shouldn't he? He's an officer and a gentleman after all, and that's what officers and gentlemen are for.

'That young chap Patterson did well too,' said Lovell, and seemed to find the fact puzzling, which, Jane knew, was because Bob was neither an officer nor a gentleman.

'Better than you know,' she said, and told him about Pardoe. Lovell laughed aloud. 'Oh why wasn't I there?' he said.

'Because we don't like to be seen out together in public,' she said, 'and quite right too.'

'Yes.' His laughter died. 'Patterson turned up with rather a stunner, you say?'

'The most incredible body I've seen in years,' said Jane. 'Even Lionel –'

'I don't believe it,' said Lovell.

'– said he could understand what men could see in women. – That was after she'd finished dancing with him.'

'In a tizz, was he?'

'All of a doo-da.' Charles spread foie gras on a biscuit.

'Bower mention America at all?'

'Just that he wants me to go,' said Jane. 'There's rather a complication there. They've announced their wedding date. Twenty-second of October. And they want me to be there. Naturally. And so do I. So I may have to make this New York trip rather earlier than was planned.'

'That's perfectly all right,' Lovell said. Jane swallowed the last of her asparagus. 'Charles darling,' she said, and her voice was sweet. 'I know nothing about your relationship with Jay Bower, nor do I want to know, but if you think that you can tell me when to go and when to stay, then you are wrong. Believe me you are wrong. Now either you accept that or I leave.'

'Oh my God,' said Lovell. 'I didn't mean – honestly I didn't. Of course I was wrong. I'm sorry.'

'I expect it's all those financial Himalayan peaks you climb,' Jane said affably. 'You looking down and seeing all the kingdoms of the world spread out before you.'

'I do not believe I'm God,' said Lovell, 'so don't blaspheme.' He moved closer to her, and his hands began to touch.

'Would you like me to take my pinny off?' she asked.

'Not just for the moment,' Lovell said.

Jane telephoned her mother the next morning. Mummy told her that she was dressing for Ascot – it was Gold Cup Day – but that she'd look in on the way back home. Then began the long and wearisome business of trying to get hold of Jay Bower. When Bower wanted her, she thought bitterly, he simply rang and that was that, but getting hold of *him*. . . . Somehow she had the feeling that if she asked Charles Lovell to find Bower for her, Bower would phone back at once. There'd be no talk then of appointments and conferences and don't know when Mr Bower will be free. The thought disgusted her. Jay Bower was in many ways a bore, but he should never have to be under another man's control.

He phoned at last, at noon.

'You got something for me?'

'For you, yes,' said Jane. 'I doubt if it's for the *Daily World*; though the *Daily Wail* or the *Daily Depress* might like it. It's a letter from your sister.'

'Erika? What on earth does she want to write to you for?'

'Not on the phone,' said Jane.

'Come to lunch then,' said Bower. 'At the flat. I'll ask Catherine, too. The pair of you can chaperone each other. I'll send a car.'

He hung up and Jane sighed and rang for Truett to borrow her copy of yesterday's *Daily World*. As she thought, Bower had phoned in a few paragraphs for the 'Wicked World' and she had no doubt they had all been accepted. After all, Bower owned the paper.

A lot about Catherine of course, 'beautiful daughter of Lord and Lady Mangan, at present cruising in the Greek Islands': a photograph of Catherine too, but with Lilian Dunn in the background, which rather spoiled the desired effect. Of course she and Lionel were there, again: 'well-known writer and philanthropist' and 'much-decorated flying hero'. The *World*'s readers must be wondering if they'd ever get engaged. Brenda Coupland was there, of course. Even Bob was there: 'prominent young Northern business man accompanied by Miss Lilian Dunn, the lovely and talented artiste'. In fact the only one who wasn't there was Francis, which ruined the object of the exercise.

The car came and took her to Fleet Street, and the *World* building, but not for her the big room and the shrilling telephones, the galleys coiling like snakes over battered desks: not this time. For her the express lift and the private lift, and the flat door opened by Bower's servant, Crabbe, who had never seemed to be there when she and Bower were lovers. Bower was in the drawing room, alone, and motioned her to the sofa, but she chose a chair instead. The naked portrait of Georgina had once rested against that sofa, and Jane found that she still hated the whole episode, and yet she still wanted Bower to be free. It didn't make sense, but then love never did make sense, nor did the amusing and civilised lust they'd shared.

'Isn't Catherine coming?' she asked.

'Later,' said Bower. 'She's shopping. She never seems to do anything else these days.'

'That's what happens when you get married,' said Jane. 'Or so they tell me.'

'And you can cut that out for a start,' said Bower. 'You could have married me any time you wanted. Only you didn't. And I bet I wasn't the only one.'

He's fishing, Jane thought, and we can't have that.

'Oh heaps of times,' she said. 'As a matter of fact I nearly got a proposal at the ball. – Of marriage I mean.'

He looked at her. 'That don who could dance?' he said. 'At Piers's table?'

'What a good reporter you must have been,' said Jane. 'You don't miss a thing.'

'I still am a good reporter,' said Bower, 'but there isn't a story in a don's amours, not unless he got himself accepted.'

'And speaking of Bower as reporter,' said Jane, 'why has my poor brother been left out of "This Wicked World"?'

'He's a don too,' said Bower. 'And he didn't get engaged either.'

'He was the host,' said Jane.

'In a pig's eye,' said Bower. 'You invited the guests, and I bet you paid for the party as well.'

There was no point in getting annoyed, because it was true. Well almost true. Francis had paid for the food, unless Mummy had helped. She must remember to ask her. Easiest to give in. She opened her handbag, and handed over the letter.

'Let's have a drink first,' he said, and rang the bell. At once Crabbe appeared with martinis.

Jane sipped and watched Bower read. He read the letter as he read everything he thought important: first a quick skim, then a slow and careful perusal. It took him ten minutes: her martini was half finished.

'You knew nothing of this?' he asked, and then, 'Of course you didn't. Damnfool question. Excuse it please.'

He drained his martini, replenished her glass and poured himself another. 'Aunt Trudi's will should be cleared by October,' he said, 'and then I guess she'll be off to the Village.'

'The Village?'

'Greenwich Village, you nut. Have you forgotten already?'

'Won't she come to the wedding?'

'I doubt it,' said Bower. 'She'll be too busy making arrangements to have our parents hung from lamp-posts.' And then he lobbed his bomb. 'I doubt if any of my family will come to the wedding,' he said. He said it rather smugly, as if it were a source of pride to him.

'But why on earth not?' said Jane. 'Catherine's a lovely girl. Charming. Well born. Educated. And not exactly destitute either.'

'All the attributes,' said Bower, 'except the one that matters.'

'What's that?'

'She isn't a German American,' Bower said.

'Oh for heaven's sake,' said Jane.

'I know, I know,' Bower said. 'But let me ask you something. You remember how my parents treated you when they thought we were going to marry?' Her face was answer enough. 'Well that's how they'll treat Catherine if I ever take her near them. Which I won't.'

'Poor Jay,' said Jane.

'Not poor Catherine?'

'No,' said Jane. 'She's got the only Bower she wants. . . . Have you told her, by the way?'

'Yes,' said Bower. 'She isn't worried. Or she says she's not.'

'And her family?'

'I haven't had the guts,' said Bower. 'Not yet. Catherine says she'll do it, but I know it's my job. I'll get round to it soon.' He sighed. 'I'd sort of hoped Erika would come. We got on pretty well when we were younger. . . . Incidentally, you were wrong about Rothermere and Beaverbrook. They wouldn't touch this thing.' He flicked the letter with his finger.

'You think not?'

'I know not. Dog doesn't eat dog. Not even when one dog's American.'

'What do you want me to do about it?' Jane asked.

'Whatever you want,' said Bower. 'It's your letter. But thanks for letting me see it.'

As he spoke, Catherine came in, followed by Crabbe who seemed bowed low with the weight of the packages he carried.

'Jane darling,' she said. 'How sweet of you to come.'

'Better bring some more of these,' said Bower, and nodded at the martini jug.

'Why are we getting sloshed so early?' said Catherine. 'Not Jane's letter? Not bad news?'

Bower said, 'Do you mind?'

'Of course not,' said Jane, 'go right ahead,' and Bower gave Catherine a resumé of what his sister had written.

'Oh dear,' said Catherine. 'How very unwise of her.'

'Could be worse than that,' said Bower. 'She probably won't even come to the wedding.'

'But Jaybird,' said Catherine, 'that means you'll have nobody.'

'Right again,' said Bower. 'Does that bother you?'

'Not me, no. How could it? But think how alone you'll look.'

'Who'll be looking at me?' said Bower, and Catherine got up and kissed him just as Crabbe came in with the martini jug. None of them seemed in the least disconcerted, thought Jane.

After lunch Catherine announced that she had more shopping

to do and Jane went with her. It was Harrods after all. Jay it seemed wanted the Fleet Street flat completely refurnished, which meant looking at everything from carpets to bath tubs. Catherine, Jane saw, had very clear ideas about what they wanted, and pretty good ideas they were. Together they ransacked the furniture department, then went to the restaurant for tea.

'It really is too bad of that – Erika, isn't it? As if my poor darling Jaybird didn't have enough to worry about. But why on earth did she write to you?'

'She thinks I'm like that, too,' said Jane. 'In fact she thinks she's going to imitate me. She said so.'

'What nonsense,' said Catherine. 'I mean you go in for good works and all that – and why shouldn't you? But plotting and planning – Jane you couldn't. All the same – it won't be very nice for Jay, will it? – No matter how sweet he is about it.'

'Does it bother you – none of his family being there?'

'Not in the least,' Catherine said. 'Apart from the look of the thing. From what I've heard they're a pretty mouldy lot. And anyway – it won't affect Jay's inheritance. That's all tied up in trusts and things. They can't cut him out of a penny.'

Carefully Jane searched her handbag for cigarettes, holder, and lighter, and found them at last.

'Then that's all right,' she said.

She was back just before Mummy arrived. Only one telephone call, a Mr Robert Patterson, and would she please call him back? She did up her dress, and rang the number he'd left. A secretary answered, – at half past six in the evening. Promising young Northern business man wasn't in it. He came on the line.

'Jane,' he said, 'can I ask a favour?'

'Ask and we'll see,' she said.

'I need a bit of advice pretty quick,' he said.

'Bob, I know absolutely nothing about wireless sets.'

'You know a sight more than anybody else about commonsense,' he said. 'Except Grandma mebbe.'

That was the accolade, and they both knew it.

'Can we talk later tonight?' he asked.

'It would have to be quite late,' she said. 'My mother's coming soon. Say ten o'clock for a brandy or something? Only ring first.'

'I'll do that,' said Bob. 'Thanks, Jane.'

She hung up and wondered, What on earth has that young man been up to? He can't have gone back to Cambridge and fought his duel with Pardoe after all? Of course he couldn't. What then? Stand for Parliament? Marry Miss Dunn? Go to Australia? . . . The doorbell rang and she hurried downstairs. When Truett admitted her mother she was in the hall waiting, Foch by her side.

Mummy made an entrance in a suit of blue and cream silk, and a large blue hat with creamy feathers. The major followed her, in dark-grey morning coat and pale-grey top hat.

'I've brought George,' said her mother, rather as if George were a dog of her own whom Foch disliked. 'I hope you don't mind?'

'Of course not, Mummy,' said Jane. 'How nice to see you, Major. It's such a lovely evening I thought we might have drinks in the garden.'

'Topping idea,' said the major, who looked as if he'd had drinks in a few other places already. Jane led them to the chairs and table by the plane tree, and left the major to open champagne for Mummy and herself while she mixed him a whisky and soda.

'I hope Ascot was a success?' she said.

'Not bad. Not bad at all,' said her mother, giving Ascot seven out of ten. 'We did quite reasonably well. Not the Gold Cup. But what's the point of tipping an odds-on favourite? Still, we had two others: a three to one and a hundred to eight, and George's each-way outsider came in second. Not at all a bad day.'

'I must say you do look dashing, Mummy,' said Jane.

'Life in the old girl yet,' said her mother, and Jane almost spilt her champagne. Never in her life had her mother talked like that. The major had his methods after all.

'Turned a lot of heads,' said the major. 'The deuce of a lot of heads. I know because I was watching. But I was the one she walked with.' He looked about him. 'Nice garden,' he said. 'Very nice. Lot of space for a London garden. I like that. You get a lot of sun, too. What you need is two or three of those what d'you call 'ems –'

'Do try to be a little more precise, dear,' said Mummy.

'Bombay fornicators,' said the major.

'I beg your pardon?' said Jane, more awe-struck than outraged.

'Sort of a chair thing they had on verandahs in India,' said the major, 'with a kind of rest for your legs so you could get the breeze up, if you follow me.'

'Oh yes I remember,' said Jane, 'but I never heard them called that before.'

'Naturally you wouldn't,' said her mother, 'but I've heard it asserted – of course I can't vouch for the veracity of it – that with a little determination and ingenuity some kind of congress could be achieved.'

It occurred to Jane that her mother also had been celebrating two winners and an each-way outsider.

'Anyway,' said the major, and rose to his feet, 'I'd better be off. The sports editor at the *World* wants a word about our expenses.'

'Now you be firm,' said his wife.

'Of course,' said the major. 'They can't expect us to live in doss houses.' He turned to Jane. 'Thanks for the drink.' He kissed her, and then his wife. 'See you later old girl.' He paused for a moment. 'Where did you say we were eating?'

'Rules,' said his wife. 'Do try to remember.' But she said it without rancour.

The major waved vaguely, muttered something about 'let myself out', and was gone.

'Dear George,' said his wife. 'A little forthright you may think –'

'Perhaps just a little,' said Jane.

'– But that's because he can't – think, you see. Not that it matters. I do the thinking. George simply follows those incredible instincts of his. Together we do rather well.'

It was quite apparent that they regarded themselves as a team.

Her mother sipped her champagne. 'How was Cambridge?' she asked.

'Great fun, but hardly a triumph from Francis's point of view.'

'So I gathered. Gwendolyn Gwatkin spent most of yesterday trying to reach me by telephone. The stupid woman should have consulted the "Racing Calendar". And when she did reach me – quite late in the evening I might add – when George and I were preparing for bed – it was to ask me whether I knew that you had been to a ball at Cambridge, and why Francis had not been included in the party.'

'She reads the *Daily World*, I take it?'

'As much of it as is within her competence. I replied that yours had been a large party, largely composed of aristocrats and heroes and millionaires, and Francis, who is of a retiring nature, had preferred to remain in the background. I then added that if she chose to read the *Express*, the *Mail*, the *News Chronicle* or the *Morning Post*, she would receive written evidence of Francis's presence, since it seemed so vital to her. I added that she might see further evidence in the forthcoming editions of the *Tatler*, *The Bystander* and the *Illustrated London News*.'

Mummy's staffwork had always been excellent, but this was worthy of the German High Command.

'How on earth did you find out?' asked Jane.

'I had already asked George to enquire at the *World* what newspapers had been represented at Cambridge, and what information the dailies had printed. And not for Gwendolyn Gwatkin's benefit I may tell you.' She put down her champagne glass.

'Will you tell me please why Francis's name was omitted in the *Daily World*? Naturally I lied to Gwendolyn Gwatkin. Every other name was mentioned.'

'I didn't know it had been until I saw the paper myself,' said Jane. 'Bower wrote the gossip bits personally. I suppose the major found that out, too?' Her mother bowed assent. 'I met him and his fiancée for lunch yesterday – there were things I had to discuss about my New York trip –' at least, she thought, that isn't a downright lie – 'and I asked him then. He was flippant about it, but what it boiled down to was that he didn't consider Francis to be important enough.'

'And do you believe that was his reason?'

'Of course not,' said Jane. 'Francis had annoyed him, and he chose to punish him by leaving him out of "This Wicked World", and a very effective punishment it would have been if the other newspapers had done the same.'

'Why does he dislike Francis?'

There was no help for it. She told her mother about the Burrowes business.

'But surely poor Francis cannot be blamed for that cad's behaviour?' said her mother.

'Bower feels that he could and should. He permitted Burrowes to come to the table where he was host, and made no effort to restrain him. Bower argued that no other man present would have behaved like that.'

'Your brother is, as you know, a homosexual,' said her mother. 'Is it possible that he is in some way captivated by Mr Burrowes?'

'I should think he must be,' said Jane.

'Then at least we have a reason for his behaviour, if not an excuse.'

'Bower is aware of that,' said Jane. 'He still thinks Francis should have tried to control him.'

'You and I both know,' said her mother, 'that Francis could not control a guinea pig, let alone a drunken and violent man with whom he is also in love.'

Jane said, 'Burrowes was controlled.'

'Of course he was,' said her mother. 'You told me. By an officer in an excellent regiment and that young protégé of yours. I have no quarrel with that. They did well. The only possible thing, perhaps, but can you see Francis taking either of their places?'

'No, Mummy.'

'Of course not. Guy and David, certainly. They would have handled Mr Burrowes with the same robust pleasure as the two who did it. But Guy and David are dead, and Francis is not. Will you ever forgive him for that, do you think?'

Oh Mummy that's a foul, she thought. A sneaking rotten foul. It isn't *fair*.

She said carefully, 'I was fond of Guy and David, obviously. We were much closer in age and spent a lot of our lives together. We were close in other ways too. When they were killed it was the hardest knock I'd ever taken – until John was killed.'

'I also,' her mother said. 'It was an appalling loss. They were men. What poor George would call "real men" – though George of course is not aware that Francis is as he is.' She mused for a moment. 'Where was I? You must forgive me. I have had rather a lot of champagne today. – Oh yes. Your brothers being killed. I did grieve for them, Jane. I promise you I did. But in the end

I found that it was wiser – and more charitable – to care for the living than regret the dead. It is a source of never-ending shame to me that you were not a part of that resolution.'

'Please, Mummy,' said Jane.

'Allow me to finish,' said her mother. 'I have thought about it often since, and the only reason I can find – reason yet again, and not excuse – is that you too were part of the war that had taken your brothers, and so very nearly taken you. You were still part of them, and even at the height of your breakdown I knew you to be stronger than Francis.' She paused for a moment, then took a deep breath. 'Besides, your father loved you.'

'He loved us all, surely?'

'Certainly not,' said her mother. 'You were the only one left whom he loved. Guy also was what George calls a "real man". Heaven knows he proved it often enough. Polo and cricket and shikari – nobody knows how many tigers he shot – or how many women he took to his bed. Your father was ruthless, clever, brave – and chivalrous according to his lights, but he could no more help chasing women than the sun can stop rising. I accept that now. It was not possible to accept it then. And he despised homosexuals. He could be very witty about them when he chose, and extremely cruel.

'He realised the truth of Francis's nature while Francis was still at school. From the very beginning he tried to "cure" him as he put it, but Francis could not be cured. He nearly broke the boy: reduced him to a condition almost as desperate as your own. I honestly believe that if I hadn't fought for Francis he *would* have broken him, and that is the point, you see. I could fight for one of you: I couldn't fight for two. It was beyond my strength.'

'And so you chose the weaker vessel?'

'Don't you believe him to be so?'

'Yes,' said Jane. 'I do.'

'And yet,' her mother said, 'despite his weakness he has made a life, achieved quite a degree of success.'

'He's a very clever young man,' said Jane. 'All my brothers were clever.'

Her mother frowned. She did not wish to invoke the dead.

'What is it you want of me, Mummy?' said Jane. 'You asked

me to get up a party for him and I got up a party. Probably the most exciting one there, in fact. I even helped him to pay for the thing, and I bet you did, too.'

Her mother shrugged dismissively. The point was not relevant, it seemed.

'I did all you asked of me,' said Jane. 'All *he* asked, for that matter. What more do you want?'

Her mother said, 'I want you to love him, but I'm afraid that's impossible.'

'You're right,' said Jane. 'I'm afraid it is.'

Truett plodded grimly to them across the lawn. She had once told Jane that outdoors was no place for a parlourmaid.

'Mr Warley on the telephone, miss,' she said.

'Tell him I'll call him back.'

'No no,' her mother said. 'I must go. George may well have remembered to go to Rules.' She got to her feet.

'Ask him to hold on,' said Jane, and Truett plodded grimly back.

'I assume,' said her mother, 'that it is not Francis's homosexuality that inhibits your love?'

'Of course not,' said Jane. 'We never have loved each other, and I doubt if we ever shall. Your point of course is that Lionel also is a homosexual – but Lionel's sexual tastes are the only thing he shares with Francis. He is witty and generous and sweet, and I like him very much.'

'I have met him, as you know,' said her mother, 'and I agree that he is all that you say, which makes him very likeable. Wouldn't there be more merit in loving someone that one didn't like at all?'

So you never liked Francis either, and yet you made yourself love him, thought Jane, which makes you rather wonderful, Mummy dear.

Perhaps her mother read the look in her eyes, for she moved at once to the house, and Jane followed. At the door her mother kissed her.

'I had four clever children,' she said, 'and I'm proud of all four.'

Truett closed the door on her, and Jane went to the waiting phone.

'Lionel darling,' she said. 'So sorry to keep you waiting.'

'Not at all,' said Lionel. 'Your mother was leaving, I gather.'

'Just left,' said Jane.

'And how is she?'

'Quite extraordinary,' said Jane, 'in the nicest possible way, and between you and me, just a little bit tiddly.'

'Gracious,' said Lionel. 'The major has made an impact.'

'Altogether for the better,' said Jane. 'What can I do for you?'

'Blessed if I know,' said Lionel. 'The thing is I had a call from Charles Lovell yesterday.'

'Oh yes?'

'He seemed to be interested in that young friend of yours.'

'Bob?'

'Mm. Asked if it was true that he'd got into some sort of a scrape at Cambridge. I told him certainly not. He'd behaved perfectly splendidly. He seemed delighted.'

'Was that all?'

'Not quite. He seemed rather curious about Patterson's partner, too. Was she really all that attractive? I told him decidedly yes. Seemed a bit odd. I just wondered if you'd heard anything.'

'Not a thing,' said Jane. 'Did he know you'd telephone me?'

'I doubt it,' said Lionel. 'As a matter of fact he asked me not to tell a soul, and I said of course not, but I crossed my fingers first, and as we were talking by telephone of course he didn't see a thing. Just thought I'd better let you know.'

'Much obliged,' said Jane, 'but I'm blowed if I can see why.'

'Any chance of our going dancing later on?'

'Not tonight,' said Jane. 'Perhaps tomorrow.'

'Mug of cocoa and an early night, eh?'

'Something like that,' said Jane, and wondered why she found it necessary to lie.

'Cambridge did rather take its toll,' said Lionel. 'I may have to reach for the Bovril myself. Phone me tomorrow?'

'Of course,' said Jane. 'Good night, darling.' She hung up. What in God's name was Charles up to?

# 15

B OB ARRIVED PROMPT at ten. He wore a day suit, which was just as well. Jane hadn't bothered to change. She'd spent too much time thinking about her brother, and the things her mother had said. Her mother of course had been right, but then Jane felt that she'd been right too, and there was no solution to that problem. Better, far better, to leave it alone. Yet she'd gnawed at it like Foch chewing the corner of a carpet.

'How nice to see you,' she said to Bob. 'Didn't you bring Lilian?'

'Lilian's in Paris,' said Bob. 'Working.' Then added not without pride, 'At the Folies Bergère.'

'Goodness,' said Jane. 'How grand.'

'Well I must say it's pretty good,' said Bob. 'On the same bill as Josephine Baker and Maurice Chevalier.'

'Of course it is,' said Jane. 'So you two haven't split up or anything?'

'That isn't the way it is with us,' said Bob. 'Just a lot of fun if and when it happens.' He stopped, then said: 'I'm sorry I didn't mean –'

'Oh don't be ridiculous,' said Jane. 'Of course you didn't mean. Have you eaten?'

He nodded.

'Then let me get you a brandy and you can tell me all about it, whatever it is.'

He sniffed at the brandy in the goblet, then sipped, relaxed. He really has learned to enjoy life, she thought.

'Funny thing,' he said, 'and I'm sorry to bother you with it, but like I said there was nobody else I could talk to. Not even Grandma.'

'Oh do get on with it,' she said.

'Yes, well.' He hesitated for a moment, like a swimmer facing a cold sea, then in he went. 'I got this visitor at the office,' he said. 'What they call a City gent. Pin-stripe trousers, black jacket, stiff collar. Said he'd called on behalf of a Mr Charles Lovell.'

Thank God Lionel told me first, thought Jane, but decided to be surprised even so. 'But I know him,' she said.

'Of course you do,' said Bob. 'He's the chap you saw at Blagdon Hall.'

'Oh yes,' said Jane. 'I told you, didn't I? As a matter of fact I think he's going to buy it.'

'So he really is rich?' said Bob.

'Extremely.'

'I see,' said Bob, then: 'This chap – name of Snelgrove – told me that Mr Lovell had heard about this business of mine and wondered whether I was interested in expanding.'

'And what did you say?'

'I said, "That depends." That's all you ever do say to the Snelgroves of this world, because pin-stripes or no pin-stripes, he was no better than a messenger boy. So I waited for him to deliver his message.'

'And did he?'

'It took a bit of time,' said Bob. 'Him having been to Rugby or wherever it was seemed to give him the idea that he was the boss, but in the end he came out with it. Lovell wants to buy in.'

'Take you over?'

'Nothing like that,' said Bob. 'I'll be the major shareholder, but he'll find the money I need to go nationwide, as you might say.'

'And could you do it? Go nationwide?'

'Oh aye,' said Bob. 'No problem there. It's what I was going to do anyway, only I reckoned it would take me a few more years. This way I could start next week. Only –'

'Only what?'

'Well it looks right,' said Bob, 'and it feels right, but why the hell should he bother? From what you tell me he's a whale and I'm a tiddler.'

'You're afraid the whale might turn out to be a shark in disguise?'

'Well yes,' said Bob. 'Only like I say, why should he bother? What's in it for him?'

'Money,' said Jane. 'If Charles Lovell has heard about you he'll have done his homework. If he wants a share he must believe he'll make money.'

'But how did he know what I'm doing?'

'How does a bee find pollen?' said Jane.

'Yes,' said Bob. 'I see. Only . . . can I trust him, Jane? Sharks is dodgy fish at the best of times.'

'You can trust him,' said Jane.

'You sound very sure.'

'You don't have to accept his offer, you know.'

'I don't have to live in a service flat in Knightsbridge either. I can always doss down in John Bright Street. . . . You're really sure?'

'Really sure.'

'Then I'll do it,' said Bob.

Jane was sure because if Charles cheated Bob, which she considered unlikely, as well as extremely difficult, she would make good whatever money was involved. Not because of altruism, not entirely, and not just because he was likeable, in her mother's phrase. A successful Bob would be far more able to take care of Grandma and Bet, and even Andy, than she ever could. It was possible to force money on them when they needed it: Bet's child, Grandma's cataract operation, the doctor for Andy after that mounted policeman had clubbed him, but oh the fuss and bother. The coy refusal changing at last into grudging acceptance, like a courtship doomed to failure. What a bitch I am, she thought. All the same how much easier it would be if she could just make them a weekly allowance; a sort of pension. She had suggested it to Grandma once, and Grandma had been horrified.

'Something bothering you?' said Bob. 'You've gone very quiet.'

'I've been thinking,' she said.

'Oh aye?'

'About the Patterson brothers,' said Jane. 'How different you are from your father. . . . What was your grandfather like?'

'Grandma's husband? Typical pitman, I'd say. Liked his pint and his pipe, and daft about bairns. He could lick any man in the street, but when we were little we could climb all over him. – Jump on him, even. All he'd do was laugh.'

'What happened to him?'

'Silicosis,' said Bob. 'You know, that dust disease you get down the pit. He lasted six months. The doctors said he wouldn't make three, but he wouldn't let himself be beaten. Not Granda.'

So there was something of their paternal grandfather in them, all three.

'And your mother's parents?'

'I didn't know them all that well,' said Bob. 'He got a job as a coal heaver at Tyne Dock, so of course they had to move.'

'Coal heaver? A big man?'

'When I was a bairn I used to think he was a giant,' said Bob. 'But he was a Primitive, same as Da. He wouldn't hurt a fly, any more than his wife would.'

'And what happened to them?'

'The Spanish 'flu happened,' said Bob. 'Back in 1918. They were both dead in a week.'

So the rest of it was all Grandma. Her husband had supplied some of the fire, but she had supplied the rest of it, and the brains.

'What you up to?' said Bob. 'Going to write our family history?'

'My God no,' said Jane. 'That would be a life's work. I was just thinking about you.'

'What about us?'

'There can't be very many like you in Felston.'

'Oh I don't know,' said Bob. 'A pretty good average, I'd say. Maybe a bit luckier than most.'

'I should have thought in Felston you'd have to make your own luck,' said Jane. 'You got out, Bob. You escaped, all three of you. How many Felston men have done that?'

'There's some goes to sea,' said Bob. 'Some's emigrated – Australia, Canada, South Africa. . . . But that's not what you mean, is it? You're seeing us like three Dick Whittingtons, off to London to make our fortunes, and not a cat between us.'

'Exactly,' said Jane.

'Well John was like that, I grant you,' said Bob. 'He'd have been doing well by now if he'd been spared. And I suppose I'm like that, too. But Andy? He's got nowt, Jane. Not a tosser.'

'He goes to Cambridge,' said Jane. 'He dines with the dons. He attends meetings, makes speeches, goes to parties –'

'*Parties?*' said Bob. '*Andy?*'

'Oh not the sort of parties you go to,' said Jane. 'Pretty girls and foxtrots and champagne. Andy goes to the serious parties. Sherry and biscuits and earnest talk with a lot of really quite important people. Oh – Andy's making his fortune, too, but with him it isn't money.'

'Power,' said Bob. 'Like I told you before. But who told you all this?'

'Francis,' said Jane. 'He goes to those parties too.'

'My brother's not a poof,' said Bob. 'He hasn't got much time for women, but he's got no time at all for men. Not that way. – I'm sorry, Jane, but I had to say that.'

'Of course,' said Jane. 'And I didn't for one moment think he had. But as you say – his driving force isn't sex. It's power. But he's still broken free. You're a remarkable trio.'

'I'll tell you a funny thing,' said Bob. 'When our Bet was single and I'd started making a few bob working for Bower, I had the idea she could maybe come down to London and take care of us. Be my housekeeper.'

'What did she say?'

'She was horrified,' said Bob. 'Even the thought of leaving Felston and she was well nigh hysterical. There was me couldn't wait to go, and her terrified I'd drag her off.'

'She was afraid of being alone.'

'We're all alone when we set up on our own.'

'Which is why she didn't want to do it. Hated it so much in fact that Felston seemed like paradise.'

'Aye,' said Bob. 'You're right. Grandma in the kitchen, and next-door neighbours, and the wives in the corner shop. . . . She couldn't be alone. Not even if she wanted to be. Now our Andy, he hates Felston. The only place he said was worse was prison.'

'Prison?' said Jane. 'Oh . . . when he was a Conscientious Objector?'

'Six months in Durham Gaol,' said Bob. 'He took more bashings in those six months than the rest of his life put together. The prisoners didn't like conchies any more than the warders did.'

'But why doesn't he like Felston? I don't mean the place, but the people –'

'Andy's not much of a one for people,' said Bob. 'Not individuals anyway. The workers, the proletariat, the masses arising from their slumber, that's fine. But show him a girl like Lilian or a chap like your pal Lionel – he'd run a mile.'

'That doesn't explain –' said Jane.

'I'm getting there,' said Bob. 'Give us half a chance.' Jane begged pardon. 'Our Andy hates the town of Felston for what it is, and the people for letting themselves be beaten by it. There's masses there all right, but you can't tell me they're arising, now can you? So he hops off to Cambridge to find out how to make them arise. That's how I see it anyway.' He looked at his watch. 'I'd better be off,' he said, 'or I'll end up making a speech meself.' He hesitated. 'You're sure I'll be all right with Lovell?'

'Positive,' she said.

'Thanks pet,' said Bob, and kissed her cheek.

And there was Bob for you. Show him an advantage and he took it. Anybody else would be painstakingly grateful, even grovel a bit, for what she'd told him: but not Bob. Doing him a favour made you one of the family, which probably meant another favour.

They had dined in Trinity. He and Francis Whitcomb and Pardoe, in the rooms of a Trinity economics don called Antrobus, their host. Thank God Burrowes hadn't come, Andy thought. He was sick to death of that bugger Burrowes. Pity Bob hadn't landed him one when he had the chance.

'More port, Andy?' Antrobus's voice was gently reproving. The decanter was in front of him, and the rules said nobody else got any till he'd made his move. Rules for everything: even having a drink.

'No thanks.' Andy pushed the port on to Pardoe, who promptly filled his glass, and Andy looked about him as he did so. Nice room. Books all over the place – but then every room he'd seen in Cambridge had books all over the place: even the lavatories. This room had oak panelling as well, and little sporting prints that looked old and valuable, and a statuette of a girl with no clothes on that was probably older and more valuable still. . . .

'Penny for them, Andy,' said Antrobus.

'Pardon?' Andy looked across at him. Forty would he be? Grey hair, a bit of a stoop, but very fit. Played a lot of squash, they said.

'Just wool gathering,' Andy said.

'We can't have that.' Antrobus accepted the decanter and filled his own glass, then pushed it on to Francis, who refused, and pushed it on to Andy who passed it to Pardoe, who left it where it was. Like Musical Chairs, thought Andy. Or Pass the Parcel. Musical Decanters. He wondered what Grandma would say if he ever started playing Musical Teapots.

'Tonight you must sing for your supper,' said Antrobus. 'You did promise us a few words, you know.'

'Oh aye,' said Andy. 'Lock-outs.'

He could just as easily have said oh yes, but Andy had early learned that a little roughness of speech went down well.

'Lock-outs is something we haven't seen a lot of in Felston. Not recently,' he said.

'Oh come now,' said Pardoe. 'You can't expect us to believe that. From what you say the town is seething with exploitation.'

'If you don't mind, Pardoe,' said Antrobus, 'we'll hear what Andy has to say.'

And there was another thing, Andy thought. Everybody else gets called by their surname, unless they're really close friends like Francis Whitcomb and Cuthbert Pardoe, but I'm Andy to everybody. Like I was their little lapdog: Andy the proletarian poodle.

'The reason there's been no lock-outs,' Andy said, 'is because there's been no work. You can't lock fellers out of unemployment, even in Felston.'

'Verily thou art answered,' Antrobus murmured.

'They closed us down after the Miners' Strike,' Andy said. 'The one that led to the General Strike three years back. . . . I had a brother in the army. He was killed in 1918.'

'Another poor private,' said Pardoe. 'Martyred in the Great Capitalist War.'

'He was a captain,' said Andy, and this time Antrobus sniggered. . . . 'There was an expression he'd picked up – used it all the time. "Surplus to requirement". Well that's what Felston is. Surplus to the bosses' requirement.

'The mines is old and hard to work, so they closed them. There's no great need of ships now we've caught up with the losses of the war, so they've closed the shipyards an' all. And the heavy industry we had was mostly ships' engines and equipment and armaments, and you can't find a buyer for them. You couldn't give it away. So we're not locked-out any more. How could we be?'

'Terrible,' said Antrobus. 'Terrible, terrible. But when there was work – how was a lock-out organised?'

'Say it was a pit,' said Andy. 'One of Lord Blagdon's, say. One day the manager would put up a notice there'd be a cut on the hourly rate. Or mebbe the bonus. Or both. Mind you he was never as blunt as that. Oh dear me no.

'Very much regret to announce, he would say. Unprecedented drop in demand. . . . Foreign competition keener than ever. If the pit is to continue in production we must all make sacrifices. . . . Like hell. Catch him giving up his Morris or the owner his Rolls-Royce. When he meant all, he meant all the pitmen. Five bob a week – the difference between just enough, and hunger.'

'What then?' Francis Whitcomb asked.

His eyes were glittering with excitement. You'd think he was at the pictures, thought Andy.

'There'd be lodge meetings,' he said aloud.

'All over the district?' Antrobus asked.

'Certainly,' said Andy. 'One pit cutting wages was like testing the water. If they got away with it all the others would do the same. So the men would meet and talk things over, and usually that was enough hot air to lift a Zeppelin.' Francis Whitcomb looked shocked. 'Then likely they'd send a petition to the manager to ask for discussion of his terms, and the manager would say that means you reject our fair and just and self-sacrificing offer, and that means you're on strike, so I hereby declare this pit well and truly closed. And out they'd go.'

'But the owners would lose money, too,' said Francis Whitcomb. 'What about their profits? Their shareholders?'

Andy shrugged.

'Coal owners aren't daft,' said Andy. 'They're bastards, but they're not stupid bastards.'

'My uncle's one,' said Pardoe.

'Then you'll know what I'm talking about,' said Andy.

'Precisely,' said Pardoe, as if they had both made the same important point.

'They could plan the thing because they always had the initiative.'

'The money,' said Francis Whitcomb.

'Exactly,' said Andy. 'They could start one of their little games any time they were ready, and the men never knew when that would be. They were never prepared. And even if they were, they never had the money put by to match what the owners had. . . . So the owners would make their demands in February say, or just before Christmas – that was a popular one. No presents for the bairns, no treats. And no coal either, when the ground was freezing. Chaps soon got fed up when the cold got to them. And their families.' He paused for a moment. 'Is there any coffee left?' he asked. Antrobus got up and poured him a cup.

'So that's a lock-out,' he said. 'Force the wages down, and if the men want to talk about it tell them they're on strike. That way you don't have to pay any wages at all for a bit. . . . The men'll call it a lock-out, but the papers'll say what the owners say. And even if the papers did call it a lock-out, what's the odds? How many people in a town like this would know the difference?'

'And I suppose the hardship involved would be considerable?' Pardoe said.

'Oh, aye. Considerable.' Andy's voice was dry.

'And where would it end?'

'In defeat,' said Andy.

Francis Whitcomb looked like a child who's had his sweets taken away. 'Always?' he asked.

'Pretty near,' Andy said. 'Even in the '26 strike, the miners went back on the owners' terms.'

'But surely,' said Antrobus, 'there must have been exceptions. An unexpected world demand for coal, say –'

'It could happen,' said Andy. 'And the men would know

about it and tighten their belts and think – This is one we can win.'

'What would happen then?' asked Francis Whitcomb.

'Scabs,' said Andy.

'Illicit labour,' Pardoe said sagely.

'Not illicit, no,' said Andy. 'Scabs don't break the law.'

'They betray their comrades,' said Antrobus. 'That's worse, surely?'

'In principle it is.'

'In principle?' said Pardoe. 'You can find it in your heart to justify such scoundrels?'

'You don't justify,' said Andy. 'Not when your belly's empty and you haven't had a cigarette or a pipe of baccy for as far back as you can remember.'

'But the others – the ones who hold out – surely they suffer equally?'

'A chap has a sick bairn,' said Andy, 'or a wife with TB, or a load of debt to a moneylender. He'll do the best he can. And scabbing's the one thing he can do.'

'So it's a story without villains,' said Antrobus.

'Except the owners,' Andy said.

'Capitalism,' said Francis Whitcomb. 'In the dock as usual.'

'Only it isn't,' said Andy. 'It never has been. If we could once get capitalism in the dock we'd get a conviction. Bound to.'

'You're in a hurry, Andy,' said Antrobus.

'Felston hasn't got much time,' said Andy, and the don winced.

He doesn't like being bested by a pupil, Andy thought. Well he'll have to lump it. I might not like being teacher's pet all the time, but there's been some good days here. Learning, discussing. . . . And some good men here an' all. But it's time I said Thanks and got back home. Among my own. To look for a way to get things started. . . .

'We're obliged to you,' said Antrobus. 'That was a very cogent, very lucid exposition.'

If only he didn't sound so surprised, thought Andy.

'We like to think we may have taught you something while you've been among us –'

'Indeed you have,' said Andy.

'– And you have paid us back in full. We're grateful.'

'Hear hear,' said Pardoe. 'When I compare Andy here with that appalling brother of his –'

Andy put down his coffee cup. 'That'll do,' he said. 'He's my brother – and I'll do the criticising – when I think it's needed.'

'Yes really, Pardoe,' said Antrobus. 'There are more serious matters to consider.'

'My application to join the Communist Party.'

'Yes,' said Antrobus, and then: 'We'd rather you didn't.' For the first time, Andy's face betrayed him. His disappointment was obvious.

'Can I ask why?'

'Certainly,' said Antrobus. 'You're a public man, you see.'

'You mean you'll make me one?'

'Not at all,' said Antrobus. 'There's nothing else you could be. In fact you are one already. In Felston at any rate. Orator. Folk hero. Man of the Left. I'm not being ironic, just stating a fact. But it's thought you should be ready by now for a bigger stage.'

'Fine with me,' Andy said. 'But couldn't I do that and join the Party?'

'Not unless you kept your Party membership a secret, and denied it if somebody challenged you. Somehow I don't think you'd like that.'

'I'd hate it,' said Andy.

'Then wouldn't it be better just to go on as you are – a Fellow Traveller if you like – and help us when you can, just as we'll help you when we can?'

'I believe in the Communist Party,' Andy said.

'We know you do, and the Party believes in you. That's why you're asked to make this sacrifice, – and believe me, Andy, we know it's a sacrifice – because we want you out in the open, a man respected, a leader of the people. Not many people respect a member of the Communist Party. Not yet. Not even the members of your own class.'

Andy nodded. He knew it was true.

'What had you in mind for me?' he asked.

'Local councillor – Labour Party Executive – MP,' said Antrobus.

It was what he'd just decided to try for, anyway. On his own. All the same.

'We've got an MP,' he said. 'Jimmy Wagstaff.'

'What you've got is a clown,' said Antrobus. 'A beer-swilling, chuckle-headed clown.'

'I did some research on him,' said Francis Whitcomb. 'His speeches are a mess of inconsistencies and his voting record's appalling.'

But the voters love him, Andy thought. Crafty Jimmy. Smiling Jimmy. The only man from Felston that ever stood up in the House of Commons and insulted his betters. Fat chance I'd have of taking his place.

'Of course we're not talking about next week,' said Antrobus. 'Or even next year. But Wagstaff can't last for ever. I mean he does go the pace a bit, wouldn't you say?'

And it was true. Jimmy Wagstaff could shift his share – and somebody else's. Another reason why the men of Felston loved him.

'We just want you to be ready when the time comes,' said Antrobus. 'We need a voice in the House. We want you to be that voice. . . . Well?'

Andy thought for a moment. To deny the Party he believed in, that really was a sacrifice, but as Antrobus had said, sacrifice was part of it, part of what would make it triumphant.

'All right,' he said.

'Good man,' said Antrobus. 'Now – there is just one other thing.' He looked to his left. 'You don't mind, Whitcomb?'

'Not at all,' Francis Whitcomb said. 'Go ahead.'

'Whitcomb's sister, Jane,' said Antrobus. 'At one time it looked as if she might have considerable influence in Felston. You may recall that we found it necessary to diminish that influence.'

'It's not something I'm proud of,' said Andy.

'It wasn't a question of pride,' said Antrobus. 'It was a question of necessity. Would you say that the measures that were taken were effective?'

'Aye,' said Andy. 'But I'm still not sure why you did it.'

'Because Jane Whitcomb is an impossible woman: an interfering little bourgeoise who tried to placate her social conscience by playing Lady Bountiful,' said Antrobus. 'She has no more idea of Marxism than I have of the moons of Jupiter – and I have no doubt that in her own egocentric way she enjoyed every second of her time in Felston.' Again he looked to his left. 'I'm sorry, Whitcomb,' he said, 'but –'

'Quite all right,' said Francis Whitcomb. 'It's all perfectly true.'

Andy thought so too, but he had also seen Jane at his father's funeral. 'I don't see what you're driving at,' he said.

'A question, no more,' said Antrobus. 'Can you see Jane Whitcomb as a threat to you if we tried to make you Felston's next MP?'

'Not now,' said Andy. 'You did too good a job.'

'Then we must get to work at once,' said Antrobus.

'You want me to go back to Felston?'

'You don't want to go?' Pardoe this time, ready to bluster, to bully.

'I can't wait,' Andy said, and Antrobus winced once more.

'There'll be money problems,' he said, 'particularly as you won't accept financial help.'

'I'll get the dole,' said Andy. 'I'll manage better than most. There's only Grandma and me.'

'You can do a little better than that,' said Antrobus. 'There's a comrade near Felston who runs a small workshop. It just so happens that he needs a fitter. You can start next Monday.'

Andy looked quickly at his hands. Soft as a lady's. Next Monday wouldn't be any picnic, but at least he'd be among his own. 'I'm obliged to you,' said Andy.

'Not at all,' Antrobus said. 'I only wish it could have been something better.'

'Something better wouldn't do for Felston,' said Andy. 'But at least I won't be going home with me tail between me legs. Folks respect you for that up there.'

'Splendid,' said Antrobus, and rose. 'Well, we mustn't keep you. You'll have a lot to do, I'm sure. I'll get your railway ticket round to you in the morning.'

Suddenly hands were thrust out at him like swords, and Andy found himself outside the door of Antrobus's set. Slowly and thoughtfully he walked down the steps. They might be Communists, he thought, but they were bosses to a man. On your way, Andy. Sling your hook, Andy. You've said you'll do what we've told you, so bugger off. Suddenly he felt gladder than ever to be going home, and ran down the stairs, his footsteps clattering.

# 16

L OVELL SAID, 'HOW pleasant to run into you like this, Miss Whitcomb.' They were at Henley. Cucumber sandwiches, strawberries and cream and Pimm's Number One, while on the river the boats went by, crews straining at their oars, eight enormous men chivvied and yelped at by a bad-tempered gnome: like Foch bullying a pack of mastiffs, she thought. Not really her sort of thing at all, though Lionel adored it, which was why she was here. Lionel was at the river's edge, with field glasses.

'Very pleasant indeed, Mr Lovell,' she said.

'Would you care to move into the shade?' said Lovell. 'The sun's quite strong here.' Move out of earshot was what he meant.

'Yes of course,' said Jane. 'At my age one must take care of one's complexion.'

Firmly he took her elbow, and led her to two chairs in an elm tree's shade. There was nobody else for at least twenty yards.

'You're a bitch,' he said, but he was laughing.

'Well what do you expect?' said Jane, 'trotting out your lines like a bad actor at country-house theatricals. – But what on earth are you doing here? You didn't row for your college or anything.'

'Well yes,' said Lovell. 'As a matter of fact I did.'

'I bet you looked sweet in those dinky little shorts. Lionel would have been quite smitten.'

'As a matter of fact he was,' said Lovell, and then, as Jane opened her mouth: 'But I wasn't.'

'You should have worn your blazer,' said Jane, 'and one of

– 167 –

those gorgeous pink caps. What school are they?'

'Not a school at all,' said Lovell. 'Leander.'

'Oh yes?'

'Oxford University Boat Club,' said Lovell. 'As if you cared. Jane darling –'

'No endearments,' she said. 'Not here. People are on the move all the time.' Lovell scowled. 'They're your rules, remember.'

'Yes yes,' said Lovell. 'It's just – oh blast. Let's change the subject. I'm going up to Blagdon Hall soon, to see how the work's getting on there. I wondered if you'd care to come with me.'

'For a clever man,' said Jane, 'you can be very stupid, Charles.'

'I don't see what's stupid –'

'You would if you'd use your brain for a minute. . . . Who else would be there? Nobody, I suppose.' His silence told her that she was right. 'Just the two of us in our dear little love nest as big as the Ritz. And scores of gossiping servants to spread the merry tidings.'

'But who could they tell?'

'What does it matter? They'd tell people who'd tell people who'd tell people. And soon or later the *Express* would get it, or one of the others.'

'Not the *World*?'

'Jay would keep my name out of it,' said Jane. 'He owes me that much. But the others don't owe me a damn thing. Or you.'

His eyes went to hers then, but she kept on talking. 'Then there's Felston.'

'What does Felston matter?'

'Gossip in Felston hurt me once before. Very badly,' she said. 'You know that. And I won't let it happen again. There's some-body there I love very much. I won't have her upset.'

'That old woman?'

'That old woman. Anyway, when did you mean to go?'

'Next Wednesday,' he said. 'It has to be then because –'

'Oh well that settles it,' said Jane. 'I couldn't possibly go on Wednesday. I have a luncheon engagement on Wednesday.'

'May I ask where?' he asked. Really he's more prickly than a porcupine, bless him, thought Jane.

'Certainly you may,' she said. 'The House of Commons. With

Dick Lambert. We used to toil together for Jay Bower during the General Strike.'

'What does he want?' said Lovell.

'Doubtless he'll tell me over the pudding, if not before.' She said more softly: 'I'm very fond of you, Charles, but not when you want to put barbed wire round me.'

'Sorry.' But it came out like a snarl. He added more gently: 'I'm due in New York in September. Taking the French Line for a change. I thought of going over to Paris first. Wondered if you'd like to come?'

'Paris in the summer,' said Jane. 'It'll be a desert.'

'Exactly,' said Lovell.

'Oh very well,' said Jane. 'I just hope you can find somewhere decent that's open.'

Lionel came hurrying across to them.

'Did you see that last eight?' he said. 'Stroke had thighs like Michelangelo's David. I simply must have another Pimm's.'

Dick Lambert said, 'It was good of you to come.'

'Not at all,' said Jane. 'It's all absolutely scrumptious. How grandly you great men do yourselves.' She looked from the majestic restaurant on the terrace to the Thames, alive with shipping, barges, tugs. Smoky and evil smelling close to, but pleasing enough when seen through a window. Not a Canaletto, but pleasing.

'Great men?' said Lambert. 'Bargain goods in the talking shop, more like.' He looked about him. The Terrace was almost empty. 'Especially during recess.'

He's looking better, she thought. He's put on a bit of weight, which he needed, and his hairline's still receding, but it doesn't matter. Makes him look thoughtful. And he's altogether more confident.

'I had a bit of news,' he said.

'Good news I hope.'

'Couldn't be better,' said Lambert. 'I'm to be Minister of State for Home Affairs.'

So that was it. Sort of apprentice Home Secretary. 'How marvellous.'

'Aye. . . . Mind you I'd been their Number Two spokesman for long enough.'

'So why the leg up? Not that you don't deserve it. I didn't mean –'

'No no, Philip's retiring, so we all move up one. To tell you the truth his health's not all that good. He'll probably go to the House of Lords.'

Jane giggled. She couldn't help it.

Lambert looked puzzled for a moment, then smiled. 'Only place he's fit for, you mean? No no. Philip's all right. But it's hard graft on the front bench.' He gestured to a waiter. 'Coffee?' he asked Jane. 'Something with it?'

'Just coffee.'

'Me an' all,' said Lambert. 'Two coffees – and I'll take a cigar with mine.' The waiter left.

'Where were we?' said Lambert. 'Oh aye. My leg up, as you call it. That's probably because of my other bit of news. I got married.'

'More congratulations,' she said, and thought: You wanted to marry me once. I wonder if she's like me? 'Have you got a picture?' she asked.

Lambert's hand went at once to his inside pocket, to extract a snapshot from his wallet, and handed it over.

'Oh I say,' said Jane, for Mrs Lambert wasn't like her at all. Big and blithe and bonny Mrs Lambert was, with a big wide smile and eyes that would take no nonsense.

'She's awfully pretty,' said Jane.

'Well she is,' said Lambert, with the air of a man well suited to his topic of conversation. 'Not a beanpole, like some you see nowadays, but a lovely smile as you can see for yourself, and a Yorkshire lass through and through. Just the wife for a tyke.'

'A tyke?'

'Yorkshireman. Tynesiders call themselves Geordies: we call ourselves tykes. And can Alice cook.'

There was obviously much more he would have told her, but the waiter brought coffee, the wine waiter brought cigars.

When his cigar was drawing, Lambert said: 'There's rules and what you might call tribal customs in politics, same as anything else, and some of them is just plain daft – or I used to think so. Being wed is one of them. I asked you to marry me once, you remember?'

'I was there at the time,' she said.

'You were,' said Lambert. 'You were always there in those days. In my mind, I mean. I couldn't get you out of it. – Don't worry. I'm over it now.'

Why oh why did the thought annoy her?

'But that was a load of romantic nonsense on my part. Like a cart horse proposing to a gazelle. Just plain daft. Alice now, she's my sort. I mean look at you.'

Chanel suit, hat by Marthe Callot, and the little Cartier leopardess in her lapel.

'We had exciting times though, didn't we?'

'We did,' said Jane.

'That strike was history,' said Lambert, 'and we were a part of it. And that's where I was wrong, you see.'

'To fall in love with me?'

'I couldn't help that,' said Lambert. 'No man could. But I had no business to ask you to marry me.'

Not another Lovell, she thought, another Bower. Not my dear Dick Lambert.

'I should have kept my mouth shut,' said Lambert. 'Only I couldn't help myself.'

Not another Lovell.

'You were never cut out to be an MP's wife,' said Lambert. 'Dances in drill halls, chats at the Labour Ladies' Guild, sitting beside her man and smiling because he's so marvellous. You could never have done that, now could you?'

'Not for a moment,' said Jane.

'Exactly,' said Lambert. 'And I'll tell you why. It's because you were born to be an MP yourself.'

This child is born to do great things, the saddhu had said. Was being an MP a kind of greatness? There was no doubt that Dick Lambert might make it so, in time, or Andy Patterson: but she, Jane Whitcomb –

'I?' she said.

'Why not?' said Lambert. 'You've got presence. You've a grand way with words and you're a lovely speaker. And you care about people. I know that. I've watched you. And it shows. People *want* to hear you. You make them feel better. More concerned. More caring. And you've got something else. I don't know what it is but you've got it. Maybe there isn't a word for it. A kind of magic.

'There's not many's been given it in the talking shop. Winston has it, and I wish to God he was on our side. That old goat Lloyd George has it too. Turns it on like a tap. And Ramsay has it sometimes. Not always.' Suddenly he stopped, appalled. 'The things you can still do to me, Jane Whitcomb. Running down my own leader.'

'I can keep a secret, too,' she said, and looked in her handbag for her cigarettes. 'No one better.'

Lambert looked relieved. 'And that's another rare quality in this place,' he said. 'But the thing is this, you see. When Ramsay sent for me to give me the good news – and very nicely he did it, I'll say that for him – first he congratulated the lucky bridegroom and then it was oh by the way you're a junior minister. Very nice. As if there was no connection between the two and we both knew very well there was.

'Anyway after a chat and a smoke he just happened to mention something that's been bothering him a lot lately. Our party's opposed to privilege of any kind, and yet half of it has hardly any voice at all. I mean women, of course. It bothers him, Jane, and I'm glad it does, because it should.'

'My name was mentioned?'

'By me,' Lambert said at once. 'Of course he'd heard of you –'

'How decent,' said Jane.

'– And that's enough of the polished irony. Of course he'd heard of you. All those pieces in the *Daily World*, and then *Striking for Beginners*. Only one thing bothered him.'

'And what was that?'

'How was your working-class background.'

'What did you tell him?' Jane asked.

Lambert waited as she fitted her cigarette into the jade holder, and lit it with her gold Dunhill lighter.

'Non-existent,' he said.

'So there goes my parliamentary career,' said Jane.

'Not at all,' said Lambert. 'Ours isn't a Party of privilege – either working class or any other kind. Anybody who wants to work towards a new social order is welcome – no matter what his background. Or hers.' He grinned. 'Especially when it seems likely that he or she can get themselves elected. So he asked me to have a word with you.' He blew smoke from his Havana.

Jane said, 'Are we just talking about this in general, or did you have a particular constituency in mind?'

'A constituency, naturally.'

'Which one?'

'Well Felston, of course.'

'Felston,' said Jane. . . . 'You know, when the General Strike was on, when you and I worked together, I'd have jumped at it. I might even have won – if there'd been a by-election – which there wasn't, by the by.'

'We'll come to that,' said Lambert. 'Go on.'

'That was three years ago,' said Jane. 'Now it's different.'

'How different?'

And so she told him, about Paris, and the Quart' Arts Ball, and the Cleopatra costume. He listened, impassive. When she had done he said, 'But that's ridiculous.'

'To you and me, yes,' she said. 'But not to the ladies of Felston. To them I'm a fallen woman, Dick. Beyond the pale.'

'You're sure?' She nodded. 'Then we'll have to find you somewhere else then.' But already his eyes were staring at the Chanel suit, the Cartier leopardess, the jade cigarette holder. Finding her a safe seat would have its problems.

'Anyway, Felston's got an MP,' she said.

'Well of course,' said Lambert. 'But we'd have had to lead up to it. You couldn't just walk in, so to speak.'

'We can forget Felston,' said Jane. 'Believe me.'

'Then it'll have to be somewhere else,' Lambert said again. 'Let me think about it.'

She had the feeling he would think for a very long time.

Suddenly she noticed a man coming towards them across the almost empty dining room: a man she recognized: chubby, smiling, with a toddling walk entirely his own. James Wagstaff, MP. He came up to the table, and gave a well-rehearsed bow, like a courtier in a play.

'I heard Miss Whitcomb was here,' he said, 'so I thought I'd better pay me respects. I hope you don't mind, Dick?'

'Not at all, Jimmy. Not at all,' said Lambert.

Three years ago the sudden appearance would have flustered him. Now he didn't even blink.

'Have some coffee or something?' Lambert said.

'Something,' said Wagstaff, and summoned a waiter, ordered brandy.

'Always a sight for sore eyes, Miss Whitcomb,' Jimmy Wagstaff said. 'But what are you doing cooped up in this place on a fine day like this?'

If he's heard rumours, Jane thought, he's not going to take them lying down. On the attack straight away.

'Miss Whitcomb may be doing a few political articles for the *Daily World*,' said Lambert. 'She wanted to pick my brains, such as they are, so I asked her here for lunch.'

'Of course nothing's settled yet,' said Jane. 'Just an idea, really.'

'You can pick my brains any time,' said Wagstaff, and his brandy arrived. He swallowed half of it and said, 'What sort of a political idea is it, Miss Whitcomb?'

'Profiles, really,' she said.

'Both sides of the House?' She nodded. 'That's one idea that never goes far wrong,' said Wagstaff. The dig was a hard one, but deserved, too. She should have come up with something a little more imaginative than *that*.

'The thing to bear in mind if you don't mind my saying so,' said Wagstaff, 'is that you can't do a real picture of an MP without looking at his constituency. His frame, you might call it. The two have to match – belong together as you might say. Horses for courses. You have a think about it, Miss Whitcomb.'

He finished the brandy, stood up and took Jane's hand. 'It was lovely to see you again,' he said, 'but I'll have to be off. 'Bye, 'bye, my dear. Ta-ra, Dick.' And off he trotted.

All the time he'd sat there he'd never stopped smiling, twinkling away like a working-class Pickwick.

'Somebody's told him,' said Lambert.

'It would seem so.' Jane lit another cigarette. 'I gather he's telling you he won't give in without a fight.'

'That's it.'

'But why should he give in at all?' asked Jane. 'The Felston people like him very much, and he's got a mind like a razor. He just proved it.'

'He proved something else as well,' said Lambert, and nodded at the empty brandy goblet. 'Even when he thought he was fighting to survive, he had to have one.'

'Poor man,' said Jane.

'There's not many take that view,' Lambert said. 'He's got

away with it so far – just – and he still manages to stick to beer when he goes up to Felston. In public, anyway. But from what I hear it won't be long before he does something daft in public, and then he'll have to go, no matter how sharp he is. Throwing him out won't do the Labour Party any good, either.'

'I'm glad I shan't be the one to replace him,' said Jane, and began to draw on her gloves. 'Thank you for a lovely lunch.'

'It was nice to have your company again,' said Lambert. 'But we needed you. We really did. . . . I'll walk you to the door.'

Does Alice know you gave me lunch? she wondered. It was a question she found impossible to ask.


'Indescribable chaos,' said Lovell. They were lunching at a place Lionel had recommended in Soho, where the food was Italian and excellent, and all the waiters were beautiful.

'Paint everywhere, carpets rolled up, furniture stacked. I must have been mad to ask you to go.'

'That isn't the only reason,' said Jane. 'And you know it.'

'Don't nag,' said Lovell. 'Please don't nag. I've been through quite enough without that.'

'My poor darling,' she said. 'What?'

'Blagdon,' said Lovell.

'Good God,' said Jane. 'What did he do? Break in and start praying again?'

'Break in be damned,' said Lovell. 'Drove up to the Hall as bold as brass. Drove up in a lorry, what's more. He was wearing dungarees, and he'd brought a ladder and brushes and a what d'you call it? – a vacuum cleaner. Said he'd come to help.'

Jane giggled. 'Oh I wish I'd been there,' she said.

'He was all over the place before I could stop him,' said Lovell. 'Spilling paint, knocking workmen off ladders, chucking plaster about. . . .'

'Poor Charles,' said Jane. 'What on earth did you do?'

'Only thing I could do. Ordered him out. On which he gave me a saintly smile, all sweet forgiveness. "Only trying to help, old chap," he said. I practically had to *throw* him out. And when I got him into his lorry he looked down on me and said, "You'd better not go back in there and tell them I'm mad – because I'm not. I've got two doctors' certificates to prove it, which is more than you have." Then he stuck his tongue out at me and drove off. I wish to God I'd never bought the place.'

'Surely there's nothing more he can do?'

'I wouldn't bet on it,' said Lovell. 'He'll think of something. How was your Commons lunch?'

'I'm not going to be an MP,' said Jane.

'Was there danger that you might?'

'A gleam in Dick Lambert's eye, no more,' she said. 'He thought I might represent Felston when the present incumbent retires.'

'What a revolting idea,' Lovell said.

'I wouldn't have called it revolting, exactly.'

'I would,' said Lovell. 'You kissing babies and opening bazaars and taking tea with the mayoress. Talk about an eagle in a cage.'

'Dear Charles,' said Jane. 'How sweetly you put things.'

'Well it's true,' said Lovell.

'It isn't going to happen,' said Jane, and ate more spaghetti arrabiata.

'You mind telling me why?'

'Paris,' she said. 'The Four Arts Ball. Me dressed up as Cleopatra. The best scandal Felston ever had. They don't want the sort of MP who goes to bed with Caesar and presses asps to her bosom.'

'Bower certainly made a mess of things for you,' said Lovell.

'Charles darling,' said Jane, and her voice was sweet: 'do at least try to be consistent. It wasn't Jay who dragged my name through the Felston mud, it was that oaf Burrowes. I told you. Jay did his best to play the whole thing down – and a jolly good best it was. If it hadn't been for him, things would have been even worse. And another thing – you're supposed to be *against* my being an MP, and if it hadn't been for that scandal I would have been.'

'Made a fool of myself again, haven't I?' said Lovell.

'Afraid so.'

'You have that effect on me,' said Lovell. 'Nobody else has – at least I don't think so. I love you very much you see, and that's one of the ways it shows. . . . Shall we talk about Paris?'

'Do let's,' said Jane.

Grandma said, 'It's nice to have you back, I must say.'

Andy put down his fork. 'Nice to *be* back,' he said. 'You don't get stew and dumplings like that in Cambridge.'

'No need for flattery,' said Grandma. 'There's plenty left for second helpings. Are you staying up here for long?'

'Looks like it,' said Andy. 'I got a job.'

'You never,' said Grandma.

'Factory out on the Newcastle Road,' Andy said. 'Mike Deegan's. They do engine repairs.'

'It would be,' said Grandma.

'And just what's that supposed to mean?' Andy asked.

'Moscow Mike,' said Grandma. 'That's what they call him round here. Spends more time on a soap box than he does in his factory. Even his Church threw him out.'

'What Church?' Andy asked.

'That's a daft question coming from you,' said Grandma. 'What Church would it be with a name like Deegan? The Romans of course. Showed him the door and told him not to come back till he stopped telling folks God didn't exist. And quite right, too.'

'Logical, anyway,' said Andy. 'Our Party wouldn't have much time for a member who went round saying that capitalism was our only hope.'

'And what Party's that, may I ask?' said Grandma.

'Well the Labour Party of course.'

'Not the Russians? The Communists?'

'No, Grandma.'

'Somehow I always thought you'd go the whole hog.'

'Well I haven't,' said Andy.

'Mike Deegan did.'

'That's his business,' said Andy. 'Mine's the Labour Party. Deegan gave me a job, that's all. Looking after another Lefty. All right. But I'll do a fair day's work – he'll sharp find that out. I'm grateful to him an' all, but that doesn't mean I have to join his Party.'

'Thank God for that,' said Grandma.

Deceiving her, Andy found, was the worst part of the whole business.

He took a walk. There wasn't much that was free in Felston, but walking was, unless you counted the cost of cobbling your boots after you'd worn the soles out. Down to the Market first. The Salvation Army was there, and doing good business, brass blaring, bass drum booming, ha'pennies and pennies trickling in from the few people with a bit left over after they'd bought their weekend food from the stalls lit by softly hissing acetylene lamps. But there was nobody at the other end of the square shouting out for Socialism. Saturday night and not a soul. It was as if folks didn't care any more. Manny Mendel, Felston's Labour Party secretary, had gone off to London to a new job and a posh new wife, and it didn't look as if anybody had taken his place. Just as well you've come back, Andy Patterson, he told himself. There's work crying out to be done here.

He walked down Queen Street to the Eldon Arms, and the trams swayed past him. The Eldon was where Jane Whitcomb stayed when she was in Felston, which wasn't often, not these days. He'd felt bad about Grandma, and he didn't feel all that great about Jane Whitcomb either. All that tittle-tattle about how much bosom she'd been showing. What did it matter anyway? You saw worse at the pictures. But it had been necessary, that was the point. Jane was a nice woman, even a good woman, in spite of the talk, but she wasn't a proper Socialist. She didn't *believe*. The inevitability of history. Evolution towards a classless society. Nationalisation of the means of production, distribution and exchange. He doubted if she even knew what it meant, though she'd sharp find out if she had to. A smart woman, Jane Whitcomb. Well, now she wouldn't have to. She could go back to her London Season and May Balls and dancing half naked in Paris – and that's quite enough of that, Andy Patterson. Keep your mind on what you're here for.

He crossed the road. It became Sea Road now, and he slogged on past the park with the lake where the swans majestically sailed, the town's only aristocrats, loftily ignoring the squabbling bourgeois seagulls, on to the sea at last: harsh bent grass, then sand dunes, and then the sea, green as a bottle, the lazy waves slapping the hard sand at the tide line, white foam like froth, that now and then glittered as the sunlight caught it. The sea that was always there, always waiting: ready to carry him away when things got to be more than he could bear.

That's what he'd thought when he was a bairn, anyway. There'd be a ship and he'd be on it: a sailing ship with brass cannon and a skull and crossbones at the mast head, and him with a cutlass swarming up the side of a Spanish galleon, then away back home with a fortune in pieces of eight – whatever they were – to pour them all into his mother's lap, and Grandma's. He'd still believed in private fortunes then, and Bob still did. That was obvious. Obvious too that he was making one and, being Bob, spending it as fast as he made it. Not that he hadn't offered him some as well. He was a good brother – but he had no place in the world that was coming.

There was a stone in his boot. He limped over to a seat facing the sea, and eased off the boot. Not a stone, he discovered: a tiny seashell, brown mottled and rounded. The pride of some bairn's collection, maybe, till it fell out of his bucket on the way to the tram. . . . It was his da who'd first shown him the truth about Socialism, but being Da, he'd got it all in a muddle. He knew nowt about the communes, or Engels or Marx: for Da it was all the early Christians in the New Testament and how they had shared everything, just like Jesus and his disciples had, and because it was Jesus then sharing had to be right, because Jesus was God. And that was Da for you. Always in a muddle with his thinking. Still, he'd shown his son the right direction. But Andy had seen straight off that the key to the thing was power, not prayer and hymns: the power to get things done, to right wrongs, to enforce the one just law: 'From each according to his ability: to each according to his need.' And the way to power was knowledge, and that had been a hard and bitter struggle. He'd left school at fourteen to work as an errand boy. Two years of that, then a five-year apprenticeship serving his time, then out of his time and straight into Durham Gaol. Not much opportunity for book reading there. He'd persevered, but it had been a hard slog with nobody to teach him, nobody to talk to, nobody to tell. I'm sounding like a chap in need of a lass, he thought, and maybe I was, but the lass had never turned up, not the one he needed, and there had been times when he'd looked upon the sea as quite another form of deliverance, the times when he couldn't see the point of staying alive: the times when he feared he'd never be of use to anyone.

But those days were long since past. If he hadn't met a lass he'd at least met Manny Mendel, and Manny had taught him to think: to read, analyse, make notes, and fit ideas together like bricks. And that had been the making of him, because Manny had been the one who had prepared him for Cambridge, even if he had buggered off down South first chance he got. . . . Cambridge, now. Cambridge had been marvellous in a lot of ways, because it turned out that he really did have a brain, and brains were the only things that lot really cared about. 'Possible alpha material', Antrobus had called him. They'd even offered to get him through Common Entrance and into a college so he could study for a proper degree. But a Part One alone would take two years, and he didn't have that much time. In two years he might be an MP.

Jimmy Wagstaff was the problem, because Jimmy Wagstaff *was* the MP, the sitting tenant so to speak. But Antrobus must know something. He wouldn't hold out a hope like that if he didn't think he could fulfil it. And there was a funny thing. How could Antrobus know, and Andy Patterson, man of Felston, not know? That was obvious too when you thought about it. It was Jimmy Wagstaff, Westminster MP, that Antrobus knew about. Plenty of chaps in London ready to pass on gossip to the Communists. You could hardly call it spying – and even if it was spying, the Party had to come first.

In the meantime Felston had to know he was back: good old Andy, always ready with a speech: pillar of his union and the Labour Movement, fearless champion of the oppressed. Get on the council, get on the committees, get your name in the paper, make things hum. He stood up stiffly: he'd walked too far. And Mike Deegan's factory was a good step from the tram an' all. He'd have to buy a bicycle out of the fiver they'd given him at Cambridge to tide him over, only come to think about it he'd better pay for it on the never never. Owning a bike in Felston was like owning a Daimler anywhere else.

Lionel said, 'Did I ever tell you that I once played this foolish game?' They were at the Eton and Harrow match at Lord's. Eton were batting and not doing terribly well.

'You played for Eton?' Jane asked.

'Sounds incredible, doesn't it?' said Lionel. 'I scored fifty-two not out in this very game, and took three wickets. I was quite a decent slip fielder too – though I don't suppose any of that makes sense to you.'

'If you think I came only for the cucumber sandwiches you're wrong,' said Jane. 'My father played for Oxford University, and he reckoned Vinney was one of the best off-break bowlers he'd ever faced.'

'I'm afraid I've never heard of him,' said Lionel.

'Vinney,' said Jane, 'was my governess. She batted quite well, too.'

'I'd adore to have met her,' said Lionel.

The Harrow fast bowler appealed for leg before, and Eton's number seven was given out.

'It looks as if Eton could do with your governess now,' said Lionel. 'Or even me.'

'Did you play at Oxford?'

'No,' said Lionel. 'By then it was quite obvious what kind of creature I was, and so I became an aesthete. Aesthetes don't do anything as dangerous as run the risk of being struck by a hard leather ball.'

'They get into dangerous little aircraft and fire machine guns at Germans instead,' said Jane.

'Only when they must,' said Lionel. 'I do wish Jay Bower would stop calling me the heroic World War Fighter Pilot. My friends don't like it. It sounds so – so meaty.'

'That's only when you join me in the gossip columns,' she said. 'He knows that deep down you're not in the least like that.'

'Yes he can be perceptive when he tries,' said Lionel. 'How is his engagement?'

'How should it be?' said Jane.

'I merely asked,' Lionel said, 'as an acquaintance of Jay's.'

'Has there been gossip?'

'No no,' said Lionel. 'Not a word, I promise you. It's merely that it's – well – hardly the most predictable of pairings, is it?'

'Well no,' said Jane. 'It's not. All the same they appear to get along together jolly well. You know, the way engaged couples do. Pet names and lovey dovey and all that.'

'Pet names,' said Lionel. 'Jay Bower. Oh do tell.'

'Certainly not,' said Jane. 'It seems to me that being engaged's a trying enough time without you planting your little barbs.'

'Oh please,' said Lionel. 'I shan't plant a single barb, I promise you. Girl Guide's Honour.' And so she told him, and it was time for tea.

Lionel was awfully good about things like tea. He never seemed to bestir himself very much, but their tea always appeared before anyone else's, and stewards and waitresses adored him, seeming to know in advance how lavish his tips would be. . . .

Brenda Coupland came over to them, a red-faced man in tow with a body shaped rather like a pineapple. Could this be Fruity Metcalf? Jane wondered.

'Darlings how lovely to see you,' said Brenda Coupland. 'You haven't met Hugo Meldrum, have you?'

But the man with the body like a pineapple was staring at Lionel, transfixed.

'Good Lord,' he said. 'You're LCS Warley, aren't you? Pettifer's House.'

'The same,' said Lionel.

'You made a half century in this very game. Years ago.'

'Fifty-two not out, actually.'

'When was it?' said Meldrum. ''o8? 'o9?'

'Somewhere back there,' said Lionel. 'I think it was the year Hadrian finished his wall.'

Meldrum looked puzzled, and then his face cleared. 'Oh yes,' he said. 'I remember. You used to make jokes, too.'

'Do get us some tea, Hugo,' Brenda Coupland said, and then to Lionel: 'Would you mind helping him, darling? He isn't awfully good at it.'

Lionel lounged off after Meldrum.

'Really, Brenda,' said Jane.

'Yes I know,' Brenda Coupland said, 'but I simply had to speak to you. It's *important*.'

'Oh Brenda,' said Jane. 'Not the little man again?'

'Who? . . . Oh HRH. Darling, of course not. I told you it was important. It's Jay Bower.'

'What about him?' Jane asked.

'When did you see him last?'

'With you. At Cambridge. Three weeks ago.'

'Did you know he'd been to New York and back since then?'

'*What?*'

'On the *Mauretania* out, and back on the *Berengaria*. I know because Sheila Biffen was on the *Mauretania* and – and another friend came back on the *Berengaria*. Not the happiest of mortals, they both said.'

'Probably had to go on business,' said Jane, trying and failing to think who Brenda Coupland's friend on the *Berengaria* could be, and why he or she must remain anonymous. 'Business often makes men glum.'

'Not this business,' Brenda Coupland said. 'It was Georgina Payne.'

'Oh now really, Brenda,' said Jane. 'Georgie's in Hollywood.'

'Not when Jay Bower was in New York,' said Brenda Coupland. 'Bunty Fairweather saw them having dinner at the Plaza together. Of course I told them there was nothing in that – two old friends meeting by chance in a strange land –'

'And what did Bunty Fairweather think?'

'She thought it was just too, too romantic. And as a matter of fact so do I. Do you suppose the wedding's off?'

'Of course not,' said Jane. 'Bower owns a chunk of World Wide Studios, the one Georgie works for. It was probably just business, as I said.'

'Business?' said Brenda. 'All that way for three days?'

'It's too much time and trouble for anything else,' said Jane. 'He's to be married in October. They've set the date.'

'I do hope it wasn't just business,' said Brenda Coupland, then: 'Oh look. The boys are bringing tea.'

Hugo Meldrum said, 'The most extraordinary thing. Lionel was in the Royal Flying Corps.'

'Were you in it too?' asked Jane.

'Me? Oh good Lord no,' said Meldrum. 'Much too fat to squeeze into an aeroplane, even then. I was in the Leicestershire Yeomanry. Too fat for a horse come to that, but one did what one could.'

'Then why is it so extraordinary?' Brenda Coupland asked.

'A cousin of mine was in the same squadron,' said Meldrum. 'Makes you think, doesn't it? Played in the Eton and Harrow match, shot down God knows how many Huns. Quite a life Lionel has had, eh?'

'I do hope you aren't about to write my biography?' said Lionel.

'Good Lord no,' said Meldrum, appalled. 'I never was much of a hand at scribbling.'

'Perhaps it's just as well,' Lionel said.

# 17

THE FIRST DAY he'd taken the tram and walked the rest. It was the first tram of the morning, and the walk was more of a half trot, but he'd arrived only just at knocking-on time at that. The factory wasn't much more than a big shed; half a dozen journeymen and two apprentices, but even so the work looked interesting. Engines for overhaul mostly; engines still just valuable enough not to be thrown away, but hardly worth shipping back to the big firms that made them, which was where Mike Deegan came in. Low overheads, low costs, and chaps that knew what they were doing. Chaps that didn't have much chance of working anywhere else, either, thought Andy. Militants to a man, the first to get the push when one of the big yards was looking for redundancy. Well, he thought, I should be right at home here, and so he was, but he hadn't expected quite such reverential treatment.

Moulsher, the one who seemed to be acting as charge-hand, actually asked him if he'd mind giving him a hand with the turbine he was working on. It wasn't a problem: he'd worked on a dozen turbines like it, but this was the first time he'd been asked if he minded; and it wouldn't do. Wouldn't do at all. He was here as one of the workers, not the Chairman of the Board.

The thing was, he was a hero. Mike Deegan told him so when he finally came to the factory. Eleven o'clock that would be, when the rest of them had already done three hours and more. Mike Deegan was big, raw-boned, with coppery hair and beard and a high-priced suit that looked as if it had been made for somebody else. He came up to Andy at once, shook hands, and invited him to the office for a chat, that is if Moulsher could spare him, and Moulsher said of course. He didn't mind at all. The trouble was, thought Andy, he meant it.

Deegan's office was a cubicle partitioned off from the main shed, just big enough for a roll-top desk, a filing cabinet, a couple of chairs and a table for plans of whatever work was being done. Behind it was a sort of hatch where a girl clattered at a typewriter.

'I hope you'll be happy here,' said Deegan.

'I'll be all right once me hands harden,' said Andy. 'It was good of you to take me on.'

'A pleasure,' said Deegan. 'An honour. Man, I didn't know what a speech could do till I heard you. You've been an inspiration round here.' His face took on a look of sly cunning, the cunning of a child. 'Further South, too.'

'I don't think I'm with you,' Andy said, and Deegan yelped with laughter.

'You're ahead of me,' he said. '1926 in London. The Elephant and Castle. There's chaps that was there say they never heard a better speech in their lives. And then the mounted police charging like Cossacks, and you the first to be attacked, standing at the head of your followers.'

'Who told you that, Mr Deegan?' Andy asked.

'Comrade Deegan.' His voice sounded reproachful. 'Chaps that was there. Good Party men, all of them. Andy, they were proud of you, and so am I.'

'It's just that I've heard if the London police knew who I was there'd be a warrant out in no time.'

'Not a word will they get from us, Andy,' said Deegan. 'But we have our instructions, and we're the boys to carry them out.'

'Instructions?'

'The working class is entitled to its heroes the same as anyone else,' said Deegan. 'More in fact, and it's just too bad we can't pay you proper homage in the *Daily Herald*, say, or even in the *Daily Worker* itself. Only we can't. But there's nothing to stop a bit of gossip, is there? Just to let folks know there's a legend among them – a legend come to life.'

'I see,' said Andy, and wondered who had thought up that idea. Burrowes, most likely.

Suddenly Deegan ceased being a romantic revolutionary, and became a knowledgeable and capable factory owner instead. He knew every detail of the engine Andy was working on, and every trick that would give it a few more years of life. He was every bit as much a fanatic when it came to machines, thought Andy, but with them his fanaticism was shrewd and practical, the key to money and jobs. Suddenly the romantic took over again.

'And you did time in Durham Gaol, too, God love you,' said Deegan. 'And all for refusing to fight the bosses' war. It's an honour to serve with you. It is indeed.'

Andy went back to the shop floor wondering how much Deegan had been told about why he was back: wondered too if Deegan had been told to keep his mouth shut, because if so he doubted whether he'd made much of a job of it.

He laboured on with the rest until knocking-off time at half past five, and a scurry for a tram that took him to the bike shop in South William Street. He got a second-hand Hercules – five bob down and a half a crown a week, and rode it uneasily back to Grandma's. She had his tea ready in no time – fried sausages and egg and bread, and apple pie. He had forgotten how hungry he could get after a hard day's work, which Deegan believed in every bit as fervently as he did in dialectical materialism.

'I hope you don't mind my saying so, but you look tired,' said Grandma.

'Why should I mind? I am tired – I'm out of practice.'

'Hard work never killed anybody,' Grandma quoted.

'But it wounded a canny few.' Andy finished the quotation and they both smiled.

'Who was it used to say that again?' Grandma asked.

'Our John.'

'Our John. Aye. D'you ever see that lass of his?'

'I told you, Grandma. We had a bit chat at Cambridge.'

'Been to a dance, you said. I remember. She'd be a good dancer, by the look of her.'

'So they tell me.'

'But she deserves a bit more than that. A wasted life hers is now.'

'Nowt to do with me, Grandma.'

The old eyes looked at him; dark and clear and needle sharp, but she let it lie. 'You haven't taken your boots off,' she said.

'Didn't seem worth the bother,' said Andy. 'I'll be changing after I've finished me tea.'

'Off out your first day back?'

'Fitters' Union,' said Andy. 'Number Five Branch meets on a Monday. That's my branch. I'd better let them know I'm back.'

'Well at least you won't finish up in the pub like some,' said Grandma, and reached for the washing-up bowl. 'Quarter past six in the morning mind, and not a second later, so make sure you set your alarm.'

His bones and muscles would ache and he knew it, and it would be nice to sit in the American rocker and read the *Felston Echo*, but there wasn't enough time. There was never enough time. He had to go to the meeting of Number Five Branch and let them see he was back, caring Andy, for whom nothing was ever too much trouble.


'It's sweet of you to come with me, darling,' Catherine said.

'Never a hardship to look at clothes,' said Jane.

They were in Molyneux's salon to look at trousseaux, but the great man had suspected appendicitis, which meant that they had been fobbed off with the head fitter, which in turn had made Catherine decidedly cross, until Jane had pointed out that this was no more than a preliminary reconnaissance, after all. Nothing could possibly be settled until Catherine's mother came back from the Greek Islands, and old Lady Mangan left Ireland to struggle on as best it might without her for a while.

'Let's just enjoy ourselves,' said Jane, and thought Please God help me to make sure that everything's all right between them. Thy will be done, of course, but why did You have to let Brenda Coupland tell me that bothersome story? Why couldn't she have been tactful just once?

'Jay is well, I hope?'

'Jaybird is perched on the highest bough,' said Catherine, 'piping blissfully.'

'It doesn't sound awfully like him,' said Jane.

Catherine laughed. 'As a matter of fact he seems to spend every waking hour dreaming up schemes to make more people read his beastly paper,' Catherine said. 'He won't be happy till every family in the country takes it.'

He needs the money, thought Jane, and said aloud: 'You're not very kind, are you, considering how much work I do on the *World*. Not to mention my stepfather. Beastly indeed.'

'Oh I didn't mean that,' said Catherine. 'Honestly I didn't. But it's such a strain being engaged, and when one's fiancé disappears for weeks at a time –'

'Does he?' said Jane, and tried to look startled.

'Well only once,' said Catherine, 'and it was only fifteen days. He had to go to New York to sign some papers.'

'Very impressive,' said Jane.

'It sounded pompous to me,' said Catherine. 'Why couldn't he have them posted over like everybody else?'

'Well why couldn't he?'

'He *said* it was because they all had to be checked on the spot by lawyers and things.'

'No doubt they had.'

'I don't think it was that at all.' Jane braced herself, and continued to smile.

'What then?'

'He finds being engaged as big a strain as I do, and he suddenly had an excuse to disappear for a couple of weeks and grabbed it like a shot.'

She began to scrabble in her handbag for cigarettes, and its contents spilled. Jane helped her pick them up, and gave her a cigarette from her case.

'Oh why don't they get on with this beastly charade?' said Catherine, then took a long, determined breath. 'I'm sorry,' she said. 'That wasn't worthy of even me. It's just that I'm nervous.'

'Brides are supposed to be nervous,' said Jane.

'Yes, and we know why, don't we?' Catherine said. She looked about her, then moved her spindly, gilt-legged chair closer to Jane's.

'Darling,' she said, her voice lowered, 'I am sorry to do this to you, but there's no one else I can ask, and quite honestly I'm petrified. I mean you are a woman of the world after all.'

'Am I?' said Jane.

'Well everybody seems to think you are,' said Catherine, then gasped: 'Oh my God I didn't mean *that*.'

Before Jane could ask what she did mean the head fitter returned, followed by a maid with coffee, and promised that the presentation would begin almost immediately.

'Promise me you'll tell me,' said Catherine.

'If I can,' said Jane. 'But not now.'

And certainly not about Bower, she thought. He promised me he'd never tell, and if he has I'll bloody well murder him. Suddenly she realised that she had quoted John, the first man in her life, when a waiter had splashed his shirt with soup. What could she possibly say to Catherine that would help? It was words, not deeds, that were important on such occasions. Bower's deeds and her own.

The mannequins swayed in the way mannequins do: languid, disdainful, and each of them about seven feet tall, or so it seemed, while the head fitter chatted away furiously, eyes flicking from clothes to her notes, then back to the clothes. Evening dresses, day dresses, cocktail dresses, suits: heavy silk, fine silk, linen, cashmere. On and on it went: really a most impressive trousseau, thought Jane. But then this was Lord Mangan's daughter. Bridesmaids' dresses followed, in a blush pink that effortlessly avoided insipidity, and last of all, the bride, in a short dress of ivory silk, cloche hat trimmed with ivory roses, and the sheerest veil that Jane had ever seen.

'It's gorgeous,' she said.

'That's just the point,' said Catherine. 'The wrapping's fine, but what about the contents? *Please* can't we go somewhere and talk?'

They went to South Terrace, where they could sit in the garden and not be overheard. No doubt Truett would consider her eccentric, but then she thought that anyway.

'This woman of the world business –' she said. 'I suppose I shouldn't have said that.'

'Not at all,' said Jane. 'It's just that – who told you?'

Catherine flung up her hands. 'I don't think anybody *told* me exactly. It's just – well – the friends you have.'

'What friends?' It was hard not to sound like a prosecuting counsel.

'Sarah Vane and Georgina. I remember the three of you together when you arranged that concert at Felston. I mean just seeing you. The way you were. It was obvious that you knew all the things I didn't. Then there's Brenda Coupland.'

'There is not Brenda Coupland,' said Jane. 'She's an acquaintance, but she's not a friend.'

'It's all so much easier for Piers,' said Catherine, not quite irrelevantly.

'Young men don't get pregnant,' said Jane.

'Neither do you.'

'There's luck,' said Jane, 'and there's management. Best to have both. . . . Do you want children?'

'Oh yes,' said Catherine.

'But at decent intervals?'

'If it can be arranged.'

'Then you'd better go to see a friend of mine.'

'Oh dear,' said Catherine. 'You don't mean an abortionist?'

'Of course I don't,' said Jane. 'A highly respectable lady doctor.'

'Sorry,' Catherine said. 'I can hardly see you visiting one of those crones you read about in the *News of the World*. Using an instrument, they always say. What instrument? When I was younger I used to think it might be an oboe.'

'Never mind that now,' said Jane. 'If you want a baby fairly soon, Harriet – my friend – will take care of the rest.'

'And Jaybird, I suppose. He ought to know what he's doing.'

'I should imagine so.'

'I mean it wouldn't do to have two virgins fumbling about on the night.'

'I should consider that most unlikely,' said Jane. 'And do stop trying to shock me.'

'Sorry,' said Catherine once more. 'It's just that I'm so scared.'

'Listen,' said Jane. 'There'll be pain because there has to be pain, but a civilised person like Jay will do his best to make it as little as possible, and after that he'll show you what fun it can be too.'

'You seem awfully sure,' said Catherine.

'I once knew a man very like Jay Bower,' said Jane. Truett stumped towards them, carrying a tray of martinis. 'Here endeth the lesson,' said Jane. 'I hope it was helpful.'

'Oh yes,' said Catherine. 'Gosh yes.'

'And confidential?'

'But of course. Mummy would wallop me just for asking.'

'And your grandmother?'

'Granny would kill me.'

Truett put the tray down, not aggressively, but with a contrived awkwardness that said as plainly as words that cocktails, like young ladies, belonged in the drawing room at that time of day.

'Tell Cook that there'll be two of us for lunch,' said Jane.

'Yes, Miss Whitcomb.'

' – which will be served in the dining room.' Truett left them.

'How she hates outdoors,' said Jane.

Catherine sipped her martini. 'I feel very grown up with you,' she said.

'Grown up? You'll be married in four months' time.'

'Yes, but –' again the gesture with the outflung hands. 'It's all very well for Piers. I mean he's been through Sandhurst and he's got his regiment *and* he's a full lieutenant. You only have to watch him chivvying his riflemen to know that he's grown up.'

'But you went to Oxford. Like him. You got just as good a degree.'

'Ages ago. I was a debutante ages ago, too.'

'Shortly after the flood, as I recall.'

Catherine grimaced at her. 'You know what I mean. But since then I've done nothing at all. Danced a bit, hunted a bit, gone shopping with Mummy, stayed in Ireland –'

' – And got engaged.'

'And that's nothing you do, either. It's just something you are. But marriage –'

'Well?'

'Marriage is something to work at,' said Catherine. 'Something I can do well, I know it – once I get the hang of the carnality.'

'What sort of work have you in mind?' said Jane.

'Not sure,' said Catherine. 'Not a hundred per cent. But I know that Jaybird isn't finished yet. He still has more mountains to climb.'

'And you're going to climb with him?'

'Roped together,' said Catherine. 'In sickness and in health.'

'For richer for poorer?'

'There won't be any poorer,' said Catherine. 'Not while I'm tied to him.' She brooded for a moment. The martini was beginning to bite. 'He's going to get richer, the devil of a lot richer,' she said at last, 'and so am I, because I'm going to help him.'

I know a man who can't wait to push your Jaybird off his peak, thought Jane: a man who's climbed even higher – and if you two are roped together, you'll crash, too. But at least she knew what Catherine would work for in her marriage. It was power.

That Saturday night he'd offered to speak in the Market Place and give the Sally Ann a run for its money. He'd been a bit nervous about it, but they'd been all for it at the Branch, and in the Labour Hall too. Councillor Billy Caffrey had introduced him. Voice that could have flattened Jericho's walls. 'Sounding Brass', Da would have called it. Whatever it was it brought them over from the market stalls and the pub doorways, and even from the Army's hymns.

'Ha'way over here,' Billy Caffrey yelled, 'and learn some sense for a change. Never mind jam tomorrow and pie in the sky. Here's a feller who's going to tell us about what we're entitled to now, this minute – and how we're going to get it, what's more. We've all heard him before, and now he's back. Now's our chance to hear him again. So come and listen, friends and comrades. Come and hear that great warrior of the working class – that champion of social justice – Andy Patterson.'

Like I was a turn on the music hall, thought Andy, but all the same Billy had done his stuff. Some of his audience was already clapping as he climbed on to the makeshift platform, hands tight clenched as they always were at the beginning, so that he wouldn't show his nervousness.

But it was like it always was. Once he'd started, there wasn't time to be nervous. He had to get them and hold them, and pour the truth into them, a truth so alive it would take root in them, and grow and flourish, and never die. He could do it, too. They had taught him a few tricks at Cambridge, honest tricks that justified the cause, but that was just icing on the cake. What was real was in himself. He praised them, prophesied, wheedled and cajoled, and they listened, men and women alike: he was reaching out to them, touching them. He could feel it. He gave them the lot: the heroic class struggle, the working-class martyrs gone before, the dignity of labour, loyalty to one another, and how unity is strength. Finally, when they all inched forward as his voice lowered, and the thunder of the Sally Ann's drum seemed no more than the pulse of his blood, he gave them his vision of the future, the fair and just society where children ate every day and were warmly clad in a city shining clean, where there was work for all and exploitation for none. He took them by the hand and led them to it, and when he had done the crowd roared its applause, as he came back to the reality of acetylene lamps and shouting stall holders, the Sally Ann playing 'There Is A Green Hill', and two policemen, their capes rolled up in the summer night, watching it all.

When he climbed down he was soaking in sweat and the crowd swarmed round him, shaking his hand, pounding his back, until Billy Caffrey and a couple of his mates had to rescue him, drag him round a corner, and into the snug of the Lambton Arms.

'I know you're not much of a hand at drinking,' Billy Caffrey said, 'but you'll have one tonight if I have to choke it down you.'

'To tell you the truth,' said Andy, 'I could do with one.'

One of Billy's pals went off to get them.

The beer tasted unpleasant, as it always did, but he had needed something for his parched throat, and beer meant the least fuss. The others, all three, drank theirs as if life held too few such pleasures.

Billy Caffrey said, 'You've left us to look after ourselves for too long.' Andy could sense no irony in the statement, but for the first time he thought he could detect a kind of wariness.

'It was a chance, Billy, and I took it,' he said.

'Chance for what?' That was one of his pals, almost a replica of Billy, short and squat and hard all through, the way so many miners were.

'A bit of education,' said Andy. 'A chance to learn things the bosses know. That way they can't have it all their own way.'

'I thought only toffs went to Cambridge,' said the other pal.

'Well so they do,' said Andy, 'but a few of them have got a political conscience. The ones who taught me had, anyway.'

'There's toffs there supporting the workers?' said the second pal, and Andy nodded. 'I'm buggered if I can see why,' he said.

'Like I said, conscience. They've come to see how wrong capitalism is – and these are clever men. They've read all the books.

They know we're bound to win in the end.'

'So they want to be on the winning side,' Billy Caffrey said.

'We all want that, Billy,' said Andy. 'Especially when it's the right side.'

'The books,' Billy Caffrey said. 'That's what bothers me.'

'They've got no practical experience, you mean?'

'There's that an' all,' said Billy Caffrey. 'Though God knows there's enough of that about. But it's the kind of books. Marx and Engels would it be? And Lenin, mebbes?'

And then Andy remembered. This wasn't just Councillor Caffrey, a good Labour man, he was ex-Corporal William Caffrey as well. Durham Light Infantryman. Military Medallist. 'Your Country Needs You'. Kitchener had no need to ask him twice. Billy Caffrey was off first call. Always there at the Cenotaph on Armistice Day, and on Empire Day off to some elementary school or other to lecture innocent children on the Glories of Empire and The White Man's Burden. Billy Caffrey was a patriot, God help him, and a moderate. It's time to watch your step, Andy, he thought.

'Well that's part of it,' he said. 'Of course it is. These fellers are scholars, you see. They read everything. Not just Germans like Marx, but Frenchmen like Rousseau and our own writers an' all: Shaw and Blatchford and William Morris. But it isn't just the books about Socialism. They already know Socialism's right – just like we do. It's the technical stuff: the legal side, the economic side. That's where the bosses have always beaten us in the past – because they had the education and we hadn't.'

The second pal said, 'Your father used to reckon that the New Testament was all he ever needed.'

And look where that got him, Andy thought.

Aloud he said, 'It may have done for him. It's not enough for me. We're fighting a war.' It was the right word for Billy Caffrey.

'You're right there, Andy,' he said. 'The greatest war of them all. Man, the Somme's not in it. This one's for all mankind. Only –' Andy waited. 'Only we're Englishmen as much as we're Socialists,' Billy Caffrey said, 'and we're proud of our country, just as I hope you are, too. We don't want to look away from our own when it comes to building the New Jerusalem.'

That's part of a speech you've made before, and more than once, Andy thought.

'There's more than one road to Socialism,' he said. 'There has to be. It stands to reason. I mean we're all Englishmen, as you say: not Italians or Germans or Chinese. We have our own traditions, like you say. We'd be daft to chuck them away just for the sake of change.'

As they listened to this twaddle, the faces of the men around him relaxed. Only help me to get on, he thought, to become your MP, and I'll tell you anything you want to hear.

'I'll tell you another thing,' he said. 'It came up during a discussion we were having at Cambridge. What they call a seminar. We'd been arguing the toss over this very subject – "Socialism and the British Way of Life", it was called, and in the middle of it it seemed to me I'd found the answer. Being Labour and being British and proud of it. It's there in one word.'

'What word?' Billy Caffrey's great voice boomed like a shout of command.

'Moderation,' said Andy.

They were all over him. They felt so pleased, so relieved, that it was almost indecent. He wondered how the Cambridge chaps would have reacted to his description of that non-existent seminar. Francis Whitcomb would have been as nauseated as he was himself. Burrowes would have shouted with laughter.

Billy Caffrey said, 'Man, that's marvellous. Would you mind if I was to borrow it some time? It says it miles better than I ever could.'

There is no need for you to sit here feeling like a bastard, Andy lad. Your business is to shin up the political ladder best way you can.

They danced that night at the Embassy, Catherine and Bower, Jane and Lionel, and Jane decided that, like Lionel, she must be growing old. The dancing bored her. All through the Twenties this had never happened. She'd had bad partners, drunken partners, clumsy partners, but the dance itself had never palled. There was always the hope that the next man would dance like Lionel. They rarely did, but even so she'd enjoyed it. But that night the enjoyment was non-existent. She had much preferred her few moments of chit chat in the powder room. (Underwear and nighties this time, and where to get them. Only one answer to that, of course, Paris. But at least Catherine no longer seemed to regard her Jaybird as a weird mixture of Torquemada and Santa Claus.)

Bower said, 'You are very far away indeed.'

She forced her mind back to the present. 'Sorry,' she said.

'And you're not dancing very well either,' said Bower. 'Way below standard.'

'I'm surprised I'm dancing at all,' she said, and told him why.

He heard her out in silence, then laughed. 'Old age be damned,' he said. 'You're bored. Your trouble is you've done nothing but dance for weeks and weeks. You only enjoy dancing when you're working. It's how you relax. You wait till you get to New York. You'll dance your shoes off.'

It occurred to Jane that he was right, and her quickstep improved at once. 'I've been thinking,' she said. 'About New York. My articles.'

'Go ahead.'

'They ought to be letters,' she said. 'To a friend. A girl friend. The kind of letters where I pour out all my girlish secrets and tell her about all the fabulous people one keeps meeting. You know – all the millionaires and film stars and diamonds and champagne.'

'No champagne,' he said. 'Not at bootleggers' prices. Not unless one of those millionaires is paying. And anyway the film stars are all in Hollywood.'

'But they must visit New York sometimes, surely? I mean business and so on? Publicity? That sort of thing?'

He looked down at her.

'Yeah,' he said. 'I guess they must. Who told you I'd seen Georgie Payne?'

'Brenda Coupland,' she said at once. There was simply no *point* in prevaricating.

'And who told her for God's sake?'

'Sheila Biffen and Bunty Fairweather and some other lady who for some reason she didn't wish to name.'

'When I was in New York Bunty Fairweather was thrown out of the Colony Club,' said Bower. 'You've got to be pretty bad to be thrown out of the Colony. I mean 21 or the Stork Club, sure – but the Colony –'

'All the same, she saw you.'

'Yeah,' said Bower. 'She saw me.' He sounded tired. 'You're telling me this because of Catherine?'

'Because of you both.'

'That's nice,' he said. 'I thank you for that. I love her, Jane. Surely you know that. She's far too young and our backgrounds are poles apart and all that. But I love her. I'm going to marry her.'

'All the same,' Jane said, 'Georgie does have a way of popping up in your life.'

'So you knew that, too?'

'I saw Michael Browne's picture of her,' said Jane, 'in the Fleet Street flat.'

'And you said nothing?'

'What on earth was there to say? What happened to the picture, by the way?'

'I gave it to Georgie.' The dance was nearing its end. Bower spoke more quickly. 'It was what you said. Business. And that's all. I'll swear it if you like.'

'No need, my dear,' said Jane. 'I've already told Brenda Coupland so.'


'Goodness how serious you both looked,' said Lionel. He had escorted her home and she'd asked him in for a nightcap.

'So I should think,' she said. 'We were talking business.'

'You certainly weren't concentrating on your dancing. Really, my dear, I positively blushed for you.'

'But I was better later, wasn't I?'

'Indeed you were,' said Lionel. 'Otherwise I should never have asked you to tango.' She hung her head, and for a moment he looked disconcerted. Then she laughed.

'You bitch,' he said, and then: 'I saw Cynthia Townsend yesterday.'

For a moment Jane looked puzzled, then, 'Mrs Agricultural Machinery,' she said.

'The very same. She's getting up a party for Cap d'Antibes in July. She'd like you to be one.'

'I daresay,' said Jane, 'but it's hardly my sort of thing, is it?'

'Do you know it might be,' said Lionel. 'I know I'm going, and so is Michael Browne. And a little bird has told me, in the merest whisper of course – that Georgina Payne may also be among those present.'

'Georgie?' said Jane. 'Does Michael know?'

'I doubt it. Don't you think it might be fun?'

'It might be a matter of life and death,' said Jane. 'But I have to go to Paris –'

'In July?' said Lionel.

'Shopping,' Jane said vaguely. 'For New York, you know.'

'I ran into Charles Lovell the other day,' said Lionel. 'Cynthia adores rich bankers – so useful for Mr Agricultural Machinery. I asked him if he'd like to go to Cap d'Antibes. He said it depended.'

'There's not a thing that happens to me that you don't know about,' said Jane. 'Thank God you can keep a secret.'

# 18

CHARLES SAID HE'D see, and they ought at least to give Paris a try first, but Paris, for the most part, was closed, and the bits that were open were full of the wrong sort of people. The Boeuf sur les Toits for example was crammed to the doors with tourists, all forced to look at each other instead of the celebrities they'd come to see. But she did drag Charles off to the Folies Bergère to look at Lilian Dunn, and decide just how special her speciality dance was.

'Remarkable,' he said when it was over. It required an effort of will on his part, she noticed, not to mop his forehead.

'All of that,' she said. 'Bob's lucky, wouldn't you say?'

'Bob?'

'My young friend from the North East,' she said. 'The one who rents wireless sets.'

'Oh him?' said Lovell. 'The Cambridge dance and all that. I should rather think he is lucky.'

It seemed that she was to be told no more, at least not yet. Instead she asked him over dinner about Olivier Lefèvre.

'Able young chap, so far as I know,' he said at once. 'Good banking family. Why do you ask?'

'A girl I know seems rather keen on him.'

'Then I hope she's got a title, or pots of money,' Lovell said. 'Both would be even better.'

'Suppose it's neither?'

'Not a chance,' said Lovell.

Zelli's was closed, and Bricktops, and La Butte, and the Boeuf sur les Toits might as well have been. The end came when Charles discovered that the Opéra was closed, and even the Louvre.

'This is preposterous,' he said.

'I did warn you,' said Jane. 'Shall I telephone Cap d'Antibes?'

'Nothing else for it,' said Lovell. 'Two whole weeks before the boat leaves.'

'Shall I drive you down?'

But that it seemed would never do. They must arrive on different days.

Jane went first, on the Blue Train from the Gare de Lyon, a kind of Eighteen-Nineties hotel drawing room on wheels. Paris was grey and heavy, with a damp and sweaty heat that made her itch, and the lunch large enough to send her to sleep, but when she woke up, heavy eyed, a headache ready to begin, the sun shone on olive trees and orange groves and the headache was forgotten. She ordered tea and it was dreadful, but the sun continued to shine, and the train clanked and blustered its way at last into the station, where Lionel was there to meet her, in beret and striped sailor's jersey and sailcloth trousers.

'My dear you look divine,' she said.

'Ageing chorus boy,' he said, 'but I enjoy it – and anyway it's expected.' He turned away to organise, in rapid, accurate French, the porters who took care of Jane's luggage. 'We have a car,' he said. 'Rather a grand de Dion. I do hope you'll drive it back. It terrifies me.'

And indeed it should, she thought when she saw it. It was the size of those ambulances she'd driven, a dozen or so years ago, but much more co-operative when it came to gears and clutch. Lionel guided her through the town, and told her the necessary gossip. Michael Browne was there and spent most of the time painting, but they'd put him in a sort of out-house, so that was all right, and there were an American writer and his wife who were drunk rather a lot of the time, but every villa party has to have one, Lionel explained.

'And Georgie?' Jane asked.

'Not yet,' said Lionel.

'And does Michael know she's coming?'

'I doubt it,' said Lionel. 'I warned Cynthia, I truly did – best to let Michael know. But Georgie wants it to be a surprise.'

'What on earth for?'

'Because she'll enjoy every minute of it,' said Lionel.

'But why did she decide to come in the first place?' asked Jane.

'I told Cynthia to tell her you'd be here,' said Lionel.

'Good gracious, is that all it took?' said Jane.

'She really is awfully fond of you.'

I was a flop as Cleopatra in Hollywood, she thought. *Not* like the Four Arts Ball. And Georgie came along and was a sensation in the part, and went straight on to stardom. No wonder she likes me. No. That was bitchiness. I'd have loathed being a film star, and we really do like each other.

The evening dawdled by. The Great American Writer and Wife were apparently too drunk to appear in public, but not too drunk to have martinis sent up at regular intervals. Cynthia Townsend looked perfectly dreadful in the sort of orange crepe that made even other people feel hot, and Agricultural Machinery, or AM as Jane had learned to think of him, wore at dinner the sort of white monkey jacket that only looks good on a very thin cocktail barman. Michael Browne had been painting hard all day and seemed about ready to sleep. The only other guest was Cynthia Townsend's sister, with the macaw screech that seemed to run in the family, so that when the two conversed the effect was like the Tropical Bird House in Regent's Park Zoo.

The villa, however, was delightful, all blue and white, spacious and cool, and the gardens magnificent: jacaranda, magnolias, oleander, hibiscus, reminding her of Hollywood and India. There was even a pool. Georgie would feel at home. But why wouldn't she warn Michael of her coming? The poor darling was obviously dying to talk about her yet again. It was really a relief when he fell asleep instead.

She and Lionel took a stroll in the garden. The scent of flowers was overwhelming, cicadas chirred, and not too far away the Mediterranean gently sighed, like a baby sleeping.

'This,' said Jane, 'is what money is for.'

'It's what other people's money is for,' said Lionel. . . .

She went to her room early. Down the corridor, the Great American Writer, or his Wife, or both, appeared to be taking an axe to the furniture, but even that sound receded when she shut the door, and went to watch the sea sigh in its sleep, before taking out her notebook and pen.

Dearest Daisy [she wrote],
Paris was absolutely dead. A desert. No one there at all. I mean the place was full of Parisians of course, but nobody one knows. I went to Zelli's and it was closed. Can you imagine? So I fled down here to Cap d'Antibes instead. . . .

Georgie arrived after breakfast. She arrived in a simply enormous Bugatti, which was followed by a van that seemed stacked with suitcases and steamer trunks. Thank God she drove neither of them – Georgie was a terrible driver. Instead she relied on two chauffeurs dressed like Ruritanian generals, two giants who appeared to be twins. Cynthia Townsend and her sister rushed to meet her, the macaw screech already high in decibels, and Lionel followed more slowly. Michael Browne had already gone off to paint, and the Great American Writer and Wife were apparently sleeping amid the wreckage. Jane continued her letter to Dearest Daisy. Georgie would look in when she was ready.

It didn't take long. Jane had just written, 'You'll never guess. The most exciting news. A fabulous film star is coming. . . .' when the fabulous film star appeared. The two women embraced, then stood back to look at each other, each face wearing a look, appraising, critical, yet loving, that they wouldn't bestow on anybody else.

'Darling, you haven't changed a bit,' said Georgie.

'My very words,' said Jane. Georgina Payne's beauty retained its almost preposterous perfection, a fact that Georgina exploited brilliantly when playing comedy.

'Darling, it's been ages,' she said.

'Well if you will live in Hollywood –'

'No one lives in Hollywood,' said Georgie. 'Even existence is barely possible.'

'Then why do it?'

'Well the mun of course,' said Georgie. 'I really am most frightfully rich.'

'Me too.'

'Georgeous, isn't it? One of these days I shall chuck it all up and travel *everywhere*. I may even look up my mother and her viscount in Happy Valley. Kenya can't be worse than Beverly Hills.'

'They're still married, then?'

'Still married. I'm not quite clear whether it's to each other or not.' She looked at Jane's hands. 'But you're not. Married I mean.'

'Nor likely to be.'

'Got a nice chap, though.'

'Very nice.'

'Oh dear,' said Georgie. 'I wish I had. I mean just look at me.' She swept her hand down her body, ruffling the blue and white of her dress. Blue and white, thought Jane: as if the house's décor had been designed only for this.

'I mean the way I look you'd think I could land just one nice chap.'

'I thought you did, once,' said Jane.

'Michael? Well yes, he was nice. He really was. For a while he was absolute bliss, even, but then he began to get that look – you know. Roses round the door, the patter of tiny feet. I couldn't have that, darling. I mean – could you see me like that?' Jane shook her head. 'And so I left him.'

'Broken hearted I may say,' said Jane.

'Is he indeed?' Georgie looked pleased.

'You do know he's here?'

'Well of course I do,' Georgie said. 'That's why I had you all sworn to silence. You see – I could do it all over again with Michael, I really could – if only he's got over this parenthood nonsense. – And there's no reason why we shouldn't do it all over again – I mean I've got enough for both of us –'

'He's doing quite well for himself,' said Jane.

'There you are then. So I had this idea. I thought if I walked in on him – out of the blue and unannounced so to speak – before he had time to put on an act, then I would know.'

'Whether he'd changed or not?'

Georgie nodded. 'Do you think I'm absolutely crackers?'

'Not at all,' said Jane. 'It might be the only way that you ever would know – I mean to be absolutely sure.'

There was a tap at the door, and the maid came in. She carried a tray on which were a shakerful of martinis and two glasses.

'Monsieur Warley made these,' she said. 'He hopes you like them,' and began to pour.

'That man,' said Georgie, 'is a saint.'

When the maid left, Jane said, 'What happens if Michael's still Roses Round the Door?'

'In that case I fear,' said Georgie, 'I very greatly fear, that it will be Murray's plan after all.'

'Murray?'

'Murray Fisch,' said Georgie. 'My not very nice chap. Far from nice, in fact. You met him, surely?'

'Aeons ago,' said Jane. 'He gave a party in Hollywood that I went to. Isn't he the owner of World Wide Studios?'

'Well not exactly,' said Georgie. 'Jay Bower owns twenty per cent, and a man in Texas owns thirty per cent, and the bank owns fifty per cent, but he is Chairman of the Board. His plan is that I should get married.'

'But do you want to marry him?'

'Of course not,' said Georgie. 'Nobody would. Well that's not strictly true, exactly, because somebody did. Mrs Fisch. Mrs Magda Fisch. Poor soul.'

'Then who does he want you to marry?'

'Dan Corless.'

Now this was real Dearest Daisy stuff. Dan Corless was the other great star in the World Wide firmament; Douglas Fairbanks's only serious rival. He'd begun his acting life as the ninth cowboy in the posse, moved up to Tarzan parts, somewhere learned how to fence and wear period costume, and now he buckled swashes all over the place: Scaramouche. D'Artagnan. Robin Hood. He was also, for this was Hollywood, very, very handsome. It would be hard to imagine a more photogenic pair, which was what this must be about: a marriage arranged not so much in Heaven as in the Public Relations Department.

'You could do worse,' said Jane.

'Could I?'

'But surely – I mean just look at him.'

'That's all I could do,' said Georgie.

'What on earth do you mean?'

'Well surely it's obvious –' Georgie stopped for a moment, then said, 'No, not to you of course, because it's a secret, and if

– 204 –

I tell you must swear you won't. Tell I mean – least of all to Jay Bower.'

'All right,' said Jane, hand on heart. 'I swear.'

'Dan Corless is as queer as a coot,' said Georgie. 'An absolute screaming pansy.'

For some reason Jane found herself giggling helplessly, and after a moment, Georgie started, too, until in the end they clung to each other and wailed.

'The studio makes him go out to nightclubs,' Georgie said at last. 'Another guy and two other girls. Dan arranges it so that it's another pansy and a couple of lesbians. That way everybody's happy.'

'You wouldn't be.'

'They'd have to pay me,' Georgie said. 'One hell of a lot of money.' She thought for a moment. 'Murray's been clever, hasn't he?' she said at last. 'America's favourite hero gets the girl – never mind the rumours, folks. This is the original femi*nine* article – and the studio gets the publicity. And at the end of the day it's Murray who gets the girl anyway.'

'But why on earth should you –?'

'Sometimes I'm bored,' said Georgie, 'and he's good at it. It takes my mind off things.' She held out her glass and Jane filled it. 'But not a nice chap, any more than Jay Bower's a nice chap.'

'Jay's going to be married,' said Jane.

'So I heard,' said Georgie, 'but don't interrupt. I've had too many martinis and I'm about to lose the thread. Where was I? Oh yes. Murray not nice and Jay not nice. As enemies they were made for each other.'

'Are they enemies?'

'Oh boy,' Georgie said, and sipped her martini, then: 'But Charles Lovell is nice.'

Fish away, thought Jane. I'm not ready to tell you yet.

'But how extraordinary,' she said. 'I've met Charles Lovell, too. How did you two meet?'

'Socially,' said Georgie. 'Just socially – at one or two of Murray's little business get togethers. Yes . . . Charles Lovell is very nice indeed. But when I think of him on the one side, and Jay and Murray on the other, it's like a very nice lion deciding which of two dreadful bull terriers he'll have for lunch. Except that he's already made up his mind.'

'Jay?'

'Well of course Jay. Murray's come up with a scheme that could give Charles thirty per cent of the studio – Jay only has twenty. Life would not be all that sweet for poor darling Jay.' She finished her drink. 'Oh my God,' she said. 'Forgive me. But somehow I thought you might be interested.'

'I am,' said Jane. 'It's fascinating.'

'It's all rather hell,' said Georgie. 'All this plotting and scheming, and assassinations and ambushes, but so long as I'm making money I don't bother too hard. Except –' Jane waited. 'Except that they're all killers, deep down. Including Mr Lovell. Especially Mr Lovell,' said Georgie. 'If he'd carried a gun for Capone, Al would be dead by now and Lovell would be running Chicago.' She paused for a moment. She was just the tiniest bit drunk. 'Does any of this matter to you?' she said at last. 'I mean really matter?'

'Jay's going to be married in October,' said Jane.

'Oh yes. You told me, didn't you? – and Murray mentioned it too. Lady Catherine – Hilyard is it?'

'You met her at Felston,' said Jane.

'Good Lord, yes, so I did. Young enough to be his daughter. Will they be happy, do you think?'

'Jay wants to be. So does she, but as you say she's young, and he spoils her.'

'Spoiling costs money.'

'Exactly,' said Jane.

'As we both know.'

'We do indeed.'

Georgie got to her feet. 'I'd better be off while I can still walk,' she said. 'That cockatoo in green and pink – can you believe it? – told me where Michael's studio is. I'd better get it over with. . . . They taught me a poem at school. Well as a matter of fact they taught me dozens, but this is the one I remember.' She began to declaim, lustily:

> He either fears his fate too much,
> Or his deserts are small,
> Who dares not put it to the touch,
> To win or lose it all.

'. . . See you later.'

Jane watched her go, and went back to her note book, but somehow she could think of nothing she wanted Daisy to know.

Lionel said, 'I do hope you're not bored.'

'Not in the least,' said Jane.

'The thing is,' said Lionel, 'that the Great American Writer is working again, and his Wife has discovered an interest in one of my sailors – I do wish women would leave them alone. – He's in Toulon,' he added. 'It's not too far by express train. I think she wants a jersey like mine.'

'And AM?'

'Gone to an exhibition of harrows and ploughs and things in Lyon, and taken the macaws with him.'

'Thank God for that.'

'As for Georgie –'

'I know about Georgie.' Lionel looked at her. 'It's all a bit complicated, but I think I understand,' said Jane.

'Michael Browne?'

'Maybe,' said Jane. 'She's not sure.'

'I do hope that Georgie isn't going to mess up his future as a painter,' Lionel said.

'So do I,' said Jane. 'Of course I do. But Georgie has her problems too.'

They drove into Cap d'Antibes and came back to a villa still deserted. The Great American Novelist still laboured, sustained by sandwiches. His Wife, it seemed, continued her infidelity, their hosts still looked at ploughshares, and Georgie was still in the studio. They were sitting on the verandah, lazily gossiping, when the telephone call came. Cynthia Townsend was addicted to telephones: indeed found life impossible without them, so that the villa had, as well as the usual telephone system, an internal one between rooms, with an extension to the gazebo that Michael Browne used as a studio. It was from there that Georgie called Jane.

'I want you to come over here at once,' she said.

'Are you all right?' said Jane.

'Pretty nearly. But it's important you come now.'

'Shall I bring Lionel?'

'Perhaps later.' Georgie hung up.

'Very cryptic,' said Jane. 'I'm to go at once to the studio.'

'But not me?'

'You will be summoned later.' Jane rose. 'I'd better be off. Georgie never fusses about nothing.'

There were paths between scented flowers, and the same whispering sea sound, and at last a little square building of stone: a tiny retreat for any artist, poet, composer of genius who felt the pressures of villa society had become too much. She went inside, and was instantly back in time and space to a studio in Fulham, years ago, with paintings all over the place, Michael and Georgie very much together, and Michael's wife attempting to slash the nude portrait of Georgie with a bread knife.

But this time there was no wife, and the paintings were different in style, in concept. Jane found she didn't like them nearly so much. Michael Browne stood in the full glare of sunlight before a portrait of a woman that owed a little to Picasso, rather more to Modigliani and nothing at all to Michael Browne, who stood like a sentry on guard. To his right, in deep shadows, Georgie stood waiting until Jane came into the room.

'Darling, how sweet of you to come so quickly,' she said. 'I couldn't bear you to miss this. History has just repeated itself.'

She moved out of the shadows to the light: in one hand she held a palette knife that she threw on to a table cluttered with paints and brushes. She had a black eye, the right one: or rather it was already beginning to show that rich mixture of colours, from grey to purple, that is called a black eye. Georgie with a black eye, Jane discovered, had something of the same effect as a moustache on the Mona Lisa.

'Darling, what happened?' she asked.

'I hit her,' said Michael Browne, and Jane waited. There had to be more to it than that.

'Well he did,' said Georgie, 'and I've no doubt that he'll say it was entirely my own fault, although others might argue that I was trying to help him.'

'Help!' said Browne, still wary, alert, even though she had dropped the palette knife.

'Georgie,' said Jane, 'you didn't attack Michael, surely?'

'He'll probably say I did,' said Georgie.

Firmly Jane moved a stack of sketches from a chair to a table, sat on the chair, and produced cigarettes and holder.

'Oh that's divine,' said Georgie. 'Where did you get it?'

'Van Cleef and Arpels,' said Jane. 'Now stop changing the subject and tell me what happened.'

Georgie looked at Browne. 'Ladies first,' he said.

'I told you,' said Georgie. 'History repeated itself. I tried to slash that.' She nodded at the Picasso-Modigliani by Browne. 'There wasn't a bread knife handy so I had to use the palette knife, only he clocked me one before I could do any good.'

'Good!' said Browne.

'I mean just look at it,' said Georgie. 'Didn't I do the right thing?'

'Well of course not,' said Jane. 'You had absolutely no *right*. Don't you remember how you carried on when Mrs Browne went for that portrait of you?'

'Mrs Browne had no right,' said Georgie, 'but I could argue that I might have had. It was a portrait of me, after all.' She nodded at the picture on the easel. 'Well that's a portrait of me, too.'

This time, mercifully, Jane managed not to giggle. Georgie turned to Browne. 'Would you say that's what happened?' she asked.

'Pretty well. Are you going to tell Jane why you decided to take up vandalism as a hobby?'

'You're the one who did that,' said Georgie. 'To your own talent.'

Suddenly they began to yell at each other, until Jane took off her shoe and banged it on the table.

'Children, children,' she said. 'A little more decorum or I shall clear the nursery.'

'All right,' said Georgie. 'I'll tell you. It's all wrong, what Michael's doing. It isn't him at all and I doubt very much if it's the chaps he's deriving from either. That's why.'

'But surely,' said Jane, 'you didn't propose to slash every painting he's done like this?'

'Just give me the chance,' Georgie said. 'Which of course he won't. But this one. This one was too much. This one's supposed to be *me*.'

'Now we're getting to it,' said Browne.

Jane said, 'Georgie, your eye's a mess. We ought to get some-one to look at it.'

'It can wait till we've finished.'

Jane made a pad of her handkerchief, went to a sink with a tap, and soaked the pad. 'Hold that to it,' she said, 'and get a move on. We'll have to do something about that eye.'

'That's about it, really,' Georgie said. 'When he told me that was me, looking all smug and self-satisfied, as if I should faint away at the sheer joy of the news – I just couldn't bear it. I thought of that first portrait he did of me, and – oh hell!' Suddenly, without preliminary announcement, she began to cry. She does even that beautifully, Jane thought, and put her arms round her.

'Come on, darling,' she said. 'I doubt if that's doing your eye any good.'

Georgie shook her head and wept on, and Jane looked across at Browne. The man was clearly in turmoil: appalled at what he had done and yet convinced that he was right to do it.

'I didn't mean to hurt her,' he said. 'Honestly I didn't. I was just defending my work.'

'Because you believe it's good?' said Jane.

'Because I know it's good.' There was no arguing with that.

'Doctor,' said Jane. 'Now.'

'Just one more thing,' said Georgie, still sobbing, and her body stiffened as Jane tried to move her. She waited till the sobs had died.

'I had an accident,' she said. 'I wasn't looking where I was going – too many martinis I expect – and bumped into a door.'

'If you think I'm going to hide behind your skirts –' said Browne.

'It isn't that, you bloody fool,' she yelled, in what Jane suspected must have been her palette-knife voice, for Browne was instantly back on guard duty.

'What then, darling?' she asked.

'Murray,' Georgie said. 'He'll be here tomorrow.'

'Who the hell is Murray?' asked Browne.

Georgie said wearily, her anger gone, 'Murray Fisch. He's the head of World Wide Studios.'

'What on earth's it got to do with him?' asked Browne.

Georgie looked at him as if he were the last of a species she had thought extinct. 'I'm the most valuable piece of property the studio owns, and you've just damaged it. That's what it's got to do with him.'

'But what can he possibly do about it? Kill me?'

'He can hurt you,' said Georgie', and he will hurt you. People don't damage World Wide and get away with it. He says that at least twice a day.'

'But that's barbaric,' said Browne.

'Well in a way Hollywood is barbaric,' said Georgie. 'Wouldn't you say so, Jane?'

Jane thought of the tantrums, the screaming and the yelling. 'Yes, I would,' she said.

Georgie turned to Browne. 'For instance, that picture. He'd hate it.'

'Don't tell me he's an art critic, too,' said Browne.

'Murray hates every kind of critic there is,' said Georgie, 'and especially the kind who would praise that picture.'

'But why, for God's sake?'

'Because it isn't beautiful.'

'You may not think so,' said Browne, 'but –'

'Forget about me,' said Georgie. 'All I'm telling you is it doesn't look like me, and this –' her hand swept down her body in the same embracing gesture, '– is what gets people into the picture theatres. Not *that*.' She gestured at the portrait.

'I bumped into a door,' she said again.

Michael Browne said obstinately, 'I can look after myself.'

'You've got a pretty handy left jab, I'll say that for you,' Georgie said, and giggled. Then, incredibly, Browne giggled too.

'All right,' he said. 'You bumped into a door.'

Jane telephoned Lionel to make an appointment with a doctor, then come to the gazebo. When it was done she drove Georgie to Antibes in the Bugatti, to its chauffeur's loud and prolonged distress, but Jane was firm. She had never driven a Bugatti. It proved to be every bit as testing an experience as she had been told. Maybe she wouldn't buy a Bentley after all.

Dr Bessonard was as courteous, skilful and sympathetic as the most expensive doctor in Antibes should be. Without a blink he accepted the open-door story, applied Merchurocrome, and suggested tinted spectacles. The famous Miss Payne, he implied, should not appear before her public with even the slightest blemish: and so, when Jane drove back to the villa, her passenger wore the most intriguing glasses with gold and tortoise-shell frames.

'If I may ask –' said Jane.

'Well I expect so,' Georgie said. 'I tell you everything.'

'How was the lovey-dovey bit? The roses round the door?'

'The sad thing is he seems to be over that,' Georgie said. 'In fact at first I thought it was going to be a round-the-world trip for two – and then art went and reared its ugly head.'

'You can't get together again? I mean, when I heard you both laugh like that –'

'That's just because of the way we feel about each other,' said Georgie. 'A script writer would call it love, I suppose. But we couldn't possibly live together – not the way we feel about each other's work. It'll have to be Dan Corless, after all.'

'Have to be?'

'Well if it isn't him it would have to be somebody else – unless I gave up the movies, which I don't intend to do on my own. It's a terrific feeling – all those people loving you and envying you at the same time. Besides if I take on Dan it'll keep Murray happy, which isn't such a bad idea at the moment.'

'Is he *so* awful?'

'Well yes, I suppose he is,' said Georgie. 'Not that it's entirely his fault, poor lamb. I mean he was born in the most terrible slum in New York's East Side. He was Morris Fischtein or something then. Got into the garment business, like so many Hollywood Jews, and sort of clawed his way into the movies. All the people who'd got to where he wanted to be tried to keep him out of course, and so he had to fight his way in, thinking up even dirtier tricks as he did so. Michael wouldn't stand a chance.'

'I get the feeling that Michael's done his share of that in his time,' said Jane. 'Like my very first nice chap.'

'Oh but that was the war,' said Georgie. 'There were masses like them during the war, but once it was over they went back to being nice chaps. Murray wouldn't even begin to know how to be a nice chap.'

Jane parked the car, and the chauffeur at once examined it for damage, seeming vaguely disappointed that there wasn't any.

'How men do hate competence in a woman,' said Jane.

'Depends what she's doing,' said Georgie.

They walked to the gazebo, where Lionel had somehow procured gin, vermouth and ice, and was already making martinis.
He adored the dark glasses.

'My dear,' he said. 'They're totally and utterly you. It almost
makes one glad that that damn door got in the way.'

Georgie kissed his cheek.

'Too sweet,' said Lionel, then went back to telling Browne
about naked wrestling at La Ruche before the war.

'He's too gorgeous, isn't he?' Georgie said. 'I wish I could do
something for him.'

'You might get him a date with your fiancé,' said Jane. Georgie
snorted into her martini.

# 19

JANE AND LIONEL walked back to the villa, leaving Georgie and Browne together.

'Well,' said Jane.

'Well indeed,' said Lionel. 'Well well well. Here's a how d'you do, in fact.'

'He told all?'

'Pretty well, I should think. Old sparks rekindling, and then the fury with the palette knife.'

'That just about sums it up. Is he any good?'

'Now?' Jane nodded. 'There's nothing wrong with Picasso, or Modigliani, but they're not ones I should choose to imitate. He shouldn't have either, because he can't do it.'

'What about his earlier stuff?'

'Old fashioned,' said Lionel, 'but enormously competent, and really rather good.'

'Then why doesn't he stay with it?'

'He's ashamed of it,' said Lionel. There wasn't much one could say about either.

Agricultural Machinery was back, with his two macaws, feeling rather good because there was nothing he had seen in Lyon he couldn't make better in Birmingham. He seemed prepared to analyse this in depth, and Lionel asked rather hastily where the Great American Writer was.

Mrs Townsend screeched, but it was her sister who answered.

'Gone to look for his Wife,' she said.

'To rescue her from the sailor?' Lionel asked hopefully.

'She's taken all his money.'

Jane thought it time to break the news of Georgie's accident. 'Horror and shock were registered by all.' That had been one of her favourite sentences in the *Daily World*, and it exactly conveyed what she witnessed now. A shrine had been desecrated.

'But how perfectly dreadful,' said AM.

'Ghastly, ghastly,' screeched the macaws.

'But she's being very brave about it,' said Jane.

'Of course, of course,' said AM. 'Makes you proud to be British.'

Then Georgie appeared, with Browne, and there was a reverent hush as the two women digested the impact of dark-lensed glasses of tortoise-shell and gold.

'Oh you clever, clever thing,' Mrs Townsend screeched and soon there was dancing to the gramophone, followed by dinner, and plans to visit a nightclub.

Dearest Daisy [wrote Jane],
 Such uproar here in Cap d'Antibes. One of my dearest friends, Georgina Payne – yes, the film star, the one and only – sustained a very nasty accident to her eye, so bad that none other than little me had to whisk her away in the Bugatti to see the most handsome and distinguished eye specialist. . . .

Why on earth did Jay have to allow me to attempt this tripe? she wondered, but the answer was all too obvious. It would help sell papers. The Paris one it seemed had already gone down well, according to his telegram. Some people thought it was funny, some thought it was just gossip, and some, a minority, even thought it was trash, but he, Bower, didn't give a damn so long as it sold newspapers and let's have the next one quick. So Jane laboured on and tried not to think how much more fun it would be to lie in the sun beside Lionel, exchanging gossip with Georgina in the shade. Georgina's complexion was so delicate that she must not get sunburned. It was in her contract. Better put that in too, she thought. Georgina didn't mind. Write what you like, she'd said. I expect you'll have to clear it with Murray anyway. That would rather depend on how Murray Fisch and Jay Bower got on these days, she thought, but that's nothing to do with me. She plodded on.

Murray Fisch arrived at teatime in a chauffeur-driven Cadillac. (Soon the chauffeurs will outnumber the guests, thought Jane.) But Fisch had brought a passenger, Charles Lovell. Jane settled down, delighted to watch the impact of AM and his aviary, but really Charles was awfully good at that sort of thing: amiable, correct, and just the tiniest bit flirtatious with the ladies. Perhaps it had something to do with the fact that he had a very good tailor. . . .

Murray Fisch excused himself from his hosts at the first permissible moment and went to Georgie. The dark glasses were like a magnet. When she took them off, he yelped like a dog that was trodden on. Georgie murmured explanations. 'A door?' he yelled. 'How could you do a stupid thing like that?'

More murmurs from Georgie and then: 'Martinis? How many times have I told –' Georgie's voice became audible then, cold and precise. 'You tell me lots of things, Murray,' she said. 'Interfering things. Personal things. Mercifully there's nothing in my contract that says I have to listen to them. Now either talk sensibly, or go away.'

'You've had a shock,' said Fisch. 'I should have realised. Come, my dear. There's someone here you've met before. In New York.' He took her hand and led her over to Lovell.

'Why Charles,' she said. 'How nice to see you.' She offered her hand and Lovell took it. Even Charles, thought Jane. Even with me here. Even when she's got a black eye. There could be no doubt that Georgie was registering hits. Does she really know she's doing it? Jane wondered. With Georgie one could never quite be sure.

'You know Jane Whitcomb, I believe?' she asked. 'She's a very dear friend of mine.'

'Oh yes indeed,' Lovell said. 'Jane, my dear, how are you?' He released Georgie's hand at last and reached out for her.

'Remarkably well, all things considered,' said Jane. 'But what on earth brings you here with Mr Fisch? I didn't know you two were chums.'

And such unlikely chums, she thought, for already Fisch was running to fat and his tailor, though no doubt expensive, was not good.

'We met in New York,' said Lovell. 'I found the film business quite fascinating.' He bowed to Georgie. 'And in certain aspects very beautiful. Do I gather that you've hurt your eye, Georgina?'

'Nothing serious,' Georgie said. 'I had a fight with a door and lost. Jane did her old wartime heroine routine and drove me to a doctor. I'm OK. Really.'

'Wartime heroine?' said Fisch.

'She was the bravest girl in Britain, I should think,' said Georgie.

'Nonsense,' said Jane. 'There were dozens of us.'

'But what did she do?' Fisch continued to question Georgie, as if Jane had no valid reason to be there in the room.

'Drove an ambulance at the Front,' said Georgie. 'Right up to the forward dressing stations, then back to the field hospitals.'

'Was she shot at?'

That was too much. 'Yes I was,' said Jane.

Fisch turned and blinked at her, amazed, as if some figment of a script-writer's imagination had achieved both physical presence and articulate speech.

'Shot at and shelled,' said Jane, 'and machine gunned, too. By an aeroplane. Only I think that was a mistake. It was probably too dark to see the Red Cross.'

'Any Americans?'

'It was a Fokker, actually.' Again the puzzled look. 'The aeroplane,' said Jane. 'It was a German.'

'In your ambulance,' said Fisch impatiently. 'Did you ever give a ride to American troops? Doughboys?'

'Certainly,' she said. 'I drove a relief ambulance in the Argonne Forest. Some of your chaps had been strafed, and –'

'Great,' said Fisch. 'Great, great. Have you sold this to anyone?'

'Sold it?' said Jane. 'This was my life.'

'Your life story,' he corrected her, and turned back to Georgie. 'It's exactly what I need for you,' he said. 'Ladylike and upper class, but sort of brave and tough, too. Hell, she must have been. I mean machine gunned. From the air. What a sequence that'll make. You know – cat and mouse. Of course we'll use more than one plane. – A squadron do you call it?'

Jane noticed that Lionel had wandered in, and was searching in vain for tea and cucumber sandwiches as he drifted towards them.

Fisch turned to Lovell. 'Hey wait a minute,' he said. 'Didn't you tell me this lady is a writer?'

For the first time, Lovell looked uneasy. 'Well yes,' he said. 'She is, as a matter of fact, but I hardly think –'

'It gets better. I swear to God it gets better,' said Fisch, his excitement so intense that the macaws ceased their screeching, as Fisch turned back at last to Jane.

He really is the rudest man, thought Jane, or has he honestly forgotten that we once met, or was I too unimportant for him to bother – until now? She had remembered Murray Fisch as a little brusque, no more, but Georgie had told her that the higher a studio chief climbed, the ruder he became. Well now Fisch must be a very big chief indeed.

' – cable the studio tonight,' he was saying. 'Tell them to send somebody over to crank the publicity. What do you say?'

'We've met before,' said Jane. 'At a party at your house in Beverly Hills. *And* at the studio.'

'Impossible,' said Fisch. 'I'd have remembered. A woman like you.'

'I did a screen test,' said Jane, 'as Cleopatra. Tom Waring directed.' That did set the macaws off again, but Fisch wasn't interested in the past. The present was too important.

'Waring would be great for this picture. He knows how to handle class – and action. . . . What do you say?'

'About what?'

'About *what*? About making this movie, for God's sake. About Georgie starring in it and Waring directing it and you writing it and me producing it. No no I mean it.' He raised a hand as if to quell a non-existent hubbub of voices telling him he was too much in overall control, too busy, just too plain *important* to do anything on such a pigmy scale as the production of a single picture. 'I've got a feeling about this one,' he said. 'An Academy Award sort of feeling. This one I produce myself.' He dismissed the crowd of protesting well-wishers, and came back to Jane. 'What do you say?'

Jane looked at him, awe-struck. Of his kind, she thought, he must be a perfect specimen.

'You see?' Fisch told the others. 'She's so excited she's speechless.'

'No I'm not,' she said. 'I'm never speechless, Mr Fisch, and

rarely excited. But I need to think about this.'

'What's to think about?' said Fisch. 'We're talking real money here. Oh I get it. You want to speak to your agent first. OK. Go right ahead. But make it quick, Miss Whitcomb. I need this one now.'

'As it happens,' said Jane, looking squarely at Lionel, 'the gentleman who advises me on these matters is here. What do you think, Lionel?'

It was Charles who reacted to this, dropping the cigarette he had just taken from his case. Lionel took it without a blink.

'I think you and I should have a chat in private,' he said, and Fisch nodded graciously: a king giving two courtiers permission to withdraw. 'But I must point out to Mr Fisch that while Jane is a talented, brilliant and extremely well-paid writer, she has not as yet written for the screen.'

'That's not a problem,' said Fisch. 'She said herself she's done a screen test, so she knows the way it works. One of the guys under contract can help her, and Waring will handle the technical stuff. But it's her I want. The Living Legend. So she's expensive? We're thinking big here.'

'First my client and I will talk,' said Lionel firmly. 'Tomorrow we'll let you know.'

'Tomorrow?' Shock, outrage, reproach, were all in that one word.

'Tomorrow,' said Lionel. 'You have to cable the Coast; I have to cable London.' At once Murray Fisch looked more relaxed. Long distance cables, thought Jane, must have a reassuring effect.

She and Lionel went into a small room that AM used as an office. 'A pleasure, an honour,' he said, and the macaws agreed. AM had to become aggressive to keep them out, and the entire villa hummed with the knowledge of Hollywood deals. Browne, Jane discovered later, came over from the gazebo expecting at least the possibility of a row, only to find himself ignored.

Lionel said, 'What do you want me to do?'

'I think I want you to accept,' said Jane. 'For every last penny you can get. For Felston.'

'I can see that,' said Lionel, 'but aren't you the teeniest bit worried your mother may cut up rough? Family name and all that.'

Jane said, 'She isn't Lady Whitcomb any more, she's Mrs Routledge. I rather think she'll love it. I know her George will. He adores the pictures.'

'And that's another thing,' said Lionel. 'Talking of the major. – There's the *Daily World*. How do you suppose Jay will feel about this?'

'He should be jolly glad,' said Jane. 'After all he's one of the people who pay Fisch to produce pictures that make money – and he usually does. So all Jay will get out of this is profit – and free publicity for one of his writers.'

'All the same,' said Lionel, 'he may not like it.'

'Then he's at liberty to lump it,' said Jane. 'But there's just one thing.' Lionel turned to her. 'This film either ends on Armistice Day or it's off. No mad scenes.'

'No Ophelias?'

'I was thinking more in terms of Lady Macbeth.'

'My dear girl,' said Lionel, 'from the way Fisch was going on, you'll end up in California or New York or somewhere, lending tone to the home of the handsome young millionaire you rescued from shot and shell.'

'You think I could do that? Lend tone to a millionaire?'

'You could lend tone to a duke,' said Lionel.

'What a gorgeous big sister you are,' said Jane.


For Charles to find his way to her bed had taken both patience and perseverance. They were on the same floor, which at least cut out the need for climbing trellis work, but the whole household had stayed up late, which meant a constant procession to and from bathrooms, but at last he managed it, and she relaxed at once to the touch of familiar hands.

Later he said, 'You don't have to do it if you don't want to.'

'But I thought you enjoyed it.'

He snorted with laughter and she covered his mouth. 'Shh!' she said.

'This picture,' he said. 'This movie. They can't make you.'

'It'll be good for Felston.'

'They'll get some of the money?'

'They'll get the lot,' she said.

'It could be – well – vulgar,' he said.

'It's almost bound to be. But just think of the fuss and the interviews and the publicity. It could be fun, you know. I might even enjoy writing the thing.'

'And your mother?'

'She'll love it,' said Jane. 'I bet she'll tell Gwendolyn Gwatkin the first chance she gets.'

Georgie had a suite in the villa. Everyone else had a sumptuous bedroom, but Georgie had the only suite, which was fair enough, thought Jane, since she was by far the most famous person there. How nice of dear Georgie, she thought, to invite me to breakfast on its terrace; coffee and croissants and brioches, two kinds of jam and a view of the Mediterranean.

'It's good of you to come,' Georgie said.

'Not at all. I love your view.'

'It's good, isn't it?' said Georgie vaguely. 'So sweet.' As if the Townsends had arranged it specially for her.

Jane buttered a croissant and waited. It didn't take long.

'Jane,' said Georgie, 'I just can't bear it any longer. I simply can't. . . . Are you going to let Murray do this movie or not?'

'Yes,' said Jane. 'Within limits I am.'

'Oh you darling,' said Georgie, and jumped up and embraced her. 'I couldn't sleep last night for worrying about it.'

'It's that important? I thought you were always turning parts down.'

'So I am,' said Georgie, 'but I wouldn't turn down this part. Murray's right, you see. Oh, I know he's ghastly, but he usually is right. Perhaps that's what makes him so ghastly.'

'So you'll be me?'

'Do you mind?' Georgie asked.

'It's a bit much,' said Jane. 'Like thinking you're going to see a pit pony and it turns out to be a gazelle. . . . But I don't *mind*. Of course I don't.'

'I'll do you justice, you'll see,' said Georgie. 'Usually I hate working, I mean the actual acting – but this time I just can't wait.'

'Who'll play the doughboy?' asked Jane.

'What doughboy?'

'Oh come off it,' said Jane. 'You know perfectly well there'll be a handsome Yank you'll rescue, then marry in the last reel. Probably turn out to be a millionaire's son.'

'Oh that doughboy,' said Georgie. 'I give you one guess.'

'*Dan Corless?*' Suddenly the two women were giggling again.

'He'll be awfully good,' said Georgie. 'He'll look marvellous in uniform and be terribly brave: jumping out of trenches and charging about all over the place.'

'The ones who did that usually got shot,' said Jane.

'Not if they were the hero,' said Georgie firmly, and then: 'Talking of the Corlesses of this world, Lionel can't really be your agent, surely?'

'I didn't say he was,' said Jane. 'I said he was my adviser, and so he is.'

'Murray's awfully impressed by him. So English.'

'Tell him he was in the Royal Flying Corps,' said Jane. 'That might impress him even more.'

'Was Charles Lovell an airman, too?'

'Infantry,' said Jane. 'The Rifle Brigade. Very smart, but not pompous like the Guards. Just the right niche for Charles.'

'He's your nice chap, isn't he?'

After a moment, Jane said, 'Well yes, he is as a matter of fact, but who on earth told you?'

'Nobody,' said Georgie. 'Chaps are just something I happen to be good at. . . .' There was no denying that one.

'How long have he and Murray known each other?' Jane asked.

'They've been seeing each other off and on for ages,' said Georgie. 'It's to do with Charles buying those shares I told you about. That's all I know about it – and all I want to know. The only money I care about at World Wide is my monthly pay cheque. But he must be terribly important.'

'Why do you think that?' Jane asked.

'Murray's scared of him. Last night after you'd all gone to bed we sat up talking, you remember? All about the picture – till three in the morning.'

'You poor darling,' said Jane.

'Oh no,' said Georgie. 'I loved it. But he kept on worrying about how Charles Lovell might not like it.'

'Because of me?'

'He doesn't know about you and Charles. I swear he doesn't. It's just that he thinks Charles may think it rather vulgar.'

'He does. He told me so. And he could be right, I suppose.

But that doesn't mean he'll interfere. I want the money, Georgie. For Felston.'

'It'll be quite a lot, if your Lionel's as tough as he talks.'

'The more the merrier,' said Jane. 'It's ghastly up there.'

'I remember,' said Georgie. 'When we did the concert.'

'Now it's worse.' She kissed Georgie, left her, went to her room and took note book and pen to the verandah. From below she heard the murmur of Lionel's voice, followed by an anguished yell from Murray Fisch. Lionel, it seemed, was being as tough as he talked.

Dearest Daisy [ Jane wrote],
  Here I am, still at darling Cap d'Antibes, and *the* most *incredible* thing has happened. . . .

And somebody around here had better tell Jay Bower about it soon, she thought, because it isn't going to be me.

# 20

T HEY HAD ARRANGED to meet at the buffet of the Central Railway Station in Newcastle. It was something he often did on Sundays: take the train to the city then wander among the secondhand book stalls by the quay, looking for bargains. Grandma liked him to do that. It gave her time to go to eleven o'clock Holy Communion before cooking the Sunday dinner. But this time he'd had to cut short his time at the book stall. All he'd managed to find was a battered collection of Shelley's poems. The wife at the stall had wanted a tanner for it, but he'd got her down to fourpence. Not much demand for Shelley, it seemed, and he wasn't surprised. The one time he'd tried to read him he couldn't make head nor tail of the stuff. Still Antrobus had said Shelley was important, so he'd better have another try, but not in the station buffet. He had gone to the buffet to meet Burrowes, and of course Burrowes was late. Andy sat at a marble-topped table and drank tea. As he moved his book away from the slops somebody else had left, he noticed his hands. Hardening up nicely: callouses where the blisters had been. Canny bunch of blokes to work with an' all. That Moscow Mike wasn't a bad feller either, Andy thought. A bit jealous because I'm a better speaker than he is, but a hard worker for the Party. When he was away from the works it was nearly always Party business. Well it had to be. He didn't see much of his own kind once the priests had spoken against him. . . .

Suddenly Burrowes appeared beside him. He had a large glass

of whisky in each hand. 'Mind if I join you?' he said. 'It's rather crowded in here.'

As he sat, Andy said, 'I don't want that.'

'It isn't for you,' Burrowes said. 'They're both mine – to help me combat the horrors of the English Sabbath. Do you know they don't open the pubs till midday on Sundays? But of course you do. You're English too, God help you.' He drank off one of the whiskies at a gulp.

That suit he's wearing must be worth ten times the price of mine, thought Andy, but he's got an egg stain on his lapel and there's a button missing. Mine's spotless. Grandma sees to that.

'Well,' said Burrowes, 'anything to tell me – or do you just want the name of my tailor?'

Andy reached for his book. 'I've got nothing to say to that tone of voice,' he said. Burrowes crouched then, as if he were preparing to lash out.

'Show some sense, man,' Andy said, and after a moment Burrowes drank the other whisky, went back to the bar and returned with two more.

'I'm sorry, Andy,' he said. 'It's just – Sunday, as I say. It really depresses me.'

Lovers' quarrel and a hangover more likely, Andy thought.

'That's all right,' said Andy. 'Come to find out about Felston?'

'Fire away,' said Burrowes.

'There's not much to tell except more of the same,' said Andy. 'The town's dying, and if you ask me there's no hope of a cure.'

'No signs of unemployment falling off?'

'Not one. The only reason it doesn't get worse is that it's as bad as it can be.'

'Trading estates?'

'The buildings are there, but the employers won't come.'

'Whyever not?'

'Because Felston makes the wrong things the wrong way. The old-fashioned way. That's the only way they know. To make the right things we'd need re-training, and why should the bosses bother with that when there's plenty of blokes in the Midlands knows the right way already? Felston's finished.'

'So what will happen?'

'What always happens when there isn't a cure. The patient dies.'

'Try to forget your metaphor for a moment,' said Burrowes.

Now that was fair enough. He deserved that. Far too preoccupied with his own despair to give a proper report.

'The best men – and women too – will emigrate,' he said. 'The single chaps that are fit enough will try for the army – or the navy or the air force if they've got the skills. The rest – it'll be the dole and then the workhouse, I'd say.'

'Dole?' Burrowes asked.

'Unemployment Benefit.' What sort of a champion of the proletariat was it who didn't know what the dole was. 'The bairns' health will get worse – rickets and undernourishment, and their parents will die prematurely.' He grinned bitterly. 'The only thing we won't have is the Means Test, because nobody'll have any means to test.'

'You make it sound like Hell.'

'That's what it's beginning to feel like.'

'And you?' said Burrowes. 'What's happening to you?'

'I'm secretary of Number Five Branch of the Fitters' Union,' said Andy, 'and I make speeches in the Market Place every Saturday night.'

'Party speeches?'

'*Labour* Party speeches,' said Andy. 'It isn't easy.'

'No, but it's vital,' said Burrowes. 'Stay at it. Anything else?'

'There's talk of me putting up for the council,' said Andy. 'But that's all it is so far. Just talk.'

'Make it happen.'

All very well for you coming up here dishing out your orders, thought Andy, but I'm the one who's got to do it.

'I'm doing me best,' he said.

'It's a Party instruction,' said Burrowes. 'That means it's an order.'

'It's more than that,' said Andy. 'It's what I want an' all. But to get on the council there has to be an election. When there is, I'll know what to do.'

'It could be months,' said Burrowes.

'It could be years,' Andy said. 'But in the meantime I'm getting meself talked about. Even had my name in the *Felston Gazette*. "Fiery if misguided orator"' he quoted. 'A couple of chaps wrote to the paper about that.'

'What did they say? You'd gone too far?'

Andy chuckled. 'They said I wasn't misguided one bit. If folks would only listen to me Felston would be out of trouble.'

'And what was the panacea that impressed them so much?'

'Go and get yourself two more whiskies while I remember what panacea means,' said Andy, and Burrowes did. He had his own armour, and it was almost impenetrable.

When he came back, Andy said, 'Panacea. . . . Oh aye. That's kind of a universal cure-all, isn't it? The one for Felston is work.'

'But you just said –'

'I know what I just said. Re-training. Well we've got a Labour Prime Minister now, haven't we? Let's ask him to come up and see for himself.'

'Do you think he would?'

'Depends if we shout loud enough. Jimmy Wagstaff's good at shouting.'

'We don't want Wagstaff turned into a hero.' Andy stayed silent. 'Any chance of a rally? A protest meeting?'

'And shop windows broken, and a few heads cracked by police batons?'

'If necessary. Well?'

'There might be one good fight left in them, but not more,' said Andy. 'I'd hate to waste it on something that's not important.'

'Not important?'

'Me,' said Andy. 'Anyway, it mightn't be a good idea for me to get mixed up in another riot. They're still after me for the Elephant and Castle business – I wouldn't fancy another six months in Durham Gaol.'

He looked at the clock on the buffet wall, only just visible through a haze of tobacco smoke and steam from tea urns.

'Before you go,' said Burrowes, 'take a look at this.'

He sorted through his pile of newspapers, and came up with the *Sunday Globe*, the *Daily World*'s sister paper, and opened it at an inside page, then gave it to Andy.

Dearest Daisy [Andy read],

Sunday's the perfect day for writing letters, isn't it? Nothing exciting ever happens on Sundays, even at Cap d'Antibes. . . .

On and on it gushed. Famous film star. Famous producer. Great industrialist. All spending their time in nightclubs and swilling champagne, or else lolling about in the sun half naked and complaining about the servants. . . . Clever though. The kind of stuff you had to finish. Andy reached the end of the piece, and handed it back. While he'd read the paper, Burrowes had picked up the copy of Shelley and read that. All alike, those Cambridge fellers. They couldn't sit beside a book and not open it.

'Well?' said Burrowes.

'I think I'll stay with Shelley,' said Andy.

'I didn't mean that,' said Burrowes. 'What you've just read, it's one of a series. The rest have all been in the *Daily World*. Next week she's off to America to write some more.'

'That'll mean a few more quid for Felston,' Andy said.

'Nothing more than conscience money, even if it's true,' said Burrowes. 'Don't you understand? Isn't it obvious – the way she writes? She's finally left the working class to struggle on its own.'

Andy didn't see that at all. To him, this piece of Jane's suggested something entirely different: a deft and knowledgeable caricature of the very worst excesses of the idle rich, neatly disguised as gossip. But he'd had enough of Burrowes. He wanted to get back to John Bright Street and his Sunday dinner.

'Ah,' he said.

'So that's one obstacle out of the way.' Burrowes threw the book back on the table, where it landed in the tea puddle.

'He was a bit of a windbag,' said Burrowes, 'and of course he'd never heard of dialectical materialism, but he could ring the bell sometimes. Try the "Ode to the West Wind". Some pretty pictures there.'

Carefully Andy wiped his book on Burrowes's copy of the *Sunday Globe*, then got to his feet. Burrowes didn't turn a hair. 'I'd better be off,' he said.

'Remember what I've told you,' said Burrowes, reaching for his newspapers and his whisky. 'Cheerio, Andy.'

'Ta-ra, Burrowes.'

He read the 'Ode to the West Wind' on the train going home. Burrowes was right, as he usually was about things that came out of books. The pictures were beautiful.

He got back to John Bright Street to find that Grandma had invited Bet and Frank to Sunday dinner, and forgotten to tell him. Afraid he would stay away because of the bairn, more like, but young Frank was asleep in his pram, thank God, and the dinner was undisturbed. Bit of beef, Yorkshire pudding, potatoes, cabbage and carrots, and suet pudding with apple and rhubarb. Nobody could cook a Sunday dinner like Grandma, and Frank had brought a couple of bottles of beer along as well. He didn't mind a glass of beer while he was eating. In Cambridge they'd mostly drunk wine.

Frank said, 'I've got a favour to ask, Andy.'

'Ask away.'

'Well I'm a driver now,' said Frank. 'Have been for nigh on a year, and I was thinking of trying for tram inspector, only you have to pass exams for inspector. Book learning and that. I was never much good with the books and I wondered if mebbe you would give a hand?'

Good old Andy. Always there when he was wanted.

'Going to become a bourgeois are you, Frank?' he asked.

His sister glared at him. 'Allow me to tell you, Andy Patterson, there's nowt wrong with getting on.'

'There's nowt wrong with the pudding either,' said Grandma, 'so shut up and eat it.'

They ate, inevitably, at the captain's table; well-known writer, not very well-known millionaire, seated away from each other and trying to act like social acquaintances, no more. The food and wine were superb, not only because they had to be on the *Ile de France*, the newest and most illustrious of the French liners, but because the captain, a fat little Breton, had a passion for gastronomy. He also had a passion for conversation, or perhaps it was just his technique for coping with the succession of strangers he was obliged to eat with. Whatever the reason he had a series of questions to be put to each passenger in succession: about one's work, one's home, and one's pets. Foch had been a problem: an honour certainly to invoke the name of a great soldier; but to bestow it on a dog, and a small dog at that. Really the French could be very po-faced about such things.

'You do not take – the dog – with you when you travel, Miss Whitcomb?'

'Not abroad,' said Jane. 'Quarantine, you know.'

'He does not miss you?'

'Almost as much as I miss him,' said Jane. 'He's getting old, too. I really do hate to leave him – and yet I must. . . . My work, you know.'

'Yes, you have told us about that. Most interesting.' The captain turned to the man sitting next to her, a Scottish earl. 'I expect you have many castles,' he said.

Foch, thought Jane, cannot be expected to live for many more years. He's in late middle age now. Soon he will be old and then he'll die, and that will be terrible. I can't even talk to Lionel the way I talk to Foch. Without that stern, self-righteous terrier I'd still be crazy. She gulped at her claret and instantly the sommelier filled up her glass. Easy, she thought. Don't gulp. You have to work this afternoon. Once this is over, no more trips for a while, except the ones where Foch can come with me. She looked at the menu. She'd already had the consommé, the crêpe de fruits de mer and the gigot d'agneau. That left only the cheese board, the bavarois and the coffee, no doubt with petits fours. How on earth could she write to that cow Daisy after that?

Dear Daisy [she wrote],
   Here I am, all at sea (ha ha!) and oh it is such fun. The most fabulous people to travel with. An earl who owns three castles (though only one is fit to live in, poor thing) and a junior minister in the late *lamented* Tory government who's off to stay with his sister. She's married to a rancher in Colorado who owns simply millions of acres and a silver mine. Just imagine. All those cowboys and prospectors, just like one sees in the cinema. And talking of the cinema –

She threw down her pen and sat back for a moment. When she'd finished this guff she'd have to take it to the wireless operator and ask him to transmit it for her, and he'd look, first at the guff, then at her, just as he'd done last time, as if he couldn't believe what he was seeing. But it was selling newspapers, that was the point, and helping the picture too, the picture that wasn't even written yet. She wondered how Bower was taking it. In the end Murray Fisch had sent him a vast cable that covered sheets and sheets, but if Bower had replied she had not been told. Her mother had replied by telegram, immediately. She was delighted, George was delighted, and Gwendolyn

Gwatkin was the fourth person in England to be informed. George had had two winners and an each-way double the preceding week, her mother added. The family was doing well. Did that include Francis? Jane wondered. Is he now embarked on a round of giddy pleasure? Because if so, it's more than I am. She sighed, and picked up her pen.

'I had no idea that this movie would take up so much of your time,' said Lovell.

Jane looked at him, her eyes glittering. 'I hope you're not about to add "Or I should never have allowed it",' she said.

'Of course not.' Charles it seemed had learned his lesson. She snuggled into him.

'Anyway what you really mean is it keeps you out of my bed.'

'Not just your bed.' He began to stroke her in the way she liked, once the heaving and gasping were over.

'Don't you have any work to do?' she asked.

'Not till we get to New York, then I won't have anything else.'

'Not even one night at the Cotton Club?' she asked.

'Perhaps just one.'

'Who will you be seeing? Just Fisch's bankers?'

'All sorts of people. Fisch's money men, of course. Fisch too when he gets back. But a lot of others too.'

'Doing what?'

'Buying,' said Lovell. 'Selling.'

'Buying and selling what?'

'Stocks,' said Lovell. It was the tone of voice that meant, 'What else?'

'Not things,' said Jane. 'Not wheat or motor cars or gramophone records or pork chops. Just bits of paper.'

'It's the bits of paper that own the things,' he said. 'How much American stock do you hold?'

'You mean what we call stocks and shares?' He nodded. 'None.'

His hand stopped. 'None?'

'Not one,' she said. 'When Uncle Walter died he left his money so that my aunt couldn't get at the capital. "Make an idiot of herself on the stock exchange" was what she told me. And when she died she left it all to me the same way. I couldn't play the market – isn't that what the Yanks say? – even if I wanted to.

Which I don't. And why have you stopped stroking me? I haven't finished with you yet.'

'Oh God,' he said.

'It'll come,' she said. 'You're not as young as you were, but it'll come. You'll see.' And then: 'Were you sort of hinting that now might be a good time to sell?'

'Why do you ask?'

'Because my mother said the same thing a few weeks ago.'

'Your mother must be a remarkably clever lady,' said Lovell. Then other matters intervened, and it was all the answer she got.

The approach to the Statue of Liberty was splendid: a clear morning, already hot, with bright sunlight, and Manhattan beyond it, posturing its welcome. For once she could tell Daisy something worth hearing, she thought, but she mustn't overdo it: 'exquisite prose', Bower would call it if she did, and impale it on the spike.

'Ilion like a mist rose into towers,' said Lovell. 'You know it was only when I first saw Manhattan like this that I realised what he was trying to say.'

'And Tennyson never saw it,' she said, 'which explains why he's a genius.'

'You writers always stick together,' said Lovell. 'Would you like me to take you to your apartment?'

'No no. I cabled Barry Golding. He'll be there complete with car, I'm sure.'

'Who's Barry Golding?'

'Didn't I tell you? He's that pansy friend of Bower's.'

'Bower has pansy friends?'

'Everybody does,' said Jane. 'That doesn't mean he is one. Barry's a sort of Lionel, only he doesn't dance quite so well.'

'Would you like to dance with me tonight?'

'Love to. The one and only night off?' Barry would want her to dance too, but he could wait. There'd be lots of time.

'I might play truant once in a while,' said Lovell, 'when you're not writing.' There was the sound of voices behind them, and he lifted his hat and moved away.

Really Charles is too much, she thought. Half the time he goes through the motions of pretending we're just friends – like a bad actor: darling Charles is a terrible actor – and the other half he's throwing caution to the winds, and either way it's delightful. Just to show that there's life in the old girl yet.

Once past the snarling aggression of customs and immigration there were reporters: rather a lot of reporters, and photographers too, organised no doubt by the New York office of World Wide Studios on Murray Fisch's orders, and really it was all very pleasant, not like the drubbing she'd received last time, when the Four Arts Cleopatra scandal broke in New York. She was a part of Hollywood, and therefore she was news: Georgina Payne was going to portray her on the screen, and therefore she was big news, important news, and she was a woman to be treated with respect, even deference. Lovely stuff. But there was no Barry to meet her, just a note delivered by a chauffeur to say that he was prostrate with a migraine but that Bexley, the chauffeur, was hers to command until he, Barry, could come to pay homage personally, so that was all right. Bexley found porters for her luggage and superintended them in a lofty way while they filled the limousine, then drove her to the rented apartment on Park Avenue where George and Martha had already been installed by Barry, migraine or no migraine. Charles telephoned while she and Martha were unpacking and asked her where she'd like to go that evening. Still watching Martha, she suggested the Cotton Club. New York, she thought, was going to be fun.

Burrowes got his protest. He got his broken glass and broken heads, too. It was the miners that started it, but then it usually was. There was one pit left working in Felston, the Benton, where once there had been seven, and its owners organised a lock-out that was a classic: exactly the way he'd described it to Antrobus in Cambridge, and the miners' reaction was equally classic. They asked for talks, the chance of arbitration, and that was that. The pit was closed. Its owners called it a strike and the men called it a lock-out, but whatever you called it two hundred and sixty-eight more men were out of work. It wasn't his fight of course: the miners took care of their own struggles; but he did what he could, which was mostly talking in the Market Place on Saturday night, but talking moderately, cautiously, the way the Party had instructed him to talk: more in sorrow than in anger; Hearts and Flowers stuff.

Inside he wanted to yell with rage because this was one they should have had a chance of winning. It was August, after all, and the weather was warm, the need for coal in the miners' houses low. But the employers had allowed for that, too. The scabs were in within days, stockpiling the coal for winter demand at rock-bottom prices. The union men could stay out for ever for all the owners cared, and all he could do was stand there and prate about how wicked and unjust it was, how men's rights were being denied. He'd have done more good banging the drum for the Sally Ann.

Then Bob came. It was nice of him, Andy wasn't denying that, but trust Bob to arrive in a brand-new Yankee Buick and park it outside Grandma's house. Andy saw it when he came home from work, and at first he thought Grandma had been taken ill, because who but a doctor would drive a car to John Bright Street? But what doctor in Felston could afford a grand car like that? He pedalled hard, then pounded up the stairs, and there was Bob, at ease in the kitchen, taking tea and a slice of Grandma's seed cake. He grinned at Andy.

'What fettle, kidder?' he said.

'What in the world –' Andy began, and then as Grandma glowered: 'How are you, Bob?'

'Never better.'

'Still making money?'

'Coining it.'

'Funny how folks gets the habit of listening to the wireless,' Grandma said. 'Seems like they cannot do without them. I know I couldn't.'

'It's a habit a lot of folk round here can't afford,' said Andy. 'You wouldn't get fat renting sets up here.'

'Now that's where you're wrong,' said Bob. 'I'll make a copper or two round here.'

'The town's one long dole queue,' said Andy.

'Not all of it. There's bank clerks and teachers and local government workers – and a few chaps like Frank Metcalfe that can afford their eighteen pence a week.'

'Is that what you charge?'

'That's all.'

'And you're opening up here?'

'Well not me personally,' said Bob, 'but I've come to have a look at a shop I might buy in Queen Victoria Street. That's why

I'm here. And to see you and Grandma of course. How's things? Grandma says you've got a job.'

'And we've got a wireless set an' all,' said Andy. 'So don't start.' The two brothers grinned at each other. Grandma relaxed, and began to prepare Andy's tea.

'Moscow Mike Deegan's taken me on,' Andy said. 'The devil looks after his own as you might say, but it's still a job. Hard work and a living wage. Just.'

'I could give you a better job than that,' said Bob.

'No thanks.'

'Wirelesses are dead easy,' said Bob. 'Honest. You could learn the lot in a month.'

'Do you have the union in your firm?' Andy asked.

'Don't have to,' said Bob. 'I pay over the minimum anyway. And a bonus.'

'*Do you have the unions?*'

'No,' said Bob. 'It's a waste of time. I can get far more blokes than I need –'

'And you have the nerve to ask me to work for you?'

'Aye,' said Bob. 'I wasn't thinking. Sorry about that.' He bit into his slice of cake.

There you have him, thought Andy. The perfect employer. Gives his workers just enough to keep them happy, but takes damn good care to bar trouble from his gates. All the same, he's not a bad brother, and he did say he was sorry.

'You've got a bit of trouble in Felston at the moment, I hear,' said Bob.

'Not me, thank God,' said Andy. 'The pitmen. Lock-out at the Benton pit.'

'The last one,' said Bob.

'Like you say,' said Andy. 'And now there's none.'

'Rough, is it?'

'The owners brought in scabs two weeks ago. The miners don't like scabs.'

'There's been fellers shouted at,' said Grandma, 'and spat at an' all, by women mostly, and three that's had a bashing to my knowledge. One was taken to the clinic.'

'That wouldn't go down well,' said Bob.

'It didn't go down at all,' said Grandma. 'The women helping there didn't want to let him in. From what I hear, Bella Docherty came out from the kitchen with a carving knife.'

'They turned him off?'

'No,' said Grandma. 'They didn't. And I'll tell you for why. Because Canon Messeter came in then and said he'd carry the chap in himself if nobody would help, and Dr Stobbs came out of the surgery and said he'd close down the clinic if he wasn't allowed to treat folks that needed treatment. "I'm here to help anyone that needs it," he says. "I don't care who they are." And him and the canon carried the poor chap into the surgery and patched him up.'

'Poor chap, Grandma?' said Bob.

'Anybody that's had a bashing from a pack of miners is a poor chap so far as I'm concerned,' Grandma said. 'And there's talk they'll give him another one when the first one's healed up.'

'Dear God,' said Bob.

'It won't help their case at all,' said Andy. 'It's stupid.'

'It's sinful,' said Grandma, 'and it'll lead to more sin. Mark my words.'

'Who is it?' said Bob. 'Anybody I know?'

'A feller called Arthur Burn,' Grandma said. 'You might remember him.'

'Of course I do,' said Bob. 'I used to sit next to him at school. Why on earth did he want to go scabbing?'

Andy was silent.

'Dr Stobbs's treating his wife for TB,' Grandma said at last, 'though I doubt it'll be for much longer, and he's got three bairns. Three more mouths to feed. So he did what he thought was best.'

'Would you have done that?' Andy asked.

'I doubt if I'd have had the guts,' said Bob.

'The scabs are victims every bit as much as the chaps on strike,' said Andy. 'All the same –'

'Let's have it,' said Bob.

'There has to be solidarity.'

'Against the likes of me?'

'Exactly.'

'Eat your tea,' said Grandma. 'Before it gets cold. It's sausage and chips. You're always on about how you like them.'

# 21

AFTER THE TEA Andy had to go to Frank's and Bet's to help Frank learn how to read a timetable, and Bob was going there to make them a present of a wireless set. Frank certainly was getting his money's worth out of the Pattersons, Andy thought. They drove to Frank's and Bet's in the Buick, and the whole street turned out to watch.

Not that he could blame them, thought Andy. The Buick was big and black and gleaming, like the kind you saw on the pictures, with gangsters on the running board firing Tommy guns at the coppers. Bet was nearly hysterical. The car belonged to *her brother*. And then the wireless. Another sensation. The only one in the street. It was a long time before Frank could turn his mind to timetables.

Bob went to the clinic. It was exactly as he remembered it: dilapidated, in need of paint, but glittering clean. The kitchen was closed, there was only one volunteer nurse on duty, the doctor was out, and Canon Messeter was at a meeting. Bob sat down to wait, and at last Canon Messeter came in, lean and brisk as always, then checked at the sight of Bob, noting the well-fed look, the expensive clothes and shoes. Not many like that visited Felston Clinic.

'Good heavens,' he said at last. 'Aren't you Bob Patterson?'

'That's me,' said Bob, and rose to his feet. 'How are you, sir?'

'Well enough,' Messeter said, 'and very glad to see you. Extremely glad. Do come along in and tell me what I can do for you.'

They went into the room that Messeter called his office, that was just big enough to contain two chairs, a desk, and a filing cabinet. On one wall was a calendar with an advertisement for somebody's laxative: on another was a crucifix.

'It's Arthur Burn,' said Bob, and Messeter's face changed, acquiring a sort of wariness.

'What about him?' he asked.

'I'd like his address.'

'Forgive me,' Messeter said, 'but may I ask why?'

'I want to offer him a job.' He told the canon about his business.

When he had finished the canon said, 'Well that's perfectly splendid of course, and I do congratulate you most sincerely, but I doubt whether Arthur Burn will be able to work for quite some time – for you or anybody else.'

'Then I'll give him some money.'

'Why should you do that?' Messeter asked.

'I sat next to him at elementary school,' said Bob, and then he added, 'He needs it.'

Canon Messeter consulted an index, then opened a ledger. 'Hayman's Buildings,' he said. 'Number twenty-eight. You know where it is?'

'Aye,' said Bob. 'I do. . . . God help poor Artie.'

'Amen to that,' said Canon Messeter.

Hayman's Buildings was a tenement that seemed to be slowly but inevitably falling apart: paint long since dried away, here and there a broken window blocked with cardboard, tiles missing from the roof. It seemed to have developed a tilt as well. Artie's flat was on the third floor, and Bob climbed the stairs in a cautious duck waddle, using the outside of the treads. The middle of each stair would be worn paper thin. One tap, one stinking lavatory on each stair-head. John Bright Street was a palace compared to that. . . . He found Number 28 by the light of a flickering gas lamp with a broken shade (nothing like a fire to cheer things up) and knocked softly once, then again. There was silence, then a sort of scraping sound, the door was flung open, and Artie Burns was facing him, one hand clutching the door frame, the other holding a crutch like a weapon.

'Who are you, then?' he said. His voice, thought Bob, was a heart-rending mixture of courage and fear.

'Santa Claus,' he said. 'It's me, you daft bugger. Bob Patterson.'

'Bob Patt –' He peered more closely. 'By God, so it is. Ha'way in, man.' He led the way into the room, bobbing precariously on his crutch.

The room was Artie Burn's mansion. Here human beings slept, and cooked when there was food, quarrelled, made love, became sick and then well once more. Or maybe not, he thought, as he saw the faces that watched him. A woman so thin her skin stretched tight over her bones, the pallor of her face off-set only by a hectic red splash on each cheek, like the face of a doll, that told its own story. Grandma was right. This woman was going to die, and no amount of food or doctoring or change of climate could save her. Not that she'd get any.

She lay in a bed in the middle of the room, and round her sat three bairns, two girls and a boy, the eldest eleven, maybe, but it was hard to tell. They were desperately undernourished, all three, and yet somebody – Artie? She herself? – had made an effort to keep them clean. The woman held the tattered remnants of a picture book: she'd been reading to them.

'Mary,' Artie Burn said, 'this is an old friend of mine. Bob Patterson.'

'How d'you do, Mr Patterson.' The voice was hardly more than a whisper, but it had once been a very pretty voice. This had once been a very pretty woman.

'Nice to meet you, Mrs Burn.'

'I'm sorry I can't get up,' the woman whispered. 'I haven't been all that well, you see.'

'Don't you worry about that, missis,' said Bob. 'I gather Artie hasn't been all that well, either.'

'Scabbing, that's what I've been doing,' said Artie. 'And the reason I walk like this is that some fellers that know better than me were good enough to show me the error of me ways.'

'Artie, man,' his wife said.

'No no,' said Artie Burn. 'Bob has to be warned. It's only fair. He might catch something, breathing the same air as a scab like me, a feller that's so bloody selfish he takes a job his mates wouldn't touch, just because he wanted to take care of his wife and bairns.'

'Artie!' This time his wife's voice was like a whispered scream. 'Please.'

Bob looked at him more closely. Artie's face was still puffy and bruised from the beating he had taken, and one arm was bandaged. He'll be like one great walking ache, thought Bob.

'Just listen to me,' Artie Burn said at last. 'I'm sorry, Bob. I get a bit carried away sometimes.'

'That's all right,' said Bob. 'Maybe we'll all feel better when we've had something to eat.'

'Eat!' Artie Burn couldn't have been more surprised if he'd suggested a trip to Monte Carlo, thought Bob, and put his hand in his pocket to bring out a handful of change.

'Eat,' he said firmly. 'Does fish and chips sound all right?'

'Sounds grand,' said Artie. 'But why should you?'

'Because you let me copy off your sum book,' said Bob. 'I was hopeless at arithmetic.' He turned to the children. 'Very clever man, your father,' he said, 'and I hope you take after him because I'm going to send you out shopping.' He turned to Artie. 'Can they go on their own?'

'Certainly,' Artie said. 'Young Mary's thirteen in a couple of weeks, and Betty's eleven.'

'And the young feller?'

'Frankie'll be ten in December,' Mrs Burn whispered. It didn't seem possible.

They found a couple of shopping bags and decided what to buy. Fish and chips five times, and eggs, milk and bread from the corner shop for their mam. Bob sent them off with two half crowns. It was the most money they had seen in weeks.

'It's good of you Bob,' said Artie. 'I can't say when I can pay you back –'

'Shut your gob. I told you I was Santa Claus,' said Bob. 'And I'm here to prove it. . . . How bad are you hurt?'

'Hard to say,' Artie Burn said. 'Me leg's not broken – just a bad sprain to the ankle – but me ribs is. And I cut me arm on something or other when I went down, and Dr Stobbs thought it might be blood poison. Whatever it is, it's in no hurry to heal.'

'It'll just have to wait, then,' said Bob.

'What'll have to wait?'

'Your job.'

'Bought yourself a coal mine, have you?' Artie Burn said.

'Mind you – you look as if you could afford one at that.'

'Nowt so old fashioned,' said Bob, and told him about the wireless business, Mrs Burn listening as if she were Cinderella in her glass coach on the way to the ball. When he'd done, Artie said: 'You're serious, aren't you?'

'Certainly I'm serious.'

'And you think I could do it?'

'Good at sums. Clever with your hands. Of course you could do it.'

'How about the union?'

'No union.' That it seemed made it even better. 'The only snag is you might have to move away from Felston.'

'Mr Patterson,' Mrs Burn whispered. 'You know what's wrong with me?'

'I think so,' said Bob.

'Of course you do,' said Mrs Burn. 'Well the one thing I've prayed for is this. If I'm spared for a while please God help me to get away from Felston. And now you come along and tell me I *have* to get away.' She smiled, and the former prettiness flickered in her face. 'Maybe you really are Santa Claus,' she said.

He gave them money. It wasn't an easy thing to do for any of them, but at last he did it; sufficient money to keep them fed and housed and to pay the woman next door to shop for them, and clean. Then the children came back with the fish and chips, and for them it really was Christmas. He'd never seen bairns eat like it before.

When he left the street seemed deserted, but somehow he knew that it wasn't. Somebody he was sure was following him to where he had parked his car on a piece of waste ground. Somehow it hadn't seemed a good idea to park it outside Hayman's Buildings. Bob unlocked the car door and as he did so a voice called out, 'Hey. Just a minute.' Deliberately, forcing himself not to hurry, Bob reached inside the car before he turned to face whoever it was. He was holding the Buick's starting handle, and it had a very comforting feel to it, he thought, especially as there were three of them standing in the shadows away from the gaslight.

'You've been seeing Artie Burn.' The same voice as before. The leader.

'That's my business,' said Bob.

'You're not his doctor.' Bob waited. 'You come to tell him he can have his job back when he's better?'

'In the pit?' Bob tried and failed to keep the incredulity from his voice.

'Where else?'

'He's never going back to the pits,' said Bob.

The man moved forward a little, peering, and Bob lifted the starting handle.

'Not too close,' he said. 'I can hear you fine from where you are.'

The man stopped. 'You're not working for the owners then?'

'Pit owners? Me?' said Bob. 'No fear. I'm Bob Patterson. Andy's brother. You'll have heard of Andy, surely? I'm in the wireless business.'

'You're a boss? Andy Patterson's brother?'

'Right both times.'

'And you're taking on scab labour?'

'When he's fit,' said Bob. 'That won't be for a while.'

'Folks won't have no dealings with scabs round here,' said the man.

He won't be round here, thought Bob, but he kept the thought to himself.

'Too bad he had to get himself a belting,' said the man, 'but there has to be solidarity.'

Dear God, another Andy, thought Bob, and got in the Buick and drove back to Grandma's. There was room in John Bright Street now; no excuse to stay at the Eldon Arms, and anyway, John Bright Street had the better cook.

The cook was alone in the kitchen. Andy had a visitor in the front room, she said, and Bob could hear the low rumble of voices, but not what they said. He told Grandma where he'd been, what he'd done.

'Feel better for it?' Grandma asked.

Bob shrugged. 'Me good deed for the day.'

But it hadn't cost him much. Not even the price of that dance in Cambridge. Nothing like.

'Anyway Artie'll do well if he comes in with me,' said Bob. 'Like I told him, he's handy and he's smart. He'll do well for both of us.'

'Good news for his wife,' said Grandma.

'It could have been,' said Bob, 'a year ago.'

'She's that bad then?'

'She knows it herself,' said Bob. 'All she wants is to live long enough to get out of Felston. – Like she doesn't even want to die here.'

'Dear God,' the old woman said, 'what a thing to say. But how can you blame her after what they did to her man?'

The voices grew louder, and there was the clatter of footsteps going downstairs. Grandma reached for the kettle.

'Andy'll be ready for his cup of tea,' she said. 'He starts early in his job. Not like the ones that goes to work dressed.'

She means the ones that wear suits, he thought. The bosses.

'I do me share of grafting,' he said.

'Brainwork,' said Grandma. 'Just like our John. He always reckoned it was the hardest work of the lot.'

Then Andy came in, and Bob thought: Something's bothering him. Something's bothering him really bad.

'You know who that was?' Andy asked.

'I think so,' said Grandma, 'but if you don't want to tell us that's your business.'

'And it's none of my business anyway, I don't suppose,' said Bob.

'I want to tell you,' Andy said. 'It's too big a thing to carry on me own, but I'd be obliged if you'd keep it to yourself.'

'Well of course.'

'That was Billy Caffrey,' said Andy. 'You remember him?'

'Councillor Caffrey,' said Bob. 'Bigwig in the miners' lodge.'

'That's him.'

'He ought to do something about that voice of his,' said Grandma. 'Even through a brick wall I knew who it was.'

'He's not one of the wild ones,' said Andy. 'Very steady man, Billy Caffrey. I reckon that's why the police sent for him.'

'The police?' said Grandma. 'He's never in trouble?'

'Not him, no. The Miners' Union. It was the Chief Constable sent for him, very nice and polite. Sorry to trouble you and would you mind dropping in. They even sent a car.'

'What was it about?' said Grandma.

'Two more scabs took a bashing last night,' said Andy. 'The police told Billy it has to stop.'

'Well so it has,' said Bob. 'That isn't the way.'

'And maybe letting other people tell you what to do isn't the way either,' said Andy.

'Oh get on with it,' said Grandma, 'and less of your interrupting, our Bob.'

'So Billy says he quite agrees,' said Andy. 'He was having a beer by this time, and the Chief Constable was on whisky and soda. All very civilised. What was needed, Billy said, was a peaceful protest, bands and banners, and speakers from across the country, to show the nation the bitterness we felt at being exploited. How the miners in their righteous wrath –' Here Andy paused and grinned. 'Oh he was well in his stride by that time. He can churn that stuff out like it was piece work. Only the Chief Constable wasn't having any. Billy said if he could have taken his beer back off him, he would. No protests, he says. Peaceful or otherwise.

'So then Billy says, very grand, that he wasn't aware that freedom of speech had been abolished in this country, and anyway he'd already invited Mr James Wagstaff, MP to a meeting of miners and their sympathisers next Sunday, and Mr Wagstaff had sent a telegram to say he'd be delighted, and what was the Chief Constable going to do about it? Because Billy knew as well as the Chief Constable, that there's nothing he *could* do about it, so long as it was peaceful.'

'So what did he say?'

'That he'd take the necessary precautions, and if Councillor Caffrey didn't mind there was rather a lot to do. So Billy finished his beer first, then shoved off.'

'Will it be peaceful?' Grandma asked.

'Not all of it,' said Andy. 'They never are.' He turned to Bob. 'You remember the General Strike?' Bob nodded. 'Ninety per cent of the workers – ninety-five even – never threw as much as one stone, never even clenched a fist. Strike pickets and coppers even played football matches. But the other five per cent –'

'Attacks on food lorries,' said Bob, 'then what they called incitement to riot, and then the mounted police. Is that what it'll be like?'

'If it is there'll be some blood let,' said Andy. 'That Chief Constable's not exactly Francis of Assisi. And there's a few of our lads ready to let off steam an' all.'

'Who'll win?' said Grandma.

'Not the workers,' said Bob. 'They never do.'

'And why not?'

'Because they talk all the time about solidarity and Party Discipline, but that's all they do. Talk about it. The police do it.'

He waited for Andy to explode, but this time it didn't happen. 'That's nearly always true,' he said. 'But this time – I'm not so sure.' More than that he would not say.

When Grandma had gone to bed at last, and Bob drank one last cup of tea, Andy said, 'Did you see Artie Burn?'

'Aye,' said Bob. 'He's in a right mess. Bad arm, busted ribs, walking on crutches. His face is bruised all colours.'

'Did you do anything for him?'

'Loaned him a few quid. Offered him a job.'

'Will he take it?'

'Away from Felston he will.'

'You're a proper Good Samaritan,' said Andy, but he was smiling. Bob let it lie. 'Trouble is,' said Andy, 'it won't help Felston much, will it?'

'It'll help Artie Burn,' said Bob.

He stayed on. There were other places to see near by: Newcastle, Sunderland, Tynemouth, South Shields, and they all held enough promise to make it worthwhile setting up a branch of Patterson's Wireless Rentals: one and six per week per set: thirty-three per cent net profit, which meant threepence each for him and Lovell. It didn't sound like much, but it was if you rented enough sets. So he drove the Buick all over Tyneside and Wearside, looking at premises, drafting newspaper advertisements, seeking out likely employees, going to work dressed, in fact, and bloody boring work it was, but all the same he wanted those threepenny bits. By Saturday morning he had done enough: there was nothing more he could do until he sent a sales team from London. If it had been winter he would have gone to a football match: in August it might as well be fishing, he thought, and asked Andy to go too, and to his surprise Andy accepted.

He still had tackle stored in his bedroom: rods, sinkers, hooks, lines, and there were plenty of places to buy bait. He bought beer and lemonade too, and Grandma had cut sandwiches the way he liked them: corned beef and tomato with a lot of mustard. At the quayside he hired a rowing boat and the two of them pulled out to sea, using the long, easy stroke they had used so many times before.

'This'll do us,' Bob said, and they let the boat drift on the almost windless sea. Andy looked at his brother's hands deftly baiting hooks.

'You haven't let yourself go soft,' he said. 'You can still row a boat and your hands are as hard as mine.'

'I play a lot of golf,' said Bob.

'*Golf?*' Andy's yelp was like a seagull screaming, but it could have been worse, thought Bob. I could have taken up polo.

'Exercise, kidder,' he said aloud. 'When you sit around as much as I do you need all the exercise you can get.'

'I suppose so,' said Andy, and cast his line. 'When Moscow Mike's promised delivery in a hurry I get more exercise than I need.'

'Is he speaking tomorrow?'

'No,' said Andy, and looked away.

'Who then?'

'Me for one,' said Andy.

Bob cast his line. 'Taking a bit of a risk, aren't you?' he said.

'I don't think so,' said Andy. 'I speak most Saturday nights in the Market Place.'

'Not to thousands of people you don't,' said Bob. 'Not to mention hundreds of coppers and the chance of a riot.'

Andy shrugged. 'There isn't anybody else that can speak,' he said. 'Not to a crowd like that. Anyway they all know how I'm fixed, so all I do is introduce the main speaker.'

'Jimmy Wagstaff.'

'The one and only. Billy Caffrey kicks off, putting the miners' case so to speak. Then there's Canon Messeter. He'll talk about the real meaning of charity, and the rich man and the camel and the eye of the needle –'

'How on earth do you know?' Bob asked.

'He always does,' said Andy. 'It's a real good turn. Folks always likes it. Then there's me. On behalf of all the good people of Felston, not just the miners, but all the working people gathered to show their support, et cetera et cetera – a hearty welcome to our MP come here all the way from London – then I get down quick and leave the rest to Jimmy. What's to worry about in that?'

'You,' said Bob. 'I know you. You get carried away. Next thing we know you'll be telling your lot to fix bayonets and sounding the charge.'

'Not any more,' said Andy.

'That crack on the head?'

'That and Durham Gaol,' said Andy, and hated himself for the look of approval on his brother's face, because he was lying to Bob just as he'd lied to Grandma. It was true he'd told Burrowes he didn't want a useless protest, but this protest wasn't useless: it was about everything he held sacred: the right to work, the brotherhood of the workers, the dignity of man. This time a battle would be justified, and there would be men in that crowd ready for a battle, a battle they could win: and what would he be doing? Introducing Jimmy Wagstaff. And what Jimmy Wagstaff would do would be to stand there oozing charm like an oil leak and telling them how it was all terrible, terrible, but one day, mark his words, one day, one wonderful day, and who knew how soon it would come. . . . That wasn't the way to tell men to fight. It was the way to tell them to surrender.

Bob said, 'I've got one,' and began paying out line.

Not a bad day's fishing, really: a couple of codling, some haddock, and a few flatties. Grandma kept what she wanted for their suppers and sent the rest round to the clinic. Even on a Saturday afternoon there would be somebody there who needed a meal, so Andy took them round on his bike. He wanted a word with Canon Messeter anyway.

When he'd gone Grandma said, 'He's speaking tomorrow,' isn't he?'

Bob looked up from the fish he was cleaning. 'Aye,' he said.

'Will he get into trouble?'

'Not if he sticks to what he told me he's going to do.'

'And what's that?'

'Introduce Jimmy Wagstaff. Tell the crowd what a fine chap he is.'

'It'll go hard with him to do that,' said Grandma. 'He can't stand the feller.'

Bob made no answer.

'You're worried, aren't you?' the old woman said.

'Andy'll be all right,' Bob said at last. 'He doesn't fancy another spell in Durham Gaol, and I can't say I blame him.'

# 22

NEW YORK WAS as busy as Paris had been idle: frantically, frenetically busy. The summer was officially over: they were now into what Americans called the fall, but the heat was still intense, and yet there the New Yorkers were, busily buzzing, like a hive of overturned bees. Business or pleasure, it was all the same to them: they worked at it, and while they worked they drank, in their homes, in nightclubs, in speakeasies, even in the cars and taxis that took them from one party to the next. It was very, very difficult to stay sober in her study and write when there were all those New Yorkers itching to dance with her, drink with her, tell her how things looked in the market.

The market was the only thing in their lives with more power than the need for a good time, because it was the market that paid for the good time. Stocks, they told her. Bonds. Going up every day. Hurry, hurry. Get in before it's too late. Come and meet my broker. The one man more potent than their bootlegger. And all because Barry Golding had recovered from his migraine, and took her to all the places they'd gone to years ago, which was just as well, since Lovell was true to his word and hardly saw her at all.

But really it was all too exhausting, and she wrote to tell Daisy so. After all, if they really believed that this boom of theirs was going to last for ever, why did they always act as if there were only five minutes left? Still it was fun to meet people like Jack Dempsey and Mayor Jimmy Walker and Cole Porter and all the World Wide Stars who had strayed across from the West Coast, but even so, one had to have some time to one's self. She had a movie to write, after all.

The thought amazed her. She, Jane Whitcomb, was to write a movie, and everyone concerned in it, including Murray Fisch – including Charles for that matter – was absolutely certain that she could. Everybody that is except Jane Whitcomb. But she had said she would do it, and she must. Georgie phoned her from Hollywood every other day, or so it seemed, and so at last she began to work in the only way she knew how, treating her service in the war as she had treated the General Strike: quick impressions, vignettes, the thousands of memories all clamouring to be written down, but not a word about John: not one single solitary word. Not that it would have mattered. The Jane Whitcomb of the silver screen was to have a very different lover. Then one day as she wrote down her memories of General Haig and the battalion that sang the bawdy song, she thought of Jabber Lockhart. What would he think of what she'd chosen to do? she wondered. He'd be angry, she was sure, and yet it simply hadn't occurred to her that reliving her life in the war might bring back the nightmares and the madness. All she had thought about was how her life would look on the screen. The power of Hollywood was immense, and she must write to Lockhart and tell him so. World Wide's publicity department would be banging their drum very soon, and Lockhart was an obsessive reader of newspapers.

Tom Waring came to call; a far more elegant and opulent Tom Waring than the bright young director who had helped her through her screen test years ago.

'You look well,' she said.

'You mean well off?'

'That too. Are you in New York to direct a play?'

'To do what?'

Whatever has happened to that sunny nature, she wondered: the gentle patience that could coax some kind of performance even out of a hopeless amateur like me?

'You divided your time between Hollywood and New York when we last met,' she said. 'Between the movies and the theatre, in fact. I take it you've given that up?'

'You take it correctly,' said Waring. 'After my divorce I made an interesting discovery. I was making more money than I'd ever made in my life, and I couldn't afford the thing I wanted most.' He smiled, and for a moment it was the younger Waring who faced her. 'But that's enough about my life,' he said.

'It sounds as if it's been eventful since I saw you last,' said Jane.

'Oh boy.'

Jane rose. 'Let me order some drinks,' she said.

'One of the events,' said Waring, 'is that I've developed an ulcer. I can't drink.'

'Coffee?'

'Milk,' he said. 'It doesn't improve my disposition, but it doesn't hurt either.'

Jane rang for George and ordered milk for him, and a martini for herself. There was such a thing as being too considerate.

When the drinks came Waring sipped, grimaced and said, 'Didn't Murray Fisch tell you I was coming?'

'He wrote to tell me you'd be in New York. It didn't occur to me that I could be the only reason.'

He looked at her. 'You mean that, don't you?' he said. 'I remember. You generally do mean what you say.' He took one more sip of milk then put it down. 'God I hate that stuff,' he said, and then: 'Have you any idea what you've done to World Wide?'

'What *I've* done?'

'What you – your story has done?'

'No doubt you'll tell me.'

'You'll either have raised the studio to the very first rank – right up there with Metro and Warner Brothers – or else you're going to sink it without a trace. Have you any idea of the money Murray Fisch is talking? Battles, trenches, airplane shots, thousands of extras, stars from other studios? – Murray Fisch, the guy who counts his change when he spends a nickel. I tell you –' Waring shook his head in bewilderment. 'The crazy thing is he's never been happier. He's blindfold on a tightrope and he doesn't even know it.'

'You don't like the idea?'

'I didn't say that.' The anger was back in his voice, but this time there was a trace of fear, too. 'You see it's like this. Murray is all excited about the movie he imagines: the one he fell for that night in France.'

– 251 –

'But why shouldn't he –'

'Because it's all in his mind. He's got your story and he's got Georgie. Put them both together and he can't miss – or so he thinks. But that's the movie he imagines. I'm the guy who has to make the real one: the one the cash customers pay to see.'

'But – forgive me,' said Jane, 'but from something Georgie said I got the impression that all producers were like that.'

'So they are,' said Waring, 'but this one is going to cost millions.'

'You don't want to do it?'

He looked at her: his face portraying his emotions like a silent movie actor's – rage, fear, ambition, all fighting for the mastery.

'I have to do it,' he said. No wonder he has an ulcer, thought Jane. They got down to work.

Jimmy Wagstaff wasn't coming. He sent his regrets, *sincere* regrets – nothing he'd have liked more than to stand up and be counted when his beloved Felston demanded its rights – but it was not for man to dispose.

'He really said that?' said Andy.

'Certainly,' Billy Caffrey said.

'On the telephone?'

'On the telephone.'

'Well I'll be damned,' said Andy. 'Was he sober?'

'Of course not,' Billy Caffrey said. 'It was just after dinner time. What he would call lunch, seeing he was in London.'

'So I says to him, just what is it man can't dispose, Mr Wagstaff, and he says me ankle, bonny lad. I've been and gone and busted it. Can't even hop as far as the bar.' Billy Caffrey sniffed. 'Not that he has to,' he said. 'They bring the bar to him. Anyway, then he goes on to say how he bitterly regrets being unable to be present on this momentous occasion –'

'It'll be that all right,' said Andy.

'Aye,' said Billy Caffrey. 'It will. Even without our wonderful MP to lead us.'

'Do you believe him?'

'About the ankle? It would be a bloody silly thing to lie about – and anyway, why should he?'

'Jimmy Wagstaff's got an instinct for trouble like a fox has for hens,' said Andy. 'And trouble's bound to happen tomorrow.

That Chief Constable as good as told you.'

'Not if we protest peacefully,' said Caffrey, but Andy made no answer. 'Anyway, that isn't the point,' Caffrey said. 'What we have to do now is decide who's to speak in his place.' He brooded on the unfairness of it, then said at last, 'Rotten sod. Why couldn't he bust his ankle next week?'

Andy shrugged. 'What about Comrade Deegan?' he asked.

Caffrey sighed. 'I was afraid you'd say that.'

'Why afraid?'

'Because he's not up to it – not a big meeting like that; and you know fine well he's not. Good enough for a street corner and a soap box, but that's about it.

'Tomorrow's the Market Place, and bands and banners. There'll be thousands there. Man, can you not visualise it? Moscow Mike up on his soap box and half Felston looking at him – and what'll he do? Either lose his place in his notes or else start telling us who Engels was when he should be talking about starving bairns. And there's another thing. That "comrade" business.'

'It's what he likes to be called.'

'Certainly,' said Caffrey. 'But it's Communist, don't you see? It's Russian. And we're all good English Labour men here.'

Andy thrust his hands into his pockets. They might start to shake, and he didn't want Billy Caffrey seeing that.

'It's like you said that night in the pub. Moderation,' Caffrey continued. 'Moscow Mike could never give us that –'

'You're right there,' said Andy.

'– But you could.'

'Now wait a minute,' Andy said.

'We haven't got a minute. The meeting's tomorrow. Now listen. I've been keeping an eye on you recently, and so have a few other fellers, important fellers. And the way we see it is this. When you first started you were a bit wild. A bit young shall we say. But young fellers is like that. Rise up! Smash the bosses! End Capitalism Now! Today! Nowt wrong with that so long as you outgrow it, and I reckon that's what you've done. That spell at Cambridge did you a lot of good. Taught you to think straight.'

He's talking to me as if he were my father, Andy thought, and he's just five years older than me, if that. And if my Cambridge friends heard what he was saying, he'd be condemned as a class enemy out of hand.

'It's very nice of you Billy,' he said, 'but –'

'Nice be buggered,' said Caffrey. 'You can do it, and you're the only one who can. There'll be no need for any of that Moscow Mike stuff. Just put the case fair and square.' He hesitated, then added: 'I know you wouldn't do this for your own gain, Andy. You're not like that. Not like some. But there'll be important men at that meeting tomorrow – and I want you to show them you have a future in the Labour Party. Maybe a big future.' He rose. 'Think about it. I'll let myself out.'

Andy let him go. It was gloomy there in the front room, and the memory of his father was all too fresh, but all the same he had to think.

It was all very well for Billy Caffrey to say he could make a speech better than most. He knew that. He'd always had the gift, even before Cambridge had coached him, but this was the wrong speech.

He'd told Burrowes that the Felston men had one fight left in them, and it was true, but only for a little while. Tomorrow they would fight, in a month's time they might not even bother to come to the meeting. . . . Moderation wouldn't rouse them. For the people of Felston moderation was the overture to despair. And yet it was what both his counsellors wanted, Caffrey and Burrowes, it was what Jimmy Wagstaff would have given them anyway. (He must find out how bad Jimmy Wagstaff's ankle was.) – And he would get on. The Labour Party wanted him, that was obvious, and if he did it right, became Felston's MP, there'd be other struggles, other fights. Fights he could lead. . . . He went into the kitchen. Grandma and Bob sat waiting, on either side of the fire. A kettle simmered; a sure sign that there would be tea shortly.

'So you're going to do it,' Grandma said.

'I might as well have invited the pair of you in with us,' said Andy. 'Is nothing private?'

'You can't turn Billy Caffrey down like the wireless,' said Grandma. 'All the same he's got a good persuading tongue on him.' She looked grim.

'You didn't hear me, by any chance?' said Andy. 'You didn't hear me say I'd call for moderation?'

Bob looked up quickly, and Andy cursed himself for allowing the bitterness in his voice to show. Grandma too had noticed it.

'You don't want to preach moderation?' she asked.

'I want to lead them into battle,' said Andy. 'I want to use words like bullets. Smash the system. Let the workers rule. Only I tried that once.' He turned to his brother. 'You remember?'

'The Elephant and Castle, 1926,' said Bob. 'I remember.'

'And all I got to show for it was a cracked skull,' said Andy. 'And if it hadn't been for you and Jane Whitcomb I'd have got another spell in gaol an' all. – So moderation it'll have to be.'

But in his heart he knew that this time they could win, and no matter how many times he told himself they'd live to fight another day, he knew also that moderation was a kind of betrayal.

The marshals had done a marvellous job: three bands, the four surviving pipers of the Tyneside Scottish, and every Miners' Lodge banner from miles around. They came in by the busload, men and women: the bairns left behind because in a crush like this would be bairns were a risk, *and* a nuisance. The buses drove off to the promenade where the marchers could buy a cup of tea and eat their sandwiches, then form up behind the banners of their unions, and march to the Market Square. It had been eleven years since the veterans had marched, but they remembered how to do it, and the young chaps did their best. Here and there on the promenade policemen patrolled in pairs, but there weren't many of them, and all they did was watch and smile. Two mounted policemen were there too, one at each end of the promenade, but they kept well away, sitting at ease, their horses' skin shivering in the last of the autumn heat. There was a car, too, with four men in it: a car that was battered and in need of a wash; altogether a Felston sort of car. Reporters, the marshals thought, if they thought anything at all, for away in the distance they could just hear the sound of the Felston contingent arriving in the Market Square.

Grandma hadn't come. She had said that she would sooner go to Evensong and say more prayers. Bob hadn't come either. Riding around in his posh car, thought Andy, looking for a lass. But the thought didn't worry him. Ahead of him was the St Oswald's Prize Band, and then the St Oswald's Banner, its bearers marching like the soldiers they once had been, and behind them were Billy Caffrey, and the other lodge leaders, and the mayor of Felston, gold chain twinkling, and with them Andy Patterson, up there among the archangels, so why aren't I feeling on top of the world? But the answer was obvious. He was about to betray his class. Better, far better, to listen to the band.

They were playing 'Tipperary'. Now there was something to think about. Tipperary. The happiest, most jaunty march of them all. 'There's A Long Long Trail A-winding' would have been far better, he thought. It was always a long long trail once you started to preach moderation. . . . He looked about for coppers. The way Billy Caffrey had told it there should have been a shoal of them, but there weren't. They were there all right, and a lot more of them than you'd expect on the average Sunday evening, but not that many, not enough to make the marching men feel threatened. For the men were marching, the way his brother John and Billy Caffrey had described the way men marched in 1915, when they still believed that they were going to win, and they would all be home by Christmas. (One of Billy Caffrey's friends, an ex-prisoner of war, had said that the Germans marched that way too.)

In his mind he began to go over the speech he had so painfully composed. 'Brothers – not comrades – ours is a legitimate struggle. The right is on our side.' No no. That wouldn't do. The Right to this lot meant the Tories. 'Truth and Justice are on our side. Only hold on. Only endure. We will win because we must. . . .' Twaddle. But at least he could make it sound good.

They arrived at the Market Square. In the centre a dais had been erected, draped in scarlet, but no hammer or sickle, thank God, just one of those new-fangled microphones that Billy Caffrey at least would never need. The band moved off to one side as Andy and the rest of the leaders moved towards the platform and climbed its stairs to the accompaniment of a Strauss waltz. 'Morning Papers' would it be? What in the world – then Andy remembered that the St Oswald's Prize Band played in public parks all over the country on Sundays, and 'Morning Papers' was part of their repertoire.

There was a shout and then a cheer as the other contingents arrived; first the rest of the Felston lodges, branches, clubs, and then the visitors, cheered as they marched in behind their banners. The marshals got to work at once, urging men to move up, packing them in. A hell of a lot of men, and women too, for the Market Place to hold, thought Andy, but then a hell of a lot of people had come to show support, and he should be glad of that at least. A nervous man in a blue-serge suit began to gabble into the microphone: 'Testing. Testing. 1-2-3-4-5-4-3-2-1. Testing.' And the crowd looked on indulgently. The microphone was working. The nervous man said, 'We're ready, Mr Mayor,' and the words boomed round the whole of the square. This time the crowd laughed, but it was indulgent laughter: a kindly giant watching a pigmy trip on a banana skin. The mayor went slowly to the microphone, waiting till the laughter died.

'It gives me great hope to see so many of you here this day,' he said, 'and not just our own folk, either. Brothers, fellow workers, from all over the North East. Brothers-in-arms you might say.'

You might, Mr Mayor, thought Andy, but I may not, as the home crowd applauded their visitors.

'Now before we begin I have one apology for absence,' the mayor said. 'It seems that our esteemed MP, Mr James Wagstaff, has suffered an accident. Something to do with his ankle, I understand.' He looked at Billy Caffrey, who nodded, and there were murmurs of disappointment from the crowd, and a ripple of laughter too from those who knew him best.

'In his place – and we're extremely grateful that he should agree to address us at such very short notice – we have that man of Felston and Labour stalwart, Mr Andy Patterson.'

Applause then from those who knew him, and massive indifference from those who had never heard of him. It was up to him to remedy that.

'So without more ado,' said the mayor, 'I'll pass you on to the first speaker, Councillor Caffrey.' He turned to the man in the blue-serge suit. 'I don't think we'll need that contraption just yet,' he said, and once again a voice boomed round the Market Square and the crowd laughed as blue serge switched off the microphone and Billy stood up, hard, unyielding as rock, and faced his audience.

'Justice doesn't need any contraptions to state its case,' he said, and the crowd yelled its delight.

'Brothers, fellow workers,' Billy roared, as the applause faded, 'I won't waste your time by going over the facts of the case. If you didn't know them you wouldn't be here. Am I right?' He waited, and the crowd roared, 'Aye.'

'What I'm going to talk to you about is the first word I used,' said Billy. 'Justice. That's all we want, but by God we do want that, because brothers, we are not just miners – we are men.' Again the crowd roared.

'Ignorant pitmen the bosses might say, too daft to do anything but go down into the darkness, get on our hands and knees as if we worshipped the bloody stuff – and cut coal for a bit wage that's handed to us like charity.

'But there's more to us than that. A lot more. There's musicians among us – and good ones –' he gestured to the band, 'and politicians and writers, and the chaps who run our lodges as efficient as any colliery manager. And there's sportsmen an' all. It was a Felston miner who was lightweight champion of England not long ago, and another that played football for Sunderland and England. And there's heroes too. Chaps that marched away fifteen years ago, and a lot that never came back. A Victoria Cross, three Distinguished Conduct Medals, and God knows how many Military Medals. All Felston miners. These aren't ignorant bloody miners, these are *men!*'

The crowd roared this time, delighted by the portrait of itself that Billy showed. He held up his arms for silence.

'And there were other heroes too,' he said, 'the ones who looked beyond our country's danger and our country's enemies, and saw that this was a bosses' war, a profiteers' war, and refused to fight to put even more money into the hands of the wealthy – and were persecuted for it and went to prison for it, where even their fellow prisoners, the thieves and murderers and rapists, turned against them. I've never been able to agree with them but I'll say this: I had just about enough courage to go to France – but I'd never be brave enough to endure what they endured. These too are men. Real men. The flower of Felston.'

Again the great beast bellowed its approval, until Billy raised his hand and the beast was still.

He's making the speech of his life, Andy thought; and then, I'll have my work cut out to match him.

'There's a piece of writing in America called the Declaration of Independence,' said Billy, 'and it contains words so important that I got them off by heart.' His eyes narrowed, and he spoke the words in a great booming chant. 'We hold these truths to be self-evident, that all men are created equal, and endowed by God with certain inalienable rights, and that among these rights are life, liberty, and the pursuit of happiness.' He paused, and the beast waited in silence, until, 'All men are created equal,' Billy thundered. 'Not just the bosses, the toffs, the capitalists and the aristocrats, but all men! All! Pitmen and fitters and labourers and bus conductors and sailors and the ones who have no work at all because the bosses won't give them any. All men! Created equal! With the right to a job and the freedom to bargain for it and the happiness that only work and a wage can bring. It doesn't sound much when you say it like that, does it? But brothers it's everything. It's what mankind was created for. It's justice! And we've come here to demand that justice this day.'

He stepped back then, and the applause was deafening. Billy had never been so good before, Andy thought, and perhaps never would be so good again, but the hour for once had found the man. If only he, Andy could have spoken first. . . . It was when blue serge switched on the microphone again and the mayor began to introduce Canon Messeter that the idea came to him, and he went down the platform steps to speak to the band's conductor. Nobody reacted, nobody bothered. Folks on platforms were always up and down conferring. Their eyes were on the tall, white-haired man who towered above them, his eyes glinting with madness, or religious ecstasy, or both: a sanctified Lear.

The band leader was happy to oblige. The band had to stay there anyway to play 'The Red Flag' at the end and, since Billy Caffrey was there, 'God Save The King'. As a piece of music 'The Red Flag' bored him, and the band knew the National Anthem backwards. What Andy Patterson had asked for was tricky, a bit of a challenge. Keep the lads on their toes, he thought. Do them good. He moved across to his cornet players.

Andy stayed at ground level, looking up like the rest of the crowd at the platform. The priest, he thought, had a magnificent presence, and knew it, and used it, and by the strength of that presence alone forced the crowd to ignore the educated voice, the long and unfamiliar words. The crowd listened to him carefully, and understood enough. He had reached the Beatitudes. 'Blessed are they that mourn, for they shall be comforted.' . . .

Well that was one for Councillor Caffrey's theory of 'all men' if you like, for all men had mourned in those terrible years of war they all remembered so well. And all women, too. Perhaps the women even more than the men. Rich and poor. Dukes and dustmen. In the war God had chosen no favourites. There were the meek, of course, but no one wanted to be thought of as meek – not even though it might mean patient, long suffering. There was surely more to life than that, said the canon, and indeed there was, and the earliest Christians had seen it, inspired by God, and acted on it. Living together, sharing together. In their community neither man, woman or child could either starve or grow rich at the expense of his neighbour. And what was that but Socialism? the canon asked, an idea sanctified by God on earth. Had not Jesus said: 'Sell all thou hast, and give it to the poor'? And had not the rich man gone away heartbroken, because his wealth was more important even than God? And had not Jesus and his disciples lived together and shared together, as a model for the early Christians? Jesus's own words had said it all. Easier for a camel to pass through the eye of a needle than for a rich man to enter the kingdom of Heaven. To be rich, therefore, was to be wicked, because how could anybody be rich except at the expense of others? It seemed that the French writer had hit on a profound truth: that property really was theft.

On the outskirts of the crowd Bob, wearing an old raincoat long since discarded and left at Grandma's, listened and marvelled. The old priest was saying far more hair-raising things than ever Billy Caffrey had done, wiping out not just an entire class but an entire social system, and all the crowd did was listen politely and applaud the bits where the rich took a hammering. It wasn't so much that they didn't believe it as they didn't fancy it. They were far keener on Billy Caffrey's justice and equality. But then Billy Caffrey hadn't spoiled it all by bringing God into it. . . . Canon Messeter took one last swipe at the rich and was applauded for it, then sat down smiling as Andy climbed back on to the platform and the mayor introduced the last speaker.

# 23

ANDY TOOK HIS time getting to his feet. He made himself look grave, concerned, passing to the crowd the pain of the sadness inside him.

'Before we start,' he said, 'the band has agreed to play a piece of music for me: for all of us. Bear with me please. It is part of my message.' He looked at the conductor, who raised his baton. Softly, and with the kind of sweetness only well-played brass can achieve, they began the Evening Hymn.

> The day Thou gavest, Lord, is ended,
> The darkness falls at Thy behest;
> To Thee our morning hymns ascended,
> Thy praise shall sanctify our rest.

The man next to Bob turned to his neighbour. 'Worse than the bloody Sally Ann,' he said, but already the canon had risen to his feet and the rest of the men on the platform followed, and here and there voices in the crowd began to sing, and the men who served in the army remembered what was to come, and unconsciously their shoulders straightened. For as the last verse came,

> So be it Lord, Thy throne shall never,
> Like earth's proud empires, pass away, –

three cornets took on the rôle of bugles, and sounded the Last Post in mournful counterpoint to the melody of the hymn. When the last echo of the bugle call, pure, sad, achingly sweet, faded and died, the whole Market Place was still. He had them now, and he knew it. In the first place it had pleased them: the remembrance of other times, the splendour of the music, and in the second place he had aroused their curiosity: why bring God and music into a speech about lock-outs?'

'First I want to thank the band for the way they played that,' he said. 'I can't remember when I last heard anything more beautiful.' The applause was deafening, and stiffly, awkwardly, the band's conductor bowed. 'And next I want to tell you why I asked for it to be played,' Andy said. 'My elder brother was one of those heroes of the war that Brother Caffrey mentioned. Enlisted as a private soldier in 1914, and died a captain, DSO and bar, on 10th November, 1918.' There was a deep sigh from the crowd. 'That's right,' Andy said. 'One more day and he'd have still been with us – might even have been here in my place.'

And that's a lie for a start, thought Bob. John was as big a capitalist as me, but I think I see what you're after, Andy lad, and good luck to you.

'He was not like me,' said Andy. 'I'm one of the other lot that Brother Caffrey mentioned – the ones that thought it was a bosses' war, and refused to oblige them by getting themselves killed. . . . I went to Durham Gaol for it. Six months I did there – six months that felt like six years, and I've still got the scars to prove it.' His voice rose to a shout. 'And I still think I was right.' His voice lowered. 'The trouble is that nowadays I think my brother was right an' all. He died for what he believed, and I took a daily beating for what I believed. It's just like Brother Caffrey said: at least we tried to act like men.'

The crowd became the great beast once more, purring compassion.

You crafty sod, thought Bob. You've got them in the palm of your hand. Good for you, kidder.

Slowly, patiently, Andy set to work on the crowd's emotions. The sublime optimism of the hymn, the strangely triumphant melancholy of the bugle call were still with them. They were all he had, and he must use them to the full. Life was desperate, cruel, unfair: it had been so for years, so many years that they were beginning to think it was inevitable. But that wasn't true.

All over the country, all over the world even, people were beginning to believe that the world could be changed. Must be changed, and they were the ones to change it: they, the working men and women of this country. The great majority, that was the point. The masses. Their rights would come soon, soon. Only hold on.

By God they're listening to him, Bob thought. They're swallowing every word. – And then from deep in the crowd a voice called out, 'Pie in the sky. Is that the best you can offer?' From the other side of the square a voice yelled, 'No guts, man. That's what's wrong with you. No wonder you wouldn't go to fight.' And then, cruelly, unbelievably, a voice stentorian enough to rival Billy Caffrey's: 'And where were you in the General Strike? Snug and warm with your pals in Cambridge?'

Andy gripped the rails of the platform. 'I can assure you,' he said, swallowed, then said again, 'I can assure you –'

But what could he assure them of? That he'd led a riot in London? That he was still wanted for questioning by the police?

'I did my share,' Andy said.

The great beast groaned. It had expected rather more than that.

'Well do a bit more,' the Geordie Stentor roared. 'You keep telling us we'll get our share in time. Well tell us how we can get a bit on account, and not next year, either. Now.'

'Let's see some action. That's the only way this world will be changed,' another voice yelled, and scattered through the crowd the voices began to call out 'Action', and more and more voices joined in until the call became a rhythmic chant: 'Action! Action! Action!'

Behind him Bob could hear the rattling sound of a vehicle's engine. He looked behind him: a bus had drawn up at the street that led to the river, and from it policemen were coming out quickly, silently, and not Felston police either, not this lot. The Chief Constable had sent for reinforcements even before the battle began. When the bus's engine was silenced, Bob heard another sound: the clatter of horses' hooves – and mounted police moved into position behind the ones on foot. It seemed the Chief Constable didn't want just a battle: this was all-out war. The only thing missing was the artillery.

Bob looked to where his brother was desperately trying to

explain, argue, persuade. But the chant went on: Action! Action! Action! His brother looked in agony, thought Bob. All that hard work, all that good speaking, wrecked and smashed by the repetition of a single word. Andy had been so near to persuading them to postpone their miseries for just a while longer, but hunger cannot be postponed.

From within the crowd there came a loud bang, and Andy thought, Dear God – they can't be daft enough to start shooting? And then – you stupid bugger, of course not. It's a firework. Then another, and another, all over the crowd: and it might as well have been guns, because wherever the bangs came, people shied away, anxious to leave the tightly packed square and unable to move. One more bang, louder than the rest, and above the yells a woman's scream. More milling, more shoving, more yelling. As Bob watched, the great beast disintegrated, became terrified individuals with only one obsession: the need to get away. The band conductor led his men to the space beneath the platform, and they crouched there as if it were a trench. The only sensible men in the place, thought Bob, so long as the platform holds. . . .

He looked at Andy, still yelling, but the microphone no longer worked. No one could hear. He even tried to go down the steps and into the crowd, but the mayor and Billy Caffrey held him back. Behind Bob an inspector of police began barking orders.

This is no place for you, bonny lad, he told himself, and moved away, as others about him moved away, avoiding crowd and police alike, glad to be able to escape, but reluctant, too. Felston had never seen anything like this before. Election nights were nothing to this.

Bob hurried down a back lane and turned into Hotspur Street, where he had parked his car, taking off his raincoat as he did so, carrying it folded over his arm, and just as well as it happened. Nice little street, Hotspur Street. Semi-detacheds, with a bit of garden. Schoolteachers' street, bank clerks' street. But even here the police were waiting, strung out the length of the street. Big lads, heavy built, and they had that look about them, the look he'd seen on the faces of the London coppers in the General Strike. He wouldn't want to ask the time off this lot. In the distance he could hear the crowd still roaring: like a football match, he thought, but he had been right the first time. It was more like a war. He took out his car keys and the nearest policeman watched him as he opened the car door, taking note of the expensive suit and hand-lasted shoes, the big, expensive car. Nothing to fear from this one. This one's on our side, the policeman's look said. Bob drove away, for the first time in years unsure of himself.

It should have been a nightmare, except that it was still happening. People, *his* people, were still shoving against each other, fighting to get out, and the fireworks were still being lobbed, *by their own side*, into the crowd. That was bad enough, being stuck up there, isolated, unable to do something, but then the police appeared, and suddenly it was three years ago, outside the Elephant and Castle. Not a damn thing had changed.

It was true that from a distance the crowd looked like a rioting mob, but that was because of the fireworks and the panic they caused. Even so, he thought, they must have looked like a problem to the police, outnumbered by – what? Ten to one? Twenty? Then there was the noise and the women screaming, and the young, hard activists shoving their way to the Market Cross, their rallying point, listening to the orders of their leader. Not a Felston man, thought Andy, though I've met him somewhere near. The police did their job well. Two columns heaved their way into the crowd and opened up a kind of funnel into Queen Victoria Street. The crowd poured through and the coppers let them go, except for the ones they'd had their eye on anyway. Easy enough to pick them up.

And so, at last, the Market Square cleared, except for the mayor and the parson and himself on the rostrum, and the diehards round the Market Cross. Maybe a hundred of them, he thought, and remembered a dinner with Antrobus one night when he'd talked about a place called Thermopylae, where a handful of Greeks had held up the whole army of Persia and been wiped out to a man. Only after Thermopylae the rest of the Greeks had won.

The mayor said, 'It's over. Can't they see that? It's over. Finished. We've lost.'

Billy Caffrey, a far better judge of combat, said, 'They don't see it like that, Mr Mayor.'

'Then how the hell do they see it?' the mayor said.

Canon Messeter said, 'Who's right and who's wrong doesn't bother them. That isn't the point.'

'Then what is?'

'These are men who have come for a fight. They think they can win, but win or lose – a fight is what they must have.' And Billy Caffrey nodded.

The police marched in like the Brigade of Guards, and as they came closer, the activists formed up to face them, first and second ranks. From their coat sleeves appeared the short handles of the picks that miners used, and the police column halted at a barked command.

'Dear God,' said the mayor. 'I think they're serious.'

'Of course they are,' said Messeter. 'We've heard a great deal about what men do – well this is one of the things they do best. Get themselves hurt – even killed – painfully and messily.'

Another barked command, and the police column began to move into line.

'They can't do this,' the mayor said. 'This is a riot, don't you see? Somebody has to read the Riot Act. And it's got to be a magistrate. How in the world can I read the Riot Act? I wouldn't even if I could. And anyway I'm stuck up here.'

Then as if to answer his question more police appeared, a solid phalanx, and in the centre of it the Chief Constable and a small, irate man who strutted like a bantam cock.

'I might have known,' said the mayor.

'Who is it?' Andy asked.

'Major Reginald Theobald,' said the mayor. 'Runs a timber yard beyond the docks. Major Reginald Theobald, MC, JP.'

'If you listen carefully,' said Messeter, 'I've no doubt you'll hear the Riot Act.'

Theobald moved forward from the phalanx of police, opened a folio volume and began to read, his voice carrying clearly on the still air. When he had done he waited, but the men in line made no move, and he stepped back into the phalanx of police.

'Tricky,' said Messeter.

Caffrey said, 'You think so, sir?'

It was amazing, thought Andy, it was well-nigh incredible, that within minutes the two of them were re-enacting the rôles of officer and NCO, and yet there it was.

'Going to be messy,' said the canon. 'Both sides look like

they mean business. Same numbers, same equipment. Like the Somme. . . . What the Duke of Wellington said about Waterloo. A pounding match.' Then there came the slithering sound of iron against stone, and Messeter looked up. 'Perhaps our Chief Constable is a military historian,' he said. 'Whatever he is this won't be the Somme. It will be more like Waterloo.'

Andy watched, and three years disappeared as if they had never been. Twelve horses ridden two by two clattered into the Market Square. The sergeant in charge halted them, and once more the Chief Constable called out to the militants to surrender.

'Ah,' said Messeter.

'And what does that mean?' the mayor asked.

'It means our heroic friends cannot possibly win. Not against horses.'

'But there's only twelve of them,' said the mayor.

'Two could do it,' Messeter said. 'All they have to do is breach the enemy line and let the infantry in.'

The police horses began to edge forward. Horse and rider together looked, as they always looked, invincible. Again the Chief Constable barked the summons to surrender. There was no answer, and the Chief Constable called out to the horsemen, who drew from their scabbards the long batons of the mounted police, and let their horses sidle nearer still.

'They can't do this,' Andy said.

'Perhaps,' said Canon Messeter, 'if I were to go down: offer to mediate –'

But as he spoke one born fool threw a firework at the police horses. It landed neatly behind the sergeant's horse, and exploded like gunfire. The sergeant's horse took off at once, and at once the others followed, hitting the ranks of men who were prepared to resist, clubbing down everyone in their way, then re-forming at the other end of the square.

The sergeant watched and waited. What was left of the enemy had re-formed. There was no sign of surrender. He looked to the Chief Constable, who raised his hand for the agreed signal, and they charged once more. Again the double line was smashed to pieces, and when they had galloped through the infantry moved in. Even the Germans hadn't had it as easy as this, the sergeant thought: not even at the Somme. . . . A man in a cloth cap loomed up in front of him, dazed, bewildered, but still clutching a pick handle. The sergeant brought his baton down on the other man's collar-bone, heard the crack as it broke. No sense in giving the poor bugger a fractured skull. It was all over anyway.

From the platform Andy, the mayor, the canon and Billy Caffrey looked down. To Messeter and Caffrey at least it was a familiar sight, except that there did not seem to be any dead.

Caffrey said to Andy, 'Will you be still now?'

'Aye,' said Andy. Caffrey let him go.

Andy straightened his clothes. Billy Caffrey had a good grip on him he thought. A real strong feller, but then all miners were strong. He looked down at the men in the Market Place. Some lay unconscious, others sat hunched on the cobblestones, nursing broken heads or limbs, and a few stood upright, guarded by police. Already other police had begun taking names.

'It all happened so quick,' he said.

'Inevitably,' said the canon. 'Cavalry invariably triumph over infantry in line. To receive cavalry they should form square – or so a great-uncle of mine told me. They were very foolish, poor fellows.'

Billy Caffrey had knowledge of only one war, his own.

'Those horses were like tanks,' he said. 'I saw it at Cambrai. They just smashed on through and kept going – and we just strolled in. Proper Sunday outing.' He looked down and came back to the present. 'But what on earth did they do it for? You warned them, Andy. I warned them –'

They were under orders, Andy thought: orders they were proud to obey – but how can I say so?

The Chief Inspector moved to the base of the platform and called out, 'Would you mind coming down please, gentlemen?'

As they did so a contingent from the St John Ambulance Brigade arrived, and with them Canon Messeter's vast, ancient Lanchester. From it stepped Dr Stobbs and three of his nurses. They got to work at once.

'Now then gentlemen,' the Chief Inspector said. 'If I might just ask you to wait here till the Chief Constable –'

'Where's Major Theobald?' the mayor asked.

'What does it matter?' Canon Messeter said. 'His job's done.'

'I might have known they'd bring a bloody Tory,' said the mayor.

'Well yes,' Messeter said. 'I suppose you might. He gives money to our clinic, you know. If he's going to provide us with patients at this rate I must ask him to increase his subscription.'

Andy said, 'How many policemen were hurt?'

'None,' said the Chief Inspector. 'One of the horses was scorched a bit by a firework, but nothing serious.'

'What you might call an overwhelming victory in fact?' said Andy.

'More like the preservation of law and order,' said the Chief Inspector. 'We finished with victories eleven years ago.' Like many of his men, he wore a line of medal ribbons on the left breast of his tunic.

Canon Messeter looked at the bleeding, bewildered men. 'But not defeats, it seems,' he said.

A Daimler moved across the Market Square, and the Chief Constable got out. He wore a dark-grey suit and a regimental tie, and had a neatly clipped, greying moustache. He'd finished the war as a lieutenant-colonel, so Andy had been told, had hopes of becoming a brigadier, was bitterly disappointed when he'd been discharged instead and forced to become a policeman, in Felston of all places. Still, he'd had a bit of luck today. One more battle for his scrapbook. And damn pleased with himself he looked, an' all.

'Sorry to keep you, gentlemen,' he said. 'I had to chase up these St John Ambulance chappies. Their bus broke down. Just as well we had one to lend them.'

'You seem to have been remarkably well organised,' said Andy. It was a very Cambridge form of words, he thought, but then it was a very Cambridge kind of statement: probing, testing, demanding an answer.

'We were,' said the Chief Constable.

'You expected a riot?' The Chief Constable made no reply.

'I think we've got a right to an answer to that,' said the mayor. Officially at least, the mayor was his superior, and could not be ignored. The Chief Constable resorted to official jargon.

'I acted on information received, Mr Mayor,' he said, 'which I'm perfectly entitled to do.'

Gossip? Andy wondered. Bribery? Betrayal?

'What happens now?' Billy Caffrey asked.

'To them?' The Chief Constable nodded towards his prisoners.

'We take statements. Press charges where necessary.'

'Against all of them?' asked Messeter.

The Chief Constable shrugged. 'Depends what they have to say for themselves. But what happened here – breach of the peace, riot, incitement to riot, these are all serious offences, wouldn't you say, Mr Patterson?'

Andy said carefully, 'From where I was the whole thing was serious, but why ask me particularly? We all saw the same thing.'

'Because you were the one making a speech when it happened,' the Chief Constable said. 'I'd appreciate a word about that if I may.' He turned to the others. 'I don't think I need detain you gentlemen any further.'

'We all saw the same things,' Canon Messeter said. 'I think perhaps I should stay, just in case Mr Patterson needs corroboration.'

'Me an' all,' said Billy Caffrey. 'Day of rest, Sunday, and anyway, it's our duty to help the police.'

'I've got a meeting,' the mayor said. 'Temperance League, over at the Ebenezer Chapel. They'll just have to manage without me. Law and order's more important than beer.'

The Chief Constable sighed.

# 24

'H E DIDN'T START it?' Grandma said.

'Not this time,' said Bob. 'He did all he could to stop it.'

'Then why isn't he home?'

'There'll be statements,' said Bob. 'Eye-witness accounts. All that.' And so there would, he thought, but that was all hours ago. Somebody was taking their time.

'He should be home by now,' said Grandma.

And there you had her, thought Bob, and there was no sense in trying to pull the wool over her eyes. Not her.

'Yes, Grandma,' he said. 'He should.'

'You hungry?' Grandma asked. He shook his head. 'Me neither. Let's see what's on the wireless.'

Being Sunday there was nothing on the wireless but a church service, so Grandma made the best of it and joined in the hymns.

It was halfway through the service when the knock on the door came. Bob got up at once, and pulled the cord that opened the door. Beneath him stood Canon Messeter, and a policeman in uniform.

'I hate to bother you –' Canon Messeter said.

'No bother,' said Bob. 'Come on up.' He hurried into the kitchen. 'It's your friend the reverend,' he said. 'He's got a copper with him. You want to go into the front room?'

'If this kitchen's good enough for Canon Messeter,' said his grandmother, 'it's good enough for any policeman.'

Bob looked at her anxiously, but she seemed calm enough:

strong enough too, for most things, but with Andy sometimes you needed all your strength.

The canon seemed to have floated up the stairs by a process of levitation, but the policeman, a Chief Inspector, was panting slightly. Too much beer, thought Bob. But I've seen you before. And then he remembered. That busload of policemen, and the mounted police behind them. This had been the man in charge.

'Mrs Patterson,' Canon Messeter was saying, 'and her other grandson, Mr Robert Patterson. I have some rather unpleasant news for you, I'm afraid.'

'If you don't mind, sir,' the Chief Inspector said, and turned to face the Pattersons. 'Andrew Patterson is in custody,' he said. If he was waiting for a reaction he was wasting his time, thought Bob.

'Has he been charged?' he asked.

'Certainly.'

Bob sighed. It was like pulling teeth. 'Well?' he said.

The Chief Inspector bridled. People who lived in John Bright Street were not supposed to say 'Well' to Chief Inspectors.

'Incitement to riot,' he said at last.

'And he's in the cells?' Bob asked. He remembered Andy's horror when he had last spoken of prison.

'Not yet,' the Chief Inspector said. 'He's still being questioned.'

Grandma stirred then, but Bob's hand came down on her shoulder. She was still.

'Any chance of bail?' Bob asked.

'Incitement to riot's a serious charge,' said the policeman. 'I doubt whether you could manage the money we'd ask.'

'How much?'

'Five hundred – maybe a thousand pounds.'

Bob's hand disappeared into his breast pocket and came out with a cheque book. 'Which?' he asked.

'Unfortunately we'll have to make sure that you've got enough funds in the bank to cover your cheque,' the Chief Inspector said. 'It's a pity it's a Sunday. We'll have to hold your brother until tomorrow.' He didn't sound as if he thought it a pity.

Canon Messeter said, 'I am myself totally devoid of funds, but I have two friends who I feel sure would guarantee Mr Patterson's cheque. Mr Patterson is a successful business man, you know. The kind they call self-made.'

'And your friends, sir?' The Chief Inspector was one of those who fought to the end, thought Bob: just like Andy.

'Mr Roger Renfrew of Renfrew Shipbuilders and Shiprepairers,' said the canon, 'and Mr Timothy Heron, of Heron, Shadwell, Hicks and Heron. The solicitors, you know. Shall I bring them to call on you?'

The inspector was a realist, as well as a diehard. 'That won't be necessary, sir,' he said.

'I think perhaps you should see Mr Heron at least,' said Messeter. 'Mr Andrew Patterson will need legal representation after all.' He turned to Bob. 'Perhaps we can call on him now, in your Buick?'

The Chief Inspector had driven to John Bright Street in a commonplace Morris. 'If Mr Heron could have a word on the telephone with the Chief Constable, that should do it,' he said. 'We're rather busy this evening as I'm sure you'll appreciate. Perhaps you could come round in your Buick and let me have your cheque when it's all settled.'

'Be a pleasure,' said Bob. The policeman left.

'Did he do that?' the old woman asked.

'Do what, Grandma?'

'Incitement to riot or whatever it was.'

'He did not,' said Canon Messeter.

'Not the way I heard it,' said Bob.

The old woman looked at him: quick, appraising. 'Tell us again what you heard,' she said.

'He talked about our John being killed, and how he went to prison,' said Bob. 'And how maybe they were both right to do what they did. And then he talked about the future, and how the world must be changed, and soon. And it would be, and we would all get our rights. – And then those madmen started yelling for action and our Andy was yelling back at them, only nobody could hear him.'

'I thought you said they had one of those contraptions,' said Grandma.

'A microphone? Well so they did, but it wasn't working by then. Smashed by one of the daft uns most likely. Anyway Andy was yelling fit to burst and then he tried to get down amongst it, only the mayor and Billy Caffrey held him back.'

'A good lawyer would have a field day with that,' said Grandma.

'Mrs Patterson I assure you –' said the canon.

'Excuse me reverend,' said Grandma, 'but all you're thinking about is the truth, and that's not the way lawyers work.'

She began to tick off points on her fingers: 'Our John died fighting, but he was right. So fighting's right, and Andy went to prison because capitalism's wrong. But don't you worry, comrades. The revolution will come soon. We'll get our rights no matter what.' The fingers clenched into a worn, work-hardened fist. 'Then the hot heads start yelling for action and a couple of well-known moderates has *to hold him back*.'

'But it wasn't like that,' said the canon. 'He wanted to stop the fighting. I shall tell them so.'

The old woman's look was pitying. 'Chances are you won't be asked,' she said. 'It'll be Billy Caffrey they'll pick on. A good lawyer could run rings round him. Can you see a middle-class jury taking Billy Caffrey's word when the lawyers have done with him?'

Canon Messeter said, 'I think perhaps we should call on Mr Heron at once.'

'Aye,' said Bob. 'I think perhaps we had.'

In the Buick the canon said, 'Your grandmother is a most remarkable woman – and highly intelligent.'

'Aye,' said Bob. 'If she'd been born a man she'd have been a lawyer – and she'd have got our Andy off.'

The work was going well, even though Tom Waring yelled and bullied and swigged milk by the quart, because he wanted to get back to Hollywood, which was quite amazing, she thought, when one considered what Hollywood had done to him. On the other hand the apartment was air-conditioned and there was Barry to take her to the Galway Slasher's or the Hotsy-Totsy at night, and then on to 21 or the Cotton Club, or just come over and mix cocktails and play the piano so very prettily: 'Blue Skies', 'Mountain Greenery', 'Button Up Your Overcoat'. The trouble was she got to bed late every night, and Tom Waring arrived early every morning. He'd declined Murray Fisch's offer of a screen writer, too, on the grounds that he would only slow things up and anyway she was learning so fast she didn't need one. Didn't want to share the credits more likely. On top of it all, Jay Bower had started cabling for more Dearest Daisy stuff.

The end came the night Barry brought her back from a party. Actually it was the early morning that Barry brought her back from a party, and not all that early either. The place had been full of musicians and, since it was a private party, black and white could play together. The gorgeously evocative names: Louis and Frankie, and Bubber and Earl and Red, and the matchless music they made, which that night had been like happiness distilled to its very essence, so that they had stayed until everyone was too tired to play any more, and drunk too much and smoked too much. In the taxi on the way to her apartment they sang 'Show Me The Way To Go Home' and their driver, whose stocks were doing well, joined in. They got out of the car just in time to see the sun rise.

'Oh dear,' said Jane.

'Rather a nice sunrise I think,' said Barry.

'It isn't that,' said Jane. 'I have to start work in three hours.'

'*Work?*' said Barry, horrified.

Really he makes it sound like prostitution, thought Jane, and in a way perhaps it is. 'The screenplay,' she said.

'May I come up for coffee?' said Barry. 'I don't think I could live another hour if there were no coffee.'

She took him up to the apartment, made him coffee and left him playing 'Lady Be Good' on the piano. What else? she thought. She hadn't even heard from Charles for days. Since there seemed no chance of sleep, she took a bath, followed by a shower, then put on lounging pyjamas and fresh lipstick before going back to the living room, to find that Barry had left the piano for what the Americans called the davenport, which was a simply enormous sofa on which he lay snoring gently. And why not? He didn't have to go to work in a couple of hours. She picked up the script. They had reached the point where she went to visit Lieutenant Lambert in the hospital to which she had driven him after he had been wounded. She read it through and grimaced in disgust. The rest of the script didn't bother her, but this bit she detested.

It had nothing to do with John, at least she didn't think it did. What she detested was that the script made it all so easy. When you were wounded – if you were the hero that is – all that happened is that you had a neat hole just below whatever it was men used instead of a left breast, and a matching and equally neat hole in your back. Beautiful nurses bandaged you up and fed you broth, and a month later, smiling bravely, you went back to the Front Line and won the Congressional Medal of Honour. It didn't work like that: at least it hadn't for John, who had been wounded twice before he was killed. It hadn't worked for any of the Americans she had met either. And yet Tom Waring was set on it: wouldn't budge. . . . Suddenly she realised that she was falling asleep and must make more coffee, strong and black, and then George came in and asked her if there was anything she wanted. His glance flicked over to Barry and then back to her, seeming to say no more than that it was unfortunate to be sure, but it could happen to anybody. Really, she thought, George and Martha are the best servants I've had since Peggy Hawkins took up Modern Languages. She decided it was time to make a stand.

'Tea,' she said. 'Earl Grey if we have it. And orange juice and ham and eggs and toast and marmalade. You'd better do the same for Mr Golding, but I think he'd prefer coffee to tea.'

George bowed and left, and she prepared to wake up Barry. Be a pleasure, really. It was all very well for the idle rich: they didn't have to go to work. And then she thought: No more do I, really. I don't *have* to work. I'll eat my breakfast and sleep, and work tomorrow. She stood over Barry and prepared to pounce.

They were finishing off the last of the toast and marmalade when Tom Waring arrived. By then Barry had shaved with George's razor, and borrowed one of his shirts. George was much larger than Barry, who looked like a very tired refugee. Jane made introductions, but Barry was too sleepy, Waring too angry to care.

'There's a hell of a lot to do,' he said. 'A hell of a lot. We haven't even started the sequence where those Fokkers shoot up the ambulance.'

Barry blinked. Jane said, 'Have some milk,' and rang for George, who came in at once with a bottle and glass.

'Fokkers?' said Barry, but George's hand remained steady as he poured.

'Eat your nice toast,' said Jane.

'What time can we start?' Waring asked. 'I mean I could go

somewhere else and start roughing out the scene –'

'As a matter of fact,' said Jane, 'I was considering the possibility of not starting at all today.'

'Oh come *on*,' said Waring.

'All my fault,' said Barry, contrite. 'I took the darling girl to a party where the music was absolute bliss. We lingered, rather. Came back at dawn. I doubt whether Jane has closed her eyes.'

'I haven't,' said Jane, 'but I think I'm about to.'

'For God's sake,' said Waring, and proceeded to throw a tantrum modelled, Jane was prepared to bet, on those of Murray Fisch. Barry watched, fascinated, and tried not to yawn, and Jane leaned across to offer him a cigarette.

'Are you all right, darling?' she asked.

'Oh fine,' said Barry. 'Fine. – If you could just persuade your friend not to shout so much.'

Suddenly Waring stopped shouting and began to laugh instead.

'OK,' he said. 'OK. You need your rest. Suppose I went away now and blocked out that scene on my own and came back around tea-time? We could do three or four hours then.'

'We could try,' said Jane, but Waring was already leaving. Barry turned to her.

'Fokkers?' he said, and Jane explained.

'I should have known,' said Barry. 'For a moment I thought Cocteau had gone to Hollywood.' But already Jane was asleep.

When Waring came back, Jane had slept enough to be able to cope with the ideas he had brought with him. The trouble was that she didn't want to. While she slept she had dreamed, she was sure, and the dream had been of John. Why or how, she had no idea, but John had come to her, and they had been happy together: no sex (she usually remembered if there was sex), but contentment, being together, a drink in a café perhaps, or a walk in woodland behind the Lines. It was ridiculous, and hopelessly unprofessional, but after that unremembered dream she had no time to spare for Lieutenant Lambert.

'You don't think love's important?' said Waring.

'Of course it is,' said Jane. 'Even if by love you mean mostly sex. But there are other things.'

'Those aircraft shooting you up.'

Men with no arms, horses with no heads, she thought. But

– 277 –

you weren't there, and if you weren't there, how could you possibly know?

'A moment of tenderness,' Waring said. 'We don't have to call it love except on the screen. You and I both know that love's the most overworked word in the language. But tenderness: compassion. Surely they must have happened?' A man with a facial tic he couldn't control, and a need for whisky that in peacetime would have appalled him: a man who had wept as she cradled him to her, his tears trickling down her naked breasts.

'Of course it happened,' she said, 'but not like that.' She slammed her hand down on the script.

'Of course not like that,' he mocked her. 'But this is the movies. This is war that's been to the cleaners: all blood and guts removed. The trick is to slip in some of the truth when nobody is looking.'

She began to like him again, but before she answered George tapped at the door and came into the room.

'Mr Charles Lovell is here, Miss Whitcomb,' he said. 'He says it's urgent.'

Waring was gathering up his papers at once, but she motioned him to be still.

'I'll see him,' she said, and Charles came in at once, elegant and cool despite the New York heat. She waited to find out who she was.

'Forgive me for butting in like this, Miss Whitcomb,' he said.

So that was who she was. 'Not at all, Mr Lovell,' she said.

'Winthrop Lyneham asked me to remind you.'

'Remind me?'

'You promised to join us all on his yacht for the weekend on the twenty-third.'

'I hadn't forgotten,' said Jane.

'Miss Whitcomb, today is the twenty-third,' said Lovell.

Tom Waring shovelled papers into his briefcase. Winthrop Lyneham was the tenth, perhaps the ninth richest man in New England.

'I guess maybe you do need a break at that,' he said. 'When can we start again?'

She looked at Lovell and, as she did so, George came in.

'Telephone, Miss Whitcomb,' he said. 'It's Felston England on the line.'

She went at once to the telephone in her bedroom. A call from Felston, England could only be bad news. When she put the earpiece to her ear, the telephone moaned and sighed like the sea before a storm.

'Hello?' she said.

'Jane? . . . This is Bob Patterson. Can you hear me?'

'Very well,' she said. It was as if she were talking to him against a freshening wind. 'What's happened?'

Out it all came. Andy's arrest. Bail at six hundred pounds. Incitement to riot. Summoned at the next Assizes.

'How's he taking it?'

'You know Andy,' said Bob. 'Never lets on. But I reckon he's scared. Another prison stretch would break him. What are we going to do?'

The use of the word 'we' touched her. 'About the bail –' she said.

'I've settled that,' said Bob. 'It's Andy going to court that bothers me.'

'Have you spoken to Jay Bower?'

'I've tried,' said Bob. 'He never seems to be there.'

'Dick Lambert? Jimmy Wagstaff?'

'Now there's a thought,' said Bob. 'This government should be on Andy's side after all he's done to get them in.'

'Go and see them,' said Jane. 'I'll get after Jay Bower and call you next week.'

'I'll get back to London,' said Bob. He gave her his numbers, home and work.

'How's Grandma?'

'Fighting mad,' said Bob. 'She gave me a message for you.'

'Oh yes?'

'Says you're never there when you're wanted,' said Bob. 'And she sends her love.'

She went back to her sitting room and looked down at the scurrying, unending traffic by the park beyond. Tom Waring had gone: George had mixed Lovell a scotch and soda.

'Bad news?' he asked.

'Exactly what I thought,' said Jane. 'I was right.' He heard her out in silence.

'A hot head?' he asked when she had finished.

'On occasion.' She didn't tell him about the Elephant and

Castle. It was not, she told herself, that she didn't trust him: it simply wasn't his business. 'But I think Bob's right when he says Andy was against the fighting.'

'May one ask why?'

'Because if he'd been for it he'd have done it. He'd have been down there bashing the constabulary, not up on a platform preaching jam tomorrow.'

'Bob of course,' said Lovell. 'Your young embryonic tycoon. Going to make a million out of wireless sets, was it?'

'Renting wireless sets,' said Jane. It seemed that Charles had his secrets to keep, too: at least he thought he had.

'You'll fight for his brother?'

'Of course.'

'Forgive me,' said Lovell, 'but from what you've told me he doesn't always seem to have been a friend of yours.'

'He was John's brother too,' she said.

'Quite right,' said Lovell. 'You must fight. You've no choice. Need any help?'

The thought of an indecently rich merchant banker offering to wade in on behalf of Andy Patterson was so bizarre that she almost said yes, but she shook her head. 'No Charles,' she said. 'Bless you, but no. What we have to do is get the case dropped, and that means loud speeches and the kind of journalism they call forthright. You were born to blush unseen, my darling. What's needed is Jay Bower.'

'I thought you said Bob Patterson couldn't reach him.'

'I can,' said Jane. 'I owe him an article. Now tell me about this Lyneham.'

'He wants some of my money,' said Lovell.

'Most people do.'

'You're about the only one I know who doesn't,' said Lovell. 'Lyneham wants some to invest in a cotton mill in Alabama.'

'How much?'

'Two million dollars.'

'As Andy's Grandma says, "Not much when you say it sharp." Will you invest?'

'No,' said Lovell.

'Bad idea?'

'A very good idea,' said Lovell. 'Build your factory next to your raw material. But the timing's wrong.' He finished his drink. 'The timing's wrong for just about everything,' he said.

'You must be the only one in America who thinks so.'

He looked up quickly. 'You haven't been buying stocks?'

'And risk your wrath – and my mother's? Of course not. Am I really going aboard this yacht?'

'If you want to. It could be rather fun.'

'Then I'll go. What shall I wear?'

'From what I hear the *Pocahontas* looks like a good-sized chunk of the *Mauretania*,' he said. 'Your very best should just about do. How's the writing?'

'The movie,' she said. 'We're making progress. Mr Waring's not the easiest of collaborators.'

'I could have him changed if you like.'

'So you could,' said Jane. 'I must try hard to remember just how powerful you are. But if it's all the same to you I'll stay with Mr Waring.'

'But if he's difficult –'

'He's also the best, Charles. Give me another two months with him and I could be a producer myself.'

'Is that what you want?'

'Now you just stop that,' she said lazily. 'We'll smoke one more cigarette together then I'm going to throw you out and get some rest.'

'Late night?'

'Early morning,' she said. 'I haven't been to bed at all.'

'Good God,' he said. 'Did that idiot Waring –'

'No, no,' she said. 'He can't go to parties. He has an ulcer. It was the most divine little pansy who took me. The one who had a migraine when we docked. We went to hear some jazz.'

'What's that?' Lovell asked.

'Those strange noises you took exception to at the Cotton Club.'

'You listened to that all night?' said Lovell, incredulous. 'Good God.'

# 25

IN THIS DREAM she was back at the party with Barry, and in the next room the band was playing 'Some Day Sweetheart'. The sound was elegant, inventive, and totally satisfying, and she was happy just to be alone in a little, empty room and listen. Then John came in, wearing his captain's uniform. (Later she was to wonder why she always dreamed of John in uniform, until she remembered that she had never seen him wearing anything else.) Behind John came Andy and Bob, and they stood in a line facing her, and began to sing a folk song that John said he had been taught at school:

> Oh come you not from Newcastle;
> Come you not there away?
> Oh saw you not my true love,
> Riding on a bonny bay?

They sang it even though the jazz continued to play, and the strange thing was that it all blended perfectly: happy, relaxing sounds that eased her deeper and deeper into sleep – until it was all over like a curtain coming down, and she was aware of a hand pressing her shoulders and a voice saying, 'Miss Whitcomb. Miss Whitcomb.'

She opened her eyes and knew at once that it was a mistake. She felt terrible. Above her Martha towered, her hand still shaking her.

'Miss Whitcomb, I hate to do this,' she said, 'but you've got a phone call.'

'Must I?' said Jane.

'I certainly don't want to bother you,' Martha said, 'but the young lady says her name is Erika Bauer and she's sure you'll want to speak to her on account of her brother. Whatever that means.'

'How long have I been asleep?' Jane asked.

'Four hours. Maybe four and a half,' Martha said.

'It isn't enough,' said Jane.

'No *ma'm*,' said Martha, meaning it. 'But the young lady said she needs to talk. A matter of life and death,' she says.

'I'd better talk then,' said Jane. 'Bring me a cup of tea, will you Martha? Earl Grey. No sugar. Milk, not cream.'

'Yes miss.' Martha handed over the handset.

'Hello?' said Jane.

Erika Bauer said, 'Your maid said you were asleep.'

'And so I was,' said Jane.

'In the afternoon?' The accusing voice said it all. Afternoons were not the time for slumber. Afternoons were for meetings, movements of votes of no confidence, open letters to the President.

'I have had a migraine for seventeen hours,' said Jane, 'and so I took my pill.'

'Oh God,' said Erika, 'I'm so sorry.'

'Not at all,' said Jane. 'It may still work. How can I help you, Erika?'

'Your stupid maid should have told me.'

'My maid is quite intelligent,' said Jane. 'Unfortunately she is also far too black to risk the wrath of people who phone from New England castles. – You are phoning from home, I take it?'

'Oh God,' said Erika. 'Oh God! I'm doing this all wrong.'

'Then take a deep breath and start again.'

To her surprise, Erika Bauer did precisely that. 'I talked to Joachim,' she said. 'He told me where you were. . . . He said it would be all right to call you. I mean how was he to know you had a migraine?'

'How indeed?'

'I mean he said you'd been in New York for days now – and I happen to know you've never even bothered to call me.'

'You're at home, you said?' Jane asked again.

'Why – yes –'

'But – forgive me,' said Jane, 'when you wrote to me you said you were about to get a place of your own.'

'I will,' Erika said. 'Believe me. It's just that –'

'What?'

'I haven't got my aunt's money yet. Don't you find that shameful? I want to live as a Socialist and I can't do it without capitalist investment.'

Well yes and no, thought Jane. I don't want to live as a Socialist, but without *my* aunt's money Mummy and I would both have been doomed.

'We must use the world as it is if we want to change it,' she said.

'That's marvellous,' said Erika. 'Would you repeat it please?'

Jane did so. It seemed that she had produced an aphorism, or at least a cracker motto.

'How's your migraine?' Erika asked.

Jane took pity. 'Better,' she said, then added hastily: 'A little.'

'Can I come to see you?'

'Next week,' said Jane.

'Not now?'

How to explain to this aspiring tricoteuse that she was off for a weekend of giddy pleasure?

'No,' she said. 'Not now. I'm just going off to Maine to study social conditions there.'

'There isn't a lot of poverty in Maine,' Erika said. 'Not real poverty.'

'I can only do my best,' said Jane.

'Oh I know you will,' said Erika, and then, 'Joachim says you are busy writing.'

Was there anybody in the world but his family who called Jay Bower Joachim? Jane wondered. And why does it annoy me so?

'I'm writing a movie,' said Jane. 'About my life.'

'For *Hollywood*?'

'Yes.' Jane awaited denunciations, accusations of betrayal, demands for repentance. They did not come. Erika Bauer's obsession with Hollywood was at least a match for her obsession with the suffering masses.

'Oh Jane,' she said, 'I think you are just wonderful. When may I come to see you next week?'

When Jane finally got rid of her it was too late to go back to sleep. Instead she rang for Martha and began to assemble the sort of clothes appropriate to a yachting weekend: Chanel, Patou, Fortuny, Paquin. . . .

Charles Lovell collected her in a Cadillac sedan complete with speaking tube and sealed-off chauffeur. It was painted white, with here and there a touch of gold: on the door handles, the swooping eagle mascot on the bonnet, the number plates, the chauffeur's buttons on his white uniform. No doubt they *were* gold, she thought.

'How thoughtful of you to bring such a discreet car,' she said. 'We British must make it clear how much we deplore ostentation.'

Lovell chuckled as he watched the chauffeur load a steamer trunk, two suitcases and a dressing case, while Martha loftily supervised.

'I borrowed it,' he said.

'From another gentleman who wishes you to invest in a brilliant but ill-timed scheme?'

'So sharp it's a wonder you don't cut yourself,' he said. 'But you're right.' He led the way to the car, and Jane kissed Martha goodbye. Lovell blinked, and so did the chauffeur, but it was ridiculous. Martha was no darker than her ayah, and Jane had kissed her ayah every day.

The chauffeur drove off at once, heading north, accelerating through the poorer districts so as not to hurt the Cadillac's feelings, thought Jane: speeding past the El and the buses and the motor cars, and pedestrians who seemed to move in swarms, like ants.

Lovell said, 'The man who owns this car has an idea for a new canning process: soups, all kinds, stews, even pies. It would have made a lot of money.'

'But not for you.'

'He's overstretched,' said Lovell, 'just as Lyneham is overstretched. Buy buy buy. They seem to think it'll go on for ever.'

'Whereas it may end quite soon?'

Lovell looked at the chauffeur, but the speaking tube was not switched on. 'I doubt if it will last the year,' he said.

'And yet you've bought into World Wide Studios?'

'I thought about that,' he said. 'Long and hard. But it seems to me that people will always find money to go to the cinema.'

'What makes you think so?'

'It's where they're happiest.'

The car moved on, across the bridge that took them to the countryside at last.

'I hope you don't mind,' said Lovell, 'but I've told this chap –' he nodded at the chauffeur '– to make a bit of a detour, let you see the woodland. The fall hasn't really begun yet, but it's still pretty spectacular on the high ground, and we'll be there in good time for dinner.'

'That's a marvellous idea,' she said.

Lovell said at once, as if it were part of the same conversation: 'I've missed you terribly.'

'That's nice,' she said.

'I wasn't joking.'

'Neither was I,' said Jane. 'It is nice to be missed by a man like you who turns down investments and borrows Cadillacs and makes detours all over New England.' She looked at him. What she had given was obviously not enough. 'And makes love so sweetly,' she said.

'That's what I want to do now,' said Lovell.

'In the old days we would have frightened the horses,' said Jane. 'We can't possibly frighten the chauffeur instead. Do you think we might manage something of the sort after dinner?'

'We'll manage something of the sort after dinner,' said Lovell, 'if I have to buy Lyneham's bloody yacht and put the rest of them overboard.'

She relaxed against the leather of the Cadillac's cushions, and looked out of the window. No need to let Charles know how close she was to purring. They had moved into Massachusetts and the highway to Vermont: maples and redwood, and conifers on the high ground; and now and again a little clapboard township that looked like a Cotswold village redesigned in wood.

Lovell said, 'How long before you finish your script?'

'Two weeks maybe,' said Jane. 'Three at the most.'

'And then?'

'I have to go back to England – Catherine's wedding. Have you been invited?' He nodded. 'And will you go?'

'If I can,' he said. 'Bower's my partner after all.'

The words were unexceptionable, but all the same she said: 'You really do detest him, don't you?'

Lovell said, 'It's very foolish to detest anyone who makes money for you,' and then again as if he were pursuing the same topic: 'We should see the White Mountains soon.'

'And will that be a treat for me?'

'It would be a treat for anyone who can see,' said Lovell, and he spoke no more than the truth. They left the highway and took a by-road into the woodland.

Dense green at the base, then outcrop higher as the trees thinned out, and then the snow line, and the leaves already turning red, yellow, grey, until the conifers took over: and glimpses of deer, of beavers, of kingfishers and mocking-birds.

'I see what you mean,' she said.

Lovell reached for the speaking tube and gave the chauffeur instructions. It was time to go yachting. . . .

The *Pocahontas* was moored at Portland, and it really did look like a chunk of the *Mauretania*, and quite a sizeable chunk at that, with a suite for every guest. Only the crew it seemed had cabins. Jane's was a very splendid suite, with a sunken bath, a shower like a fire hose, and a bed so comfortable it seemed to beckon. But she mustn't, she told herself. If she lay down she would sleep for hours. Instead she rang for her stewardess, her *personal* stewardess, Winthrop Lyneham had told her, and watched her unpack while she thought about her host.

All twinkling and genial was Winthrop Lyneham, a little too plump and a little too rosy, with a wife as genially twinkling, as plumply rosy as himself. What the Americans called Old Money, so Lovell had told her, but Lyneham's eyes were shrewd; he had more than doubled his fortune in his lifetime. And with an eye for a pretty woman too – if one could call oneself pretty. Mrs Winthrop Lyneham in her day had been very pretty indeed.

The stewardess said, 'All done, madam. Would you like to choose your dress for this evening?'

Jane said at once, 'The Paquin.' Short in the front, dipping into a train at the back, and in two shades of green, one like creamed asparagus, the other like aspidistras, but put them together and they looked very fetching: just the thing in fact to show off a few emeralds.

'Very good, madam.'

Interesting to note that the stewardess had no need to ask which was the Paquin dress. Jane opened her handbag and took out her notebook and pen. 'Darling Daisy,' she wrote, 'It's the life on the ocean wave *again*'. . . .

Cocktails were taken on deck, which made her glad that she had brought a Kashmiri shawl, also of green, but flecked with gold. Far too early in the season for furs. Yet some of the women wore them, the rest were bare shouldered. Sweat or goose pimples. Jane knew at once that she was disliked, and for no other reason than forethought. Only Mrs Winthrop Lyneham seemed pleased to see her.

'My dear,' she said, 'how absolutely gorgeous you look. And those emeralds. Where did you get them? Or shouldn't I ask?'

'Ill-gotten gains,' said Jane. Lovell, who was bringing her a cocktail, checked for a moment then ploughed on grimly. Mrs Winthrop Lyneham chuckled, but no one else did. The temperature on deck dropped perhaps five degrees.

'What on earth's going on?' Lovell asked.

Jane smiled at him, but her voice was angry. 'Did you see those bitches?' she said. 'I was tried, condemned and sentenced in fifteen seconds.'

'Well can you blame them?' said Lovell. 'Rosie Lyneham's the only one who can even remember what it's like to be like you.'

She sipped her martini and began to feel better, but even so it was a long and dreary dinner. Lyneham did his best and so did his wife, but he had been unlucky. His guests were all the sort of rich men who might be persuaded to invest in an Alabama cotton mill, and their wives were the sort who rated respectability as only slightly less important than dividends. Lovell might well get away with it on such an outing, but for her there was no hope at all, and she was out-numbered six to one, or six to two if you counted Rosie, but poor Rosie had her poor husband's fund-raising drive to think about.

Lovell said, 'I rather think we're about to sail.'

'Why not?' she said. 'It's a ship, after all.'

'I meant,' said Lovell, 'that there simply isn't time for you to go ashore, although they are most certainly bitches. I could ask Lyneham to cut the voyage short if you like.'

'Certainly not,' she said. 'If they want war, they shall have it.

I belong to the bulldog breed after all.'

'Anything less like a bulldog than you in that dress I cannot imagine,' said Lovell. 'A tigress, certainly –'

She smiled up at him, meaning it this time, yet knowing the other women still watched. The saddhu all those years ago had called her a leopardess, and tomorrow she would wear the brooch to prove it, but tigress was close enough.

'Darling Charles,' she said, 'you always know what to say. But now you must excuse me. I must mingle.'

'Among the bitches?'

'Certainly not,' she said. 'Among their husbands.'

Cocktails were fun, and the dinner excellent, with a lobster cardinal almost as memorable as the Meursault that accompanied it. Prohibition it seemed meant all things to all men except the very, very rich, to whom it meant nothing at all. When they had finished the men drank port and the ladies left them to it. Lyneham had spent some years in an English merchant bank, and found the custom not only agreeable, but good for business: and so the ladies found themselves in the saloon drinking coffee. Jane waited for the opening salvo.

'Are you to delight us with your company for long?' the first matron asked.

'Miss Whitcomb,' Rosie Lyneham said firmly, 'is here in America until she has finished her movie. It is a real-life story based on her adventures as an ambulance driver in the Great War.'

And that was all it took. Jane Whitcomb was a celebrity, and to a celebrity all things were forgiven, even ill-gotten emeralds. Jane remembered Erika Bauer. Hollywood really did have its own magic. Even so, she thought, Charles as a liaison officer was unbeatable.

It turned out to be rather pleasant, in a shame-making sort of way, being fawned on by all those rich bitches. Suddenly it dawned on her that even though she was the best dressed and best be-jewelled woman present, she was also almost certainly the poorest, if a husband's wealth could be counted, and why not? Her wealth had been made by her uncle. How Uncle Walter would have hated the idea of her being the poorest person present, but he'd have enjoyed the fawning, she thought.

When the gentlemen came in there was talk of bridge, and

she got up at once and said good night. Tomorrow, she explained, she must get up early and go over a very tricky scene. She left in a sort of reverent hush. In her state room the stewardess was turning down her bed, and Jane sent her away, then took off her make-up and her clothes, before putting on a nightgown that she knew Charles liked, of black translucent silk. The body showing through it was still not bad, she thought, even though she had to do more and more exercises and second helpings were unthinkable, even of that heavenly lobster cardinal. But no matter how self-sacrificial she was, it couldn't last much longer, and then what would she do?

That made her think of the boom. That, it seemed, couldn't last much longer either, according to Charles. And then what would anybody do? Not just people like Winthrop Lyneham and Jay Bower, but the people at Felston. They couldn't survive a boom. What chance would they have in a slump? She found herself yawning. Thank God she had finished before Charles came in.

'Have you come to help me finish my scene?' she asked.

'I said I had some figures to go over.'

'You didn't lie. . . . One figure anyway.'

He took off his dressing gown. 'I love your dress,' he said.

'Oh you do, you do. But before we embark on this act of depraved carnality, may I ask a question?'

'If it's a short one,' he said.

'If not stocks, what should one buy?'

'Real estate. Gold.' He drew her to her feet.

'Should I do that?'

'You're safe,' he said. 'You have no holdings at risk.'

'Only you,' she said.


'Dearest Daisy,

'Last night I had dinner with six hundred million dollars.' Well that's how much Charles had reckoned they were worth, excluding himself. Charles was always a bit coy about saying how much *he* was worth. One of the lesser peaks of the Himalayas, he'd told her once. That put him behind the Rockefellers and the Mellons and Carnegies, but not all that far behind.

Always talk big money when you can, Jay Bower had told her, and so she talked six hundred million, and the yacht and the

Cadillac and the lobster cardinal. Then the view from the boat deck: not the sunlight on the water or anything like that, since Jay would denounce it as poetry, and delete it. What she described was an event. Charles had dragged her off to see it, forcing her to abandon Dearest Daisy, which wasn't all that hard to do.

'I really have to finish this piece,' she said.

'You will,' said Lovell. 'This may even give you a couple of paragraphs.'

In the distance she could see another craft coming towards them, moving at a quite astonishing speed.

'What on earth is it?' she asked. He handed her his field glasses, and when she adjusted them she saw a big boat, half decked, stacked with crates. It had twin propellers that whipped the sea to froth, and roared towards the *Pocahontas* like a privateer to an East Indiaman.

'My guess is she's a Motor Torpedo Boat. Ex-navy.'

'She's very dirty for a navy boat.'

'*Ex*-navy boat. She doesn't fire torpedoes any more.'

'I'm delighted to hear it.'

'What you're looking at is a rum-runner, said Charles. 'At least that's what they're called. They also run whisky and champagne and gin that hasn't come out of a bath tub.'

'But it's coming here,' she said.

'Certainly. You might want an extra martini tonight.'

The motor-boat roared in, the helmsman cut his engines, and the motorboat nestled under the big yacht's lee. A lot of men aboard her, Jane noticed, and a machine gun, mercifully unmanned, mounted in the stern. Sailors threw lines to the motor boat and almost at once a donkey engine coughed, then bellowed, and a net swayed out from a winch on the yacht's main deck.

Jane watched fascinated as the man on the boat loaded crates into the nets, one of them first moving aside a stubby little gun with a cylinder attached to it. A Tommy gun! Of course! He handled it as casually as if it were a fishing rod. The net swung in, then back, over and over, until there were no more crates to be loaded.

'We must be going to have a remarkable party,' said Jane.

Lovell snorted. 'Winthrop's brother is running for governor again,' he said. 'He needs supplies.'

'But supposing we're caught?'

'How can we be?' said Lovell. 'At the moment Winthrop's brother *is* governor.'

Someone on the motor boat waved, the lines were cast off, and again the propellers churned, the smaller craft moved off, trailing its white wake.

'But where would it come from?' Jane asked.

'Nova Scotia,' Lovell said. 'Probably Yarmouth or Clarke's Harbour.'

'Are there many of them?'

'America's a thirsty country,' said Lovell. 'This is the only expanding industry Canada's got. What do you think?'

'I've never seen anything quite so cynically corrupt,' said Jane.

'That's not how they see it.'

'You'd better tell me,' she said. 'I can't see it any other way.'

'Your host and his friends see an unworkable law – so unworkable that the judiciary flout it, and the police cash in on it, and murderous animals in the big cities make fortunes when they're not too busy killing each other. When a law is unenforceable what can you do but ignore it?'

'Become teetotal?'

'It was the teetotallers who started it,' said Lovell. 'They were going to create a cleaner, healthier America. What they did create was a monster. Will you write this for Jay Bower?'

'Would my host be pleased?'

'Oh dear,' he said. 'Probably not. Excuse me. I didn't think – I just wanted you to have a what d'you call it? A scoop.'

He meant it, bless him, but really to use it was unthinkable. Instead she wrote about the time she had seen Machine Gun Jack McGurn at the Hotsy-Totsy Club – at least somebody had told her that was who it was. But Jay disliked the word 'probably' as much as he disliked poetry. So far as Dearest Daisy was concerned, it was definitely Machine Gun Jack McGurn, and it rounded off the article very nicely.

When it was done she rang for tea, and the stewardess brought Earl Grey. Winthrop Lyneham really had enjoyed his time in England. She wondered what would happen to him when the boom ended: whether he had enough gold bars and real estate. The answer was probably yes, since his family had been so rich for so long. The same should be true of Jay Bower, and yet she wondered. Jay had always been in a hurry: buy whatever it was and let the dividends catch up later. It wasn't surprising. He had always been rich, and saw no reason for that state of affairs to alter, and yet – if he weren't rich would Catherine still want him as a husband? Come to that, would Catherine's grandmother accept him on any terms at all? Catherine's grandmother, delightful though she was, had been so rich for so long she considered that if you didn't have enough money it was your own fault. Lack of money was the one sin she would never forgive Jay.

Which brings us to Charles, she thought. Charles is rolling in it. An earl's stately home, a Russian count's emeralds, it was all the same to Charles. How much? the only question, and then beat down the asking price. Was that part of the attraction? Not beating down, just the fact that he was so enormously rich? She had read somewhere that wealth and power could act on women like an aphrodisiac. Men too, no doubt, if they were pansies. Some psychiatrist, no doubt of the Freudian school, had written about it at some length. Carefully she thought about Charles: how he looked, the way he made love, what was wrong with him and what was right; then asked herself if she would feel the same about him if he were poor. She decided that it depended on what one meant by poverty. Never to dine at the Closerie des Lilas again, or dance at the Cotton Club. . . . What a greedy bitch you are, she thought, but then whose fault is that? Even when you try to go in for good works they won't let you. She waited till six then went to the saloon to help Wynthrop Lyneham drink some of the crates of gin he'd shipped aboard that morning.

'Come again, you really must come again,' Rosie Lyneham said. 'We did so enjoy meeting you,' and for once the voice seemed to mean it: no 'Please God help her to understand I'm just being polite.' And this after Charles had turned down her husband's offer. What a useful weapon Hollywood was. A whole armoury. The stiletto that could puncture the most monstrous ego: the bludgeon that could fell six dowagers at a stroke.

'It has been fun,' she said, and embraced her hostess. Rosie

Lyneham had been specially designed to be embraced, she thought, and even at fifty accepted it as no more than her due.

Lovell said, 'I have to get straight back to New York.'

'Me too.'

'Mr Waring is restless?'

'Rampaging I should think,' said Jane. 'And you? More figures to check?'

'Not like yours.' He picked up the speaking tube and spoke to the Cadillac's chauffeur. Later he said, 'I hope you enjoyed our little jaunt?'

'Oh yes,' she said.

'I know the guests were boring, but Lyneham's quite fun and Rosie even more so. And you did see the rum-runner.'

'You mean you knew I would?'

'Of course,' he said. 'Why else would I take you?'

'Lust,' she said.

'You don't need a yacht for that.'

She looked at him. For once his face had no defences. He would marry her if he could as soon as she said yes. But what would be the point? To be married to a hundred, maybe even two hundred million dollars? She already had more than enough, and the freedom to pick and choose, to say no and mean it whenever she wasn't in the mood. 'Dear Charles,' she said.

Tom Waring was already at the Park Avenue apartment when she arrived. She was early, but even so Waring managed to convey the impression that he had been kept waiting. It didn't worry her. This time she was rested, and she'd done her homework between spasms of Dearest Daisy. They settled down to a long and amicable wrangle about the love scene, and what Waring thought the cinema public wanted, and Jane thought they could have, and reached agreement at last with the minimum of yelling. Waring looked at her, surprised. He had barely sipped his first glass of milk.

'I never dreamed it would be that easy,' he said.

'Nor I,' said Jane. 'The worst's over, isn't it?'

'The rest's mostly action,' Waring said. 'Technical stuff. All we have to do it block it out – the stunt men and the flyers will break it down with me. Say two or three more days on the dialogue and you're free to go.'

'That's marvellous,' she said.

He looked at her, appalled. 'Was I that bad?'

'Of course not,' she said. 'It's just that a friend of mine's getting married. She wants me with her.'

Waring said, 'Getting married, huh? I guess it takes all kinds.' He sipped at his milk. 'Can I ask you something?'

'Of course.'

George came in. 'Excuse me, Miss Whitcomb,' he said. 'I have London England on the line for you.'

Twice in one week, his voice seemed to say. Boy, are we at the hub of things.

She hurried out. Waring was beginning to look as if he needed milk again.

Jay Bower said, 'Do you think you could persuade Bob Patterson to stop bothering me?'

'No,' said Jane. Bower sighed.

'That means you won't,' he said. 'OK. Maybe Brother Andy's a good story, and maybe I'll run it, but you'll have to come back here to write it.'

'Done,' she said.

'How soon can you get back?'

'I'll sail next week. The first boat I can get.'

'You still working on that script?'

'Almost finished.' There was a silence, and she knew exactly what he was doing: shrugging his shoulders in a way that was his equivalent of Pontius Pilate washing his hands. He had made his decision: he wanted no part of her life story, even if he still owned a chunk of the studio. Just as well, she thought, considering how soon he'll be a married man.

'You haven't written to Daisy lately,' he said at last.

'Yes I have. I finished one yesterday. I'll get it on the next boat.'

'What's it about?'

'Bootleggers. Speakeasies. Machine Gun Jack McGurn.'

'Cable it.' He hung up on her for the twenty thousandth time, and she went back to the drawing room. Waring was still there. George had plied him with milk. 'Not bad news I hope,' he said.

'No,' she said. 'Just a reminder that there is life after movies.'

Waring looked as if he didn't believe it. 'I was meaning to ask you,' he said, then hesitated. 'It's kind of personal,' he said.

'I'm not awfully good at personal questions.'

Waring swigged at his milk as if it were brandy before a battle. 'All I wanted to ask you is this,' he said. 'If you should happen to see Charles Lovell, would you mind telling him that you think I'd make a good director for this picture – that is if you do think I can do it, of course.'

'Why should I happen to see Charles Lovell?'

'He's a friend of yours.'

'An acquaintance at best.'

'But he listens to you – takes your advice. Murray Fisch said at Cap d'Antibes you were the only one he did listen to.'

On that basis: soothsayer, wise woman, sybil – she could commit herself. 'If I run across him I'll tell him you'd make a good director, because you will. It's all settled, surely? Murray Fisch wants you –'

'The word's out,' Waring said. 'This is going to be a big one. Everybody wants it. Raoul, King, Howard. Everybody. If I do it and get it right I'll be up there with the best of them.'

'Then I shall say my lines as soon as I meet my audience. But is Mr Lovell really that important?'

'Murray Fisch thinks he is,' said Waring, 'so he must be.' He rose. 'Nine o'clock tomorrow?'

'Make it ten.' Waring owed her a favour, and anyway Barry was going to take her to the Stork Club.

# 26

Some of the lads thought he should just run away. Billy Caffrey made it sound like it was his duty to run away: get on a boat for South Africa or Australia or somewhere – and leave his brother with six hundred quid's worth of bail to cough up. Billy Caffrey reckoned he could afford it, and maybe Bob could, but that wasn't the sort of thing you could do to your own brother. Mind you, I can see what Billy's after, thought Andy. Embarrassing to have a platform speaker inciting a riot, and even more embarrassing to have a platform speaker whose only defence was he was telling the rioters to stop rioting. Our brave comrades having their heads cracked by the Tyneside Cossacks and him safe up on the platform telling them to knock off. Either way he couldn't win.

He was all right for the time being, certainly. Magistrates' court, remanded on bail, up at the Assizes first chance they got. The bosses and the coppers couldn't wait to get him up in front of the judge. He'd got a good chance his lawyer had said, but he'd said it like he had no chance at all. Suddenly Australia didn't seem like such a bad idea. . . . Now that's enough of that, he told himself, and accelerated his pedalling, trying to use physical effort to blot out thought, and often enough it did at that, especially if you worked for Moscow Mike Deegan.

He took off his boots in the backyard, then climbed the stairs and washed up in the sink while Grandma set the table for his tea. Pie and peas, one of his favourites. So at least she was on his side.

'Heavy day?' she asked.

'Heavy enough. Deegan's given us a ship's generator you could sell for an antique. First owner must have been Noah.'

Grandma chuckled: 'What's he think of you now?'

'Same as always. Working-class hero. I only hope he isn't daft enough to go boasting about what a hero I was at the Elephant and Castle. That really would put me inside.'

'You're sure you tried to stop it this time?'

'Word of honour,' said Andy. 'Canon Messeter, Billy Caffrey, the mayor.'

'Well then –'

'They'll say they're prejudiced,' said Andy, 'that they're lying for me.'

'The canon wouldn't lie.'

'They'll say that after what he got in the war he's a bit confused – and anyway they've got their own witnesses.'

'Who?' Grandma snapped. 'Who've they got?'

Like she was ready to eat them, he thought. 'The coppers.'

'And they're not prejudiced?'

'Gallant defenders of our liberty,' said Andy. 'Boots polished, medals right across their uniforms, hands on the Bible. The jury'll believe them, I bet.'

Grandma snorted. 'I forgot,' she said. 'This letter came for you.' She brought it from the mantelpiece to the table. 'Finish your pie first, can't you?' But already he had snatched at the envelope, slit it open. London postmark, college crest on the writing paper. Burrowes wanted to see him. He would.

It was a Sunday-morning meeting again, in Newcastle railway station buffet. Andy could see the sense of it – the place was always busy, and if he and Burrowes were to meet as if they didn't know each other, the station buffet was as good a place as most: always busy, and always thronged with incurious transients whose only worry was the time of their train. It just seemed so childish: 'Is this seat taken?' 'Not at all. Please sit down.' 'Pleasant weather for the time of year.' They'd be using passwords next.

To Grandma the whole business was obviously suspect, and the less he told her the more suspect it became, but she made no comment about it, merely smiled indulgently, which made it even worse, as if he were once more the little boy who had found a bar of chocolate in the streets, and neglected to share it with John and Bob. She thinks I like all this posturing, he thought, so she lets me do it for a treat, to take my mind off what's to come.

Only once did she refer to it, and that was just before he set out for Newcastle: suit well brushed, boots polished.

'I'm not asking you what you're up to,' she said.

'Thanks, Grandma.'

Beyond ignoring him totally, she showed no reaction to that.

'That's because I know you've got more sense than to get into real mischief, but I can't help wondering why you can't invite him here instead of gallivanting off to Newcastle. Does he think this place isn't good enough for him? It's always been good enough for Jane.'

This place hasn't got a wine and spirits licence, he thought, and even if it did I wouldn't let him in here to make fun of you. Not that he would succeed, but he would try. Of course he would. Mockery's one of the things he likes best. So why do I bother seeing him? It's because awful as he is, he's right, and wonderful as you are, he thought as he watched her assemble handbag, gloves, prayer book and hymnal, you're wrong. Off to Sung Eucharist or whatever it's called, he thought, and not totally angry I'm going out because it'll give you time for a gossip before you come back here and start on the Yorkshire pudding.

'Half past one and not a minute later,' she said. 'I'm not spoiling a good Sunday dinner, not for anyone.'

He walked with her to the end of the street, where she turned off to go to the church. Neither said a word to the other.

He was first, as usual. Time keeping had been an anxious duty for him since his first day's work. For Burrowes it seemed always to be a matter of choice: he arrived on time only if something more agreeable didn't happen to delay him, and that Sunday something more agreeable must have happened, since Burrowes was twenty minutes late and looked pleased with himself. He came up to Andy and went through the ritual, and Andy removed his raincoat from the seat he had managed to keep, so that Burrowes could dispose himself and his two large whiskies in front of him.

'Nice to see you out and about,' he said.

'My brother did it for me.'

'Yes,' said Burrowes. 'Family pride's an outmoded concept of course, but it does have its uses. Exactly how rich is your brother?'

'I've no idea,' Andy said.

'Find out, will you?'

'No.'

The flat refusal surprised Burrowes so much that his hand shook, the whisky slopped in his glass.

'You refuse to comply with an instruction?' he asked.

'I refuse to satisfy idle curiosity,' Andy said.

Burrowes nodded. A point had been made and accepted. 'Curiosity is never idle, not if you use it properly,' he said, 'and it's the most enormous fun, but if you don't think so, I shan't press you. Tell me about the riot instead.'

'What about it?'

'The brutal attack on protesting workers, the vicious cruelty of capitalist police.' The tone of voice is still mocking, but he means every word, thought Andy.

'And what you said to urge them on – or warn them off.'

Andy told him. When he had done, Burrowes said: 'So the famous Patterson eloquence urged restraint?'

'The famous Patterson eloquence did as it was told,' said Andy, 'like the rest of me. Act like a moderate. Look like a moderate. Talk like a moderate.'

'Did it not occur to you that the position might have changed?'

'Why should it?'

'Because comrades were there, armed, disciplined, and ready to fight.'

'Nobody told me that was what they were,' said Andy.

'You must have heard something at Deegan's.'

'Rumours,' said Andy. 'That's all you ever get at Deegan's. What I expect from you is instructions.'

'I don't like your tone,' said Burrowes.

'I'm not all that happy about yours,' Andy said. 'Never have been.'

Suddenly Burrowes smiled. It was a smile any actor could have been proud of, thought Andy: polished, effortless, and yet with just a hint of modest manliness. The smile that bowled them over, he thought. Them, but not me. All the same, play along Andy lad. We can't have a slanging match in the station buffet.

'I'm afraid I got rather carried away,' Burrowes said. 'The thought of those poor fellows being beaten like that –'

'That's all right,' said Andy, and for a moment Burrowes's smile flickered. By offering forgiveness Andy was guilty of a presumption almost impossible to prevent. Even so, Burrowes carefully reassembled his smile.

'The thing we must consider,' he said, 'is what happens next.'

'To me you mean?' Burrowes nodded. 'Don't you have instructions?'

'Not instructions, exactly. In view of the circumstances the Party can hardly instruct you. We *do* have a suggestion, however.' He finished his second whisky, then looked at Andy's empty cup. 'More tea?'

Andy shook his head. 'Let's have the suggestion.'

'All in good time,' Burrowes said, and went back to the bar.

Being kept in suspense. My punishment for talking back to my betters, Andy thought. Like being kept in after school. In many ways Burrowes would have made a good school teacher. The need to instruct, the need to dominate, the need to punish; they were all there. Burrowes came back at last with two more glasses of Scotch.

'Sorry to keep you waiting,' he said. 'Such a crush. Now where were we?'

'You were about to make a suggestion,' Andy said, and Burrowes giggled.

'How naughty you are,' he said, then the camp archness vanished. 'The Party has considered all the known reports of the Felston riot. It has considered you and your usefulness to the Party, as well as your highly successful endeavour to pass yourself off as a Labour moderate.'

'Which the Party instructed me to do.'

Very softly Burrowes said, 'The Party line can change, comrade.'

'You're telling me it's changed for me?'

'I'm telling you that you are requested to plead guilty to the charge of inciting a riot or whatever the mumbo jumbo is.'

'That means I'll go to prison.'

'You've done it before,' said Burrowes.

'I won't do it again.'

Burrowes leaned towards him until Andy could smell on his breath a mixture of garlic and whisky.

'This is a suggestion, a request,' he said. 'But it's an extremely urgent request. Permit me to tell you why.' Andy waited. 'In the first place you are almost certain to be found guilty anyway.'

Andy didn't waste time arguing about witnesses. He'd already disposed of that argument with Grandma.

'You seem very sure,' he said.

Burrowes lit a cigarette, and the smell of Virginia tobacco joined those of garlic and whisky.

'The Party has friends in all sorts of places, as you know,' he said. 'They include lawyers and civil servants, some of high rank. The kind who can get access to all sorts of papers. The law wants you, Andy, the way a gamekeeper wants to nail a weasel to a tree. You'll go to prison anyway – but if you plead guilty at least it won't be for quite so long.'

'I don't want to go at all.'

'Of course you don't,' said Burrowes. 'But it's quite inevitable, I'm afraid. I really mean that.'

What you mean is that you want me in prison, Andy thought, which means you want to take the coppers' eyes off somebody else, and I wonder who that is?

'But if you plead guilty,' Burrowes continued, 'you're announcing to the world how deeply committed you are to the militant workers' cause. That should be of great advantage to you when you come out of prison and back to political life.'

'And to hell with moderation?' said Andy. 'And anyway, it's the moderates that get elected. You know that as well as I do. That's why you made me one.'

Burrowes said gently, 'I've already told you. The Party line has changed. We're asking for a sacrifice, I know that, but the Party never forgets its loyal servants. And after all, you do believe in the militant struggle. You've already demonstrated the fact.'

Andy said, 'The coppers don't know it was me at the Elephant and Castle.'

'And we'll do our best to keep it from them,' said Burrowes. 'Of course.'

And there you had it, Andy thought. Either you go quietly,

or you go resisting arrest. But you go.

'This needs a bit of thinking about,' he said.

'Not too much,' said Burrowes. 'The Party wants an answer soon.'

'When?'

'Tomorrow night,' said Burrowes. 'But not here. We've used this deplorable milieu often enough for the time being. Felston has a ferry service I believe?'

'That's right.'

'It takes one across the Tyne. Fifteen minutes, would you say?'

'Ten.'

'More than adequate time to accept the Party's suggestion. The eight-thirty ferry, comrade. . . . You can point out the sights to me as we go.'

Erika Bauer came to tea. She had travelled in by train, she said, then on to Jane's apartment by cab. She made it sound like Hannibal crossing the Alps with his elephants, thought Jane, but then Erika wasn't allowed out unaccompanied all that often.

'How did you get away?' Jane asked.

'Daddy's away on business with the tourer,' said Erika, 'and Mama went to visit friends in the sedan, so there weren't any more chauffeurs. And Mama wanted a new book to read so I said I would get it.' She held up the book. Thomas Mann's *Buddenbrooks*, in German of course.

'Won't someone be suspicious that you've been away so long?'

Erika said, not without dignity, 'I'm allowed some time on my own, you know, to stroll in the park, go to galleries, take tea. In the afternoon, of course.'

Train rides like safaris, the occasional free afternoon, and this woman was setting out to turn the world on its head: though Jane could well understand why she should want to.

Erika had put on weight, which, despite the convention of the times, made her look prettier: cheeks more rounded, figure more apparent, the blue eyes more noticeable, but dear oh dear, thought Jane, someone must tell her about clothes and make-up, and soon. From what Barry had told her, they could be quite cutting about such things in the Left-Wing intellectual enclaves in Greenwich Village.

'You haven't got your money yet, I gather?' she said.

Erika shook her head. 'Next month,' she said. 'Lawyers take for ever. It's why they're so rich.'

'Next month is October,' said Jane. 'Rather a good month for revolutions.'

'Is it?' said Erika, and thought about it for a moment, and looked pleased. 'So it is. We'll show them, Jane. I promise you.'

That 'we' was a little disconcerting. 'What do you propose to do?' Jane asked.

'I have a friend who was at Bryn Mawr,' Erika said. 'She feels exactly as I do. Once I can get my hands on the loot we're going to start a magazine together. Oh Jane – do say you'll write for us. We're going to call it *Red Awakening*. Rather neat, don't you think? Not "rude". "Red".'

'Very witty,' said Jane, 'but do tell me, who's going to finance your magazine?'

'My friend,' said Erika. 'She's rolling in money.'

'Not you?'

'How could I?' Erika said. 'All I've got is a hundred thousand dollars.' For the first time she looked like Jay Bower's sister.

'Always remember,' said Jane gravely, 'that we live under a capitalist system. Until it's destroyed it isn't just commonsense, it's our duty to hang on to our money.'

'Oh I will remember that,' said Erika. 'I promise you. Which reminds me – do tell me about Hollywood. – Your movie.'

'*My* movie? Well I suppose it is in a way. It's certainly my life – or a piece of it. We've just about finished the first draft script.'

'Who's we?'

'Tom Waring and I. You know – the movie director.'

'I saw his production of *Much Ado about Nothing*,' said Erika. 'It was summer stock – quite close to our house. There was a party afterwards and I met him. Such a sincere man. Not the Hollywood type at all.' She blushed. 'What I mean is he's like you. He uses Hollywood to say what he has to say in terms of technique – but he hasn't forgotten Shakespeare.'

Well not completely, thought Jane, but the memory's beginning to fade, I fear.

'And you know Georgina Payne, too,' Erika said.

'We're old friends,' said Jane, and hoped that Erika wouldn't mention her brother. It was just possible that she might blush.

'I admire her so much,' said Erika. 'So elegant and aristocratic.

I suppose as a Socialist I shouldn't say that, but art is different from reality, isn't it?'

'Totally.'

'I'm so glad you think so. But it's a little worrying sometimes.'

'What is?'

'Seeing Georgina Payne on the screen. I remember once she wore a ball gown and sables and a diamond tiara, and suddenly she saw herself in a mirror and just threw back her head and laughed. It made being rich seem –' She hesitated.

'Seem what?' asked Jane.

'Wonderful,' said Erika. 'And you and I know it isn't like that at all.'

I know no such thing, thought Jane, but how can I say so? She's having the time of her life, so how can I spoil it?

George came in, and said, 'Refreshments, Miss Whitcomb?'

'Ah teatime,' said Jane. 'What would you like to drink, Erika dear?'

Erika looked bewildered. 'Why tea of course,' she said.

'Tea for two,' Jane said to George. It wasn't the Sligo Slasher's after all.

Bet had made a bit of a scene. She'd got her head bitten off for it by Grandma, but she'd made the scene first. That man of hers, Frank, had been working on the trams and thank God for that. He'd been in no mood for teaching him how to be an inspector, so that left just Bet and her bairn, and the bairn was asleep in its pram. Pity Bet wasn't an' all. He'd got back from his cosy chat with Burrowes to see the two of them sniffing at the Yorkshire pudding, and Bet had taken one look at who it was and sniffed at him instead, and not as if he smelled like Yorkshire pudding either. At least she'd let him get his dinner down before she started on him, but then out it came, with the first mouthful of baked apple and custard. Head on like a charging bull.

'I suppose you're proud of yourself,' she said.

'Not always,' said Andy.

'Very funny I'm sure,' she said. 'Well I'm not proud of you and no more is Frank. A gaol bird for a brother-in-law and him working for the council.'

'I was a gaol bird before you even met Frank.'

'That's not what I mean and you know it,' said Bet.

'Now listen,' Grandma said.

Andy put down his spoon and fork. He'd enjoyed his dinner and there was nowhere else to go. Might as well let her get it over with: if it wasn't now it would be later, and it wasn't the sort of thing you wanted to hang about waiting for. More like a ride on a ferry.

'Let her get it off her chest, Grandma,' he said. The old woman sat down, watching, listening.

'You had no right to behave like you did,' said Bet.

'So you were there, were you?' said Andy. 'Go on, then. Tell us how I behaved.'

'I was *not* there,' said Bet. 'The idea! . . . But I've talked to plenty that was. You ranting and carrying on, and telling those dafties to stand firm and fight the coppers.'

Well there was still one industry left in Felston, he thought. Everything else might have shut down, but rumour mongering was full-time round the clock. Like always.

'Suppose I was to tell you that's not true?' he said.

'Why should I believe you when there's hundreds say it is? Can't you ever think of anyone but yourself?'

This last question was so breathtaking in its stupidity that for a moment he couldn't even try to understand it.

'Well?' said his sister.

'You'd better explain yourself,' he said.

'Don't you understand anything?' It was obvious that Bet found him as incomprehensible as he did her.

'You've got a family,' said Bet. 'There's Bob that's a respectable business man getting on in the world, and he has to find hundreds of pounds to get you out of a police cell. Not that it'll be for long, mark my words.

'And there's me and Frank and the bairn.' Now we're getting to it, thought Andy.

'Frank's getting on an' all. He's a driver now, and he'll be an inspector one day, you'll see, and then we'll have our own house with a bit garden, or we would have done if you hadn't started your antics. Do you think the Tramways'll make a man an inspector when his brother-in-law spends his time with thieves and pickpockets and murderers?' Rather belatedly she added: 'And what about Grandma? A fine thing for her, the age she is, to be left on her own and the neighbours gossipping about her grandson the convict?'

'Never mind Grandma,' the old woman said. 'Grandma can take care of herself. Always could. Not like some. Just you answer me this. Andy's spent hours and hours trying to get into Frank's head how to pass his inspectors' exam. Timetables and costs and passenger liability and I don't know what. I've sat here and listened to them, so I know.

'Your Frank's not the brightest man in Felston, not by a long chalk, but Andy was that patient with him. "I don't think you've quite got the hang of it, Frank," he would say. The patience of Job. If it was me I'd have belted him with a flat iron.'

'My Frank's not –' Bet began.

'You'll listen to me, my lady,' Grandma said. 'You've had your say, now it's my turn. If working on Frank isn't caring for the family I don't know what is. I tell you if that man of yours ever does get promoted to inspector he'll owe Andy half his wages.'

'That's as maybe,' Bet said, 'and I'm sure Andy did his best for Frank with the book learning. But prison! None of the rest of us was in trouble. Never. I mean look at our John. He was an *officer*.'

'And now he's an angel if he's lucky, having a bit crack with your father, so we needn't start worrying about *them*. Show some sense, girl. Andy's not a murderer, or a parson had up for interfering with a choirboy come to that –' Bet flinched as if the old woman had struck her. 'He's a chap that wants to do good by everybody. And they're putting him in prison for it.' She turned to Andy. 'One of these days,' she said, 'you'll realise that what you're after is impossible; that you've wasted your time. I hope I'm not here to see it.'

The knowledge she carries inside her is like pain, he thought, and he longed to embrace her, to tell her that she was wrong, and that one day he would prove it. Then Bet had to go and spoil it. As usual.

'Other men get married and take care of a family,' she said. 'Get married and keep themselves respectable. Why can't he?'

'Being respectable,' said Grandma. 'That's what you're after, is it?' She looked hard at her grand-daughter. 'Come here.' Bet made no move. 'Come here, me lady.'

Bet went to stand in front of her, like a much younger Bet

accused of stealing sweets, the charge not yet proved.

'You're pregnant again, aren't you?' she said, and waited. 'Well?'

'Yes, Grandma,' said Bet.

Grandma turned to Andy. 'That's all it is,' she said. 'Another bairn on the way. So naturally she's worried about her man's job and the things folks is saying about her. We all do that, especially in the early months. It's as natural as breathing. A bit hard on the rest of us, but if you had any idea of what's coming, you wouldn't hold it against her. Not for a minute.'

27

T HE FIRST LINER back was the *Majestic*, and World Wide had
   got her a state room and notified the press, so that a platoon
of photographers and reporters fussed her most politely before
the *Majestic* sailed: the surest way to inform the rest of the world
that Jane Whitcomb was important, and more than that. She
was news. Flowers, champagne and chocolates in the state
room, and already there were invitations, too: passengers' parties, ship's officers' parties, and a seat at the captain's table. All
very gratifying, but the best thing of all was that she could be
alone for a while. New York had been exhausting, and she must
write to tell Daisy so.

Even last night, just before they sailed, Barry had taken her
to yet another speakeasy, The Onyx, and really it was most
awfully sweet. Like so many, it was in the basement of one of
those tall, narrow houses they called brownstones, which had a
second staircase at the back, just in case. Some were awful, but
this one was rather elegant: upholstered banquettes and linen
napkins; glasses even. Glasses really put it at the top of the
league. The cheap places used teapots and cups, but the good
ones had glasses, bottles, and booze that didn't make you blind.
They weren't raided, you see, Barry had explained to her,
because they paid the biggest bribes. They had music, too: the
kind of jazz that Charles still found incomprehensible, and
which for her was now an essential part of life.

Charles. . . . Now there was a tricky one if you like. He'd
reacted as if her decision to go home had been made only to

punish him, which was droll when one thought about it. She hadn't even seen him since that admittedly fascinating trip on the *Pocahontas* until three days ago when he'd rung up to say he was all alone in a suite at the Plaza and would she like to go over? She'd worked extra hard on his behalf, too – all that squirming and yelling – because she'd thought the poor fellow might miss her, and jolly smug he'd been about it, which was her own fault, really, for encouraging him. Still, it had helped when she'd put in a good word for Tom Waring. But when she'd broken the news that she was off – well – he'd reacted all over the suite at the Plaza. Too bad she couldn't tell Daisy about that. It merely went to show, she thought, that if you gave a dog a bone all he would do would be to eat it there and then, and immediately start to make a fuss about where the next bone was coming from. That made her want to think of Foch, but first she must finish with Charles.

It wasn't as if he had condemned Andy out of hand; far from it. Yet again he had grasped Andy's point of view, even saying that if he had been in Andy' shoes he'd have done exactly as Andy had done. He hadn't even worried too much about whether Andy had urged his fellow workers to riot or not, beyond saying that he hoped it wasn't true because it was stupid, and Andy didn't sound stupid. What he'd done to annoy her was to suggest that she get somebody else to look after Andy. Bob had been his first choice. 'Smart young fellow', he had called him, and then added hastily, 'from what you tell me'. Then because Bob couldn't possibly handle it on his own he had given her the names of a couple of lawyers, which she had written down as soon as she got back to the apartment, but even so she'd insisted that she must go home. First he had been incredulous, then indignant, then hurt. 'But why?' he kept asking. 'There's loads of time before the wedding.' And at last she had told him: 'Because I must. Because I adopted the whole family and it's turned out to be just like a marriage: in sickness and in health.' In the end she'd made him see it, because he was both fair according to his lights, and the right kind of gentleman. But it had been touch and go. Three whole weeks without her, he had said. Not that I can see you all that often, I admit, not like this, but you've no idea what a good feeling it is just to know that you are there.

That last remark had touched her so much she had let him reach out to her again, but this time she made him try harder.

Jane rang for the stewardess to come to help her unpack, which meant to do the unpacking, then went on deck to watch the departure. That was always one of the best things about the crossing, the sight and feel of that massive lump of metal easing away from the pier; the tugs fussing and the crowd yelling. . . . There was a big crowd on the pier, jaunty and rich for the most part, and privileged inhabitants of that juggernaut America that would roll on for ever towards greater and greater wealth – except that Charles, like Mummy, said that it wouldn't. Suddenly there was Charles, pushing his way forward just too late, for already the gangway was being hoisted clear, and all he could do was scan the line of passengers until he saw her, then wave and yell. The yelling was useless: somebody had brought a band to the pier and they were playing 'Give My Regards To Broadway' fortissimo, but the wave said all she wanted to hear. He was sorry and had come to tell her so, and so she waved back and blew kisses, and this time he didn't even try to pretend that they were just good friends; just stood there waving until he was no more than a speck on New York's lengthening skyline. She turned to look at the Statue of Liberty, alas facing the wrong way for poor old Andy, then went back to her cabin.

Her unpacking had been done, neatly and carefully, and yet the poor woman must be rushed off her feet – she must remember to give her something nice when they got to Southampton. There were more presents too: a vast bouquet of roses from Barry, and a magnum of champagne 'from the crowd at Sligo Slasher's'. 'Wish we could be there to help you drink it.' What would her stewardess make of that? Not a thing she told herself. Speakeasies would be no novelty in her life. . . . She forced her mind to think about what she would write to Daisy. The band on the pier should go well, and there must be a few on the passenger list worth a paragraph or two, but not The Onyx, she decided. Daisy and her friends had already been told enough about the perils of bootleg gin.

There was a knock at her door, and she called 'Come in.' It was her stewardess, looking impressed, even awe-struck, which was odd indeed. Stewardesses were usually the most impassive of God's creatures. She carried a package that was taped and sealed.

'This came for you, madam,' she said.

'Good gracious,' said Jane. 'How on earth did it get here?'

'By motor boat, madam. Somebody radioed to say it was coming.'

'How exciting,' said Jane, and put it on a table by her chair.

'Yes, madam,' said the stewardess, abandoning any hope that she would see what the package contained. 'Is that all, madam?' she asked.

'Yes,' said Jane. 'Thank you for unpacking for me. I couldn't have done it nearly so well.'

The stewardess didn't doubt it for a moment.

To open the package required the combined efforts of her nail file and a fruit knife that somebody had provided with a basket of fruit. Charles was a dab hand at taping and packaging. And no wonder, she thought, when she opened it at last. More sapphires, ear-rings this time, and once again by Fabergé.

My darling [Charles wrote],

The count had a disastrous run at the races at Hialeah. Bad news for him, good news for me. I told him they were going to a good home. He said he wished he was.

As a proof that I love you they are dubious at best, but bankers don't write sonnets – at least this one doesn't. I'm going to miss you like hell, but things are madder than ever here, and I daren't leave for at least three weeks. Tell your mother if she ever wants a career in banking that I hope she will offer me first refusal.

Our times together in and out of bed have been the most joyous of my life.

I love you.

Charles

PS I should never have thought myself capable of writing those last twenty words – until I met you.

She folded up the letter, and put it in her dressing case. Sonnets were all very well, she thought, but prose too had its points. It was a beautiful letter. . . . She opened her jewel case and locked away the ear-rings. No sense in announcing that they had just arrived. If anyone were ill mannered enough to ask she would say that it was additional material from Hollywood. She looked out of her port-hole. Sunshine, calm sea. Time for a stroll on deck before she bathed and changed to go to the purser's party.

It was raining, which was no novelty in Felston, but all the same he couldn't get rid of the feeling that Burrowes had arranged it. His boots didn't leak, thank God, but his raincoat was sodden and his cap like a sponge by the time he got to the ferry landing, paid his tuppence and clicked his way throught the turnstile to the gas-lit shelter adjoining the floating dock. Close by, a couple of cars and a van were waiting to be ferried, their owners snug inside them, but in the shelter on the quay he stood and shivered and watched the handful of passengers huddling like sheep. Only one other man stood apart and that was Burrowes, in a trench coat that was stained and torn yet obviously waterproof, and expensive, and carrying an umbrella he must have bought that morning, as soon as the rain began to fall.

Andy turned away to watch the dark mass of the ferry moving up to the quayside. A couple of deckhands in oilskins stood poised, massive mooring ropes ready in their hands. There came the sound of the engine-room bell and the rhythm of the propeller changed, its wake boiled and thrashed in the dusk as the ferry sidled in, and at the exact moment needed the deckhands threw the mooring ropes and two men scurried from shelter into the rain to loop them round their bollards. The ferry heaved and shrugged like an overgrown whale, and the ropes round the bollards creaked, as the gangway came rattling down, the cars and vans drove aboard, and the foot passengers followed, Andy hanging back, watching where Burrowes went.

Of course he went on deck. Everybody else went into the saloon out of the wet, but not him. They couldn't talk in the saloon, so Andy went on deck too and took what shelter he could against the saloon's bulkhead. At least he wouldn't be treated to other folks' cigarette smoke if he stayed outside.

The ferry's horn made a kind of groan, and the gangway came up, the men on shore cast off. Once more the ferry's propeller boiled and thrashed, and they set off north across the river. Not a bad old tub, Andy thought. Big and beamy like a fat old woman, but the engines still sang sweet, her brasswork gleamed. Da had worked on this one, back in the days of Edward VII. He'd have liked to know how well she was wearing.

'Filthy night, isn't it?' said Burrowes.

He'd come up from behind – trust him! – and Andy turned to face him. Burrowes buttoned up in his expensive shabbiness, raindrops bouncing from his posh umbrella.

'I've seen better,' said Andy.

'Sorry about that,' said Burrowes. 'I simply thought that it would be such a convenient place to talk. And rather a bonus for me, too.'

'Bonus?'

'To discover that one can trust one's self to such an antiquated piece of machinery.'

'Not even a bar,' said Andy.

Burrowes's voice grew sharper. 'Have you made up your mind?'

Andy took a deep breath. He mustn't sound too scared, but he daren't risk a head-on clash either. If he did, Burrowes would simply tell the Party that he was of no use to them, and the Party would let him go. He couldn't bear that. The Party was his life, even if it could find a place for sarcastic upper-class pansies like this one.

Burrowes moved closer, and he could smell the garlic. 'Well?'

'You see it's a bit difficult,' said Andy.

'It's a simple yes or no decision.'

'Not in prison,' said Andy. 'Nothing's simple in prison. You'll not have been inside, I daresay.' He kept his voice matter of fact: no irony this time.

'Not yet,' said Burrowes. 'One of these days I may have to.'

Let us know and I'll give you a few tips, Andy thought. I *don't* think.

'Well once you're in they don't question you any more,' said Andy. 'Just give you a good belting if you get cheeky. It's before . . . when the coppers have got you –'

'Go on,' said Burrowes. He seemed excited, like a kid looking forward to a treat, Andy thought. 'Tell me what happens with the police.'

'When you're in custody,' said Andy. 'That's the worst time – from the Party's point of view. You see the police have already arrested you and charged you, so naturally they want a conviction. That always helps when you want to be promoted, and I never met a copper who didn't.'

'Get on, man,' said Burrowes.

'And it always looks good for them if they make a prisoner confess to other crimes as well.'

'How could they do that?'

'Give him a belting.'

Burrowes said, 'A beating, you mean? It would be severe, I take it?'

'That's where the luck comes in,' said Andy. 'Some coppers are decent. They wouldn't touch you at all unless you gave them lip. Some might or might not, depending on how they were feeling. Some –' he shrugged – 'some would really hurt you.'

He looked at Burrowes. In the deck lights the other man looked slightly sick, and yet somehow still gloating.

'But that would make no sense,' he said. 'You have nothing more to tell them.'

'Oh but I have,' said Andy. 'That's what's worrying me.'

'What on earth do you mean?' Burrowes asked.

'Cambridge,' Andy said.

'*Cambridge?*'

'The people I met, talked to. The plans they had. The things they were going to make happen. Pardoe, Whitcomb, Antrobus.'

Burrowes looked appalled. 'But those were privileged conversations,' he said. 'You couldn't betray them.'

'Anybody can betray anybody,' said Andy, 'if the pain's bad enough.'

'They would deny it. It would be your word against theirs.'

'I should hope they would deny it,' Andy said. 'Do you think I'd want this to happen to them? . . . And then there's you.'

'What about me?'

'Messages, secret meetings, always there to tell us what the Party thinks. Of course you'll deny it too – you'd be daft if you didn't. I'd bear you no grudge, but when folk get about as much as you do, you wouldn't be hard to trace. The waitress at the station buffet might well remember a chap buying all that whisky, the price it is, and that umbrella and raincoat doesn't exactly make you invisible, not when you could be in the saloon.'

'Don't forget we know what you did at the Elephant and Castle,' Burrowes said.

'You haven't been following me,' said Andy, and his voice was reproachful. 'I wasn't saying I'd do it – I'd sooner die – I'm saying I might be made to do it.' He paused for a moment. 'Oh,' he said. 'I see what you mean. You're thinking you might get arrested and the coppers would get it out of *you*. If they did I wouldn't bear a grudge, I promise you. Only it would go a bit harder on you, wouldn't it?'

'Why should it?' said Burrowes.

'Because all I'd be doing was turn in a few Cambridge toffs, whereas you – you'd be betraying a working-class hero.' He moved back, away from Burrowes's garlic-laden breath. 'That's why I said it takes a bit of thinking about.'

The voyage was quick: easy seas, no head winds and a bright sun almost all the way. By rationing the time spent at parties, she managed to get a good deal of work done, too. Dearest Daisy had never had so many letters. . . . Three people actually had the temerity to ask what her package had contained. Goodness how news spread on board ship, but who were these creatures who had the gall to ask such personal questions of a stranger? Not that her lie did her any harm. Scripts from Hollywood could only enhance her prestige.

The parties were fun of course, and she never lacked dancing partners, although the Americans always looked unhappy until they received cables from their brokers, which affected their dancing. It was just that she had no man to look after her: no Charles, no Barry, no Lionel. (She did not include Jay, who devoted his entire life to looking after himself.) It might be shame-making to admit it but men did have their uses, even their attractions. Georgie would have made no bones about it. There were three aboard who would have been at least adequate, and Georgie would simply have made her choice, whereas she, Jane, could not. Far better to work, and dance in between whiles, or sit on deck and watch the promenaders while pretending to read her script.

She didn't have to read it properly. Thanks to Tom Waring she knew it almost by heart. Not that it was all that bad, she assured herself. It was just that it had almost nothing to do with

Jane Whitcomb, not even the Jane of the war years. And that all-American hero instead of her dear John? Or would Jay Bower think it was meant for him? Almost she giggled aloud at the idea – Jay's fury would have been epic – but she held it back. The promenaders were watching Jane Whitcomb at work.

Soon it would be the wedding, she thought, and time to hand over that nice little Georgian tea service she – or rather Lionel – had chased all over London. Jay Bower never drank tea, but Catherine must. She had lived half her life in Ireland. How would it work out? she wondered. Disaster? Ecstasy? Bit of both probably. Those two together could never be humdrum. . . . She found herself wanting to yawn and that would never do, not in front of her audience. Go indoors or whatever they called it on ships and take a nap, she thought, then off to whoever's party it was, and dinner at the captain's table between the Romanian conductor and the rajah who had been to Harrow. It would be nice to get to Southampton, and even nicer to get to London. Knightsbridge would be bliss.

And indeed it was. She'd worn her sari yet again at the fancy-dress ball, and from then on everything had moved like a speeded-up film: packing, cabling Lionel and over-tipping the stewardess, and then suddenly docking, and positively sprinting through customs and on to the train. She had shared a carriage on it with two rather nice Americans, who, like all Americans in Europe, nice or not, couldn't wait to get to Paris, but in the meanwhile they insisted on buying her lunch and she told them what to drink at Bricktop's. There had been a headline in the *Daily World* she'd wanted to follow up: 'Irish Bomb Outrage Sensation', but the nice Americans asked too many questions, and when she got to the station Lionel was there to meet her, complete with a chauffeur who loftily supervised the porters handling her luggage. Just like Martha in New York, she thought, except that Lionel had borrowed the Hispano-Suiza again. For once she was glad she didn't have to drive, though the chauffeur was no more than competent; much better at being bossy with porters.

'Was it enormous fun?' Lionel asked.

She leaned back into the Hispano-Suiza's seats, and a smell of leather and perfume and cigars. She found that she had to think before she answered. Charles had been wonderful, and great fun: and so soon after she had thought he could be neither. Or was that simply because of wealth acting as the aphrodisiac it was supposed to be? But for the rest?

'Hectic,' she said. 'Extremely hectic. There is a black man called Louis Armstrong who plays the best jazz trumpet I ever heard.'

'Better than Beiderbecke?' Lionel sounded shocked.

'Different anyway. I brought you his records so you can judge for yourself. The music was fine, but the parties – oh darling, when do they ever *sleep*? Speakeasies and parties and nightclubs and ticker-tape. On and on and on. I'm quite exhausted.'

'Not too much, I hope,' Lionel said. 'I've booked a table at the Gargoyle. I want to hear everything.'

'Very well,' said Jane. 'But not too late. I'll probably have to lunch with Mummy.'

Foch was pleased to see her, which was a relief: not over-demonstrative of course, and certainly not fussy, but tolerant about such matters as being picked up and caressed, watching benignly as this time it was the chauffeur's turn to unload the car, while Lionel loftily supervised. When she put him down he moved at once to Truett, the parlourmaid, and Jane knew then that he had been well fed, perhaps too well fed, while she was away. He certainly wasn't moving very fast – and then she remembered why. Foch was getting old. He was ten, which didn't sound too bad, but then one multiplied it by – seven was it – and that made him old: really quite vulnerably old.

Lionel stayed to drink one cup of tea, then promised to come to collect her at eight, and left, which was just as well. She really had to telephone her mother. Mrs Routledge was at home, and prepared to chat. Nowadays she treated 'the instrument' as a delightfully simple means of exchanging gossip rather than an affront to the usages of polite society.

'Quite well, thank you,' she said. 'George also. The beginning of the National Hunt season is always nerve racking, but he bears up well.'

Really Mummy, one would think you had entered him for the Gold Cup, thought Jane.

Aloud she said, 'I've loads to tell you.'

'I shall be an avid listener,' said her mother. 'The boom continues?'

'For the moment.'

'Ah,' her mother said. 'My suspicions are well founded then?'

'You know they are, Mummy. The richest man I know says you can work for him in his merchant bank at any time.'

'Racing,' said her mother, 'supplies me with all the excitement I need. And George of course. But thank him. I take it I know to whom you refer? – Oh, Gwendolyn Gwatkin asked me when the cinematographic film of your life is to be made. I told her that my lips were sealed. How she enjoys pompous phrases.'

Her mother chatted on, conveying a sense of physical happiness so complete that Jane could have wept for the joy of it. Only after the luncheon invitation – her turn this time, Jane insisted – did her mother talk seriously.

'Have you read today's *Daily World*?' she asked.

'Not yet, Mummy.'

'I should do so at once. It contains some quite disquieting news about Ireland. Goodbye, child. I look forward to luncheon tomorrow.'

As Jane hung up she realised that not one word had been said about Francis. No doubt that was Mummy being tactful.

The article in the *Daily World* was exactly what she had feared, after her mother had exhorted her to read it. Mangan Castle had been dynamited by members of the IRA, and the Dowager Countess of Mangan, who had been in residence at the time, was now in a Dublin nursing home, suffering from a heart attack. Jane read the piece through twice, then phoned Jay Bower. He was available at once.

'You've read the piece?'

No time for how are you, nice to hear your voice, did you have a nice trip?, but how could she blame him for that?

'It's ghastly,' she said. 'I phoned at once. How is Lady Mangan?'

'We're still waiting word on that,' he said. 'It could be a stroke.'

'And Catherine? And Piers?'

'Catherine flew out this afternoon. It'll be in the paper tomorrow. Piers is with his regiment in India. He's asking for compassionate leave.'

'And their parents?'

'Cruising like always,' said Bower. 'Norwegian fjords? Iceland? We're still trying to reach them.'

'But how on earth could those idiots do that?' said Jane. 'Lady Mangan used to help them, find them jobs.'

'Because they're idiots,' said Bower. 'No. Not idiots. Crazies. At least you and I would call them that. To them the jobs weren't important. What they cared about was the principles.'

'Even if they starved?'

'Sure. These guys don't get their kicks from bacon and eggs and Guinness. What makes them feel good is righteousness.'

'By blowing things up?'

'Certainly.' For once, it seemed, Bower was prepared to talk; perhaps he even had to talk. 'You've seen things blown up.'

'Yes,' said Jane, 'but not like that. Gun limbers. My own ambulance. A farmhouse once, where we were billeted.'

'A farmhouse isn't bad,' said Bower, 'but it doesn't compare with a Georgian mansion.' There was a brief silence.

'I saw Hill 60 go up,' said Bower.

'Before my time.'

'Yeah,' Bower said. '1916. You Brits tunnelled under the hill like badgers and packed it with dynamite. Thousands and thousands of tons. Then you blew the top off the hill like you would take the top off an egg. They say they even heard it in London.'

'They did,' said Jane. 'I was there. I heard it. I even heard the windows rattle.'

'The nearest mankind ever got to Krakatoa,' said Bower, 'and it wasn't the Germans who did it; it was you Limeys. The good guys. God knows what we'll do next time.'

'There can't possibly be a next time,' she said, for this was 1929. Another war was unthinkable.

'We haven't time to make bets,' said Bower. 'How soon can you go to Ireland?'

'You want me to do a piece about this?'

'Well of course,' he said, and then his voice softened; almost he pleaded. 'I guess Catherine could do with some help, too.'

'I can't go tomorrow,' she said, 'but the next day almost certainly, if you can arrange a plane.'

'What's wrong with tomorrow?'

'I have to see my mother,' she said, 'and do something about Andy Patterson.'

'For God's sake,' said Bower, 'forget about them. This is important.'

'You have your family to worry about,' she said, 'and I have mine. And anyway, what's happening to Andy could sell papers too.'

'Blackmail, huh? Write up the working-class martyr or else?'

'It isn't even necessary,' she said. 'The way I write it, Andy will sell. I promise you.'

'So long as you go,' said Bower.

'Just get me a plane.'

Bob was a little harder to reach – just left the office, seeing a technician, and then a meeting with his suppliers and not to be disturbed, not for anything. 'I'm sorry, Miss Whitcomb.'

'You will be,' said Jane, 'if you don't get him out of that meeting.'

He came to the phone at once, and listened to Jane's instructions, but she could tell that his meeting was important, and kept her message short.

'I'll get on to it right away,' he said when she had done. 'Nice to have you back. We could do with a bit of help.'

She went to bathe then, and to choose a dress suitable for both Lionel and the Gargoyle.

# 28

SHE HAD LONG ago decided that it was by no means her favourite nightclub, despite all that fuss about the Matisse décor and those thousands of bits of broken eighteenth-century mirrors. Lionel on the other hand adored it (something to do, so he said, with it being the only nightclub one went up to in a lift), and he approved the dress: Hartnell, and just the right pink for Aunt Pen's ruby set. He ordered champagne, and she told him all about the rum-runner. He was enchanted.

'My dear you're a positive pirate,' he said. 'How can we stay-at-home girls begin to compete?' Then he added softly, 'Take your time. Three tables away.' Jane looked. Brenda Coupland was sharing a table with someone vaguely familiar: a man who looked like a pineapple.

'Haven't we met that man?' she asked.

'*You've* met him,' said Lionel. 'I went to school with him.'

'The Eton and Harrow match,' said Jane.

'The very same. Hugo Meldrum. Please God Brenda wants him all to herself.'

'How could she possibly?' said Jane, and she was right. Brenda beckoned them over as soon as she saw them.

'Darlings how divine to see you,' she said. 'Hugo do wake up and order more champagne. You can't possibly nod off before midnight.'

Hugo ordered a magnum and blinked sleepily at Lionel.

'But I know you,' he said. 'You're L. C. S. Warley. You made a half century against Harrow.'

'Fifty-two not out,' said Lionel.

Meldrum turned to Jane. 'I've met you, too,' he said. 'How spiffing.' He waited as the waiter brought more chairs.

'Bit of luck for me being here with Brenda,' Meldrum said. 'She usually goes nightclubbing with the Prince of Wales.' There was no resentment in his voice, only pride.

'Not on Tuesdays,' Brenda Coupland said, 'and not at the Gargoyle.'

'She's a great one for the chaps,' Meldrum confided. 'Her latest's a subaltern in the Rifle Brigade. Makes a change from all those guardees.'

'Must you reveal all my girlish secrets?' Brenda Coupland asked.

'Proud of you,' said Meldrum. 'Proud of myself, come to that. One night it's the Prince of Wales, the next it's a fat oaf like me. Damn it, I've got a right to be proud.' He looked across the room. 'Babcock,' he said.

'I beg your pardon?' said Lionel.

'Miles Babcock,' said Meldrum. 'Over there.' He gestured to where a thin and obviously bad-tempered man was apparently about to quarrel with a woman Jane was sure was his wife. 'Batted number five in the same team as you against Harrow. Didn't do awfully well as I remember.' He got to his feet. 'Come and say hello to him, Warley. Be a treat for him seeing you again.'

'I hardly think –' Lionel began.

'Oh do go with him,' Brenda Coupland said. 'Hugo does so adore reminiscing.'

Reluctantly Lionel rose and followed Meldrum. The waiter had just opened the champagne.

'Last time you sent them both off to get us tea,' said Jane. 'What girlish secret are you going to reveal this time? Not Jay Bower again?'

'Jay Bower? Of course not. He's getting married, isn't he? It's his grandmother, or rather his grandmother-in-law.'

'Lady Mangan?'

'You've met her?' Brenda Coupland asked. 'But of course. You know the twins quite well.'

Jane said firmly, 'She's awfully sweet.'

Brenda Coupland shrugged. Being sweet, it seemed, was

what grandmothers were for. 'You heard about her house in Ireland and the bomb or whatever it was?' Jane nodded. 'One gathers Lady Mangan is quite ill,' said Brenda Coupland. 'And my rifleman – although why Hugo insists on calling him mine I've no idea – the poor boy's in India – except he enjoys going on about me – Hugo I mean – really the Town Cryer isn't in it.' She paused and looked bewildered, which somehow made her even more beautiful. 'What was I talking about?'

'Your rifleman. Would it be Piers Hilyard?'

'That gorgeous May Ball,' said Brenda Coupland. 'Well of course it's Piers. Oh I do wish he wasn't in India.'

'He'll be back for the wedding.'

'My dear I'm counting on it. But he'll be frightfully upset.'

'Well of course he will,' said Jane.

'Not just in the ordinary way,' said Brenda. 'He adores his grandmother. Apart from his twin she's the only one he cares about.'

'And you, of course?'

'Me?' Brenda Coupland smiled. 'I'm just about level with that spaniel bitch of his. The two of us nose about under the table, looking for scraps.'

Jane realised then that it was possible to feel pity even for Brenda Coupland.

From Babcock's table there came a strange sort of keening sound. Babcock won over to laughter, Jane thought: delighted to relive the Harrow triumph. She looked across the room to find that it was nothing of the kind. Babcock's face had turned a sort of cerise colour; he was far more bad tempered than when Meldrum and poor Lionel had joined him, and was making dismissive gestures of an almost frantic urgency. Only his wife seemed to be enjoying herself. Jane watched as Meldrum made one more attempt at explanation before Lionel dragged him back to his table.

'Well,' Meldrum said. He reached for his glass and drank thirstily.

'What happened?' asked Jane.

'Words fail me,' Meldrum said, and refilled his glass.

'Surely not,' said Brenda Coupland. 'And do leave some for the rest of us, Hugo, even if you are upset.'

Meldrum signalled for another bottle.

Lionel said, 'We were not a success. I was afraid we wouldn't be.'

'He didn't care to relive your triumph together?' Jane asked.

'The triumph was mine alone,' said Lionel. 'He made the grand total of three runs. Moreover he claims that I ran him out.'

'And did you?' Brenda Coupland asked.

'I did not. He called for an impossible run and I sent him back. It was while I was attempting to explain this to him that he made that extraordinary noise.'

'But we won that year,' said Meldrum.

'That didn't console him in the slightest,' said Lionel.

'Chap's a cad,' said Meldrum. 'He should never have been included in the team.'

Lionel took Jane off to dance.

It was as she brushed her hair that night, Foch watching, at ease on the carpet, that she remembered what Brenda Coupland had said about Piers. His love for his grandmother was both profound and obvious, like Catherine's. But unlike his sister's, it was violent also: the violence rigorously controlled, but obviously there, waiting to be unleashed, or perhaps even to break free when, for once, it proved stronger than the control.

Her mother came in state: by taxi, wearing her violet silk with the cameo brooch and a neat little pair of diamond ear-rings. New, Jane thought. The major must be doing well.

'How pretty you look, Mummy,' she said. 'And such ear-rings too.'

'George is most generous,' said her mother, and gave a smile that on any other woman would have been a grin. 'He spoils me.'

'A labour of love,' said Jane. 'You deserve it.'

Her mother's smile became more conspiratorial than ever, but she declined champagne and asked for sherry instead. Just as well, thought Jane. I drank quite enough champagne last night.

Her mother said, 'You look well.'

'Sea voyages are very recuperative,' said Jane.

'You found New York exhausting?'

New York had not succeeded in exhausting her only because she had declined to accept its terms. She had told Lionel it was hectic, and so it was.

'Hectic,' she said, 'and far too demanding.'

'Then it was time you came home,' said her mother, 'even to such disturbing news.'

'Lady Mangan? Or Andy Patterson?' asked Jane.

'Both surely,' her mother said. Jane loved her for it.

'There isn't much I can do for Lady Mangan,' she said, 'except go to see her, but I can fight for Andy Patterson, and I will.'

'I don't doubt that for a moment,' said her mother. 'The *Daily World*?'

'Yes, Mummy.'

'I had never realised just how stimulating journalism can be,' her mother said. 'Do please call on me if I can help in any way.'

'I certainly shall,' said Jane.

Her mother sipped her sherry, and Jane saw the change of mood at once. Francis, she thought.

'Your brother called on me during the long vacation,' she said. 'En route to Berlin, as usual.'

'On his own?'

'If he had a companion,' said Mrs Routledge, 'he at least had the good sense to keep him hidden from me. Why must he always choose Berlin for his amours?'

Lionel had told her the answer to that one, and her mother needed to know the truth.

'It's cheap, Mummy,' said Jane.

'Oh dear,' Mrs Routledge said. 'Will I never learn to stop asking foolish questions?' She sat for a moment, then said, 'He referred to you.'

'Not another attempt to widen his social horizons?'

'The ball it seems was a success – whatever the purpose for which it was given.'

'Does he intend to tell me so? Perhaps even to say that he's grateful?'

'I should think it most unlikely,' said her mother. 'What he referred to was what he called your obsession with Felston. He suggested that I might persuade you to give it up. I told him that few things were more unlikely, and on two counts: a) that I might make the attempt, and b) that you would take the slightest heed if I did.'

'Thank you, Mummy.'

'Not at all. I am, I hope, a realist, and I have two children, both

dear to me. But why should he persist in this? Your obsession –
as he calls it – does nothing but good, after all.'

'Burrowes,' said Jane. 'He must still be seeing Burrowes.'

Her mother thought for a moment, then said, 'Conditions in
Felston should be made to get worse, not better?'

'Clever Mummy,' said Jane.

'And how will this affect Andy Patterson?'

'Badly,' said Jane, 'unless I make enough noise. Mind you
with Jay Bower's help I can make quite a din.'

Next morning she flew to Dublin. This time the flight was,
by Bower's standards, conventional inasmuch as she landed at
Dublin's new airport. The plane was a Lockheed Vega, rented
from a South African diamond dealer, and its seats were
upholstered in leopard skin, the authentic Bower touch. Six of
them, and all for her.

Catherine met her at the airport, and the two women
embraced. Catherine's embrace was at once fierce and yearning,
the touch of a strong child who has learned vulnerability for the
first time.

'How is she?' Jane asked.

'They think she may die,' Catherine said. 'They didn't want
to tell me but I made them.'

She led the way to a waiting Bentley, the same car that her
brother had driven in a way that had made Jane wonder whether
he had ever considered death to be even a possibility, however
remote. A porter loaded her luggage into the car, and she
handed over a shilling.

'Far too much,' said Catherine, and Jane looked at her. She
was perfectly serious.

'You mustn't be nice to them,' Catherine said. 'That only
makes them worse.' Then she added in the same, socially conscious voice: 'Would you like to drive?'

'Yes please.'

'Granny can't see us just yet. Visiting times are limited. She
wants you to go to her this evening.'

'If that's all right.'

'It is if Granny says so,' Catherine said, and smiled. 'In the
meantime I thought you might like to drive over and see what's
left of the house. They left us a kitchen, so there'll be food, and
a glass of wine. They stole only the whisky.'

'You'll have to navigate,' said Jane.

The car was as big a brute as she remembered, strong, arrogant, and a devil to go, but once you got the feel of it, the power was always there, and the control, once you learned how to apply it. Like a big horse, she thought, that's only been ridden by the wrong sort of man. The right sort of woman could take a bit of getting used to.

'It was good of you to come over so quickly,' Catherine said.

'I like her too,' said Jane. 'Have you heard from Piers?'

'A cable from India,' said Catherine. 'They've given him a little more leave. Compassionate, they call it. That's a funny word to use in this country.'

'And your parents? And your older brother?'

'We cabled Mummy and Daddy. They'll leave the ship at Oslo and come home overland. Desmond's on his way to visit Piers. He's in the middle of the Indian Ocean. God knows when he'll get back.'

'How ghastly for him.'

'Isn't it?'

She says the words as if they have no meaning, thought Jane: as if her world had narrowed to her grandmother and her twin.

'I talked to Jay before I left,' she said.

'Oh yes?'

Jane realised that even Santa Claus Bluebeard was of little importance compared to Granny.

'He's very upset.'

'Yes of course,' said Catherine, with a note in her voice that suggested that the whole world should be upset when Granny was so desperately ill. Jane reminded herself that Catherine was still very young, and hoped that Piers wouldn't take it like this.

But that Jay Bower had been upset she had no doubt. She had seen him at the *Daily World* building where she'd gone to meet the driver who would take her to Croydon. The driver had been Bower's chauffeur, and the car Bower's Bentley, newer and even more powerful than the one she now drove. Bower had come to the aerodrome with her, and reeled off the messages to give to Catherine: not to worry too much, to stay calm, to let him know if anything was needed, just to say the word and he'd fly out the best heart man in the country. All that would keep.

His upset, Jane thought, was partly because of Lady Mangan,

whom he genuinely liked, and much more because Lady Mangan's illness could well mean postponement of the wedding. There was another worry too, gnawing away at him like the Spartan boy and the fox, but like the Spartan boy he kept that one hidden. . . . And he'd found time to think of Andy, which was nice of him. Make Andy a working-class martyr and he'd pull out all the stops.

They were through the suburbs now, and into the first fields: horse-drawn coal waggons replaced by donkeycarts loaded with turf; grass and more grass, the richest, lushest grass in the world. She wondered how Bridie's Girl and her foals were doing. It would be the hunting season soon: she must go to see them.

'Left at the cross roads,' said Catherine.

She eased the great car at the turn, changing down and accelerating, and it leaped forward like Bridie's Girl when she'd clapped her heels to her. Through a village, ugly church, ugly cottages, and one, bigger and uglier than the rest with a name outside: Mulligan's. The pub, thought Jane, and the grocer's shop, and probably the post office too, and all of it and the people in it belonged to Lady Mangan, for this was the village that served the estate. Horses not cattle on that grassland now; Mangan horses: one of them no doubt the promising youngster that Piers had coaxed his grandmother into paying for.

'Pull up at the top of this rise,' said Catherine.

Jane did so. From the hilltop what was left of Mangan Castle was clearly visible, and from a distance it didn't look too bad. It was a ruin of course, broken walls pointing up at the sky, stables burned down to their foundations, but it was set in formal gardens and parkland, and even the wreckage of the house had a kind of symmetry, like one of those pictures of ruins that Italian was so fond of. Piranesi, was it? Salvator Rosa?

'What happened to the horses?' she asked.

'They made the grooms turn them out into the meadow. They're all safe. Can we drive on now?'

Jane drove on. From close to it was all different. From close to it was just wreckage without shape or form, a lovely object transformed by fire and explosion into ugliness. Part of the portico survived, dangerously tilted, and a section of the great staircase still made its elegant swirl before ending in firewood. The upper floors had collapsed completely. In the hallway Jane could see the charred remnants of the bed she had slept in, partly covered by the charred remains of books. The library too, and the great state rooms; all that superb Irish Chippendale, smashed or burned or both. And the pictures? Had they all gone, too? The Persian carpets, the Purdey shotguns, the Waterford crystal?

'Did you ever see anything like it?' Catherine asked.

This would not do. The girl was awash with self-pity.

'Oh yes,' said Jane. 'Many times.'

'How could you possibly –'

'In the war,' said Jane. 'In northern France. It wasn't all just coal mines and peasant farms. There were châteaux too. Some almost as big as this, and a lot of them took direct hits. I've seen troops using bits of Louis Quinze furniture to light a fire and brew tea. What's happened is awful, darling. But it isn't unique.'

And there aren't any smashed horses, she thought, entrails steaming, heads six feet from the bodies. If there were I wouldn't be here.

Catherine said, 'Of course it's not unique. It's happening all over Ireland, even now. It's just –' she gestured. 'This is our *place*. The place that Granny made – restored, anyway. And destroying it's like destroying us.'

'I think we'd better go,' said Jane.

'No! No, please. Not yet.' Awful as it was to stay, it seemed that it was even worse to go.

'Some of the back of it is still standing,' Catherine said. 'Kitchens, and the room where the servants ate – the servants' hall. I sent word we were coming. There'll be food prepared.'

The staff were like survivors everywhere: butler, cook, footmen, housemaids, grooms; they each one had their story, and each one wanted to tell it, like troops after a particularly vicious trench raid, or an attack that had been repulsed. In the end it was the butler, like a good sergeant-major, who called the others to order, then took Catherine and Jane to what was left of the housekeeper's room, and offered them sherry, which Jane made Catherine drink.

The housekeeper's room had been blasted less completely than most of the house. A tarpaulin covered the gap in its ceiling, and the wrecked furniture had been replaced by survivals from the rest of the house, so that they sat in leather armchairs rescued from the library, before eating eggs and bacon at a deal worktable at which two Sheraton dining chairs were placed.

Catherine looked about her. 'I can't tell you how ghastly I feel,' she said.

'You don't have to.' Jane sipped at her sherry. 'But you'll have to – what was it the Tommies said? – "soldier on", you know. Your grandmother needs you, can't you see? There isn't anybody else. Not yet.'

'I'm going to try,' Catherine said. 'I really am. And it's all because of you. If you hadn't come here I don't think I could have. Granny's had a stroke.'

'A bad one?'

'Very bad. If she weren't so strong she would have died. She was all right when it happened –'

'Maybe you had better tell me about that first,' said Jane.

There had been arrangements to guard the house, but that night the guards weren't there. And so – there had been six of them, the butler said, in one big car. Yankee, he thought it was. Not one he recognised. They all carried either automatic pistols or shotguns, and had scarves tied over their mouths. Not local men. All the servants had sworn to that. Dubliners probably, and not the kind, the butler had said loftily, who could find their way around a place like Mangan Castle. They had locked up Granny and the rest of the servants, and made the butler take them on a tour of the place. They had hated every foot of it.

'But why?' Jane asked.

'It wasn't Irish,' said Catherine. 'It was the seat of the English exploiter, the occupying power, and so of course it had to go.'

Some of them went back to their car and brought dynamite and petrol, and set the dynamite in place. The butler thought that they acted like men who knew their business. And as they worked, Granny had jeered at them, congratulating their courage on tackling a gaggle of women and unarmed men, and only pistols and shotguns to protect themselves with. They hadn't liked it – no doubt they were more accustomed to be feared than mocked – but they had gone on with their work. The last word would be theirs, anyway.

The house was destroyed. Lady Mangan stood and watched, apparently unmoved, as first the explosions came, one after another, and then the flames. The wreckers got into their car then, and she watched them go with no more than an ironical bow, then she turned to watch their car as it climbed the hill, and there on the rise, watching the great house burn, were the men and women of the village, and some of the children too. It was then that Lady Mangan had her stroke.

'The butler sent a groom to ride to the post office and phone Dublin for a doctor,' Catherine said. 'Mulligan wasn't at all keen on the idea, but the groom's a big chap. He can be persuasive. And so they took Granny away.'

'Is she conscious?'

'Most of the time,' Catherine said. 'It's just that her left side is paralysed, and she can't always remember words – or even people. She's so damn helpless. . . . *Granny!*'

'Perhaps we should go to see her,' said Jane. 'We can do no good here. And anyway, I've got to find somewhere to stay.'

'But you're staying with us,' said Catherine. 'We've got a house in Merrion Square. – Unless they've burnt it down.'

A house in Merrion Square, thought Jane. The most exclusive, expensive square in Dublin, unless of course they had burnt it down.

'But maybe we shouldn't stay there,' Catherine said. 'It's been closed for absolutely ages, and I don't think I dare trust the servants. Could you bear it if we went to the Shelburne instead?'

Jane said she could, and the butler came in. 'Father Foley's here, Lady Catherine,' he said. 'He's cycled up from the village. He says he'd like a word.'

'No,' Catherine said, and the butler turned away.

'Wait,' said Jane. 'Father Foley's the parish priest?'

'Yes, miss.'

'Then of course we must see him. Bring some tea if you can manage it.'

'Yes, miss.' The butler waited, but Catherine had nothing more to say, and he left.

'You shouldn't make me do this,' Catherine said. 'He was probably up on the hillside with the others.'

'He's the most influential person in the village,' said Jane. 'At least you can listen.'

Father Foley was short and dark and in early middle age, but already running to fat. A clever man by the look of him, thought

Jane, and accustomed to dealing with people by no means as clever as himself, which might explain his pomposity.

'Lady Catherine,' he said, 'this is a terrible thing. A terrible thing indeed.'

Catherine said no word, merely looked at Jane, and Father Foley knew at once that he would have to do better than that.

'Father,' Catherine said at last. 'This is my friend Miss Whitcomb. She has flown over from England to help me through this appalling time. We are shortly going to Dublin to see my grandmother, who is very ill.'

'I'm sorry to hear that,' Father Foley said.

'You didn't know?'

'At times like this,' Father Foley said, 'there are always rumours. I find it best to ignore them.'

'Quite right,' said Jane. Father Foley looked surprised.

'I came,' he said, 'to offer you the sympathy of the entire village. None of us was involved, Lady Catherine. I can assure you of that.'

'My grandmother,' said Catherine, 'had arranged for the house to be guarded by the sons of friends: young men who were perfectly capable of resisting that rabble who – did what they did. But on the night it happened there was a ball in a house twenty miles away and the young men went to it because my grandmother insisted that they should. The whole house knew about that, Father. The whole village knew – but no one else did.'

'The village has no grudge against your family, I promise you.'

'But they enjoy a good bonfire. Were you there too, Father?'

The butler came in with a tea tray: silver teapot, milk in a pottery jug, and sugar in what looked like an ashtray. The only cups available were half-pint pots. Jane poured, as Father Foley tried again.

'It must seem morbid to you, I can see that,' he said, 'but look at it from their point of view. Nothing like that had ever happened in their lives. Nothing like it could ever happen again.'

'I must remember to tell my grandmother that our loss wasn't totally in vain,' said Catherine. 'At least the village enjoyed it.'

'They did not enjoy it.' Father Foley was now angry enough to raise his voice. 'They feel for you as a family at this time, but the sight was irresistible. Surely you can see that?'

'All I can see is that one of them betrayed us,' said Catherine.

'Lady Catherine, please –' the priest began, but Catherine interrupted him.

'My grandmother is seriously ill and may be dying,' she said. 'That is what you came to ask me, isn't it?'

'One of the things.' The priest put down his cup, tried and failed to appear at ease. 'Whether you believe me or not, I'm sorry to hear it. I shall pray for her. The whole congregation will pray for her.'

'And the other thing you have to ask?'

'It's the wrong time,' Father Foley said. 'I should have realised that.'

'Please ask me anyway,' said Catherine. 'Is it about the jobs my grandmother used to find for your parishioners?'

'Yes,' said Father Foley. 'It is. Those jobs are vital to this village, as I think you know. If they are to finish we'll have to look elsewhere, though God alone knows where that can be. Will your family still help us, Lady Catherine?'

'If my grandmother survives the decision will still be hers,' said Catherine. 'If it's left to the rest of us then it would be wrong of me to hold out any hope.'

'I bid you good day,' the priest said. He was a clumsy man and he set the pots clattering on the table, but he did not slam the door when he shut it.

'Well,' said Jane. 'You certainly told him.'

Catherine shrugged. 'He deserved to be told,' she said. 'For all I know he could be the one who betrayed us.'

'A priest?'

'A patriot too. From what our nurse used to tell me his most popular sermon was all about driving the wicked English out of Holy Ireland. Well it seems his prayers are answered.'

'You're leaving?'

'What is there to stay for?' said Catherine. 'If Granny dies I shall never come back, and I doubt if Piers will, either.'

'She's really so ill?' Jane asked.

'So the doctors say.'

Jane remembered Bower's message about flying out a specialist.

'It's sweet of him,' said Catherine, 'and I'll ask, of course. But

I doubt if it will do any good. It's typical Jay, isn't it?'

'I'm not quite sure that I follow you,' said Jane.

'*Daily World* stuff: Top Doctor Flies To Dying Peeress's Bedside. It really is sweet of him – I mean that – but whether she lives or not is rather up to Granny.'

When Jane saw Lady Mangan she thought that her granddaughter was right. The old woman lay on her back, stiff and unyielding, watched by a nun who rose and moved away as the two young women and the doctor came in.

'No change,' the doctor said. 'As you can see.'

'Is she –' Jane had to force out the words '– completely paralysed?'

'We're hoping not.' The doctor looked at the nun. 'And praying, too, I might add. But the shock was tremendous. It's really a matter of will power now, though of course we'll try everything.'

'Bringing out a specialist from England wouldn't help?'

'Your privilege if you want to,' said the doctor, 'but I doubt it.'

'Then I won't,' said Catherine. 'You've done everything possible, I'm sure.'

Jane moved closer to the bedside. Lady Mangan's body lay still as death, the wide grey eyes unblinking. Then suddenly as Jane watched, an eyelid fluttered: it was as if the old woman had winked at her. Jane stifled the impulse to mention it. It had been such a tiny movement after all, and to raise false hopes at such a time would have been cruel indeed. Instead, she bent to kiss Lady Mangan's forehead that was as hard and dry as a memorial statue's.

Catherine had taken a room at the Shelburne, and booked another for Jane. As they walked in it was obvious that everyone in the place knew who Catherine was, but even so Jane made her sit down in the lounge and ordered cocktails.

'Quite right,' said Catherine. 'Thank you, darling. So degrading just to run away and hide.' Jane produced cigarettes and the big lounge buzzed. Cocktails and cigarettes while her own grandmother lay at death's door!

'Listen to them,' said Catherine. You know what they're saying, don't you?'

'We're a treat for them,' said Jane. 'We may as well let them enjoy it.' She produced her jade cigarette holder and the buzz intensified.

A young man came up to them, not a very well-dressed young man by the Shelburne's standards.

'I'm from the *Irish Times*,' he said. 'I wonder, do you have a statement you'd care to make?'

Catherine stirred in her chair, and Jane reached out and touched her arm.

'My name is Jane Whitcomb,' she said. 'I'm a close friend of Lady Catherine. At the moment she has nothing to say except that her grandmother is in a critical condition, and that if she dies she will consider the ones who attacked the house as no better than murderers. And so do I.'

The young man made a note.

'Are you the Miss Whitcomb who's doing her life story for Hollywood?'

'I am.'

'If I may say so, Miss Whitcomb, you got here awfully quickly. I heard you were just back from America.'

'Naturally I came quickly,' said Jane. 'I flew here. A friend loaned me a plane. This is a terrible, disgusting thing.'

The young man made another note, and left. I've hogged the limelight, thought Jane, but Catherine won't mind. At least he left her in peace.

## 29

'Like a little girl who's lost her two best things at one go,' said Jane. 'Her doll's house and her granny.'

Jay Bower scowled at the cigar he was about to light. He didn't like what he was hearing, and indeed, thought Jane, it was a poor return for lunch at the Ritz.

'That's not a very nice way to put it,' he said.

'It wasn't a very nice thing to watch. But it didn't last long. Catherine's far too nice to hate for more than a week. And anyway, she hasn't lost her granny.'

'You're sure?'

'If she had I wouldn't be here.'

She thought of Lady Mangan. The old woman had seemed almost as big a wreck as the palace she had created, but in the end the eyelid flutter had been repeated, and then her left hand had moved. Half of her was useless, and always would be, so the doctors said, but even half of Lady Mangan would be enough for most people to cope with, especially her doctors and nurses.

'She's coming back here,' said Jane, 'as soon as she can travel. She's finished with Ireland.'

'The house in Eaton Square?' Jane nodded. 'And the wedding?'

'Goes on,' said Jane. 'She's even talking of being there herself.'

Bower lit his cigar at last. Now, she thought, was the time to warn him.

'Catherine's her own sweet self as I say,' she said, 'but she's had a dreadful shock.'

'Oh sure,' said Bower.

'I mean really dreadful,' said Jane. 'Apart from you, Piers and her grandmother were the most important people in her life. More than her parents, even.'

And what a whopper that is, she thought. To have her granny back as she had been, Catherine would have tossed Jay Bower away like an empty tube of lipstick.

'You saying we should postpone the wedding?'

'How could I?' said Jane. 'All I'm saying is she's moody. On edge. You'll have to be patient.'

'Well of course,' he said.

'Don't say it like that,' said Jane. 'When I first talked to you about being patient I had to explain what it was – and even then you thought I was kidding.'

'I can do it,' Bower said. 'For her.' He was completely serious.

'Mind you do,' said Jane. 'Catherine will stay with her grandmother at least till her mother gets back. Then they'll travel over together.'

'Should I go to her?'

'Lady Mangan's not quite ready for visitors yet, and Catherine won't leave her.'

'I respect her for that,' said Bower. 'I really do. Any news of her twin?'

'On his way back home,' said Jane. 'He hopes to pick up Desmond on the way.'

'Do they know who did it? The bombing I mean?'

'Do who know? The police?' Bower nodded. 'If they do they're not saying. It's believed it was what's called an Active Service Unit based in Dublin, but Catherine reckoned it all began with a tip-off from Mangan Village – or maybe even from the castle. One of the servants.'

'And it's all gone?'

'Just about. A shelf full of books, a few chairs, a Canaletto and quite a large part of a Velasquez. And that's about it.'

'Dear God,' said Bower.

'Don't let it worry you too much,' said Jane. 'She can buy more pictures, even build another castle if she felt like it.'

'It isn't that,' said Bower.

'What then?'

'It's the utter waste of it all.'

'Hill 60 was worse,' said Jane. 'Or so you tell me.'

Bower signalled for more coffee. 'You're a tough one, aren't you?'

'I prefer realist,' said Jane. 'A realist who cares more for people than things. I've got more than enough things as it is.'

Bower smiled. 'OK, OK,' he said. 'So I'm a snob, and you're not. . . . People, humh? Like Andy Patterson maybe?'

'Exactly. I had a word with Andy yesterday.'

'You went to Felston?'

'Of course not,' said Jane. 'That would never do. Besides, I was on that plane till lunchtime. No . . . I had Bob bring him down here.'

'How is he?'

Difficult to answer that, she thought. Scared and defiant, and of course she had expected that, but there was something else: a suggestion of bewilderment, and a suggestion of betrayal, neither of which she could explain. Not yet.

'Another spell in prison could kill him,' she said.

'That would be news too,' said Bower.

'Crusading's better,' she said. 'The *Daily World* To The Rescue.'

'If we can do it.'

'We must,' she said.

Again Bower smiled at her. 'You really do care about people,' he said.

'The ones who deserve it.' She sipped her coffee. 'Does Dick Lambert still work for you?'

'Not on the pay roll,' said Bower. 'He's Junior Minister at the Home Office – only the King's allowed to pay him. But he writes me an article sometimes. You getting Dick involved in this?'

'Maybe.'

'It could break him.'

'Or make him,' said Jane. 'He'd be a crusader too.'

'Take it easy,' said Bower. 'I have a feeling you're on the edge of a minefield.'

'I'll be careful. Do me a favour?' Bower nodded.

'If I can,' he said.

'Could you find out what my brother is doing these days? His social life, I mean – now that we've all launched him into society.'

'Nothing easier,' said Bower. 'And talking of social lives, I heard from Erika the other day. She reckons she'll get her money any time now. She says how soon can you let her have an article for *Red Awakening*?'

'Not till I've done something about Andy,' Jane said firmly.

Bob Patterson said, 'You didn't tell her the half of it, did you?'

'I can't even tell you,' said Andy.

'Oaths sworn in blood? The Black Hand Gang?'

Andy smiled. 'A bit like that.' He looked around the living room of the South Molton Street flat. The only time he'd ever seen luxury like that had been at Jane Whitcomb's house or at the cinema, he thought. Or Cambridge. . . .

'So you want Jane to fight for you with one hand tied behind her back?'

'I don't want her to fight for me at all,' said Andy, then: 'Don't look at me like that, man. I didn't mean it the way it sounds.'

'How did you mean it then?'

'I'm grateful to her, God knows,' Andy said. 'She's been marvellous. But I'm a man. Like you. I fight me own battles, always have. Only this time I can't.'

The doorbell rang, and of course it was Jane. Trust *her*, thought Andy, and then: What on earth's the matter with me? She's doing her damnedest to keep me out of prison. It's just the way she does it, he thought, but please let her go on.

'Champagne?' said Bob. 'Dry martini?'

'Champers, please.' Bob went out to get it.

And there's another thing, thought Andy. Our Bob offering posh drinks in a posh flat, and to the manner born as Hamlet said. Though mind you, John had made himself at home in the officers' mess. Come to that I didn't do too badly at Cambridge.

'That's where we start,' said Jane.

'Pardon?' Andy cursed himself for day dreaming.

'Cambridge,' said Jane. 'The people you knew there.'

'Your brother was one.'

He was trying to protect her, and she knew it.

'We'll use him if we must,' said Jane. 'But there were others. Burrowes, for instance, Pardoe. Antrobus.'

'Antrobus isn't –'

'Isn't what?'

'Like Burrowes,' Andy said at last. At least he hadn't said like Francis. What a gentleman he was.

'Neither is Pardoe. It's not obligatory, you know. Not even at Cambridge. But Pardoe's a clown. Let him stay with the Rude Mechanicals.'

Bob came back in with champagne and an ice bucket, twisted the cork from the bottle of Pommery, and poured out three glasses. Jane took hers: Andy hesitated.

'Go on, kidder,' his brother said. 'Suffer for your faith.'

Andy took his glass and sipped. To his dismay he found he liked it.

'Antrobus is quite normal,' Jane continued. 'That isn't the point.'

'What is then?'

'He has a sister,' said Jane, 'who is married to a cabinet minister.'

'Gossip,' said Andy. 'Muck raking. Is that it?'

'You did it to me once,' Jane said. 'You thought it was in a good cause, so I bear you no grudge. It just so happens I think you're a good cause too.'

Andy nodded. He had no words to thank her, nor did she expect any.

'Two more things,' said Jane. 'One – you and I will write an article about the riot for the *Daily World*, and if it goes down well, we'll write another.'

'So long as it's the truth,' said Andy.

'There'll be truth in it,' said Jane, 'but what will keep you out of gaol is the innuendo. Now you either accept that, Andy, or I'm off now.'

'I accept,' Andy said.

She let it pass without comment.

'One last thing,' she said. 'Did you lose money from your job to come here?'

'I haven't got a job,' Andy said. 'I got the push.'

'This model Communist employer fired you?'

'In person,' said Andy. '"Here's a week's wages and your cards," he said. "Now bugger off."'

'No,' said Jane. 'You resigned.'

'I tell you he –'

'You resigned,' said Jane. 'You found the atmosphere unbearable.'

'But why on earth should I?'

'Men of the Left,' said Jane, 'running a capitalist enterprise. The hypocrisy became too much for you, even although it was your only livelihood.'

'He'll deny it.'

Bob chuckled. 'Who'll believe him?' he said. 'He's a Communist.'

Andy stood up. 'I don't like this,' he said.

'Prison's better?'

Jane said, unheeding, 'What do you do now?'

'Same as the rest of Felston,' Andy said. 'Nothing.'

'We can't have that,' said Jane. 'I'll phone Dr Stobbs. You'll be volunteer handyman at the clinic. . . . You can do that, can't you?'

'Of course I can.' Andy seemed annoyed at the idea that he could not. 'But that's charity work – and you know how I feel about charity.'

'It's helping your fellow man – and woman and child,' said Jane, 'with the threat of false imprisonment hanging over you, and no thought of gain. It's news, Andy. A good story.' Her voice softened. 'And if you do it at all you'll do it well. I know that.'

'Keep me out of mischief I suppose,' said Andy.

Bob said, 'What we need's a spot of dinner.' He looked at Andy. 'We're not dressed for anywhere posh.'

'Soho?' said Jane.

'Suits me,' said Bob. 'What do'you say, Andy?'

'I'm not hungry,' Andy said.

'You've got to eat, man. We all have.'

'You two go,' said Andy. 'I'll get meself a sandwich.'

'Do you good to get out for a bit,' said Bob.

'I tell you I'm not hungry.' Andy was yelling the words. 'Leave us alone, can't you?'

Bob opened his mouth to speak once more, but Jane touched his arm. 'Andy's right, you know,' she said. 'He's got a lot to think about. He should be on his own for a while.'

Andy looked at her. There was neither irony nor derision in

her face. She had simply stated what she believed to be true. 'Thanks, Jane,' he said.

They went to the Deauville, in Frith Street. Jane refused the à la carte. The set meal of five shillings was more than adequate, she said, so Bob was reduced to ordering the most expensive wine in the house, a Château Margaux at thirteen and sixpence.

'That brother of mine,' he said. 'He's a hard man to shift.'

'If he wasn't he wouldn't be in this mess,' said Jane. 'But he's worth fighting for.'

'You really believe that, don't you?'

'Of course I do,' said Jane. 'I don't always agree with him, but I've never doubted his goodness from the moment I met him, any more than I doubted your father's. It's a rare quality. Your grandmother has it too. Three generations . . . that's rare indeed.'

The waiter brought their potage Solferino. When he had gone, Bob said, 'You didn't say I had it. Thank goodness.'

'Because you haven't,' said Jane. 'Not like theirs.'

'Did John?'

'Not all the time. No successful soldier could.'

'By successful, you mean efficient?'

'I mean good at his trade, which was killing people.'

'Our John,' said Bob. 'It's hard to imagine he would be like that. . . . Ruthless.'

'Not with me,' said Jane. 'Never with me. With me he could put all that out of the way. But it was there. John was more like you.'

'Is that a compliment?' he asked.

'Just a fact.'

Bob sipped and approved the Margaux. 'I heard from Lilian Dunn the other day,' he said.

'How is she?'

'Fine. Still prancing around the Folies Bergère in the altogether. She said something about you.'

'Do tell.'

'If you ever give me a piece of advice, I'm to take it.'

'And will you?'

'If it's good advice,' said Bob. 'And if I want to. She also sent you her best regards.'

'Please give her mine. As a matter of fact I do have some advice.'

'Let's have it.'

'Leave Andy to his sulks. He thinks the whole world's against him just at the moment.'

'Maybe it is,' said Bob, 'except for you and the Pattersons. And not all the Pattersons.'

'Bet?' Jane asked.

'No prizes for that one,' said Bob. 'Still, like Grandma said, she's expecting, and that does make a difference.'

'Somebody must keep her away from Andy,' said Jane.

'Don't fret,' said Bob. 'She won't go near him – not till he's acquitted.'

Next morning Jane wrote to Daisy once more.

Dearest Daisy,

Here I am back in dear old London. So quiet and peaceful after New York. But goodness me how respectable everyone is becoming: not a breath of scandal about anyone, not even the politicians. In America the politicians are always in trouble and everyone loves it because it gives the voters such lovely things to gossip about, but here – What on earth is going on?

Here in England the politicians aren't just virtuous, they boast about it. Even the government. Is there *no* scandal in high places any more? . . .

Two days later she received Andy's piece about the riot. Postmark Felston, she noticed. He'd wasted no time in getting back. Funny how they all clung to the place; except Bob. And John. Andy had written his article on four sheets of a cheap writing pad, which meant that it was far too long, but there was good stuff in it. She reduced it to manageable length before Bower could reach for his butcher's cleaver, then went through it again.

Nice, visual stuff. The view from the platform, the band playing – 'The Evening Hymn'. That would go down well – and then the chanting of the militants, the fireworks thrown, the Riot Act and the police. Andy had been very fair about the police. No lurid descriptions of blood in the gutters, smashed heads, broken limbs. He seemed to have written down what he saw, no more – and what he had seen was heroic workers fighting against authority, and doing pretty well – till the cavalry came. Then Andy really did let himself go – but just far enough. Bower liked a dash of Leftism in his paper's politics, but no more than a dash, and Jane edited the words to make them acceptable: the hint that many workers and police alike were ex-soldiers; the courage on both sides; the almost even match until the mounted police arrived, and Canon Messeter's reference to Waterloo. That was good, bringing a parson in on the workers' side, and not only an upper-class parson, but a heroic parson, a war hero. Or had Andy merely written down what he had seen and heard, with no guile at all? With Andy one could never be sure.

He had made the mounted police the villains, which of course they were, breaking collar-bones, trampling down everything in their way. But there were far too many references to Mongol hordes and Cossacks. She took them all out but two, and sent it off to Bower. He telephoned her almost at once.

'Good stuff,' he said. 'How much is yours?'

'Mostly the editing.'

'He did a nice job. You want your half for Felston Clinic?'

'No,' she said. 'Give him the lot. And the by-line.'

'The poor devil's going to need it,' Bower said. 'Think he can handle the other one?'

'No,' said Jane. 'He'll try, but the other one is going to need a real bitch like me.'

Bower hung up.

Andy did his best, but as a gossip he was useless. Too nice, too good even, as she had told Bob. Time for a bitch to go to work, and it was a bitch's job, far below the dignity of the leopardess the saddhu had predicted she would become. Even so she took out the little Cartier leopardess that Aunt Pen had given her and pinned it to her lapel. Extra claws were always useful. 'What Cambridge Taught Me,' she wrote, by Andrew Patterson, as told to Jane Whitcomb.

It came out as smoothly as toothpaste from a tube: so easily in fact that she was worried: no frantic reassessments, hardly even a hesitation: but when she read it through again she knew that she had got it right.

What a marvellous opportunity it seemed I had been offered, from the grimy poverty of Felston to the majestic wealth of Cambridge. . . . The great colleges with their superb libraries: the elegant rooms of the dons. . . . Smoked salmon and claret when you wanted it, instead of fish and chips when you were lucky. . . . And such men to instruct you, to teach you all the wonders of a life you hadn't even known existed: men related to the highest in the land, who had been to the great public schools before ever they set foot in Cambridge, living in monastic seclusion for seven long years of their boyhood and young manhood, acting out the rituals of their cloistered lives before taking the fruits of their studies to Cambridge, bringing to perfection the knowledge that adolescence had taught them.

And passing it on to me, that was the wonder of it: me, Andy Patterson, an ignorant proletarian with rough hands, and an accent they could barely understand. Yet how hard they worked to teach me what they knew, even vied with each other, to use a word they taught me.

And the things they could teach. These elegant and educated men knew more about industrial strife than any street orator I had ever heard: about Marx and Engels, Lenin and Trotsky, the Russian Revolution and the French. Not just politics, either, but the pleasures of life, the elegancies, the things the men of power will continue to enjoy long after the revolution is over and the dictatorship of the proletariat has begun. One day, I have promised myself, I shall write a book about it – if ever I have the opportunity and time. I learned far too much to tell in just one article. . . .

Bower telephoned her two hours after he had received the piece; the fastest reaction from him that she had ever known.

'Bitch is right,' he said. 'Congratulations.'

'Thank you.'

'It's with the lawyers at the moment,' said Bower. 'They'll take their time – they always do – but I'll bet good money they won't find anything. You didn't put a foot wrong. But you said nothing about Dick Lambert.'

'Should I have done?'

'You asked me about him.'

'I'm going to send him a copy,' said Jane. 'I doubt if he reads the *World* when he's not writing for it.'

'A *Daily Herald* man if ever I saw one, and *The Times* because he must,' said Bower. 'But why pick on Lambert?'

'Reasons.'

'OK. Be like that,' Bower said. 'But watch your step. I don't like being sued, even when it sells papers, and I don't want the government on my back.'

'Who would?' said Jane. 'Don't worry. I'll watch my step.'

She waited for the phone to slam down. Instead Bower said, 'About your brother.'

'Yes?'

'He's still living the high life. Like when we went to Cambridge, you know? Country house weekends, City dinners, Hunt Balls.'

'Not politics?'

'Hell no,' said Bower. 'He's even taking dancing lessons. Tangos and foxtrots.'

God knows he needs them, thought Jane, but what in God's name is he up to? 'I'm obliged to you,' she said.

'Don't be. I want a favour too. Catherine's coming back from Ireland next week. Her mother and father finally made Dublin. She wants to see you.'

'That's hardly a favour.'

'You're her friend and I appreciate that, I really do,' said Bower. For once he sounded unsure of himself. 'The favour is – I want you to find out how she feels about me and tell me the truth, whatever it is.'

'She's said something to upset you?'

'She hasn't said a damn thing,' said Bower, 'which is why I'm upset. You'll do this for me?'

'Of course.' Bower hung up, and this time she didn't blame him. The poor man was in love after all.

# 30

THREE DAYS LATER, Truett tapped at the door of the study and said, 'There's a Mr Lambert on the telephone asking to speak to you, Miss Whitcomb.'

Easy, she told herself. Don't rush.

'Lambert?' she said, and then, 'Oh yes,' and went into the hall. 'Dick,' she said. 'How nice of you to call.'

'We've got to talk,' said Lambert.

'Delighted,' said Jane. 'Another lovely lunch? – My treat this time.'

'No!' His voice, a light tenor at the best of times, came out like a yelp. 'What you're doing – it's serious. I hope you realise how serious.'

'You're not telephoning from your office I take it?'

'Of course not.'

How soon those politicians learn the value of deviousness in the face of adversity: the ones who know how to survive, Bower had told her. Lambert it would seem was a born survivor.

'You could come here,' she said.

'I might be seen.' Even the thought seemed to frighten him.

'You could wear a false beard.'

'I tell you this is serious,' Lambert said.

'Then you suggest a place.'

He at once suggested an address in Fulham. 'Hotel?' she asked.

'It's a flat. You just walk into the building and up the stairs. Nobody will bother you. How soon can I see you?'

'Not till next week,' she said.

'Whyever not?'

'Catherine Hilyard's on her way back from Ireland. I said I'd look out for her. You remember Lady Catherine? She came to the Felston ball.'

'Hilyard?' he said. 'Oh yes. Lady Mangan's grand-daughter. Are you mixed up in that, too?'

'Politicians are the ones who are mixed up,' she said. 'Surely you know that Lady Catherine and I are just innocent bystanders – and that's never the right thing to be.' They agreed a date at last, early in the next week, and she gave her word she would be there.

'And there are to be no more articles for the *World* till I've seen you,' he said. 'Do I make myself clear?'

'As crystal,' she said, but she did not say she would obey his commands: and when she told him so by way of explanation he would be aggrieved, she knew, because men always were. On the other hand it couldn't be helped.

She went to her work room to think about Dick Lambert, the coming man, and Foch emerged from the kitchen and followed her up the stairs. He finds them much heavier going than I do, she thought. Really I must tell Truett to put him on a diet. She sat on the chair in front of the typewriter table and Foch, still expert at choosing his moment, clambered on to her lap. Her hands stroked the harsh fur, massaged the tough little body, and Foch shivered, then sighed.

'Yes I daresay,' she said severely. 'It's all very well for you, stuffed to the bung with dog biscuits and leftovers, but what about poor old Andy? What about poor old Dick Lambert, come to that?'

Dick, she was sure, was every bit as worried as Andy, and it was important to know why. The fact that he had once proposed to her must be important to him, she supposed, but she doubted whether it would worry his wife. It had been years ago, after all, and when all was said and done Mrs Lambert was the one who had got him. No. It had to be more than that. Dick Lambert the coming man. The insolence of office. Shakespeare might be full of quotations, but they were always apt. Dick Lambert, it was clear, liked office, and the insolence that went with it. Even on the phone he'd enjoyed chucking his weight about, so long as she'd let him. Her hands grew still, and Foch yapped, aggrieved. Jane apologised and scratched the small of his back, the one place Foch couldn't reach, no matter what contortions he performed, and the yap became a sigh.

What I'm writing must be important indeed, she thought: so important that poor old Dick's been told to put a stop to it. That will mean bluster, threats. But Dick wasn't the kind to use bluster – he had far too much intelligence – and his threats would have teeth to them. The target would be Andy. It had to be. Andy was the only one who was vulnerable. It was time to think how he could be attacked, and hence how he must be defended. Soon it would be time to use the typewriter, which would lead to sulks. Foch hated the typewriter. So she rang for Truett and ordered tea, and Foch went off with Truett. Far better chance of a biscuit from Truett, as Foch well knew.

'There Is A Happy Land' by Andrew Patterson, as told to Jane Whitcomb, she typed.

I have a new job, up here in Felston, and it's a job I like very much: handyman to the Felston Clinic that takes care of the poor and the needy and asks for nothing in return, because nothing is all those poor folks have. It's a grand job, helping to care for those who need it, putting my skills to proper use. In fact there's only one thing wrong with it. It doesn't pay any wages.

Not like my last job, working as a fitter for Mike Deegan. That paid wages. Nothing lavish, but never less than the basic. Trouble was I couldn't stay on there when I found out what went on. That place was a hotbed of Communism, and Russian Communism at that. Now don't misunderstand me. I'm a working man, and I'm all for the working man, but the working man I'm for is the British working man. I don't need a bunch of pro-Russian Reds to tell me what's good for my country – or my fellow workers. Why, even the chap who ran the place was known as Moscow Mike. So I left. Resigned. And glad to. With the job I have now – it means tightening my belt now and again, but it means helping them that needs it an' all.

On and on she wrote, but this time she had to fight the words to make them do what she needed. Even so, when it was finished, she knew she had achieved what she wanted. She also knew that Andy would hate it. . . .

When Catherine arrived in London, she went to Eaton Square and telephoned Jane at once, begged her to come round. Really there was no need to beg, thought Jane. I *want* to see her, but all the same she knew why. Catherine was still very much on edge and afraid to be alone. She went out and found a taxi, and took Foch with her. Foch was very fond of taxis: Jane let him sit on the seat.

Another butler to let her in, but this one was English. No Proudfoot he, but a sad and disapproving man who looked at her, sighed, then led her in to Catherine. She sat in a light and airy drawing room with furniture by Sheraton; cheerful, elegant furniture, and yet the tone of the room was melancholic, and Jane knew at once why the butler sighed. He was echoing his mistress's mood. Brown dress, Jane noticed, and a single strand of pearls. Catherine should never wear brown. Even so she jumped up at once, ran to Jane and kissed her.

'How quickly you came,' she said.

'I said I would,' said Jane. Foch snorted. 'How are you, Catherine?'

'All right.' Already the girl was bending down to Foch, fondling the neat curls at his neck. 'What a handsome fellow,' she said. Foch snorted again.

'Doesn't he know it,' said Jane. 'How's Emily?'

'They say she's better,' Catherine said.

'Say?'

'Well how can she be better, lying there like that, her speech all slurred?'

'At least she's speaking,' said Jane.

Catherine stepped back from Foch. 'You sound like my mother,' she said.

'That may not necessarily be a bad thing.'

Catherine flushed scarlet. 'Oh dear God, I'm being beastly,' she said. 'Jane darling, do forgive me. I'm so – so *bloody* confused.'

'Of course you are,' said Jane. 'How could you not be? Just try to remember that I'm fond of Emily too.'

'She sends her love,' Catherine said. 'It took for ever, but she did it.'

Suddenly Jane understood Catherine's confusion. Emily Mangan was a remarkable old woman, as remarkable as Grandma, and with the same ability to move her to tears.

'Have they caught the ones who did it yet?' she asked.

'They never will.' Catherine looked into Jane's eyes. 'Please don't think I'm being melodramatic or anything. It's just what everybody says. Granny's solicitor, the people we dine with, everybody.'

'People are so afraid of the IRA?'

'Unless they love them,' Catherine said. 'But it doesn't matter. We're leaving Ireland. We're never going back.'

'And the house?'

'It was insured,' said Catherine. 'The insurance people are going to contest it of course – it's an insane amount of money – and we'll sell the land.'

'And the jobs in the Midlands for the village?'

'That's over,' said Catherine. 'Just as I told Father Foley.'

'Emily's had enough?'

'She said she wasn't strong enough to make decisions,' Catherine said. 'It was the only time she cried. In the end Daddy just told Father Foley to stop pestering us. . . . He's not awfully good at it, you know. Not like Piers.'

'Who's staying with you?' Jane asked.

'Aunt Margaret – Mummy's sister – was supposed to be coming up from Chippenham, only she phoned to say her arthritis won't let her.' Suddenly, unexpectedly, she giggled. 'What a gorgeous way to put it.'

'Which explains why you summoned me here so briskly.'

'Well yes,' said Catherine. 'I mean I can hardly stay here on my own, can I? Mummy was adamant.'

'You want me to move in?'

'It's either that or a hotel,' said Catherine, 'and I hated it in the Shelburne on my own.'

'Why not stay with me then?'

'Oh yes,' said Catherine, and then, 'Oh I say. Would you mind awfully? You must have masses of people coming to see you.'

Lovers, thought Jane. She's worried about my lovers. The

thought of poor Charles as part of a queue, perhaps not even at its head, almost gave her the giggles.

'They're mostly quite civilised, I promise,' she said.

'Oh I didn't mean –' Catherine hesitated, then stretched her hand out to Foch, who went to her at once. 'May I really come?' she said.

'Well of course,' said Jane, 'but not in brown.'

There were problems, of course. Clothes just unpacked had to be packed again, and there was Catherine's maid to be considered. Truett would resent Catherine's maid, the more so as Jane didn't have a lady's maid of her own, and Mrs Barrow would detest her. Better to give her a holiday. Catherine looked uneasy at that.

'You *can* look after yourself, I suppose?' said Jane.

'I had to at Oxford,' Catherine said. 'I wasn't all that good at it.'

'Truett will help you.'

'Won't she mind?'

'The only thing Truett minds,' said Jane, 'is serving drinks in the garden, and it's getting a little chilly for that now.'

The butler came in, sad still, but resigned. Mr Bower was on the telephone.

'Jaybird,' Catherine said. 'Well it's about time.'

But she doesn't exactly run to the phone, thought Jane. She ran faster to Foch and me. She wondered what would happen when Piers came home. Would he and Catherine move even closer together after what had happened, and how would Jay Bower handle it, on top of all his other worries? At least Brenda Coupland would be glad to see Piers.

She went ahead to soothe ruffled feathers, but there were none. Truett at least was the most colossal snob, and Catherine was not only a lady, but a refugee from terrorists, who would doubtless be good for a sizeable tip. Mrs Barrow too declared herself to be delighted, and promised something extra special at dinnertime. Jane went to her bedroom and sat, with Foch beside her. A bath, she thought: a long, hot bath before her guest arrived. So much to think about, so much to regret. A bath was the only way to make such things tolerable. She turned on hot water, poured bath salts lavishly, and went back to her bedroom to undress. Foch yawned. 'You're no gentleman,' she told him.

Truett tapped at the door. 'Mr Bower, madam,' she said.

'I'm in my bath,' Jane called, '– or about to be. Tell him to call again in half an hour.'

That made her bath even better, and the water was so hot she yelped as she got in. Cautiously she leaned back, then soaped the sponge.

So much to think about, she thought: Catherine and Jay, Lady Mangan, Andy. Yet if you took the saddhu's viewpoint there was nothing to think about. Catherine would marry, Lady Mangan would stay crippled, Andy would or would not go to prison. It was all in their karma, their fate: and nothing either God or man could do could alter that. Which is why I shall never be a Hindu, she thought: grateful to the saddhu though I am. If I accepted my karma I wouldn't even be in this delicious bath. I'd be shivering in four inches of tepid water in that awful bathroom in Offley Villas, which I used to share with Mummy, and now even Mummy doesn't live there; but then Mummy too had refused to accept her karma.

Andy would never accept his. If he escaped prison he would fight on, and if he went to prison he would be broken; but he would never bend. He must not go back to prison. Other people might be inconvenienced, even hurt, if he were to be kept out, but if so other people must lump it. Andy was not only family; he was, she realised, necessary for the good of his country, just as the goad is necessary to the ox. It was what made him different from all the others. The goad and the ox knew each other.

She stirred the water with her foot. It was cool enough now not to sting. Jay and Catherine, she thought. Bluebeard and Snow White. Was that really how it was? Surely Catherine had come to terms long enough since with her innocence: accepted it under the plane tree in her garden? That would have been fine – if it had been the point. But it wasn't. Catherine had shelved the problem of her maidenhead as unimportant. The only matters of urgency in the world were her grandmother – and how soon her twin would get to her to share her grief. Compared with her grandmother and her twin, Jay Bower was no more than an acquaintance: rich, eligible, indulgent, but not part of the family: not one of one's own.

Lady Mangan . . . Jane pulled the plug from the bath, and drew the shower curtain, turned the shower on full, and the water hit hard. It was a very American shower. Lady Mangan might well have invoked her karma, she thought, but she had winked instead. Like Grandma she would have found the idea of karma as indulgent, if not downright sinful. She turned off the shower and put on a bathrobe, to walk into her bedroom. Foch looked at her, then away.

'You can be as snooty as you like,' she said, 'but it's your turn tomorrow.'

Truett tapped at her door. Mr Bower was on the line again. Jane picked up the phone by her bed.

'You don't make it easy to say thank you,' he said.

'Are you saying thank you?'

'Certainly.'

'Whatever for?'

'Taking care of Catherine. I really appreciate that. Now listen. I can't give her dinner tonight. I'm dining at the House of Lords. – But I could stop by and pick her up later. Take her dancing. The Savoy or somewhere.'

'No,' said Jane.

'What do you mean, no?'

'Lionel's at a party with his friends, and I can't possibly find another man at such short notice.'

'Who asked you to?'

'In a sense you could say Lord and Lady Mangan, and her grandmother. Perhaps even her twin brother. I'm her chaperon.'

'But that's ridiculous.' She said nothing. 'I wouldn't do anything like that. I'm going to *marry* her.'

Jane said, 'I don't suppose they think you would. But this is the aristocracy, my dear. Substance doesn't matter a damn. Form is everything.'

Silence, then at last Bower said, 'Is it OK if I stop by for a nightcap?'

'Not too late,' said Jane. 'She's had a very tiring journey, and she's still feeling the strain of what happened to her grandmother.'

'God yes,' said Bower. 'I keep forgetting how vulnerable she is.'

'Not like us,' said Jane.

'Hell no.'

She found herself wishing that his agreement had not been quite so wholehearted.

Bob called; the least civilised of all her friends. Catherine was still in her room, changing for dinner, and Bob showed no desire to linger, but he had had a letter from Andy, and it worried him. When Jane read it, she understood why. Andy was depressed, which was not surprising, but he also resented bitterly the third of Jane's articles, the one about Mike Deegan. He thought it made him into a sort of Judas. Would he be in order to ask Jane to arrange some sort of retraction?

'At least he asked for your advice,' said Jane.

'And that's the most worrying thing of the lot,' said Bob. 'Andy needing a second opinion – and from me of all people.'

'But he agreed to this when we first talked about it,' said Jane. 'You were there.'

'Certainly he did,' Bob said. 'But now he's back up there. If you ask me he's been got at by some of his own side.'

A letter from one of the dons? she wondered. A visit from Burrowes or Deegan himself? Andy had a very tender conscience.

'Newspapers aren't all that keen on retractions,' she said at last, 'even when they're in the wrong. And this time we were right – for the most part. And anyway if we retract it's as good as saying we lied about Deegan.'

'Which would mean that he's on Deegan's side,' said Bob. 'Sound grand in court that would. But you can see how miserable he is.'

'Tell him he can be miserable in prison or miserable out of it,' said Jane. 'But if he wants to stay out he'll have to stand by what I say.'

Bob looked up at her then. There was surprise in his eyes, and wariness too. 'You're a hard one, aren't you?' he said.

'When I have to be.'

Just like my mother, she thought, and Mummy was right as usual when she told me I was very much her child.

'I have a meeting soon with a man who could stop this court case of Andy's – if he can be made to.'

'And you can make him?'

'Only if Andy sticks by what he said. Tell him to hang on for just one more week. Surely he can chloroform his conscience till then?'

Bob winced. 'Hard isn't in it,' he said. 'All the same you're right, and I'll get a letter off to him and tell him so.'

Then Catherine came in. No nonsense about brown velvet and pearls. The dress she wore was of blue and white, demure, but elegantly cut, and she wore Jane's gold bangles on her arm, gold hoops in her ears. Bob shot to his feet like a private when his colonel comes in, she thought.

'Lady Catherine,' he said.

'Mr Patterson,' said Catherine. 'How nice to see you.'

At least she sounds as if she means it, thought Jane.

'I was sorry to hear about your trouble,' he said. 'I know how you must feel.'

'Do you?' Catherine asked.

'Aye,' said Bob. 'I do. I lost my father a few months back. He was a grand chap, wasn't he, Jane?'

'He was indeed,' said Jane.

'But that's not the same and I know it isn't. It just gives you an idea of what can happen, that's all. What I mean is – my grandma's still alive, and well, thank God, and I love her very much, and if anything happened to her – I reckon I know how you'd feel.'

'What would you do, Mr Patterson?' Catherine asked.

'Do?'

'If somebody blew up your grandmother's house and caused her to have a stroke.'

Bob thought for a moment. 'Nothing nice,' he said at last. Catherine smiled. 'Do sit down, Mr Patterson,' she said.

Jane rang for drinks. It seemed that Bob was going to stay for dinner.

He was good company for Catherine: close enough in age to make him a contemporary, but very much the business man, the man of affairs, from the world that linked with her fiancé's rather than her own, a world exciting in its novelty. He answered her questions in a way that made her laugh, and in the sitting room after dinner Catherine sipped her coffee and said: 'You know I can still remember that night when you danced with me in Felston. You had nothing then, had you?'

'Not a thing,' said Bob.

'And then you bobbed up in Cambridge, and you and my brother made that terrible little tick stand up for "God Save The King". You've come a long way, Mr Patterson.'

Bob smiled. 'But it isn't journey's end, Lady Catherine,' he said. 'Not by a long chalk.'

She was smiling at him again when Truett came in and announced, 'Mr Bower.'

Bower came into the room, checked for a moment, then walked up to Jane. 'Nice of you to ask me here,' he said.

'Not at all,' said Jane. 'Let me give you some brandy.' She began to pour cognac as Bower went to Catherine.

'Hi,' he said.

'Jaybird,' said Catherine, 'how sweet.' She offered her cheek for Bower to kiss. 'You remember Mr Patterson, don't you?'

'He should,' said Bob. 'He used to pay my wages not all that long ago. How are you, sir?'

He offered Bower the cognac Jane had poured, and Jane thought that he'd done very well until that last word, that 'sir'. It only served to emphasise the difference in their ages.

'Fine, just fine,' said Bower. 'And you?'

'Mustn't grumble,' said Bob.

'That means he's coining it,' Bower said. 'Maybe I should resent that. The more people listen to the radio, the less they buy newspapers. But it would take more than that to make the two of us fall out. Wouldn't it, Bob?'

Bob blinked for a moment, then said, 'Why quarrel when we can both make money?'

And there you had them, thought Jane. One relaxed, the other tense, and both equally dangerous.

Bower turned to Catherine and began to ask questions about her grandmother as Bob finished his brandy. Time he was off, he said. He hadn't meant to interrupt a private party. Meticulously he took his leave of Catherine and Bower, then Jane walked him to the door. 'I'll write to Andy first thing,' he said. 'Thanks, Jane.' He kissed her cheek.

'Give my love to Grandma,' said Jane.

'I always do,' he said.

In her drawing room it seemed that Catherine and Bower had run out of conversation. It was not a problem that Bower encountered often.

'Nothing wrong with young Patterson, is there?' he asked.

That 'young' could be a mistake, too, thought Jane, but all she said was, 'Andy's got stage fright, but it isn't serious. All will be well.' To Catherine she said, 'Bob's brother's in a bit of trouble. Not of his making, I need hardly say. He's been accused of a crime he didn't commit, and the *Daily World* is helping him – which means that Jay is.'

Catherine gave him her best smile of the night. 'Oh Jaybird,' she said. 'What a darling man you are.'

'That's what the *Daily World* is for,' he said.

'That and making money,' said Catherine.

Bower looked up from the cigar he was about to light.

'We're all for that,' he said.

'Even me,' said Jane. 'Even if I do give it all to Felston.'

'Which reminds me,' said Bower. 'I need a couple more pieces from you – just to ram it home. "My Friend The Parson", should go well.'

'Canon Messeter?'

'Give us his DSO and all that. What school he went to. You Limeys love a gent.'

'He'll hate it,' said Jane.

'It'll keep him out of prison,' said Bower, 'so I guess he'll learn to live with it. . . . Does he have a dog?'

'Of course he doesn't have a dog,' said Jane.

'Whyever not?' Catherine asked.

'Because he can't afford one,' said Jane.

'Good God!' said Lady Catherine Hilyard.

For the first time, thought Jane, she is learning what poverty means, and tried her best not to smile.

'Do me a piece about "My Dream Dog",' said Bower, 'and why he can't have one. You Limeys love a dog almost as much as you love a gent.'

'You're very American this evening,' said Jane.

'I need the practice,' said Bower. 'I'm going there.'

'Before our wedding?' Catherine was incredulous.

'I'm coming back before our wedding too,' said Bower.

'New York?' Jane asked.

'New England anyway. I want to see my father – or rather I have to. We've got things to talk about.'

'Give my regards to Erika.'

Catherine went over to the gramophone and began to turn over the records.

Jane said softly, 'Is everything all right?'

'Why shouldn't it be?'

'"I want to" became "I have to".'

'And to think I once wanted to marry you,' said Bower.

'Are you glad I turned you down?'

'Hell yes,' said Bower. 'I bet you even sleep with your eyes open.' Jane chuckled. 'How's my bride to be?'

'A little easier,' said Jane. 'It's just as well she came to me. She needs someone to talk to.'

'She needs you,' said Bower. 'She's lucky she's got you. Her mother's not much, and her father's nothing at all. And now her grandmother needs her. You're the only one she's got left to lean on.'

'There's Piers.'

Catherine put on a record and came over to Bower.

'Come and dance with me,' she said. 'Just once. I'm quite sure Granny wouldn't mind.'

He rose, and took her in his arms, and the record played 'I Want To Be Happy'.

## 31

Two days later, Bower sailed for America. Before he left he'd given precise instructions to Jane, and to Don Cook, his editor, how to carry on with the Andy Patterson campaign. Jane asked Cook if he approved of it.

'Very nice,' said Cook. 'Righteous indignation's always a good circulation builder. Mind you, I wouldn't mind a good trunk murder as well.'

As always, she could never really be sure whether he was joking or not. Perhaps he couldn't either.

Time to go to see Dick Lambert. 19, Gregg Street, Fulham, he'd said; Flat D. She took a taxi to the top of the street and walked, in case there were nosy neighbours. It was that sort of street: never reaching out for anything much, and rather too satisfied with what it had got. Just the place for nosy neighbours. Biggish houses, five or six bedrooms if you counted the attics, with a scrap of garden front and back. Converted into flats, most of them, but the gardens were neat, the windows clean, and the brass doorknobs shone.

Jane went into Number 19, and began to climb the stairs. Flat D was on the first floor. Nice door, she thought. Mahogany, and waxed till it shone. Even Truett would have approved. By the door was a visiting card: 'C. D. Roberts', she read, and stifled conjecture as none of her business. She tapped at the door instead. Lambert opened it at once, staring at her as he did so, but there was nothing in the least lustful in his look. He merely wants to make sure I'm not overdressed for Fulham, she thought. Nor am I. Grey suit from Harrods, a hat I forgot to throw away and my Felston handbag. I could pass for a native. And so could he, she thought. Blue suit, white collar, discreetly striped tie, worn bowler hat and umbrella.

'You broke your word to me,' he said.

'Dick, how lovely to see you again,' said Jane. 'How are you?'

'Well enough,' he said. 'And you?'

'Never better.' She drew off her gloves and looked about the room. Quite a nice room. Not a great deal of money, but what there was had been well spent. Three-seater settee, two armchairs, and at the other end of the room a dining alcove just big enough for four, and a door that led almost certainly to a separate bedroom: perhaps even a separate bath. There was a sofa table too, rather a good one, its top covered with photographs: groups for the most part, gilded youth enjoying itself, but one alone, the head and shoulders of a girl quite young, and more than adequately pretty. Jane nodded to it.

'Is that C. D. Roberts?' she asked.

Dick Lambert glowered. There was no other word for it.

'Yes,' he said. 'It is.'

'She's pretty,' said Jane. 'Her flat's very nice.'

'She's my secretary,' said Lambert. 'I tell you that because it would be child's play for you, or Bower, or anybody else on the *Daily World* to find it out.'

'May I sit down?' said Jane.

'Oh for God's sake,' said Lambert, and then: 'Yes, yes. Sit down, please. I apologise. Excuse me.'

She sat, and ferreted in her handbag for cigarettes, lighter, cigarette holder. It would not help Lambert to feel better towards her but it wasn't meant to. She wanted him on edge.

'When I first came in you were about to accuse me of something,' she said.

'Aye, by God, I was,' said Lambert. 'I told you there were to be no more articles in the *Daily World* – or had you forgotten?'

'Certainly not,' said Jane. 'You made rather a thing about it.'

'And you agreed,' Lambert said, 'then went on to break your word. Lied, in fact.'

'Nonsense,' said Jane.

'You've got the face to deny it?'

'What you did,' said Jane, 'was give me a series of commands to which I said nothing. *Then* you said, "Do I make myself clear?" and *I* said, "As crystal." But I didn't make you any promises.'

'You can wriggle all you like but you broke your word,' Lambert said.

'Nonsense,' Jane said again and picked up her gloves. 'Really, Dick, if you thought I'd sit here and be a target while you sling mud – I'd better be off. I have an article to write.'

'No,' said Lambert. 'Wait.'

'Wait please?'

'All right, damn it,' said Lambert. 'Please. Excuse me. Sit down and I'll try to explain.'

Really, she thought, after Jay Bower the poor man's a pushover. She sat, and looked up at him like a schoolgirl looking at an adored instructor.

'This whole business is – it's wrong,' he said at last.

'What whole business?'

He looked furious then, and she said quickly, 'Dick, listen to me. Either we're precise about what we're talking about, or there's no point in talking.'

He pushed a hand through his hair. Suddenly he looked very tired. 'All right,' he said. 'That's fair. We don't want any misunderstandings. What I'm talking about is the riot in Felston Market Place.' She nodded. 'The police are satisfied that Andy Patterson started it.'

'The police wanted a scapegoat and Andy was the nearest,' she said. 'Go on.'

'The police don't lie,' he said.

'We both know that's not true,' she said, and fitted another cigarette into her holder. 'Stick to the facts, my dear.'

Lambert flushed a dark and ugly red. 'For whatever reason you and the *Daily World* take up Andy's case,' he said, 'and to get what you want you start a kind of moral blackmail.'

'I?' she said. 'The *Daily World*? Who did we blackmail? When? Where?'

'There's only the two of us here so I'll tell you,' he said. 'All those hints about goings-on at Cambridge. And one of the chaps involved has a sister who's married to a cabinet minister, as well you know. You're setting it up to be a cabinet scandal. You even wrote a letter about it to that friend of yours. That Daisy. Why aren't there any scandals in politics any more? You just leave it to me, Daisy darling, and I'll find some. That's what you were saying.'

'What sort of scandals?' said Jane.

Lambert looked away. 'You know,' he said.

'Cards on the table,' said Jane. 'Face up.'

Lambert took a deep breath. He hated what he had to say. 'Homosexuals,' he said at last. 'Running loose in Cambridge colleges. Corrupting the young. Besmirching the Labour Party. That's what you're on about – and it's got to stop.'

'No it doesn't,' said Jane. 'Not unless somebody sues me – and the *World*.'

'Likely isn't it?' said Lambert.

'Not at all likely,' said Jane, 'because it's true. But even if somebody did find the guts to sue me, they'd have a hard time proving it.'

'Hasn't it occurred to you that your brother's one of them?'

'Of course it has,' said Jane.

'You'd risk your own brother?'

'Francis would never sue.' Jane smiled. 'Believe me I know. He's much too fond of the quiet life.'

'He could still wind up in prison.'

'Homosexuals take that risk every day of their lives.'

'Who told you that?' Lambert asked.

'He did.' I lie of course, she told herself. It had been darling Lionel. But I'd never risk him.

'There's talk already. It'll get worse. You're damaging the Party. Damn it I thought you were on our side. You did your bit for Felston after all.'

'These men care nothing for Felston – or the Labour Party.'

'Oh come now,' he said.

'They're Communists.'

'They're men of the Left,' said Lambert. 'They share our ideals.'

'Felston doesn't think so. Not all of it.'

'You still keep in touch then?' Jane nodded. 'And yet you can write this – this innuendo, and those rubbishy letters to Daisy. You even drag a parson into it. Even a bloody dog.'

'It's what sells papers,' said Jane. 'I forgive you for the "bloody" by the way.' Lambert flushed.

'It just slipped out,' he said.

'Of course.'

Lambert tried again. 'My Party needs these men, Jane. We need their brains, their ideas, their vision if you like. There's more than one road to Socialism, of course there is – but these are the men who'll know what to do when we get there.'

'I've written five articles,' said Jane. 'I've only mentioned them in one.'

'Does that mean you won't mention them again?'

'Of course not.'

Lambert sighed. 'The cabinet minister's furious,' he said. 'And his wife's worried sick.'

'I can hardly blame her,' said Jane, 'but there is a way out, you know.'

'What is it you want?' said Lambert.

'That you drop all charges against Andy Patterson.'

'Out of the question,' said Lambert. 'How can I possibly? That's the Attorney General's business. I can't just walk in and tell him what to do, any more than I can tell Felston's Chief Constable to forget the whole thing.'

'What you say is not entirely true,' said Jane. 'What you really mean is you don't want to do it: not that you can't.'

'I don't want to interfere with the course of justice,' he said. 'It's wrong.'

Because he means it, she thought, I will answer him in kind: 'As wrong as sending an innocent man to prison?'

'He's not there yet,' said Lambert, then before she could answer he said, 'All right. I know things are bad for him. . . . You are quite sure he's innocent?'

'Quite sure.'

'Then I'll have to do what you ask. But no more articles.'

'Not for a week,' she said.

'You're not giving me much time,' said Lambert.

'You don't need much time. A couple of confidential chats: that's all it will take, surely?' Reluctantly he nodded. Even the thought of those confidential chats was hateful to him.

'There'll be something in it for you – or rather your government. Sort of a quid pro quo.'

'What'll that be?'

'A little piece in the *World* to say how quickly you acted to see that a wrong was righted. A government ever vigilant to protect the rights of even the humblest.'

'I'd want to see it first,' he said.

'Of course.' She offered her hand and he took it. 'We have an agreement then?'

'Aye,' he said. 'Only call it a deal, because that's what it is.'

Jane rose and began to pull on her gloves.

'This is a pretty room,' she said. 'Thank Miss Roberts for letting me use it.'

His face assumed a wary look, one that she had never seen on him before. 'I'll do that,' he said. 'Now if you don't mind I'm going to ask you to go out first. I'd rather we weren't seen together.'

'Of course,' said Jane, and then: 'I honestly think you'll go a long way in politics. I know you deserve to.'

First the stick, then the carrot, she thought, as she walked up Gregg Street, but it was true. Dick Lambert did deserve to get on, because he still wanted to help people. Needed to, even. It was part of him. But goodness how quickly he had learned to enjoy the perquisites too. She wondered what C. D. Roberts's first name was. Cecilia? Cynthia? Chloe?

She arrived home to find that Catherine was already back from shopping. 'Goodness,' she said. 'How – how monochrome you look. Not like you at all.'

'These are my working clothes,' said Jane.

'Have you been working?'

'That's what your fiancé calls it.'

'Jaybird would never make you dress like that,' she said. 'Come and see what I've bought.' It was a riding crop.

'You have been busy,' said Jane. 'What about all those curtains and bath towels and things?'

'I found I can't make up my mind on my own, and you were working,' Catherine said. 'And anyway Emily Plumtree phoned from Woodstock – got your number from Eaton Square – and offered us a couple of days' hunting.'

'Us?'

'I said I couldn't possibly go anywhere without you, just at the moment.' Suddenly the airy manner faltered. 'It's true, you know.' Jane waited. 'And we could take out Bridget's Boy and

Bridie – they're not all that far away. Perhaps even Bridget herself if she's not feeling her years.'

'And always supposing they're up to it.'

'Oh they are,' said Catherine. 'I promise you. I phoned Mr Benson at the farm and he told me so himself.'

'I could do with a couple of days' hunting,' said Jane. 'Where will we stay?'

'Emily's got masses of room and she's dying to meet you. First meet of the year, too. Oh darling, it will be fun.'

'We'll drive there,' said Jane. 'In my new car.'

'What new car?'

'The one I've been promising myself ever since I drove in yours.'

So they drove to Oxford in what Signor Bugatti had described as one of Mr Bentley's very fast lorries, and that just about described it, thought Jane. It was a pig to drive, but it was very fast. Catherine adored it. She adored the trip to Oxfordshire too. Emily Plumtree was a chubby, middle-aged widow with a passion for hunting that matched Catherine's own, and a delight in newspaper gossip that made Jane a very welcome guest.

'And your horses,' she said to Jane. 'Benson and a groom brought them over this morning. They're in tremendous shape. Even the old girl looks a devil to go. Do come and see.'

They went to the stables. Benson really had done a good job, she thought, although one day, maybe even half a day, would be enough for Bridget. But her offspring looked as if they could go for a week.

'I like the gelding,' Emily Plumtree said. 'No chance of selling him, I suppose?'

'None.' Jane hesitated. 'I'm sorry, that was rude. But I'd much sooner keep him.'

Emily Plumtree chuckled. 'Who wouldn't?' she said, and then: 'I've ordered dinner early. We'll be up by six.'

The first day was perfect. Like something out of Surtees, she thought. Cold, crisp air, the going firm, and Bridget glad to be back doing what she did best. All Jane had to do was hold her back to a canter, and give her her head when she came to a fence. There was nothing she or anybody else could teach Bridget about taking fences, but all the same she handed her over to Benson's groom at mid-morning, and took out Bridget's Boy instead.

The gelding was a match for the Bentley, she thought. Just as strong, just as pig-headed, and with the same turn of speed. It took all her strength and cunning to control him. This was a horse that deserved rather better a hunt than this, she thought: farmers, lawyers, doctors, even the squire, mounted on horses that were Ford Model T's to Bridget's Boy's Bentley. She must ask the major if he was ready for a point to point: perhaps even an outing over hurdles. By the end of the day she was exhausted. They had found and killed just before sunset, and it had taken every trick she possessed to stop the gelding from over-running the hounds. Catherine said that Bridie was a wonderful mare, but her eyes were on Bridget's Boy.

'Piers would be after you for that one,' she said. 'So am I.'

Jane said firmly, 'You won't get him.'

'But I may ride him?'

'If you ask him nicely.'

But not the next day. Next day the hunt didn't meet, though it brought its own excitements. Emily Plumtree's copy of the *Daily World* trumpeted the news: Justice Triumphs. Charges Against Our Andy Withdrawn. 'Today,' the editorial said, 'our government (in the person of its Attorney General) displayed a care and compassion entirely British. . . .' All the charges against Andy had been dropped. He was a free man once more. 'A government that can make decisions such as these,' boomed the *World*, 'deserves our warmest support and applause. . . . Common man . . . no class distinction . . . momentous decision.' Don Cook had rather laid it on with a trowel, she thought, but politicians had no objection to trowels: not even Dick Lambert. Cautiously, mindful of aching limbs, she relaxed in her chair and read it through again. It seemed that the bargain had been kept.

The day afterwards they met again, and this time Catherine asked for Bridget's Boy. Jane could see no reason to refuse her. If anything Catherine was a better rider than she was, and in far better practice. Besides, it was time she tried out Bridie, and so she agreed. The trouble was that better rider or not, Catherine was far more reckless, and put Bridget's Boy at a fence the gelding decided just wasn't on, and proved his point by throwing her at the last minute. She landed on iron-hard ground and her left knee slammed against a tree stump. When she tried to stand up she found she couldn't and had to wait until a couple of grooms happened along, and went at once to phone an ambulance.

Jane found out about it when she rode in at last. Bridie had done well, she thought, though not so well as her brother. She was mildly surprised to find Bridget's Boy in the stable – until Emily Plumtree's head groom told her why; then she dashed for the house, to find Catherine in her nightgown, stretched out in bed, an ominous lump in the bedclothes showing where they were lifted from her knee.

'Of all the damn fools,' she said.

'I beg your pardon?' said Jane.

'Me,' said Catherine. 'To put your lovely horse at a fence like that in such a stupid way. I deserve this. I really do. I might have killed him.'

'Darling, what happened?' said Jane, and Catherine told her, and there was no doubt that Catherine had been stupid. On the other hand the horse had a kind of inevitable power that made one think he could do anything.

'He'll get over it,' said Jane. 'You both will.'

'I won't get over this,' said Catherine. 'Take a look.'

Jane drew back the bedclothes. Catherine's left leg, copiously bandaged, rested on a sort of basketwork cradle of a kind Jane hadn't seen since the war.

'Oh my God,' she said. 'It's not broken, is it?'

'Look at my knee,' Catherine said. It had swollen to the size of a cannon ball. 'Nothing's broken,' said Catherine, 'but I put my knee out and some doctor or other put it back again. I'm afraid I yelled rather a lot.'

'I've no doubt he'll understand.'

Catherine glowered. 'This isn't funny,' she said.

'No love,' said Jane, 'but you're not exactly a country doctor's typical patient, are you?'

'I suppose not,' said Catherine, and looked at Jane again. Mannish hacking jacket and jodhpurs, and yet she looked as feminine as if they were a ball gown. She glowered at her knee.

'The thing is,' she said, 'that it may take rather a long time to go down.'

'You mean –'

'I shall probably have to march down the aisle on crutches, if not a bath chair.'

Jane waited. She was quite sure there was more to come.

'Jaybird sent me a cable from the *Mauretania*,' Catherine said. 'He'll be home in three days.'

'But how did he know you're here?'

'He didn't,' said Catherine. 'Piers told me. *He's* home already. Truett told him where to call. When I told him he couldn't stop laughing.'

'Laughing?'

'The thought of me coming off. He thinks it's a hoot. If he tells that Coupland bitch I'll kill him, and so I told him. Oh I'm so *bloody* miserable.' Suddenly and disconcertingly she began to cry, and Jane somehow managed to get her arms around her without hurting her leg.

'There there,' she said. 'It'll be all right. You'll see.' Which was ridiculous, but what else could she say? and at last the sobs diminished to shuddering sighs.

'Jaybird will be furious,' the girl said at last.

'You can handle that.' Catherine looked up at her.

'Yes,' she said, 'I suppose I can. But as for Piers laughing at me –'

'Never mind,' said Jane. 'He'll be off to Ireland soon.'

'That's just it,' said Catherine. 'He won't. Granny's told him not to. She's coming here instead.'

'Is she fit for a sea voyage?' Jane asked.

'I doubt it,' said Catherine. 'But she isn't going to take a sea voyage. She's going to fly.'

'Good God,' said Jane. 'They'll let her?'

'I don't who know "they" are,' said Catherine, 'but if you mean the doctors and my parents – they'll do as they're told – like everybody else. Anyway Granny says there can't be all that much to flying from Ireland. You do it all the time.'

'Doesn't sound much of a compliment,' said Jane.

'I don't suppose it was meant to be. She's hopping mad, which means she must be lots better. . . . She's really rather wonderful, isn't she?'

'She really is,' said Jane.

'All the same that damn twin of mine better have no more fits of the giggles.' There was no doubt that Piers's laughter meant far more to her than Jay Bower's wrath.

# 32

THEY HIRED AN ambulance to take Catherine back to South Terrace, with Jane following in the Bentley, a convoy impressive enough to bring all her servants out to the street, and quite a lot of other people's servants too. But at least she'd let Don Cook know, and it had appeared in the next day's 'Wicked World' column. 'Lady Catherine Hilyard, the beautiful fiancée of our proprietor, sustained a slight accident on the hunting field. "All my fault," she said, laughing merrily. "Bridget's Boy was faultless." Bridget's Boy is a hunter belonging to our contributor Miss Jane Whitcomb, the well-known philanthropist and script writer.' . . . And the even better known scapegoat, thought Jane, once Jay Bower gets his hands on me.

But it was Piers she saw first. He came at cocktail time, with roses and champagne. Jane mixed gin and vermouth as Lionel had taught her, and Piers sipped cautiously.

'Good Lord,' he said. 'That's delicious.'

'There is no need to sound quite so surprised.' He nodded towards his gifts.

'Sorry,' he said. 'This is a joint offering, by the way. Me and brother Desmond. – But I didn't think she was quite ready for Desmond yet. How is she?'

'Resting,' said Jane. 'Feeling her aches and pains a bit. I called in a specialist from Harley Street and he prodded rather. Had to, poor man. I say – where on earth did she learn all those dreadful words?'

'The hunting field,' said Piers. 'Mind you – she doesn't understand the meaning of half of them. Where did you?'

'The Somme and Ypres mostly,' said Jane, 'and I understand the meaning of all of them. She doesn't want any jokes, Piers.'

'Jokes?'

'About falling off horses. If her knee doesn't heal she may have to postpone the wedding.'

'No jokes,' said Piers at once. 'Not from me, anyway. Was her language really bad?'

'Foul,' said Jane, and Piers grinned, delighted. 'Truett gave notice. Truett's my parlourmaid, by the way. She was brought up a Baptist, she tells me.'

'I'll have a word with her then,' said Piers.

'You?'

'Certainly,' said Piers. 'Catherine's my sister. And anyway, I've a sergeant who's a Baptist. Damn good man. Very devout.'

'Doesn't that make life rather difficult for him?'

'Not really,' said Piers. 'He's also battalion boxing champion. Middleweight. . . . Did Catherine tell you about Granny?'

'She said she was flying over.'

'It worries me a bit,' Piers said. 'Not the flying – Granny would swim over if she felt like it. It's why she's doing it.'

'I need rather more than that, Piers.'

'There's bags of time before Catherine's wedding. Why is she coming? Because she wants to be here? – or to keep me out of Ireland? I think she knows something.'

'How could she?' said Jane. 'An old woman, seriously ill –'

'They'll be in and out, all the cronies,' said Piers. 'Servants, neighbours. And all with tongues going wag wag wag. If they had something – even if they didn't know it themselves, Granny will know. Ah well – she'll tell me when she gets here – or she won't.'

'When will that be?'

'Next week. Desmond and I are to go out to Croydon to meet her – and Mummy and Daddy of course.'

Attendant lord and lady indeed, thought Jane.

'Will Catherine see me now do you think?'

'Not now,' Jane said. 'She's sleeping, I hope. Come round in the morning and gravely sympathise.'

'Be a pleasure,' said Piers. He got to his feet. 'Tell her not to start the champers without me.' He looked at his watch. 'Good

Lord,' he said, 'I'll be late for my appointment.'

'Not a word to her,' said Jane. 'Not even a hint. Or Catherine will kill you, she told me to tell you.'

Again Piers grinned. 'Of course not,' he said. 'We're keeping this one in the family. Just let me ring for Truett will you, then I'll speak to her in the hall.' He took her hand, bowed over it and was gone. He really was a formidable young man, she thought. Poor Brenda Coupland, what has she let herself in for?

He did come back the next morning, and for many mornings after that, playing acrimonious games of backgammon, ludo, and even snap, as if they were back in the nursery, but never once did he tease Catherine about her horsemanship. Sometimes he brought their elder brother, Desmond, but she preferred him to come alone, no matter how loud their quarrels. Jane began to feel like a maiden aunt in her declining years, until Lovell's cable arrived. 'Home on Thursday, Regards. Lovell', she read. Just that. It seemed to be enough. Jane looked at Truett, who had brought the cable.

'Do I take it that you have withdrawn your notice?' she asked.

'Oh miss,' said Truett, 'I was hoping you'd forgotten. Poor Lady Catherine – she must have been delirious.'

'Who told you that?'

'Her brother, miss. He explained it all to me. He's ever so nice, miss. I mean I made a right fool of myself, but never once did he say so.'

You and Brenda Coupland, thought Jane, but had no time to develop the idea. Almost at once Truett was back again, to announce Mr Bower. He came quickly into the room. He was in a towering rage, his impatience all too evident as he waited for Truett to leave.

'Jay, my dear,' said Jane, 'what a delightful surprise. How are you?' She offered her hand, and because Truett was there he had to take it.

'Shall I bring the ice, miss?' Truett asked.

'No cocktails for me,' said Bower.

'For me, then,' said Jane. 'Thank you, Truett.' When the parlourmaid had gone, she said, 'Really, Jay.'

'Never mind the etiquette,' said Bower. 'I want to know what the hell you think you're playing at.'

'Chaperoning your bride to be,' said Jane. 'What else would I be playing at?'

'Chaperoning?' said Bower. 'You damn nearly killed her.'

'Please don't shout, Jay,' said Jane. 'This is not Madison Square Garden.'

'You had no right to take her hunting.'

'Any more than she had a right to take me hunting,' said Jane. 'It was her idea, by the by.' Truett came in with a bowl of ice. 'Thank you,' said Jane. 'I'll mix the drinks myself.' Truett left, disappointed, and Jane began to construct her martini.

'You had no right,' Bower said again. 'There was nobody else to turn to so I left her in your charge and you damn near got her killed. As it is it looks like you've screwed up my wedding. Do you suppose I went back States-side for fun? It was business. I told you it was. If you bothered to listen. I *had* to go and why not? I thought I could rely on you.'

On and on and on like a crazy man. Trust and innocence and betrayal, over and over as she sipped her martini.

'No right,' he was saying. 'No goddam right.' They were back to that again. – 'I hate to say this but it seems to me you've turned into a selfish bitch who thinks more of her next martini than the girl I trusted you with. Did it never occur to you –'

It was then that she slapped his face, a quick and vicious blow with all her weight behind it and a sound like a whip crack. For a moment he was silent, then, 'Well,' he said, 'you punch your weight. I'll say that for you.' Jane made no answer, because she couldn't. It was ridiculous, but she had no idea how she felt, none at all: except that she was glad that the tirade had stopped.

Bower said, 'I'll change my mind, if I may. I'd like a martini.'

'Certainly.' She filled a glass for him, topped up her own.

'That's the first time you hit me,' he said. 'I ought to drink to that.'

'I suppose most of your women do, sooner or later,' she said.

The fist of his free hand clenched, and she knew that if he wanted to hit her, he would. A houseful of women couldn't stop him. But he gulped at his martini instead, then replenished his glass from the shaker.

'Boy you take your chances,' he said.

'You don't leave me much choice,' said Jane.

'No,' he said, 'I guess I don't. What I said about you was all wrong. Stupid and wrong. I'm sorry.'

It was then that she realised the emotion she felt. It was pity. 'I'm sorry I hit you,' she said.

He shrugged. 'Like you say – it's happened before. I thought I'd learned to control myself, only –'

'Something happened in New England.'

'You're clever,' he said, 'but not that clever. Nothing happened in New England. Nothing I wanted, anyway.'

'Your parents won't come to your wedding?'

'My parents won't do a damn thing for me, and Sister Erika's getting her money, so don't bother her. Marriage is a bourgeois institution and she's got a revolution to start. But she sent you comradely greetings.'

'What on earth are they?'

'God knows,' he said. 'I'm just the messenger boy. . . . I really am sorry, Jane.'

'It's all right,' she said. 'Honestly.' There was a lot more to this – whatever it was – than persuading his parents to attend his wedding, but he wasn't going to discuss it with her. Nor should he. Catherine was the one he should discuss it with, though she doubted whether he would.

'Am I still working for you?' she asked.

'Why sure.' He even sounded surprised, but then Jay was a remarkable man.

'Because if I am I think you ought to see this,' she said, and took an envelope from her handbag, handed it to him. Bower took out the single sheet of paper, and read it once, then again.

Dear Miss Whitcomb [he read],

You are quite right to say that Andrew Patterson is innocent so far as the Felston Riot goes. The man you want is Tom Lynch from Eggleston.

And that was it. No signature, no nom de plume. Just a straightforward betrayal. Typewritten by somebody who didn't type for a living, with the same kind of typing on the envelope. Newcastle postmark.

'Eggleston?' he asked.

'About ten miles from Felston,' said Jane, 'and very similar. A little smaller, that's all.'

Bower sat down and took out his cigar case. All his own troubles were forgotten. This, after all, could be a story.

'Think it's true?'

She shrugged. 'I can't answer that till I know something about Tom Lynch.'

'What do you think?' he asked. 'Put the stringer on it?'

Mills, the Newcastle stringer, was a good enough reporter, but this might need something more.

Before she could answer he said, 'No. Not just Mills. We need a real snooper for this one.'

'You think it's worth it?'

'Could be,' he said. 'If there is a story it'll be a good one.'

'The *Daily World* Unmasks The Man Behind The Riot.'

'Sure,' he said. 'It would be nice to know who the Judas is as well.'

'Mr Pinner,' she said. 'He's the one we need.'

'Who in hell's Mr Pinner?'

'He's a private detective,' she said. 'He helped me to trace the Pattersons. He knows a good firm of private detectives in Newcastle.'

'Discreet?'

Jane remembered Mr Pinner's investigation of Major Routledge. 'Absolutely,' she said.

'You handle it then. Give him a week. If he can't come up with something by then we'll pay him for his time. If he does we'll scoop the *Depress* and the *Wail*.' He's grinning as if it's his birthday, she thought, after all that misery. Let's try not to spoil it.

'What did they tell you about Catherine's accident?' she asked.

The smile vanished. 'Don told me,' he said. 'Displaced knee-cap, severe swelling. We may have to postpone the wedding.'

'The specialist thinks otherwise. He thinks she'll be fine – if she stays away from horses for a while.'

'She will. Is he any good?'

'According to Harriet Watson he's the best.'

'He'll have to do then.' Bower got to his feet. The anxious look was back. 'Are you sure I can't see her?'

'Turn your face to the light.'

He did so, and she examined him carefully, from very close,

but still felt only pity. The mark of her blow was gone. 'I'll go and see,' she said.

'Just a minute.' She waited. 'Have you heard from the Coast?'

'Hollywood? No. Am I about to?'

'I should think so. The script's been OK'd and they've started casting. They've even signed up flyers for some airplane sequence or other. Looks like it's going to be a big one.' But you haven't seen a script, thought Jane. I bet Charles Lovell has. 'I wish you luck,' Jay Bower said.

She preceded him up the stairs.

The next day she telephoned Mr Pinner, and arranged for him to come to her at the *Daily World* building. It was a pleasant enough room, but its brown furniture and sporting prints were aggressively at odds with the clothes she wore. Mr Pinner blinked, and Jane knew why. All that was missing was the spittoon. He read the letter slowly and carefully.

'You want to trace this Tom Lynch?' he said. 'Shouldn't be too difficult.'

'We'd rather like to trace the person who wrote this letter as well.'

'Ah,' said Mr Pinner, 'that might be possible – then again it might not. I'll know better once I'm up there.'

'I'll let you get on with it, then,' said Jane, and Mr Pinner rose.

'I'll be in touch as soon as I've got something,' he said. 'If I may say so, it's nice to be working with you again, Miss Whitcomb.'

From the *World* office she went to her mother's house for lunch. Mrs Routledge listened carefully to the description of Catherine's accident.

'Poor child,' she said. 'But impetuous, one gathers. Wayward even. I take it the horse was undamaged?'

'Absolutely,' said Jane.

'I wonder if George might take a look at him? He sounds as if he might have potential, and George would know.'

'Yes please,' said Jane. 'Thank you, Mummy.'

Over coffee her mother said, 'Have you any other excitements for me? I have none, I fear, except that Gwendolyn Gwatkin is most anxious to meet your friend Daisy.'

'*Daisy*?' said Jane. 'Mummy you know that's impossible.'

'Gwendolyn believes that nothing is impossible,' her mother

said. 'You have to be very stupid indeed to believe that.' She bit cautiously into a petit four. 'Have you no news at all, child?'

'Well, yes,' said Jane, and told her mother about her encounter with Jay Bower.

'Money,' her mother said at once. 'Don't you agree?'

'Certainly,' said Jane. 'Only money – or the need of it – could make him like that. You know. Really quite awful, and then suddenly rather pathetic.'

'Certainly I know,' her mother said, 'but I never saw the need to relent at once.'

'Nor did I,' said Jane. 'When he was rude I slapped his face.'

'Excellent,' her mother said. 'It is a comfort to know that one's daughter has learned to look after herself. There is no danger of a relapse, I trust?'

'None whatsoever, Mummy.' Mrs Routledge threw back her head and trumpeted her laughter, and Jane began to tell her about the anonymous letter.

'Interesting,' her mother said. 'Extremely interesting, wouldn't you say?'

'You mean who sent it?'

'Certainly,' her mother said. 'There are two obvious factors, I think.' Jane waited. 'Who knew of the involvement of this man Lynch, and who disliked him enough to betray him?'

'There is perhaps a third,' said Jane. 'The reason why this person disliked Mr Lynch so much.'

'Your father would have been proud of you,' said her mother. 'I know that I am – and extremely grateful that you should discuss it with me.'

'Why not?' said Jane. 'It's the *World*'s business after all. We do owe Jay Bower something.'

'It is nice to have a brain,' said her mother, 'and even nicer to use it. I am grateful that you give me the opportunity. When does Mr Lovell return to us?'

Darling Mummy, thought Jane. You've never fought fair in your life.

'Two or three days,' she said.

'In time for the wedding,' said her mother. 'Oh, good. I do hope that all goes well for Mr Bower.'

'At the moment hoping is all we can do,' said Jane.

Her mother looked at her sharply, then began to discuss conditions at Wincanton. The major was not happy: far too firm. A trip to Oxfordshire to look at Bridget's Boy would do him good. Jane offered them both a lift there in the Bentley and she accepted at once.

'George can give us lunch at Oxford,' she said. 'The Mitre was always considered agreeable, and he can well afford it.'

There was a cable from Hollywood which Truett delivered on a silver salver. Truett rather enjoyed delivering cables from exotic places, and Hollywood rated very high among the places she considered exotic. . . . World Wide Studios. Where else? Murray Fisch was thrilled and delighted to tell her that the script was finished, the casting well advanced, and the flying sequences begun. Jay Bower had already told her that, though he had sounded neither thrilled nor delighted. But her good friend Murray (she knew that was what he was, because that was how he signed himself) was also delighted to tell her that Georgina Payne was on her way to Europe to observe the battlefields at first hand, and would no doubt call on Jane at the first opportunity. Jane found the idea of Georgie observing eleven-year-old battlefields hard to accept, but looked forward to seeing her.

In the meantime there was Mr Pinner to be considered. He telephoned her one evening from Newcastle and was concise and direct, as always. Eggleston had yielded a fair crop of Tom Lynches, ranging in age from six months to seventy-seven years, but only one that had shown any promise, although it would be fair to say that he was promising indeed.

Irish by extraction, as his name implied. There had been a massive emigration of Irishmen into the north east in the preceding century, when the demand for labour and muscle had seemed insatiable, but then the boom times passed, and the labour and muscle were still there, but not the demand. Tom Lynch was a miner and the son of a miner, who had served for two years with the Tyneside Irish in the war. Risen to sergeant, said Mr Pinner, which showed he was a leader, and in two years, which showed that he had brains, too. Good speaker, and a power in the local Miners' Lodge, their union. Mr Pinner thought he must be about thirty-seven, though he looked older, but then everybody in Eggleston looked older than their years.

Mr Pinner had used the local men, the two detectives and the stringer, to ask the questions, since his own London accent would have betrayed him at once. Tom Lynch was well liked; a bachelor who lodged with his widowed sister, a man whose only interest would seem to be politics, and yet apparently without political ambition of any kind. Twice asked to stand as Lodge Secretary, and declined: only last month asked to stand as councillor, and declined that too, and yet he was extremely knowledgeable. The stringer had asked him about his political views and he had quoted Marx, Engels, even Lenin, fluently, and as far as the stringer could tell, accurately.

'I hope our man didn't give himself away, Mr Pinner?' said Jane.

'No no.' Mr Pinner was indulgent. 'I suggested he talked to a lot of other chaps too, and very boring they were, he told me, though he got a piece out of it for his local paper.'

'Very nice,' said Jane. 'Was Lynch at the Felston riot?'

'It is not an easy question to ask,' Mr Pinner said. 'People here aren't exactly wishful to discuss it.'

'I suppose not.'

'But my guess is that he was. There's a lead I'm following. I can probably have an answer in say three days, if that isn't stretching things too far.'

'You carry on,' said Jane. 'Nothing on who sent the letter I suppose?'

'Not yet,' Mr Pinner said, 'but I've got a feeling. I really have. Play this one right and we'll find the answer.'

'I wish you luck then.'

'Thank you, miss.'

She hung up as Piers was admitted. Catherine was by then allowed to sit up from time to time, and they played chess together. It was every bit as acrimonious as their ludo had been. Before he went up to her she invited him on the expedition to look at Bridget's Boy. He was delighted.

'And in your Bentley, too,' he said.

'I shall drive,' Jane said firmly.

He grinned. 'Call on me if you're tired,' he said. 'Oh by the way, I had a telegram from Dublin. Granny and her courtiers fly over next week. You and Catherine will be summoned to the presence.' He went up the stairs as the phone rang again. It was Lionel, ringing to complain that she was neglecting him. . . . She invited him round for dinner next evening. Really, she couldn't stay in the rôle of chaperon for her entire life. Not yet, anyway.

The trip to Oxfordshire was a success. Her mother approved of Piers at once, and the major approved of the Rifle Brigade, so all was well. For his part Piers knew exactly how to flirt with a lady of her mother's age, and was massively impressed by the major's knowledge of horses. The meal went well. After it she drove them to Hyde's Farm, where the farmer, Benson, kept her horses. He directed her to the field where they were grazing. Jane left the others to inspect her treasures, while Benson appeared with a saddle, stirrups and reins, and she went into the farm to change into the jodhpurs and jacket she had brought.

When she came back Piers and the major were already deep in discussion, if not argument.

'I want him,' Piers was saying.

'Before you've even see him go?' the major asked.

'Yes!'

The major clapped Piers on the shoulder. 'You're no fool, my boy,' he said, then looked to Jane. 'Ah, my dear. All ready to go, I see. Think you can manage –'

His wife cleared her throat. '– to show us what he can do?'

'Do my best,' said Jane, and went into the field, where Benson held Bridget's Boy, and swung into the saddle. Bridget's Boy did his Bentley act, shying, fidgeting, like an engine responding to the starter, then she clapped her heels into him and he was off, the smooth power rippling beneath her as she took him from canter to gallop across the field, then on to the fence. The gelding took it flying, neat and sure footed as a cat, and across the next field she went, then brought him round once more. She could have galloped all day, and Bridget's Boy seemed to welcome the idea, but she brought him round at last, took the fence once more, and back to where the others waited. Bridget's Boy snorted. A little outing like that was by no means his idea of an afternoon's ride, but when Benson led him off to be rubbed down he went at once.

Apples, thought Jane. Maybe even sugar lumps. And doesn't he know it. She turned to the major. 'Well, sir?'

The major was on the surest ground he knew. For once he even looked wise, as he turned to Piers. 'Well?' he asked.

'I've never seen a horse like him,' Piers said. 'Not close to. I said I want him, and I do. But it would be a crime to try to get him. He's yours – and I congratulate you.'

Jane turned to the major.

'You may be on to something remarkable,' Routledge said. 'My bet is you are.'

'He'll make a good hurdler?'

'Hurdles?' The major sounded indignant. 'Handle that horse right and he could win the Gold Cup.'

'You think so?'

'I know so,' said Routledge. 'Of course he's young yet – needs schooling. But give him time – would you like me to find him a trainer for you?'

'Oh yes please,' said Jane. Her mother's smile was worthy of the Spirit of Christmas Present.

She drove Piers back in time for him to change and take Brenda Coupland to the Gargoyle, dropped off her mother and the major, and returned to South Terrace. The telephone had been busy, Truett told her, and indeed it had. Both Mr Lovell and a Miss Payne had telephoned her, and both would like to see her that evening. She sent at once for Mrs Barrow, who could see no problems. To cook for a famous film star would never be a problem, not even at two hours' notice. Then there would be two extra meals to be taken upstairs, where Catherine and Piers were playing recriminatory chess, but that didn't worry Mrs Barrow either. She liked Catherine and Piers, and she loved to cook. Jane telephoned the Ritz and Lovell's flat, and invited her extra guests.

Charles she invited earlier than the others. If he had a story to tell or excuses to make it was better that he should do it in private, but after Truett had announced him and left them alone, she went to his arms at once.

'Well well,' he said. 'You are glad to see me.'

'Cupboard love,' she said. 'Those heavenly ear-rings.'

'But you're not wearing them.'

'Not yet,' she said. 'The first time's a private view. You know that.' His arms tightened round her. 'Such a sweet letter, too.'

'Do we have to dine with the other two?'

Jane thought: I'd bet those same ear-rings that not once since she grew to womanhood has a normal male wished Georgie elsewhere.

''Fraid so. She says you travelled over together?'

'On the *Majestic*. Same table,' he said. 'She's awfully fond of you. Never stopped talking about how sweet you were.'

'And what did you do?'

'I listened.' She pressed closer to him, her arms about his neck.

'Soon I'll show you the ear-rings,' she said. 'Very soon. I promise.'

Then the doorbell rang, and just in time, she thought, before my lipstick is utterly ruined. It was Lionel, and if he was overjoyed to see Charles Lovell, he hid it well. On the other hand Georgie was coming, and when it came to film stars Lionel was the most colossal snob, thought Jane, besides being my agent. She set him to mixing martinis as the doorbell rang again.

That evening Jane had chosen to wear a dress by Paquin of a pink so subtly strong it could even support the rubies Aunt Pen had left her. One look at Georgie, and she was delighted with her choice, not because she could hope to compete, but because there was no fear of competition. Georgina had chosen to appear as an ice princess, in an Erté dress that shaded from palest blue to icing-sugar white. Her only jewellery was pearls: about a thousand of them, thought Jane: looped round her neck and wrist, and threaded in the unbelievable gold of her hair. All this, Jane thought, for a cosy dinner à quatre, then caught the flash of her rubies in the mirror and grinned. Girls like us are bound to be aware of each other, she thought, even when we can't win. Once we stop, we'll take up knitting. She swept towards the ice princess.

'Darling,' she said. 'How lovely to see you.'

But Georgina would have none of that. She laughed and threw her arms around Jane, as she had done in France.

'How grand you look,' she said.

'Not bad for a writer,' said Jane. 'You're scrumptious as ever, I see.'

'No black eyes, anyway,' said Georgie.

'How is Michael by the by?' Lovell asked, then: 'Don't look so alarmed. Murray Fisch told me.'

'From what I hear he's still making a mess of good canvas,' said Georgie. 'Found himself a new sparring partner, too. I hope she learns to roll with the punch. Lionel, darling. How divine to see you. Will there be dancing?'

'After dinner,' Jane said firmly. 'The poor darling can't dance on an empty stomach.'

'Just give me the chance,' said Lionel. 'I know just the stomachs I would choose.'

Mrs Barrow had laboured lovingly and long, and Lionel as always was loud in her praise when Jane took Georgina away and left the two men to strictly rationed port.

'I haven't seen you since the boxing match,' Lionel said. 'How upset that feller Fisch was.'

'Been in the States,' said Lovell.

'Business?'

'Trying to raise the money you gouged out of Fisch for Jane.' He grinned.

'For Felston, really. From what Jane tells me they need it. How are things over there?'

'Have you got investments there?'

'Not a sou,' said Lionel.

'Don't.'

The doorbell rang, and Bower came in, watched dourly by Truett, who did not approve of uninvited guests.

'Miss Whitcomb said in the drawing room,' she said.

'Sure.' He handed her his overcoat and hat. 'I just wanted to say hello to these gentlemen first.' Truett left, still disapproving. 'Good to see you, Lionel,' said Bower.

'You too. Would you care for a glass of port?'

'Better not,' Bower said. 'I'm in enough trouble with Truett as it is.' He turned to Lovell. 'How are you, Charles?'

'Well.'

'And prosperous, I hope?'

'Bankers are always prosperous,' said Lovell. 'When they're not, they cease to be bankers. You thrive, I trust?'

'I do my best.'

'You always will, Jay, I'm quite sure of that.'

Lionel said firmly, 'We really should join Jane and Georgina.'

'Georgie, too?' said Bower. 'I just wanted a word with Jane about the paper. I'd no idea there was a party.'

'Come along,' said Lionel, and walked to the drawing room,

wondering as he went if all the telephones at the *Daily World* were out of action.

The carpet was already turned back and Georgina was winding the gramophone, but Jane at once suggested they go to the study. Before they could move, Piers and Catherine came in, Piers carrying his sister.

'I told you we'd come up after dinner,' said Jane.

'Yes, but it looks as if all the fun's going to be down here. Do let me stay.'

'Please do,' said Piers. 'She's getting damn heavy.'

'Pig,' said his sister. 'I could recline on that sofa like Madame Récamier. Hello, Jay darling.'

'Hello darling,' said Jay. 'Put her down, Piers.' To Catherine he said, 'But not like Madame Récamier. She married a banker.'

Jane took him to her work room.

'Not your most tactful remark,' she said.

'Not all my jokes work,' he said. 'Sorry.' She left it. So often post-mortems achieved nothing.

'You came to see her, of course,' said Jane. 'That was why you didn't phone. You knew I might have guests but you came anyway.'

'I had to see her,' said Bower. 'I very often do.' Bower vulnerable was a rare sight indeed, and perhaps he knew it, because he continued, 'Anyway I haven't had any news of your guy Pinner yet.' She told him what Pinner had reported.

'The Judas,' Bower said at last. 'It couldn't be Andy Patterson could it?'

'Good heavens, no.'

'Think about it,' said Bower. 'This Tom Lynch – my guess is he was one of the death-or-glory boys at that riot – maybe even the leader.'

'He wasn't arrested.'

'Some guys got away. Some guys always do – and it's usually the smart ones.'

'But –'

'Let me finish. This guy Lynch is the fighter, the leader – just the way Andy Patterson was three years ago at the Elephant and Castle. But this time Andy's the onlooker. No. Not even that. He's the one who has to say, "Please don't fight, fellers. Please don't be rough" – while the cops and the men he admires most are beating the daylights out of each other. Andy's what they call a direct action man. Having to watch could make him jealous. It would sure make me jealous. And it's mostly jealousy that makes Judases.'

'I hadn't thought of that aspect,' she said.

'It only just occurred to me. Not that it matters. Either way it's a good story.' He looked at his watch. 'I have to go. I've got a meeting.'

'At this hour?'

'Newspapers never sleep,' he said. 'What time will Catherine go to bed? Before eleven?'

'I doubt it,' said Jane.

'Tell her I'll stop by and say good night to her,' said Bower. 'If that's OK?'

'Of course,' said Jane.

'That girl,' said Bower, and then: 'Love's a kind of madness. Did you know that? The kind that makes you want to stay crazy for the rest of your life.'

They danced, and gossiped: about Hollywood and London and Cap d'Antibes: about the Prince of Wales and Mussolini and Greta Garbo; and always they danced, one of the men for ever cutting in while Catherine watched and made far-reaching plans about the kind of dresses and the kind of jewels she would have as soon as she was married.

When Bower came back they were drinking champagne, but Bower asked for whisky and Truett, outraged once more, trudged off to fetch it. Not a good meeting, thought Jane, trying and failing to think of an excuse to leave the love-birds alone. They couldn't all march off the dance floor, even one as tiny as her sitting room. But Bower wanted no more than to sit on the edge of her sofa where she elegantly reclined, and murmur softly, listen to her murmured replies. When his whisky was finished, Jane said to Catherine, 'Bedtime, I'm afraid,' and Catherine agreed at once. 'Time for a real lie down,' she said. 'I don't see how that Récamier person stuck it.' Jane waited, but Bower was silent until Piers got to his feet, then: 'No,' he said. 'I'll do that.'

He went to Catherine and picked her up, gently and easily. She wore what was called a 'sensible' nightdress, and on top of it a dressing gown of nannylike respectability, but as she put her arm round Bower's neck, Jane became aware for the first time of the sensuality in the girl, the pleasing femininity of her body despite at least two layers of cotton, and rose. 'I'll come and tuck you up,' she said.

Bower could not have been more decorous or correct, she thought, but even so, his love really was a kind of madness. The sooner they were married the better. He went as soon as he had put Catherine in her bed, kissing her cheek before he left.

'Jaybird's awfully strong, isn't he?' said Catherine.

'Every bit as strong as Piers,' said Jane.

'Piers doesn't count, not this time,' Catherine said, 'but don't tell him I said so.'

In the drawing room they were talking of Catherine and Bower.

'It *always* works, that being carried by a big, strong man,' Georgie was saying. 'I've had it done to me in three pictures that I can remember. Of course in the movies it's different.'

'How?' Piers asked.

'Well in the first place you may not like the man who's carrying you,' said Georgie, 'and after three or four takes he'll start to sweat rather a lot. It's awfully hot in a studio – all those lights and things. Then unless he's a weight lifter or something, he'll start to tire – I mean a full-grown woman's a pretty solid lump – and once they've tired they get mad because heroes aren't supposed to get tired. All the same, the directors like it.'

'Why?' asked Lovell.

'Because it does their work for them. There it is, love, passion, you in his arms, and the message couldn't be more obvious, and yet the censors can't touch him, because all our hero is doing is helping out a lady in distress.'

'A clear case of virtue being its own reward,' said Piers, and walked towards her.

She backed off warily. 'If you want me to dance, OK,' she said, 'but no heavy lifting. We're neither of us up to it.'

Soon after that Georgie decided to go back to the Ritz, and both Piers and Lionel offered to escort her, and she accepted both offers.

'He has come on well, hasn't he?' she said, as she put on her coat, for all the world as if he were a promising horse, thought

Jane. 'I really must make sure he keeps in touch.' Once again Jane felt sorry for Brenda Coupland.

When the three of them had left, Lovell said, 'I mustn't stay long.'

'Not tonight,' said Jane.

'But I must see you soon.'

Oh Lord, she thought. Another Jay Bower. Crazy with love for a girl who accepts every gift he offers.

'Of course,' she said. 'I'll come to you whenever you say. You know that.'

That made him feel much better.

Whenever he said was two days later, and she was just about to leave when Mr Pinner telephoned.

'Lynch was at the riot,' he said. 'He organised that fight with the police.'

*Bower was right.* 'You're quite sure?' she asked him.

'I made contact with one of the rioters,' said Mr Pinner. 'Out on bail. In hospital till a couple of days ago, which is what held me up. Broken head.'

'He agreed to talk to you?'

'For twenty pounds he did,' said Mr Pinner. 'You know what things are like here, Miss Whitcomb. Desperate.' There was a pause. 'I'm not saying I'm proud of myself, but at least it worked. Lynch drilled the men. Just like the army, my chap said. Out on the moors where nobody could see them. Chaps from miles around. Ex-soldiers most of them. He handled them well too, but in the last mounted-police charge he managed to slip away. They were all under orders to do that, but he was one of the few that managed it.'

'Will this man say this in print?'

'If we give him enough money to get out of Eggleston he will.'

'I'll speak to Mr Bower. Any luck with our Judas?'

'My chap said Lynch had got very pally with a stranger just recently,' Mr Pinner said. Stranger, Jane knew, would mean a man from anywhere but Eggleston. 'Posh bloke,' said Mr Pinner. 'But a bit odd.'

'How odd?'

'Drank a lot,' said Mr Pinner. 'Niffed a bit too, if you'll pardon the expression.'

'His name is almost certainly Burrowes,' said Jane.

'No almost about it,' said Mr Pinner. 'Burrowes it is. With a bit of luck he might lead us to this Judas of ours. . . . When can you let me know about the money, miss?'

'Tomorrow,' said Jane. 'Call me at any time.' She thought for a moment, then added: 'Except the early morning.' She hung up and thought how bad things looked for Andy.

# 33

NEVER STAY THE night, Georgie had told her, and so far she had made it an invariable rule, but that night she had needed all her will power to get away. Showing off the ear-rings had been a great success, and his need for her, his joy that they were back together, delightfully apparent. She had enjoyed it all, not as much as Charles, she thought, but enough, and she had worked jolly hard at it too, which perhaps explained the lassitude that overcame her, that and the bed's all-embracing comfort. So easy to sleep, but in the end she had got up, showered and dressed, and allowed Charles to escort her to a taxi, as she always did. When she went into South Terrace Foch was waiting for her as he always was: another invariable rule. Only idiots believed that dogs can't possibly know, she thought. Foch knows everything. He followed her up the stairs with his fussy, scrambling hop, then into her bedroom, and slumped down on the carpet, his button-black eyes unwavering.

'Yes I know,' she said. 'But it's become a sort of habit that's rather hard to break, and it really is fun.' She began to undress – yet again, she thought. 'Don't you remember what fun it was?' Foch snorted.

'Don't you try that elder-of-the-tribe look on me,' she said. 'I remember what a fool you made of yourself over that spaniel bitch in Offley Villas.' Foch looked reproachful.

'Mind you,' said Jane, 'if you're thinking about the sapphires you have a point. That makes me his kept woman. Is that what you're saying? But I honestly don't think it does. After all – I keep myself, thanks to Aunt Pen.

'On the other hand there is a certain amount of value received or services rendered or whatever the jargon is – when it comes to the gymnastics, I mean. Then again one could argue that if I were his wife it would be a perfectly normal and natural thing to do, but as you sagely observe, I'm not his wife, and never will be.' She slipped her nightgown over her head, then bent to tickle Foch behind his ears, which he adored.

'You're too clever for me, mon brave,' she said. 'You always were.'

She got up then, to sit in a chair and light a cigarette. At once Foch scrambled up beside her so that she might tickle him once more.

'Yes, all right,' she said. 'But just for a couple of minutes. We both need our beauty sleep these days.' Foch nudged her to get on with it, and she did so.

'Then there's Jay,' she said. 'Charles hates him, he really does. I'm sorry if I sound melodramatic but I honestly believe he's out to destroy him. I'm quite sure Jay's vulnerable. That trip to New York didn't achieve a thing, if you ask me, and I rather think Charles noticed it. Charles really is awfully nice, and a super lover and all that, but oh dear he gloats. I never met such a gloater. Poor Jay.' She tickled Foch once more, then put him down on the floor and got into bed. 'He'd better not be poor Jay,' she said. 'Not if he hopes to wed the fair Catherine. Booty is what she wants. Loot. . . . And she'll have to get it. Goodness how vulnerable you poor chaps are.' She thought for a moment. 'He wants my child,' she said. 'But I don't.' She turned off the light. 'Good night, darling Foch.'

Lady Mangan had enjoyed her flight. Her one regret was that she had discovered aviation so late in her life, but she intended to make up for it. She intended to fly, she told Jane, all over the place. Her speech was as slurred as a bath-tub gin drinker's and now and again she failed to remember the words she needed, and either sought for a substitute or glowered at her son until he supplied one, for all the world as if he were a sort of walking thesaurus, thought Jane. Her face had altered too. Like the right half of her body it was frozen, immobile, so that her words came out of the side of her mouth that still worked, like a bad actor's in a gangster film. Yet she was neither comic nor pathetic, but formidable still. She sat on a large, upright chair, her feet on a stool, and a rug over her knees: her son, his wife and their children stood around her. Her court, thought Jane. But what am I? The messenger? 'News, news my liege.' But I have none, not for her. Prisoner at the bar? 'Jane Whitcomb you are charged that you did wilfully and with malice aforethought allow my grand-daughter to damage her knee on the eve of her wedding.' Yet Catherine was standing, like the others.

'They say Egypt's nice,' said the dowager. 'You fly to Paris, then on to Nice and other – locations.'

'Places,' said her son.

'You're slow, Edward,' said his mother. 'Far too slow. Anyway I shall be off to Cairo for the winter. You and Felicity had better come with me.'

Lady Mangan made protesting noises.

'Nonsense,' said the dowager. 'You love to travel. Both of you.'

'By ship,' said Lady Mangan. 'Travelling on liners – that's what we like.'

'Travelling in an aeroplane is much more exciting,' said the dowager. 'I think I shall buy one. When is my appointment with the – the clothes maker.'

'Couturier,' said her son. 'Four thirty, Mamma. Half an hour from now.'

'Then I shall talk with Jane,' said the dowager. 'The rest of you can go.'

Dismissing her son from his own drawing room, thought Jane, and yet he goes like a lamb.

'Catherine, better sit down for a while,' the dowager said. 'Piers, see that she does.'

'Yes, Granny.' The two voices chimed together in mocking chorus, and the old woman waited till the door closed.

'You think she's all right?' she asked.

'The specialist seems to think so.'

'Good of you to look after her.' The old woman looked up at her. 'Sit down,' she said. 'I forget my manners, you know. In fact I forget the devil of a lot of things. . . . That horse of yours must be a –'

'Brute?' said Jane.

'A damn good un,' said the dowager, 'if he can throw my grand-daughter. Will she be happy?'

'My goodness I hope so,' said Jane.

'That's no answer,' the old woman said, 'but a foolish question doesn't deserve one. How can you know? How can anyone? So long as he's rich. . . .'

You too, thought Jane. Hurt as you are, you've seen exactly where Jay's vulnerable.

'Piers,' the old woman said. 'He's off to Rutland for a few days. Hunting. That's good. Hunt in England by all means. But he must never go back to –'

'Ireland,' said Jane.

'Never,' the old woman said. 'You can't tie him up, but try to make sure he never does. Promise.'

'I'll do what I can,' said Jane, 'but I shouldn't think he'd ever want to go back there.'

'Not want to,' the old woman said. 'Have to. The place across the water.' Suddenly, disconcertingly, she fell asleep.

Mr Pinner contemplated his glass of stout, and told himself that he had earned it. Nobody rose up to protest the motion, and why should they? Mr Pinner asked himself. He'd done all that he had been asked to do, and in the time allotted, and for one of his favourite clients, Jane Whitcomb. A glass of stout was the least he was entitled to. When it was done he might even treat himself to another. Nice pub, after all, clean and neat; in what they called the Bigg Market in Newcastle, that seemed to attract a lot of chaps like himself: middle aged, bowler hat and raincoat, and on their own, a newspaper their only company; the only company they seemed to need. . . . A shadow fell across his copy of the *Daily World* and he looked up at once. Oh Lord, he thought, trouble, and laid down his newspaper, pushed the table away from his legs.

'You know who I am?' asked the man standing over him.

'Andy Patterson, isn't it?' said Mr Pinner. I've seen enough photographs of you, this last few weeks, he thought. 'Take a seat. What can I get you?'

'Nothing thanks.' Andy Patterson put a glass on the table as if it were a written excuse for not wearing boots on parade.

Shandy, Mr Pinner thought, and a very light shandy at that. The brewers won't get fat on this one. Then, to his relief, Andy Patterson sat down. 'I thought we better have a word,' Andy said, and Mr Pinner waited. 'About Tom Lynch,' Andy said at last.

'Who's he?' Mr Pinner asked.

Andy Patterson sighed. 'He's the feller you've been asking questions about all over Eggleston. You and a couple of New-castle 'tecs and that newspaper chap.'

'I can hear you,' Mr Pinner said. 'No need to raise your voice.'

'You want him for the riot in Felston, don't you?' said Andy. Mr Pinner drank stout. 'It's nice in a way,' said Andy, 'because if you're after Tom Lynch it means you're another one who doesn't believe it was me. All the same –'

'Read tomorrow's *Daily World*,' said Mr Pinner. 'It's all in there, so they tell me.'

'So you really are after Tom Lynch?'

'I've got him,' Mr Pinner said.

'Somebody split on him?'

'Somebody didn't want to go to prison,' said Mr Pinner. Andy winced.

'Nobody wants that,' he said. 'All the same, Tom Lynch was fighting for his class. The ones that trusted him – the way he trusted them.'

'There were two he shouldn't have trusted,' said Mr Pinner.

'Two?'

'How do you think we got on to Tom Lynch in the first place?'

'It was a Judas who told you?' Mr Pinner nodded. 'Why didn't you spend your time finding out who he is, instead of going after a man that was only doing his best for his class?' Andy drank some of his shandy. 'I know who the Judas is,' he said at last.

'May I ask how?'

'Snooping,' Andy said. 'Talking to informers. Using me brains.'

'And maybe talking to a man from London, too? An educated man? A posh sort of feller, even if he is fond of a drink?'

Andy's hand clenched round his shandy. 'Maybe,' he said at last. 'Can you prove who the Judas is?'

'Of course,' said Mr Pinner. 'Which is more than you can, I bet.'

'Where in the world did you get proof?'

'A typewriter,' said Mr Pinner. 'Clever bit of machinery, a typewriter. It can tell you things even when you're not using it. You won't tell me who you think the Judas is?'

'Any more than you'll tell me,' said Andy.

'Or what made you come here to find me?'

'I don't mind that,' said Andy. 'This is a funny part of the world, Mr Pinner. Half the men round here have nothing to do – or ever will have, by the look of things. But that doesn't mean they won't lend a hand to help one of their own. You've been watched ever since your pals started asking questions.'

Mr Pinner sighed. He had been so confident, and so wrong.

'You were good,' said Andy. 'I'm not denying it. There were just too many of us. And besides –'

'Yes?' said Mr Pinner.

'Nothing,' said Andy.

*They've had a tip off*, Mr Pinner thought. He'd have to phone London again, before he caught his train.

Andy Patterson rose. 'I'd better be off,' he said.

'It was nice to meet you, Mr Patterson,' said Mr Pinner, meaning it.

'Something I had to do,' said Andy. 'Find out what we're up against.'

'Am I so terrible?' Mr Pinner asked.

'No,' said Andy. 'You're not. That's just the trouble.' He turned. 'Ta-ra then.'

Mr Pinner said, 'Better not go to Tom Lynch's sister's house, Mr Patterson. The police have already been, and they'll be watching the house – and his visitors.'

Andy Patterson left. His glass of shandy, Mr Pinter noticed, was scarcely touched.

Some folks would say it was a waste of a bus fare: Felston to Newcastle and back, and a glass of shandy he'd left untouched because of – what? Righteous indignation? But he didn't see it like that. He had to know; it was part of his nature. To sniff out the enemy and face him, head on. Only this time the enemy had turned out to be a nice man, and a kind one: kind enough to warn him not to visit Tom Lynch. He got into the bus, where the tobacco smoke hung like gauze, and once again thought how glad he was he didn't smoke. All that money saved, to help Grandma to keep him fed. . . . To pay the bus fares for stupid outings like this one.

The thought came back again, unbidden. Burrowes would be angry he'd acted on his own, and Burrowes was the one who had told him the Party might need him again. But that was a joke. He'd been ditched because the Party had preferred Tom Lynch, and the only reason they might need him again was that Tom Lynch would be going down for five years hard labour at least, poor bugger.

He still wanted to serve, he told himself. That was what his kind of politics was. Service. Sacrifice, even. He was beginning to think like his father, but there was no avoiding the fact. Sacrifice it had been. He too had been in Durham Gaol. . . . And it wasn't as if he were after anything for himself. All he wanted was to lead the poor and the downtrodden, and the misguided too, if only they would see a bit of sense, into the land of milk and honey that was theirs for the taking, if only they'd listen to him. I hope you're enjoying this Da, wherever you are, he thought. I'm going on like an Old Testament prophet.

The Bible meant betrayal, too. Jacob and Esau, and Uriah the Hittite, and the top of the bill, Judas. Well it looked as if the Party had a Judas too, and maybe more than one. Somebody in London had tipped off Burrowes that the *World* was after Tom Lynch. Well the Party wanted him back on the job, and he'd oblige them, not because of Burrowes – that 'tec Pinner was worth a dozen of him – but because the Party was right. So it was back to the union meetings and the good, solid Labour men with their Union Jacks and their patriotism and their Land Of Hope And Glory. At least he wasn't going to prison.

'I'm afraid you've got a Judas, too,' Mr Pinner said. 'It was somebody in London who tipped off Burrowes. It had to be. He'd never make five yards up here.'

'You think so?' said Jane.

'I know so, miss. They were on to me in no time at all, and I know a lot more about keeping my head down than Burrowes.'

'You did a good job, Mr Pinner.'

'Thank you, miss.'

'Can you tell me – do you think Andy Patterson's involved now?'

'Not to say involved, miss. He's got more sense. I think Burrowes just went to him for some local advice – and being the chap he is he came to have a look at me. As good as told me he's a better detective than I am. I'll be getting the night-sleeper, miss,' Mr Pinner said.

'No urgency,' said Jane. 'We can stand you another night in a hotel.'

'I think I'd better come back,' said Mr Pinner. He sounded smug. 'I know who tipped us off. I can even prove it if you want me to.'

'Who was it?' said Jane. Mr Pinner told her. 'Good God,' she said.

'Excuse me asking, miss,' said Mr Pinner, 'but are you going to the *Daily World* offices today? Because if so –'

'Not a word,' said Jane. 'I promise you.' But she crossed her fingers as she said it, the way the Americans did.

'I'll call on you tomorrow morning then,' Mr Pinner said.

'Here,' said Jane. 'At South Terrace. Thank you so much, Mr Pinner. You've done splendidly.'

She telephoned Dick Lambert then, at the Home Office, and was not surprised to be told that the minister would call her back. And not from the Home Office, she thought. Yet his call did not keep her waiting long.

'I trust this is important,' he said.

*How very like Jay Bower he's become, now that he has power.*

'Of course.'

'Please be quick, then. I have a very urgent meeting –'

'Not on the phone.'

'Oh,' said Lambert. At least one didn't have to draw pictures. He wasn't a fool. 'I have a meeting in Kensington at six,' he said. 'Could you be at Kensington Gardens at five? The Round Pond?'

'An old haunt of mine,' she said. 'And Foch's. We shall look forward to seeing you there.'

He was there before her, although she was there exactly at five, Foch straining at his leash as if there weren't a moment to lose.

'That spaniel bitch,' said Jane, 'was years ago.' Foch slowed to a trot, and they reached the edge of the pond, where ten-year-old admirals launched their yachts against the might of their country's foes.

'Hello,' she said, and he spun round at once, wary as always of what exotic creature would confront him, clamouring to be admired, but all he saw were well-cut tweeds and the right sort of dog.

'How nice to see you,' he said, relieved, and shook her hand – as if I were a voter, thought Jane. 'I don't wish to sound pompous,' he said, 'but I really don't have much time.'

'Perfectly all right,' said Jane. 'You'll have been told about tomorrow's article – about this man Lynch?'

'Yes indeed,' said Lambert. 'We're all most grateful about the way the thing was handled.'

I bet you were, Jane thought. No individual member of the government singled out for praise. Just 'The Government's Firm Stand': 'The Government Insists On The Rule Of Law'. But never once was an individual minister named. To praise one single minister of this government for attacking a Left-Wing activist would be rather like praising King Herod as he slaughtered his first child. But the government – that plump cushion of anonymity – there was nothing wrong in praising that. Somehow it was even reassuring.

'But if that's all you came to see me about,' Lambert said, 'I'm most grateful as I said, but I really do have a meeting –'

'It isn't,' said Jane. Foch pulled at his lead, and she looked down at him and said, 'No, Foch.' He snorted, then sat. Lambert waited.

'Somewhere in your side,' said Jane, 'you have a traitor.'

'My side?' said Lambert. 'Traitor?' He sounded bewildered, which was far better than a blanket denial. Slowly, omitting names, she told Dick Lambert what Mr Pinner had told her.

'But –' said Lambert. 'But – what you're saying is that whoever this person is must have got their information from me.' Jane nodded. 'But that's impossible. The only ones I talked with were the Home Secretary – whom I presume consulted the Prime Minister, but even so – and a couple of senior civil servants.'

'Not even your wife?' said Jane.

'She prefers not to know about such things,' Lambert said, 'and in any case I resent what you're implying.'

'I'm implying nothing,' said Jane, 'except that talk breeds talk.'

'I quite agree,' said Lambert, 'but in this case it couldn't have. I promise you.'

Jane's hand tightened on Foch's lead, and he stood up at once.

'That leaves us with C. D. Roberts of Gregg Street,' she said.

'What on earth are you suggesting?' Lambert said.

'She's rather fond of photographs,' said Jane. 'Nothing wrong with that – except that one of them was of a picnic somewhere. Nothing wrong with that, either. Golden lads and girls. All that. Except that C. D. Roberts's golden lad was a chap called Pardoe, who's rather a chum of a chap called Burrowes.' She twitched at Foch's lead. 'Goodbye, Dick. Take care of yourself.' She left him to the yachts and the ten-year-old admirals.

Mr Pinner arrived in time for coffee, and some of the biscuits Mrs Barrow had baked. He ate rather a lot, which would please Mrs Barrow.

'You must be exhausted, Mr Pinner,' she said.

'Not at all,' Mr Pinner said. 'I like to keep busy – and I slept like a top on the train. First Class sleeper. Lovely.'

'Success is always rewarded at the *World*.' Jane sipped her coffee. 'You're quite sure we've got the right chap?'

'Positive, miss,' Mr Pinner said. 'I've even got a sample of his office typewriter.'

'What put you on to him?'

'That chap I gave the hundred quid to. He heard the two of them quarrelling. Dead give-away, that was. You know him, do you miss?'

'I know of him,' said Jane. 'Michael Deegan, better known in Felston as Moscow Mike.'

'Quite so, miss. He's very Red from what I hear.'

'Then why on earth did he do it?'

'Jealousy, miss. You wouldn't believe it, would you? In a grown man. Smart one too, they tell me.'

She thought of Charles Lovell. 'Oh yes,' she said. 'I'd believe it.'

'The way my chap told me about the row – it was funny. Strange, you might say. Deegan going on and on about how it wasn't fair, and Tom Lynch saying he was sorry, but that was the way the Party wanted it.'

'What wasn't fair?'

'Tom Lynch being OC rioters, so to speak, and Deegan not even being allowed to make a speech. Like the kid that didn't get a sweet, my chap said. And Tom Lynch seemed genuinely sorry for him. And that made Deegan even angrier. He'd wanted a row. Comes of being Irish, I suppose.'

'But surely they both are?'

'Lynch doesn't act it. Apart from being RC.'

'But surely his priest wouldn't allow him to be a Catholic and a Communist?'

'He didn't tell his priest he was a Communist,' said Mr Pinner. 'Came as a bit of a shock by all accounts.'

'Anyway, that set me wondering. An awful lot of anonymous letters start with jealousy.'

'But Andy Patterson did make a speech. Shouldn't Deegan have been jealous of him, too?'

'I've no doubt he was, miss. But Patterson had gone back in the betting so far as the real Reds were concerned. It was Lynch who was the blue-eyed boy. And so Deegan sent you that letter.'

'And you got a sample of his typewriter?'

'I have it here, miss.' Mr Pinner handed it to her, and she compared it with the original. They were identical.

'How on earth did you get it?' she asked.

'I had a look at that workshop of his. There's a bit of an office at the back and I heard a typewriter going. So I broke in one night and took that sample, just to be sure, as you might say.' He looked at her enquiringly. 'Are you all right, miss?'

'A little dazed, perhaps,' said Jane. *'You broke in?'*

'Only way, miss.' Mr Pinner delicately brushed crumbs from his waistcoat on to his plate. 'I had my skeleton keys of course, so the lock was undamaged. In fact nothing was damaged, and all I took was that one sheet of paper. And you did say it was important, miss.'

'Indeed it is,' said Jane.

'May I smoke my pipe, miss?'

'Please do.'

Mr Pinner lit his pipe as he did everything else, neatly and efficiently. Jane had no doubt he had been an excellent burglar.

'Your informant gave you an awful lot for a hundred pounds,' she said.

'It's a fortune where he is,' Mr Pinner said. 'I asked him if he wanted it in fivers, but he said pound notes. He didn't even know of a place that handled fivers.'

'And he's going away?'

'If he knows what's good for him,' Mr Pinner said. 'I suggested Canada. Will you be using it, miss? In the paper?'

'Rather up to Mr Bower,' said Jane.

'If it's all the same to you miss,' said Mr Pinner, 'I wouldn't bother Mr Bower with any details – you know. Like how I got the sample.'

'Of course not,' said Jane. 'Mr Bower hates details. It'll be our secret. After all you keep plenty of mine. Why shouldn't I keep one of yours?'

'Always a pleasure to work with you, miss,' said Mr Pinner.

# 34

SHE TOOK A taxi to Fleet Street. Bower had invited her to
lunch, which meant martinis, and the Bentley was a big
enough handful without them, the Riley an invitation – if he
saw it – for Bower's mockery. Gone back to your roller skate?
he would say. That Bentley was too much for you, was it? A taxi
was a much better idea. Besides, she could count it among her
expenses, all of which went to Felston.

He listened to her carefully, then compared the two sheets of
paper. 'No doubt about it,' he said. 'We've got the facts. The
thing is do we have a story?'

'That's up to you,' said Jane.

'I'm asking you what you think,' he said. 'I know that's not
what I pay you for, but you do it anyway.'

'I don't think it's us,' she said. 'Tom Lynch, now. What he
did was wrong, but it had stature, attack. The man was a class
warrior, true, but the emphasis was on the warrior. He was
almost a tragic hero. But Deegan – that's only muck to be raked.
A small man's envy of a big man's stature. That's not us.'

'Tom Lynch as Prometheus, or even Milton's Satan,' said
Bower. 'You could maybe work that up into an article for my
sister. But not for the World. We won't publish his secret.' He
reached out for the cocktail shaker and filled up their glasses.
'Too bad Bob Patterson stopped working for me. He'd have
known how to handle Deegan.'

'Because he's a Geordie, you mean?'

'Sure,' said Bower. 'What else? But I guess you're right. We'll let it lie. All the same your Mr Pinner did a first-class job. We'll use him again.' He stretched and yawned. 'Three days,' he said.

'Three days what?'

'To my wedding,' said Bower. 'Had you forgotten?'

'Would the Archangel Gabriel forget the millennium? Of course I hadn't forgotten. I tried on my hat and dress yesterday.'

'Catherine said she asked you four times to be a bridesmaid.'

'Did she?' said Jane. 'I rather lost count.'

'Why did you turn her down?'

'On the grounds of age,' said Jane. 'A more than adequate excuse.'

'There were others?'

'I considered it inappropriate,' said Jane. 'I rather thought you would, too.'

The other luncheon guests arrived.

'Do you often go to Bluebeard's chamber?' Georgie asked.

They were dining together in her suite at the Ritz: caviar and foie gras and Dom Pérignon, all of which World Wide would pay for. What pain Murray Fisch must feel when he received the bills.

'Now and again,' said Jane. 'When he needs to add a little tone.'

'All be different when he marries her ladyship.'

'Goodness, I should hope so,' said Jane.

'It's his bachelor do tonight.'

'A bit early isn't it? There are still three days to go.'

'Jay wouldn't want a hangover on his wedding night. Piers is master of the revels, so he tells me. Offered to scratch if I'd go with him to the Savoy to dance. But I said no. I was jolly firm. Somebody's got to keep Bower in order.'

'You think Piers can do that?'

'Piers can do a hell of a lot,' said Georgie. 'Not my type, but very persuasive.'

*Good news for Brenda Coupland?*

'We went to the Kit Kat Club the other day,' Georgie said. 'Ran into that protégé of yours – Bob Patterson. He's very persuasive, too. What are you wearing for the wedding?'

Jane told her. 'Sounds like a dowager's outfit,' Georgie said.

'I'm not exactly in my first bloom,' said Jane. 'Are you going?'

'To the wedding? Wasn't even asked. But I should have declined if I had been.'

'Inappropriate?'

'The very word,' said Georgie.

St George's, Hanover Square, was no place for harems, thought Jane.

Georgie poured more champagne. 'Did Murray send you a script?' Jane nodded. 'And?'

'I rather liked it,' said Jane. 'It had far more of what I'd written than I'd expected.'

'That's because Tom Waring's directing,' said Georgie. 'Any other director would start tinkering the minute he got the script – but Tom had OK'd it already. He was stuck with it – and a good thing too. It's a damn good script. We'll do you proud, Tom, Dan Corless and I.'

'You think he can do it?'

'Certainly. It's all he *can* do. Play the hero. You'd think he'd be like the principal boy in panto, wouldn't you? All tights and slapping his thigh and come on Puss, only another eleven miles to London, and clasping Alderman FitzWarren's daughter to his bosom when he'd far sooner clasp Alderman FitzWarren. But it doesn't work like that. On the screen he'll look good. Tom and I will see to that.' She smiled at Jane. 'You didn't seem surprised when I told you Tom was our director.'

'Should I have been?'

Georgie nodded approval. 'That's right,' she said. 'Play it close to your chest. That's one of the things chests are for. The thing is I phoned Murray yesterday – how that man goes on about money! – and he told me that Charles Lovell thought Tom was a good idea, and so of course Tom got it.'

'Charles is that important?'

'The biggest cheese of all – except the bank. He bought out that Texan I told you about. Didn't he tell you?'

'I didn't ask,' said Jane. 'I never do. Any more than he ever asks about me. It works very well.'

'Try telling that to Murray,' said Georgie.

The wedding was what St George's Hanover Square weddings always were: chic and fashionable, and run with a precision any crack regiment would have been proud of, which wasn't really surprising since officers of the Rifle Brigade formed the Guard of Honour, and the regimental band played at the reception. Jane sat with her mother and the major, her mother in a dazzling suit of blue and silver, and the major in a morning suit of a rather daring grey, and a gardenia in his lapel. Jane wore a dress made by Vionnet, and pearls, the silk of the dress deepening in colour as it descended, from the palest pink at the shoulders to a glowing burgundy red at the hem. Her mother had stared at her long and hard.

'Very nice,' she said. 'Very nice indeed, child. Simple but not demure. What I enjoy most about your choice of clothes is that they mirror your sense of fun.' The wedding service was a treat after that. . . . Demure indeed.

An organ, of course, and a choir: to Bower any less would have been unthinkable. Only a threat of tantrums from his bride had avoided the presence of trumpeters, and a fanfare, but at least he had a bishop, to whose episcopal charities Lady Mangan contributed largely. The dowager had had him flown over from Ireland the day before. Soon she would be considering an airline of her own, thought Jane. He was a ruddy, healthy-looking prelate, with a voice that boomed round the church like cannon. No doubt he spends a lot of time in the hunting field, she thought, and settled down to enjoy the service, but it was thin stuff compared with the Burial of the Dead. Those bishops that Elizabeth had summoned all those years ago had been far more concerned with the life hereafter.

'. . . an honourable estate, instituted by God in the time of man's innocency'. . . . Nothing wrong with that, they were both honourable enough, according to their lights: but where was the excitement, the sense of urgency? When it came it was all on the debit side.

'. . . and therefore is not by any to be enterprised' (what on earth could that mean?) 'nor taken in hand inadvisedly, lightly, or wantonly,' the bishop boomed, 'to satisfy man's carnal lusts and appetites, like brute beasts that have no understanding.'

Suddenly she began to think of Lord Blagdon. He had preached a sermon once in York Minster, according to Charles. Had he found happiness in a house with only twenty rooms? Would that be mansions enough? Her mother nudged her. It was time to stand and sing a hymn. 'The Voice That Breathed

O'er Eden.' Well obviously. A girl couldn't consider herself properly married till that had been sung, with 'O Perfect Love' to follow. At last the bishop joined Bower's hand with Catherine's, and this time the great voice was matched by the splendour of the words: 'Those whom God hath joined together let no man put asunder.' But would it work like that? Maybe it all depended on the words Jay had spoken earlier: 'With all my worldly goods I thee endow. . . .' Not cynicism, she told herself. Not witty Jane in her sense-of-fun clothes. Just Jane with her deplorable ability to look a fact in the face.

More prayers, and Catherine's father, having given his daughter away, buried his face in his hands as if it had been altogether too much. Piers, she noticed, knelt to pray bolt upright, the best man – lieutenant perpetually on the alert to make sure that his charges behaved, which they all did splendidly until the organ pealed out again, the inevitable Mendelssohn, and Mr Joachim Bower and Lady Catherine Bower set off for the vestry.

'Very nice,' said her mother once more.

'It's a pity we had to miss Chepstow,' said the major.

The reception was at Eaton Square. The dowager, persuaded at last not to attend the church, had no intention of missing the reception. She sat in her favourite chair, her feet on a stool, and received homage. A new dress, thought Jane. Hartnell by the look of it, and an emerald set she hadn't seen before. She stood in line to kiss the bride, be kissed, chastely, on the cheek, by the bridegroom. There was no time for more: the queue behind her was vast. She went over to the dowager instead, and bent to kiss her.

'Catherine looks gorgeous,' she said. It was true, and both women knew it.

'You chose the dress,' the dowager said.

'I helped, anyway.'

The old woman snorted. Really she snorts almost as well as Foch, thought Jane. 'Don't go away without seeing me,' the dowager said. 'I'll have a word when I take my rest.'

'Delighted,' said Jane. 'May I introduce my mother, Mrs Routledge, and my stepfather, Major Routledge?'

The dowager nodded to the major, who stepped back, relieved, then looked at his wife. 'You have a very fine daughter,' she said.

'I know,' her mother said. 'I'm so glad you think so too.'

'Always there when she's needed,' said the dowager, 'and always gone before you can say thank you. Go and get yourselves some champagne. Tell Piers you're to have some of mine – not that grocers' stuff.' The grocers were Fortnum and Mason.

'Well of course,' said Piers. 'Granny told me you're on the First Team. And quite right too.' Cobb, the dowager's own butler, came up to them, and offered glasses. 'On the list, Cobb,' he said.

'Very good, sir.' They each took a glass, and sipped.

'Good God,' said Major Routledge. Piers grinned at him.

'Quite right, sir,' he said. 'Not for all and sundry, is it? Not that Granny's mean. It's just that there isn't an awful lot left.'

'Nectar,' said Major Routledge. 'Absolute nectar.'

'All that stuff in the service about the miracle of the wine at Cana,' said Piers. 'Set me thinking. At Cana the host was hauled over the coals for keeping the good wine till the last.' He sipped from his glass. 'It makes a lot more sense if most of the guests don't even know there is good wine. Not this good.'

'I've never drunk its equal,' Jane's mother said.

'Probably not.' Piers spoke on easy terms as one connoisseur to another. 'As I say, there isn't an awful lot left, but all the same it's there to be enjoyed. It's just that she's rather fussy who she enjoys it with.' He nodded to them, and went to talk with the seemingly endless supply of guests.

'How gratifying,' said Jane's mother, 'to be – as the Presbyterians say – numbered among the elect – if it was to this that we were elected.' She drained her glass, and looked about her for Cobb.

At last they were summoned to eat. The major and her mother on her right, and Don Cook on her left. Very much the *Daily World* contingent. Dick Lambert was there too, but far, far away from her. Jay Bower being tactful, she wondered?

Don Cook followed the direction of her eyes.

'He turned up at the Stag Night, too,' he said. 'Just a glass of wine, then back to the House of Commons. Junior ministers can't be too careful. We might have booked an exotic dancer.'

'And had you?'

'Of course not.' Did Don Cook sound wistful for once? 'It was

– 408 –

all very respectable. Good food, good wine, and everybody off home by eleven.'

Not wistful: outraged.

'He didn't seem all that keen on you,' Don Cook said.

'My name came up?'

'Young Hilyard just happened to mention what good work you and Lambert did together during the General Strike. Lambert turned sniffy. Very sniffy.'

'What did Piers do?' Jane asked.

'Laughed at him. Lambert couldn't bear it.'

'Whyever not?'

'It was like being flogged. He knows how to hurt, that young man.'

Jane turned to the major. Cobb it seemed was his friend for life. His glass had never been empty.

The meal finished at last, coffee appeared, and at once Piers was on his feet. It was time for the telegrams: from New York, New England, Hollywood, Ireland, Catherine's college at Oxford, Piers's battalion in India. One by one Piers read them, tolerant of their leaden humour and upper-class prurience. Yet another hope that all their troubles would be little ones, and he shook his head ruefully as he picked up the next.

'Regret to advise you,' he read, 'that funds are –' He broke off and read the rest of the telegram in silence.

'Oh dear,' he said. 'That one was for me, from my bookmaker. Whatever is the world coming to? Have these chaps no respect?' There was a ripple of laughter, and he went on reading. More speech-making, and at last Bower rising to reply: 'On behalf of my wife and myself,' and then laughter and applause, as there always was. Yet he did not seem happy, thought Jane. He seemed enormously pleased, like a business man who had finally brought off a hugely difficult and lucrative contract, but he wasn't happy. . . . Piers announced that there would be dancing in the ballroom at the back of the house, and the guests drifted out to the sound of music from the military band playing 'Lady Be Good', 'My Blue Heaven', 'Ain't We Got Fun'. Well and accurately played, thought Jane, but they did sound like marches. Piers came up to her at once, and asked for a dance. She looked around for her mother, but already Mrs Routledge and the major were progressing round the floor, as stately as two liners in a stream of pleasure craft. She and Piers moved on to the dance floor.

'Thank God that's over,' said Piers. 'I love my sister, God knows, but now it's up to Jay.'

'Quite right too,' said Jane. 'That's what marriage is all about – or so they tell me.'

'You think they'll be happy?'

'Of course they will,' said Jane. 'He adores her.'

'I was adored once,' said Piers, and then: 'Who said that?'

'Sir Andrew Aguecheek,' said Jane. '*Twelfth Night*.'

'Oh yes of course. Not making much sense, am I? Too much of Granny's best champers.'

'You sure you didn't come off too?'

'Come off?'

'Your horse,' said Jane. 'Hunting. In Rutland. Goodness – you have been hitting the fizz.'

'No no,' said Piers. 'But I didn't get a ride on Bridget's Boy – or anything like him.'

'Nice people you were with?'

'Oh the nicest,' said Piers. 'But not the sort you would know.' He reached back among the champagne bubbles for an explanation. 'Very dull,' he said at last.

'Then I almost certainly don't know them.'

He nodded gravely. Jane found that although she wasn't holding him up precisely, it was necessary to push him in the direction he ought to take.

'I say,' he said at last. 'About Granny. About Mangan Castle.'

'What about them?'

'Hanging's too good for them. Wouldn't you say hanging's too good for them?'

'They didn't kill her.'

'Not yet,' said Piers. 'She looks better than she is as a matter of fact. It's all will power and guts now.'

'She's got plenty of those.'

'She had,' said Piers, 'but it's mostly used up by now. What's left is magnificent of course, but there isn't very much, I'm afraid. Dear old Jay –' He hesitated.

'What about him?'

'He'll have to take over when Granny goes. Fill the bill. All that. For Catherine I mean. It won't be easy for him.'

'And you?'

'I'll have to start looking after myself. God knows I'm old enough.'

The music stopped, and she went to where Jay and Catherine were sitting, and once more offered her congratulations.

'It's fun, isn't it?' Catherine said. 'I can't think when I –' she stopped just in time. Enjoyed herself more? Jane wondered. It was not the sort of thing to say at your own wedding, no matter whose champagne you had drunk.

'When I saw such a cheerful crowd,' Catherine said. 'Thank you so much for all that scrumptious silver, darling. Just the thing for the Berkshire house.'

A couple of old-school chums approached her, screeching congratulations as the band struck up again. Bower rose to his feet.

'Let's dance,' he said, and they moved on to the floor.

For a little while they danced in silence. The happiest day of your lives, thought Jane. It may be for her, but not for you. A little gaiety if you please, sir.

Aloud she said, 'She really does look beautiful.'

It was like giving water to a man dying of thirst.

'She does, doesn't she?' said Bower. 'A credit to me.'

'A credit earned,' said Jane. 'You deserve her.'

'I don't know about deserve her,' said Bower. 'I love her –'

'Well of course.'

'The funny thing about love,' said Bower, 'is that it hurts. I hadn't realised that. It isn't like what we had – what the French call *une amitié amoureuse*. That was almost all good times and laughter. It isn't like that at all. There's pain. There's a great deal of pain.'

Another casualty of Granny's champagne? Jane wondered, but Bower was steady on his feet, his leading automatic and sure.

'Jay, my dear,' she said. 'This isn't one of my little pieces to Daisy –'

'Let me finish,' said Bower. 'Please.'

'Very well.'

'The telegram that Piers nearly read out loud,' said Bower.

'What about it?'

'He's a very smart young man, my brother-in-law. The kind I could have found a place for if he ever wanted to quit the army.'

'Could have?'

'You're being smart again,' said Jay Bower. 'That's OK. I like it when you're smart. That telegram wasn't for him. It was for me, but it wasn't to say congratulations. It was from my old man, and he isn't the sort to squander two bucks to wish his son happiness when he doesn't even approve of the bride. . . . I asked him for money. Money's not something he throws out of windows.'

'A lot of money?'

'Half a million dollars.' Jane missed a beat, then recovered. 'Things are going wrong States-side,' said Bower. 'Badly wrong. A lot of people are going to go very, very broke very soon, and I could be one of them.'

'You shouldn't be telling me this,' said Jane. 'Not here. Not now.'

'On my wedding day,' said Bower. 'The happiest day of my life.'

'Have you talked it over with Catherine?' she asked. He shook his head. 'We must have five minutes together, but not on the dance floor.' They danced on.

'When do you leave?' she asked.

'For my honeymoon? Five o'clock. We'll spend the night in Fleet Street. Tomorrow we were supposed to go to Paris, then Cap d'Antibes.'

'Tell her you want a word with me. Another letter to Daisy.' Bower nodded. 'And try not to let it show.' He led her from the floor.

Lionel had just arrived and was showering excuses like confetti as he congratulated first Catherine, then Bower. Such a mistake to visit friends in the country, he told them. Owls hooting all night and not a wink of sleep till four in the morning, when he dropped off at last and missed the milk train and not another one for hours. The two school chums were looking at him as if they had paid for admission and getting their money's worth and more. She took him off to dance.

'Was I contrite enough?' he asked.

'Contrite, yes. Honest, no,' said Jane. 'Are you in love again?'

'Well yes,' said Lionel, 'only it isn't that. Well I expect it is in a way. The poor darling's in the sort of trouble we poor pansies rather specialise in.'

'Blackmail?'

'Exactly. It follows us about like a faithful hound. It's because our idea of fun's illegal, you see.'

'Have you managed to straighten things out?'

'Do you know, I rather believe I have,' said Lionel. His voice was as gentle as ever, but Jane was suddenly aware of the other Lionel, the one who had wrestled in the mud in the gardens of La Ruche, climbed into the cockpit of a Sopwith Camel, time after time, never knowing whether he would climb out again.

'That's all right, then.' They danced on, Lionel, as always, the best dancer in the room.

'Poor old Jay's not exactly the life and soul,' he said. 'He's supposed to be happy.'

'He *is* happy,' said Jane. 'He's just found out that marriage has its responsibilities, that's all.'

When the dance ended, Jane took him over to see her mother and the major, and her mother was gracious: she approved of Lionel. The major was gracious, too. He approved of the Royal Flying Corps, and of the grocers' claret, of which there seemed to be an endless supply. Cobb came across to them, and asked if Jane were free to visit Lady Mangan. At once Lionel asked her mother to dance. Another proof of his courage? she wondered, and followed Cobb across the dance hall to the staircase, on and up to the bedroom where Lady Mangan lay, and knocked gently. A nurse appeared at once, ready to take over, but Cobb would have none of it. He was the chief servant of the household, whose privileges matched his responsibilities: he marched on in. 'Miss Whitcomb, my lady.'

'Come in my dear,' said the dowager, and Jane went up to the bed. The old lady, still in her Hartnell dress, lay on the bed. She looked much older and more frail than she had at the reception, and it seemed to Jane that Piers could well be right.

'You can – can leave,' Lady Mangan told the nurse. 'Not too far, mind.' The nurse left, white starched uniform crackling like snow underfoot. 'Are they – pleased with themselves down there?'

It seemed that the word problem was back again, thought Jane.

'They're enjoying themselves very much,' she said.

'My new son-in-law takes great pains not to show it.'

Another sharp pair of eyes, even after a stroke.

'It's just the way he is,' said Jane, and it was true enough.

'I hope he hasn't got the – the notion –' the old woman looked mildly triumphant at the alternative word she had found '– that Catherine is an heiress.'

'But surely,' said Jane.

'Let me finish. *You* were an heiress because Penelope and Walter decided to make you one. Anybody else who might have had a claim they just ignored.'

My brother Francis, Jane thought.

'It was their money to do what they liked with, and in my opinion they did the right thing. But I can't do what I like with my money.'

'Whyever not?'

'My son's an earl,' said the dowager, 'and so will my grandson Desmond be. In time. My other son's in a regiment that's very –'

'Fashionable?'

'Expensive,' the dowager said. 'Earls are expensive, too. Very. Catherine can only get what's left over. It'll be a tidy sum, but it won't be what she's used to. I hope Mr Bower realises that.'

'But he's rich,' said Jane.

'He's American. How do I know he can hang on to his money?'

Before her stroke the dowager, or someone close to her, had been alerted. The wealthy could scent ruin the way a deer could scent a leopard, it seemed.

'I love Catherine,' said the dowager. 'Always have. That's why I spoiled her, and now she's used to it. Maybe if I'd have loved her more I'd have given her less.'

'You're starting to fret,' said Jane. 'It won't do.'

'Quite right,' the dowager said. 'Up to him, now.' Then she added surprisingly, 'Seems the right sort of feller. Hard worker.'

'All of that,' said Jane. 'I know. I work for him.'

'Tell him to keep at it. . . . Give us a kiss, then. It's time for my – my –'

'Nap,' said Jane, and bent to kiss her. ''Bye, 'bye, Emily.'

'Goodbye, lass.'

She went out softly. The bride and groom were dancing together. While his arms were around his wife he seemed easier, altogether more carefree. He even smiled. Then the music stopped, and he saw Jane, and led Catherine over to her.

'Jane,' he said, spacing out the words, 'I've had an idea for another Dearest Daisy. Come into the library and I'll tell you about it.'

Oh dear, thought Jane. More lines from a bad play. He's as bad as Charles.

Bower turned to Catherine. 'It'll only take five minutes,' he said.

'Well make sure it does,' said Catherine, and looked about her. 'Oh look – there's Lionel. It's about time he danced with the bride.'

She moved away, and Jane and Bower went to the library.

'Some of my father's cable was in code,' Bower said at once. 'It made sense – but not the right sense, if you follow me. The inner meaning was this: in his opinion the jig's up. The boom's going to burst like a balloon.'

'How soon?'

Bower shrugged. 'Any minute.'

'You're in deep?'

'Deep enough. I sold Lovell my share in World Wide. Or maybe you know that.'

'I heard rumours.'

'Georgie loves to chatter,' he said. 'Just like everyone else in Hollywood. . . . I told you I need half a million bucks.' She nodded. 'It's just possible my old man may give it to me.'

'Well then –'

'At a price,' he said. 'My uncle – the one who got me started – left me some real estate in Boston. Prime location. My old man might feel generous enough to buy it from me for half a million.'

'It's worth more?'

'About double. Dear old Dad's been after me to sell for years.'

'Isn't there another way?'

'I can raise a quarter of a million outside the family, but that's it,' he said. 'Unless I sell the paper, but it would take too long.'

'You mustn't sell the paper,' said Jane, and then: 'My money's all tied up –'

'I couldn't ask you,' he said.

*Couldn't you? Then why tell me so urgently? Why all this Dearest Daisy?*

'But I might manage something. Let me talk to my solicitors and see,' she said.

'Do you mind if I ask who they are?'

'Medlicott and Rubens,' she said.

'What they call in vaudeville a real class act. Tell them you can have a quarter of a million bucks' worth of my business.'

'I'll tell them.'

'I don't want to rush you,' he said. 'But this really is urgent. How soon can you go?'

'Now,' she said. 'Just let me say my farewells and go home and change. And – oh, Dearest Daisy. What sort of article am I going to write?'

'Tell your public about what real smart cookies we are,' he said. 'How we exposed an enemy of our society, when even the police suspected the wrong guy.'

'But we've already done that.'

'Sure,' said Bower, 'but we haven't taken enough bows yet. – And thanks, Jane.'

'I haven't done anything yet.'

'You're in my corner,' said Bower. 'I don't deserve it, but you're there.'

# 35

MEDLICOTT AND RUBENS had offices in Knightsbridge, not far from Harrods, which Aunt Pen had always considered very convenient. 'Whenever I visit my lawyers to see how much money I have, I can go round the corner afterwards and spend some of it.' . . . Jane had telephoned from her house before she left, and Mr Medlicott was able to see her. Mr Medlicott was always able to see clients worth half a million pounds. Jane went to business at once, and Medlicott listened carefully, courteously, as he always did, as befitted a tall and elegant patrician, ageing well. When she had done he said, 'I think we'd better have Rubens in on this,' and picked up the desk telephone. Jane had no objection; Rubens had only two fields of expertise: chorus girls and money.

While they waited they talked of the theatre and hunting, and Aunt Pen's airedale Bob, now Medlicott's airedale, and one of the reasons why she trusted Medlicott, cunning though he was. When Rubens arrived Medlicott at once began to explain Jane's problem. He did it accurately and objectively, not once betraying where his own sympathies lay. As he talked she watched Rubens listen, his whole being concentrated on what his partner was saying. Neat and tidy and self-effacing was Rubens: nothing patrician about him. Nothing plebeian either. Just an air of enormous competence and expertise. When Medlicott had done Rubens said, 'So it's come, then.' He might have been talking about frost in January: an expected and therefore obvious fact. 'Your friend Mr Bower is to be relied upon, I take it?'

'I explained to Mr Medlicott that this conversation is between lawyer and client. What I believe you call privileged,' she said, and Rubens nodded vigorously. Of course, of course, the nods said. Do get on. We are talking about money. We are talking about *vast sums*.

'Mr Bower had it from his father,' said Jane, 'who is a very important banker, so I believe.'

'Bauer Brothers and Martens,' said Rubens. 'If such a thing were to happen, he would know.'

'If?' said Jane. 'He talked as if there were no time at all.'

'You must excuse me,' said Rubens. 'It's not every day a pretty lady walks in and tells me that someone's world is coming to an end.'

'Really Rubens,' said Medlicott.

'Not yours, not mine, I agree,' said Rubens, 'and not Miss Whitcomb's either. We have no dollar holdings – or very few.' He turned to Jane. 'You won't mind if we get rid of the ones we have?'

'So long as you do it discreetly,' said Jane, and Rubens smiled. Money was a serious matter, and Miss Whitcomb took it seriously. A client to cherish.

'Quarter of a million dollars,' he said. 'Say sixty thousand pounds or a little more. I have your file with me.' And indeed he had, she thought. A great wodge of papers that might have slowed down a Samson, but he lifted it almost casually, though with respect. It too was money. He began to leaf through it.

'Current account,' he said. 'You can do as you wish with that – and there's the quarterly dividend due in a couple of months. You could borrow against that. . . . Nothing in private savings. The trouble is you spend it as soon as it comes in, Miss Whitcomb.'

'Just like my aunt,' she said. 'What about the sale of her house in Mount Street?'

'All part of the estate,' said Rubens. 'Not to be touched, I'm afraid.'

'There are these,' said Jane. She opened the leather case she had brought with her, and took from it one by one the little jewel cases, then opened them. Diamonds, sapphires, rubies, emeralds, winked and gleamed on Medlicott's desk.

'Good Lord,' said Rubens, and went to them at once.

'None of them are Aunt Pen's,' said Jane. 'I promise you.'

Rubens went first to the sapphire necklace and ear-rings Charles had given her.

'These are incredible,' he said.

'Fabergé,' said Jane. 'I don't want to sell them unless I must –'

'I should think not,' said Rubens.

'– but I'll pawn them if I can get a good price.'

'Pawn?' said Medlicott. He made the word sound like an obscenity.

'We need an expert valuation,' said Rubens. 'Obviously you are in a hurry. There's a jeweller I know not far from here –'

There are a dozen at least, thought Jane, and I bet you know them all. You'd have to, since your hobby is chorus girls.

'– If you wouldn't mind waiting I could go to see him at once.'

'Of course,' said Jane.

'Let me order some tea,' said Medlicott.

Earl Grey and rich tea biscuits, and a cigarette. She needed the cigarette.

Medlicott said, 'You realise that when this happens it won't be just your friend Bower?'

'The whole of America,' said Jane. 'I know.'

'Not just America.' He stirred in his chair. 'I hope to God Bower's wrong,' he said, and she looked at him, surprised. It was the first time she had ever seen him portray a human emotion.

Rubens came back at last, and put the leather case beside her like a man getting rid of a live coal.

'Not enough, I'm afraid,' he said, and grimaced. 'My friend the jeweller thought you'd do better in New York, poor fool. But if you wouldn't mind waiting a few moments longer, I'd like a few words with my partner. – If you'll excuse us.'

'Of course,' said Jane. It took them an hour, but at last they came back in.

'You can sell the rest of the stuff for twelve thousand and pawn the Fabergé for five. If you sold it as a set you could get fifteen at least.'

'I don't want to do that unless I absolutely must,' Jane said again.

'Even if you did it still wouldn't be enough. With what you've got in your current account you'd still be only half way there.'

'I'd better be off then,' she said, and rose.

'No, no,' said Rubens. 'Please hear me out. Cigarette?' He offered the box on the desk and she took one.

'Medlicott and I can arrange for you to have the money on a short-term loan,' said Rubens, 'if you were to receive an agreed share of Bower's newspapers as security. It would be rather a large share – from what you tell us Bower is not a very good risk at the moment – and of course there would be interest on the loan.' Jane lit her cigarette and inserted it into the jade holder, taking her time.

'It's a good offer,' said Rubens, 'perhaps even a happy one. Everybody benefits.'

She looked at Medlicott. 'I agree with Rubens,' he said.

'Interest?' she asked.

'Five per cent per month,' said Rubens, 'to be shared between us.'

'I couldn't –' said Jane.

'You are not a charitable institution,' said Medlicott, 'any more than we are, and your friends must be made aware of the fact.'

'But five per cent per month –'

'I've no doubt he'll be glad to pay it.'

Her next problem was to tell him. She looked at her watch. They would be on their way to the Fleet Street flat by now: perhaps already there: for her to ring was impossible.

'You'll have to call him,' she said, and gave them the number. 'If you don't mind, I'd rather not hear it.'

'Of course,' said Medlicott. 'We'll use Rubens's office.'

While she waited she looked again at the jewellery. So much of it, and nearly all the wages of sin. She would sell Jay Bower's ear-rings, she thought. If Bower didn't need the money, Felston could have it, and the way things were going Felston might need it. And Lovell's ear-rings were far nicer. That was an unforgivable thought, but there was no denying its truth.

The two lawyers came back at last. Their expressions told her nothing.

'He said he didn't want to mortgage his paper.'

'He turned us down?' Almost she was glad.

'It was touch and go,' said Rubens. He looked bewildered. 'The one chance he had to save his neck – and he admitted it – and he didn't want to take it.'

'But in the end he did?'

'When we told him that the share in his paper would be held by you – if it came to that,' Medlicott said. 'Then he agreed.'

'Was he angry?'

'Not angry,' said Rubens. 'Bewildered. At first at any rate. I've seen it happen before, with rich men who lose their money. At first they can't believe it. They know it's true, but they just can't accept it – and even when they can, they still have the idea they're in control. He saw sense quicker than most, I'd say. Couldn't wait to start calling New York.'

'I can leave it to you then?' she asked.

'Certainly,' Rubens said. 'It's a straightforward enough transaction.'

Jane rose. She desperately needed to get away.

'Just one thing,' said Medlicott. 'Mr Bower did happen to say that this was the first night of his honeymoon.' He looked reproachful. 'I do think you should have mentioned that.'

An early night. No more champagne, not even another martini, just a bowl of soup and a cup of coffee, then up to her bedroom with Foch for company. She wouldn't sleep anyway, but she had to lie down, and with Foch beside her at least she could talk. She undressed and put on her dressing gown, and Foch looked at once to the chair.

'Oh all right,' she said, 'but I must lie down soon. I feel as if I'd just finished a ten-mile walk.' Then she sat and Foch clambered on to her lap, ready to be stroked.

'Jay of all people,' she said. 'Like that clever clogs Rubens said, he was so used to being in control. And now he's going to have to be nice to me. No. . . . Not Jay. He doesn't know how to be nice. . . . And the first night of his honeymoon. Poor Mr Medlicott. I wonder what they were doing when he phoned?' Foch sighed. Her fingers had found the precise spot behind his ears that he could never reach.

'He'll be happy now,' she said. 'At least I hope he will. Enough cash to survive and his bride in his arms. Will Catherine be happy too, do you think?' Foch gave a sort of canine shrug. Lady Catherine Bower was no concern of his. Who was Bower to her at the moment, she wondered. Bluebeard or Santa Claus? But she did not say it aloud, not even to Foch. She continued to stroke him. The feel of the harsh hair was soothing to them both.

'But it isn't as if it was just Jay Bower,' she said. 'As you are well aware, there is now another gentleman in my life – and he and Mr Bower are *not* friends. And yet I was going to pawn his gift to me – to save a man he detests. He wasn't at the wedding either. I do hope they haven't had another row. He'll have to be told, by the way. He'll find out anyway. He always finds out everything about Mr Bower – but it isn't that. He has a *right* to be told.

'You may well ask,' she told Foch, 'if I ever loved Jay Bower. If the way he feels about Catherine is love, then I never did, any more than I love Charles. . . . I did love John Patterson, but that was more than a dozen years ago, when you weren't even a pup. You can like a man and perform the most extraordinary antics with him, without being in love with him, thank God. Do you feel the same about ladies? That spaniel bitch in Offley Villas, for instance?'

Foch made an indeterminate noise at the back of his throat. His love life, it seemed, was his own concern. Jane picked him off her lap and laid him down on the carpet, where he fell asleep almost at once.

'Lucky for some,' she said, and took off her robe, lay down on the bed and lit a cigarette. No chance at all that she would sleep.

It had been the devil of a day. A marvellous start, no doubt about that: her suit a success, and Mummy's, and Mummy in terrific form. But then it had all started to go wrong. Piers for instance: he had been much too drunk, and rather shifty about that hunting in the shires. Had he taken Brenda Coupland off for dissolute purposes instead? She rather doubted it. He wouldn't have looked shifty about that. Then Jay and his shattering misfortune which had turned her into a usurer, not to mention the betrayer of Charles. . . . Hussy. Jezebel. . . . But unless she betrayed Charles she couldn't have saved Jay Bower. She wanted to cry, but there was no point in crying if you didn't know what you were crying *about*. And then there was Catherine. . . .

Truett was saying, 'Telephone, Miss Whitcomb. Telephone.'

Jane opened her eyes. Why was it that they always woke you just when sleep came lapping like the waves at Cap d'Antibes?

'He insisted, miss,' said Truett.

'Who did?'

'Mr Bower, miss.' Truett sounded surprised that Jane should ask such a question.

'Did you tell him I'd gone to bed?'

'Yes, miss.'

'What did he say?'

'He said it was important, miss. Get her to the phone, he said.'

Jane toyed with the idea of telling Truett to hang up, but what would be the point? He would only ring back.

'Tell him I'm coming,' she said.

'I've got to talk to you,' said Bower.

'Truett did mention that I was sleeping?'

'This is important. First off I have to thank you for arranging the loan.'

'Write me a letter,' said Jane.

'No . . . wait!' He was back in the editorial chair again. 'You've just about saved my life.' She said nothing. 'My married life, anyway. Maybe you didn't know it, but the *World*'s in hock to a lot more people than you.'

'I didn't know it.'

'Bankers mostly.' He left it at that. 'I was living high on the hog because of what I had in the States. Thanks to you I still have a few bucks in the States – not as much as before, but enough.'

'Jay I'm glad, honestly,' she said, 'but I'm also terribly sleepy.'

It was as if she hadn't spoken. 'I want you to do me another favour,' he said. 'There's a good reason, believe me.'

'What reason?'

'Because if you do you'll get your money back quicker.' Debtors as well as creditors had their own kind of leverage, it seemed, and besides, Jay Bower knew perfectly well that she wanted no share of his newspapers.

'What do you want me to do?'

'Go to New York,' he said. 'I've told Don Cook to forget about that Daisy piece. You can do some more about New York instead.'

'That's all?'

'Of course not. I want you to see my creditors are paid. I've got the money to pay them, but I need the right kind of receipts.'

'Won't your lawyer do that?'

'He will if you're watching him. I tell you New York is about to go crazy.'

That would be worth seeing, she thought. 'Very well.'

'Thanks,' he said, and paused, then said again, 'You've just about saved my life. How soon can you leave?'

'The first boat I can get. And you? What will you do?'

'Us?' said Bower. 'Go on off to Paris and Cap d'Antibes. Catherine would be very upset if we didn't.'

Jane blinked at the handset. The ramifications of love still managed to surprise her.

'Yes,' she said. 'I expect she would. Where is she, by the way? I mean, how did you manage to get to the phone?'

'She's asleep,' said Bower. He sounded smug. Santa Claus all the way, she thought.

'I think I'll follow her example.' For the first time since she'd known him, Jane hung up first.

The first thing, the most important thing, was to talk to Lovell. She had no idea how he would react: roar, beat her, walk out on her or simply shrug. With Charles one never knew, which was a considerable part of his attraction. It would have to be at his flat in Mount Street, she thought, on account of the roaring. The beating was something she'd have to take a chance on. Mornings were tricky for him, she knew, but she phoned early next day, and told him it was urgent, and he postponed two meetings.

He had heard nothing, not yet. The very way he held and kissed her told her that. Lovell let her go at last and led her into the drawing room, offered to make coffee, but she refused. She wanted to get it over with.

'It's always a pleasure to see you, you know that,' he said, 'but I've a feeling I'm not going to enjoy this very much.'

'Why do you say that?'

'Because I know you,' he said. 'I know you better than I thought it was possible for one human being to know another – and I've never known you quite like this.'

She told him, fully, completely, reeling it off as if it were a letter to Daisy, because that was the way she had learned to tell things. When she had done she took from her bag the two little shagreen cases that contained the Fabergé jewels, put them on the sofa table beside her.

'Naturally I've brought them back,' she said. 'I'm glad I didn't have to pawn them. . . . I can't say I'm sorry for what I did, but I do regret the necessity. Honestly.'

She was about to rise, to leave, but he said, 'Sit still. We haven't finished.'

'No,' she said. 'I suppose not.'

'You would have pawned my jewels and sold his,' he said. 'Why is that?'

She told him half the truth. 'His aren't important to me.'

'No?' Lovell was incredulous. 'And yet you saved his skin for him.'

'Because he's a friend, a colleague,' she said. 'Because he's just married a girl who thinks poverty's having only two sable coats.' He sat silent. 'It was only money after all,' she said.

'Only?'

'And not even mine. My lawyers found it.'

'Medlicott and Rubens,' said Lovell, and smiled. 'I'd hate to be Bower if he got behind with the payments.'

'He won't.'

Lovell shrugged. Whatever happened to Bower, it seemed, would be inadequate. 'You think I'm responsible for this?' he asked.

'Yes,' she said. 'I'm afraid I do.'

'You're wrong.' He got up, paced the room and turned to face her, still taut and trim, like the soldier he once had been. 'I could have done it – nothing easier, but I didn't. Breaking him would have been too much. All I did was take his movie business from him. The rest he contrived for himself.'

'Why did you take his movie business?'

'I could get it cheaply. It was worth having.'

'That isn't the only reason, is it?'

'As we're being honest, no. I took it because I detested him, and it seemed the most appropriate of his possessions to deprive him of.'

'Appropriate?'

'It involved you,' he said.

'The Serpent of Old Nile,' she said. 'Cleopatra,' and smiled in her turn. Almost she added, 'Really, Charles,' but stopped herself in time. For Lovell this was deadly serious.

'It was all over long before I met you,' she said. 'My word on that.'

'Of course,' he said, 'but to be jealous is to be stupid. I am aware of that, but I'm also jealous. And so I robbed him. Legally of course, but it was robbery.'

'Just because we were lovers?'

'Yes.'

'But that's worse than stupid,' she said. 'It's crazy. Do you suppose he was the only other man I ever slept with?'

He stormed across to her, and she waited for the blow.

'You'd better explain yourself,' he said.

'I don't have to,' she said. 'But I will – since we're being honest. . . . There was one other, and only one. You met him.'

'I did?' He was bewildered.

'John Patterson,' she said. 'My captain in the Royal Northumbrians. He told you to carry a rifle instead of a revolver.'

'But he was your fiancé,' said Lovell. 'It was in the middle of the war. You were going to marry. Of course you –' He broke off.

'Bower asked me to marry him,' she said. 'Again and again. Showed me the house in Berkshire by moonlight, turned up the volume on the nightingales. It worked with Catherine. It didn't with me.'

'He wanted to marry you?'

'He made quite a point of it,' said Jane. 'And why sound so surprised? *You* want to marry me.'

'And you refused him?'

'Every time. But at least he offered.'

Lovell went back to his chair and sat. Above everything else he seemed bewildered.

'You swear to me this is true?' he said.

'No,' said Jane. 'I don't swear. I tell you so – as one would between friends, which I hope we still are.'

'It's just – I thought he'd taken advantage of you, you see,' said Lovell, unheeding. 'There was this one thing I wanted – the only thing I wanted and couldn't have, and I thought he hadn't even bothered to ask.'

'Well now you know,' said Jane.

'Now I know,' said Lovell. 'But I'm damned if I know how I feel.'

'Better, I hope.'

'Very possibly,' Lovell said, 'but it doesn't matter. I'm still in love with you. And now you tell me you're off to New York?' Jane nodded. 'Would it bother you to tell me the names of the people Bower asked you to see?' Jane stared at him. 'Don't worry,' Lovell said testily. 'I'm not up to my evil ways again. It's just that if I knew the names I might be able to make life easier for you, that's all.' He smiled. 'My word on it.'

She gave him the names.

'I can help you,' he said.

'Help Bower, you mean.'

'And Medlicott. And Rubens,' said Lovell. 'I might even save you all some money. At least I know a man in New York who will. But don't ever tell them I did it. . . . Am I forgiven?'

'If Jay Bower was silly enough to take you on and lost, that's between the two of you,' said Jane. 'There's nothing to forgive.'

'And we'll go on seeing each other?' he asked.

'I'm here,' she said. 'It's up to you when I go.'

'If that were true,' he said, 'you'd never leave.'

She managed to obtain a suite on the *Aquitania* two days later, and Bower of course tried to pay for it, which was ridiculous. How could he even consider suites on luxury liners when he was going broke? He still had no concept of what it was to be poor, or even moderately well off, and Jane had no time to teach him, except by sending back his cheque.

# 36

THE NEWS BROKE when they were three days out. Every day the ship published its own newspaper and every weekday the bulletin contained the Wall Street stock market quotations. For years now those quotations had recorded a climb so steady as to seem inevitable, but on Wall Street the firework display was over at last: the final rocket exploded and the golden dreams began to fall.

The first reaction was incredulity, the second a rush to the bar, and then an urgent need to send a cable, and a rush to the wireless operator. Jane went and watched, and memorised. The notes would have to wait till later. Millionaires forming a queue, she thought. What they called standing in line. And not only millionaires. Their maids and valets hovered beside them, as desperate for news as their masters. One at least of the millionaires was drunk, one had a heart attack just as it was his turn. The bar was packed, the dining room almost deserted. Jane went to her suite and ordered soup, sandwiches, champagne.

'Not many people have your appetite, miss,' the steward said. 'Not today.'

'The bar seemed to be doing well,' said Jane.

'Funny thing about Americans, miss. They have to go abroad to do their drinking and leave all their money at home – and then they find out they haven't got any.'

'You too?' said Jane.

'I dabbled,' said the steward. 'I was saving up to buy a pub and then I went and dabbled instead. I didn't lose the lot, touch wood –' he rapped his forehead '– but it'll be a long time now before I buy a pub.'

He's been drinking too, thought Jane, and who will blame him?

The steward opened the champagne and poured her a glass.

'Is it so very bad?' she asked.

'Cables,' said the steward. 'Ship to shore telephone. The big banks intervening. Multi-millionaires like Morgan and Rocke-feller going to steady the market. All be fine next week. So they say.'

'You don't believe it?'

'Not what they're saying,' said the steward. 'I believe what they're doing, though.'

'What's that?'

'Selling,' said the steward. 'Or trying to. Only they can't find any buyers. . . . Steady the market. You might as well try to put Niagara in reverse.' He served the soup for her, opened his mouth, then shut it again. 'I hope I haven't talked out of turn, miss,' he said.

'Not at all,' said Jane. 'This has been a terrible day for you.'

'All of that, miss,' said the steward. 'I think I'll go and lie down for a bit if you don't mind.'

Next morning brought news of a suicide. A Mr Golding, owner of a chain of hardware stores around Newark, New Jersey, had shot himself in the head while alone in his cabin. His wife said she couldn't understand it. He had no reason to be depressed. The market was bound to steady. Everybody said so. Suicide, Jane was to discover, would become a common-place, but this was the first. It seemed to her that every passen-ger aboard held their breath, trying to decide who would be next. It was not the sort of thing one usually wrote about to Dearest Daisy, but it had its own excitement, and it was disgrace-fully easy to moralise. The ship finished its voyage in a kind of drunken gloom.

At Pier 90 Barry for once was not there to meet her – more financial woe, she thought – but there was no shortage of taxis. She found that there was no shortage of tables in expensive restaurants either, or nightclubs, or seats in theatres. America was going broke, and the first casualties were luxuries: a Cadil-lac, an Isotta-Fraschini, a Manet or a seventy-roomed cottage in

Maine, the For Sale columns in the newspapers told her, she could have taken her pick; except that she found she couldn't bring herself to do so, that it seemed wrong: but it had been hard to turn down the Isotta-Fraschini. Only the cinemas were doing well, but the cinemas were offering three hours of oblivion for as little as a dime, and so the queues stretched round the block. Charles had been right yet again.

George and Martha seemed to her the only happy people she saw for the first few days, and she knew them well enough to ask them why. They looked at each other, and Martha chuckled.

'We talked it over last year, George and me,' she said. 'The way we figured it, it couldn't last and it shouldn't last.'

'Shouldn't?' said Jane.

'If it had lasted that meant it would have gone right on getting better,' said Martha. 'Every day till the end of the world. And that didn't sound like the will of God to George and me, so we sold all the stocks and bonds and put the money in the bank.'

'I hope it's a big one,' said Jane.

'First National,' said George.

'Big enough,' said Jane. She had an account there herself, and didn't doubt for a moment that George and Martha knew it.

The next day the cables arrived. The first was from Georgie: 'Returning New York Thursday Mauretania,' she read. 'On no account lend money to MF. Hugs and kisses. Georgie.' MF must be Murray Fisch, thought Jane. Had he been caught by the market too? But why not? It seemed that everybody else had, except George and Martha.

The second cable was from Bob. 'Bet's had a daugther,' Jane read. 'Please say whether OK to call it Jane.' She cabled 'Yes', and thought vaguely of a christening mug, but money in the bank would be a better idea. She wondered then who had advised Bet to call her child Jane. Bob was certainly clever enough, but too far away to be bothered. Andy and Grandma were clever enough too, but they would have regarded the idea as no better than begging. It must have been that husband of hers, she thought, and not a bad idea either. A father should provide for his offspring in every way he can.

A friend of Lovell's came to see her; or at least that was how he described himself on the telephone. Andrew Fairweather, banker, and Groton and Harvard, so Charles had told her.

Fairish shot, good with a rod, rode to hounds from time to time in Virginia, but after twenty minutes Jane was quite sure that he was not Charles's friend: his slave perhaps, but not his friend. Charles owned him.

'So after Charles cabled me I naturally held myself in readiness to do anything I could,' Fairweather said. 'Always a pleasure to help my friend Charles – or indeed any of his friends who may need my poor services.'

It sounded all right – the slightly over-enthusiastic bonhomie, the all-pals-together-at-the-Ivy-League-Club stuff, but there was something wrong with it, and at first she couldn't quite place what it was, and then it came to her. Beneath all the hearty booming Andrew Fairweather was furious. Charles had snapped his fingers and he'd jumped, to fetch and carry for a woman he had never even heard of, a woman who was far too friendly with her servants – and a couple of Coloureds at that – a woman who Charles had insisted must be treated with respect and instant obedience. If she'd told him to grovel he'd have got on his knees at once: he had no choice.

'There are debts that I've promised to see paid,' she said.

'Charles told me in the cable,' said Fairweather. 'He sent me the names – and the amounts.' Jane looked at him. 'In code of course.'

'Of course.'

'My instructions are to settle for less than the amounts stated, wherever possible. It shouldn't be too difficult. Ready money is a rare commodity in New York these days.'

He should have enjoyed that, she thought, but in fact he was still furious, and in the end she realised why. There was nothing in it for him. He got to his feet, still booming away with furious camaraderie.

'Better get on with it,' he said. 'Mustn't keep a friend of Charles's waiting.'

'So nice that you're a friend of his too,' said Jane. 'It makes a sort of bond, wouldn't you say?'

For a moment she thought that he might hit her, then George brought him his hat.

Jane tried and failed for the twentieth time to phone Barry, then began another letter to Daisy: jewellers' shops for sale and men selling apples on the street and Georgie due in on Thursday. A tricky mixture, but she was getting it to blend when Martha knocked and came in.

'Miss Erika Bauer on the phone for you,' she said. Jane sighed. 'It would be,' she said.

'Yes, miss.' Martha stood impassive. 'Last time I had to wake you up.' Suddenly the two women laughed out loud. 'Better take it, I suppose,' said Jane, and went into the drawing room.

'Erika darling,' she said. 'I was going to call you in a few days and surprise you. How on earth did you know I was in New York?'

'You're in the *Star*,' said Erika, 'and the *Herald and* the *Tribune*. Why in a few days?'

Crisp, thought Jane. Extremely crisp. 'Because I'm working, darling,' she said reproachfully. 'Some of us do, you know.'

'Certainly I know,' said Erika. 'I do myself. That's why I want to see you. Can't you come to the party tonight?'

'All the way to that castle for a party?'

'No no.' Erika's voice became indulgent, as if Jane's ignorance, though obvious, was excusable. 'I live in the Village now. Do say you'll come.' In the end that was the easiest thing to say.

The address was 73 Chestnut Street, and once again it was all too easy to find a cab that would take her. Number 73 turned out to be a small neat house in a small, neat street, but house and street alike were beginning to show the first, ineradicable signs of decay. Suddenly Jane found herself homesick for South Terrace, and paid off her driver with far too large a tip, walked up a brick-paved path and pressed a bell that at once exploded into life with a noise like a fire alarm. Nothing happened. Jane looked at her watch: seven fifteen. She had been invited for seven. Once more she pressed the bell, and then, being conscientious, a third time. If there was no answer she would finish her letter to Daisy, and Martha would cook her a steak. Martha cooked steaks superbly. . . . The door opened and Jane found herself looking at a young woman wearing pyjamas that weren't all that clean.

'Why Erika,' she said, 'I hope I didn't wake you?'

'A nap,' said Erika Bauer. 'So *sorry*. We had rather a late night of it. Krominski was here. Just back from Russia.'

'How exciting,' said Jane.

'So I thought I would have time for a nap. It seems I didn't.'

My fault? Jane wondered. 'But come in anyway.'

Jane followed her down a hall painted white, and hung with artefacts that seemed African in origin, and were uniformly black. Each one was of a quite staggering ugliness. Beyond the hall was a living room, large and elegantly proportioned, and decked out with a squalor that only the very rich can achieve, and probably only very rich females at that, thought Jane. A man would have hired servants.

The furniture was good: solid, American traditional, and the lamps came from Tiffany's. But the ashtrays overflowed, dirty, empty glasses seemed to be everywhere, and a pretty blue-and-white carpet was stained with something that might have been scrambled eggs. Nobody had done anything about it, Jane was sure, because nobody had hired any servants. Sooner or later Erika would have to hire servants. Either that or she would have to move.

'Make yourself at home,' said Erika Bauer.

Jane chose a chair that bore no visible evidence of either food or drink. She was wearing a silk Poiret suit of which she was rather fond. Erika went to a pile of magazines in a corner of the room, and brought the top one to Jane, who looked at the cover. '*Red Awakening*', she read. 'The American Road to Socialism.' There followed a list of contributors, and then the words: 'Edited by E. Bauer and J. Klein. J. Klein and E. Bauer Publishers.' The cover of the magazine was of course red, with something that might well have been a rising sun embedded in the middle. Erika waited. Something, it seemed, had to be said.

'How exciting,' said Jane.

'Yes, isn't it?' Erika's voice held no trace of irony. 'Our very first edition and it appeared on the day – the very day – that American capitalism went into terminal decline.'

'Didn't that rather affect sales?' Jane asked.

'By no means.' Erika was triumphant. 'Almost the whole edition was given over to articles saying that that was precisely what would happen. So far as we can discover, we were the only magazine in America that dared to print that very obvious truth. How exciting that you'll be writing for us.' Exciting for whom, Jane wondered, but it was not yet the time to quibble. She took out her cigarette case, lighter and holder instead, and Erika at once looked disapproving. What on earth does she expect? Jane wondered. A corn-cob pipe?

'You don't mind if I smoke?' she said aloud.

'Not at all,' said Erika, 'but forgive me. Isn't all that gold and jade rather bourgeois?'

'Not when I use them,' Jane said firmly. 'But speaking of the bourgeoisie, I bring you greetings from your brother.'

'Joachim of *course*,' said Erika. She sounded pleased that she should have remembered his name. 'How is he?'

'Married.'

'He wrote to tell me,' said Erika. 'Such a pity I couldn't go myself.' She looked at the pile of magazines. 'So much to do. But you must know how it is.'

A voice from the door said, 'Does your friend really know about work, Erika darling?' Jane looked towards the sound. Another woman in pyjamas – was it some sort of uniform? Or maybe it was to be a pyjama party? This must be J. Klein, she thought, tall, slender, almost beautiful in red silk pyjamas that were grubby and coffee stained. Obviously Jewish, too, and Jane wondered whether Erika's father had met her. Jay Bower certainly hadn't: he would have said so.

'Of course Jane knows about work,' said Erika. 'She's a very successful writer. Hollywood, too. Jane – this is my friend Jennifer Klein – Jane Whitcomb.' Jane offered her hand, and Jennifer Klein accepted it, reluctantly, Jane thought, releasing it almost at once.

'But hardly a worker,' she said. 'More of an intellectual like us. Unless you classify yourself as a bourgeois?'

'I don't classify myself as anything,' said Jane. 'I'm not the sort of writer who needs a label.'

'That's a shame,' said Jennifer Klein. 'From our point of view, I mean. We're the sort of editors who believe in commitment.' She walked to the sofa and sat, and just missed treading on the carpet's scrambled egg. Jane waited. 'You look rich,' Jennifer Klein said. Jane found that she had nothing to say to that, either. It was Erika who scurried into speech.

'Jennifer is very well known for her openness,' she said. 'It's part of her commitment, being honest and direct. She has a hatred of hypocrisy.'

'I'm sure Miss Whitcomb will discover that for herself – if we are to work together,' said Jennifer Klein, and then to Jane:

'I'm rich, too, as it happens. And Erika isn't exactly poor. It's amusing, don't you think, in an ironic sort of way – two women of the Left who have managed to hang on to their money –'

'While all around them the bourgeoisie are losing theirs?' said Jane. 'It has a certain irony, certainly.'

'But it also means that we can continue to publish,' said Erika. 'The time has never been more ripe for what we must do.'

'America – perhaps almost the entire capitalist system, in ruins,' said Jennifer Klein. 'Now is the perfect time to tell the world what must be done.'

'You're proposing a revolution?' Jane asked.

'It may not come to that,' said Jennifer Klein, 'in the sense that the revolution may come from within.'

'So many people who thought themselves secure,' Erika said. 'Little people. Workers. With a few hundred dollars of savings they worked for all their lives. And now they have nothing. Their lives are shattered. They have no idea what to do –'

'And so we must tell them,' said Jennifer Klein. 'There is no good – no *value* in being shattered. They must be angry. It's their duty to be angry – angry enough to overthrow what caused their downfall and build again, build a new system in which they are the masters. Anger alone will do it, if they are angry enough. And if they aren't, then it will have to be revolution. Obviously. We have a shining example after all.'

They mean it, thought Jane. These two mad women really mean it. But then are they really so mad? The system they hate so much *is* close to collapse. People *have* lost their savings. There'll be anger soon enough.

'Will you help us?' Erika asked. 'Will you write for us?'

'Subject to certain conditions,' said Jennifer Klein. 'Party discipline we can't demand – not yet. But we do insist on an orthodox Left-Wing viewpoint. What you call a label.'

'Will I be paid?' asked Jane.

'On acceptance,' Jennifer Klein said at once. 'We aren't lavish payers. We can't afford to be. The magazine eats money – but we have to keep it going.'

'Two dollars a thousand words,' said Erika. 'Five thousand words maximum. We try to use people who are good at their craft, as well as idealists, but that's all we can afford – and yet very few people turn us down. Don't you think that's wonderful?'

'It's because of their faith in what we are trying to do,' said Jennifer Klein. 'Their contribution to the cause of Socialism.'

And now it's up to me to make mine, thought Jane. Aloud she said, 'Three years ago in England we had what we called a General Strike. For a brief while the workers shut the whole country down. I could do you a piece about that.'

'A strike that failed,' said Jennifer Klein. 'Hardly inspirational, is it?'

'I'm not sure it did fail,' said Jane. 'It may be that it could happen again, especially after what's happened here, in America. And if it does – it will be violent.'

'Was there violence the first time?' Jennifer Klein asked.

'Yes.'

'And did you see some of it?'

'Quite a bit,' said Jane.

'Then go ahead and write your piece. Sometimes there is a need for violence. Now is such a time. It isn't that I – that any of us – enjoy violence. It's because there's a need. Until we destroy, how can we possibly rebuild?' said Jennifer Klein, then turned to Erika. 'Already the workers are making jokes about the rich men who lost their money,' she said. 'And that's a good sign. A joke can be the beginning of anger. There is one I heard today. Two bourgeois are discussing a third who has lost all his money in the stock market crash, and killed himself because of it.' To Jane she said, 'I suppose you've heard there have been a great many suicides?'

'I've heard,' said Jane.

'And one rich bourgeois says to the other – "How did he do it? Jump off the Chrysler building?" That's the tallest building in New York. In the world probably. . . . And the other rich bourgeois says "Good heavens no. He didn't lose nearly enough money to jump off the Chrysler building."' Jane decided not to stay for the party.

On the way home in a taxi she thought about the two of them, as cocooned against the world outside as caterpillars waiting to be butterflies. And yet they were so absolutely sure. Was it possible for them to be so wrong, here in a city where everything that gave delight was closed already or waiting for the end, a city where the Goths were only two days' march away at best?

In the apartment George was waiting for her, obviously unhappy, as if he too had heard about the Goths.

'You've got visitors, miss,' he told her. 'I told them you weren't home, but nobody seems to listen any more.'

She went into the drawing room. Barry was sitting there with Murray Fisch. Each seemed to be looking at the other with a kind of incredulous horror.

'Gin,' said Jane firmly, 'and vermouth. It's well past the cocktail hour.'

George went at once, before Murray Fisch could finish saying 'Nothing for me thank you,' and Jane went across to kiss Barry and say, 'Darling where on earth have you been? I've phoned and phoned.'

Barry was looking quite beautiful: Sulka shirt and tie, and a suit that even Lionel would have approved. Suddenly Jane was sure that Barry had lost every cent he ever had.

'So I gathered,' he said. 'I've been away. Staying with friends. Lucky to have them the way the world is now. Friends, I mean.'

'Yes indeed,' said Jane, and turned to her other visitor. 'And you, Murray? I do hope you're well. How is everything on the Coast?'

'Never better.' Fisch spoke as firmly as if he were denying the nastiest kind of rumour. 'The motion picture business is absolutely fine.'

'Well that's good news for those of us who rely on it,' said Jane, as George brought in the laden tray: gin, vermouth, ice and shaker.

'I'll mix them myself,' she said and George bowed and left them to it.

'Nothing for me,' Fisch said again. 'I've got a lot to take care of in no time at all. I was just hoping for a few minutes' talk about our movie, if that's OK?'

'Of course,' said Jane, and made cocktails for three, then shook and poured. 'We'll just have one tiny drink together in the study, and leave Barry on his own till we've finished.' She turned to Barry. 'We won't be long, darling. I know we've got simply masses to talk about.'

Murray Fisch said, 'It's my belief that that man is not a normal male.'

'Mine too,' said Jane, 'but it's a pity you can't dance with him. Is that what you came to talk about, Murray? Homosexuals?'

'I came to talk about our movie,' said Murray Fisch.

'Oh lovely,' said Jane. 'I saw Georgie in London only last week. She told me how well it was going.'

'I thought Georgie was in France, looking at battlefields,' said Fisch.

'Not last week she wasn't. She was in Bond Street, looking at diamonds.' Murray Fisch shot up in his chair, as if I'd just jabbed him with a hat pin, thought Jane.

'She's right, of course,' he said at last. 'The movie's going ahead just great. The flying sequences are almost finished, and we're nearly ready for the scenes in the trenches. Once Georgie gets back we'll go right to work.'

'Thursday,' said Jane.

'I beg your pardon?'

'That's when Georgie gets back.'

'Oh,' said Murray Fisch, and then: 'Oh great . . . great. This is going to be a winner, Jane. I promise you. Maybe even an Academy Award winner. Best actress and best writer, even. I tell you with a story like that anything's possible. The trouble is, there's just one snag.'

'Oh dear,' said Jane. 'Nothing too dire, I hope?'

'Nothing we can't handle between us,' said Fisch.

'What sort of snag?' said Jane.

'The one that's always with us,' Murray Fisch said. 'Money.' Then he held up his hand as if to stem a torrent of words Jane had no intention of unleashing. 'But it's nothing you and I can't solve in this room, right here and now.' Jane waited.

'It's like this,' said Fisch. 'The Depression has been a disaster here, as you can imagine.'

'I can indeed.'

Murray Fisch took heart at that. The English woman had spoken at last, and her words were encouraging.

'Even in Hollywood,' he said.

'Good gracious.' Murray Fisch felt better by the minute.

'My word on it,' he said. 'As you know we raise a lot of our finance through the banks, and just at the moment the banks haven't all that much money to lend – not even for a project as sure-fire as ours is, which means our budget is just a little short up front. Nothing too awful, and if we waited a while we'd get it anyway, once things settle down, but Georgie's on her way back home as you know and we want to get things started. The sooner we get our hands on those Academy Awards the better.'

'Yes indeed,' said Jane. 'How much is World Wide short?'

Murray Fisch winced. Such forthrightness he found upsetting. 'It's not the company,' he said. 'The company's in pretty good shape, considering those shenanigans on Wall Street. It's me that has the responsibility – as producer I make the budget one million three, and as things are I'm exactly twenty-seven thousand dollars short. Say seven thousand of your pounds. Isn't that ridiculous? Twenty-seven thousand short in a budget of over a million? But if I don't get the money in place our movie could be put back for months – maybe even to next year.'

'Oh dear,' said Jane.

'So what do you say?' said Murray Fisch.

'What can I say?' said Jane. 'It's simply terrible. . . . How on earth are you going to tell Georgie?'

'If you were to lend me the money I wouldn't have to tell her,' Murray Fisch said.

'I?' One word. Not even that. Just a letter. But it told him with utter clarity that she wasn't going to lend him a dollar, or even a dime. 'I'm afraid I couldn't possibly lend you money, Murray,' she said. 'My lawyers handle all that sort of thing for me, and of course they are in London. You could cable them, I suppose. Medlicott and Rubens.'

'No lawyers,' Murray Fisch said. 'I was hoping to keep this on a personal basis.'

'Money's never on a personal basis,' said Jane. 'That's why I make my lawyers handle it. Oh dear. . . . It does seem a shame. A mere twenty-seven thousand dollars, as you said.' Her brow wrinkled, then cleared. 'I tell you what,' she said. 'Why don't you ask that nice Mr Lovell who stayed at Cap d'Antibes? He's a banker, so they tell me, and he seemed absolutely fascinated by the movie business.'

Murray Fisch said, 'I just might do that. In fact if you'll excuse me I'll get on to it right away.'

'Of course,' said Jane. 'We must save the picture before Georgie gets back.'

'Yeah,' said Murray Fisch. 'But you won't tell her, will you?

We don't want her worried –' He smiled bravely. '– and I'll find the money somehow.'

'Of course you will,' said Jane. 'And I've no intention of worrying Georgie.' Murray Fisch fled.

The nerve of the man, she thought. The sheer bloody nerve. But that wasn't it, not really. For whatever reasons he desperately needed to get his hands on twenty-seven thousand dollars, probably to meet those mysterious margins Charles was always pontificating about – and when you're desperate you either find the nerve or go under. But that was not why she was so angry. It was because he had considered her fool enough to fall for a cock and bull story like that one. That didn't just hurt: it stung. She went to the mirror and used powder and lipstick.

'Calm down,' she told herself. 'This is none of it Barry's fault – and if you're right the poor boy's going to need all the sympathy he can get.' She went back to the drawing room and poured Barry another drink.

'That producer left as if you'd tied a rocket to him,' he said. 'I hope he didn't upset you too much.'

'He didn't upset me at all,' Jane said. 'On the contrary.'

'Was he trying to raise a loan?'

Somehow she didn't leap out of her chair. 'Why on earth should he?'

'Everybody is,' said Barry. 'Everybody's poor. Everybody owes their broker and their bank, and the banks and brokers want to be paid now. This minute. Just because he's a Hollywood big shot doesn't make him different from anybody else.'

'You too?' she asked.

He smiled. It was the smile, she would have sworn, of a man without a care in the world.

'Sure,' he said. 'When it comes to money – or the lack of it – I'm as normal as the next guy.'

'You're broke?'

'Totally.'

'But – forgive me – I don't mean to pry – but what happened?'

'I bought too much stock with money I didn't have. Like everybody else. And like everybody else I tried to borrow. Only unlike everybody else I *did* borrow. I found a guy who loaned me the money I needed. He's called a loan shark.'

'Loan shark?'

'Sort of high rates of interest. Like twenty per cent. Per month.'

'But that's ridiculous,' said Jane. 'No court would –'

'Honey,' Barry said. 'We're not talking about courts. We're not talking about law – or even order. We're talking about a man who will break your arm if you miss one payment. That's what a loan shark is. Fortunately I got lucky. Or I thought I did. I got enough money to pay him off.'

'But how –?'

'I sold my apartment, which in these days is incredible. Sold it for cash – to a widow who thinks it might be a nice place to rehabilitate a few unfortunates down on their luck, provided they don't mind doing their rehabilitation lying down. Then my uncle in Chicago died and left me his collection of gold coins. Gold, Jane. It's about the one stuff people still stand in line to buy. And then –'

'Yes?'

'I became what the song calls an old man's darling. Mind you that could be worse. It could be a hell of a lot worse, as a matter of fact. He's rather sweet. . . . But even if he wasn't, I have to eat. Oh – and starting tomorrow I'm also playing the piano in a bar. Not our sort of bar, I'm afraid, but it's three dollars a night and all the gin I can drink without falling over.'

'I can lend you some money,' said Jane.

Barry held up his hand in rebuke. 'What do you take me for?' he said. 'A film producer? I'm OK, Jane. Honestly. In fact compared with some I'm laughing. I just wanted you to know why you hadn't heard from me. Please don't look so sad. The whole United States is broke. At least I've still got a silk shirt left. Do you know anybody who's better off than me?'

'Four,' she said. 'In the whole city I know four. Two are Christians who believed that the boom was sinful and got out of it last year, and the other two are – I think – a couple of lesbians who're so Left-Wing they knew the boom would fail and so they never got into it in the first place.'

'So the moral of our story is to be a believer?'

'The moral is to let me lend you some money.'

'No darling,' Barry said.

'I wouldn't break your arm.'

'And so you'd never get your money back – and we both know

it.' He looked at his watch: a gold Cartier. He had chosen the most extraordinary way to be destitute.

'I'll have to go,' he said. 'The man who keeps me will be home soon, and he hates to be kept waiting. But impatience can be a virtue too.'

'You won't just disappear?' she said. 'You'll call me?'

'Of course.' Once more the brilliant, carefree smile, and she knew that she would never see him again.

# 37

IT REALLY DID need a lot of thinking about – or else no thinking at all, because there seemed to be no answers, no explanations. Maybe Charles Lovell could explain it to her, or just possibly her mother, but aside from them she could think of nobody who might tell her why bright young men were selling apples, middle-aged executives were jumping out of windows, a pretty homosexual to whom wealth was as natural as the air he breathed had resorted to prostitution. The one thing that seemed obvious in the whole sorry mess was that it was only just beginning, and would therefore get worse. And not just in the United States. She tried not to think of Felston, because thinking would do no good.

Martha said, 'Miss Bauer is on the line.'

'Again?' said Jane.

'Yes miss,' said Martha. 'She's sorry to disturb you, she says. But she needs to speak to you.'

Just like her brother, thought Jane.

'You didn't stay for the party,' Erika said.

She could hear it in the background: glasses tinkling, music that made no sense to her, and a lot of laughter, very little of it male.

'I wanted to get on with the article,' said Jane.

'You've started?'

Really she made it sound as if I were about to write *War and Peace*, thought Jane.

'Mm,' she said. 'Mm' was a meaningless noise after all.

'But that's wonderful,' said Erika. 'At least – has my father spoken to you?'

'No,' said Jane.

'I'm afraid he will,' Erika said. 'You won't let him upset you, will you?'

'Do my best,' said Jane.

Something else to think about: something else to which there was no answer. All one could do was wait.

Mr Bauer (it required a strong effort of will on Jane's part not to think of him as Herr Bauer) phoned after dinner, while she worked on her letter to Daisy.

'I wish to see you,' he said. It seemed that they all had the same conversational style: father, daughter, son, but father's was by far the most obnoxious. She waited.

'For me to come to New York is inconvenient,' Bauer continued. 'It will be simpler if I send a limousine to bring you to me.' Still Jane waited. 'Why do you say nothing?' Bauer asked.

'What is there to say?' said Jane. 'You want me to visit your castle in the country, and I don't. Presumably you think you have matters to discuss with me. I cannot imagine what they may be, but whatever they are I shan't visit you in New England.'

'Why not?'

'I can't spare the time, and anyway I didn't like it there.'

This time it was Bauer who created the silence. 'Tomorrow,' he said. 'Four o'clock. Apartment D, the Marmont Towers on Park Avenue.'

'What about it?'

'I want you to be there,' said Bauer.

'Then invite me,' said Jane.

'Please Miss Whitcomb,' said Bauer, 'will you do me the honour of calling on me there?'

'Certainly,' said Jane, 'though I'm afraid I shan't be able to stay long.'

Bauer hung up. It was remarkable, it was downright incredible, thought Jane, how good they all were at doing that.

The Marmont Towers was much as she would expect a haunt of Bauer's to be. A commissionaire to open the taxi door, a canopy to shield her complexion from the sun, and waiting on her slightest whim a receptionist who telephoned Apartment D at once, and told her that she was expected, she could go up right away, smiling as if this were glad tidings indeed, as if her rich uncle in Australia had died and left her a million. Another attendant flunkey all but carried her to the elevator, which seemed to be designed in Italian Rococo style, took her up to Apartment D and rang its doorbell. At once a parlourmaid appeared, blonde and pretty, with a self-assurance one didn't see in New York all that often these days, thought Jane, and led her down a corridor hung with stags' heads to a room almost big enough for the schloss, or whatever it was, and far too big for Park Avenue. Fifty people at least could have danced there, she thought, and still left room for the band, but that was ridiculous. No one would ever dance in a room that Mr Bauer owned. It was a room for a shareholders' meeting, even if all the shareholders turned up. Black leather furniture, minor masters on the walls, a stand of arms above the fireplace, and a vast chair and desk for the chairman of the board, who rose as she came in, neatly squared the papers he had been reading, and advanced to face her. He made no offer to shake hands.

'I have ordered coffee and cakes, or would you prefer tea?'

'Tea, please.'

Bauer turned to the maid. 'Tea and coffee at once, Gretchen,' he said, and the girl left, not quite running. Bauer gestured to seats by a window, and they sat and looked down. Beneath them the traffic moved with no sense of urgency, none at all, and the pavements were crowded with people who seemed neither to know nor to care where they were going. At a corner a man was playing a harmonica, another was holding out a cap, begging for money. In all the time she watched, no one gave any.

'Like the end of a war,' Bauer said. 'A war with no winners.' But that was untrue. Bauer would always be a winner.

Gretchen came back, pushing a trolley, poured tea and coffee, and offered cakes, which Jane refused. Bauer chose something vast, chocolate coated and stuffed with cream, and attacked it with a neatness she found fascinating. Not a crumb escaped.

'I hope you have the time to finish your tea,' he said. 'What I have to say won't take longer than that.'

'Go ahead.' Jane took cigarettes, holder and lighter from her bag, and Bauer frowned. Permission had been neither asked nor given.

'I wish you would tell me,' he said, 'whether you deliberately set out to alienate me from my children?'

'Of course not,' said Jane.

'And yet since you have met them my daughter has left her home to pursue a political career as dangerous as it is degrading, and my son has declined to act with me in a very lucrative business deal, has in fact acted against me – and you are helping him. You and that understrapper Fairweather.'

I must remember understrapper, she thought, for next time he's in a rage.

'Your daughter is old enough to make her own decisions,' she said, 'and so is your son.'

'Erika is the sort of girl who never made a decision in her life,' said Bauer. 'Until she met you. God didn't put her in this world to make decisions. Marriage, children, the welfare of the poor and church on Sunday. That is what Erika is here for.'

How utterly wrong you are, thought Jane, and how unlikely it is that I shall tell you so. Especially the bit about marriage and children.

'And then she met you,' said Bauer, 'and you filled her head with your Socialist nonsense, and your strikes and newspaper articles – and she left us – her mother and me, left us to live in a slum.'

Well not exactly a slum, thought Jane. Nothing that a good charwoman couldn't cure.

'Are you saying that I put Erika up to this?' she said.

'She told me that she talked with you, that she admired you. Some people it's good to admire. I don't think you are one of them.'

Jane said affably, 'At least you're honest. But do be sensible, Mr Bauer. I hardly know Erika. If she admires me I'm flattered, but I've hardly been in a position to influence her. I doubt if we've had more than four or five hours' private conversation together in our entire lives. And she isn't doing what I do anyway.'

'Of course she is,' said Bauer. 'She's modelled her entire life on yours.'

'She may say she has, she may even think she has – but she

hasn't. I'm a spectator, Mr Bauer, a watcher of the scene, very occasionally a commentator. Erika's a participant – because that's what she's always wanted to be, and now she's wealthy enough to do as she pleases.'

'She isn't wealthy at all,' said Bauer. 'You can forget about that.'

Jane looked out of the window. The man with the harmonica played doggedly on: the pedestrians still ignored the proffered cap.

'To those poor men down there she's a millionaire,' she said. 'And anyway, why put it all on me? You visited her yesterday?' He nodded. 'Then you must know she has another friend with far more influence than I could ever hope to have.'

'A woman called Klein,' said Bauer. 'A Jewish woman.'

He didn't speak the words aloud, but she knew what he was thinking: There are so many things wrong with you, but at least you're not Jewish.

'Then why blame me?' asked Jane.

'Because I don't believe what you're telling me. Maybe *you* believe it – I'm not so sure about that any more – but I know that for Erika you were the model – the star for her waggon. It was because of you she left us.'

That should make me feel sorry for you, she thought, but it doesn't. Nothing can.

'I have very little tea left,' she said. 'Perhaps we should discuss your son.'

'He married,' said Bauer. 'I expect you know that.'

'Certainly.'

'Married another protégée of yours.'

Jane shrugged. That was something they could debate all evening. 'It was a very splendid wedding,' she said.

'You were there, no doubt?' Jane inclined her head. 'And I was not. Nor was his mother – or his sister.'

'That was rather obvious,' said Jane. 'But it was a *splendid* wedding, even so.'

'To a lady, I understand.'

'In every possible way,' said Jane. 'But I know what you mean. Her father's an earl.'

'An Irish earl. I'd expected him to marry a German girl. So

– 447 –

had his mother. We could have arranged the daughter of a graf
– a count – if that's what he wanted.'

'He didn't,' said Jane. 'He wanted Catherine Hilyard.'

'And now he's got her? It's upset his mother very much.'

'He's happy,' said Jane. 'If you and his mother had come to
the wedding you might understand why.'

'You're impertinent,' said Bauer.

'Naturally you would think so.'

Bauer's fists clenched, but his voice stayed calm. 'But I don't
want to waste any more time discussing what is no concern of
yours. Why do you employ this idiot Fairweather to pay off my
son's debts?'

'Because your son asked me to.'

'I find that hard to believe,' said Bauer. Jane stubbed out her
cigarette, put the holder back in her handbag.

'No, wait,' Bauer said. 'Let me finish. I've no doubt that
Joachim did ask you to act for him, but where did he get the
money?'

'Even suppose I knew,' said Jane, 'why on earth should I tell
you?'

'Did he not even mention the fact that I had offered him the
money he needed? That we could do business together?'

'Oh that,' said Jane.

'Yes, that. . . . Well?'

'Are you sure you want to know?'

'Of course I'm sure.'

'He mentioned it,' said Jane. 'Made quite a speech about it in
fact. What it amounted to was that if he was going to be robbed
blind he would rather it happened outside the family.'

Three minutes later she was in Park Avenue, putting fifty
cents into the cap of the harmonica player's friend. The weather,
she noticed, had turned distinctly chilly.

'He phoned me in London,' said Georgie. 'God knows what
that cost World Wide.'

She and Jane were drinking cocktails at the Plaza, looking
down at the aimlessly meandering crowd in the Park. Surely
there were more mounted policemen on duty than there used
to be? Jane remembered the mounted police baton charge in
London, at the Elephant and Castle, and looked away.

'He wanted you to lend him money?' she asked. 'But Murray told me –'

'Of course not,' Georgie said. 'He knew I wouldn't lend him a cent. What he wanted was to find out where you were. It didn't dawn on me why until afterwards, so I sent you that cable.'

'It's the market I suppose?' said Jane.

'From what I hear he's lost his shirt.'

'Does that mean World Wide will fire him?'

'I doubt it,' Georgie said. 'He really is a very good producer. They're far more likely to lend him the money and stop it out of his salary.'

'Then why come begging to me?'

'Because you'd have been a damn sight cheaper than World Wide's board.'

Jane thought of Charles Lovell and knew that Georgie was right, as her friend looked down at the crowd once more.

'This town's ghastly,' she said. 'I wonder if the Coast will be any better.'

'Ghastly?' said Jane.

'Sad,' Georgie said. 'Not just sad. In mourning.'

'For the good times?'

'For optimism,' said Georgie. 'For American know-how. For the brave new world.' She looked down again. 'That hath such people in it.'

'Gracious, you are feeling bad,' said Jane.

'I have a right to be,' Georgie said. 'I'm getting married next month.'

'Dan Corless?' Georgie nodded. 'Oh you poor darling,' said Jane, then got up and kissed her. 'Congratulations.' No doubt it's all the fault of Georgie's martinis, she thought. But what else could I say?

'Thanks,' Georgie said. 'Murray broke the news when he phoned me. Seemed to think it was funny. It was the only time in the entire chat he seemed to be enjoying himself.' She turned her head slowly into profile, and the lovely features seemed at first perplexed, then resolute, almost stern. She was acting again.

'He seems to think we'll go on seeing each other, just like

before. But I couldn't possibly do that. I mean I'll be Mrs Dan Corless.'

Jane giggled. 'You and Murray will be just good friends?'

'Of course not,' said Georgie. 'Who on earth would be friends with Murray Fisch? Still you know what they say when you've just missed a bus. There'll be another one along in a minute.' Jane looked at Georgie's still flawless beauty. The queue would be of cinema proportions.

'Murray's settled on a title for our little effort, too,' she said.

'Tell me the worst,' said Jane.

'Well at first he said it was going to be *Ministering Angel*, but I screamed so loud we didn't even need the telephone, and so he said it would be *Angel of No Man's Land* and I said OK.'

'It's better than *Ministering Angel*,' said Jane. 'Not that he told me.'

'He wouldn't,' said Georgie. 'He's mad at you. You want to eat?'

'Not really.'

'Nor me,' Georgie said. 'But we do have to have something to soak up all these martinis. I have a Personal Appearance this afternoon. In Brooklyn.' She made it sound like Siberia. 'Will you come to my wedding?'

'I'm afraid I can't,' said Jane. 'I have to go back to England.'

'And who will blame you?' said Georgie. 'It'll all be choreographed by the Publicity Department, including the bridal night. Pity we couldn't film that, too. It would be better than Laurel and Hardy.'

'Darling, do you have to do it?' asked Jane.

'No,' Georgie said. 'I don't. But it'll help our careers – and the movie. And at least we won't get in each other's way.'

'Unless you fall for the same chap.'

'Darling,' said Georgie, 'the ones Dan goes for make me look like Tarzan.'

The room service waiter arrived with the blotting paper.

Mr and Lady Catherine Bower had invited her to Berkshire, but Lady Mangan was unwell and Catherine thought it best not to leave, so she lunched at the Fleet Street flat instead, and a very pleasant lunch it was, with no need to worry about whether the wine in her glass bore even the remotest relationship to the label on the bottle.

Jane asked about Lady Mangan's health.

'It's always the same problem,' said Catherine. 'She's had a stroke and she refuses to accept it. She just wants life to go on as if it had never happened.'

'It's what keéps her going,' said Bower.

'It's what will kill her,' said Catherine.

Then at least she'll die happy, thought Jane, but she kept it to herself.

'Aeroplanes indeed,' said Catherine.

'They're still her passion?'

'She's obsessed by them,' said Catherine. 'She insists she's off to Egypt as soon as she's fit to travel, and she's taking Mummy and Daddy with her. Mummy and Daddy hate aeroplanes. . . . But we want to hear about New York.'

'I don't think you do,' said Jane.

'Just like Dearest Daisy?'

'They were the best bits. It really is quite ghastly, especially as it was all so wonderful before.' She turned to Bower. 'I met your sister.'

'Did she mention my marriage by any chance?'

'She said she was sorry she couldn't come. She's in publishing these days. A magazine called *Red Awakening*.'

'Did she coax an article out of you?'

'I did a piece about the General Strike in London. She paid me six dollars for it.'

'Six bucks?' Bower was horrified.

'But surely,' said Catherine, 'that's not much more than a pound. Oh Jane, how could you?'

'Felston,' said Jane. 'It all helps. And anyway, I very nearly wasn't published at all.'

'Erika was going to turn you down?'

'Not Erika,' said Jane. 'Her partner. A woman called Jennifer Klein.' Bower looked blank. 'They're sharing a house in the Village.' She turned to Catherine. 'That's a sort of Chelsea.'

'Oh,' said Catherine knowledgeably. 'Bohemian.'

'Well they do have painters and poets,' said Jane, 'but they have what Erika calls intellectuals, too.'

'Is that what Erika and this Jennifer are?'

'Well . . . yes,' said Jane. 'Anyway, this Jennifer for some reason decided she didn't like me or my work, and tried to give me rather a bad time, so I sent them back my six dollars. The next thing I knew the piece was published and Erika sent me my six dollars back.'

'That was jolly decent of her,' said Catherine.

'Yes,' said Jane. 'It was. But then in many ways she's a very decent sort of girl, which is why I wrote the piece in the first place.' She hesitated, but there was no point in putting it off. It would have to come out sooner or later. 'I also saw your father,' she told Bower.

'You went out there?'

'Certainly not,' said Jane. 'He told me to, but I wasn't in the mood. We met at an apartment in Park Avenue.'

'Marmont Towers?' Bower asked. Jane nodded. 'What the hell does the old ba – the old fool think he's playing at?'

'Jaybird,' Catherine said. 'Please. Jane's our guest.'

'Jane's our friend,' said Bower, 'and yet my father had the gall to invite her to his – his –'

'Love nest?' Jane suggested.

Bower grinned. 'Yeah,' he said. 'I guess that's it. Who was the maid? Heidi?'

'Gretchen,' said Jane.

'She must be new. . . . And he really asked you there?'

'For tea,' said Jane. 'Nothing more. Except to tell me he disliked me.'

'But why on earth should he do that?' said Catherine.

'He seemed to think that I was the reason he was no longer on good terms with his children.'

'He's the only reason for that,' said Bower, then Crabbe came in and called him to the telephone. Mr Cook, it seemed, had a problem. Jane turned to Catherine.

'Well,' she said, 'at least you look happy.'

'Well of course,' said Catherine. 'Cap d'Antibes, and that lovely house in Berkshire – and the whole week here in Fleet Street. So exciting. If only Granny were better.' She paused for a moment. 'Or did you mean all that sex stuff?'

'I meant everything,' said Jane.

'I remember I asked you about it – under the trees in South Terrace. Your maid was cross because she had to serve the drinks in the garden.' Jane waited. 'My dear there's nothing to it,' Catherine said. 'It's just like riding a bicycle. Once you've got the knack you don't even have to think about it any more.'

At that point Bower came back – perhaps it was as well – and Catherine left them to prepare to visit her grandmother.

Over coffee Bower said, 'I gather the old man was pretty rough?' Jane nodded. 'About Erika too?'

'That was foolish, I agree,' said Jane. 'But angry people are often foolish. He had to blame someone and I was the nearest.'

'From what you say – I gather she's a lesbian, and my father knows it – or at least suspects it?'

'Almost certainly,' said Jane. 'Perhaps I should add that Erika's friend is Jewish.'

'Dear God,' said Bower. 'I'm glad I wasn't there. . . . And then there was me.'

'You of course were accused, tried and condemned for not marrying a German girl. If you'd wanted a German earl's daughter, that could have been arranged, too.'

'*What?*'

'But I don't think that was it, not really,' said Jane. 'Your real crime was to get yourself into trouble, then get yourself out – and hang on to the Boston real estate.'

'I didn't do that,' said Bower. 'You did.'

'It's what old friends are for. You've read the papers I sent you?'

'Everything's fine,' said Bower. 'I owe you one. A big one. The biggest.'

'Never mind that,' said Jane, 'but if I may ask –'

'Almost certainly,' said Bower.

She appreciated that 'almost', at such a time. It was pure Jay Bower. 'How on earth did you know about your father's love nest?'

'My dear girl,' said Bower, 'you don't suppose he kept it a secret, do you?'

From Fleet Street lunch, Jane went to her mother, and Kensington tea. Meticulously her mother established that her daughter was in good health and had lost no money in America. She even behaved creditably about the title of her film, wincing visibly but offering no comment. Both she and the major were well it seemed, and George had taken a trainer-friend to see Bridget's Boy. The trainer-friend had declared himself delighted to take him on.

'And now what are you going to do with yourself?' her mother asked, then added, not quite inconsequently, 'You look sad.'

'Do I?' said Jane. 'I must try to hide it. New York's a very sad place.'

'One sees pictures,' said her mother. 'A hundred men queuing for one job: rich men – formerly rich men – jumping out of windows. Homeless people living in shanties built out of petrol tins. Hoovervilles they call them. After their President, no doubt. – Did you see such things?'

'It was everywhere,' said Jane.

'But there are still wealthy people in America.'

'Not so many as there were,' said Jane, 'but the well-established money has survived. It always will – short of Communism.'

'I imagine that the same will be true of England,' said her mother. 'There can be no doubt that in England too things will get worse.'

'So everyone says.'

'Everyone for once is right. But your friend Mr Lovell will survive, as will Mr Bower, one supposes.'

'With him it was touch and go,' said Jane, 'but he'll be all right.'

'I'm delighted to hear it,' her mother said. 'George is far too set in his ways to join another newspaper. Young brides can be expensive, I'm told.'

'Very.'

'Especially when the husband, the rather older husband, is besotted.'

'Just so, Mummy.'

Her mother poured more tea. 'We still have not resolved the problem of what you are to do with yourself,' she said.

'I don't think there's anything I can do,' said Jane. 'The movie script's completed. Georgie wants me to go to Hollywood but I'd only be in the way. There's nothing more boring than watching other people work and being idle oneself.'

'Especially when the work they do is congenial to them,' said her mother. 'I have frequently experienced the same emotion when accompanying George to a race meeting. There is nothing else you wish to write?'

'Not at the moment.'

'Your friendship with Mr Lovell?'

'It continues. But that's all it is really. It doesn't fill my life.'

'I'm sad to hear it,' her mother said. 'I don't mean that I disapprove – at least I don't think I do. I have never considered the matter with any thoroughness – but you were never meant to be idle, child. At least you have Felston.'

'But that's just it,' said Jane. 'I haven't. Except that I do send them money from time to time. Whenever I've earned any, in fact. Which reminds me.' She told her mother about Erika and Jennifer, and the six dollars gleaned from *Red Awakening*. Mrs Routledge enjoyed it hugely, but called her to order at once.

'Very amusing,' she said, 'but you digress, Jane, and you know you do. Six dollars will not solve Felston's problems.'

'Perhaps nothing will,' said Jane, 'but if there is a solution I won't be consulted.'

'Whyever not?' asked her mother.

'I'm considered frivolous,' said Jane.

Mrs Routledge considered her daughter: hair cut in the latest style, shoes and dress from Paris, ear-rings from God knew where, but shockingly expensive. 'I am quite sure that Captain Patterson's grandmother does not think so,' she said.

'There aren't an awful lot like Grandma,' said Jane.

'I used to think,' said her mother, 'that your affaire with Felston – it seemed to me then nothing less – was both foolish and humiliating.'

'Did you, Mummy?'

'For someone whom God endowed with intelligence,' said her mother, 'I have occasionally contrived to behave with the most shocking stupidity. That conclusion of mine was the best – or worst – example.

'It should have occurred to me that what you had set out to do was admirable, heroic and Christian: on a par with your service as an ambulance driver in fact, of which I was also stupid enough to disapprove. Idealists, heroes and heroines, self-sacrificers, are not the easiest people in the world to live with – dear George is far more restful – but you are – what can be the opposite of a necessary evil? A necessary blessing. Yes, that's it.

My own particular necessary blessing. I do most earnestly beg you not to give up now.' She waited for a moment. Jane was silent. 'Have I offended you, child?'

'Of course not,' said Jane. 'I'm trying very hard not to cry, that's all.'

'It's taken me a long time to tell you that I'm proud of you,' said her mother, then added in a voice very like the major's: 'The devil of a long time.'

Then Jane did cry, and her mother got up and embraced her, a clasp of maternal comfort she had last received when she was ten years old, and about to be sent home to England from India, that was her entire world.

'There isn't any reason for me to go there,' said Jane at last.

'No reason, no,' said her mother, 'but an adequate excuse perhaps. Didn't you tell me that Mrs Patterson's grand-daughter had a child who is to be called Jane? Might it not be polite of you to attend the christening? Perhaps even obligatory?'

'Perhaps it would,' said Jane.

'Then do so.' Her mother hugged her once more, and returned to her chair. 'Powder and paint yourself,' she said. 'I have no wish to see my daughter look as you do.'

Jane produced lipstick and compact, and set about repairing the damage.

'I have news of your brother,' Mrs Routledge said.

'How is Francis?'

'He is Dr Whitcomb now,' said her mother. 'Reader in Comparative Economics, fellow of his college. Very much the coming man.'

And yet she is proud of him, thought Jane, because she loves him at least as much as she loves me.

'He's been to see you?' she asked.

'He wrote to me,' said her mother. 'His visits here are infrequent, no doubt because he considers George a frivolous person, too.'

'He's still at the same college?' Jane asked.

'Certainly,' said her mother, surprised. 'Why do you ask?'

'He did once hint to me that he might become a fellow of King's.'

'That particular height has yet to be scaled,' said her mother.

'And his social life? Does that flourish too?' Jane asked.

'Do you know, I believe it does,' said her mother. 'One reads about him in the *Tatler* and so on. One reads about him at dinners and concerts and first nights. A very odd taste for Francis to develop. Mind you – I've been in the *Tatler* myself – or did I tell you?'

'You know you didn't,' said Jane.

'At Ascot, inevitably,' said her mother. '"Mrs George Routledge, stylish and popular adherent of English racing."'

'Mummy,' said Jane. 'Show me at once,' and Mrs Routledge did so. And there her mother was, stylish certainly, in a Hartnell suit and a hat from Paris, and popular too, if the group around her were anything to judge by: and beautiful still. Jane felt that for two pins she would cry again, but that would mean more lipstick, more powder: and anyway there was no need to cry when she could smile.

## 38

Tom Lynch was to go for trial before the end of the year, so Jay Bower had told her. In the meantime he was remanded in custody. There wasn't a great deal in it for the *World* whether he was found guilty or not, and he almost certainly would be: perhaps a couple of paragraphs on an inside page. In the meantime Andy Patterson was safe, a free man, and totally lacking in interest, so far as the *World* was concerned. Moscow Mike Deegan was in hospital: broken ribs, black eyes, teeth missing, so the Newcastle stringer had reported. Neither he nor anybody else, including the police, seemed to have any idea who had done it, or why. Nothing in that for the *Daily World* either. Jane telephoned Bob and asked him to dine, but dinner it seemed was difficult, and they settled for drinks. Lovell, she knew, would be perfectly happy to feed her.

Bob arrived in splendour: white tie, topper, brand-new evening dress. 'My we are grand,' she said, and went at once to pour martinis. 'Business must be good.'

'Folks can always find money for the wireless,' said Bob. 'It takes their mind off things.'

'There's a lot to take their minds off, no doubt.'

'Not so bad down here,' said Bob. 'Here folks just listen and pay up. They've still got jobs, you see. But up in Felston –' He shrugged. 'Best day's work I ever did, getting out of that town.'

He wasn't a bad man, she reminded herself: not even a callous man; just incapable of understanding why Felston's problems should be any concern of his.

'How's Grandma?'

'Fine,' said Bob. 'Feeling her age a bit, but don't tell her I said so. Otherwise fine. I'm making sure of that.'

The other side of Bob. Felston was hardly more than a memory, but Grandma could have his last shilling.

'And my namesake?'

'Surprised you, did it, that cable?' said Bob, and accepted the martini she poured him. 'Surprised me an' all when they asked me to send it.'

'Frank's idea no doubt?'

'You're a sharp one all right,' said Bob. 'Aye . . . it was Frank. Mind you I didn't see the harm in it. Otherwise I wouldn't have sent the cable.'

'No harm at all,' she said. 'When's the christening?'

'Week after next. I said I'd go. What choice have I got? Grandma would give us no peace.'

'Would you like a lift in a Bentley?'

'You going too?'

'I'd like to see my namesake,' said Jane.

'She's worth seeing from what I hear,' said Bob. 'A real bonny bairn. About all there is worth seeing in Felston – till they get a look at the Bentley.'

'Andy won't like it,' said Jane.

'Andy? He's gone very quiet these days,' said Bob. 'After the riot and Tom Lynch and all that. Grandma's a bit worried about him. But he's not making a lot of noise, not just now. Your Bentley will be safe with him.'

She topped up his glass. 'Where are you dining?' she asked.

'Theatre,' said Bob. 'Then supper. I've booked at the Savoy. She likes the band.'

'New lady friend?'

'Newish.'

What a family, she thought. His brother on the dole in a dying town while Bob danced in London's most expensive restaurant, and no doubt thousands of people would listen to the Savoy's band on their wireless sets, just as he too had done one night when he also had no job: listening on a set he had made himself, one night when she had danced there.

'Have fun,' she said.

'Have fun. That's American, isn't it?'

'Probably,' said Jane. 'Their language is awfully catching.'

'I may be going there,' said Bob. 'There's a chance of a deal. A lot of their stuff's going cheap these days. Did you see your friend the film star while you were there?'

'I did as a matter of fact,' said Jane. 'Before that she was here in London.'

'Aye,' said Bob. 'I think I read it in the paper. I was up in Scotland at the time, renting wireless sets. Is she still as good looking as ever?'

'Every bit,' said Jane.

'And to think I once found the nerve to ask her to dance,' said Bob.

'As a matter of fact she's going to be married quite soon,' said Jane.

Bob drained his glass and put it on a tray. 'Film stars is always getting married,' he said.

They ate at Lovell's flat. She had so much she wanted to tell him, and their bodies needed each other so. He doesn't fill my life, she had told her mother, and it was true, but from time to time he could provide her with an oblivion she desperately needed. As I do for him, she thought. At least I hope I do. My God how tired he looks. Not the body, he's just proved that. But in his mind –. She reached out to touch his face.

'Are you all right?' she asked.

Lovell smiled. 'Showing my years, am I? These last few weeks haven't been easy.'

'But you are all right?'

'I've made a lot more money I don't need – but it's a habit I can't break. Now my doctor says it's time I played some golf or shot some pheasants or something.

'I'm flattered you should worry about me,' he continued, 'but I'm tired, that's all. Mentally tired, I mean. And I hate golf. On the other hand I do have rather a lot of pheasant at Blagdon Hall.' He reached out to touch her in his turn. 'I'm having a house-party there quite soon. Is there any chance you could be a part of it? I'll invite some other women as well.'

Jane said cautiously, 'There wouldn't be much chance for any of this.'

'None whatsoever, I should imagine,' said Lovell. 'We'll just have to make up for it when we get back to town.' She moved back into his arms.

Later he said, 'I gather you saved Bower's skin for him?'

Just how do you gather it? she wondered, but was far too shrewd to ask.

'I hope Fairweather made himself useful,' said Lovell, and she told him about Bauer and the word understrapper. Lovell was enchanted. 'It would be too cruel to let poor Andrew know,' he said.

'Yes, it would.' Jane was firm. 'It's odd, but Mr Fairweather reminded me of someone, and it took me simply ages to realise who it was. . . . Lord Blagdon.'

'I wouldn't let Blagdon near any money of mine,' said Lovell.

Jane and Bob drove off to Felston one Saturday in late October. Over breakfast she had read the *Daily World*, checking her latest letter to Daisy. Not a single error, she noticed. Sub and copy-taker alike had done a good job. She turned the page and the headline leaped at her: 'Accused Rioter Commits Suicide In Prison. Lynch Found Hanged In Durham Gaol.' It was a good piece: far more than a blown-up version of an official statement: Bower would have seen to that. A quick résumé of the Felston Riot, a modest self-compliment to the *World* for unmasking Tom Lynch, regret that he should have chosen such an end despite his Catholic upbringing. All this was to be expected. What was not was the thinly veiled reference to the brutality of the prison, the hint that Lynch had been assaulted by his fellow prisoners, and by warders too in the hope of further information. Just what will Dick Lambert make of that? she wondered, then her eye moved down the page to another, smaller headline: 'Murder In Ireland?' the headline wondered, and she read on. The bodies of two men had been found in a bog in County Dublin, by a farmer cutting peat. The bog was near a village called Storrs. Both men had been shot dead before being dumped in the bog, and both were known to have IRA connections. Jane got up and consulted her atlas. Storrs was perhaps ten miles from Mangan Castle.

She phoned Bower at the *Daily World* office, and for once was put straight through.

'Saw the piece about poor Lynch, did you?' he asked.

'Sounds nasty,' she said.

'It is nasty. I thought about letting you tell Daisy about it, but with her there'd have to be glamour as well. And there isn't any. Still you could do me a piece about it. We Name The Guilty Men. Kick off with Dick Lambert, then all the way down to the prison warden.'

'I'm going up there today as it happens,' said Jane. 'For a christening.'

'In Felston?'

'Even in Felston children get christened.'

'Yes, of course,' said Bower. 'It's just that I got the idea you've been avoiding the place recently. Care to do me a piece? Five hundred words.'

'All right.'

'Make it quick then,' said Bower. 'You're not working for Erika.'

'I'll expect rather more than six dollars,' said Jane.

Bower snorted. 'Usual rates,' he said. 'Anything else?'

'Those two men found shot in Ireland,' said Jane.

'Nothing there for you,' said Bower. 'Just a little fraternal blood letting between fanatics.'

'You know this for a fact?'

'It's what the local cops say,' said Bower. 'And anyway, what else could it be?' He hung up.

When Bob arrived Truett was loading Jane's luggage into the boot. There were four cases. He had brought one.

'Staying for a month?' he asked.

'I've been invited to Blagdon Hall,' said Jane. 'There's a shooting party there.' And anyway she had her reputation for frivolity to live up to.

The Bentley liked the Great North Road. It had room, and long, straight stretches, and in the towns traffic tended to get out of its way.

'You don't believe in hanging about, do you?' said Bob.

'I phoned ahead and booked dinner at the Eldon Arms,' said Jane.

'Oh God.'

'I know,' said Jane, and her voice was sympathetic. 'But we can't spend all our time in roadhouses.'

'Perhaps just once?'

'We'll see,' said Jane.

They stopped for tea in Durham, then the great car snarled its way through the north east's private preview of Hell: pit heaps and mine shafts and factories, all idle, all deserted. When at last they saw the sea it was like a vision of escape.

'And our Bet wonders how I can bear to live in London,' said Bob.

They went through Newcastle, trams and buses more often than cars, shops with no customers, and on to the Felston road.

'What will you give the new baby?' asked Jane.

'Money,' said Bob. 'She'll need all she can get to survive up here. And you?'

'The same.'

'I thought fifty,' said Bob.

'So did I.'

'A hundred quid's not a bad start. All the same I think we'll tie it up so her da can't get his hands on it.'

'Good gracious,' said Jane. 'Do you think he might?'

'And lead us not into temptation,' said Bob. 'That's good advice whichever way you look at it. I know a lawyer in Barrington Street. I'll put him on to it.'

They had reached the town, and she eased off on the Bentley's throttle, threading her way among more cars, more buses, and horsedrawn carts. We couldn't be more conspicuous in a chariot with zebras, she thought, but at last they reached the Eldon Arms, and drove round to its coach yard. The manager appeared, took one look at the Bentley, and told them how happy he was to see them again.

Bob took one look at the dress Jane wore for dinner and announced that they would go to John Bright Street by taxi. The Bentley would clamour for trouble as much as her clothes, and a tram was out of the question. Jane agreed without argument. She had driven enough for one day, she didn't know if Andy was ready for the Bentley yet, and Felston didn't seem the sort of place to find out. So they went and rattled their way to Grandma's house and half the street turned out to watch, because taxis in John Bright Street were almost as rare as Bentleys.

Grandma was glad to see her and said so, and hugged her, and for a moment there was the old fierceness in her grip, but only for a moment. She is looking old, thought Jane. She has been an old woman for a decade at least, but now she looks like one.

'By we are grand tonight,' she said. Jane's coat was a heavy wool ready made she had bought from Bergdorf Goodman in New York, that was just right for a cold day in the country, but beneath it she wore a dress from her favourite Chanel, blue and white silk cut to her figure, and diamond drops in her ears.

'Draw up to the fire,' Grandma said. 'You'll catch your death.' She turned to Bob. 'You've been splashing out as well, I see,' she said, and her hand grasped the lapel of his suit. 'Pure wool is that, and don't tell me it's ready made.'

'Well of course it's not,' said Bob. 'Savoy Tailors is this – made to measure. – But don't go telling our Andy. Where is he, anyway? Doesn't he know we were coming?'

'Meeting,' said Grandma. 'It always is. Don't you remember? He said he'll get back as soon as he can. He's a bit down, so try to be nice to him.'

'That's up to him,' said Bob.

'Aye, I know,' Grandma said. 'But try.' She turned to Jane. 'You've eaten?' Jane nodded.

'We had a bite at the Eldon Arms,' said Bob.

Grandma shook her head. 'Proud as peacocks, the pair of you.'

'We didn't want to put you to any trouble,' said Bob. It had been a terrible meal. Grandma would have done one much better at a tenth of the price.

'You two's never any trouble,' said Grandma. 'In fact I don't know how we could manage without you.'

'If you start on about money we'll go back to the Eldon Arms,' said Bob. 'Tell us about our Bet. Why isn't she here?'

'Frank's on late shift, said Grandma, 'and she couldn't leave the bairns. And anyway she's got to get things ready for tomorrow.'

'Bit of cake, is there?'

'I made that,' said Grandma.

'Then I'll have some.' She aimed a blow at him and he dodged it, laughing. They were still laughing as Andy came in, and then the laughter died.

'Hello, kidder,' said Bob.

If Grandma looked old, then Andy looked ill, almost ready for death.

'Hello,' said Andy, then turned to Jane. 'You're looking grand.' But it was simply a statement of fact: there was no sarcasm, no attack.

'Thank you,' she said, and got up and kissed his cheek. He accepted even that.

'Andy,' said Bob, 'are you all right?'

'Well yes,' said Andy. 'Why shouldn't I be?'

'You look poorly,' said Bob. 'You don't think you should see a doctor?'

'Had a lot on my mind, that's all,' said Andy. 'I'll get over it. Sorry I wasn't here to meet you, though. The branch meeting went on a bit and I couldn't just leave. Not now I'm chairman.'

'Do you want something to eat?' Grandma asked. 'These two have eaten.'

'Just a cup of tea,' said Andy. 'I'm not hungry.'

The old woman's eyes looked at him, appraising, but all she did was swing the kettle closer to the glowing coals. Jane got up to fetch cups and saucers, and Grandma made no protest. She had long accepted Jane as one who belonged. 'Maybe we could all do with a cup,' she said.

'Things look bad round here,' Bob said.

'Never worse,' said Andy.

'You still out?'

'Haven't done a day's work since I got the push from Deegan's.'

'I heard he's in hospital,' Bob said.

'You heard right,' said Andy. 'Somebody gave him a proper belting. Broke his ribs, kicked him in the mouth –'

'That's enough,' said Grandma.

'Aye,' said Andy. 'It is.'

'There's a chap I was at school with got a belting an' all,' said Bob. 'Artie Burn. He was caught scabbing. His wife had TB.'

'I mind you telling me,' Grandma said. 'You gave him a job, didn't you? Renting your wirelesses?'

'That's right,' said Bob. 'Out Ripon way. He's doing very well.'

'What happened to his wife?' Grandma asked.

'She died,' said Bob. 'When they're that far gone, there's nothing else they can do.'

He is not a brutal man, thought Jane. Generous and easy going and wrapped up in his business, but not brutal, not even uncaring. It's just that he's lived with the fact of tuberculosis all his life. Once it reached a certain stage then you were doomed.

'How did he take it?' Grandma asked.

'It hurt him,' said Bob, 'but he had to go on. What else could he do? He's got three bairns.' He said it as one stating another obvious fact.

'Deegan wasn't like that,' Andy said.

'All I know about Deegan was he got belted,' said Bob.

'Deegan wasn't a victim.'

'Not even when somebody stuck a boot in his gob?' Bob looked at Grandma, rigid with wrath. 'Sorry.'

'Not even then,' said Andy. 'He was being punished. At least the chaps who did it thought he was.'

'The chaps who belted my pal thought the same,' said Bob. 'The stupid –'

'Bob!' Grandma's voice was a yell.

'Fools,' said Bob.

'Folks get ideas,' said Andy. 'They seem right and maybe they are right, but once folks start to act they come out wrong.' He looked at once suffering and bewildered. 'Jane knows what I mean,' he said.

'Do you, pet?' Grandma asked.

'Yes, I think I do,' said Jane, and turned to Andy. 'But I can't discuss it. Not this one. It's what is called privileged information. I'm sorry.'

'Too late to talk about it anyway,' said Andy. 'I was just trying to explain what's got into me. Only I can't.'

'You look about ready for your bed,' said Grandma, and Bob looked at his watch. 'We all do,' he said. 'Jane's had a long drive and I've got business to see to tomorrow, Sunday or not. I asked the taxi to come back for us at ten. Just time to finish our tea.'

'Business,' said Grandma. 'On a Sunday.'

'Only time I've got,' said Bob, 'but I'll be here in time for the christening.'

'You'll be here in time for Sunday dinner,' said Grandma. 'One o'clock sharp.'

In the cab Bob said, 'She looks older.'

'Yes,' said Jane. 'She does.'

'An old woman,' said Bob. 'She never looked like one before.' He looked from the taxi's window to the narrow, half-empty streets. 'Ten o'clock on a Friday and the town's dead,' he said. 'There was a time you wouldn't have been able to move for drunks.'

# 39

B OB WAS GONE as soon as breakfast was over, on a round of
visits to shop managers, with the local area manager to drive
him. There was an appointment for sherry too, with a solicitor.
Jane gave him her cheque for fifty pounds, then sat in her room
with the Sunday newspapers. More suicides in America, more
unemployment in Wales, in Scotland, in Northern England.
Georgina Payne and Dan Corless announced their engagement.
Was that disaster too? she wondered.

A maid tapped at her door and told her there was a Mr Patterson to see her. He was waiting in the lounge. That could only
be Andy, she thought. Not even the threat of death would get
him to come up to her suite. 'Tell him I'll be down soon,' she
said, and looked at her watch. Eleven forty-five. Still time for
coffee, but not the Eldon Arms' coffee. She checked the fit of
her suit, put on her hat and slung the Bergdorf Goodman coat
over her arm. Plain and simple and discreet, she thought. She
would do. Only she mustn't put on any more weight.

Andy looked ill at ease waiting for her, but then anybody
would in that huge, deserted room with its dark and pompous
furniture and musty smell, the curtains drawn against the daylight as if to acknowledge a death.

'I wanted a word,' he said.

'Of course.' She motioned him towards a chair.

'Here?' He sounded horrified, as if the lounge of the Eldon
Arms was no place for the likes of him. No place for the likes of
me, either, she thought, but where else is there?

'Andy, it's far too cold to go for a walk,' she said, and pressed the bell. 'Will you take a drink with me?'

'Tea,' he said. 'I could do with a cup of tea.'

Jane ordered tea for him, and a whisky and soda for herself: the only alcoholic drink the Eldon Arms could handle. They came at last, and she poured out the tea for Andy, added soda for herself. He added more sugar, she noticed, three more spoonfuls, and she thought, shock. The poor devil's in shock.

'I expect you know what I want to talk about,' he said.

'I think so. Mike Deegan. . . . And Tom Lynch.'

'I can understand why you couldn't discuss it last night,' Andy said, 'but can we talk about it now? On our own?'

'Probably,' she said. 'Let's see.'

'It was to have been me,' said Andy. 'The working-class hero: the fearless opponent of the bosses. They thought I was made for it.'

'Who did?'

'Why – the Party. They knew I'd done it before – and they knew the way I could speak because they trained me. Only I didn't fancy going inside again.'

'Inside?'

'Durham Prison. I'd been a martyr for the faith once, and I found that once was enough. They tried their best to get me to do it again –'

'Burrowes?' Jane asked.

'You know an awful lot about it,' said Andy. 'But then of course you do. That 'tec you sent up from London – was he really a private investigator?' Jane nodded. 'Well I'll go to France,' said Andy. 'Like a character in a book. And I stood there and had a drink with him. Whoever would have thought I'd meet one of them? Or Cambridge dons, for that matter? Or lords and ladies?' Piers and Catherine, she thought.

'And I owe it all to politics,' Andy continued. 'And very nice too. Broadening me horizons, all that. But I couldn't take another dose of Durham, not to meet the King of England. So I said no thanks.'

'And then what happened?'

'They changed the Party line. Altered the plot if you like. To hell with making speeches. Let's have a bit of direct action. Bring in the Class Warrior.'

'Tom Lynch?'

'Tom Lynch. Don't misunderstand me. He must have been a hell of a good chap. . . .'

'You never met him?'

'Not to say met him. We spoke at the same meetings a few times. He spoke well. But words weren't what he was made for. Not like me. Like I say, he was a fighter. Like our John.'

'I would have thought there was a lot of you in him, too,' she said. 'Faith. Idealism. Compassion. He must have felt them to have taken such risks.'

Andy looked at her warily, but it was plain that she meant what she said. 'You understand us then,' he said at last. 'The daft fanatics that don't know when to stop because their only aim in life is to put an end to Felston.'

'I understand,' said Jane. 'But I also understand that where there are men like you, there are lovable rascals like Burrowes.'

And pompous prigs like Pardoe, she thought, and high-minded intellectual snobs like my brother.

'Lovable rascal,' said Andy. 'By heck that's good. He's a rascal all right, and the way he tells it he's been lovable often enough.' He flushed. 'I'm sorry.'

'Don't be ridiculous,' said Jane. 'Do you suppose I didn't know?'

'Aye, you're right,' said Andy. 'I'm being ridiculous, and we don't have time for that. When Grandma says one o'clock she means it.' He drank his now-cold tea.

'So Tom goes off and recruits his Merry Men because they've told him this was one we could mebbe win and he agreed with them, only they didn't put enough stress on the mebbe, not to my way of thinking. The meeting comes, the crowd assembles, and I get up and do my Betrayal of the Workers act, and Tom Lynch starts his war, and loses. The coppers had all been in the army too. . . . But at least he gets away, and I'm set up to take his place – only I don't blame him for that. It was all part of what you might call the overall strategy, and a bit of a novelty for me – being the injured innocent. But I was terrified of prison.

'And then Canon Messeter stepped in, and our Bob, and the *Daily World*. I tell you, I was never more relieved in my life. I was that grateful –'

'You wrote and told me so,' said Jane. 'It must have been a terrible time for you.'

'And then it all came out in your paper about Tom Lynch and I started blaming you for it – that's the kind of daft state I was in. It took a five-mile walk to make meself see sense. I've still got the blisters. – You got an anonymous letter, didn't you?' Jane nodded. 'But you know it was Deegan.'

'Yes . . . our private investigator found that out for us. And I take it that it was Tom Lynch's Merry Men who beat him up?'

'Who else?' said Andy. 'But he's still dead.'

'Do you know why Lynch killed himself?'

'I think so.' He shifted in his chair, and Jane waited. 'There's no reason you shouldn't know,' he said at last. 'In fact I wish you could get it in your paper – but you would never be able to prove it. Not a bloody thing.' It was the first time that she had heard him swear.

'Tom Lynch would take a belting,' Andy said. 'He knew it was coming and he took it, because what else could he do? And then he'd take another, and another. And then the screws would tell the other convicts things about him – how he'd been a sergeant in the army and treated the men rough, especially the ones who'd been inside, and if any of them felt like giving Tom Lynch another belting, well the screws had no objections. There might even be another plate of porridge for them at breakfast.'

'You know all this?'

'It's what happened to me,' said Andy. 'Only when I got bashed it was for being a conscientious objector. . . . But I do know it as it happens. Through a chap I met. He's just got out after doing a stretch.'

'And that's why Lynch killed himself?'

'No,' said Andy. 'Like I said, Lynch was a tough nut. Like our John. Not the kind that cracks easy.' He paused, struggling for words that would explain. 'Tom Lynch wasn't married,' he said.

'He lived with his sister.'

'In prison,' said Andy, 'if you're a grown man and you haven't got a wife, that can only mean one thing.'

'Oh,' said Jane. 'I see.'

'Not like the Nancy boys,' said Andy, 'the ones that are inside for unnatural acts or whatever it is. A lot of them are married off so to speak before they've been inside five minutes. But there's others. Not like them. Chaps that would just as soon have a woman on the outside – but when there aren't any women, a man will have to do. Tom Lynch was a good-looking chap. Suppose somebody fancied him, a feller with a lot of power outside and a lot of pals inside? What chance would one man have if the screws weren't even interested?'

'None whatever,' said Jane.

'Unless he hanged himself.'

'How ghastly,' said Jane, and then: 'I realise that's a most inadequate thing to say, but then anything one said would be inadequate.'

'You're right there,' Andy said. 'I know. I've tried.'

They did it to you, too, she thought, which goes a long way towards explaining why you are as you are. But now isn't the time to think about that.

'I'm glad you told me,' she said, 'but what you said at the beginning is true. Without proof, there's nothing the *World* can do.'

'It isn't that,' said Andy.

'What then?'

'I had to tell somebody. I had to hear myself say it aloud. It's a terrible burden to put on anybody, especially a woman, and I apologise for that, I really do. But I had to tell it. I couldn't help myself.'

'Please,' she said. 'Don't apologise. What are friends for?'

He looked across to her and smiled. 'Thanks,' he said.

Jane looked at her watch. 'We'd better be off or Grandma will be angry,' she said.

Bob was already there when they arrived, smug with virtue, but the kitchen clock said three minutes to one. Almost Jane put out her tongue at him. He had brought wine to drink with their meal, but Grandma wasn't in the least annoyed: he had also brought whisky and sherry and Grandma adored sherry.

'Jane Anne,' he said, as he poured out drinks. Andy wanted lemonade, and he had brought that, too.

'Who's she?'

'The bairn,' said Bob. 'Canon Messeter said Jane's a nice enough name, but she needed a saint on her side as well. Right, Grandma?'

'He didn't say it as common as that,' Grandma said repressively, 'but it's pretty well what I told you. And there's nowt wrong with being named for Jesus's grandmother.'

'Nothing at all,' said Jane.

'There's nowt wrong with being named for our Jane, either,' Andy said. Again the sharp old eyes looked at him, and again no word was said. Roast beef, Yorkshire pudding, roast potatoes, carrots, leeks, cabbage, then apple tart with cream instead of custard, because of Jane. The claret Bob had bought from the Eldon Arms had no reason to feel superior. All Jane wanted to do when it was done was to find an easy chair and doze, but that was a privilege reserved for men. She and Grandma did the washing up.

When it was finished Grandma said, 'I thought we might walk to the church. It'll help us get our dinner down.' Even Bob thought it was a good idea.

The church was the brick-built box she had been to twice before with Canon Messeter, with its look, from the outside, of a factory in the middle of a recession. Inside it was still the same: the worn deal chairs, the table for an altar with its allotment of flowers and gleaming brass cross. Above the altar the crucifix still hung: a small masterpiece of wood and ivory, worth as much as all the rest of the church put together. The Sunday School was about to finish as they came in, but already Bet and her husband were there, and young Frank, now a fractious two-year-old who saw no reason why he shouldn't run around the church and turn over the chairs. Frank's parents were there too, and a youngish woman introduced as 'my friend Norah'. The Sunday School children sang lustily – their ordeal was approaching its end, and they knew it.

'There's a home for little children/Above the bright blue sky,' they roared, but even so the grown-ups spoke in whispers. It was only then that Jane realised that she and Norah were to be the godmothers, and that Bob was godfather. Frank, it seemed, was leaving nothing to chance.

The Sunday School children filed out decorously enough. It was only when they were outside that they knew they were safe and the yelling began. Canon Messeter, in cassock and surplice, made his way to the font, and the others went to join him, the baby asleep in her mother's arms. Jane looked at her once more. She really was a very pretty baby, and with an astonishing resemblance to Grandma, which argued that once Grandma had been very pretty too. The thought did not surprise her.

In the tiny, gimcrack church there was none of the grandeur of St George's, Hanover Square, but the Elizabethan bishops had still worked hard at that astonishing and heart-lifting prose, and Canon Messeter recited it for all it was worth, like an actor who believes every word of his part. She discovered that she was expected to hold her namesake, and almost panicked at the baby's lightness, even with a christening robe and shawl. Canon Messeter handled the baby far more deftly, but then he had had far more practice. As the water touched her forehead, baby Jane woke, blared once in a yell that echoed round the church, then went back to sleep. Canon Messeter continued placidly, rolling out the splendid words as if Jane's yelling was the most beautiful music, and perhaps to him it was, thought Jane. The baby's soul now belonged to God, and soon she would be given a certificate to prove it.

Bob had provided refreshment at Bet's house too, whisky and sherry and beer, to accompany the sandwiches and cake. Frank's parents and Norah and the Pattersons made up the party, or so she thought, until Canon Messeter arrived in a clerical suit of astonishing decrepitude, which had nevertheless, Jane was quite sure, been made in Savile Row. He accepted sherry and cake, and chatted placidly about the baby's good behaviour while undergoing its ordeal. Jane turned to Bob.

'Have you given them the chque?' she asked.

'It's a trust account in a bank,' said Bob. 'If you feel like giving more – on her birthday say – you just send it to the solicitor.'

'What did Frank say?'

'He said thank you,' said Bob. 'He may even have meant it.' He looked across the room. Norah, the other godmother, was on her own. 'Better have a word,' said Bob.

'Who is she?' asked Jane.

'"My friend Norah"? Lived round the corner from us when Bet was a bairn. Used to push her in her pram. Lost her man in 1917. Drowned at sea. A "U" boat got him, poor feller.'

'How on earth does she manage?'

'Best way she can,' said Bob. 'She's got a job in a chip shop so she's better off than most. Excuse me.'

He went over to Norah, and soon the woman was laughing,

and in doing so looking much prettier.

Canon Messeter came up to her. 'It was good of you to travel so far,' he said.

'To see my namesake? Not at all,' said Jane.

'Mrs Metcalf tells me you have been most generous,' said the canon.

'No more than I can afford,' said Jane. 'Bob Patterson did the same.'

Canon Messeter looked to where Bob was. Norah was now giggling as Bob poured out more sherry.

'A remarkable young man,' said the canon. 'And an able one.'

'Just so,' said Jane. 'Patterson's Wireless Rentals.'

'He's rich, it would seem.'

'Quite adequately,' said Jane. 'You must talk to him.'

Messeter looked at her squarely. 'Yes,' he said. 'I must.'

'I'm sorry,' said Jane, 'but I had no intention of being offensive.'

'Merely realistic?'

'Yes, of course. You need money and so you ask for it. It's the only way – and it worked with me, after all.'

Canon Messeter said, 'I would be pleased if you could call on Dr Stobbs and me at the clinic.'

'I don't see the point,' said Jane. 'I'll always contribute – you know that.' Messeter nodded. 'I don't need visit your clinic to do that.'

'There is more to this venture of ours than simply money,' the canon said. 'Your ideas could be useful to us, I'm sure.'

'I think not.'

'They were in the past,' said Messeter. He sounded almost testy.

'Oh in the *past*,' said Jane. 'But I've changed, you see. My ideas wouldn't be of the slightest use now. I'm far too frivolous. All I'm good for is money.'

'What nonsense,' said Messeter. 'Who on earth put that idea into your head?'

'Dr Stobbs,' said Jane.

Messeter flinched. 'We hurt you very badly, did we not?'

'Not you,' said Jane. 'But I'd much rather leave things as they are.'

Andy came over to them. 'I hear the hot water's giving trouble again.'

'We need a new system,' Canon Messeter said, 'but it will take rather more than a whist drive.' The two men looked furtively at Bob, then Messeter hurried into speech. 'Andy here is our plumber-carpenter-electrician-upholsterer,' he said.

'Handyman,' said Andy.

'But of course you knew that,' said Messeter. 'You wrote about it in your paper, didn't you?' Jane nodded.

Indeed I did write about it, she thought, but it never occurred to me that he'd still be doing it – though I should have done. Andy wasn't the kind to offer a gift and then renege.

'I'll look in tomorrow morning,' Andy said. 'See what I can do.'

'Most welcome,' said Messeter absently. He squared his shoulders and set off towards Bob. The look on his face was that of a rider approaching a particularly nasty fence.

'It was good of you to listen to me this morning,' Andy said. 'It helped me a lot.'

*I don't help people any more. I'm too frivolous.*

Jane took out her cigarettes and holder, and Frank's parents did everything but stand on a chair to get a better view.

'It's a heavy load,' she said. 'I realise that. But only you can put it down. It is your choice, you know. No one else's.'

Then Bet came up to thank her for her gift, and dragged her husband with her. He'd been doing rather well at the whisky, thought Jane, and hoped he wouldn't be driving his tram till the morning.

On the way home, Bob said: 'You've got a new admirer. "My friend Norah". She thinks you're a bobby dazzler.'

'A what?'

'Lovely, grand, elegant, super,' said Bob.

'But I hardly exchanged five sentences with her.'

'Six,' said Bob. 'She's pretty well memorised them. "A real lady," she said. "No side at all."'

'Condescension?'

'Exactly,' said Bob. 'And the way you wear your clothes – and such clothes –'

'She thought you were a well-dressed bobby dazzler, too,' Jane said.

'She's lonely,' said Bob. 'I can't bear seeing that.'

Any more than I can bear to watch Andy suffer, she thought. But once you leave them to it, it all starts again.

'That parson,' said Bob. 'That Messeter. You know him pretty well, don't you?'

'Not recently, no.'

'You know him better than I do. You didn't give him the idea I'd be good for a touch, did you?'

'Certainly not,' said Jane. 'He asked me if you were rich and I said adequately, but that's all.'

'He wants me to donate a new heating system to that clinic of his.'

'And will you?'

'Of course not. Not just now, anyway. Every penny I've got's tied up in the business. Apart from what I squander on what Da used to call riotous living.'

'Quite so.'

There was Bob for you: giving and taking with equal ease.

'And another thing,' said Bob. 'What's our Andy doing running after a parson? I thought he was an atheist.'

'He mends his current heating system.'

'Oh,' said Bob. 'I see. . . . Somehow I didn't think it would be prayers.'

The last taxi of the day rattled to a halt outside the Eldon Arms.

'Paperwork for me now,' said Bob. 'I'm too full of Grandma's cake to face the dinner here. Pity Norah's chip shop's closed on Sundays. . . . What about you?'

'Certainly not dinner,' said Jane. 'I think I'll do some paperwork too.'

# 40

THEY WENT TO the roadhouse where Blagdon had seen them both. Bob seemed very keen on the idea, and she was still mad about dancing anyway, but even so she telephoned Lovell in London to tell him where she was going.

'Roadhouse?' Lovell said. 'What on earth for?'

'It isn't exactly a giddy round of pleasure up here,' she said. 'I thought I might just risk one valeta before my rheumatism sets in for the winter.'

'Poor old thing,' he said. 'Don't forget to dip your red flannel vest in camphor. . . . But why on earth tell me?'

'Lord Blagdon might be there.'

'Oh,' he said, and then: 'I'm doing my best, you know. Honestly.'

'I do know, Charles,' she said, 'which is why I'm phoning you.'

After that he got rather personal, which made her feel much better.

It had not been a pleasant three days after the christening. Most of it she had spent with Grandma, when she wasn't working on her piece for the *World*. Usually Grandma was alone, since Andy was working at the clinic and, like most old people, she talked about the past: Blagdon Hall and her husband, the children she'd borne, the Boer War which always somehow became mixed up with the Great War of 1914. John. She had so many memories of John: his mischief, his obstinacy, his ambition. Her memories were far clearer than my own, thought

Jane, but maybe if I live to be so old, I too will remember clearly.

Twice they walked round to Bet's house, and Jane learned how to hold so tiny a child; still pretty, still like Grandma, with a grave, unwinking stare: and once Andy stayed away from the clinic because the pipe he needed hadn't arrived, and they talked about Cambridge. Grandma listened, enthralled.

'And you were a part of all that,' she said.

'You know I was,' said Andy. 'I told you.'

'But I never realised it was like that,' she said. 'I'd no idea.'

'Like what, Grandma?'

'Like Blagdon Hall,' the old woman said, and turned to Jane. 'Is it like that?'

'I suppose it is,' said Jane. 'Old and massive and reeking of money.'

Grandma turned back to Andy. 'And you were there,' she said. 'Arguing with those nobs.'

'They call them dons, Grandma.'

'I daresay,' Grandma said. 'I just hope you gave as good as you got.'

The rest of her days were spent on the article, one of the most difficult she had ever written: so much hearsay, so much guesswork, however much she believed it to be true. The charge of homosexual rape was out. No newspaper would touch it, not even one owned by so progressive a proprietor as Bower. The all-male society, that was the thing to stress: the young and healthy males cloistered like monks, with no desire to take monastic vows, and not just chastity. Poverty and obedience were equally abhorrent to them. Yet there they were, day after day: making mailbags, slopping out, attending chapel because they must: the murderers who had escaped the gallows, the conmen and the thieves. There too was Tom Lynch, the only one who was there, not for doing what he knew to be wrong, but for what he believed to be right: and there he killed himself. At last it was done, and she wrote one more piece – a seaside postcard to Lionel of a fat lady wading in the sea, and being nipped by a crab in a most unseemly manner. The fat lady had just smacked the face of the bewildered little man next to her.

'Not in the sea,' she was saying. 'How many times must I tell you?' 'See you after the slaughter,' she wrote. 'Please take me dancing.'

The roadhouse was as it had been before: the same rough-hewn look, above-average food, well-above-average drinks, and a band that knew its business. No Lord Blagdon, which did not surprise her. His modest new dwelling – fifteen rooms was it? twenty? – was over three hundred miles away.

Bob was an attentive and agreeable host, but then he was always that, she thought. Good champagne, and claret carefully chosen, but without fuss. He had learned a lot, but made no show of what he had learned. His dancing had improved, too. More lessons, she wondered, or were they all from the exotic dancer herself, Miss Dunn? Whoever had taught him had done an excellent job. He was almost as good as Lionel – an appalling, almost a treacherous thought.

In one way only he was not like Lionel. The reason Bob danced with a woman was not convention: it was sex. She didn't doubt it from the moment he first held her in his arms. His flow of small talk was easy and unforced: the clinic's heating system, the night he had helped Piers make Burrowes stand for the National Anthem, his yearning for a Bentley, but as the talk flowed and she laughed appropriately he was, she thought, assessing her, as if she were a sort of problem that he could, given time, not only solve, but solve to his own advantage.

All this without pawing her, without putting his hands even fractionally beyond permitted areas, or letting his knee push between hers as if by accident. Never a hand or foot wrong, in fact, and yet, simply by holding her, by touch, he was obliging her body to be aware of his. Not forcing: forcing implied an approach he would never have considered for a moment. Coaxing, guiding, persuading. . . . And the devil of it is he's doing far too good a job, she thought. It would even be possible to succumb, despite her friendship with Charles: despite Bob's total reliance on him, come to that. What a reckless young man he was. If Charles even suspected, he would destroy him without hesitation. When the music stopped she turned at once and went back to their table.

'Gosh, I'm thirsty,' she said, and the waiter poured more wine. When he had gone she took out her cigarettes. No more dancing, not quite yet. 'Tell me about your girls,' she said.

'Girls?' He tried and failed to sound puzzled.

'Oh come on, Bob,' she said smiling. 'You know what girls

are. That ravishing creature in Paris. That new one in London.'

'Newish,' said Bob at once. 'I distinctly said newish. I remember. She's divorced. Wants to go on the stage. Only she shouldn't.'

'Whyever not?'

'She can't act.'

Jane laughed. 'And Lilian Dunn?'

'Fine, so she tells me. I pop across whenever I get the chance – just to keep in touch, you know.'

'I know.'

He looked at her then, but her face was impassive.

'The trouble is she's met another chap,' he said. 'Well there was never any doubt she would, with looks like that. The trouble is this one owns a bank – or a good piece of one.'

'Just like Charles Lovell,' she said.

There was a pause. At last Bob said, 'That's right.'

After that they merely danced together. Whatever current Bob used had been turned off. It was only on the way home that she remembered to ask the name of Lilian's banker. When Bob told her she thought: 'Poor Peggy Hawkins,' and tried not to yawn. Suddenly she was very tired.

She was first to arrive at Blagdon Hall, and Lovell came out at once to admire the Bentley, making all the right noises like a dutiful host, then taking her into the house for tea while her cases were carried upstairs. She looked about her. The hall had been restored superbly, and so had the little drawing room. No doubt the rest of the house was now splendid too.

'Tell me about your other guests,' she said, as a new butler brought in tea. An imposing enough presence, she thought, but not a patch on Proudfoot.

Lovell listed five Americans, two of them with wives. Among the very few left with readily available money, he thought. An Australian cattle millionaire with his wife, and a Spanish marquis who had left his wife at home made up the list.

'He always does,' said Lovell. 'Damned if I can think why. Except that she's extremely ugly.'

'Will any of them be difficult?'

'I shouldn't think so,' said Lovell. 'There are a couple of things I want their money for, but they're reasonable risks. I don't see any problems.'

'Then what's upset you?'

'It shows, does it?'

'Probably not to your millionaires, but I know you better than that.'

'You do indeed, thank God.' He paused for a moment. 'It's Blagdon.'

'What about him?'

'He wants his house back.'

'But that's ridiculous,' said Jane.

'So's Blagdon ridiculous. One minute he's threatening law suits, the next he's offering to buy it back.'

'But he hasn't any money.'

'By instalments,' said Lovell. 'Two hundred pounds a year from the produce of the home farm –'

'You did away with the home farm.'

'He'll get it back. Please don't interrupt. Two hundred a year to be paid by him and his heirs for ever. He's even sent me a contract.'

'But it's crazy.'

'Exactly,' said Lovell. 'I got on to my lawyers. They say they can probably get an injunction against further harassment and it may come to that. But I can hardly do it just before a shooting party. The newspapers would splash it all over the place. I hope to God he doesn't come here.'

'Is it likely?'

'He did once before,' Lovell said. 'Remember? Said he'd come to help with the decorating. Buckets of whitewash all over the place. Charlie Chaplin wasn't in it.'

Jane found that she wanted to giggle. Never before had she seen Charles terrified. 'To get back to your house guests,' she said. 'How have you explained me to them?'

'I want your money too.'

This time she laughed aloud. 'Clever Charles,' she said. 'I'd better wear the sapphires.'

The terror vanished. Suddenly he looked furtive instead. A most untypical look for Charles.

'The staff are all busy with dinner,' he said, 'and none of the guests will arrive before seven. My valet has a day off. I was wondering if I might –'

'Might what?'

'Come and look at the sapphires.'

Bob had aroused her, there was no doubt of that, but it had not been Bob she wanted. Maybe it wouldn't be Charles for much longer, furtive, frightened, greedy Charles – but all the same: 'Very well,' she said. 'But just this once.'

The true Charles look came back then: the chairman of the board calling the meeting to order.

'Good,' he said. 'Marvellous. You haven't got a maid so I've sent one of ours to help you unpack. She'll do all the lady's maid stuff while you're here. Her name's Mary. Perfectly reliable, Clegg tells me.'

'Clegg?'

'The butler. Mary will be gone by five to help with the dining-room table. I'll look in about a quarter of an hour after. If Mary's still there for whatever reason, I'll bring some papers for you to sign.'

More acting, she thought. I do hope it doesn't come to that. He's so bad at it. 'I'll get rid of her,' she said.

She was in the bath when he arrived; not quite by chance. After all not every room at Blagdon Hall had its own bathroom. He deserved an extra treat.

'You locked the door?'

'Of course,' he said in his chairman-of-the-board voice, but already he was tearing off his clothes. She stood up and reached for a towel, and he looked at her.

'I don't know what I've done to deserve this,' he said, 'but I swear to God I'm grateful. I'll always be grateful.'

He reached out for her, and carried her to the bed.

It was a good one, an especially good one. Together they had learned how to pace themselves, to make it last and linger, but this one was especially good: so good that she yelled out loud.

'And you're the one who keeps telling me to be discreet,' said Lovell.

'It's your own fault,' said Jane. ' – And you needn't look so smug about it either.'

'One does one's poor best,' said Lovell. She threw a pillow at him, and he grabbed her again. As he dressed she said, 'You didn't even see the sapphires.'

'Put them on,' he said, and looked at his watch. 'We've just about got time.' So she put them on and posed as Lilian Dunn and that black girl Josephine Baker and the rest of them did at the Folies Bergère. Next time she must try to get some ostrich feathers, she thought. After all he really did seem to enjoy it, and it was a pleasure to show off her body. At her age it was a pleasure to have a body worth showing. . . . He looked at his watch again. Time to go.

'Better be off,' he said, and went to the door, then came back to collect a neat file of papers from the table. The chairman of the board left nothing to chance.

As he left she said, 'Thank you, Mr Lovell. A most interesting demonstration, but I think perhaps we'd better go over it all again before we make any firm decisions.'

He tripped on the door sill and nearly dropped his papers. Fifteen all, she thought, then went to run a bath before Mary came to help her dress.

The shooting party had met for drinks in the hall. The Americans, male and female, were the sort she had met aboard the *Pocahontas*, to whom money was as necessary – and available – as water to a fish. They had come from London to Newcastle by train and were intrigued by its smallness, as if it had been constructed by Hornby, she thought. The cattleman looked like a cattleman, and so, unfortunately, did his wife, lean and leathery, and tanned to the colour of one of their own short-horns. Not the sort of body on which to hang a Poiret gown, thought Jane, which was what she had done. The Spanish marquis, the Marqués de Antequera, would one day be lean and leathery too, but in his early forties he still had a kind of horsy elegance about him.

Jane had swept in last, babbling excuses about her lateness: she had no intention of appearing as temporary acting hostess, even if Charles had made her yell. The two American women at once looked at the sapphires, blinked, then looked again. If Charles were to look smug now he'd give the whole game away, she thought, but being a banker as well as a man he was discussing hog-belly futures with one of the husbands.

Of the two women, one was quite young – wife number two, or possibly three – thought Jane, the other, like her husband, in her fifties. Money of her own? All of them, and the three who had arrived unencumbered, looked easy and relaxed, as if jump-

– 484 –

ing off the Chrysler building were something that happened on another planet. She was in the presence of money notable not only for its quantity but for its endurance also.

'Do you shoot, Miss Whitcomb?' the Australian woman asked. Laura, was it? Lorna? Louise? She really must concentrate: no matter what fun she'd had.

'No,' she said. 'I never have. Do you?'

'Well yes,' said the Australian woman. 'I sort of have to in the outback. On account of the dingoes. . . . Wild dogs?'

She had the trick of making a statement a question, like some Southern Americans.

'Have to,' said her husband. 'Laurie's a better shot than I am. She's got cups to prove it.' Higgins, that was it. Fred and Laurie Higgins.

'You're not interested in sport, Miss Whitcomb?' the young wife asked. Cardwell. Joyce Cardwell. That was it.

'Not shooting,' said Jane, and turned to smile at Charles. 'I ride when I can.' Lovell somehow managed to avoid choking on his drink.

'Miss Whitcomb is an excellent rider,' he said, and so thirty fifteen became thirty all.

Dinner was good, of course; that was inevitable. Trust Lovell for that. After it the men sat over their port, and the women were herded out by the older American lady.

'What barbarity,' Joyce Cardwell said, and looked at Jane, who shrugged. She had no great need of port.

'At least we won't feel liverish tomorrow,' she said, and helped herself to coffee. There was brandy, too. Rather a good one.

'Have you known Mr Lovell long?' asked the older American lady.

'Quite a while,' said Jane. 'He's awfully clever about money, isn't he?'

'So my husband says,' said the older American lady.

'And mine,' said Laurie Higgins.

'And what else do you do?' said Joyce Cardwell. 'Apart from riding, I mean?' Really this can only go on for so long, thought Jane.

'I'm a writer,' she said. 'Or rather a journalist.'

'Ought I to have read you?'

'Not unless you read the *Daily World*,' said Jane, 'which is the paper I write for. But as it's an English paper I doubt if that's likely. On the other hand it's possible that you may see me. My work, anyway.'

'See you?'

'I've written a screenplay,' said Jane. 'For Hollywood. They've just started shooting it.'

'Who's in it?' Joyce Cardwell asked. 'Anyone I should have heard of?'

'I've no idea,' said Jane. 'The stars are Georgina Payne and Dan Corless.' Laurie Higgins hitched her chair a little closer.

'You know them?' she asked.

'Not Dan Corless,' said Jane, 'but I've known Georgie for absolute ages.'

Not another word from Joyce Cardwell, but the other two women were avid for details. What was she really like? and was she really so beautiful? and why had she never married?

'She was engaged a long time ago,' said Jane, 'to a painter called Browne. Only it didn't seem to work, unfortunately. But I've heard a rumour – this is just between ourselves of course –'

'Of course,' said Laurie Higgins, from whom 'Cross my heart and hope to die' would not have been in the least surprising.

'Well I've heard,' said Jane, 'that she may be going to marry Dan Corless.'

'*No*,' said Laurie Higgins, and even Joyce Cardwell was impressed. The senior American lady said, 'Well what could be more appropriate? Kind of like your royalty, wouldn't you say? King and Queen of Hollywood?'

'It is rather like a fairy tale,' said Jane. 'One can only hope they'll be happy.'

'Bound to be,' Laurie Higgins said. 'And starring in your movie, too.'

The gentlemen joined them at last, still talking money, until the older American lady told them to stop. There were other matters far more interesting, she said, and told them Jane's news.

The marquis said, 'You really know Georgina Payne?'

'I really do.'

'Tell me then, please, is she really as beautiful as she appears on the screen?'

'Every bit.'

The marquis sighed with relief. An illusion had not been shattered. 'It has been one of the dreams of my life to meet her,' he said. 'But then every shepherd hopes to meet a goddess.'

But not every shepherd owns a hundred thousand acres and a couple of castles, thought Jane.

'Has she ever been to Spain?'

'Never,' said Jane.

'Then I invite her,' the marquis said. 'I invite you both.' As an afterthought he added: 'And her husband of course. At any time.'

'I shall tell her so,' said Jane. 'Next time I see her.'

'She will be welcome,' said the marquis. 'Most welcome. And you too, Miss Whitcomb. Of course. If only –' Jane waited. 'Spain is such a restless country,' said the marquis. 'Strikes, riots, demonstrations. Miss Payne I think is the sort of lady who seeks tranquillity.'

Jane thought of black eyes, and a palette knife ready to rip up a painting. 'She's quite tough, really,' she said.

The marquis was appalled. He said, 'I cannot agree with you, no matter how well you know her. I have seen her on the screen many times. A dove, a gazelle could not be more vulnerable.'

Lovell said, 'In any case, the whole of Europe is restless these days. Look at Italy, look at Germany.'

One of the unaccompanied Americans began at once to talk about the price of Saar coal, and Jane went for more coffee. When she came back Laurie Higgins said, 'You really like horse-riding?'

'Very much,' said Jane.

'The reason I ask – I don't want to sound pushy or anything – but I sort of get the idea women don't shoot much. Pheasants, I mean.'

'It isn't usual.'

'Right. And Mr Lovell has some horses? Good horses?'

'So he tells me.'

'Then I'd sooner ride,' Laurie Higgins said, 'if he'll let me have a horse.'

'You have riding gear?'

'All I'll ever need,' said Laurie Higgins. 'Had it made in London just before we came here. You should have seen Fred's face when we got the bill.' She smiled, but there was no malice in her smile. Jane thought how easy it would be to like her.

'Do tell me, Miss Whitcomb,' the older American lady said, 'where did you get those absolutely wonderful sapphires?'

Charles was deep in discussion about the world effect of the stock market crash, but Jane was sure that he had heard the question. 'They belonged to the wife of a Russian nobleman,' she said. 'I heard they'd come on the market, and a little man in New York got them for me.' Forty thirty.

Then it was match postponed. Charles Lovell wanted a prompt start next day, and the marksmen decided on an early night. Mary, big and bustling, was there to help her undress, and Jane got rid of her as soon as possible. She was a heavy-handed girl with a large clumsiness rather like Lord Blagdon's. Very like Lord Blagdon's in fact, but there was simply no point in exploring that one. As she drifted off to sleep she remembered that the older American lady was called Mary, too. Mary Robinson. Not an easy name to remember.

# 41

S HE ATE BREAKFAST alone. Every other guest had gone to the
shoot, Clegg told her reproachfully, but there was no need.
As she ate her boiled egg she could hear the persistent popping
of small-arms fire. Add a few rounds of artillery and it would be
quite like old times, she thought, and ate up quickly. Clegg had
quite enough to do preparing an outdoor lunch. She swallowed
the last of her coffee and set off for the stables.

They had been renovated too: the stable yard was weeded,
and the stable clock was working. Lovell had warned the head
groom that she would be coming, and he eyed her warily. She
was far too elegant to match his idea of what a clipping lady
rider should look like.

'Let's see what you've got,' said Jane, and settled at last on a
bay mare with a white stocking and a white blaze on her forehead: Daisy Bell.

'The mare's a bit fresh, miss,' the head groom said.

'Bring her out and let's have a look at her.'

The head groom obeyed because he had no choice. All the
same the poor man's worried, she thought, and rightly so. If I
come a cropper Charles will blame him. Much better not to come
a cropper, for both our sakes.

Daisy Bell came out, looked at Jane, and snorted. At once
Jane's hand went to her pocket and offered sugar lumps pur-
loined at breakfast. The mare accepted them daintily and from
the look in her eye decided to postpone judgement and allow
herself to be saddled. Jane stroked her soft muzzle as she waited,

then swung herself into the saddle. The mare danced a few steps as a matter of form, but the hands on the bridle knew their business, and she moved off out of the yard at a walk, the head groom watching them go, still far from easy in his mind.

She walked the mare along the stable path to open ground, away from the shot guns' popping. Daisy Bell was much too fresh to ignore loud bangs. She chose a bridle path through a spinney, hardwoods ablaze with red and golden brown and yellow, and remembered the seemingly endless miles of New England in the fall. Had that really been only a year ago?

The spinney ended and there was open ground before her, wiry grass with here and there a clump of grazing sheep. The mare began to pull and Jane gave her her head, wary of rabbit holes. The mare's stride lengthened and Jane indulged her. Daisy Bell was a goer all right. She wondered if Charles would sell her and knew he would not, any more than she would sell Bridget's Boy.

Making love with him had been really rather gorgeous, and so had the wordplay afterwards. That part of her life was fine, so long as Charles could control his jealousy – and really he must stop buying her sapphires from the Russian nobility, though she rather doubted if there were any left. It was her other life that was hopeless: that suffocating need to be of use: practical, organising, striving for a goal worth achieving. Writing for the *World* was all very well, and writing the screenplay had been enthralling (and very good for Felston) but they were not what she was *for*. She had held her namesake in her arms and knew with complete certainty that motherhood was not for her. She was meant to be an aunt, and a damn bossy one at that.

Daisy Bell snorted, and Jane pulled her to a halt. They had reached the crest of a hill, and before them more hills unfolded, stretching on and on to the horizon, gorse covered, bleak, and already very cold. The mare danced once more.

'Goodness, you're a glutton for punishment,' Jane told her. 'Come on then.' She turned Daisy Bell downhill and resumed the canter. It still seemed effortless. She must ask Charles how good she was over jumps. . . .

To be useful was all she needed, but she might as well have demanded the moon. She was totally untrained, as Harriet Watson had told her so tactfully, and too damned old to begin training. She was, in fact, completely useless. When Dr Stobbs had called her frivolous he had just about got it right. Change the subject, she told herself. Think about something else. You can't burst into tears when you're riding a horse. On the way back to the stables she planned another letter to Daisy.

Lunch was the traditional first day of shoot fare at Blagdon: mulligatawny soup, shepherd's pie with sprouts and carrots, and rice pudding and cream. Men and women alike ate ravenously: the cold and exercise had seen to that. When Jane walked over from the stables she was barely in time to claim her share. They ate at trestle tables and sat on benches, but the wine was a first-growth claret; not that there were many takers, Jane noticed. Steadiness of hand and eye were far too important.

'Wine, miss?' asked Clegg.

'Please.' Jane had no intention of shooting anything.

From across the table Laurie Higgins asked, 'Good ride?'

'Very,' said Jane. 'I thought you were coming too?'

'Next time,' said Laurie Higgins. 'I've never seen a shoot like this before, and I thought now I'm here I ought at least to take a look.'

'Impressed?'

'I never saw anything like it.' The Australian looked at the great mound of birds awaiting the game cart. 'That's a shoot? Back in Australia we'd call it a massacre.'

Her husband said something to her and they got up and walked to where his loader stood waiting with the shot guns. Really she looks much, much better in tweeds, thought Jane. I wonder how good she is on a horse?

One by one the others left the table, and Jane waited alone for her rice pudding, until Charles came to her and sat beside her.

'There's a business matter I'd like to discuss with you,' he said at once. She looked at him warily, but he seemed to be speaking the truth.

'Certainly,' she said. Clegg brought her pudding.

'Finish that first,' said Charles. 'It's rather a good one, if I may say so.'

It was delicious: fragrant with cloves and cinnamon, stuffed with sultanas, drowned in double cream.

'You're quite right,' she said. 'It's heavenly – but do talk business while I eat.'

He looked about him. There was no one within earshot. 'It's about Felston,' he said.

'More bad news?'

'I'm afraid so.'

'Dear God,' said Jane. 'What else can anyone do to the wretched town?'

'It has one shipyard still working,' said Lovell.

'Beech and Calthrop,' said Jane at once. 'Andy Patterson served his apprenticeship there.'

'I'm sorry,' said Lovell, 'but Beech and Calthrop is closing down as soon as their last ship is finished.'

'*What*?' said Jane. 'Who told you this?'

'I'm even more sorry to tell you that the decision was mine – partially mine at any rate.' Jane pushed her plate away. 'Would you care to walk a little? I very much want to explain what I was obliged to do. I and some others.'

'Yes, of course,' said Jane, and rose to her feet.

'I'll walk you back to the house,' Charles Lovell said, and they set off together. 'Please believe me, it wasn't an easy decision.'

'Just tell me,' said Jane.

'Britain has too many shipyards,' said Lovell, 'and especially too many old ones, just as it has too many of the wrong sort of factories, too many coal mines that are hard to work. Nobody wants to buy ships just now, or if they do they can afford to pick and choose. Guaranteed price, quick delivery. You follow me?' She nodded.

'Some of our yards can do that, but not many. Shipowners are beginning to look elsewhere more and more, and a shipyard needs money even when it isn't working. Maintenance, repairs, skeleton staff. They all need investment, and for that the shipyard owners look to the banks.'

'To men like you.'

'To men like me. Just as the factory owners do. And the mine owners. Now I know that people like your friend Andy Patterson think our wealth is unending, but we both know that's not true. There are limits – and I'm one of a committee set up to decide what those limits are.'

'And one of them is Beech and Calthrop?'

'I'm afraid so. We'd begun to fear as much at our meeting last week, but we gave our accountants instructions to go over the figures again, and they did. I phoned them just before lunch. Beech and Calthrop hasn't a hope of survival, I'm afraid.'

Lovell paused. He expects me to say something, thought Jane. He even expects there's something I want to say, but there's nothing. How can there be? – if what he tells me is true. And why should he lie?

'So what should Felston do?' she asked at last. 'Take Job's wife advice? Curse God and die?'

'There's nothing Felston can do,' he said, 'except hope for another war.'

'But that's appalling,' she said. 'And in any case there can't possibly be another war.'

He shrugged. 'Industrial towns like Felston are old and out of date,' he said. 'They can't make things at a profit, not any more.'

'And profit is all that matters?'

'It's the only thing that works,' he said. 'I honestly and truly believe that.' He hesitated. 'What money the banks have must go to the towns and factories that can make a profit, survive the depression.' He paused once more, but this time she had no comment, no question.

'I told you as soon as I could,' he said at last. 'Perhaps you would treat it as a confidence – at least until the press announcement?'

'I promise,' she said.

'Forgive me,' he said. 'This isn't the time for personal matters – not for you at any rate. But I must ask you this. I can't help myself. What I've done – been a part of – does that mean we're finished?'

'Of course not,' said Jane. 'You did what you thought had to be done. I don't know enough to judge whether your decision was the right one or not, but I know you think it was. If you'd done it out of malice, cruelty, vindictiveness, I'd leave you now. But you didn't. Some people die so that others may live. That's your creed, isn't it Charles?'

'More or less.'

'It's pretty drastic,' said Jane, 'but at least it's honest. My word on it – this doesn't affect us. Not a scrap.'

But it was match abandoned when it came to laughter.

Felston knew almost as soon as she did; days before the press announcement. Andy had the news from Burrowes, and for once even Burrowes seemed appalled. They met once again in the Newcastle Station buffet: tea urn steam and cigarette smoke and the clatter of thick china cups.

'I can't believe it,' Andy said.

'But it's true.' Burrowes' voice, for once, was gentle.

'Yes,' Andy said. 'It must be. There's one ship on the stocks – general cargo for some French line or other. She's almost ready for launching. Then she'll go for fitting out, and that will be the end.'

'What sort of job loss would that be?'

'Seven – eight hundred,' Andy said. 'Even more if all the stages were full.'

'They'll never be full again, I'm afraid,' Burrowes said.

'Gates locked, bolted, barred, just like the others,' Andy said, and counted off the casualties in his mind.

'Not a factory left open with more than fifty men in it,' he said. 'Not a shipyard, and one mine, just the one – and that's only because they need it to ventilate the shafts. Those bastards in London have murdered the whole town.'

'Your friend Jane Whitcomb is currently visiting one of the killers,' said Burrowes.

'Jane's at Blagdon Hall,' said Andy.

'Charles Lovell's place,' said Burrowes. 'He's one of the merchant bankers who made the decision.'

Perhaps she's even sharing his bed at this moment, Burrowes thought, but he decided to save that one for later, when Andy might need further goading.

'You –' Andy hesitated. 'Forgive me for asking, but you really are sure about this?'

'Positive,' said Burrowes. 'You shouldn't doubt me, Andy. You must know by now how reliable my sources are.'

'It's just –' Andy threw up his hands. 'I just can't take it in. But why are you telling me all this anyway?'

'I could hardly tell Deegan,' said Burrowes, 'and poor Tom Lynch is beyond telling. You're all the Party has left up here – if we still have you.'

'You shouldn't need telling the answer to that,' Andy said.

'We worry about you,' Burrowes said, 'and you must agree that we do right to worry. But I do owe you an apology about one thing. You were right when you refused even to consider going back to prison. Poor Tom's death proved that.'

I'm hurting him, Burrowes thought, but now and then he needs to be hurt, and I'm entitled to some amusement after all.

'You want me to do something,' Andy said.

'Obviously. We want you to start being active again. Working at the clinic is very good, too. It shows how compassionate you are. Now don't get excited. I meant that sincerely. But we want you to speak out as soon as this is known.'

'Don't worry,' said Andy. 'I'll speak.' He brooded for a moment. 'The only trouble is I've been asked to stand as a Labour councillor.'

'Not as good as an MP,' Burrowes said, 'but it's a start.'

'Labour,' Andy said. 'Middle of the road. Patriotic, even.'

'Just what my comrades and I want,' said Burrowes. 'On the surface at any rate. We want you back, Andy, on precisely those terms.'

Of course you do, Andy thought. You said yourself, there isn't anybody else.

'Besides,' said Burrowes, 'even a middle-of-the-road Labour man has a duty to say what he thinks about Mr Lovell closing down Beech and Calthrop. We're compiling a little dossier on Mr Lovell. I'll send you a few gems. You may find them useful.'

The clinic knew, or rather Canon Messeter did, because a cousin telephoned him and told him, in confidence of *course*, and his cousin was married to a fellow member of Lovell's committee. Messeter at once swore Stobbs to secrecy, and told him. Stobbs too was appalled.

'It'll mean a lot more patients,' he said.

'Of course it will,' said Messter. 'And Calthrop was good for a five-hundred-a-year subscription. Now he'll probably go to end his days in Knightsbridge – if it isn't the South of France.'

'It's a swine all right,' said Stobbs, 'but I don't see what we can do about it.'

'I've been thinking about that,' Messeter said. 'Some yards receive investment, some don't. That seems to be the basis of the thing. What we should do is try to arrange things so that the decision is reversed, and Beech and Calthrop join the survivors.'

'Change places with another yard, in fact?' Messeter nodded. 'And the other yard goes under?'

'Precisely.'

Stobbs looked bewildered. 'Hardly the Christian spirit, surely?'

Messeter said firmly, 'We are fighting for survival.'

'And anyway,' said Stobbs, 'how on earth can we possibly do the thing?'

'I have checked with Andy Patterson,' said the canon. 'Jane Whitcomb is presently staying at Blagdon Hall – with Charles Lovell. Some sort of house-party, I understand. I knew Lovell in the war. We served in the same battalion – and I'm led to believe that Jane Whitcomb has some influence with him too.'

'What on earth do you mean?'

'I have no idea,' Messeter said, 'but I believe my statement to be true.'

'But how can you know?'

'Gossip,' said Messeter. 'Mine is a large family. Gossips to a man – and more importantly, woman. We must call upon Jane Whitcomb.'

Stobbs didn't like it. At least they ought to telephone first, he insisted, but when they tried she wasn't there. Messeter got out his vast, decrepit Armstrong-Siddeley tourer. For once he could drive it without pangs of conscience about petrol.

Jane had had a trying day: a combination of a broken stirrup leather, the onset of the curse and the discovery that Laurie Higgins was a much better rider than she could ever hope to be had combined to try her patience about as far as it could go. It hadn't helped that Laurie Higgins was so damn nice about it. Jane had had the better horse, but Laurie Higgins was far and away the better rider, and the knowledge hurt. It was childish, but it hurt. For years everyone had agreed that she was good on a horse, but let Laurie Higgins mount a horse, any horse, and together they became a female centaur.

She left the Australian talking to the head groom. A bath, she decided, half an hour on her bed, and two aspirins to combat the headache she knew was coming. Then Clegg met her at the door to tell her that a parson and a doctor were waiting to see her. They had telephoned for an appointment, Clegg told her fairmindedly, but he had been obliged to tell them that Miss Whitcomb was Otherwise Engaged.

Jane went up to her room. The bath became water splashed on her face: make-up and a change of clothes a substitute for the bed that looked at her so invitingly: but she took the aspirins. The two men were waiting for her in the little drawing room. What on earth are they doing here? she wondered. From the corridor she could hear Messeter's voice, its audibility magnified by years of preaching, telling Stobbs his recollections of Blagdon as a schoolboy. She waited for Clegg to precede her.

'Miss Whitcomb,' said Clegg, and left her to her fate.

Messeter was on his feet at once, and Stobbs scrambled after from the depths of a vast leather chair.

'Good of you to receive us. Most kind,' Messeter was saying.

'Not at all,' said Jane. 'You telephoned, I believe, but I've been out riding. With a friend,' she added conscientiously.

'Quite so,' Messeter said. 'I've heard you are a notable horsewoman.'

From whom? Jane wondered. And whoever it was never saw me beside that Australian cowgirl.

'Do sit down,' she said, 'and tell me what brings you here. I can ring for sherry if you'd like it.'

'No no,' said Stobbs. 'We mustn't take up too much of your time.'

He makes sherry sound like a substitute for opium, she thought, and waited. It was Messeter who told her why they had come.

'But,' she said at last, 'from what you say this information is a secret.'

'In a sense,' Stobbs began.

Messeter interrupted him. 'In every sense,' he said. 'As a gentleman I have broken my word, but not to have done so would have made me an even greater sinner than I am.'

'I see,' said Jane. 'Or rather I don't. I mean I can understand your concern – I feel it myself, believe me –' Messeter lowered his head in acknowledgement '– but I can't understand why you should come to me.' Despite the aspirin, her headache, she knew, was on its way.

'Can't you?' said Stobbs. 'I should have thought it was obvious.'

'Stobbs old chap,' Messeter said, 'I wonder if you would mind going to the car for me? I rather think I left my Bible in it. There's a passage I particularly want Miss Whitcomb to see.'

Stobbs glared at Messeter, received in return a glance of Arctic frost, then got up and went.

'He's a dear fellow,' said Messeter, 'but I think this is best between the two of us.' Jane waited.

'You have learned the value of silence,' Messeter continued. 'I congratulate you on that, not least because I never did, though I must tell you it makes it no easier for me.'

'Why should I make it easier?'

Messeter sighed. 'You've already had this news, I take it?' Again she said nothing, and he hurried on. 'Forgive me. I had no business to ask that question, but I'm concerned, you see.'

'Of course,' said Jane, and he was aware at once of the warmth in her voice.

'Intercession,' he said. 'That is what we came for, Stobbs and I. To ask you to intercede. You may think that it was a mistake to bring Stobbs, but he's as much concerned as I am.'

'I may think it was a mistake for either of you to come,' said Jane. Her head had begun to throb, but it would be impossible to skip dinner. Laurie Higgins must never believe that she was sulking. More than anything else in the world she wanted to lie down on her bed.

'I had to come,' Messeter said. 'You may think it a hopeless journey, perhaps even a foolish one, but it had to be made. Lovell will listen to you – we both know that.'

'Not about this.'

'He will, I tell you,' said Messeter. 'He must.'

For the first time since she had met him he was close to anger.

'I shan't ask him.'

'You could save the whole town.'

'No,' said Jane. 'I couldn't. The decision – from what you tell me – wasn't just his. It was made by a group.'

'Charles can dominate any group he's in,' Messeter said. 'Believe me I know. Do you want me to beg? I'll beg. Go on my knees if you like.'

'What a monster you must think me,' said Jane.

'I'm not thinking of you at all,' Messeter said. 'All I can think of is Felston. There is a passage in the Bible I should like to quote you – although there's no Bible in the car, God forgive me, and even if there were I have it by heart. It's St Paul as a matter of fact.' He continued in the same conversational tone. '"Though I speak with the tongues of men and of angels, and have not charity, I am become as sounding brass or a tinkling cymbal." I think that they are some of the most remarkable words ever written.'

'First Epistle to the Corinthians,' said Jane. 'My governess thought so too. She made me learn them by heart twenty years ago. "And now abideth faith, hope, charity, these three; but the greatest of these is charity." I've never forgotten it.'

'Then doesn't it follow –' Messeter began.

She interrupted him. Her headache was getting worse, and she had to finish what she had to say.

'Vinney – my governess – used to say that charity meant one of the aspects of love,' she said. 'The giving kind of love.'

'She was quite right,' said Messeter.

'And with Felston I've done my best to show charity,' Jane continued. 'I've helped the place whenever I could, with time, energy, ideas; and when there was nothing else to give I've at least given money. I still do.'

'We may have seemed ungrateful,' Messeter said, 'but in our hearts we were not. It was just that the town was so much more important than one individual. Miss Whitcomb we still need your money. I think we'll always need it, but now we need your indulgence, too. If you could persuade Charles Lovell –'

'I think,' said Jane, 'that you're confusing me with Mata Hari.'

'Believe me I intended no kind of innuendo –' Messeter said.

'Perhaps not,' said Jane, 'or perhaps it's only that you think you didn't – but this isn't my job. I can't do it.'

'You mean you won't,' said Messeter.

'I mean it's none of my business.'

From the door Charles Lovell said, 'She's right, you know, Rupert.'

Unhurried, Messeter looked towards where Lovell stood. Tweeds and boots. Been out shooting. Let's hope he's had a good day. But Lovell's eyes were on Jane.

'Forgive me,' he said, 'but are you quite well?'

'Just a headache,' she said. 'It's beginning to bang rather.'

'You must go and lie down,' he said. 'Shall I ring for your maid?'

'No,' she said. 'A rest should do it. I'll be all right by dinner time.' She rose, and the ache intensified with her movement.

'I'm sorry,' she said to Messeter. 'Honestly I am. Anything else – I'll do it gladly. But this – there are certain rules I can't break. Excuse me.' She moved to the door.

'I'll come with you,' said Lovell.

'No,' said Jane. 'Canon Messeter's come a long way, and you're the one he should speak with after all.'

She left them together.

# 42

'REALLY, RUPERT,' SAID Lovell. 'Bullying a lady. Hardly your style, is it?'

'I don't agree that I bullied her,' Messeter said. 'I desperately needed her help, and I was pushing her hard, that I admit – but as to bullying – I try not to bully anyone, not any more.'

'You can try bullying me if you like,' said Lovell. 'You've done it before.'

'Nonsense,' Messeter said. 'When did I ever do that?'

'When you had the battalion and I had "B" company.'

'And you wouldn't apply for leave. I remember.'

'Till you bullied me into it. You were right. I needed that leave.' Lovell took the chair Jane had sat in, and faced Messeter squarely. 'Now's your chance to bully me again,' he said.

'I hear Beech and Calthrop will close down,' said Messeter.

'That cousin of yours told you? Dalton's wife?'

'Does it matter?'

'Not in the least,' said Lovell, 'inasmuch as it's true enough – but rather confidential just for the moment.'

'I don't want to advertise it,' said Messeter. 'I want to stop it.'

'So do I,' said Lovell. 'In an ideal world I would stop it. But this world's not ideal. Far from it.'

'Charles, I beg you,' said Messeter. 'No cynicism. Not now.'

'I thought I was being honest,' Lovell said. 'Let me explain what's been decided.' Messeter nodded, then listened carefully.

'Couldn't an exception be made? Just one?' he asked at last.

'You know it can't,' said Lovell. 'Wales, the north west, Ulster, the Clyde – they all have the same problems. They're no worse off than Felston – they couldn't be – but they're certainly no better.'

'You're saying that all we can do is watch disaster happen?'

'I'm saying that there's no bank in the country, in the world – that can fund what is happening now,' said Lovell. To himself he added: And it will get worse. But there was no sense in telling the other man so. Poor old Rupert had had about as much as he could take.

'The government?' Messeter asked.

'It's your only hope.'

'The last straw, you mean.' He looked about him at the easy, elegant room, furniture and pictures alike discreetly proclaiming wealth.

'You're so rich,' he said.

'Not rich enough. And anyway I'll be punished for it. I'll never enter the Kingdom of Heaven, will I?'

'Easier for the camel to pass through the eye of a needle, you mean? We must set about making you poor, Charles.' He rose to his feet. 'I must join Stobbs. He's lurked for quite long enough.'

'Before you go,' Lovell said, 'please tell me why you approached Jane.'

'It's said she has some influence on you.'

'By whom?' Lovell asked.

'Several people as it happens,' Messeter said. 'And I have watched you together myself. You're not awfully good at dissembling, Charles.'

'I'm too much in love to be that,' Charles Lovell said.

'And she?'

'She likes me quite a lot,' said Lovell, and hoped to God that Messeter wouldn't pity him, but all the canon said was, 'You're sinning of course, but it isn't a particularly important sin – at least I don't consider it so. Tell God you're sorry – if ever you are – and do your best for Felston.'

The headache relented enough for her to go downstairs for dinner. It would have been too dreadful to have Laurie Higgins think she was sulking, but all Laurie Higgins wanted to do was discuss plans for the next day's riding to the point where the headache showed signs of returning. Mercifully the party broke up early. More birds to be slaughtered next day made a good night's sleep essential. Charles managed a few words with her in the hall, heading off the Spanish marquis by pronouncing the word 'dividends'. Dividends of course were a sacred subject, no more to be shared than the confessional, and so the marquis moved away. Earlier he had expressed an enthusiasm for joining the riding party, which Charles had deftly vetoed. She hoped that Laurie Higgins was its cause.

'You got rid of him?' she asked.

'It wasn't too difficult,' Charles Lovell said. 'Rupert and I are old friends.'

'He accepted your reasons?'

'He knows the truth when he hears it. Poor chap. The whole thing is hurting him dreadfully.'

'To be good – really good – like him, must be a terrible load to carry.'

'When I first knew him it didn't even show,' said Lovell. 'He was simply a very efficient officer who worried rather a lot about his men. And his junior officers. Since then it seems to have intensified.'

'He knows about us,' said Jane.

'Apparently quite a few people do. We've broken the eleventh commandment, my dear.'

'Thou shalt not be found out?'

'That's the one. Does it worry you?'

'I don't think so,' said Jane. 'Not now my mother knows.'

'Good God,' said Lovell. 'Does she?'

'Has done for ages. I didn't want her to find out from anybody else.'

'She doesn't disapprove?'

'She thinks I need the steadying influence of an older man,' said Jane. 'Her very words, bless her.' She held out her hand. 'Goodnight, Mr Lovell.'

He touched it lightly. 'Good night, Miss Whitcomb.' He turned to invite the marquis to one last glass of brandy, as Jane escaped up the stairs.

'This is really quite ricidulous,' said Georgina Payne.

'Not from where I am,' said Bob.

They were in bed together and the sheet had slipped and left her uncovered. She can give her ten years he thought, but she's still in Lilian's class. He leaned across to kiss her, selecting his targets, one and two and three, and Georgina tried to be impassive and found that she couldn't, and wriggled instead. His arms came round her.

Later she said, 'All the same I mean it. It's ridiculous. How long have we known each other?'

'Five years,' said Bob.

'Five years ago you danced with me. Once. In that little hall in Felston. Then you stroll back into my life and hey, presto. I mean look at us.'

'I'd just as soon look at you.'

'I mean I'm going to be married next week.'

'Congratulations.' He reached out to touch her.

'Don't do that,' Georgie said, not meaning it.

Only the first part had been tricky, and even that hadn't been exactly climbing Everest. He'd gone to New York on a ship his father had helped to build, bought all the stuff he needed at give away prices, and taken the first train he could to California. New York had been awful. Cold wind, cold rain, and gloom that was thick enough to slice like bread. But in California the sun shone from the minute he got off the train. It was all just a matter of staying calm, not losing your head.

The right hotel for a start. Nothing flash, not for a Limey business man. Somewhere quiet and discreet with a lot of class. Why not? He could afford it. He had to afford it, otherwise the game wasn't worth playing. Then the rented car, a Cadillac: grey with a touch of blue. Not memorable, but elegant. The elegance that costs money. His clothes were no problem at all. He'd bought them all in London.

Getting to her hadn't been all that tricky either. He'd thought it out on the liner going over, and it had worked as he had been sure it must. He was a partner in one of Charles Lovell's business enterprises, and Lovell's was a name that opened every World Wide door. He'd proved that from the moment he had telephoned their publicity department. After that all he had to do was lie back and let it happen: privileged tour of the studio, then lunch with some bloke called Fisch whom he hadn't liked at all, but who was important. Very. He'd told him so himself. And then a cocktail party where Georgina Payne had been guest of honour, but even she had been told to be nice to the Englishman who was Charles Lovell's partner. Not that she'd found it all that much of a chore. He knew that as soon as they had danced together. Funny thing about dancing. He'd tried it on Jane, too, and she'd known at once what he was up to, even started to respond to it. All the same she'd turned him down flat. Just as well, really. When all was said and done she'd been John's girl, and he'd have regretted shenanigans like this with his more-or-less sister-in-law, even if she'd let him. Which she wouldn't. But this one . . . lunch at a place that actors never went to: a bungalow you could rent by the day or week or year, and that was it.

Georgina Payne said, 'Don't fall asleep.'

'As if I would,' said Bob.

'No,' she said. 'You wouldn't. Not you. . . . You're awfully good at it.'

'Thanks.'

She slapped him, hard enough for him to feel it. 'Don't be smug,' she said. 'Neither of us deserve that.'

'Sorry.'

'That's better. Let's get back to the subject. I'm going to be married. Did anybody else tell you that?'

'He did,' said Bob. 'I met him at the cocktail party.'

'So you did. . . . Did you dance with him, too?'

'I was afraid he might want to lead,' said Bob.

'Dan? Not a chance in the world.'

'I'm right, aren't I?' said Bob. 'I mean he's queer, isn't he?'

'As a seven-dollar bill.'

'Blow me,' said Bob. 'The number of times I've seen him rescue maidens in distress.'

'That's just the movies,' said Georgia. 'You do it in reality. It's far better.'

'You were in distress?'

'Not really,' said Georgie. 'But then I'm not a maiden either. It's just – Dan's sweet, honestly. But there's no point in being married to him. I mean there wouldn't be any of this.' Her hand reached out.

'Then why do it?'

'Publicity,' she said. 'It helps the picture. And anyway movie stars have to be married eventually, otherwise people talk.'

'Jane's picture?'

'That's right. I keep forgetting you're a friend of hers.'

'More like one of the family,' said Bob. 'She was going to marry my brother.'

'John, wasn't it? She told me once. Was he like you?'

'He was far and away better than me,' said Bob.

'My God.'

'No,' said Bob. 'I'm serious. He was a grand feller was John. I've missed him since the day he died. Him and Jane together, that would have been something, that would.'

'She's a marvellous person,' Georgie said, 'and she's written me a marvellous part. Light me a cigarette, will you darling? I'll have to go soon.' Bob did so and Georgie said, 'You called it Jane's picture.'

'She wrote it, didn't she?'

'Indeed she did. But when Murray Fisch talks to me about it he calls it my picture, and when he talks to my fiancé about it he calls it Dan's picture – but in his own mind, when he's quite sure nobody's watching, Murray calls it his picture.'

'What on earth for?'

'Because it's going to be good. It's going to be sensational. And anything that good, that sensational – it has to belong to Murray.'

Like you, thought Bob. Georgie swung her legs from the bed and yawned and stretched like a cat. She knew exactly what she was doing.

'I'm going to take a shower,' she said. 'Care to join me?'

As he soaped her she said, 'Shall we do this again some time?'

'Just give me five minutes.'

She laughed then: a good, healthy guffaw.

'I wish I could,' she said. 'I'd like to time you, but I have a costume fitting. Tomorrow?'

'Fine,' said Bob. Her arms came round him.

'You're awfully devious,' she said, 'but you're a sweet boy all the same.'

In his mind he was thinking: two down and one to go. He was neither proud of the thought nor ashamed. It was simply there.

New Year's Day, 1933. Another year, she thought, and another hangover. She could blame Laurie Higgins for that, back to England and a winter in a rented house in the shires, now that she had discovered the delights of fox hunting. Pretty soon Fred would be an MFH, thought Jane, if she didn't take on the job herself.

On his rug by the bed Foch whimpered softly. Was it rabbits again, or the spaniel bitch from Offley Villas? He was an old gentleman now, not above being carried up the last few stairs, and either of those delights should be beyond him, but he could still dream.

Anyway, you're in no position to pass judgement, she thought. You drank far too much champagne, and you're more than old enough to know better. All very well to blame Laurie and Fred, but you didn't have to go to their party at the Ritz, and even if you did go that was no reason to put away quite so much Mumm. Lionel had put away even more, but it hadn't affected his dancing. It never did. Jay Bower had shifted his share, too, and quite a bit of Catherine's. It really hadn't looked like a madly happy new year for either of them, though both his newspapers seemed to be doing well, moving steadily Leftwards as the Depression bit deeper. He was paying off his loan regularly too. It was his marriage that had faded in the Happy-Ever-After Stakes, although he still adored Catherine. That was all too apparent.

Careful not to wake Foch, Jane stretched out an arm and looked at the bedside clock. Nearly twelve, but she hadn't got to bed till half past five. . . . Charles had been at the party, too. Not that they'd achieved much. Damn champagne anyway. Even Mumm. She got out of bed, put on a dressing gown and went to the window. The hangover resented movement and retaliated, but all the same she went, and looked out. A hard, clear day, the bare trees black in the pale sunlight. No snow, but a dusting of frost on the grass, even at midday. Too hard a day for hunting. Laurie Higgins would just have to sleep late and dream about it, like Foch. Jane lit a cigarette, took an aspirin, swallowed water, and reviewed her year. It was becoming a habit, almost a tradition: remembrance of things past and a hangover, and Foch asleep, whimpering happily.

Grandma had died. That without doubt was the main event. She had died in her sleep and Andy had found her, after knocking timidly at her bedroom door. Nobody ever walked into

Grandma's bedroom uninvited, but on the other hand it was quarter past eight and she still wasn't up. He'd sent at once for Dr Stobbs, but she was dead already, her heart too tired to go on beating. Stobbs had assured Andy that no one had ever died more peacefully, but for Councillor Patterson that wasn't the point. He was now in a world without Grandma, a world that until then had been unthinkable. All he had left was his politics and that seemed to consist largely in biting lumps out of poor old Charles.

She had gone up for the funeral of course, and even Dr Stobbs had been civil to her. Of course he had: the *Angel of No Man's Land* had made an enormous amount of money, and her share still went to Felston – and if that thought made her a bitch, then a bitch was what she was. All the same he had been civil, even gone to the funeral himself: the saddest moment of her life since John had died. She had sat in the front row, beside Bob and Andy and Bet, and Bet's husband Frank and their children, because Bob and Andy had insisted. Young Jane was not yet four, but even so she had been taken to the church. In Felston the death of a grandmother demanded everyone's presence. Heartrendingly like Grandma she had looked, too, and still very pretty. When Bob had looked at the child he had been very close to tears.

Bob – prospered. That was the only word for it. He had his own Bentley now, and even Charles agreed that he was rich. He had had some sort of affaire with Georgie too. This she was sure of: Georgina had written to tell her so. It had led to a screaming row with Murray Fisch, who had hired detectives to spy on her, a row which Georgie had inevitably won, because she had an Academy Award, which in a Hollywood studio was the equivalent of a squadron of tanks. And Bob had paid for the new hot-water system. . . .

Now come on, she told herself. Either go back to bed and sleep, or stay awake and remember. But it was too late to go back to bed, and in any case her head was beginning to clear, so remembering it would have to be, but not Bob and Georgie. That was ages ago.

Lady Mangan was still alive: no better and no worse, and still flying at every opportunity that offered, towing her son and his wife, feebly protesting. She had never gone back to Ireland, and never would. Her car components factory was on short time, and even if it weren't she would never recruit Irish labour. Her younger grandson was a captain now, and had done rather well in an Indian frontier skirmish. Mentioned in Dispatches, or whatever the phrase was. His twin had had a miscarriage brought on by a car crash, and the car had been one of which Bower disapproved, no doubt rightly, thought Jane. A Fraser-Nash was hardly the car for a pregnant female. All the same he'd made rather a mess of telling her so.

What else? Charles was still Charles, and his wife still lived: but even if she didn't I'd still be Miss Whitcomb. I'm rather bored, though, she thought. I didn't get an Academy Award and I've written no more movie scripts, and Dearest Daisy had her last letter ages ago, and quite right too. She was far too frivolous for these terrible times. All the same it would be nice if Bower would use her more often.

There was a tap at the door, and Foch rose at once, ready to defend his mistress to the death. Jane looked at him fondly.

'Were you drinking champers last night too?' she asked. 'God knows you could have been. Everybody else was.'

'Come in,' she said. It was Truett: Foch went back to sleep.

'Telephone, miss,' Truett said.

'Mr Bower?' For once the thought was agreeable.

'No, miss. A Canon Messeter.'

Felston, she thought. That could only be bad news. 'I'll come at once,' said Jane, and followed Truett to the phone.

'I think I should tell you that I'm phoning from London,' said Messeter.

'Is anything wrong?'

'Not wrong, no. I had some business affairs to arrange, and I wondered – this may sound presumptuous – I should like to see you if I may.'

'Of course.'

'The trouble is I'm needed urgently in Felston and I really should go back there tomorrow if that's at all possible.'

'Come to dinner,' said Jane. She was by no means strong enough to manage lunch. 'There will only be my mother and stepfather here. You can come early if you have anything private to discuss.'

'I should like that,' the canon said.

Toast and boiled eggs and a walk in the park, she thought, and Foch will come too, even if I have to carry him. But there, she admitted to herself, she maligned Foch. He could still move very creditably on the flat. She wondered to herself how her mother and Canon Messeter would get on, and rather thought that all would be well. With her stepfather there would be no problem. The major still held the Rifle Brigade in deep respect.

It was in fact a successful dinner party. The major was delighted to learn that Canon Messeter had commanded a battalion – something he himself had once longed to do, and yet it was part of his charm that he could wholeheartedly admire those who had succeeded where he had failed. Her mother too was impressed. Over coffee, while they waited for the gentlemen to finish their port, she said: 'I like him – if one can be familiar enough to like anyone so saintly. It enhances my respect for your power of description, too. That article of yours caught him to the life. – But tell me – is he quite well?'

'Worried,' said Jane. 'About his parish, his clinic, the entire town. He told me he had come here to try to raise money on some property he had inherited.'

'To feed the hungry, of course.'

'Of course,' said Jane.

'And was he successful?'

'He had already raised the money two years ago.'

'Very saintly,' said her mother. 'And I do like him *very* much. I hope he won't mind.'

When they came back the canon said at once how much he had enjoyed his dinner.

'There was a time in my life when I would pursue a good meal like a hunter chasing a fox,' he said, 'but this was positively Lucullan.'

'Mrs Barrow,' said Jane. 'The trick is to employ a very good cook and then obey her lightest word.'

'But Mrs Barrow – a minor genius, I agree – did not choose the port, surely?'

'No,' said Jane. 'The major did that.'

'My husband,' Jane's mother said, 'is held to be a capital judge of port.'

'Without question,' said Messeter. 'I cannot recall when my taste buds were put to so delightful a test.' His face clouded. 'It seems almost sinful – Not in you,' he added hastily. 'In me.'

Jane said, 'Would it bother you if I were to tell my mother and the major why you came to see me?'

'Not at all,' said Messeter, 'if you're sure it won't bother them.'

'It won't do that,' said Jane, and poured out coffee, offered brandy, which Messeter declined, though her stepfather did not.

'The canon is worried, intensely worried, about the state of the town for which he holds himself responsible,' she said.

'Hardly that,' said Messeter.

'Exactly that,' said Jane. 'Forgive me but I must be honest about this if we are to achieve anything. You have worked like a slave in that town for years. Nursed its sick, buried its dead, fought to save its souls – and begged, cajoled and schemed for money to support it in a way a professional conman would envy.'

'Conman?' the major said.

'Confidence trickster,' said his wife. 'Just listen, George.'

'All this for nothing, for less than nothing,' said Jane, 'inasmuch as all the money that you had has long since gone. And tonight you came to tell me that the town – I don't exaggerate – the town will perish if nothing is done, and nothing can be done. A friend of mine told you that, didn't he? No private fortune is great enough to pull the Felstons of this country out of their graves.'

'To my shame I refused to believe it, but I know better now. It's true.'

Her mother looked at Jane. 'You're saying it's hopeless?' she asked.

'Indeed I'm not.' Jane sounded indignant, and her mother smiled. 'I said no private money,' Jane continued. 'But this isn't a matter for individuals – no matter how rich. This is the entire country's business. Felston is part of our country after all.'

'You mean go after Members of Parliament, that sort of thing?' the major asked. 'But don't they know?'

Her mother said, 'A very good question, George,' and the major blushed like a schoolboy.

'They know,' said Jane. 'Of course they know. There have been reports, commissions, White Papers, and they all sing the same song. Nothing can be done. We must wait for the upturn.'

'So it's hopeless,' Messeter said.

'No.' Jane's voice was vehement. 'There's one gun we haven't fired yet.' She turned to face him. 'Andy Patterson was going to prison, you remember? You arranged his defence for him, did all you could, but you were quite sure he'd go to prison. And yet he didn't. Why not?'

'Ah,' said Mrs Routledge.

The canon took a little longer. 'There was a great deal of popular feeling,' he said at last. 'The press took it up, as I recall.'

'The *Daily World* took it up,' said Jane.

'But – forgive me –' the canon seemed diffident, but determined to have his say. 'One man is something a newspaper can write about, make a fuss of, sentimentalise even. But a whole town. Would that be a satisfactory subject for a popular newspaper?'

Mrs Routledge nodded her approval. It was good to see that sanctity too could use its brains.

'Of course not,' said Jane, 'but we aren't going to do it like that.'

'We?'

'You and I and the *Daily World*. Do you remember years ago, the *World* organised a Christmas Party for Felston? We brought up a band and entertainers – took London to Felston if you like? Well this time we're going to bring Felston to London.'

'But how are they going to get there?' Messeter asked.

'We're going to organise a Hunger March,' said Jane. 'We're going to walk.'

'From Felston to London? That's three hundred miles. It would take a month at least.'

'And free publicity every day.'

'They couldn't do it. They're nowhere near fit enough.'

'The strongest ones could – especially if they trained for it.'

'But they'd need kit, accommodation, a place to sleep.'

'The rich might not be able to finance a whole town, but one march wouldn't break them.'

'It would be presumptuous for George and I to describe ourselves as rich,' said her mother, 'but we would certainly subscribe.'

'I might ask you to do rather more than that, Mummy,' said Jane. Her mother looked at her warily.

'The Felston contingent will walk all the way,' said Jane.

'Every foot. Each man must swear to that, short of serious illness. But we'll also arrange for other people to march part of the
way: bands and banners, even individuals if they feel like it. To
show it's important to them, too.'

'I used to enjoy walking in the hills,' her mother said. 'Especially in Darjeeling. I should enjoy finding out if I can still do it.'

'Me too,' said the major. 'I was in the Piffers you know.
Punjabi Frontier Force. Marched across half of North India. Put
us both down.'

'Wait a moment, please,' said Messeter. 'Nothing's been
decided yet.' He turned to Jane. 'When did you think of this
idea, may I ask?'

'Over the soufflé,' said Jane.

'What a tribute to Mrs Barrow,' murmured her mother.

'So you have no pledges? No commitments?'

'None,' said Jane.

'Not even from the *Daily World*?'

'I'll get them,' said Jane. 'See if I don't. Jay Bower will eat this
one up.'

'You're very sure.'

'I have to be if we're going to win.'

'And are we going to win?' Messeter asked.

'Put it this way,' said Jane. 'I'll get them to London – I'll even
get them to Downing Street, and then it will be up to the talkers,
the negotiators, but I'll get them there – everyone who can still
stand – and I'll guarantee the whole country will know about it.

'Just leave it with me, canon. You get yourself back to Felston
and I'll talk to Jay Bower tomorrow morning.'

'Back to Felston?' Messeter said. 'I'm blowed if I will. Far more
important things are happening here.' He looked at the decanter
beside the coffee pot. 'I wonder if I might have a little of that
brandy?' he asked.

Bower loved it. She had never doubted that he would, and
she was quite right. His enthusiasm from the start was even
greater than hers.

'It can't miss,' he said. 'They'll be on the road for how long?'

'A month,' said Jane.

'We can dip into that story any time we want for thirty days.
Wonderful! You'll go with them for a while?'

'I rather think,' said Jane, 'that I should go with them the whole way.'

'You surely don't mean that?'

'Think about it,' said Jane. 'I'll be the one who writes about it. How can I do that if I don't take part myself?'

'You think you can walk three hundred miles?'

'I'll find out soon enough,' said Jane, 'and I'll prepare myself like the others.'

'Chanel doesn't design dresses for route marches.'

'Never mind the dresses. It's the boots that are most important. A colour sergeant told me that once. And he knew what he was talking about. He'd marched across South Africa in his time.'

'Route marches,' said Bower. 'Colour sergeants . . . like the war . . . do you care for the job of war correspondent?'

'Were you seriously considering anyone else?'

'It won't be like a party at the Ritz,' Bower said.

'You forget I once drove an ambulance,' said Jane, 'and anyway all I got from the party at the Ritz was a hangover.'

'You weren't alone,' said Bower. 'Believe me.' He pressed a button on his desk. 'Miss Praed,' he said. 'No calls till I tell you. Only the "A" list.'

Jane wondered who the 'A' list were. The Prime Minister? The Prince of Wales? The King? The only name she would have bet on was Catherine's.

'There's a hell of a lot to arrange,' Bower was saying. 'The hell of a lot, and we'll have to keep it quiet – in the early stages at any rate. I'm not letting the opposition in on this one. . . . You'll go up there yourself?'

'Of course.'

'That's all right, then.' Nice to be trusted, even if one wasn't adored.

'Money,' said Bower. 'We'll have to pass the hat. Naturally the *World* will put up a lot of it – if it's OK with you?'

Because I'm still a shareholder you mean, thought Jane. Bower didn't wait for an answer.

'But there ought to be others, too,' he said. 'Kind of a committee. The right sort of names. You know?'

'Bob Patterson,' she said.

'The local boy who made good and yet still worries about his home town. Great.'

'Charles Lovell.'

Bower looked at her. 'You think he would?'

'If we ask him politely. He's a local landowner now, remember.' Reluctantly Bower wrote down his name. 'Lady Mangan,' said Jane, then added hastily: 'I don't mean to sit on a committee, but your father-in-law could do that for her, and she's news – all that flying –'

'And all that money,' Bower said. 'OK. I'll speak to her if she'll let me get close enough.'

'I thought you got on well.'

'So did I,' said Bower. 'I guess I was wrong. But this is different.' She left it at that.

They talked on and on, and no one on the 'A' list phoned. Bower looked at his watch.

'I could use a martini,' he said. 'Want to come up for lunch?'

'It will be nice to see Catherine,' said Jane.

Bower said, 'She won't be there. She's having lunch with an old school chum, then on to a matinée.'

'Oh,' said Jane, then: 'Why don't we ask Canon Messeter?'

'We need a chaperon that bad?'

'Don't be silly,' said Jane, though her mother would have said they did. 'It's just that the canon and Dr Stobbs will be in this up to their necks – and anyway he'll be useful for the committee.'

'I thought you said he was broke.'

'He's related to half the peerage,' said Jane.

'Phone him,' said Bower. 'Tell him we'll send a car.'

# 43

THE CANON CAME to Fleet Street and refused martinis but drank red wine. As the talk continued, with Bower making notes at they ate, he began at last to believe that the thing Jane had suggested so casually might really be going to happen. Bands and banners and marching men: a war with no casualties, he thought: a war to be fought in the name of God.

'Your rôle is mostly snobbery, I'm afraid, so far as the *World* is concerned,' said Bower.

'It frequently is,' said Messeter. 'It's the only way I know how to raise money. But I do it really rather well. Let me think for a while. Would you like a duke?'

Bower gasped aloud. Almost he rubbed his hands. Perhaps, thought Jane, he needs a duke for his 'A' list.

At last Messeter left to ponder his list of aristocrats, and Jane too decided it was time to go. There were quite enough ideas to be going on with: what they needed now was arrangement. As so often after a visit to the *World*, she was going to call on her mother.

'Will you be seeing Lovell soon?' Bower asked her.

'Probably.' Her tone was cool, and he flushed, angry at his own clumsiness.

'Don't get me wrong,' he said. 'I'm not being nosy. Not this time. It's just something you maybe ought to know. . . . We got it on the wire before you came in. . . . Lord Blagdon.'

'What about him?'

'He was picked up in Oxford Street yesterday dressed like a

tramp and singing in the gutter. Begging for pennies. When the cops came for him he told them he was destitute. A wicked wizard had cast a spell on him, he said. Deprived him of his birthright.'

'Oh my God,' said Jane. 'What happened?'

'The doctors diagnosed a nervous breakdown. A nursing home, plenty of rest and no excitement. Just as well he's a lord. If he'd really been destitute he'd be in gaol right now.'

Her mother said, 'You have done well.'

'So far,' said Jane, 'but it's very early days.'

'I do not think money will be a problem. Certainly you are sure of publicity.'

'Even publicity may be a problem,' said Jane. 'Thirty days is a long time to keep a story alive. Bower doesn't think so, but then he doesn't have to do it.'

'And you do?'

'It wouldn't be fair otherwise.'

'Let us think,' said her mother, then after a pause: 'Celebrities.' Jane looked bewildered. 'Isn't that what they call them? People who appear frequently in the newspapers?'

'That's right, Mummy. Celebrities.'

'You must get all you can find and persuade them to do a day's march – or even half a day's. I'll speak to George about it.' She saw her daughter's look of bewilderment. 'Jockeys are often famous,' she said. 'Especially if they've won the Derby or the Grand National.'

Jane got to her feet, went to her mother and kissed her.

'And my rôle is to give money, I take it?' Charles Lovell said.

'I'm afraid so.'

To her surprise he said, 'Fair enough. After all I was the one who told Rupert to make the government take notice. Who else's arms are you twisting?'

'We're rather hoping for suggestions.'

'You shall have them. . . . About the men. The actual footsloggers.' She waited. 'Go for ex-soldiers. They'll be in their thirties now, but that doesn't matter. All they have to do is march. And if they're in their thirties they'll be family men, which is all to the good. They know what they'll be marching for.

'And feed them up. Men can't march day after day on bread and scrape. And keep the numbers down. Take only the best. Set off with a mob and you'll finish up with stragglers all the way back to Felston before you reach York. Go for an army company – say a hundred and twenty men – and take only the best. Make it a privilege to belong – and a matter of shame if you're told to leave. And get a few good sergeants.'

She found that it was difficult to make notes when one had no clothes on: there was no reason why it should be so: it simply was.

Later Charles said, 'Billets?'

'Billets, Charles?'

'Places to sleep,' said Lovell. 'And eat, come to that. At ten miles a day you'll need thirty at least. I know a chap who'll be useful there. Used to be an RQMS – Quarter Master Sergeant – and finished up as a captain. I can put him on to it if you like.'

'If he's discreet.'

'He works for me,' said Lovell, then suddenly he laughed aloud. 'Publicity's important you say?'

'It's vital.'

'When your chaps stay the night, what sort of places had you in mind?'

'Drill halls, Labour Party halls, places like that,' she said. 'Tents when the weather's fine. It'll be summer after all.'

'Quite right, too,' he said. 'Hardship. That's what it's all about. If it wasn't for hardship, there wouldn't be any need for a march. All the same –'

'Yes, Charles?'

'No reason why they shouldn't stop off at the odd stately home on the way. Not often. Just now and again. It would look good in your paper.'

Once again she got up and kissed somebody in thanks for a good idea, but this time the kiss lingered rather. When it was over, Lovell said: 'Heard about Blagdon?'

'Yes,' she said.

'Bower told you?' There was no point in play acting. She nodded. 'Poor clown,' said Lovell. 'We both thought he might be crazy – and how right we both were. . . . Poor devil . . . his only talent is to play the buffoon.'

'At least he didn't come up to the Hall,' said Jane.

'Which reminds me,' Charles Lovell said. 'The chaps you pick – they'll need toughening up. Exercise. All that. You could use the Hall if you felt like it.'

'You don't mean that.'

'Certainly I mean it. You can put me down for tents and so on if you like. And boots. There's nothing more important than boots.'

'A colour sergeant told me that once.'

'Colour sergeants always know what they're talking about.'

'Charles,' she said, 'forgive the question, but all this – what you're doing – it's not just because of me, is it?'

'A lot of it is, obviously,' said Lovell, 'because a lot of most things in my life is because of you – but some of it . . . no . . . some of it is because it makes sense. A lot of sense. The only sense there is to my way of thinking. A lot of chaps like me will say it's all Bolshevism, bloody fools, and they're wrong.'

'Why, Charles? Why are they wrong?'

'Because if we don't do something and get it right, the odds are the Reds will take over and make it even worse.'

His arms came round her, and they lay together: no heaving and straining, no sudden and unexpected yells. It was the most tranquil time she had spent in years.

She travelled North by train, for this time she wasn't frivolous, and the Bentley reeked of frivolity. She would hire a Morris or a Wolseley, she thought, once she got to Newcastle. Anything so long as it was dowdy. A pity she didn't wear spectacles: horn rims would have helped enormously. She would have to do the best she could with grey suit, tweed coat and a hat so sensible that even Truett had been shocked. Lionel had almost wept.

She had told Lionel because he could keep a secret as well as anyone she knew, and also because she had to give him some reason for visiting Felston, and the truth had seemed by far the best.

'I hope you won't be expecting me to march,' he said.

'Oh but I shall. Distinguished war hero? Certainly you must march,' she said. When she left his only problem appeared to be where he should have his walking shoes made.

Bob too had been with her from the start. It was the best possible memorial to Grandma, he said, and he offered her any and every assistance at once. All the same he seemed relieved to learn that Lovell would be in it, too. Lovell was the senior partner after all.

That left Andy. Andy was a councillor now, which gave him a certain amount of local power, but his real strength was in his being the man he was: caring, compassionate, and yet hard all through. The people of Felston responded to that. If the march were to succeed it would be important for Andy to be on her side. And yet how could he not be? This was a politician's dream, and beyond everything else Andy was a politician. The compassion was inviolate, and always would be, but with it went that need to be listened to, respected, and finally obeyed, that only politicians know.

He was still in John Bright Street, so Bob had told her. Bet and Frank had wanted him to move in with them but he'd turned them down flat and Bob could see his point. Two bairns yelling were two too many. . . . So Jane drove her hired car to the old, familiar street. She'd hired an Austin in need of paint, but roomy and comfortable. The glittering clean house was a reproach in itself: the doorknob shone, the front step was flawless, the windows gleamed. She had not thought Andy would be so houseproud. Nor was he. When the door opened in response to her knock it was 'my friend Norah' who looked down at her from the top of the stairs.

'Oh Miss Whitcomb,' she said. 'Come up, please. Mr Patterson said you were coming but he's not back yet.'

'Thank you,' said Jane, and climbed the stairs, and flogged at her memory like a jockey with a fading favourite. She couldn't call the poor woman 'my friend Norah'. . . . The stair-carpet was beginning to go, she noticed, but it had been swept that day she was sure, and its brass rods shone. . . . Barnes. That was it.

'Why Miss Barnes,' she said. 'What a pleasant surprise.'

'I'm in the kitchen,' Norah Barnes said. 'Mr Patterson said you were kitchen company.'

'From the first day I came here,' said Jane.

Miss Barnes moved the kettle to the glow of the coals, and it began to sing almost at once.

'Will you have a bit of cake with your tea? It's one I baked myself.'

'Yes, please,' said Jane. The only possible answer – but the cake was delicious. Jane ate it and sipped tea as Miss Barnes peeled potatoes.

'They'll go with the meat pie I made him,' she said. 'Even Mr Patterson can boil potatoes – if he's not thinking of something else.'

Which is more than I can, thought Jane.

They talked about Bet, and her children, and Frank's chances of being the next tram inspector, and then there was the sound of footsteps on the back stairs, and Andy came in.

'There you are, Mr Patterson,' Miss Barnes said. 'Your visitor's here before you.'

'Hello, Andy,' said Jane.

'Hello,' Andy said. He looks wary, she thought, but that's me. I usually bring a problem with me. Apart from that he looks better fed than I've ever seen him – and Grandma was a marvellous cook. This one must make him eat more.

'I'd better be off,' Miss Barnes said. 'Everything's just about ready for you. The pie's in the oven. All you've got to do is boil the potatoes, so I'll say ta-ra. See you tomorrow.' And then she smiled at him.

Oh dear, thought Jane. Is that how it is?

Once again feet clattered on the back stairs.

Andy said, 'She cleans the place. Does a bit of cooking for me. I suppose she's what you might call my housekeeper.'

'She seems to be looking after you very well,' said Jane.

'What do you mean?' The words snapped out at her.

'The place is spotless,' she said, 'and I'd say you'd put a bit of weight on. You're lucky to have her.'

'Oh,' he said. 'I see. I suppose I am. Lucky, I mean. There's no –'

'No what, Andy?'

'No hanky panky.'

Careful, she told herself. If you so much as smile you'll be on the next train back to London.

'Of course not,' she said. 'A man like you. And I must say she seems like a thoroughly decent woman.'

'Yes,' said Andy. 'She is. But you didn't come here to talk about Mrs Barnes. Let's have it, Jane.'

She cleared her throat, feeling like a young and nervous lawyer beginning the most difficult case of his career. May it please the court. . . . 'Canon Messeter came to see me last week,' she said.

'I knew he was in London. I didn't know he'd been to see you,' said Andy.

Because I told him not to: not until I'd seen you first.

'He's very worried about Felston,' she said. 'Very distressed.'

'He's not the only one.'

'We began to discuss it –'

'Just the two of you?'

'I invited him to dinner,' said Jane, 'with my mother and stepfather. Then at last we had what I think was rather a good idea.' Cautiously, feeling her way, she began to tell him about the march.

When she had done, he said, 'It was your idea, wasn't it?'

'Well – yes,' she said.

'Just like the Christmas Concert was your idea.' Then he astonished her. 'My God,' he said. 'I wish it had been mine.'

'You like it?'

'I think it's wonderful. You've got the *World* behind you, you say?' She nodded. 'And you can raise the money?' Another nod. 'From our Bob?'

'Some of it. He wouldn't be left out.'

'If he's not careful he'll be skint,' said Andy. 'He pays for Miss Barnes. Pays for me an' all, come to that.'

'Why shouldn't he?' said Jane. 'He's your brother.' Andy accepted it.

'You know I'm a councillor now?' he said. 'And Billy Caffrey's mayor this year? Billy listens to me. I reckon I could help you a bit – if I'm needed, that is.'

'Help?' she said. 'Help? You're going to run the whole shooting match.'

'But it's your idea.'

'Andy,' she said. 'Listen to me and don't be offended. Every newspaper Left of centre has a Socialist celebrity nowadays. And you're the *Daily World*'s. You're our working-class hero. All our readers know who you are. We don't have to introduce you. You're already there.'

'But you're the one –'

'Just listen. I'm the posh one. The toff. Screen tests and screenplays. Letters to that idiot Daisy. You're the one who's here, leading the struggle. The class warrior who refused to leave the battlefield. This march is going to be a big thing, Andy. A difficult thing – and you're the only one I can think of who can do it. That's why it has to be your idea.'

'Mr Messeter knows it isn't.'

'I've already spoken to the canon,' Jane said. 'He agrees with me.'

'You mean he'll tell lies?'

'Certainly not,' said Jane, 'but he won't tell the truth, either. He'll keep his mouth shut. Will you do it?'

He was silent for a moment. Burrowes, he thought. I should talk to Burrowes about it first. The Party doesn't like it when you make your own decisions. . . . Ah – to hell with that.

'I'll be proud to do it,' he said, and he meant every word, she thought. His only regret seemed to be that he'd have to stop blackguarding Charles.

So it began: first the meetings, with the canon and Dr Stobbs and Billy Caffrey; the selection of organisers and marshals, ex-NCOs for the most part: men still fit, still young enough to march, but with the stamp of authority, the assumption that to them obedience is a right. The committee grew in size, but it kept its secrets. The search for the marchers began. Keep it down to a company, Lovell had said. They could have had a division. Every man in the town wanted to go: Dr Stobbs had to be ruthless in his selection. There were cobblers and cooks to find, and drivers for the lorries that would carry the tents – and the men whose strength might fail them. Ex-RAMC men had to be recruited and St John Ambulance men, too, mechanics, tailors to mend clothes that were bound to wear out. The list seemed endless, but still the secret remained. The whole town kept it, and it remained a secret.

# 44

J ANE WENT BACK to London and wrote her article: 'This Town Must Not Die', then another and another, while the town itself furtively and furiously prepared, and Andy grew busier than ever; Miss Barnes glowed in a kind of reflected glory, as winter died and spring came.

It came early that year, and the local papers announced that Mr Charles Lovell, the well-known banker and philanthropist, had set aside a part of his beautiful estate as a holiday tent village for Felston's unemployed. Felston loved it, and laughed in silence.

Once more Jane discovered that she had begun an enterprise which found her redundant, but this time it had no power to hurt. There were so many other things to be done: people to see, articles to write, and in any case she was out of the enterprise only temporarily: once the march began she would be back in it quickly enough; perhaps too quickly, as mile succeeded mile.

She went to visit Harriet Watson. All that walking meant preparation, as she had told Lovell, and who better to advise her than Harriet, who could keep a secret as well as Felston itself? The doctor was delighted to be asked.

'It's a splendid idea, absolutely splendid,' she said, 'but I'd better have a look at you first.'

When she had done, she said, 'No reason why you shouldn't do it. You're almost indecently healthy. Only if I were you I'd cut back on the gaspers and martinis till it's over.'

'Yes, Doctor,' Jane said humbly.

'You can cut that out for a start,' said Harriet. 'Oh – and another thing. I'll give you the address of a good foot man. He'll tell you all about shoes and things. And start taking walks. A little longer each day. As I say you're indecently healthy when one considers the life you lead – but three hundred miles is quite a stroll. . . . Do you want to stay for gin and scrambled eggs?'

Gin and scrambled eggs was their invariable lunch together.

'Yes, please,' said Jane.

'Jolly good,' said Harriet. 'You can start cutting down tomorrow. And before I forget – tell your friend Stobbs that if he needs another doctor when he reaches the Home Counties I'll be glad to help.'

'But it'll be almost over by then,' said Jane.

'That's when they start to drop,' said Harriet. 'Don't you remember?'

Jane thought for a moment, and did. When the battle was over, the objective achieved, still they went down, and so often it was the best of them: the ones who had kept themselves going by spirit alone, till even that ran out.

'I'll tell him,' she said.

Lionel protested bitterly about her régime.

'Apollinaris?' he said. '*Here*?' They were at the Café de Paris.

'I'm in training,' said Jane.

Lionel poured champagne. 'I'm walking too,' he said.

'I'm walking for a month,' said Jane. The champagne bubbles winked at her. 'Well perhaps just one glass,' she said. Apollinaris had bubbles too, but it still tasted like water. Lionel filled her glass to the brim: he was generous even in victory.

'I have news of a friend of ours,' he said.

'Which one?'

'Two friends in fact – if one can call Hugo Meldrum a friend. More a reminder of one's lost youth.'

'Hugo Meldrum? Oh – the fat man who saw you score fifty for Eton.'

'Fifty-three,' said Lionel firmly. 'Not out. He and Brenda Coupland are going to be married.'

'*What?*'

Lionel looked smug: he couldn't help it. It was a juicy piece of news.

'But I thought Brenda was saving herself for the Prince of Wales?'

'So did she,' said Lionel. 'Not to mention the Rifle Brigade. But it seems that the Little Man has met yet another American – a lady from the Deep South this time – and no others need apply. He won't even answer Brenda's phone calls. And what with that and the Depression – she took rather a knock one gathers –'

'So Hugo's Prince Charming at last?'

'Yes,' said Lionel. 'I suppose he is. But he still looks like a toad.'

The band began to play 'Ten Cents A Dance' and they stood up together. It was still pure joy to dance with Lionel. Exercise, she told herself firmly. That's all it was: exercise. But Felston could have been at the far side of the moon.

Lady Mangan was pleased to see her: she said so. Her face was brown from the Egyptian sun, but she still looked ill, with a kind of damaged look that nothing could repair. She shooed away her son and daughter, and Catherine, who seemed disposed to linger.

'You look well,' she said to Jane.

'I am well,' Jane said. 'I'll tell you why in a minute.' And then: 'Oh Emily. Egypt again.'

'I know,' Lady Mangan said. 'But the South of France is too cold at this time of year. Even Spain is too cold. And Egypt really isn't all that bad if you take a suite at Shepherd's.'

'Then why did you come back?' said Jane. 'It's hardly the Nile here.'

'Piers is coming back from India soon,' said Lady Mangan. 'I want to see him again. I may not get all that many –' The word eluded her.

'Chances?'

'– Opportunities.' The old woman looked triumphant. 'Aeroplanes are all very well, but I love my grandson.'

'And your grand-daughter.'

'Yes, of course.' Lady Mangan sounded impatient. 'Is she happy?'

'Catherine? Why shouldn't she be?'

'I have no way of knowing. You might. Is she?'

'If she's not she hasn't told me,' said Jane. 'And I know she likes being married. She told me so herself.'

'Likes,' said Lady Mangan, as if she despised the word. 'And I thought that man could handle her.'

Jane went to the couch on which the old woman lay and knelt beside it. 'Emily,' she said. 'What is it?'

'If I knew,' Lady Mangan said crossly, 'I wouldn't be bothering you. But there's something not quite right with Catherine. I know there is.'

'She lost her baby.'

'So did I,' said Lady Mangan, 'so I had another. Why can't she?'

'Have you asked her?'

'She says there's plenty of time,' Lady Mangan said. 'Her own good time, she means. The things you young women get up to nowadays.' She looked darkly at Jane. 'Well perhaps not you,' she said, 'though I'm not so sure.'

'Emily, please,' said Jane in her most theatrical voice. 'You forget that I'm –'

'A virgin?' said Lady Mangan, then added coarsely, 'Don't make me laugh.'

Jane giggled, and the old lady guffawed, but when she had done the worried look came back.

'All the same,' she said, 'you ought to be married and having babies. You haven't got that much time left.'

'No,' said Jane. 'I was destined to be an aunt. I'm sure of it.'

'Then I wish you'd be Catherine's baby's aunt,' Lady Mangan said. 'Will you talk to her, love?'

'I'll try,' said Jane.

Talking to Catherine wasn't all that easy, not any more: so many old school friends and old college friends, so many lunches and matinées and dress fittings and race-meetings and Harrods. During her time in London they met three times, at the opera first and then a dinner party, where to talk anything but banalities was impossible. The third time was at the Fleet Street flat, after Jane had visited Bower's office to talk yet again about the march. As they did so, Bower's telephone rang. Bower scowled, but it was Messeter's duke. He's got one on the 'A' list at last, she thought.

Bower covered the telephone's mouthpiece. 'Go on up to the flat and order martinis,' he said. 'His Grace doesn't always remember why he's telephoned.'

Jane took the public elevator and then the private one, and found herself alone with Catherine.

'Darling,' Catherine said. 'Where on earth have you been hiding yourself?'

'South Terrace,' said Jane. 'Where have you?' And that was when she heard about the chums and the matineés and Harrods and things, but at least Catherine ordered martinis. Just the one, Jane told herself, and no wine at lunch. You're in training.

'The last time we met was at Granny's,' said Catherine, 'if you can call that a meeting. She booted me out as soon as you got there. Wanted to ask why no tiny feet were pattering, I suppose.'

'Yes.'

'And did you tell her?'

'How could I?' said Jane. 'I've no idea.'

'I went to see your friend Dr Watson, that's why,' Catherine said. 'She's rather a dear.'

'Not if you call her that she's not,' said Jane.

Catherine said unheeding, 'It's all sort of mixed up with my miscarriage. You knew about that?'

'I knew you'd had one,' said Jane.

'Jaybird bought me a Fraser-Nash for my birthday,' Catherine said. 'An absolutely vivid scarlet and a *vast* great strap round the bonnet. Then when he found out I was preggers he forbade me to drive it, which was foolish.'

'He should have asked you nicely?'

'He shouldn't have asked at all,' said Catherine. 'I adored that car.'

Jane blinked. Surely Catherine hadn't begun on the martinis before she'd arrived?

Catherine said hastily, 'No. That's silly. I don't mean that.'

'Somehow I didn't think you did,' said Jane.

'What I meant was being pregnant upset me rather. I didn't know how I was going to cope and when Jaybird started laying the law down – I did the other thing.'

'Was it very bad?'

'Didn't Jay tell you?'

'My mother had rather a bad dose of 'flu,' said Jane. 'I went with her to Cap d'Antibes to recuperate.'

'Cap d'Antibes is over-rated if you ask me,' said Catherine. 'Not that I saw much of it. One doesn't, on one's honeymoon.'

'I hope the honeymoon was satisfactory.'

'This one was fine.'

'This one?' said Jane.

'This particular one, I mean,' Catherine said. 'Please don't jump on me like that. It makes me nervous and I say stupid things. Where was I?'

'About to tell me about your car crash.'

'I was driving down to Berkshire,' Catherine said. 'It was a lovely day and I let it rip rather, then suddenly these two *idiots* on bicycles came out of a side road without even stopping and I slammed on everything and just missed them, then I hit a signpost and out I came. "A" over "t" as Piers says, and went straight into a ditch that was full of muddy water – and that was what saved me. But I lost the baby. – And before you start jumping on me again, it wasn't my fault. The magistrate said so.'

'No more jumping,' said Jane. 'I was just going to say how sorry I was. . . . I expect Jay was furious?'

'How could he be?' said Catherine. 'I told you. It wasn't my fault.' She offered the martini jug to Jane, who shook her head, then filled up her own. 'I say,' she said. 'This march of yours. It does tend to keep old Jaybird busy.'

'When I left him he was talking to a duke about it,' said Jane.

'Which one?' Catherine asked vaguely. To the daughter of an earl of course, dukes might not be so impressive as they were to commoners.

Jane told her and added, 'I'm sorry if I've caused him to be away so much.'

'No no,' said Catherine. 'That's fine. Absolutely. I mean what better cause could there be? I'm marching myself. Didn't Jaybird tell you?'

'No,' said Jane. 'But I'm delighted to hear it.'

'One day,' Catherine said. 'One whole day with the footsloggers. You're doing rather more, Jaybird says. The whole three hundred miles, in fact.'

'That's right.'

'Darling Jane,' said Catherine. 'You never could learn to do things by halves, could you?' But it was said with affection, even sweetness, and for a moment they were back to where they once had been. Then Bower came in and Catherine bounced to her feet, put her arms around his neck and kissed him.

'Well,' he said. 'There's a nice surprise. I wasn't even sure you'd be here by now. Do all dukes talk so much?'

'Helen's got laryngitis,' said Catherine. 'She had to get her maid to phone up and tell me so. Lunch is off, so I'm afraid you're rather landed with me.'

Jane gathered up her handbag. 'I'd better be off, too,' she said.

'No no,' Bower said. 'Catherine didn't mean that, did you honey?'

'Of course not,' Catherine said. 'All I meant was I'm sorry if I'm in the way when you talk business.'

'No business.' Bower sounded firm. 'We'll go to Boulestin's or somewhere and really enjoy ourselves.'

'Yes, do come, darling,' Catherine said.

'It's a long time since we've been all three together,' said Bower. 'This calls for a celebration.'

So much for no more wine at lunch, thought Jane. She'd have to go to a nunnery or a prison or something.

The telephone rang, and Bower picked it up at once. 'Yes?'

Catherine scowled. 'You'd think you could be hanged for not answering the damn thing,' she said, and poured what was left of the martinis into her glass.

'Yes? Yes? Yes?' Bower was saying, and then, 'Put Elliott on to it and the new guy in features – what's his name? Walters? Get out all the material we have on him. I'll be in your office right after lunch. See you then, Don.' He put the phone down. 'Don Cook,' he said. 'There's a big story breaking about Georgie Payne's husband.'

'Dan Corless?' said Catherine. 'The film star? What's happened to him?'

'Seems like he's dead,' said Bower. 'The way Don Cook tells it, somebody killed him.'

Somebody had. The Reuter's story was vague enough, and no amount of frantic phone calls and cables could produce much more. Dan Corless had been set upon by two young men in the sanctity of his home, the World Wide Publicity Department stated, robbed and shot dead, but not until he had put up a heroic resistance in the finest traditions of the heroes he had so often portrayed. Miss Payne was prostrate, and, it was feared, would remain so for some time to come. Bower, like every other newspaper proprietor and editor, did what he could with those scraps, doing his best to turn them into a feast: but Bower had one ingredient his rivals could never have. Dan Corless might be dead, but Darling Daisy was resurrected.

It was reasonable enough, thought Jane. Georgina might be upset, but she could hardly be prostrate with grief, not, as seemed probable, if Corless had been murdered by a couple of homosexuals; and she would be nice to Georgie: she'd told Bower that as soon as he asked her to write the piece, and all he'd said was 'Of course.' And Dr Stobbs would be pleased if nobody else was. When she'd done it she wondered if the next move in her career should be to turn novelist; it was far more a work of fiction than a newspaper article. All the same, Bower was delighted. She wrote to Georgie, and sent a copy of her article with the letter. Time to think about getting fit. Neither nunneries nor prisons seemed practical, so she went to a health clinic in Hertfordshire instead. No wine, no martinis, precious few cigarettes, and a quite awful diet: but she could swim, and walk in the woods, and be on her own. It was a long time since she'd been on her own and she found that she enjoyed it – for a clearly defined and limited period.

She could think, for one thing, without interruption. Think about Catherine. The girl was clearly on edge about something. The loss of her baby should have explained that, but Jane wasn't too sure it did. All that uproar about her car, and how rotten Cap d'Antibes was, no matter how adroitly she'd explained it afterwards. . . . A lover? . . . But when Jay had joined them in the penthouse flat she had embraced him in a way that owed nothing to acting. No wonder Lady Mangan was worried. Suddenly she stopped dead, and the only noise about her was that of a thrush that had suddenly decided to sing.

'None of your damn business,' she said aloud, and the thrush was silent. 'But it's just possible I love her like a niece,' she said, and resumed her walk. The thrush resumed its song.

She thought about Felston, too, waking and sleeping. (It had even begun to invade her dreams.) But Felston was out of her hands now. Dukes and councillors and doctors and mayors were all slogging away at Felston's problems, and all Jane could do was pray to God they – and she – would get it right. Otherwise she lost weight and felt hungry and broke in the walking shoes that she had bought.

# 45

I N LONDON SHE stopped barely long enough to read her letters before setting off for the North, and since she was going to Blagdon Hall and the holiday tent village, she took the Bentley. She took Foch, too. He would look splendid in newspaper photographs once the march started, and it would do him good to meet his fellow marchers. Besides, he adored the Bentley. Only one communication at all exciting awaited her. It was a cable from Georgina. 'Darling, what bliss to hear from you. Such a sweet letter. Regards to Daisy. Kisses. Georgie.'

Well at least she's not prostrate, thought Jane, but then why should she be? The whole thing choreographed by World Wide publicity. Wasn't that what she had said? She took out the dresses she would need for Blagdon Hall, and Truett snuffled her disapproval. All this gadding about, the sniff said, was not what she expected in good service, let alone her being a Baptist.

Lovell was far more pleased to see her, although the house, vast as it was, seemed to be bulging with people, and any kind of frolic was out of the question. Stobbs was there, and Canon Messeter, and experts of every possible kind, from dieticians to pedicurists. Even the duke was expected. Andy and the mayor were there too, but they slept in the tents with the rest of the men. The *World*'s photographer, Timmins, who had arrived before her, had chosen to sleep in the tent village too. It was where the best pictures were.

Andy came to meet her, and show her the village, and Foch came with them. For once he seemed almost benign, as if good works were something he approved of. Declining years, thought Jane, but not aloud. Andy was with her; it would have to wait.

'How is it going?' she asked.

It was a question she had already put to Charles and Stobbs and the canon, but it was expected, and so she asked him.

'Canny,' said Andy, meaning not bad, but then he would. The others had said 'Splendid', 'Excellent', 'First rate'.

'The lads are getting fitter every day,' he said. 'I wish you could see them eat.'

'I will,' said Jane.

'And their families.'

It had been Charles's idea that the married men should have their wives and children with them, to eat and enjoy the country-side as they did. There must be no feelings of guilt.

'I was thinking –' said Andy.

'Yes?'

'The folks here have been quiet as the grave,' he said. 'Not a word. But every day that passes it gets harder. It's got so big. I think it's time there was a statement.'

'A press release,' she said. 'I'll talk to Jay Bower tonight.'

'Thanks, pet.'

Goodness she thought, you are happy.

Page ten of next day's *World* carried a small paragraph saying that Andy Patterson of Felston, self-sacrificing as always, was organising a petition to request work for the town.

Andy was not impressed. 'Not very exciting, is it?' he said.

My goodness, he'll be demanding a press agent next, thought Jane.

'It's a start,' she said. 'A hint, that's all. If we start being exciting now the other papers will be all over the place.'

'That wouldn't be bad for us.'

'It would be bad for the *World*,' she said, 'and without the *World* there'd be no march at all. Don't worry. All the other papers will be here when the band begins to play. Even *The Times*.'

'I don't want you to think I'm ungrateful,' he said. 'Not to you. Not to Mr Bower, either. But it's our last chance, don't you see?'

'Yes, I do see. Like September, 1918. "Backs to the wall",

Field Marshal Haig said. ''The Boches had driven us back to the Channel almost.'' '

'And what happened?' Andy asked. 'I was lodging with His Majesty at the time, remember? In Durham.'

'The Germans ran out of steam and we counter-attacked. Us and the Yanks. We pushed them right back to their own border. Armistice Day happened. We won.'

'Backs to the wall's not quite it,' Andy said. 'Not this time.' He thought for a moment. 'Do or die. . . . That's our motto.'

None of the other papers bothered to send anyone, not yet, and perhaps it was as well. It was too early. Suppose something went wrong? Felston would go on keeping its secret, but by now Burrowes would know. I'll be hearing from him, Andy thought. I should have realised that when I chivvied Jane to put it in the paper. Not that it would have stopped you, he admonished himself. Obstinate bugger.

The children had a grand time. Fields to run in, trees to climb, streams just right for fishing and wading, and the women too enjoyed themselves, once they overcame their distrust of sleeping in tents and sitting in the open air. All that space: all that emptiness. It could be frightening after the comfort of a closed-in room: but the food was something else again. None of them could remember eating like that since the good times just after the war. Men, women and children alike began to put on weight.

Their menfolk worked at becoming fit, worked as hard as ever they had in shipyard or pit or machine shop. Stobbs watched them obsessively. The problem – incredibly – was that they were too keen. They wanted to do too much before their bodies were ready, and it took the combined efforts of the instructors and Stobbs himself to ease them into a routine of exercise that – if they had attempted it in the first week – would have knocked them flat.

Slowly but inevitably their bodies began to harden, until five minutes' early morning PT became half an hour, and the gentle strolls of the beginning became route marches, and all that was missing of their army days was the sound of the guns.

It was Charles who suggested that the tents be replaced by wooden huts. Bob was up on a visit at the time, discussing with Charles the expansion of Patterson's Wireless Rentals. Does he ever think about anything else? Jane wondered. – Apart from women of course. Bob was staying at the Hall, and it bothered him. He should have been in a bell tent with his brother and his mates, but how could he? He was a gaffer, a boss: a toff who travelled first class, with a car and chauffeur to meet him at the station. Huts and bell tents were denied him.

'Huts?' said Jane. 'Like a barracks, do you mean?'

'Hardly that,' said Lovell. 'Something a little more cosy.'

They were in the Great Drawing Room, looking out at the tent village with its gossiping women, and children working as hard at play as their fathers worked at physical fitness.

'I was thinking –' Lovell hesitated. 'Huts would be rather more permanent, wouldn't they? Not that I anticipate a march every year of course, but we could arrange other things – cricket, football matches, that sort of thing. Weekend breaks. Something like that. What do you say?'

'Who would feed them?' Jane asked.

'I would of course.'

'We would,' said Bob.

'Fine,' said Lovell. 'You see, at the moment these chaps haven't a lot to do. I've seen it happen in my own battalion, and I know. The thing is they're fit now – doing things that would have killed them a month ago and with a lot of energy left over. And we've got tradesmen here. Plumbers, carpenters, electricians. And when they go off on the march we'll bring another lot in. What do you say?'

'We'll have to talk to Andy first,' said Bob, 'but I doubt if he'll be any problem. Not this time.'

Andy hated to go up to the Hall. As Grandma had suspected, it reminded him too much of Cambridge, but even so Bob was right. Once Lovell had explained his idea Andy forgot his surroundings completely.

'But that's marvellous,' he said. 'That's absolutely the best idea –'

'Forgive me,' said Lovell. 'We'd rather hoped you'd be pleased, but – if I may ask – why as pleased as this?'

'Because we'll be doing it ourselves,' Andy said. 'This won't be a hand-out. A bairn's present at Christmas. This'll be what *we* made.'

'That's right, kidder,' said Bob. 'Once you get back from your bit walk you'll be Clerk of Works.'

'All work will be paid for, of course,' said Lovell.

'They'll do it for nothing,' said Andy. 'Be glad to.'

'They'll be paid. I once told Canon Messeter that even bankers can't finance the unemployed of a whole country. But we can each of us do our share, and I intend to do mine. They'll be paid.'

Andy looked at them. 'You're all in this, aren't you?' he asked.

'If we can get in,' said Jane. 'Mr Lovell seems quite determined to hog the lot if we let him.'

'We won't,' said Bob, and turned to his brother. 'Least we could do, kidder. I mean just look at them. A few weeks here and they're walking like men again. . . . And the bairns – which reminds me. Why aren't they all at school?'

'Billy Caffrey fixed that,' said Andy. 'Got the education committee to say this was an open-air school, so we brought along a few teachers. Not that the bairns get much schooling. The teachers are usually away on route marches.'

'So it's agreed then?' Lovell asked.

'Too true,' Andy said. 'I'll tell the men tonight if you like.'

'Please do.'

She couldn't believe it. That Charles Lovell was a kindly man and a humane man she knew, otherwise she could not have stayed with him, but this gift was princely. When Andy left, Bob looked at Lovell, awe-struck. He too had some idea of the size of the cheque that Lovell would have to sign. Lovell had rung for champagne.

'I've got to hand it to you,' Bob said. 'I really do.'

'Yes.' Lovell allowed self-esteen to show for once. 'Rather a good idea, though I say it as shouldn't.'

'Not the idea.' Bob was blunt. 'The money.'

'I can afford it.' The self-esteem had vanished. His bluntness matched Bob's own. 'And it will give me pleasure.'

'Split three ways?' said Bob.

'Certainly not,' said Lovell.

'We aren't to have any pleasure?' said Jane.

'Perhaps a little,' said Lovell. 'I might cut you in for twenty per cent between you – but understand this the pair of you. I'm the senior partner.' Clegg brought in the champagne, opened it and poured three glasses. Lovell carried one to Jane.

'Let's have no nonsense about Apollinaris,' he said. 'Not

tonight. Even a junior partner can manage one glass.'

She walked with Foch to Knightsbridge and called on Medlicott, and told him that soon she would be spending yet more money on Felston's poor. Medlicott at once sent for Rubens because he knew even more about money than he did, and Jane told it all again. Rubens listened with a look of grim triumph on his face. I've always known this would happen, his face said, and now it has. Ah well, at least it's over: but all he said was: 'It's rather a lot.'

'There are rather a lot of them,' said Jane.

'But even so –'

'Are you saying I haven't got it?' said Jane.

'Oh you've got it all right,' said Rubens.

'The thing is it's supposed to be our business to help you hang on to it,' said Medlicott. 'Not chuck it out of the window.'

Charles had warned her that she would run into that one, and persuaded her not to lose her temper, because it was a) true, and b) a good thing to have them on her side. Fortunately he had also provided her with a way out.

'I was thinking,' she said. 'The interest on that money we loaned the *Daily World* is doing rather well, even allowing for what I'm paying back to you. Why don't we use that?'

Simultaneously the same look appeared on both men's faces. First: Who on earth put her up to that one? and then, Ah yes, of course. It would seem that they knew about Charles, but then so did everybody else. . . . Foch snorted, and slumped down on the carpet, and Medlicott took a biscuit from the tea tray and broke it in half.

'If I may,' he said.

'Of course.' Medlicott held out the biscuit, and Foch walked over to accept it, and wagged his tail. He approved of Medlicott.

'How old is he?' Medlicott asked.

'Rising ten.'

'A good age for a Scottie,' Medlicott said, 'but he seems fit enough.' Even that slight pause had been sufficient for Rubens to do sums in his head.

'A very neat solution, Miss Whitcomb,' he said. 'Of course it would have been better if that money had been reinvested, but if you insist –'

'Oh I do,' said Jane.

'Then we'd better get on with it.' The prospect of doing so didn't seem all that agreeable to him.

After lunch (steak, salad, Apollinaris), she took Foch to the vet's. What Medlicott had said about the dog's age worried her rather. Rising ten *was* a good age for a Scottie. By then it was raining, and the vet lived in Chelsea, much too far to walk in the rain, so she drove him in the Bentley, which put him in a good mood.

He greeted the vet, McKie, like an old friend, which in a sense he was, despite a marked absence of biscuits. McKie was a shy and inhibited man, far more at ease with dogs or cats or even canaries, than people. Foch was easy: it was coping with Jane that was his problem: and if that isn't good for curbing my ego, then I don't know what is, she thought.

'How is he?'

'Very well,' McKie said. 'Getting on, of course. Ten would he be?'

'In a couple of months.'

'For ten he's in very good condition indeed. You don't over-feed him, I see.'

'It's a temptation,' said Jane. 'But no.'

'You're doing him a kindness,' said the vet. 'Exercise?'

'Rather a lot,' said Jane.

'That won't hurt him either,' McKie said. 'So long as you don't expect him to run too much. He'd try, you see – Scotties are like that – but his heart wouldn't be up to it.'

'Walks,' said Jane. 'Very long walks. If I may speak in confidence –' McKie looked surprised. It wasn't a request he received often.

'Certainly,' he said, and she told him about the march.

'Would you expect him to walk the whole way?' he asked at last.

'Oh no,' said Jane. 'Just as much as you think is good for him – and especially where people are watching. He's to be our mascot.'

'But you,' McKie said. 'You intend to walk the whole way?'

'I do,' said Jane, and he offered his hand, almost scarlet with embarrassment.

'Allow me to congratulate you, Miss Whitcomb,' he said. 'I

think it's a wonderful thing you're doing. As for your mascot, he'll let you know himself when he's had enough. Will you have a vehicle with you?'

'A couple of lorries. And a car, I think.'

'Let him ride in one. Take his basket with him. He'll be fine so long as he doesn't overdo it.'

He wouldn't even take a fee. 'My contribution to the cause,' he said. Another guinea for Felston.

Georgie's cable arrived the day before she set off for Blagdon. It was early June, and Foch had paraded in every park she could think of. It was clear that he found this passion for exercise a kind of lunacy, but he enjoyed it, and so he indulged her.

'Your friend Georgie's arriving in a week,' she said. 'On the *Mauretania*. Staying at the Savoy. You liked the biscuits at the Savoy, remember, but this time you won't get any, I'm afraid. You'll be going walkies. The longest walkies either of us has ever done. Let's hope she's staying for a while.'

Foch snorted. He really did like those biscuits at the Savoy.

At Blagdon things were moving. The site for the hut village had been cleared, foundations and trenches dug: wooden sections lay neatly piled, waiting assembly, but the work had stopped, for the moment at least. The men who had done it were preparing to move: their preoccupation now was with boots and socks and waterproof capes. The way it was, thought Jane, when troops moved up to their share of the line: except for one thing. These men, like the soldiers they once had been, were taut, on edge, nervous of what was to come; but they were also happy.

She knew many of them quite well by this time, like Corporal Laidlaw who had guarded her old Riley the first time she had visited Felston, and Billy Caffrey, who bellowed his dismay that he wasn't going to be allowed to make the whole march (but then Billy Caffrey bellowed everything).

'They won't let me,' he said. 'They say I've got to stay and take care of Felston. They say I'm too old. Me! Dr Stobbs and the canon's going. They're years older than me.'

'The canon's taking his car,' said Jane. 'They'll ride most of the time.'

'Quite right too, at their age,' Billy Caffrey said. 'But me – I was a footslogger for three and a half years. Too old, indeed. Still –' he brightened, 'I'm doing the first day with you. And maybe the last an' all, according to Andy. Or do you think that's cheating?'

'You're the mayor,' said Jane. 'You'll have to be there. You represent the whole town.'

'I'll be glad to do it,' Billy Caffrey bellowed, 'but so does our MP represent the whole town, and all we've heard about from him is his bunions.'

Foch was popular from the start. She had put on his scarlet collar and lead, that blazed against his black fur, and from the moment he arrived there was a sort of jauntiness: a swagger about him. 'A real light infantry dog,' said her friend the corporal, who was ex-light infantry himself.

# 46

They didn't set out from Blagdon Hall: that would never have done. The only possible place to start from was Felston Market Place, and so they rattled their way there in hired buses, the transport lorries and the canon's ancient Armstrong-Siddeley. In the Market Place there were, inevitably, speeches, first from Jimmy Wagstaff, their MP, who had brought his bunions and referred to them constantly, then from the duke, who read his speech in a frantic gabble, anxious only to get down from the platform and out of sight, and last of all from Billy Caffrey, who, as mayor, wished them God speed, an effect somewhat vitiated by the fact that he then took his place in the front rank between Jane and Dr Stobbs. Last of all was the canon, who prayed long and earnestly for a successful outcome to their journey. Never, thought Jane, had she heard a more profound 'Amen', and wished that Charles had been there to hear it too, but Charles had gone back to London. The presence of a duke was publicity, he argued, and well worth having, but a banker's presence could only mean that there was something in it for the banker, no matter how many huts he bestowed on the unemployed.

The banners were assembling now; the union banners, fitters', miners', shipyard workers', even shop assistants'. They would go only as far as the band that led them, the first three short miles, great splashes of colour against the sooty brick of the house, but the other banner, made by the women at Blagdon, would go every yard of the way to Downing Street. It showed a sailor, a shipwright and a miner, the town's crest, and below it the town's motto: Industria et Fortitudo – Industry and Courage. Only the courage was left, thought Jane, and they would need every scrap they had.

Ahead was the band: another great splash of colour: the scarlet of uniforms, the golden gleam of instruments. The marshals were busy now, checking the precision of each rank of men, until at last they too took their places. The band leader looked towards them, and Andy raised his hand.

'Good luck,' he said.

'Amen to that,' said Canon Messeter, and the band blared out, in a blare of invincible cheerfulness, the only possible tune: 'Tipperary'. In the front the band leader strutted, the band played as if the march were over, not just beginning, then the banners moved off, and then the men, all hundred and twenty of them, with Jane in the front rank and Foch ahead of her, straining at his lead. There was the old, familiar sound of boots on cobblestones, a rhythmic crunch like no other sound in the world.

'By lad it takes you back,' Billy Caffrey said.

'It does indeed,' said Canon Messeter.

Jane knew what they meant. Already they were back in France, on a good day when the sun was shining, and the Front Line many miles away. As the marchers moved the cheering began, small boys ran alongside the column, a couple of dogs ran too, yapping their excitement, but the men ignored it all. They marched at attention, not sad, but dignified, determined to show their town how much they believed in what they had set out to do. At last they reached the town's limits and the brass band and the banners swung away, until only the marching banner was left. Only then did they march at ease. When a mouth organ played, the words roared out:

> Pack up your troubles in your old kit bag
> And smile smile smile.
> While you've a Lucifer to light your fag
> Smile boys that's the style. . . .

Foch even enjoyed the singing. This, his every bouncing step told her, is the life. There would be trouble at the first rest-stop, she thought, but like it or not, into the canon's car he would go. She wanted him fit for the next lot of photographers. In Felston Bower had done them proud. Not just Timmins, but another photographer too, the Newcastle stringer and a man from London as well as herself. The other papers had sent reporters and photographers, too: inevitably, when a duke was there at the send-off, wishing Godspeed to the unemployed. No newspaper could ignore such Heaven-sent irony.

'Will it be like that all the way?' Andy had asked.

'It will if I've got anything to do with it,' she had told him.

He had sighed then, not angry, but disappointed that people had to be bullied, coaxed and chivvied into supporting what was right instead of doing it instinctively, because of the inherent goodness of man. He should be glad they do it at all, she thought, and glanced at him. Not singing: not Andy. Already his mind was miles away.

He was thinking of Burrowes. He'd been dead right about what his reaction would be: the letter must have been written as soon as he had read that first bit in the *Daily World*. The trouble was Burrowes had sent it off to John Bright Street, and all the time he had been at Blagdon Hall. Norah had had to send it on, and even then she'd had to get somebody to help her. Better with a rolling pin than a pen, was Norah. Already he was missing those scones she baked.

As usual, Burrowes's letter paper and envelope were the most expensive there were, and as usual they had somebody else's address printed on them, heavily crossed out and his own substituted by hand.

'Imperative we talk,' Burrowes had written. 'Unfortunately it's not possible for me to travel North at the moment, so you must phone me urgently' (twice underlined) 'at the number at the top of the page, between six and seven any evening. Reverse the charges.' Why not, since somebody else was paying for the call? 'But do it quickly.' More underlining.

It had meant a two-mile walk to reach a phone booth. Blagdon Hall was full of phones, but there was a risk he might be overheard, and anyway for some reason he didn't want any kind of link between Burrowes and the Hall and the marchers, or even with Lovell nowadays, so a walk it had to be. As if he hadn't done enough walking.

Burrowes hadn't been angry, not at first. Simply bewildered. 'This was your idea?' he asked.

'You read the paper,' said Andy.

Burrowes took it to mean yes. 'And you didn't tell us?'

'Too late,' Andy said.

'What do you mean, too late?'

'It came out in a discussion I was having with some of those Right-Wing Labour chaps you're so keen for me to get pally with.'

'Yes but even so –' said Burrowes.

'They were on to it straightaway,' Andy said, hating every lie he uttered. 'As a matter of fact our Bob was there too. He was the one that thought of telling the *Daily World*.'

'He would,' said Burrowes, and then: 'But he's a capitalist. What was he doing with a lot of Labour councillors?'

'Being sociable.'

Burrowes ignored it. 'I can see you had a problem there and then, but you could have got in touch with me later.'

'No point,' said Andy.

'What do you mean, no point?' Now the anger was beginning to show.

'You got in touch with me,' said Andy.

'Did it never occur to you that we might not approve the idea?'

'No,' said Andy. 'Why should it?'

'Because it reeks of paternalism. Dukes. Bankers. Wireless tycoons. The *Daily World*. That ghastly Whitcomb woman boohooing for her poor darling workers every step of the way.'

'Without them we'd never have even got started,' said Andy. He looked at his fist, clenched hard round the phone. He'd been all right till Burrowes had said 'that Whitcomb woman'.

'That's just the point,' Burrowes said. He was yelling now. 'This is all just fodder for the Right-Wing press. There's no Left-Wing propaganda in it at all.'

'Not unless I make some,' said Andy. 'There's nobody else.'

'All right,' Burrowes said at last, 'but do it carefully. Don't offend your Labour friends. I mean that. And for heaven's sake keep in touch.' Then he'd hung up.

Andy slogged along the Newcastle road, the rhythm of his footsteps matching that of those around him, but his eyes unseeing. Outside of prison Burrowes is the only man I've ever hated, he thought. All the same I'll do what he asks, because what he asks is right. . . . But I'm glad he won't be there on the pavement, cheering me on, when we get to Newcastle.

Newcastle sent a band of its own to meet them, that led them in to the centre of the city, where the Lord Mayor waited with yet another speech. As the days went by, the marchers became very good at being harangued: standing at ease, sharing a cigarette, while the voice droned on and on and all they thought about was their feet: but this was early days and they actually listened. He was on their side, and it was kindly meant, but oh, he did go on. Even so he ended at last and they gave him a cheer, then the band's bass drum gave an admonitory thud and cigarettes were pinched out, shoulders squared. This time they marched off to John Philip Sousa: Colonel Bogey; past the cathedral and the railway station, across the bridge and heading South. The band fell out and on they slogged down the Durham road, until at last they reached the field prepared for them. Charles's former RQMS, Mr Richards, had everything ready and waiting. Beef stew and dumplings, and apple tart and custard, and all the tea they could swallow. Trestle tables and folding chairs, too. No squatting down with your back against the hedge. And the food was delicious, especially after all that exercise. Foch finished his in minutes. Even so he made no protest when he was put into his basket and the canon's car.

They spent that night in the Labour Hall of a pit village outside Durham: another speech, of course, then tea and doorstep sandwiches, and the chance of a pint in one of the village's three pubs. The villagers were as poor as the marchers themselves, yet everybody wanted to buy them a drink, and Dr Stobbs patrolled the pubs to make sure they didn't have too many. There were still two hundred and eighty-five miles to go.

Jane slept chastely at the vicarage. The vicar and his wife approved of what she did, of that she was sure; perhaps they even admired her, but they couldn't have been more on edge if they'd agreed to put up a unicorn for the night. Perhaps it's the cigarette holder, thought Jane, or even the cigarettes. Neither of them smoked, and all they had to drink was sweet sherry. But what really made them nervous it seemed was Hollywood, and the only way to tackle that was talk about it, and so she did, and left them saucer-eyed.

Her bed was narrow, and the mattress far too soft, but even so she fell asleep at once, almost as fast as Foch, snug in his basket. Next morning the vicar's wife called her, and there were eggs and bacon – delicious. They walked with her to the Labour Hall, and even thanked her for staying.

'But I should thank you,' said Jane.

'No no,' the vicar said. 'We've never been close to something heroic, and we appreciate it. Reflected glory. All that.'

The vicar's wife kissed her cheek, and Timmins took a picture.

Then they were off. No bands this time, no banners streaming in the summer breeze: just the steady crunch of marching feet as the miles went slowly by, oh so slowly, and your body reminded you that no matter how carefully you'd prepared, the road was hard and London far. Better, far better, to limit your objective, and think about where you would eat your midday meal.

It was indoors this time, in another colliery village hall: fish and chips and jam tart, and tea in enormous enamel mugs. For Foch Mr Richards had provided a plate of mutton scraps. Bless Charles, she thought. He's even remembered to take care of my dog for me. I would never have remembered that Foch doesn't eat fish. That night they slept under canvas, Jane in a small tent primly out of earshot of the bell tents used by the men. Once again she fell asleep in minutes, and once again was woken far too early.

On and on down a road that seemed endless, as thirty miles went by, then fifty, seventy, a hundred. Not so much singing now, except when a celebrity joined them, and then the men showed off a bit. Once it was a bishop, once a music-hall comedian, and once an entire town council. . . . They reached Doncaster: another band, another speech; then the band led them through the town, out to a road that was gravel, not concrete, a winding road that led them at last to a house even larger than Blagdon Hall, the house where the duke's sister lived, and she, her husband and her brother were outside the main doors to receive them. Timmins was photographing frantically as the canon introduced first Jane, then Andy, then Dr Stobbs. Again Jane detected a hint of what she was beginning to think of as the unicorn look, but this was the British aristocracy after all. Eccentrics were no novelty.

Really a small price to pay, she thought, as she wallowed in a bath, hot and perfumed and bubbling. Foch looked at her indignantly. He'd already been bathed.

'Yes I know,' she said, 'but you can't stay with an earl and a countess and a duke when you're covered in road dust. It simply isn't done.' Foch snorted, unconvinced.

Bath salts and hot water did marvels for aches and stiffness, just as Chanel did marvels for one's morale. The countess had decided that the occasion warranted a dinner party, and invited all the neighbouring gentry who would be sympathetic to the cause. A pity she hadn't brought Charles's sapphires.

'I'm sorry that the soap got in your eyes,' she told Foch, 'but we both have to look our best – and I must say you do look grand.' He did, too: black fur tight curled after his bath, red collar glowing. Of course the dinner guests all adored him, but he was used to that. The *Daily World*'s Mr Timmins had made him the best-known dog in the country. Jane took him down to be admired, then handed him over to the butler, who led Foch to the kitchen. He would be given far too much to eat, Jane was sure, but he deserved a treat. He had been working hard.

Messeter and Stobbs were there to dine, but not Andy, and his refusal had not surprised her. Cambridge had taught him the proper knives and forks. It wasn't that. He had to stay with the men because that was where he belonged. Of that he was utterly sure, but once Dick Lambert had been utterly sure, too. Dick was doing a day's march next week, Jane remembered, and wondered how he and Andy would get on.

Over dinner the canon worked hard at selling Felston to his neighbours, and so did Dr Stobbs, but Jane had no chance to do the same. All her companions wanted to talk about was Holly-wood. . . . When it was over her hostess conducted her to a sort of study where she could make her telephone calls. Bower first. Brusque of course, he was always brusque, but obviously pleased with life.

'We'll need another piece tomorrow,' he said. 'Tell us all about the nobs in their stately home. Disraeli's two worlds. – Only don't mention Disraeli.'

'Of course not,' said Jane. 'He was a Tory.'

Bower snorted. 'March going well?'

'So far.' Jane touched the wooden rim of the telephone table.

'A few of the men are limping a little – nothing serious – and anyway tomorrow's a rest day.'

'Why?' said Bower.

'a) Because they need a rest, and b) Because it's Sunday.'

'Church Parade you mean?' Bower asked.

'Only if they want it,' said Jane.

'You might get a piece out of that, too,' said Bower. 'We've got to keep it up.'

'You sound very cheerful,' said Jane.

'I should be,' Bower said. 'The circulation's climbed every day this week, thanks to your march. If this keeps up I won't owe anybody anything.'

'Splendid,' said Jane. 'How's Catherine?'

'In the pink,' said Bower. 'She won a packet at Sandown Park. A hundred to seven – so she's taking me out to dinner. She sends her love.'

'Give her mine,' said Jane. 'She's still going to march, I hope?'

'Wouldn't miss it for the world,' said Bower, and hung up.

'What on earth are you doing, marching about all over England?' said Georgie. 'Is it some new craze I haven't heard about?'

'It's to help people,' said Jane.

'What people?'

'Poor people.'

'But darling, you've got masses of money,' said Georgie, 'and even if you hadn't you could live off me.'

Jane looked at the handset. There could be no doubt about it. 'Georgie, you've been drinking,' she said.

'Well of course. It's Saturday night. I've been dancing too, with a rather sweet soldier. His sister married the Demon Bower.' So Piers was back. 'I do wish you were here,' Georgie said.

'I bet Piers doesn't.'

'Well no,' said Georgie, then added severely: 'There's far too much of that sort of thing anyway. Maybe I should switch to good works too.'

'You could always march with me.'

'Will it be fun?'

'Just you, me, and a hundred and twenty men.'

After that she felt that she deserved a reward, and telephoned Charles Lovell at his flat.

'Dining with Messeter's duke's sister?' Lovell asked.

'Just dined. It's a vast house. Telephones all over the place.'

'Ah,' Lovell said. 'Mm.' In other words she had told him to be careful of what he said, and he had told her that he would.

'You remember that stone-exporting group we did a couple of deals with in New York?' he said. 'Chap with a Russian name.'

'I remember him very well,' said Jane. 'Those rocks were real-quality stuff.'

'I wrote you a letter agreement,' said Lovell.

'You did indeed.'

'Look up the last clause when you have a moment,' said Lovell.

'You think it's inaccurate?'

'Certainly not,' said Lovell. 'I think it's the best piece of drafting I ever did.'

'That makes me very happy,' said Jane. 'You must explain it to me in more detail next time we meet.'

He was reminding her that he had written to say he loved her in words that had amazed her, just as the gift of sapphires had amazed her – but all the same Georgie was right. Good works too had their place in the scheme of things.

She made her last call, then, to her mother, who listened to her account of the march so far, then asked about her feet.

'As a former infantry officer George has had a great deal of experience in these matters,' said her mother. 'He says feet are of the utmost importance.'

'And he's absolutely right,' said Jane. 'Mine are fine.'

'And Foch?'

'His feet are fine, too,' said Jane, 'but I don't let him walk all the way at his age.'

There was a silence, then: 'He and I are contemporaries, are we not?' she asked. 'But then I'm not walking all the way either.'

'Ouch,' said Jane, and then: 'Talking of animals, what horse came in at a hundred to seven at Sandown Park?'

'Bonny Lad,' said her mother at once. 'George gave it as an each-way selection. Such a triumph. Owned by that young brother of Captain Patterson.'

'Really?' said Jane.

'Actually it's owned by a syndicate, but Mr Patterson is one of them. Did you back it?'

'We have all sorts of chaps on this march, Mummy,' said Jane, 'but I doubt if we run to a bookmaker.' Her mother changed the subject.

'I shall say a prayer for the success of your march tomorrow,' she said. 'It is vital that it should be successful, but then of course you know that or you wouldn't be doing it.'

The gentlemen had left their port and were taking coffee in the drawing room. Canon Messeter was still pushing Felston as hard as he could. How old he looks, thought Jane. White haired and bone thin, like a saner and more kindly Lear, and yet he is not much older than Charles.

'But here is Miss Whitcomb,' he said as Jane came in. 'She will tell you herself.'

'What will I tell?' said Jane.

'How patiently our good people bear their misfortunes.'

'Well yes,' said Jane. 'They do. But they aren't crushed, you know. Not yet. Not many of them anyway. You mustn't think they're sitting about waiting for the end.' Messeter's duke began to look nervous, sensing that at any moment politics might be invoked. It was time to change the subject.

'That's why they're marching,' said Jane. 'Not for charity. For work. And that's why people are supporting them – because they want to support themselves.' She turned to the canon. 'More good news,' she said. 'Guess who's going to do a day's march with us? . . . Georgina Payne.'

'*The film star?*' the duke's sister said.

'The very same,' said Jane.

'The one who played you in the ambulance film?' The duke's sister appeared to be of the sort who like to get things absolutely clear in their minds.

'That's the one,' said Jane.

'Well I'm damned,' the duke's sister said. 'Can anyone else join this march of yours?'

The news was as big a sensation with the marchers as with the gentry, thought Jane. Even Andy was staggered. He made the annoucement after breakfast when the men assembled for Dr Stobbs's inspection of their feet, for Dr Stobbs too agreed with Major Routledge. At first they thought it was a joke, but

when they realised it was true a great roar went up, and Jane
learned that the power of the press was one thing; the power of
the screen quite another.

# 47

AFTER THAT IT was a quiet day, a day they needed. Time to write home, or gossip, or just rest your feet, or go to church. Charles's ex-RQMS had even arranged that. For the Catholics there was a bus to take them to the Church of Our Lady in the next town, and another for the Baptists, the Methodists and the Presbyterians. For those who belonged to the Church of England there was a church a gentle stroll away, where Canon Messeter celebrated Holy Communion at the local vicar's invitation. Disraeli's – and Bower's – two worlds yet again, thought Jane: the marchers' blue-serge suits contrasting with the country tweeds and casual elegance of the regular, middle-class worshippers. After church there was time for a beer before a huge Sunday dinner of roast beef and Yorkshire pudding and all that went with it, and after that a football match, then more resting of feet, more letter-writing, to the music of a radio that Bob had supplied.

Jane wrote up her notes on the two worlds, added a paragraph about Georgie, and went back to the house to telephone. The night editor was impressed.

'You've got a good piece there,' he said. 'Georgina Payne. Does Mr Bower know?'

'Not yet.'

'I'll get on to him first chance I get. He may want a word with you tomorrow. Where will you be?'

'Out walking.'

'Oh,' said the night editor. 'Oh yes, of course. Ring in when you can. I'll put you on to the copy-taker.'

South again, always South, but not always fifteen miles a day, not any more, or not for everyone. Men began to fall out, their bodies' strength no longer able to cope with the demands of their hearts and minds. Too many years of undernourishment, of too much bread and not enough meat. But none of them asked to be sent home. They took a lift in the lorry instead, and rejoined the column as soon as they felt strong enough. To have gone home would have been surrender.

Then the rain came. They had done a hundred and fifty miles dry shod, which was pretty good for an English summer, but the rain came down at last, persistent as a nagging wife. The men were ready for it – boots that for once were waterproof, mackintoshes and capes – and to Jane's astonishment they even joked about it, and then she remembered: so often it had rained in France too. It was what the marching men expected. It was only in what they sang that the rain's misery was reflected:

> There's a long long trail a-winding
> Up to the land of my dreams,
> Where the nightingales are singing
> And the bright moon gleams.

'They always sang that one when we were getting close to the Line,' Canon Messeter said. 'To me it says more about death than the Mozart *Requiem*.'

It was true, she thought, and remembered just how true it was, when the troops were going forward and her ambulance was jolting back, but this time it was different. There was melancholy of course, but it was the melancholy of a song, a story, a play, to be savoured and even enjoyed. There was no misery, not this time.

Georgina joined them in Cambridgeshire. It was one of Bower's triumphs. For days the *World* had teased its readers, coyly declining to say when Georgie would march, and the day before she did, Bower had smuggled her out of London, under the noses of his rivals, to a small country hotel which was filled that night with *World* employees, one of whom manned the telephone switchboard. It was like one of the star's own movies, and she loved it.

Jane left the column and came to the hotel in a car Bower had sent for her, Foch in his basket by her side. She didn't want him wandering in the wet, developing rheumatism. The car sloshed and waddled along sopping-wet country roads, then up a driveway that resembled a small stream, but the hotel itself was warm and comfortable. Trust Bower for that, she thought. She left her bag in her room, then went at once to Georgie's: the bridal suite, but then it would be. The hotel didn't do one for widows.

The two women embraced at once, then Georgie leaned back, her hands still grasping Jane's shoulders.

'Good grief,' she said. 'How healthy you look.'

Georgie, thought Jane, did not. A lot of her walking would be done in the canon's Armstrong-Siddeley.

'Exercise,' she said. 'Nothing like it to make you healthy. I've lost three pounds as well. Oh I do wish I enjoyed it.'

'That and good works,' Georgie said. 'It always surprises me to know you do good works. You enjoy life so. Shall I make the martinis or will you?' Jane was about to say no, then realised she couldn't, not to Georgie. On the other hand she hadn't drunk alcohol since Charles's champagne.

'Me,' she said. With any luck she could add extra vermouth to hers when Georgie wasn't looking. Georgie gestured to where gin, vermouth, ice and a shaker were waiting. Really Jay's cohorts had done them proud.

'I must say,' said Jane, 'I think it's awfully decent of you to do this.'

'Me too,' said Georgie, 'though it's probably insanity. Very likely it runs in the family. I mean to say – fifteen miles.'

'There's a car if you get too tired,' said Jane. 'Rather an antique, but it goes when it must. Foch uses it rather a lot. What does World Wide think about all this?'

'They love it,' said Georgie. 'Georgina Payne on the side of the poor and down-trodden, and acres of newsprint. – And all for free. I haven't the heart to tell them it isn't Georgina Payne at all. It's Jane Whitcomb. And if I did they wouldn't listen.' She sipped at her martini: sipped, where once she would have swigged, when they were alone. Was life catching up with her at last?

'I told you about Bob Patterson, didn't I?' she asked.

'You had a bit of a thing going, you said. But it didn't last.'

'Well how could it?' said Georgie. 'Me in Hollywood and him in London.'

'You were back in London yesterday.'

'Yes but –' Georgie hesitated. 'There's something about that young man. I mean he's good company and he's funny with that accent of his, and he's utter bliss to sleep with – but he's trouble, too. Don't ask me how I know it, but he is. So I kept away. The studios are very puritanical these days. Did he ever try it with you?'

'Once,' said Jane.

'And?' Georgie was determined on an answer.

'I turned him down, though I do see what you mean.'

'You still have your nice chap then?'

'Still the same one. He's all I need.'

'All that money and talent *and* good looks,' said Georgie. 'Commonsense, too. It isn't fair. . . . Talking of money –' She brooded.

'What about it?'

'Well it's more like talking of Danny really. He left me all his. He was awfully sweet.'

'Was it a lot?'

'Masses. He bought a lot of real estate. Apartment blocks and building lots and things. The Crash hardly touched him.'

'Nothing for his boyfriends?'

'He was going to. Eventually. But the studio dreamed up this story about how he loved me so much he left me everything and I did the same for him – and they made us do it so they could have a picture of us reading our wills. For some reason we were wearing bathing suits at the time.' She smiled, remembering. 'He looked awfully good in a bathing suit. Such a waste.'

'So he never –'

'Not once,' said Georgie. 'He just couldn't poor lamb. Of course next day I changed my will back again when no one was looking, but he – didn't. All the boyfriends were furious. They seemed to think I should hand it over to them, but I didn't see it at all. I liked Danny. He was nice. . . . Anyway it means I've got a few extra dollars for Felston.'

'You don't have to,' said Jane. 'Just being here's all we want from you.'

'Better Felston than those California fairies,' said Georgie. 'Two of them killed him, you know.'

'Did the police never find out who?'

'Never. God knows they tried hard enough. I offered a reward of twenty thousand dollars and the studio doubled it. They had to. Murray Fisch was furious. But it never got paid. . . . I hope it will, one day.' She looked at her empty glass and put it down. 'Dinner and an early night, I suppose,' she said. 'Early start in the morning?'

'I'm afraid so,' said Jane. 'We want to be on the road by nine.'

'Pooh, that's not early,' said Georgie. 'The way the studio works nine o'clock's midday.'

Next morning was a dry one, and Georgie managed four miles, which considering she never took any form of exercise and smoked and drank far too much and ate all the wrong things, wasn't bad at all, Jane admitted. How on earth did she keep her figure? But Georgie did more than just walk. She set off in the front rank of course, with Timmins and the rest of the photographers frantically busy, but after that she made sure that she walked with every rank of the marching men, so that every man could say that he'd walked in the same file as Georgina Payne. For the meal break Bower had ordered a hamper from Fortnum's, but she and Jane turned it down flat, ate corned beef sandwiches and drank mugs of tea. It was the men around them who ate the plovers' eggs and smoked salmon and caviar, and drank champagne from the bottle. After that she rode in the Armstrong-Siddeley with Foch, and Canon Messeter for chauffeur.

They spent the night at Cambridge, and the whole town turned out in welcome. Term had finished but there were still dons and undergraduates about, and they jammed in tight with the townspeople as yet another band, yet more banners, led the way for the Felston banner and the Felston men. A lot of the dons and undergraduates were Left-Wing, and strong supporters of the march and all it stood for, but even the most dedicated were there to see Georgina Payne, to gaze at a fantasy made flesh.

It was flesh worth gazing at, Jane admitted to herself. Well outside the town Georgina had rigged blinds round the Armstrong-Siddeley, changed her dress and renewed her make-up, then taken her place in the front rank once more. As they progressed down King's Parade, the crowd yelled, the sun came out, and the bells began to ring, for reasons totally unconnected with the Felston March, but that didn't matter. What mattered was that the bells were ringing.

They were staying at a house outside the town, a former manor house, now a study centre for comparative religion. Its director, a friend of the canon's, was a Trotskyite Buddhist. Georgina marched in with them, and into the building, though the *Daily World* car was waiting to take her to London. Jane mentioned the fact as they went to her room. Georgina kicked off her shoes and sprawled on a bed that was austere, even harsh, and quite unworthy of a Hollywood star.

'Change of plan,' the star said. 'It seems they've got a hall here, and a piano, and I've promised that nice parson I'd play a few tunes for the chaps. Remember I did it once before, when we were at Felston.'

'That's a wonderful idea,' said Jane, and lay back wearily on her own bed, which actively resented being lain on.

'Well I hope so,' Georgie said. 'I mean I'm madly out of practice. But I don't expect the chaps will mind.'

'You know damn well they won't,' said Jane. 'They'd go through fire for you.'

Georgie smiled. 'A hundred and twenty of them,' she said. 'And just us two. We'll never get better odds than that.'

'All the old favourites,' Jane told the copy-taker. '"Lily Of Laguna", "Roses Of Picardy", "Let The Great Big World Keep Turning". The audience can only be described as rapturous, and demanded encore after encore.

'Miss Payne had never looked lovelier, in a strapless blue-and-silver evening dress, and a deep décolletage.'

'I wish I'd been there,' the copy-taker said. I wish my brother had been there, thought Jane, but he wasn't: or if he was he hid himself well.

Next day Georgie left them, and demanded that Jane meet her in London as soon as the march was done.

'But aren't you due back at the studios?' Jane asked.

'Sort of leave of absence,' said Georgie. 'Because I'm upset, and I jolly well am. Also because the next script isn't nearly ready, but that's our secret.'

There was no concert the next night, and no rapturous applause either, but later on at Grantham they picked up Major and Mrs Routledge, and a couple of opera singers, soprano and tenor, who sang as they marched, to the men's intense embarrassment. They sang well enough, but their marching was terrible.

'Their thrilling notes lightened the journey,' Jane lied to the copy-taker. 'Also present were Major Routledge, the *Daily World*'s popular racing correspondent, and his wife, the mother of your reporter. Mrs Routledge wore an elegant tweed suit and calf-skin shoes, and proved a redoubtable marcher.'

She had, too, eating the miles as if she were hungry for them, Jane thought, and the men had admired her for it. They had liked the major too, for his vast knowledge of racing and his willingness to share it. At the end of the day's march they had left to begin a journey to Scotland. There was racing at Ayr. Before they left, Jane and her mother managed a few moments alone.

'It's going well,' her mother said. 'One can sense it.' She looked at Jane more closely. 'But it's tiring you.'

'It isn't the walking,' said Jane. 'It's the responsibility. I hadn't quite realised what I'd set out to do.'

Her mother nodded. 'You'll bear it of course,' she said, 'because you must, but when it's over you must rest, whatever the outcome.'

'Yes Mummy,' said Jane. 'I really must.'

Her mother reached out to touch her cheek, then kissed her. 'I'm proud of you,' she said. 'It's been a privilege to play even a small part in such an adventure. Oh – before I forget. George is arranging another celebrity – or trying to. He won't tell us who, in case he can't do it – but if he's successful we'll let you know.'

'So long as he's famous,' said Jane.

'He will be,' her mother said. 'I'll see to that. Goodbye, my dear.'

Another day, and another and another, till two hundred miles had passed since Newcastle, and the men finally began to believe that they would do it. Sometimes they marched alone, but more and more often they had company, to remind the *World*'s readers that they were still there, still moving steadily South: a bishop, a retired admiral, the entire chorus of a West End musical who were sped off by fast car to the railway station and put on make-up and costumes on the train, while Mr Timmins took pictures, and caught the next train back to the march, for by now Mr Timmins was as dedicated as everybody else.

Dick Lambert joined them when they reached Royston. The visit was not a success. The trouble was that Lambert was a member, and a rising one at that, of a coalition government that many considered to be a betrayal of Socialism. And yet how could the poor fellow not march? thought Jane. Bower had invited him, 'as a man of the Left and an old contributor to the *Daily World*', and Lambert was all too well aware of the sort of publicity he would get if he refused, and so he marched, with a kind of dogged determination that did him no harm at all in the eyes of the men, though Andy was barely more than civil. At the noon break he and Jane ate together.

'It was good of you to come,' said Jane.

'Strange,' he said. 'I could detect no irony in what you said.'

'There was none,' said Jane. 'I know pressure was applied, but there are such things as urgent meetings and conferences abroad.'

'I'm not such a coward,' Lambert said.

'Indeed you're not,' said Jane, 'which proves what I said is true. It *was* good of you to come.'

'It'll do me no harm, either. I don't want you to think I hadn't realised that.'

'Except among some of your colleagues perhaps?'

'Perhaps.' Suddenly Lambert was wary.

'That was just chat,' said Jane. 'Nothing for the *World* unless you say so.'

'Well then,' said Lambert, 'not for the *World* – some of my colleagues hope I'll break a leg – if not my neck.' He straightened up his shoulders. 'And some of them wish they were marching alongside of me. Still not for the *World*, this government isn't going to put the country right. It hasn't got the guts – but if and when it goes it'll be followed by something even worse – which is why I stay in it.'

He took a piece of meat from his stew and offered it to Foch, who nibbled cautiously.

'You've marched every day so they tell me,' he said. She nodded. 'My God you're tougher than I am. Maybe you should have my job. You or that disapproving friend of yours.'

'Andy Patterson? We've both of us quite enough to do as it is.'

'You have,' Lambert said, 'but Patterson would take my job tomorrow. He aches for it, does Brother Patterson. He's just like me. That's how I know. And it's no good telling me he's kept the faith, never made compromises, never dirtied his hands. No more did I till I took office . . . since then I've done nothing else.' The marshals blew their whistles and the column began to form.

'Not today,' said Jane. 'You haven't compromised today.'

'My feet wish I had,' Dick Lambert said.

Next came Lionel, in country tweeds and walking shoes, very much the warrior, the flying hero. Jane had warned him in advance, and he too wore his medals. To the men he was simply another ex-officer, but one decent enough to join them and share their food – and march every step of the way. Jane blessed him for it.

Two days after Lionel left them, the major's surprise appeared. Bonny Lad had raced at Ayr, and come home at six to one. A lot of the men had backed it, and now he appeared, complete with jockey, as the column moved on to Letchworth. Apart from Georgie's, he got the biggest reception yet.

'Cavalry,' said Canon Messeter happily. It was all that they lacked. Jane looked at him. Despite the spells in the Armstrong-Siddeley he looked very, very tired. The men were forming up for the day's march, and the waiting was hard for him.

'You should rest,' she said.

'Presently. For some reason your friend Mr Timmins likes me to be here when he takes his pictures.'

Because you look as you do, she thought. Because a picture with you in it forces the eye to see, forces its owner to acknowledge that if you are there, looking as you do, then our cause is just.

'I fear that Foch is enduring our march far better than I am,' said Messeter. 'All the same I'm glad of his company. So is

Stobbs, believe it or not, though he finds it hard to say so.' Jane led him off to his car.

Bonny Lad behaved well. 'A future Derby winner,' Jane told the copy-taker, and for all she knew it was true, mincing and sidling at the head of the column, his jockey's silks gleaming. What about her own champion? she wondered. There hadn't even been time to ask the major how Bridget's Boy was doing – but Bonny Lad, a big, handsome grey, drew crowds wherever they went and they didn't bother him. He was used to crowds and their applause.

When he left them there were just two more days to go. First Watford, and a long night's rest under a roof, an old drill hall fitted out with camp beds, and the day after that was London.

Trafalgar Square. Downing Street. Industria et Fortitudo triumphant. But the day before that Jay and Catherine Bower joined them: 'the *Daily World*'s proprietor and his lovely wife, determined to see for themselves and pay homage to the men of Felston for their magnificent achievement'. Well the men of Felston deserved it. A lot of them were limping now, but the lorries were empty of men. The end was almost there, and to ride to it was unthinkable.

# 48

B OWER AND CATHERINE arrived in his Bentley, and the men
gave them a cheer. Bower was at once drawn into conference with Messeter, Stobbs and Andy. Jane went over to
Catherine and embraced her. She was as taut as a bowstring.

'Did you see him?' Catherine asked at once.

'See who, darling?'

'Bob Patterson.' It was said impatiently, as if Jane were being
deliberately obtuse.

'Darling, didn't you know?' said Jane. 'I've been on a walking
tour.'

'Please,' said Catherine. 'No jolly jokes. Not now.'

Jane looked at her: the younger woman was very close to
tears.

'No jolly jokes,' she said. 'He didn't come here. I don't mean
he doesn't support us – it's just that he said himself this is no
place for a capitalist.'

'So he sent his horse instead?'

'You did well on it so they tell me. So did some of the chaps
here. My stepfather tipped it for a race at Ayr. That's why Bonny
Lad was so popular when he came to march with us.'

'Jay doesn't know Bob Patterson has an investment in that
horse,' Catherine said. 'Please don't tell him.'

'Why on earth should I? It's Bob's business. . . . Piers is home
they tell me.'

'You mean Georgina Payne told you.'

'Well yes. They went dancing together I believe.'

'He was rather smitten,' said Catherine.

'Most men are. Is he pining for Brenda Coupland?'

'My dear, the most extraordinary thing,' said Catherine. 'Did you *know* she was going to be married?'

'To a fat man called Meldrum.'

'You've met him? What's he like?' She seemed to have recovered, which was just as well. The marshals' whistles were blowing, and Bower was moving over to join them. It was time to go.

'Fat, as I say,' said Jane. 'And very rich.' Foch rose to his feet as Bower came up.

'Who's very rich?' he asked.

'A man called Meldrum, who is going to marry a woman called Brenda Coupland.'

'Anything in it for us?' Us of course was the *Daily World*. Catherine looked at her sharply. Bower obviously knew nothing of his wife's brother's involvement.

'I doubt it,' said Jane. 'Maybe a par in "This Wicked World".'

Bower lost interest at once, and Catherine looked relieved, as Andy gave the signal, the banner moved forward, and the column followed.

After that there was always somebody near them, and no chance to talk privately, no chance at all to talk about what was more important than anything else in Catherine's mind.

She had been Bob's mistress. There could be no doubt of it. Perhaps she still was his mistress. First Sarah, then Georgie, and now Catherine. How cunning of Georgie to spot so early that Bob was trouble, but then in her own way Georgie was cunning, especially when it came to her own survival. . . . The three girls on the platform at Newcastle Station. She could almost hear him gasp aloud when he first saw them. He'd never before seen such beauty or such wealth: a peasant beholding three goddesses, but not the Judgement of Paris, not for Bob. He'd gone for all three – and would have made it four if she'd let him. What was he for God's sake? Some kind of collector? Pretty women instead of Spode or Chippendale or American Air Mails? And what about Lilian Dunn? Did she belong in the same cabinet or was she part of another set? The Felston March was no place to work that one out, though by the look on her face Catherine was having a stab at it. When the midday break came, Bower went to her at once.

'You look tired, honey,' he said to her. 'Are you sure you're OK?'

'I'm fine,' she said. 'Honestly.' She smiled at him and at once was beautiful.

There's another thing, thought Jane. She keeps on being so nice to him. Remember in the Fleet Street flat, how she went up to him and kissed him and he looked ready to burst with happiness, just as he's looking now? Why does she do it? Guilt?

'How many miles have we done?' Catherine asked.

'About seven,' said Jane.

'Gosh,' said Catherine. 'Seven miles before lunch. Every day.'

'Not always as much as that,' Jane said. 'The men are doing well today. They want to get to the end.'

'If I was the ruthless realist I'm supposed to be –' Bower smiled at his wife, 'I'd want this march to last for ever. There's never been anything like it for selling papers. As it is – all I've got left is the grand finale, but what the heck. These guys have earned their triumph.'

'You think it's going to be a triumph?' Jane asked.

'How can it miss?' said Bower. 'Trafalgar Square. Thousands of people. Celebrities by the dozen. All the ones who marched. All except Bonny Lad, that is.' Bower smiled again. 'He's running at Worcester.'

'Oh,' said Catherine. 'That's too bad.'

'Georgie's coming?' said Jane.

'Couldn't keep her away. She's promised to lead the singing.'

'*Singing?*' said Jane. 'You're going to put a piano in Trafalgar Square?' It sounded like a job for the Surrealists, but Bower was looking indignant.

'Piano?' he said. 'Hell, no. We're bringing Felston Brass Band down by train.'

Then Canon Messeter came across to thank Bower for all he had done to publicise the march, and to thank Catherine too for turning out with her husband, and once again there was no chance of the women slipping away, to give and receive tremendous secrets. And just as well too, thought Jane. Georgie and a brass band in Trafalgar Square were quite enough to think about on an afternoon's march.

They ended the day at Hampstead, in a hostel attached to some college or other, that devoted itself in an appropriately

Hampstead manner to putting the world to rights. The men of Felston, the college thought, had given a highly commendable lead in this, and so it did them proud: a vast meal, and even an allowance of beer, although they did not approve of beer, then a gramophone recital for those who wished to attend. Not many did. They preferred more beer in the pubs near by, and the kind of tunes they were used to. Jane did her best with Béla Bartók and Schönberg, but when Honegger was announced she suddenly remembered the need of an urgent conference about the next day's march, and dragged off Canon Messeter to the office set aside for Andy's use, as the man who was in charge. It isn't a lie, either, she told herself. I do want to know about plans for tomorrow, especially about what other land mines Jay Bower's planted.

Stobbs had procured a bottle of whisky, and offered her a glass. Jane accepted. The march was almost done now: she could break training at last.

'We've got a late start tomorrow,' Andy was saying. 'Just as well, really, with the lads on the beer tonight.'

'They won't go mad,' said Stobbs. 'They know what's expected of them.'

'Let's hope so,' said Andy, 'because what's expected's a heck of a lot. March to Trafalgar Square, then a speech of welcome from Dick Lambert,' he paused for a moment '– then a couple of songs from Georgina Payne, then Billy Caffrey introduces me and I make a speech.'

'Jimmy Wagstaff?' Canon Messeter asked.

'Our devoted and caring MP's in a nursing home,' Andy said.

'Heart attack,' said Dr Stobbs. 'It might even be true.'

'Anyway, that's it,' said Andy.

'Downing Street,' Canon Messeter said.

'Not for the lads,' said Andy. 'Lambert told me himself when he condescended to join us. You'll have a petition, no doubt, he said. He knew fine well we had. The *Daily World*'s been on about it for weeks. I told him yes. "You any idea how many signatures?" he asked me. How on earth could I? The petition was in the *World*'s offices in Fleet Street. The *World* reckons a hundred thousand, I said. Shook him, that did. Say half that to be on the safe side, he said. That's still a lot of signatures. You'll be able to send it with a deputation to Downing Street. Say half a dozen. I was thinking we'd all go, I told him. Not to Downing Street, he says. Trafalgar Square, yes – so long as it's peaceful –'

'Which it will be,' said Stobbs.

'But Downing Street's not for processions,' Andy continued. 'That's what Lambert told me, and from what I hear he's right. So all we have to do now is decide who goes. I propose us four, Billy Caffrey – he's mayor after all – and one of the footsloggers. They could draw lots for it.'

'Why us?' said Messeter. 'We did no more than the others.'

'Because we're known,' Andy said patiently. 'We're the ones that have had their pictures in the papers. Right, Jane?'

'Oh absolutely,' said Jane. 'I'll even have to take Foch.'

There was a tap at the door and the principal of the college looked in. 'Sorry to interrupt,' he said, 'but there's a police inspector asking for Mr Patterson, and a Dr Watson – a lady – asking for Dr Stobbs.'

Andy rose to his feet. 'I'd better see him then,' he said.

The principal's face said it all. Capitalist lackeys, he was thinking. White Guards. Cossacks.

'I'll go with you,' Stobbs said to Andy. 'If you'll ask Dr Watson to wait –'

'I'll do that,' said Jane, and rose. 'She's an old friend of mine.'

Harriet was waiting in the entrance hall and came to her at once, kissed her, then stood back to look at her: not like Georgie appraising possible competition; more like a painter looking at one of his pictures that had turned out better than he'd thought possible.

'But you look wonderful,' she said.

'Exercise,' said Jane. 'Fresh air. The open road.'

'You should keep it up.'

'Dancing's exercise too,' said Jane. 'You've come to help Dr Stobbs?'

'He phoned as soon as you got here, I gather. There are a few of your fellows he'd like a second opinion on.'

'I was afraid there might be,' said Jane. 'They wouldn't give up. Not one.'

'Will he be long?' Harriet asked.

'I hope not.' Dear God I hope not, she thought. Why must the police come pestering Andy now?

Harriet said carefully, 'Lots and lots of celebrities turned out for you, I see, even Mr Bower and his wife. You told her to come to see me.' Jane nodded. 'And she did. She's a sweet little thing, don't you think?'

Oh how I wish I could tell her that, thought Jane. Catherine, you're paid back in your own coin.

'We've been friends for years,' said Jane.

'So I gather. She had a very bad smash you know.' Jane nodded. 'Intense ones like her really should be extra careful. Everything goes so deep.'

Before she could say more the door opened and the police inspector came in, with Andy and Dr Stobbs. The inspector was rolling up what looked like a street map.

'You just stick to that and we won't go far wrong, sir,' he said. 'Your lads will be wearing their medals, I take it?'

'That's right.'

'I'll tell my lads to wear theirs too,' the inspector said. 'There'll only be two of them with you. They won't get under your feet, but they know the way. . . . Been a pleasure to meet you both. A real pleasure.' He shook hands with the two men, and was gone.

'Well!' said Jane.

'It wasn't a handcuffs job,' said Andy. 'Just working out the route for tomorrow.'

Jane introduced them to Harriet, and left them to it. She was suddenly tired, overhelmingly tired, and so it seemed was Foch. She had to carry him up the last flight of stairs.

She had slept for perhaps an hour when the knocking began. She was at the Gargoyle, dancing with Lionel, and the drummer in the band was banging louder and louder, making his bass drum sound like the opening of a bombardment. Foch woke and began to bark and she woke too, and the bombardment became a fist pounding on her door.

'Jane,' Andy called. 'Wake up. Jane!'

'Give me a minute,' she said, and found her dressing gown (warm and sensible and guaranteed not to shock Andy) and went to the door.

Andy said, 'I'm sorry to disturb you –'

'That's all right,' she said. 'What's wrong?'

'It isn't even as if you could do anything,' Andy said. 'It's just – I felt sure you would want to know.'

'Andy, what is it?'

'Canon Messeter's had a heart attack,' Andy said. 'Dr Stobbs and that pal of yours have taken him to hospital.'

'I'll get dressed,' she said.

'No,' said Andy. 'Dr Stobbs said stay away. Rest, he said. Get fit for tomorrow. Make it a success. It's the only thing the canon wants – for us to do it right.'

'Very well,' said Jane, but before she went back to bed and sleep she phoned Charles Lovell. It was a treat she had been saving until the march was over, but Charles had a right to know.

'Rupert?' he said. 'Where is he?' Jane told him and added, 'Harriet Watson's with him.' It had been at Harriet's house that she had first met Charles. 'You'll let me know if there's anything –' he said.

'Of course.' Even two words showed how close she was to tears.

'My poor darling,' he said.

'We're so close,' she said. 'Almost there. And he –'

It was what Harriet and she had feared. When the battle was over, the object achieved, even then they went down, and so often then it was the best of them who fell, the ones who had kept going by spirit alone, till even that ran out.

'Let me know the minute there's any news,' Charles Lovell said. But there was nothing more, and she phoned the *Daily World* instead.

She telephoned Harriet the next morning as soon as she decently could: Stobbs was already busy with the rest of the sick.

'He's ill,' said Harriet. 'Very ill and of course he must have known it for ages, but he's been too damn busy looking after other people to take care of himself.'

'Like Dr Stobbs?'

'Exactly,' said Harriet. 'But at least I'm going to have a good look at him before he leaves London. As for the canon –' she hesitated. 'He's a tricky one. He doesn't want to die, and that's a good thing. I don't mean he's a coward –'

'He wants to see what good the march has done,' said Jane.

'Precisely. That will help him, but even so I shouldn't think he's got awfully long.'

'Do you think there's any point in another opinion?' Jane asked.

'Some Harley Street wizard? Why not,' said Harriet. 'I've no objection and I don't suppose Stobbs has either.'

'I'll pay, of course.'

'Of course,' said Harriet, 'but don't tell your friend the canon. He'd much rather you saved your money for Felston.'

Dr Stobbs was ruder, more aggressive even than usual, but the men accepted it: they knew why. Andy had broken the news at breakfast, and emphasised that the march would conclude exactly as if the canon were there. The men accepted that, too. Messeter had always been a mystery to them: a creature from another, unknown world, but one whose goodness was self-evident, whose prayers, they knew, were heard, whatever kind of God they believed in: more like a talisman than the sort of parson they were used to. The *Daily World* had played up the story for all it was worth, and that pleased them. The canon had always been one of the celebrities, the legends. It was right that his sickness should be known.

The Felston Brass Band arrived, and Billy Caffrey, and for the last time the marshals began to muster their men, but this time there were union banners from all over London, a great, blazing forest of them.

Billy Caffrey said, 'I was sorry to hear about the parson. You want me to mention it?'

'Better let me,' said Andy.

'Aye,' said Billy Caffrey. 'Comrades-in-arms. All that. Will he pull through?'

'If I was one for prayer,' said Andy, 'which I'm not, I'd be praying now.'

The bass drum gave a warning thud, the two policemen who would act as guides took their places beside the banners, and for the last time Andy gave the signal to march. Even just outside the college the crowd was already dense, yelling and cheering so loud that it was hard to hear the band, shouting their admiration for those men, freshly-shaved, clothes pressed, boots polished, medals glittering, who marched at attention, looking neither to right nor left, more like men marching to combat than to triumph. As the column passed each crowd broke up, many of its members hurrying for a bus, a tram, a tube, anything that would get them to Trafalgar Square.

On and on went the column, through St John's Wood and Bayswater, and from time to time other bands swung in ahead of them, sparing the Felston band, saving it for the rally, yet making sure that the music was always there. Foch stepped out jauntily. From time to time someone in the crowd would point to him, and Jane was quite sure he knew it, but all the same something was puzzling him: it was the absence of Canon Messeter.

# 49

Trafalgar Square at last. Along Pall Mall, and on to the one gap in the crowd that the police had kept clear, as people reached out to touch, to clap shoulders, until at last the police guides led them to their place at the foot of the column, and Jane, Andy and Dr Stobbs climbed up to the platform where the celebrities were already waiting: Georgie, the duke and his sister and her husband, the bishop, the comedian, Dick Lambert, Lionel, her mother and stepfather and the rest, every single one of them except Bonny Lad. About half the House of Commons seemed to be there too, she thought: the Labour half, and photographers and newsreel cameramen were already busy. Jane went to Georgie and they kissed; flash bulbs popped and newsreel cameras whirred.

'I heard about that saintly man,' said Georgie. 'My dear I could weep. Is he very ill?'

'Very,' said Jane, 'but please, darling. No sad songs.'

'No no,' Georgie said. 'Nothing like that. Not today. The band and I tried it all out last night.'

Dick Lambert went to the microphone and began to speak, and gloom descended on the duke like a London fog. His worst fears were realised: the speech was nothing but politics. He didn't recover until Georgie stepped forward to sing. Keep it cheerful, Jane had told her, and keep it short, the police had said. A crowd of this size is too big to control for long, even a crowd as good humoured as this one. Georgina stood up, stepped to the microphone, and did as she was told. Never again, she knew, would she have a living audience as big as this one, its vastness overflowing into Charing Cross; a great, dark mass sprinkled with white, the whiteness of upturned faces. She nodded to the band conductor, the opening chords were struck, and Georgie began: 'Daisy Bell' to get them going, 'Roses Of Picardy' because it was about love as well as war, and last of all 'Tipperary', because everybody knew it and they could yell their heads off. Then she sat down, and no amount of applause could bring her back. They had to make do with Billy Caffrey instead, but at least Felston's mayor didn't keep them for long. He had a funny accent, too. Furtively the police inspector looked at his watch and wished he could wipe his forehead. If Patterson didn't go on too long it should work out very well.

Andy took his time getting to the microphone, giving the crowd time to settle down. Jane looked at him, so calm it would seem, so assured, and yet with that vast monster of a crowd to please. He's actually enjoying it, she thought. *This* is what he walked three hundred miles for. 'Thou hast it all' indeed.

'Comrades,' he began, and the duke winced, the gloom came back, but not to the crowd, the monster. The monster was hearing the words it had travelled far to hear, the sacred words: 'Justice' and 'Suffering Humanity' and 'The Right to Work'. There was nothing new in what he said: there couldn't be. The message was as old as man's misfortune; but he put fire into it, and anger, and even love, and the monster took it and tasted, and devoured every scrap, as Andy in his turn kept it short and stepped back from the microphone. Then the cheering began. The chief inspector looked at his watch and then, on duty or not, took off his cap and mopped his forehead as the cheering grew louder still.

'That was the best speech I ever heard you give,' said Jane.

'It was a Bobby Dazzler all right,' said Billy Caffrey, which was generous of him, thought Jane. Against any other yardstick, Billy Caffrey's too would have been thought first class.

They were in a roomy but anonymous Daimler supplied by Bower: Jane and Foch, Dr Stobbs (already fretting to get back to Canon Messeter), Andy, Billy Caffrey, and ex-Corporal Laidlaw, who had won the lottery and was rigid with stage fright. On the seat by their driver was a huge parcel that contained their petition.

'Let's hope it works,' was all that Andy said.

He hadn't spoken much since Trafalgar Square, Jane thought. Barely enough to tell dukes and film stars and bishops how grateful he was. Perhaps great actors felt the same, once they had left the stage. The Daimler flowed on through London traffic, up Whitehall, until at last they came to Downing Street, and pulled up outside Number 10, where the press photographers already waited. No newsreel cameras, not this time, since there was no film star, but at least there was a large and splendid policeman, presiding over it all as if it were a party for which he personally had sent out the invitations. The Daimler eased to a halt and they got out. Billy Caffrey and the corporal went round to the Daimler's front seat to collect the parcel, and the others moved towards the door of Number 10. Just before they reached it, Jane put out a hand to hold Stobbs back, and Andy moved forward alone, past the policeman at rigid attention, to stand before the Prime Minister's door. Mr Timmins caught the moment to perfection. Thou hast it all, thought Jane again. Glamis, Cawdor, all. But of course that was nonsense. Andy had hardly begun: and yet, just for a second, he had seemed so perfectly at ease where he stood.

The door opened, and a suave young man appeared, looked at the five figures confronting him and was far from impressed.

'On behalf of the people of Felston,' Andy said, 'I present you with this petition, which asks for no more than work for the people who live there: a fair day's work for a fair day's pay.' He took the parcel from Stobbs and Laidlaw, and offered it to the suave young man, who passed it at once to the manservant behind him.

'I shall see the Prime Minister gets it,' the suave young man said, and that was the end of their journey. The Prime Minister was far too wily a politician to appear in person. The door to Number 10 swung shut. The march was over.

There were still things to do, of course. The marchers had been driven back to the college, where they were to stay one more night, in buses paid for by the fund. Some of them still had a few bob of their Bonny Lad winnings left, and them he had to persuade to stay sober. Then there were the sick, but Dr Stobbs took care of them. He, Andy, was in charge of the healthy ones, his main concern to get them on to the special train that would take them back to Felston. Jane had offered to help, but he had told her he could manage, and so he could. Besides, a nasty little voice inside him whispered, being seen to be working your guts out's worth nearly as many votes as making speeches. He was wrestling with the march's accounts when the college principal called him to the phone. Canon Messeter, he thought, and hurried to the office where the telephone was. 'This is Andy Patterson,' he said.

'The very man I wanted to speak to,' said Burrowes, who sounded drunk.

'Go ahead,' said Andy. 'There's nobody else here.'

'You did well,' Burrowes said. 'That speech of yours was a gem. A masterpiece. I was there – and so were others. The Party's pleased.'

'Tell them I said thank you,' Andy said.

'Keep it up,' said Burrowes. 'Get yourself talked about. Use your influence. You could go a long way. Do you know that? The Party can take you a long way.'

Only because there's no one else to take, thought Andy, and waited.

'Just one thing,' Burrowes said. 'Get rid of that woman. We don't need her and her race-horses and caterwauling actresses. Sling her out.' Once more Andy waited. 'Well?' said Burrowes.

'It won't be necessary,' Andy said at last.

'Of course it's necessary,' said Burrowes. 'It's essential.'

'I mean she's already left,' said Andy.

'Oh,' said Burrowes, and then: 'Well done. That's excellent, I must say. I never thought you could be so effective so quickly.'

And there you had Comrade Burrowes in a nutshell, thought Andy. He could believe that a person would leave a position of power only because that person was forced out, and never because whoever it was might consider that their work was done, and hand on the power to somebody else because they liked him.

The funny thing was that Canon Messeter didn't look so very much different from when he was on the march. A little paler perhaps, but just as neatly shaven, the faith still shining in his eyes. He was very ill, the specialist had said, which meant that all three doctors were unanimous, but then he'd been very ill on the march, too, and probably for weeks before that.

'It's good of you to come,' he said. 'You must have so much to do.'

'Not now,' said Jane. 'Andy Patterson's taken over now. All I do is rest my feet from time to time. It's bliss.'

'I agree with you,' Messeter said, 'though continuous lying down can be rather boring.'

'You haven't been trying to get up?' said Jane.

'What would be the point? I know I can't. The spirit indeed is willing, but the flesh is weak. Very weak in my case.'

'Is there anything you want?' Jane asked quickly.

'I have a Bible, and a prayer book,' said the canon, 'so that's all right. . . . Some Dickens, perhaps. . . . *Pickwick Papers* for preference.'

'I'll send it round at once,' said Jane. 'No food? Fruit?'

'Caviar,' said Messeter unexpectedly. 'I should like to taste caviar just once more. And champagne.'

'You shall taste it as often as you like,' said Jane.

Dr Stobbs said that the canon could have both, and the specialist and Harriet agreed, after Stobbs had delayed his departure until the last possible moment, and only just caught his train at King's Cross. The men were still concerned about the canon, Andy found, came to ask Stobbs about him, and were dismayed by what they learned, but the journey to Felston was long, and there was a bar that sold beer. Soon they began to sing.

When they reached Felston Station they lined up for the last time, for the benefit of the *World*'s stringer and Mr Timmins, but not just for them. Billy Caffrey marched past the band and the banner, moving with the strut of the sergeant he once had been, then turned to face them with the swivelling stamp the drill book decreed.

'Men,' he bellowed, 'I want three cheers for Andy Patterson. Hip hip –' The hurrahs crashed out like artillery fire, and when they had finished, Billy Caffrey's voice blared again: 'Felston marchers – Dismiss.'

They broke ranks at once, crowding in on Andy, pounding him on the back, shouting their thanks. For what? he wondered, but he knew the answer. It was for something that they themselves had achieved, and even if it was never anything more than a protest, at least it had been delivered to Downing Street.

In his turn he said, 'Thanks, lads. Thanks.' But inside himself he was thinking: Maybe this time Comrade Burrowes was right.

'Caviar?' said Lovell.

'Just once more, he said, and the doctors said Why not?'

'Sidney Smith said something about Heaven is eating foie gras to the sound of trumpets.'

'Well he was a parson too,' said Jane. 'Maybe they'll do a swop.'

'He's really bad then?' Lovell asked.

'If you want to see him I should go soon.' She pulled off her stockings and stretched out her legs. 'Not bad,' she said. 'No great hockey player's calves, even after three hundred miles.'

'Come here,' said Lovell. 'There's more to do with legs than just walking.'

'How vulgar you are,' said Jane, and flopped down beside him, rolling over as she did so. 'Thank God,' she said.

'It was the most tremendous fun,' Georgie said, 'but it damn near killed me. I don't mind good works again in moderation, but no more walking.'

They were in Georgie's suite at the Savoy, and soon they would go down to join Lionel and Piers, and dance, but for the moment it was pleasant just to sprawl at ease, and remember.

'They were so little, most of them,' Georgie said.

'Probably their diet,' said Jane. 'Feed their children properly and they'd shoot up.'

'I wish somebody *would* feed their children properly and them too,' said Georgie. 'They deserve it. They even liked my singing – or they said they did. Which is just as good really. Well at least I've done something useful at last – apart from playing you, that is.'

'Talking of which,' said Jane, 'when are you going to make your next picture?'

'We start next month,' Georgie said. 'It's a comedy this time. I hope Murray's found me a funny one. Some of it's in Spain. Have you ever been to Spain?' Jane shook her head. 'Would you like to go?'

'For the movie you mean?'

'No no. In the movie Spain will be California. It always is. So is almost everywhere else as a matter of fact. No – I was just thinking about jolly hols. We did discuss the idea you remember, as we tramped all those endless miles.'

'Why not?' said Jane. 'I've nothing else to do.'

'The trouble is I don't know any Spaniards. Do you?'

'Afraid not,' said Jane, then remembered Blagdon Hall. 'Oh yes I do,' she said, and quoted the canon. 'Would you like a marquis? He's rather a fan of yours.'

Lionel and Piers were ignored that night: it was the two women who were the celebrities, something that Georgie found as natural as breathing, but Jane still found it a strain to act as though nobody was staring at you when everyone was staring at you, including all the waiters. It was the *Daily World* that was responsible, of course. I should have brought Foch with me, she thought. He's an even bigger celebrity.

During her first dance with Piers he asked her, 'Have you seen anything of my sister lately?'

'Not since the march.'

'I thought you were great chums.'

'I think so too,' said Jane, 'but the march finished just three days ago.'

'Sorry,' he said, and then, 'It's just that I'm rather worried about her.'

'Worried?' said Jane. 'Why?'

'Because I think she's in some sort of trouble.'

'Even if she were,' said Jane, 'it isn't something to discuss on a dance floor.' The band stopped.

'I don't have to be back until lunch time tomorrow,' he said. 'Could I come for coffee to your place on the way?' She could think of no way to refuse.

'Frivolity,' said Lionel, 'is the spice of life. Oh I know that good works are the thing these days – and Jane will tell you that I strode out manfully on the Felston March, though in fairness to the others I did not sing – but all the same, there should be fun. There was in the Twenties: why not now?' He looked around him. The Savoy dance hall, as it happened, was packed out.

'People just aren't happy any more,' said Piers.

'You look happy enough,' Georgie said.

'Then my appearance belies me,' said Piers. 'Soldiers have no business to be happy – unless they're doing what they're trained to do, and you need a war for that, and how can you be happy in a war?'

'And how can there *be* a war?' Georgie asked. 'It just isn't possible. Not any more.'

'Mussolini doesn't seem to think so,' said Lionel. 'Neither does this new chap in Germany.'

'His main idea seems to be to keep the Reds in order,' said Piers.

Lionel sipped his wine. 'If that's all he does we'll be grateful to him,' he said.

# 50

P IERS WAS PROMPT to the minute next morning, and they took
coffee under the tree. Truett had sulked, but Jane was firm.
In the open air no one could hear them. Piers took one look at
the garden, and at once appreciated the fact.

'I'm jolly grateful to you,' he said.

'Not at all,' said Jane, 'but all I can offer you is coffee. You do
realise that?' She began to pour. 'Black or white?'

'White, please,' said Piers. 'I do apologise for being a nuisance,
but you must know how it is with twins – at any rate with
Catherine and me. I'm worried, Jane.'

'Perhaps you'd better tell me why,' said Jane.

'Very well.' He sipped at his coffee. 'As we're alone I'll tell
you exactly what I think – if I may?' Jane nodded.

'I think that for Catherine to marry Jay Bower was a mistake,'
said Piers. 'That isn't a twin brother's jealousy – at least I don't
think it is – I rather like the fellow, in fact. All I mean is he's the
wrong fellow. I mean for Catherine. I can't give you reasons
apart from a twin's instinct, and that's no reason at all, but I
believe I'm right. I'm sure I'm right, in fact.' Jane waited, and
Piers ploughed on.

'At first it didn't matter a damn,' he said. 'She wasn't blissful,
but then how many married couples are? She was happy
enough. But then, after a bit, she *was* blissful sometimes, but
only sometimes. The rest of the time she was miserable.'

'After she'd lost her baby?' asked Jane.

'Precisely then. You're suggesting that may be the reason of course, and a jolly good reason too. Not much worse could happen to a woman, even if it was her own silly fault. All the same, it wasn't grief that was bothering her. It was love.'

He waited, but still Jane said nothing. Piers finished his coffee and continued. 'She didn't quarrel with Jay, not when I was there anyway. If anything she was nicer to him than she'd ever been. It wasn't that.'

'What then?'

'It was being a twin that made me wonder,' said Piers. 'I know her the way she knows me – but I've never been in love. Not like that.' He smiled. 'I was adored once,' he said. 'I said that to you at her wedding, remember? But that was just a joke. – Not like Catherine at all.'

Poor Brenda, she thought.

'You're probably thinking it's none of my business,' said Piers.

'Well is it? Even supposing it's true.'

'I worry about her because there's a special bond,' said Piers. 'It's quite weird, actually, and impossible to explain, unless you happen to be a twin yourself. But she's a part of me if you like. Take one of us away, and the other is incomplete, and that's how I know her. That's how she knows me.' He paused once more, and then: 'You're not going to help me, are you?' he said.

'How can I help you?' said Jane. 'I'll listen, I'll always do that – but what more can I do?'

'Then listen now,' he said. 'I'm almost done. . . . I think I know who it is.' Jane waited. There was nothing else she could do.

'It's someone you know, too,' he said. 'Know quite well, in fact. I didn't – eavesdrop or anything. Didn't have to. I just watched them together – and being her twin, I knew.'

'But even supposing you're right,' said Jane, 'what can you do about it? What right have you to do *anything* about it, come to that. It's her life, after all, whether she's a twin or not.'

'Because I'm frightened for her. I really am,' said Piers.

'You mean she might kill herself?' said Jane, incredulous.

'Good God, no.' Piers was horrified. 'She'd be more likely to kill him.'

'A family trait perhaps?' said Jane. 'Or is it confined to twins?'

He looked at her sharply. 'We'll have to talk about that one some other time,' he said.

'We won't have to talk about it at all,' said Jane.

'You never have?'

'Of course not. It's none of my business – any more than Catherine's affaire is.'

'Now there I'm afraid you're wrong,' said Piers. 'You know the chap, you see. In fact when I had it out with her I rather got the idea she'd told you who it was.'

'Had it out with her?' said Jane. 'Wasn't that a foolish thing to do?'

'Extremely,' said Piers, 'but I couldn't bear to see her suffering like that – and so I –' he shrugged. 'I talked to her and made it worse. I should have talked to him.'

'No!'

'Somebody must,' said Piers. 'If not me – then you.'

'What could either of us possibly say to him?'

'That he must stop it.'

'Or else what?'

'Or else nothing,' said Piers. 'For heaven's sake don't get the idea I'd attack *him*.'

'You would a hundred years ago,' said Jane. 'Challenged him to a duel.'

'This is now,' said Piers, 'and all one of us can do is tell him to leave Catherine alone because he's destroying her. It should be you because you'd do it better, but if you won't then I'll have to.'

'If you do it he'll point out to you that you're no angel yourself,' said Jane.

'Brenda Coupland? That's different,' said Piers. 'You know it is.'

'Well yes,' said Jane, and wondered whether she should drop a hint about Charles, or even Bower, and discovered that she couldn't. 'All right,' she said. 'I'll talk to him. I hope I don't lose my temper.'

But when she telephoned his office she was told that Bob was in Birmingham, and not expected back for a week. She saw Catherine instead. Catherine arrived by taxi on the afternoon of Piers's visit. It was raining and Jane took her to the little room she used as a study.

'Darling, why didn't you telephone?' she asked. 'I might have been anywhere.'

'I just suddenly had to see you,' Catherine said, 'and anyway if I'd telephoned you might have made an excuse.'

'Gone into hiding? Why?'

'You've seen Piers, haven't you? Please don't deny it.'

'Why on earth should I? I danced with him last night and gave him coffee this morning.'

'He talked about me. . . . And Bob.'

'Yes.'

'He had absolutely no right –' Catherine said.

'Please keep your voice down,' said Jane. 'None of the servants are deaf. . . . Piers told me because he loves you – being a twin I suppose he has no choice – you're a part of him, too – but anyway he does, and he's worried about you.'

'I'm worried about me too,' said Catherine, and then began to cry, very softly, because of the servants. Jane took her in her arms and hushed and soothed as she had done once before. At last Catherine had done and produced a handkerchief. It would take more than that to repair the damage the tears had made, but the make-up would have to wait. 'I've done something terrible,' Catherine said.

'Gone to bed with Bob?' said Jane. Best to keep it matter-of-fact. There had already been drama enough.

'You make it sound very mundane.'

'No,' said Jane. 'I don't expect it was that.'

'As a matter of fact it was wonderful,' Catherine said. 'Every time. Not like with Jay at all.'

I shouldn't be hearing this, thought Jane, but if I stop her now she may not be able to start again.

'And now Bob wants to finish it.'

'Quite right,' said Jane.

'It's easy for you to say that – but I don't think I can,' said Catherine, and waited for a moment. 'Aren't you going to say I must?'

'Only you can say that,' said Jane.

'It's like a disease,' Catherine said. 'That's all love is, really. A disease they haven't found the cure for.'

'Just because he's good in bed –' Jane began.

'He's wonderful in bed, but that isn't it, not all of it, anyway. He's just marvellous to be with. Funny and exciting at the same time. Was his brother John like that?'

'Exactly like that,' said Jane.

'Oh darling, we didn't either of us have much luck, did we?' said Catherine, and then: 'Oh why couldn't I have met him first?'

To head off more tears Jane said, 'The first time you did meet him he was with the most devastatingly attractive girl I'd seen in years.'

'Lilian Dunn,' Catherine said. 'She was pretty, but rather common, wouldn't you say?'

'So's Bob,' said Jane.

'He's not!' Catherine was furious.

'Oh come off it,' said Jane. 'It's part of his charm.'

Catherine calmed down: even managed a smile. 'Well yes,' she said. 'All the same if I'd met him before Jay came along –'

'Do you honestly think he'd have asked you to marry him?'

'Well of course.'

'Catherine – do you really?'

'I think it would have worked – if I'd been free.'

'Bob's the biggest womaniser I've ever known,' said Jane. 'He likes pretty women the way a child likes a box of sweets. Lots and lots of them so that he can choose one at a time.'

'That's a terrible thing to say,' said Catherine.

'It's true,' said Jane, 'and I rather think you know it's true.'

There was a long pause. Tears struggled to come through, but were repressed, and Catherine looked past Jane to the rain-blurred windows and the weeping garden.

At last she said, 'I can't say that I'm absolutely certain, but I've thought it all along. You know it for a fact, I suppose.' Jane nodded. 'And you didn't tell me?'

'Would you have listened?'

'Of course not. Forgive me please. It was a stupid thing to say. And anyway, even if I had known it for a fact – I'd still have gone for him. I still do.'

'Does Jay know?'

'He knows I'm miserable,' Catherine said. 'He's had more than his share of that, poor darling, but he doesn't know why.'

'Are you sure?' asked Jane.

'It may have escaped your notice,' Catherine said, 'but Jay thinks he's absolutely irresistible to women. I don't mean that as a criticism – how can I? – It's simply a statement of fact. In other ways he's a very nice man, but he'd never suspect a wife of his could –' She paused for a moment; the words wouldn't come. 'That's how Bob and I got away with it for so long.'

'So how have you explained this miserable state of yours?'

'I told Jay it was because I lost the baby after my car accident.'

'Maybe it was,' said Jane.

'It's Bob. That's all it is. *Bob!*' There was desperation in the way she said it.

Jane took out cigarettes and lit them for them both. Catherine dragged hard on hers.

'Did Piers tell you he was going to see Bob?' she asked.

'I talked him out of it,' said Jane.

'Oh you darling. Bless you,' said Catherine. Jane didn't tell her that she had promised to talk to Bob instead.

After a pause, Catherine said, 'I take it that the next step is the time-honoured solution for women with the miserables.'

'Have you put down?'

Catherine snorted with laughter, then was serious. 'Make me have a baby, and take damn good care that my husband's the father.'

'Not make you,' said Jane. 'But if it's what you want –'

'How can I possibly tell?' said Catherine. 'I mean I quite go for the idea of offspring – in a general way – but giving up Bob seems rather a high price to pay for giving birth to someone I may not even like.'

'Can you think of another solution? Go on as you are, perhaps?'

'No I can't,' Catherine said. 'It's killing me. Perhaps I mean that quite literally.' She stubbed out her cigarette. 'So if you think it's what I should do, well, one can but try.'

Oh neat, very neat, thought Jane. Put the responsibility on to me. Even so, she had told Lady Mangan she was born to be an aunt, and what were aunts for but to accept responsibility?

'Go and wash your face, then I'll ring for drinks,' she said.

'Tea,' said Catherine. 'With lots of sugar. One sniff of a martini and I'd be flat on my back – and I can't do that till I'm alone with Jay.'

That left Bob. There was no longer any point in seeing him, but she had given her word. However, he solved her problem for her: he too came to her – but at least he telephoned first.

He called on her on this way home from the office. He looked tired, but as though tiredness was something he had learned to cope with. He also looked alert and confident, and with a sort of guarded optimism, like a talented general who is now almost certain that the battle is about to go his way. He's about to do another deal, thought Jane, as she mixed him a whisky and soda.

'I heard you wanted to see me,' he said, 'but this is the first chance I've had. I've been away.'

'Birmingham,' she said. 'Your secretary told me. I hope it was a successful trip.'

'I hope so too,' said Bob. 'It's beginning to look that way, but you didn't get me here to talk about Birmingham.'

'Don't you know why I asked you here?'

'I've seen Catherine,' he said, 'if that's what you mean. But that's between the two of us, surely?'

She knew that she was blushing and that he was aware of it.

'If you mean it's none of my business you're right,' she said, 'but the alternative would have been a most unpleasant row, almost certainly.'

'You mean Piers?'

'He came to me and said one of us must talk to you. It seemed much better that it should be me.'

He nodded. 'You know I like Piers,' he said. 'He used to like me, too. Remember the time at Cambridge we made that drunken Red stand up for the National Anthem?' He sipped his drink. 'He doesn't like me any more, I don't suppose.'

'I think he would,' said Jane, 'if you'd picked on anybody else but his sister – and his twin sister at that. No, even that's not it. I don't think he'd have been bothered if she'd been happy about all this, but she's not. She's extremely miserable – and that affects him too. A bit like the *Corsican Brothers*, if you –'

'Alexandre Dumas,' said Bob. 'I told you before. I was a great reader when I was a printer.' Another sip at his drink. 'I didn't set out to make her miserable,' he said.

'Of course not.'

'I set out to make her happy – and she was happy, until it was over. Her trouble is she wouldn't see it was over. . . . My trouble is I'm very fond of women.'

'I had noticed.'

He grinned at her. 'Aye,' he said. 'You have. But just for the moment I'm too fond of all of you to be tied down to just one. I told her that at the start. I always – it seemed the only honest thing to do.'

I always do that, he was about to say, but realised in time that it would have been vulgar boasting.

'But she wouldn't let go,' Bob was saying. 'I tried to tell her but she wouldn't listen.'

'Tell her what?'

'With me it never lasts,' said Bob. 'While it's there it's marvellous, but when it's over I want to move on. I can't help it. It's just the way I am. I'm not saying it's like a sickness – there's too much pleasure in it for that – but it's there and I can't cure it – and I don't want to.'

That is the difference between them, thought Jane. For Catherine love is a disease: for Bob, lust, or sex, or whatever he calls it, is the very opposite.

Bob smiled at her. 'But now,' he said, 'your troubles are over.'

'*My* troubles?'

'Concern then. She's finished with me. Came round specially to tell me so. From now on we meet only socially, and please don't hold me too close if we dance.'

Goodness, how bitter he sounds, thought Jane. I thought he wanted to end it. And then – of course. He wanted to end it but she has. That's one little treat he didn't get.

'So it's over,' said Bob.

'All for the best,' said Jane.

'Aye . . . It is. You know she really was a very nice lass.'

'Oh for heaven's sake go away,' said Jane.

After he had gone she poured herself a drink; one that she deserved, had even earned. Like the monkeys with the typewriters, she thought. Give them enough time and they'd type out the complete works of Shakespeare. . . . Give Catherine enough time and she solved her own problems. All she'd wanted, all that the three of them had wanted, was an audience. It really was time she thought about Spain. No one could expect her to solve problems there. She didn't speak Spanish.

*

'Not Andalucia,' her marquis had written: 'not in June. It will be far too hot. Come and stay with me in Santiago de Compostela instead. It is very beautiful, and the breeze from the Atlantic is cool. I have a house there and you are most welcome to stay as long as you like.' As an afterthought he had added: 'I have horses, also.'

But Georgie would have none of it. Andalucia was where the gypsies were, and flamenco, and the fighting bulls. At least they ought to see it, she said, before they went on to wherever it was, and Jane agreed and put in a word for Madrid, too. Georgie had no objection: there was a Ritz in Madrid. The problem was how to get there. Days and days on a train would be far too boring, and she didn't want to waste time driving through France. Then Georgie remembered that she had danced with a man who dealt in luxury cars, and he made a phone call to Madrid, after which they booked a passage on a liner that stopped at Malaga. Before they left, Georgie phoned Murray Fisch to say they were going.

'He quite liked it at first,' she told Jane. 'Publicity for the new picture and all that. "World Wide star examines locations for new picture: *A Night in Seville*".'

'Is that what it's called?'

'Probably. The point is he quite liked that. Then he asked for my itinerary – Murray loves itineraries, and arranging cameramen and press interviews – all that – and when I told him we didn't have one he started to scream. He does that, you know.'

'But surely it isn't *so* bad of us – going off on our own for a few days?'

'Not us,' said Georgie. 'Me. He doesn't give a damn where you go now you don't work for him, but me disappearing will give him nightmares.'

'But what about?'

'Kidnapping, accidents, being recognised in the company of the wrong sort of man.'

'What sort of man is that?'

'Anyone married and anyone else he hasn't picked himself. In the end he forbade me to go, and I said the line was bad and hung up just after he started to scream again. I like to listen to him scream. All the same we'd better get away before he sends somebody to stop us.'

'Would he really do that?' asked Jane.

'Like a shot.'

Her mother advised her to take some pills she had discovered on her cruise to India that were really excellent for diarrhoea.

'But this isn't India, Mummy,' said Jane.

'I expect it's much the same. Heat and vast distances and mosquitoes and dust.'

'You don't make it sound very exciting.'

'Oh no doubt it will be beautiful, India was too, you will recall. Even so I should take those pills. Before we found them Gwendolyn Gwatkin was prostrate for a week. . . . Does your friend Mr Lovell approve of this jaunt?'

Jane was about to say that it was none of his business, but that would not have been true.

'He says he'll miss me – but I shall be gone less than a month after all.'

'From your tone I gather you won't miss him quite so much.'

'I don't think I shall,' said Jane.

'It would be a kindness not to allow him to be aware of it however.'

'I never do, Mummy,' said Jane. 'He told me something in advance of publication as they say – something even the *Daily World* doesn't know yet, but they will quite soon – so I can tell you.'

'I hope it's good news,' said her mother.

'Moderately. Felston is to reopen one shipyard, and one coal mine.'

'It doesn't sound very much.'

'It isn't,' said Jane. 'Charles said the same to the man who told him – some junior minister or other. The other man said that at least it was a start, but I don't believe it. It's a gesture, that's all. A bone for those poor dogs who walked three hundred miles for it. – Which reminds me – I saw Francis the other evening. He seemed very pleased I'd been involved – with Andy Patterson's march, as he called it.'

'He said he had to come up to town for a meeting of the Left Economics Society,' said her mother.

'Which explains no doubt why I met him at the Embassy Club.'

'He came here to tea,' said her mother. 'I too was congratulated on marching.'

'I was also congratulated on going to Spain,' said Jane. 'The Left, he thinks, will seize power there.'

'It's possible,' said her mother, 'but by no means inevitable. What George would call an each-way bet. No more.'

'It's not what I'm going for anyway. If I were I wouldn't take Georgie. I'm looking forward to being frivolous for a while – Francis doesn't approve of Georgie.'

'How sad for him,' said her mother, 'but then he's a sad person, wouldn't you say?'

And you love him more than anyone else in the world, thought Jane. More than me, more than the major even. Please God don't let me be jealous any more.

'Before I forget,' said her mother, 'George thinks you should start racing Bridget's Boy soon. Quite early in the jumping season. He wants to know if you'd like him to suggest a race.'

'Oh yes please,' said Jane.

When she left, she called on Canon Messeter. He had finished *Pickwick Papers* and she had promised him *Great Expectations*. He was outside in the garden, in pyjamas and dressing gown, seated in a chair with a rug round his knees. She gave him his book, and sat down facing him.

'Still here,' he said. 'That's what I say to myself every morning. . . . Still here, I see. Why do you cling on so?'

'You're getting better,' said Jane.

'So your doctors tell me. But not much better. Never enough, if you see what I mean.'

'Enought for what?'

'To go back to Felston. Except perhaps as a patient. But they're far too busy there to be bothered with the likes of me.'

'What will you do?' asked Jane.

'I've a widowed cousin who says she'll find room for me,' said Messeter. 'She's good at looking after people. . . . Lives in Hampshire. Rather a nice part. Otherwise it'll have to be the Home for Indigent Clergy or whatever it's called. All the old black crows flapping and cawing.'

'I should stick with the cousin,' said Jane.

'That's what Charles said. He visits me when he can, you know. We talk about the war. Not the pleasantest of topics, but it takes my mind off the clinic.' He sighed. 'Very well. The widowed cousin it shall be. She's a good person. The bossy kind of good person. It will be a treat for her to have someone to chivvy. Will you write to me sometimes?'

'Of course.'

'Stobbs sends me a postcard when he can, but he's frightfully busy now, poor chap. He says he's only just discovering how indispensable I was. All lies, of course, but very nice lies. . . . You're off to Spain, Charles tells me.'

'Santiago de Compostela.'

'Where St James is buried – or so the Spaniards believe. And why not? He must be buried somewhere. There are times when I wish I were. Forgive me. I've always despised self-pity, and now I wallow in it.'

'Are you in pain?'

'Not at all,' said Messeter, 'but I realise how useless I am – and that in itself is painful. I pray most earnestly that it will never happen to you of all people.'

She said goodbye to Foch, but after all it was Truett and Mrs Barrow who fed him, so that his farewells, though warm, were not too demonstrative. She would miss him even so. The march had brought them together again after all that rushing about and leaving him behind.

Georgie called for her, and was on time. She had hired a car and chauffeur to take them to Southampton – film stars it seemed were always mobbed on trains – and the driver seemed to know his business. They could sit and gossip all the way, the dividing window firmly shut.

For much of the time Georgie talked about Dan Corless. 'Such a sweetie,' she said. 'Rather like your Lionel, and such fun to be with. If only –' the acting look appeared again. 'But it was not to be.' The look vanished. 'Murray Fisch hated him, you know.'

'But he must have made millions for World Wide.'

'Of course he did – but if he'd ever been exposed he'd never have made another cent. It was just one more thing for Murray Fisch to worry about. How that man's managed to avoid an ulcer is beyond me.' The thought seemed to depress her. 'I hope there are some nice men on the boat,' she said.

'I thought you said there was too much of that sort of thing,' said Jane.

'Well so there is,' Georgie said. 'In my case, anyway. But one still has to dance.'

They had adjoining state rooms of which they saw very little. Each day contained an invitation to at least three parties, and every party seemed to have an adequate supply of nice men, with or without wives. The wives, Jane noticed, took one look at Georgie and immediately looked either indignant or resigned, and even though Georgie was on her very best behaviour, not too outrageous, flirting not at all, cautious with the martinis, the indignant ones far outnumbered the resigned. Jane found herself remembering Michael Browne's wife years ago, and the bread knife stabbing at the canvas. Yet it wasn't Georgie's fault; not really. She just couldn't help it.

Still, it did make the time pass quickly, and she had her share of partners too: she too was famous. . . . I was adored once, Piers had said at Catherine's wedding. She had written to Piers before she left, and told him that all was well, but without offering explanations. That was her last good deed for the time being, if good deed it was. Now was the time for frivolity, and she danced until her legs ached. Frivolity, she discovered, could be every bit as exhausting as marching for Felston.

In Malaga the sun was shining; not the bland sunshine of England but heat like a blow, the Indian heat that went on and on, unrelenting, day after day after day.

'My God,' said Georgie as the ship docked. 'This is worse than California. Do you suppose they have air-conditioning?'

Stewards came to collect their luggage, and the purser himself escorted them to immigration, to explain to the officials in adventurous Spanish how very, very important these ladies were. He needn't have bothered, thought Jane. Immigration knew at once who Georgie was, and so did customs, and so did the Guardia Civil. Some of them had even seen the movie. All of them saluted, and very smartly they did it, thought Jane: especially the Guardia Civil in their dark green uniforms and black patent-leather hats.

'But how do they keep so cool all buttoned up like that?'

Georgie asked. Jane led her towards the exit, where a man in a dark business suit stood waiting.

'Collar and tie too,' said Georgina, 'and no sign of wilting. How do they do it?'

The man came up to them. 'Señora Payne,' he said. 'My name is Garcia – from Automóviles Sanchez. Your car is waiting for you. This way, please.'

Already porters were hauling their luggage after them, as Jane and Georgie followed Garcia into the glare and uproar of the street: old women in black, young women in every colour of the rainbow, sailors, soldiers, more Guardia Civil, carts, horses, donkeys, motor vehicles in every stage of decrepitude, and in the middle of it all, lording it, the aristocrat among peasants, the car that Georgie's dancing partner had found for her.

It was black, but it gleamed like a jewel, and the upholstery was white leather. It was a big car and a roomy car, but even so it had a sleek elegance of line that was utterly feminine: quite unlike the Bentley's masculine muscularity.

'Ah,' said Jane, and Garcia looked worried.

'Forgive me,' he said, 'but I was told – I beg pardon if I am wrong – that you will drive the car, Miss Welcome.'

'Whitcomb,' said June. 'That is my name. Whit-comb.'

'It is not an easy car to drive, Miss Whitcomb,' Garcia said.

'Nevertheless I shall drive it.'

'And – forgive me once more please – but I am told that in England you drive on the wrong side of the road.'

'No,' said Jane. 'Everybody else does that. But you needn't worry. The last time I drove one of these was in California.'

The only other time, in fact, but why add to Garcia's worries? He was stroking the Hispano-Suiza's paintwork as if it were the skin of a much-loved mistress. Why be angry with him? There weren't an awful lot of men she would trust to drive that car either. Offhand she could think of only two.

'I tell you what,' said Jane. 'You ride with us and direct us to our hotel. If you're not happy by the time we get there, we'll hire a chauffeur.'

The porters had finished stacking away the luggage, and Georgie was giving them money. Garcia had no choice. He bowed: a movement that was at once elegant and fatalistic, and very Spanish.

The car handled like a dream, and lived up to its name: it had a dash, a daring that also seemed very Spanish, and a precision in its engineering that seemed entirely Swiss. Just as well it isn't the other way round, she thought, as they drove through the streets, the first of so many she was to see in Spain: streets as thronged as the first one had been: flower sellers and men on mule-back, and ragged men who smoked cigars: children playing, begging, stealing, tattered women who walked like queens, angry little tramcars that charged like bulls. One had to be very wary of them. Everywhere there were posters: some elaborate, even grandiose, and very official, others with a crude, home-made look that seemed to have been put up in darkness. From every café there was music too, roaring out: the sort of music she associated with bull fights; roaring out, too, political slogans of every kind, as she was to learn later: Left and Right: Communist, Anarchist, and – a word that was new to her – Falangist too.

Her mother was right. Very like India in its heat, noise and confusion, she thought, and in its smells too: sweat and the scent of flowers and inadequate drains. They left the port and passed the cathedral, still unfinished after so many centuries, and the car climbed upwards, moving along a tree-lined road, shaded and wide, purring past other cars, and horse-drawn carriages plying for hire, like the gharries she remembered from her childhood: the sort of road where rich people lived, until they reached their hotel: old and comfortable and weathered as an English country house, and far more luxurious. Garcia got out and found the one receptionist who could speak English, then came back to Jane.

'I apologise,' he said. 'With you the car is quite safe.' There was a long pause, then he squeezed the words out at last. 'Even safer than with me.'

For a Spaniard that was really handsome, she thought, and offered him her hand. He took it, but it was Georgie's he wanted to hold.

In Andalucia they were lost. They had maps, and could always find the next road, the next town, finish the day in the new hotel recommended by the one where they had stayed the night before, but they were lost even so. It was the strangeness of it, thought Jane: a beauty and a threat of terror unlike anything she had ever seen before, and yet none the less real for that. She had not thought the poverty would be so crushing, not now, in the twentieth century, but there it was all around her, in countryside, village and town: roads that in England would evoke a sense of outrage, but here were accepted as inevitable, shacks that stayed erect entirely by chance, a landscape like a desert, interspersed with little patches of greenness where the water was; and everywhere people: far too many people for the land to feed. Men, women and children torpid with hunger as the great car swept by them. Even Felston isn't as bad as this, thought Jane, but who will organise their march? In the cafés the radios blared their music, the slogans screamed out.

There were other places too of course, quite enchanting places: the cathedral of Seville, the Alhambra at Granada, Cordoba's incredible mosque so vast that there was a cathedral inside it, but somehow they seemed like stage sets where a tenor might suddenly appear and sing the 'Flower-Song' from *Carmen*. The reality was the poverty that surrounded them. One night – Cadiz was it? Cordoba? – some gypsies came to dance flamenco in the garden of the hotel where they stayed. Two singers, four dancers, a guitarist, who performed with the same absolute faith in their talents as the dancers of the Ballet Russe. . . . They had been paid, but being gypsies they came round later and begged, and when they came closer Jane could see why. The clothes that blazed with colour and elegance on the stage looked old, fading, worn, when the dancers came close. Here, in the south of Spain, great talent too was poor.

'Did *you* think it would be as poor as this?' Georgie asked.

'Not for a moment,' said Jane. 'Are you sorry you came?'

'No,' Georgie said. 'Not sorry. The places we've seen. That dancing tonight – we ought to try to put some dancing in the movie.'

'You're far too fair to be a gypsy.'

'A pretend gypsy,' said Georgie. 'A gypsy who gets it wrong. . . . It'll be funny – but I'll still look cute.'

She says it as she might say 'Tomorrow is Thursday,' thought Jane, and it's equally true.

'All the same,' said Georgie, 'I wouldn't want to come back here until they've had their revolution.'

'What revolution?'

'Darling, this place is as poor as Mexico,' Georgie said, 'and they have revolutions in Mexico all the time. Let's go and see if Madrid's any different.'

# 51

MADRID WAS THE capital of course, and so there were streets where the shops were smarter than those anywhere else, and elegantly dressed men and women; and of course there was the Ritz. Excursions too, to the Prado museum that was filled with pictures, and made Georgie think nostalgically of Michael Browne and black eyes; to the Palace of the Escorial, which seemed to be nothing but gloom on a colossal scale: and to a cool little town one visited solely to eat strawberries, and a good thing, too: the strawberries were delicious and the heat of Madrid every bit as bad as the heat of Andalucia, and the traffic more dense, the trams more ferocious. Even so they shopped, and drank champagne from Cataluna, and ate the little snacks called tapas which was all they could cope with in that tremendous heat. The Spaniards didn't even seem to notice it. They ate as if the famine were due to begin next week.

That was of course the ones who could afford it. In Madrid too there were people who looked as if they hadn't eaten for weeks: beggars and boot blacks and prostitutes, gypsy children and ragged mothers with infants at the breast, and all with outstretched hands. Again it was so like India: just as in Bombay or Delhi the rich walked by unheeding, almost you would have thought unaware of what was happening, but they couldn't be, thought Jane, not with the bombardment of politics constantly to remind them, even here by the Puerta del Sol, the most fashionable part of the city. Even here the slogans were chalked on walls, the fly posters stuck wherever there was an empty space. Here too the voices blared from the loudspeakers of radios, and men and women stood on boxes at street corners and harangued the crowds: even in the Retiro Park, the fountain by the Prado, the great square called the Plaza Mayor. But the rich it seemed were as deaf and blind to politics as they were to poverty, and passed by with a more than pharisaic abstraction.

One evening they sat together in Georgie's living room – no air-conditioning alas but the fans on full – sipping iced drinks, for at least there was lots of ice.

'This marquis of yours,' said Georgie.

'He is not my marquis.'

'Who's ever he is, did he say what the weather is like right now?'

'Cool,' said Jane, 'which is why rich people go there.'

'We're rich,' said Georgie. 'I think we should go too. I'm sick of politics – or do they have it there as well?'

'There it's more religion,' said Jane. 'It seems that St James is buried there.'

'In *Spain*? How on earth did he get there?'

'No doubt there will be a guide who'll tell us,' said Jane.

There was a tap at the door, and she called 'Come in.' A small page boy appeared with a cable on a salver. He looked elegant enough – every Spaniard she had seen could look elegant given half a chance, and the Ritz's uniform was stylish indeed, but his face she thought looked far too sad for its years. Long hours she thought, no time for play, and an entire family depending on the pesetas he earns. She gave him an enormous tip and the sad look vanished, a smile replaced it, and he saluted her like a guardsman, then bowed himself out.

The cable was from Bower. 'Why disappear like that?' it said. 'We could use some good Spanish stuff. Phone me. Jay Bower.'

But she wouldn't, she decided. She would send him and Catherine a postcard instead, with a picture of a bullfighter or a dancer or a church. There wasn't all that much scope for frivolity in Spain, but that was what she had come for and she might as well take what there was. She had used up all her compassion on Felston, and she told Georgie so.

'Quite right too,' said Georgie. 'Anyway it's too hot for all that. Let's try Santiago de whatnot – though I doubt if it's famous for frivolity – not with a saint's tomb bang in the middle of town.

Still your friend the marquis may know a few nice men – or is he a nice man himself?'

'He's a married man,' said Jane, 'with a very ugly wife so I'm told. I suppose he is quite nice looking, but not as much as he thinks he is.'

'Doesn't sound terribly me,' said Georgie. 'And the ugly wife will be there too.'

'Bound to be. Oh – and he says he has horses. I forgot to tell you.'

'I only sit on a horse when I do cowboy pictures,' said Georgie, 'and even then I usually get somebody else to do it for me. Let's hope there's dancing.'

They walked through the evening crowd towards the Plaza Mayor. Nobody hurried. To hurry would be to get hotter: far better to stroll and enjoy what breeze there was. When they reached the plaza they sat at a table outside their favourite café and looked at the other people, which was what everyone else was doing, apart from a few little groups dotted about the square, each group surrounding a man on a box who seemed to be shouting abuse: sometimes at his group, sometimes at the next speaker.

'You know it looks like comic relief and all that,' said Georgie, 'but I get the feeling that these chaps mean it.'

Indeed they did. Two groups nearby began to jostle each other. From somewhere or other banners appeared: the hammer and sickle of the Communists and the five arrows of the Falange. Would Francis enjoy this? she wondered, or would he find it too nerve wracking to watch his theories tested like this? For now the jostling had become kicking, and some of the crowd had blackjacks, others knives.

A young man came up to them, a worker, by the look of him: cheap suit and a well-worn beret. He bowed to Georgina and spoke to her in English.

'Aren't you Georgina Payne?' he asked. 'I ask because I have been a fan of yours for years now.'

'Yes,' Georgina said. 'That's who I am.'

'Then you must go away,' the young man said. 'Soon it will get worse. I do not want you to be hurt. Or your friend.'

Already the isolated groups had merged into two opposing mobs.

'It will be very bad,' the young man said. 'Please go inside.'

They got up and went into the café. In any case the waiter had no intention of venturing outside to present their bill.

'Thank you,' the young man said, then spun on his heel and charged into the chaos. They watched him go.

'Now there is a nice man,' said Georgie, 'but I doubt if we'll see him again.' The police whistles blew, and the Guardia Civil appeared and charged into the crowd, using their batons indiscriminately. Women and men alike screamed out in pain, then suddenly the fighting mob fell apart and its members raced off to the side streets that led into the square, some of them running past its central statue to escape an otherwise inevitable beating. The Guardia it seemed had arrived to set as many examples as they could.

The far end of the square was dimly lit, alternating soft light and darkness, and they saw one running figure disappear, then return again in the lamplight until within the darkness there came a sound that Jane had thought she would never hear again: the unmistakable sound of small-arms fire. Once, then again, and again. From the people inside the café there came a long sigh, then immediately after a kind of frantic babbling. No need to speak Spanish to guess what they said: 'That was a gun.' 'Three shots wasn't it?' 'Some poor devil must have got it.' 'I wonder which side he was on?'

'Well,' said Georgie. 'We do live, don't we?' She ordered brandy for them both. They would have to wait a while before it was safe enough to leave.

When they got back to the Ritz Georgie said, 'How do you suppose Jay Bower knew you were at the Ritz?'

'He knew I was in Spain,' Jane said, 'and I told Catherine we'd be staying in Madrid, so he just phoned somebody here and told him to try all the likely hotels.'

'Yes,' said Georgie. 'I expect that's –' The telephone rang and she picked it up. 'Yes?' she said. The telephone rumbled. 'Didn't you get my card?' Georgie said. 'Oh dear. I must have forgotten to post it.' The rumble grew louder and she covered the mouthpiece. 'Murray Fisch,' she said, then into the mouthpiece: 'I wish you wouldn't set your spies on me, Murray. I came here to get away from all that. . . . Of course I'm taking care of myself. . . .

– 600 –

We both are. . . . Yes, of course. I mean apart from tonight's riot –' The rumble became a scream.

'Murray,' said Georgie. 'You shouldn't do that. You know it isn't good for you. . . . Send who over? . . . From where? . . . Seville? . . . If you really think it's necessary. . . . Yes, Murray. . . . If you say so. . . . I understand, Murray. . . . Goodbye, Murray.' She hung up the phone. 'Get lost, Murray.' Then she turned to Jane.

'That was Murray the Masterful,' she said. 'Protector of Widows, Guardian of the World Wide Sacred Flame. He must have used the same technique as Jay Bower. We'll have to make an early start in the morning.'

'I'm sorry?'

'To go to Santiago what's it. He's sending some creep from Seville to keep an eye on me. I can't be very frivolous with a World Wide creep watching. Ten more days for God's sake. That's all we've got. What can happen in ten days?' She thought for a moment. 'Well maybe that's not fair,' she said. 'We did see a riot tonight. You should have heard him. Well you probably did. I don't mind giving him an ulcer – you should watch him eat. It's disgusting. But a heart attack would be too much. At least I *think* it would.'

They got up early and packed and left after breakfast. At least that had been their intention, but when they got down into the lobby it was packed with photographers and reporters who surged at once towards Georgie. The one looking at Jane reproachfully was no doubt the *Daily World* stringer, she thought, and then one of the photographers asked her to stand beside Georgie. 'The Angel of No Man's Land', she thought, and stood beside Georgie, and smiled.

'How long does this go on?' she asked.

'As long as it takes,' said Georgie. 'Just keep thinking how much money you've got and keep on smiling.'

She didn't have to smile for long. It was Georgie they'd come 'for and they hated to let her go. Not that Georgie seemed frantic to leave. She was as relaxed and co-operative as if being harassed like this was exactly what she needed. But then Georgie refusing publicity would be like a man dying of thirst refusing water.

What seemed like the entire hotel staff had come along to

watch, and they were all smiling too, though no one took their photographs. Their page boy of last night was positively beaming. Had the little horror told the press and made even more pesetas?

At last they were done, except for the last, inevitable question. 'Where do you go next, Miss Payne?'

'Paris,' said Georgie. 'A little shopping, then back to Hollywood for my new picture.' A reporter opened his mouth. 'No no, boys,' she said. 'I've told you all I can about the picture. If you want any more you'll have to come and see it.'

Slowly, reluctantly, they left, though the appearance of the Hispano-Suiza brought them stampeding back. As Jane drove away at last Georgie blew them a kiss, then settled back in her seat and lit a cigarette.

'That should cheer Murray up a teeny bit,' she said, 'even if he wasn't here to take charge.'

They drove out of the city, moving north and west through the great plain of La Mancha. Again the sun was unrelenting, but at least for a while the road was metalled and they could lower the windows without choking in dust. As dry and hot and bare as Andalucia, thought Jane, but this time without even the green blazes of fertile land, however infrequent. Scrub and cork oaks and vineyards, producing the kind of wine, the Ritz's sommelier told them gravely, that they must never, never drink. On and on, unending, with here and there a windmill for Don Quixote to tilt at, and then at last a small miracle, a town with a petrol station, and Jane had the tank filled up. They were carrying extra petrol in cans, but stations like this one didn't seem to occur very often.

'You know the extraordinary thing is,' said Georgie, 'that I like Spain. I mean look at it.' She gestured at the landscape. 'The Dust Bowl on a bad day. And yet I like it.'

'Some of it's beautiful,' said Jane.

'Heaven,' Georgie agreed. 'And most of the rest of it's Hell. Maybe that's what I like – a country completely devoid of compromise.'

'I like the people,' said Jane.

'Me too. The ones we've met have been really nice.'

Mostly young, thought Jane, mostly male, and all admiring. She swerved to avoid a flock of goats herded by a ragged boy and girl that used the highway as if it had been designed for them.

'My God,' Georgie said. 'It's like the Old Testament or something.'

'Like a Victorian painter's version of the Holy Land,' said Jane. 'Only in his picture the children would have been better fed.'

'And a damn sight cleaner,' said Georgie.

They passed a couple of lorries, and then more emptiness, until a bend in the road showed them another town, and one other car moving towards it. Rather a nice car, she thought. A De Dion would it be? She put her foot down and the Hispano-Suiza loved it, and its engine told them so.

'Lunchtime?' said Georgie.

'I'm starved,' said Jane.

The gap between the two cars narrowed, until its driver saw them coming and put his foot down in his turn, and for a moment held them. But Jane wasn't having that. She pushed the Hispano harder, and this time the Hispano roared its approval, leaping after the De Dion like the feline thing it was. Another leopardess, thought Jane.

The De Dion driver had reached the car's limit, and edged it further into the road, daring it to challenge. He's spotted I'm a female, thought Jane, and doesn't like the idea of being over-taken. Too bad. . . . The distance narrowed steadily and just before they might have touched she sounded the Hispano's horn, an incredible fanfare like the sound of the charge and the De Dion seemed to move sideways and the Hispano sailed through: Georgie blew another kiss as they passed.

'Who were they?' said Jane.

'Bullfighters, I think,' Georgie said. 'They didn't have their pretty suits on, but they all had pigtails.'

'Goodness,' said Jane. 'No wonder they didn't want us to pass them.'

The town had only one restaurant of any merit, so the guide book said, and to it they went, and were immediately recognised, or rather Georgie was. Its owner was a film fan. They were awarded the best table in the house, which seemed exactly like all the others except for a rather better view; fresh flowers were brought to them, and wine.

I'll have to be careful with the wine, thought Jane. There's still rather a lot of driving to do. Then the bullfighters came in. There were five of them, and one was obviously a star. The proprietor was beside himself. Another star – and only one best table. . . . But he bowed them to the second best, his forehead falling lower each time. Very young, this star, thought Jane, with a thinness that was all strength, like a greyhound's, and with something of a greyhound's instincts too. This man also had killed his fellow creatures, but in his case, if he got it wrong those creatures could kill him. It was impossible to say how she knew this. He looked neither menacing nor cruel, nor even stern. At the moment he was laughing at something one of the others was saying, and the laughter gave him an innocence that made him look even younger than he was. Yet there was no escaping the fact of his preoccupation with death. It was just simply and obviously there, she thought.

'My, he *is* a pretty one,' Georgie murmured, and it was true. His face in repose had an entirely masculine beauty that matched the elegance of his movements. He motioned the others to sit and came to them.

'Excuse my impertinence, Miss Payne,' he said. 'I came only to say how much I admire your pictures.'

'Do sit down,' said Georgie.

'For a moment if I may. I want also to say how much I admired the driving of this lady here.'

'Thank you,' said Jane.

'This lady here,' said Georgie, 'is Miss Jane Whitcomb. She is the one who *really* drove the ambulance my last picture was about.'

'The Angel of No Man's Land,' he said, and stood and bowed. 'Wonderful.'

'A glass of wine?' Georgie asked.

'If you please. I should like to drink a toast.'

Georgie signalled to the proprietor, who brought an extra glass, poured the wine and started bowing again. Really if he gets any lower he'll burst his belt, thought Jane. He's far too fat for all this bowing.

The bullfighter raised his glass. 'To two beautiful and famous ladies,' he said, and drank, then added: 'I am famous too. I am Ollara.'

'How nice,' said Jane, and the young man laughed.

'You have never heard of me,' he said, 'and why should you? I am famous only where they speak Spanish: here, Peru, Mexico. Ollara who fights the bulls and wins.' He tapped the table with his fist. 'So far.'

'How well you speak English,' said Jane.

'I am Gallego, what you would call Galician, but I was brought up in Mexico – like so many Gallegos,' Ollara said. 'My father thought that if I learned to speak English I might get a job in California. Be a gardener, or maybe even a waiter. But I learned to fight bulls instead. Maybe not such a long life – but a lot more fun.'

'We wish you good luck,' said Jane, and she and Georgie raised their glasses in their turn. He looked from one woman to the other, and Jane knew precisely what he was thinking.

He had tried all his tricks: boyish charm, elegant good looks, the very real fact that he might be hideously mutilated or even killed at any time, and it hadn't worked. The two women were as nice to him at that moment as they would ever be. Even so he knew how to accept defeat gracefully: so gracefully that he gave no hint that he knew he'd been defeated.

'You go to Vigo?' he asked.

'To Santiago de Compostela – to stay with friends,' said Jane.

'Drive to Vigo on Sunday. That car of yours should take you there in no time at all. I am fighting there on Sunday. Go to the Plaza de Toros and I will dedicate a bull to you both – and I will arrange that you have good seats. Of course.'

'We'd like to very much,' said Georgie.

'If we can possibly get away we will,' said Jane.

He left them then and Jane could hear his laughter again, caught another glimpse of the innocence it brought, as the proprietor offered them asparagus. Georgie followed Jane's gaze.

'There's a lad who doesn't believe in wasting chances,' she said.

'Ollara? If I had a life expectancy like his I wouldn't waste chances either.'

'There was a time when you took risks, too,' Georgie said.

'*And* I didn't waste my chances.'

'John Patterson?' Jane nodded. 'But just the one?' Georgie said.

'Just the one. It was enough.'

'Yes, but all the same,' said Georgie, 'if a man has lots of women they call him the dashing type, a charmer, a Don Juan. But if a woman has lots of men they call her a whore. Doesn't seem fair, does it?'

'It isn't fair,' said Jane, 'but there doesn't seem to be much we can do about it, apart from not being found out.'

'I never have been,' said Georgie, 'apart from the famous occasion when Mrs Browne reached for the bread knife.'

As they left, Ollara stood up to bow to them. He made his companions stand up and bow, too.

# 52

GALICIA, THEY FOUND, was like no other part of Spain they had seen. To begin with, the month was June, and yet there were strong, persistent showers followed by sunshine, like an English April, and the poverty – because it was Spain there was inevitably poverty – was of a different kind. The best roads followed the coast line and so Jane took it as soon as she could, passing through decrepit villages crammed with dirty white hovels because there was no money for paint.

The fields were small and the soil poor and strewn with rocks that men and women alike strained to haul away to make space for whatever crop they might grow. The only other motive power appeared to be an occasional scrawny bullock. But on the ocean side there was mile after mile of golden, empty beaches, and long estuaries created by the unending battle between ocean and granite: a lively ocean, even in June, with a restless heaving of its blue-green surface, and massive, glittering waves that charged the beach like stampeding horses: beautiful, austere Galicia. No wonder, as Ollara had said, so many Gallegos had gone to Mexico. At least it was warm. What would this land be like in winter? Suddenly Jane remembered what this place reminded her of. New England. That was it. Rock and huge ocean, and dour and grudging soil. It could have been Maine.

They left the ocean at last for the road that led to Santiago de Compostela: more tiny fields, bullock carts, a man with a scythe, a man who played the bagpipes, and hamlets that seemed to be inhabited solely by old women dressed in deep mourning, but at last they came to the city.

It too was austere, and it too was beautiful, with a grey, granite beauty of its own. As they drove down the narrow, arcaded streets the rain began to fall once more. They got out for one brief glimpse of its cathedral and the majestic buildings flanking it.

'It must have taken years. Maybe centuries,' said Georgie, 'and it's wonderful. But why would they break their backs doing it?' Jane could find no answer.

She was thinking of Durham, another tiny town with a massive cathedral: another dark jewel glowing in the midst of poverty. The people there knew poverty, too, went to distant lands: in nearby Northumberland they even played the bagpipes. . . . She took out her note book and wrote down the name of the marquis's house, printing it clearly, then looked about her for someone who might be educated in this country, where so many were not. Inevitably, she settled for a priest. In this town, there were plenty to choose from.

'Casa Soledad,' he said aloud. 'So.' He produced a pencil from a pocket in his soutane, sketched busily and handed the result to Jane. 'La Casa del Marqués de Antequera?' he said.

'Sí,' said Jane, and felt like an idiot. It was all the Spanish she knew. The priest went up to the car.

'Que coche tan bonito,' he said, and stroked it with a gesture like a benediction, then strode away.

His sketch map worked. With its help they fumbled their way to the edge of the town, leaving behind the cathedral and the arcades, until they came to a park full of grim trees, determined on survival, to twin pillars that might once have supported massive gates; but the gates were gone. On top of each pillar was a lion carved in stone. They sat facing away from each other, for ever on the watch, and behind them was a gravel-strewn carriage-drive.

'We're here,' said Jane, and drove on through, easing the Hispano down to its slowest speed. The drive was in desperate need of repair. More grim, determined trees lined the path, and ahead of them was the Casa Soledad. Seventeenth century by the look of it: Spanish baroque, and a very pretty example, too.

From among the trees four riders appeared, three men and a

woman, the woman riding side-saddle. The woman was of a quite spectacular ugliness: the kind that wins bets, Georgie said later. The riders trotted two and two on each side of the car, like a cavalry guard of honour; the marquis by Georgie's door, his wife behind him. On Jane's side was a man slightly younger than the marquis, and by no means ugly, though almost certainly the marquesa's brother, and behind him a fair-haired young man, as young as Ollara, but without any sense of the urgency towards life Ollara had showed. At the moment he appeared to be sulking.

They reached the steps that led to the house, and Jane braked the car, the riders dismounted, and at once servants came running. Like something out of the eighteenth century, thought Jane: four indoor servants to carry luggage, four grooms to lead away the horses. The marquis came across to her.

'Welcome, Miss Whitcomb,' he said. 'Welcome to my house. And to your friend also.'

'May I present Miss Georgina Payne?' said Jane. 'The Marqués de Antequera.'

'The famous Miss Payne who played the famous Miss Whitcomb,' the marquis said. 'What a great pleasure it is to meet you.' Did everyone in Spain read fan magazines? Jane wondered.

'I present you to my wife, Doña Dolores,' the marquis said. Jane took the marquesa's hand, and then Georgie came forward to do the same. Fate could not have been more cruel if it had been planning the event all year, thought Jane. Georgie had had a good lunch, at which she had been flattered by a young man of considerable fame, then relaxed in a luxurious motor car before taking just enough exercise in Santiago de Compostela. Moreover she was wearing a Vionnet dress in her favourite blue and white that lived up to the promise of even her good looks. Georgie looked at her best in fact, even by her own demanding standards.

The marquesa wore a riding habit that looked as if it had been designed for someone else. Perhaps she had bought it just before going on a diet, thought Jane. Moreover it was black, and black was not a colour that could accommodate the sallowness of the marquesa's complexion. And then there was her ugliness. . . . Only malice on the part of fate could have put the two of them together. Beauty and the Beast. But this was the first time it had been suggested that the Beast too was feminine.

Georgie offered her hand. 'It's very kind of you to invite us,' she said.

'Not at all,' said the marquesa, and touched Georgie's fingers. 'You are most welcome.'

'My wife's brother, Don Ramòn Linares,' said the marquis, and the by no means ugly man shook hands with them both. 'And Mr Timothy Jordan,' said the marquis. 'Mr Jordan is from the United States of America, where he is at university with our son.' The fair-haired young man came up to shake their hands. He no longer looked sulky: simply over-awed.

'You will want to go to your rooms to rest and change,' said the marquis. 'My wife has put you next door to each other. Do not worry about your car. My chauffeur will take care of it.'

They followed a maid upstairs. Their rooms were big, old-fashioned, comfortable and cool, with no need for the electric fans that stood by each bed. As they stood by the window of Jane's room, looking down at its view of the town, the marquesa appeared.

'I hope everything is all right,' she said.

'Everything's fine,' Georgie said. 'I hope we aren't putting you to too much trouble.'

The marquesa looked puzzled. 'No no,' she said at last. 'The servants are perfectly able to cope.'

The door closed and Georgie said, 'Poor bitch.'

'Yes,' said Jane. 'Very sad.' Impossible to say that part of the sadness was Georgie's presence in the same room.

'Toss you for who bathes first.' There was a bathroom between their two bedrooms: Georgie won, and Jane began to unpack. No doubt there was a maid to do it for her, but she liked to know where things were. When it was done she lit a cigarette and inserted it into the holder. One thing about long-distance driving, she thought. It helped you cut down on the gaspers.

'Not that much scope for frivolity,' said Georgie, 'unless they bring in some outside talent,' and Jane rather thought she was right. An undergraduate, and a brother with a walk-on part who looked as if he thought frivolity should be taken in moderation even at fiestas. Not much scope for frivolity there.

Georgie yawned. 'All this charging about is exhausting,' she said. 'You must be whacked.'

'I enjoy it.'

'Of course. Or you wouldn't do it. All the same –' She changed the subject. 'Don Ramòn didn't exactly seem the life and soul, did he? Little Lord Fauntleroy looked cute though. Timothy what's it.'

'Yes, didn't he?' said Jane. 'I carried a few just like him in the ambulance. They were mostly marines. Do you suppose there will be martinis?'

There were. There was also Don Ramòn's wife, Doña Isabel, who had not been out riding because she was pregnant. As they were introduced she assessed the value of the clothes and jewellery that the English women wore, and was at once resentful and impressed. Jane and Georgie accepted martinis. Doña Isabel, because of her pregnancy, drank milk, the marquesa dry sherry, in infinitesimal sips.

'In Spain it is not the custom for women to drink alcohol,' said Doña Isabel.

'In America it isn't even the law,' said Georgie. 'Men either for that matter. It's all just a matter of how badly you need a drink. Right, Mr Jordan?'

'I'm afraid so,' Timothy Jordan said, and blushed. 'What I mean is – I think it's wrong, bringing the law into it. It should be left to the individual.'

'Quite right,' said Jane. Young Jordan blushed, and gulped at his martini, and the cocktail talk plodded on: the estates in Andalucia, the fish cannery in Bayona, the Barcelona factory.

'My brother is kept very busy,' the marquesa said.

Her money, of *course*, thought Jane, which explains why he married her. She looked across at Georgie, who was agreeing with her as clearly as if she were saying so aloud.

'In fact,' the marquis said, 'were it not for his obsession with putting sardines in tins, one might not have seen Ramòn at all.' Clearly the marquis despised commerce: a disagreeable necessity at best. 'And we are fortunate indeed to have Doña Isabel with us in her present state of health,' he continued.

He hates her being here, thought Jane. Four women, three men. It puts his wife's dinner table out.

'Isabel drove down from Madrid yesterday,' said the marquesa. From black she had changed to green. It seemed to make no difference.

'I could not resist the opportunity of meeting two such famous ladies,' Doña Isabel said.

'Oh what a shame,' said Jane. 'We could have offered you a lift.'

'Not possibly,' said Doña Isabel. 'I am sure you are both of you too fast for me.'

The hockey stick smashing on to the shins, thought Jane, and never a shin pad in sight.

At dinner she had Timothy Jordan on her right. He was perfectly polite, and answered every question she put to him, but offered nothing in exchange. Instead he ate, and in enormous quantities. She had forgotten how much the young could put away and still stay slim. Doña Isabel, on her left, ate almost as much, and the marquesa at the foot of the table, almost nothing.

Doña Isabel began to talk of a friend of hers. 'Her husband died of a heart attack,' she said. 'Such a surprise to us. He had no reason to have a heart attack. A rich man, with sons, and poor Rosaria had to go at once into black. Such a shame. Black was never her colour. But of course she must wear it. For a year at least. It is the custom. The country women wear it for the rest of their lives when their husbands die. Like big crows out in the fields.'

Jane ate on in silence. Doña Isabel was stalking her prey, but it wasn't her: not this time.

At last Doña Isabel said: 'You too are a widow, Miss Payne?'

Georgie turned to her. 'How foolish you make that sound,' she said affably. 'I am Miss Payne of course, when I'm being an actress, and I'm also a widow, but when I'm a widow I'm Mrs Corless.' She continued with her meal.

Sucks boo to you, thought Jane. My friend carries a hockey stick too. But Doña Isabel was intent on blood. 'And yet you do not wear black,' she said.

'I expect you find that strange,' said Georgie, 'especially as unlike your friend I look very good in black. But there are reasons.'

'Do please tell them,' said Doña Isabel. Georgie sighed her God-give-me-patience sigh.

'There are two,' she said at last. 'One is that it is not the custom in the United States, except for the funeral, unless one prefers to do so.'

'Quite right,' said Jordan, helping himself to a great deal of the fruit the butler offered.

'So I wore black at the funeral,' said Georgie. 'Of *course*. But Dan – my husband – he couldn't bear to see me in anything but bright colours, and once, not long before he died, he made me give my promise that I would always wear bright colours, pretty clothes – and so I did. He was my husband, you see. The man who had shown me so much love and affection –' Her voice shook a little: tears began to well in her eyes.

Like a tap, thought Jane. She can turn it on every time. What a splendid actress she is. The rest of the dinner guests were staring at Doña Isabel in horror; even Don Ramòn. Especially Don Ramòn in fact.

'I am deeply sorry that you should feel upset in my house,' said the marquesa. Doña Isabel flinched.

Carefully Georgie wiped away the welling drops. Her make-up was unimpaired.

'Please don't apologise,' she said. 'I'll have to get over it after all. It's just that it was so recent –'

'I also apologise. I had no intention to upset you,' said Doña Isabel.

A pity that her last words of the evening should be a lie, thought Jane.

'No need to apologise, really,' said Georgie, but her voice shook once more as she said it and she shuddered before bravely eating a peach. Again everyone looked indignantly at Doña Isabel.

First she knocks them down, thought Jane, then she kicks them, then she jumps on them, pregnant or not.

Doña Isabel went to bed. Since there was no rain, the others went into the garden to drink coffee.

Timothy Jordan lived in New Mexico and went to Harvard University, and that was all she knew about him, except that he belonged to the same fraternity house as Martin, the son of their host and hostess, but over the coffee he took the seat next to hers, and she learned a little more. Because he was raised in New Mexico, where his father was part-owner of a silver mine, he spoke passable Spanish, and at Harvard it was one of his subjects. Harvard was fine except there wasn't much chance to go riding – not the kind of riding you could do in New Mexico – and so he'd got leave to come to study Spanish in Spain, where there were plenty of horses. He liked the food, too.

'And the people?'

Jordan looked at the marquis, who was well within earshot. 'Yeah, I guess so,' he said. 'Very nice. Very friendly.'

Jane decided it was time to tell her host about Ollara's invitation. He seemed enchanted.

'And so you had a car race first?' he said. 'And you beat him?'

'He wasn't driving,' said Jane.

'Maybe not,' said the marquis, 'but it would be his car. How splendid that you won. But as for the bulls – of course you must go. We must all go. First lunch in Vigo, and then the bulls. I will arrange it all.'

He makes it sound like a journey to Ecuador, thought Jane, and looked at Timothy Jordan. He was sulking again. The marquis began to explain bullfights to Jane, who had never seen one, and to Georgie who had seen quite a lot in Mexico, but the marquis enjoyed talking to pretty women and would not let such an opportunity slip. He explained it all well, so well in fact that Jane was confident that she would loathe the entire preceedings.

At last Don Ramòn invited Georgie to take a stroll in the gardens, no doubt to apologise for Doña Isabel's behaviour, and the marquis rather belatedly went to talk to his wife. At once Timothy Jordan asked her if she too would like a stroll. The young man was obviously anxious to tell her something. Just as well to find out what it was. There was a moon, and there were nightingales singing, but it couldn't be that, not with Georgie there. They set off down a stone-flagged path between shrubs and scented flowers, some still glittering with raindrops. The marquis – or the marquesa – had bought well.

'I want to apologise,' Timothy Jordan said.

'For sulking?'

'It's a stupid habit. Childish, too. I'm trying to cure myself.'

'And how do you do that, Mr Jordan?'

'By meditating. And please call me Tim. Do you know about meditating?'

'A little,' said Jane. 'I was brought up in India.'

'It's a very hard thing to do,' said Tim. 'I work at it and work at it – but it's hard. But I didn't want to talk about me. That's all we *have* talked about – and I'm the most boring subject you can imagine.'

'What shall we talk about then?'

'You.'

She made herself stroll on, unhurried. Ahead of them Georgie and Don Ramòn were just out of earshot.

'What about me?'

'I read an article of yours in a magazine: *Red Awakening*. It was published in New York but I bought it in Boston. Most of it was just facts. The right facts, sure, but facts was all it was.'

'And mine?'

'You wrote about your General Strike back in England – and right away I was there. I could hear the voice of that man who told the people what the world would be one day – and the cops charged them like Cossacks. I could see that man go down when they hit him – a real hero of the people. A workers' hero.'

Oh Andy, why aren't you here, listening to your praises?

'And all in that place with that extraordinary name.'

'The Elephant and Castle?'

'That's it,' said Tim. 'What's it mean, Miss Whitcomb? What's its significance?'

'It's a pub,' said Jane, and his face fell: there was a danger that he would sulk once more. 'And if I'm to call you Tim,' she said hastily, 'you must call me Jane.'

'Oh that's wonderful,' he said. 'Jane. Thank you. You see – it isn't easy to explain –'

'Try,' said Jane.

'This may well be the most important moment of my life. What I mean is – after I read your article I remembered who you were. I'd seen the movie you see, and it was very good. I mean I thought Miss Payne was excellent – really. But that was all it was. A movie. And then one day in an English Literature class – we were analysing the rôle of Sabrina in *Comus* – it suddenly occurred to me that the woman who drove the ambulance was the woman who wrote that piece. I went to an associate professor I know – not all that old. You can talk to him – and he's English. I asked him to find out about you and he said you wrote for the newspapers.'

Not all that old. What would that be? she wondered. Twenty-eight?

'He found you'd written a book, too. He gave me the address of a bookshop in your Charing Cross Road and they got it for me.'

'*Striking for Beginners*,' said Jane.

'Right. I read it straight through. Sat up half the night. It's not just the political attitude – I'm a man of the Left. I guess you noticed that –'

'Of course,' said Jane.

'It was the compassion. In olden times I think you would have been a very religious person. Even a nun, maybe.' The thought seemed to please and appal at the same time. 'I realised then and there that you would be an important part of my life – that one day I would have to meet you. And then the marquis said you would be coming here. Can you imagine how I felt?' Before she could answer he continued, 'I was scared, you know? I mean all I knew about you was your mind, your achievements. I mean how could I imagine you would look like you do?' Suddenly his elation vanished, and was succeeded by gloom. 'There's something you should know about me,' he said.

'Nothing too personal, I hope.' Jane tried to sound aloof, and failed. She wanted to know what it was.

'I've portrayed myself as a serious person,' said Tim, unheeding, 'and most of the time it's true. But not all the time.'

'Well of course not. You –'

He continued as if there had been no interruption, flattening her words as a tank flattens barbed wire.

'I play football,' he said. 'Not your soccer. American football. And not for Harvard either. There would be some excuse if I played for Harvard – but I just play for fun. I enjoy it, you see.' Even to say it seemed to depress him.

'But why on earth shouldn't you?' said Jane.

'You really think it's OK? I mean the state the world's in –'

'It will be neither better nor worse than if you didn't play football. And if you intend to do something about the state of the world –'

'I intend to try. Sure.'

'Then you'll do a better job if you're fit and strong. From what I know of American football you will certainly be that.'

'Hey,' said Tim. 'Hey, that's *right*.'

They were coming back to the house. Tim said quickly, 'I can't tell you what it means to me, meeting you like this. I doubt if anybody could. Not Gorki. Not Dostoevski even. But I guess you know how I feel about you.' This seemed to require no answer, for he continued at once: 'Are you serious about going to this ritual sacrifice?'

'The bullfight?' said Jane. 'Certainly I'm going.'

'You'll hate it,' said Tim, and Jane wished him good night. By now she knew him well enough to see that the sulks were about to return.

# 53

'DON RAMÒN WAS gentleman enough to apologise,' said
Georgie.

'For what?' Jane was brushing her hair, and Georgie in
pyjamas and dressing gown sat and watched, and smoked a last
cigarette. Even the way she sat transferred it all into a scene
from the movies. Her next one, no doubt. The comedy.

'For what that purple cow said to me,' said Georgie.

It was true, Jane admitted to herself, that Doña Isabel had
worn a dress of a colour one might describe as purple.

'Unfortunately,' said Georgie, 'he tried to get me into the
bushes in order to do it. I very nearly went. My good deed for
the day. I mean imagine being married to *that*. How did you get
on with yours?'

'I only walked with Timothy Jordan.'

'That's the one.'

'But he's just a boy,' said Jane.

'A very big boy. Good looking, too. I saw the way he looked
at you. Talk about dog-like devotion. You ought to get him a
collar and lead.'

'Georgie,' said Jane. 'I doubt if he's more than twenty. I'm old
enough to be his mother.'

'If you started early enough, sure. But you're not, are you?
You take care, my love. The young ones are always trouble. Big
trouble.' She stretched the word big into at least five syllables.
'I've never gone in for them myself, but I've watched the ones
who have, and it always ends in chaos.' She stubbed out her

cigarette. 'I hope you don't mind the advice to the lovelorn?'

'Not at all,' said Jane. 'But I'm not lovelorn.'

'That's OK then.' She went to Jane and kissed her cheek. 'Beddy byes time,' she said. 'Big day tomorrow. The marquesa's going to show us the cathedral. Good night, darling.'

The marquesa approached the cathedral as she would have approached any other old friend: with a kind of familiar affection. For her it had its good points and its bad points, and she pointed them out with equal candour. The cathedral was a building: an exquisitely arranged pile of wood and stone, no more. The true essence of the place was in God and the Blessed Virgin and Santiago. There was no candour in her attitude to them. . . . For Jane and Georgie the place was a revelation and they had dressed with care: long skirts, arms covered, borrowed mantillas on their heads. The marquesa nodded approval, and approved even more when Jane consented to be driven by a chauffeur. For some reason it seemed to her inappropriate for a female to go to God driving her own car.

They looked at the vast cathedral square, that seemed big enough to accommodate the rest of the old town put together. At last they went inside into darkness rather than gloom, a darkness studded with soft pools of candlelight. The place was busy with pilgrims, even on a weekday morning, but the marquesa threaded her way through them, knowing precisely where she wished to go, and the other two women followed. From time to time she stopped at an altar to pray, without warning or apology, and the others knelt and tried to pray too. It wasn't nearly so easy for them as for the marquesa. Jane wondered what her mother would make of it: an attempt to pray in the midst of noise, and fairly substantial noise at that. Guides lectured, a priest said Mass, and other worshippers prayed too, some of them quite loudly. Jane's mother prayed always in a lofty Anglican silence.

When at last they came away, back into the great square and the beggars waiting, their amputated limbs on show like freaks at a fair, the marquesa handed out coins with brisk efficiency, then suggested they take coffee in the town.

Together they walked through the arcaded streets, and if the marquesa was aware of how many passersby stopped to stare at the three women together, one attractive, one beautiful, one ugly, but all three elegant, she gave no sign. The shops were small, and for the most part geared to the poverty of the region. Here and there were shops that sold lace, and for some reason quite a few that sold musical instruments: brass for the most part, and drums: mostly second-hand and battered but sparkling clean.

'The Gallegos are very fond of music,' the marquesa said.

From a nearby café a radio blared, and then a voice began to orate: the voice they had heard before in Malaga and Seville and Madrid. The marquesa's lips tightened. 'Politics,' she said, and led them into a café.

She must have telephoned in advance because the waiter led them at once into a private room. How odd, thought Jane. I've often reserved a table, but never a whole room. Was the marquesa so self-conscious?

'Forgive me,' the marquesa said. 'It is sometimes pleasant to be surrounded by people, but I thought it quite possible that Miss Payne would be recognised, and it might be inconvenient for her.'

'Inconvenient is right,' said Georgie, 'and if custom allows I'd like you to call me Georgina please.'

'Custom has nothing to do with it,' the marquesa said. 'It is a matter of individual choice, and so Georgina it will be. Georgina. Jane. Dolores.' She looked at the other two as she spoke their names, and touched her breast at her own.

'I hope we were good pupils, Dolores,' said Jane. 'So excellent a professor deserved only the best.'

The marquesa smiled. 'I have had much practice at this,' she said, 'but not many who have listened so carefully. And yet no doubt you are Protestants.' She seemed to find the thought surprising. 'In Spain we have very few Protestants, only Catholics, and atheists. Very strange Catholics who believe everything their priest tells them, and even stranger atheists who believe in nothing at all.'

'Shouldn't the Catholics believe what their priests say?'

'In matters of religion, yes, of course. But not in politics. In politics they should make up their own minds, but they do not. Nobody in Spain does. The Catholics vote for what the priests say, and the atheists vote for what they read in books: their minds made up on both sides, and impervious to change. Impervious, is that the word?'

'Exactly the word,' said Jane.

'It will of course lead to great sadness,' said the marquesa.

'You mean revolution?'

'You were in Madrid,' the marquesa said. 'Would you not say that the revolution has begun? It is a joy to me that my son Martin is in America, but when things get worse I doubt if he will stay.'

Which is he? Jane wondered. Everything or nothing?

'But our problems are one thing we should not share with our guests,' the marquesa said, and turned to Georgina. 'I must thank you for the way you handled a most difficult situation last night at dinner,' she said, then added with relish: 'Isabel has been asking for it for years, and last night she got it.'

'Is there a reason for it?' Georgie asked.

'Jealousy, I think,' said the marquesa. 'Ramòn is my half brother. My mother married twice – very un-Spanish – and it was my father who had all the money. He left it to me. I don't think that Isabel quite realised that when she married. And then Ramòn is not a marqués. That is why I – and my guests – are her most frequent target. What a splendid actress you are, Georgina – but very naughty.'

'When did you spot it?' Georgie asked.

'After my prayers last night,' said the marquesa. 'So often things come to me after prayers, perhaps because prayers help to empty one's mind of preconceptions.'

'Like bereaved widows?' said Georgie. 'But I was fond of Dan.'

'Of course,' the marquesa said, 'but it became clear to me that you were acting that fondness, and with justification. It was not your quarrel after all. I can no more help being rich than I can help being ugly. Shall we go?'

In the square, close to where the marquesa's car and chauffeur waited, a band was playing, their instruments as battered and shining as those in the shop window.

Georgie said, 'That took the wind out of me rather – her saying how ugly she was.'

'Me too,' said Jane. She was waiting for Georgie to finish her make-up so that they could go down together for drinks and lunch.

'Because she *is*, you know, but somehow it doesn't matter, not once she starts to talk. Where *did* she learn her English, do you suppose? It's marvellous.'

'English nanny, English governess, English tutor,' said Jane. 'She told me last night. She has a passion for English literature, she says.'

'Very laudable,' said Georgie. 'I wish I had.' She put away her lipstick. 'What are you doing after lunch?'

'I've been asked to go riding,' Jane said, trying not to sound defensive.

'With young Lochinvar?'

'Georgie, you stop that,' said Jane. 'Anyway, Lochinvar's English literature.'

'He was a Scot,' said Georgie. 'All I'm saying is be careful. You're far too soft-hearted for your own good.'

Tim had wheedled two good horses out of the head groom, she thought: both Andalucian, with rather too much dressage in their movement, but strong and eager, a pleasing combination. As she handed over her customary sugar bribe, Tim said: 'I like your outfit.'

She was wearing jodhpurs and had been delighted to find how easily she could get into them after the Felston March. If this keeps up I shall have to have them taken in, she thought, knowing that it wouldn't.

'Thank you,' she said. 'Where shall we go?'

'I thought across the Finistera road,' said Tim. 'There's open country beyond there. We can let them go for a stretch. They can both jump a bit too, if you want.'

'Fine,' said Jane. 'Lead the way.'

The riding part was fine. Tim was good on a horse, not just looking the part, but really riding, jumping too, the hard and dangerous stone walls that reminded her of Ireland, the Ireland of the Atlantic coast. There was even a Celtic cross standing askew in the scrubland where they pulled up at last to rest the horses. Jane dismounted and tethered her horse, then fished in her pockets for cigarettes and matches.

'You smoke a lot, don't you?' said Tim.

'I don't play football.'

It was, she learned, the wrong thing to say. In fact it was a quite awful thing to say. The fact that he played football had been told to her in confidence. When she tried to point out that there were only the two of them present, he simply kept on talking. So many men seemed to have that gift, she thought, remembering Dr Pardoe. He loved her, it seemed, and she must know that he loved her. Of course he knew that his love was hopeless, had known it from the beginning, but it was all he had to offer and he would have offered it, if she had not chosen to indulge in misplaced wit when all he had meant to say was that he cared about her health as much as he cared about her entire being. Hopeless? she thought. But what could he have hoped for in return? Love? Marriage? A kind word? All three?

He had thought, he really had thought, that he had found a soul mate: a beautiful and superior person with whom he could share his political philosophy, his ambitions for the years to come, the needs of his mind, his spirit, and yes his body, too. Now we're getting there, she thought. Charles would have said all that in one sentence, but then Charles was much much older.

Did she not realise the cruelty of what she had done? Young men were supposed to be strong, and thank God he was young as well as strong, but even so the hurt, the pain that her flippancy had inflicted wouldn't go away like that – fingers snapping like fire crackers – and she needn't think it. Lack of experience didn't mean lack of sensitivity. On the contrary. . . . Now there, she admitted, he was right. The point he made was valid: but he left her no room to say so. What she had done, he told her, would haunt his dreams each night, when at last he would be lucky enough to *get* any sleep, which in all probability wouldn't be for weeks. Four words from her, it seemed, had wrecked his life. On and on and on.

When she could take no more Jane got to her feet and unhitched her horse from the Celtic cross.

'Where do you think you're going?' Tim yelled. 'I haven't *finished*.'

'Home,' said Jane. 'You can tell the rest of it to your horse.'

He took a step towards her, and she raised her cigarette stub. 'If you put a hand on me I'll burn you. I mean that,' she said. He turned away, and she added more gently, 'Using force like that – it's only in novels that it gets a man anywhere. Honestly.'

He turned his back to her, and she ground out the cigarette, mounted her horse, and trotted off. She was almost home when she heard what that same novelist would have called the 'thunder of hooves' behind her, and Tim swept by to take the next wall at the gallop. If he had hoped for a fall, to be unconscious and pale at her feet, he was disappointed. He and the horse were well up to the jump. He cleared it neatly and kept on going. Jane lit another cigarette, cleared her last fence, and rode home at a trot.

'You won't have another?' Billy Caffrey asked.

'No thanks,' Andy said.

'Aye,' Billy Caffrey said. 'The shipyard's not all that generous with its overtime, they tell me.'

Spoils of war, Andy thought. When Felston Marine opened, he had been one of the first taken on, and there'd be a job for Billy Caffrey too when his year as mayor was over. The bosses couldn't refuse work to the Champions of the People, and fair do's, he thought, it's better than being our Bob's pensioner.

'I'll just walk you to the tram stop then,' said Billy Caffrey.

They left the Boilermakers' Arms to go into the summer night: drizzle and a spiteful wind that should have come in March, and a seven thirty start next day.

'Folks thinks a lot of you these days,' Billy Caffrey said. 'Not that I'm complaining. I agree with them.' Andy waited.

'There's talk you should be chairman of the Finance Committee.' Billy Caffrey said.

To be chairman of the Finance Committee was to be the next mayor of Felston, as both men knew. Still Andy waited. 'There had to be a catch and there was. Out it came.

'Being mayor's not an easy job,' said Billy Caffrey. 'Not bossing the council or presenting school prizes or chairing committees – nowt to that once you've got the hang of it – I mean *being* mayor. In the public eye. On display, you might say. Like Pontius Pilate. No . . . not him. The one I'm after was the one that was above suspicion.'

'That was Caesar's wife,' said Andy.

'The very one,' said Billy Caffrey as if he'd scored a brilliant point in debate. 'That's just it. You're not married, you see.'

'Well I know that,' Andy said.

'It wouldn't half help your chances if you were. . . . There's your tram coming. Ta-ra, bonny lad.'

That had been three nights ago, after a pint in the pub. Beer nowadays wasn't as big a hardship as it used to be. He could never manage more than a couple of halves, but it wasn't a fight to get it down, not any more. But marriage was something else. You couldn't go into the Boilermakers and ask for a quick half of marriage, never mind a pint. He could see Billy Caffrey's point right enough. Marriage meant kids and commitment, and a steady man in charge. It also meant the near certainty of being the town's next MP, and no more Felston Marine, even if the yard stayed open that long.

He was tired, and he knew it: the machine shop had given him a hard, long day. Even so he should be thinking straighter than he was. The first requirement of a married mayor, or a married MP come to that, was a wife.

He got off the tram and walked to the John Bright Street back lane and up the back stairs. Never do to go in the front way with his work boots on. He opened the kitchen door, and the light was still on: Norah Barnes was beginning on a pile of washing up. She turned to face him; nervous, and yet glad he was there.

'Oh Mr Patterson,' she said, 'I'm so sorry. I got in late today. Me mam's had pleurisy again. I had to sit with her till me sister came.'

'That's all right,' said Andy.

'It's just – I haven't finished, you see. I hope I won't be in the way.'

'No,' said Andy. 'You'll never be that.'

# 54

THE MARQUESA SAID, 'In many ways he's a remarkable person.'

It was Saturday. The two of them were alone in the garden, waiting for the others. The marquesa had suggested a trip to the nearby town of Cambados, and Tim had promptly disappeared, which was tiresome of him. There was no point in anyone looking for him, either, especially Jane. Despite his size Tim was adept at disappearing.

After their quarrel they had seen very little of each other, to Jane's relief. One day they had met on the stairs and he had apologised for what he now recognised to be appalling rudeness, she had said not at all, and that had been it: and now the marquesa was telling her Tim was remarkable.

'I don't mean simply that he's clever and good looking, though of course he is both. I am thinking more of how intensely religious he is – for a person who doesn't believe in God.'

'What a splendid paradox,' said Jane.

'Isn't it?' said the marquesa. 'It took me simply hours to create it. But he is, you know. Religious. In the old days if he'd been born a Spaniard he would have become a Jesuit and gone off to save the Indians in Mexico or Peru, and probably finished as a martyr.

'Now, because he feels this intense need to serve, he has become Left-Wing. It is strange to me, but all the good young people, the ones who wish to serve others, all look to the Left for their inspiration, to the books that tell them to believe in nothing.'

'He's read a piece of mine,' said Jane.

'So he told me. It was an inspiration, he said. A hymn to the courage of a leader of the working class.'

'It was meant to be,' said Jane. 'I'm glad it succeeded. – But I'm not one of those who believe in nothing.'

'My dear, of course not,' said the marquesa. 'That is why I had hoped so much that you would be an influence for good on him.'

This is a remarkable and dangerous woman, thought Jane: herding me in a direction I do not wish to go.

'I'm sorry your hopes were dashed,' said Jane.

'Jane, please,' said the marquesa. 'Don't be angry. The boy fell in love with you, I have no doubt. Is it so dreadful? It would seem to me such an easy thing to do.'

'They usually fall for Georgie,' said Jane.

'One sees why,' the marquesa said, 'but Georgie is here to tempt men like Ramòn, or perhaps my husband. In you I think Timothy sees other things as well as beauty.'

'He sees someone old enough to be his mother.'

'And yet who is not his mother. He sees a fallible human being who nevertheless has learned to help people and still keep her faith. If he has that potential in him should you not encourage it?'

The others came from the house then, and Timothy was with them. Two cars would be needed, since Doña Isabel would need lots of space, and even then there was a great deal of fuss.

'I tell you what,' said Jane, 'why don't I take Tim with me in the Hispano? He was telling me he'd love to ride in one.'

Georgie's eyebrows shot up in two exquisitely modelled arcs, but she said nothing. They went to the cars.

'This is very generous of you,' said Tim. She risked a glance at him, then eased back from the Mercedes in front. He was scarlet with embarrassment.

'Not really,' said Jane. 'I have a very nasty tongue sometimes, and I should have learned to control it by now. This gives me the opportunity to apologise too. Shake?' He touched her offered hand timidly, and she returned it to the wheel.

'I'm nineteen,' he said. 'In my sophomore year. I reckon nineteen's about as miserable as you can get. Anyway, for a – ' He hesitated. 'There, you see? I can't even tell you what I am. I can't say man and I won't say boy.'

'A chap,' she said. 'A thoroughly nice chap. That's what you are.'

He snorted with laughter. 'OK,' he said. 'It'll have to do. I'd like to tell you what you are, but I guess that's not allowed?'

'I'm afraid not,' said Jane. 'Let's talk about what you intend to do after Harvard.' It turned out to be a thoroughly pleasant drive.

Outside the restaurant Georgie was waiting, and spoke at once to Tim. 'Darling,' she said and again he blushed, though to Georgie as to any actress the embarrassment was meaningless. 'Do go and tell the others we'll be along in a minute. I must have a word with Jane. Girlish secrets, so please don't be cross.' Tim hurried off at once.

'Before you start,' said Jane, 'I just felt sorry for him. That's all.'

'I never start,' said Georgie, 'any more than you do. That's why we stay friends. I just wanted to tell you that the purple cow's been going on about you both ever since we left, and believe me I know. I was sitting next to her.'

'Oh dear,' said Jane. 'Couldn't the marquesa shut her up?'

'She was in the other car, with her husband. He's hopeless. No good at all. She talked English of course so naturally the chauffeur couldn't understand a word. But I could.'

'What did you do?'

'Pretended to go to sleep,' said Georgie. 'It worked, too. No point in insulting you when I couldn't hear. . . . And then I did go to sleep. Ramòn woke me. The only treat he's had all day.' She put her arm through Jane's. 'Let's get it over with.'

But it wasn't like that. Jane guessed that even before Tim had appeared the marquesa had spelt out all the rules. There was nothing in the way of bitchiness: not a thing. Instead they talked of the next day's bullfight, which Doña Isabel had every intention of attending, but there were compensations. It appeared that she and Don Ramòn would return to Madrid the following day.

On the way back Tim said, 'I don't wish to seem unkind, but –' he hesitated.

'Doña Isabel?' He nodded. 'But she said nothing.'

'That's just it,' said Tim. 'It isn't like her to say nothing. You must have noticed. Somebody must have told her to shut up.'

'Who could do that?'

'The marquesa,' said Tim at once. 'She can do a great deal, believe me. Look at the way she calmed things down after Doña Isabel made your friend cry. She's very beautiful, isn't she?'

'She has to be,' said Jane. 'She's a film star.'

'No kidding,' said Tim. 'She's quite the most beautiful woman I ever saw in my life. You don't mind my saying so?'

'Not at all.'

'Please let me be serious,' he said. 'Saying she's beautiful is no more than saying a redwood's a big tree, that's all. It doesn't mean I have the same feelings for her as I have for you.'

What feelings are they? she wondered. Inspiration and fulfilment? Muse and mistress? Very flattering at her age, no doubt, but hard to live up to, even the first part. Damn the marquesa anyway.

Firmly she turned the conversation to his future career. Was the law the best way to get into politics? they wondered, for politics it would have to be. Someone had to put the world to rights, no matter how unworthy that someone might be.

Sunday was dry, to the loud relief of Doña Isabel and everyone else. Rain, it seemed, might have stopped play. Once again the three-car convoy moved off, but this time it was Georgie who rode with Jane. She had explained the social reasons why to Tim, and there had been no sulks. He had gone off quite happily with the marquesa. It was clear that her conversation too was important to him, despite her ugliness, and at his age that was remarkable. Jane wondered if Doña Isabel was bitchy about that, too?

'I'm glad you took my advice and brought sunglasses,' Georgie said.

'I thought we were in the shade.'

'Well so we are,' said Georgie. 'The best seats are always in the shade. It's just that if you shut your eyes nobody can see you doing it if you wear sunglasses.'

'But why should I shut my eyes?'

'I told you,' Georgie said. 'Some of it gets pretty messy.'

'Oh,' said Jane, and wondered if Tim would be all right. It was his first bullfight too.

It was in fact dreadful. There were other ingredients too in this dreadful feast of death: the fairground vulgarity of costumes, with the tragic clown act of the picadors' horses – clumsy and expendable brutes that the bulls tossed and gored and who screamed out their agony in vain because their vocal chords had been cut. There was courage, too: the brute, head-on courage of the bulls, and the elegant, dancing courage of the matadors; but above all else there was suffering. The bulls died, two horses died, and one of the matadors would never fight again, even if he lived.

Ollara of course was superb: she had never doubted that he would be. Always closer to the bulls, Don Ramòn told them: always invading their territory instead of clinging to his own and challenging them to come to him. She had never thought that there would be territory in a bullring: a kingdom for the bull as well as one for the matador, but it seemed there was. Ollara conquered the bulls' kingdom like a Hannibal, a Napoleon, and when his enemy lay dead, strutted his way round the arena, holding on high the ears of the bull that he had been awarded, strutted his way to where Jane and Georgie sat, and bowed to them in turn: for they more than most were the cause of all this slaughter: to them it had been dedicated. The crowd to a man knew who Georgie was, and shrieked and yelled their approval. Just as well they had both worn their prettiest dresses.

When the slaughter was done, the marquesa said, 'A young man of great promise. Even Belmonte would have been impressed.' Belmonte it seemed was the greatest matador in Spain.

Jane looked at her, and could see no evidence of irony. The marquesa had enjoyed her afternoon – no, perhaps not enjoyed, as a Roman senator's wife might have enjoyed a bout between gladiators: for the marquesa a ritual had been transacted with elegance and grace, and she had been privileged to be present. Yet she had been to Mass that morning and, Jane had no doubt, prayed earnestly for compassion to all God's creatures.

She looked at Tim. He was bone-white: his whole body clenched in the need not to give way: to cry out, to denounce, perhaps even to vomit.

'Ought we to go to see Señor Ollara?' she asked.

'He will send someone,' Don Ramòn said. 'The rest of us will wait in the car for you.'

His voice was humble. For these two women death had been unleashed. Even Doña Isabel was silent.

When they got to the room where he changed, Ollara still wore his suit of lights. He was drinking red wine and seemed gloomy and pale until they appeared.

'Well,' he said, 'did I do well for you?'

'You were magnificent,' said Georgie.

'For the second bull, yes. That was perfect. Georgina Payne demands perfection. But for yours –' he turned to Jane '– I thought I lacked elegance towards the end. Did you not think so?'

'Not in the least,' said Jane. 'I never saw anything like it in my life.' And that at least was true.

One of the picadors came in, the picador who had ridden the first horse to die, piercing the bull's shoulder with his lance while the horns ripped and tore. Spanish came from his lips like bullets from a machine gun. Ollara got to his feet at once.

'You must excuse me,' he said. 'José Luis – my colleague who was injured – is asking for me. I must go to him. Thank you for coming. I am so glad it was such a good corrida.' He kissed their hands and was gone.

When next she saw Timothy his colour had come back, but she had no doubt that the bullfight was still with him: that it might never go away. Yet it wasn't that he lacked courage: of that she was sure. The sight of blood is a shock hard to adjust to. God knows I found it so, she thought, and until now mine was always the blood of men.

She lay on her bed and rested and thought of the day. Tim was now real to her, in the way that only those one likes are real. Georgie. Her mother. Andy. Lovell? Better not to think of Charles just at the moment. Tim was a sweet boy, and by almost any definition a good boy: struggling with so many things: the needs of mankind, his faith and lack of it, his need for love and the inadequacies of youth.

It could be argued that she had been nice to him; letting him ride in her car, helping him plan his future. A jolly decent aunt in fact, when the last person he needed was an aunt. He needed a lover. Old enough to be his mother, she'd told the marquesa, but that man Freud in Vienna would have seen nothing wrong with that. But supposing she did – she was quite sure she wouldn't enjoy it, though if she understood the marquesa correctly, that wasn't the point. Enjoyment would be Tim's department. The poor child seemed so unutterably sad. Child. She had thought the word 'child', not man, just as the marquesa had said boy. Was the marquesa pandering for him, making her Cressida to his Troilus? Maybe he deserves it, she thought. Tomorrow the purple cow and her husband would be going to Madrid, the marquesa and Georgie were off to town to buy lace, and the marquis had some meeting or other. The time and the place would be no problem, and the poor child loved her so. The loved one?

Georgie came in. 'It's time you changed, lazy-bones,' she said. Jane got up from the bed, and went to the wardrobe. 'You didn't enjoy it, did you?' Georgie said.

'I hated it,' said Jane.

'I suppose I should hate it too,' said Georgie, 'but I'd be lying if I said I did. All that skill – that courage – and all for us, this time. Being a woman has its compensations. All the same – we've been a little short of frivolity on this trip, wouldn't you say?'

'Just a bit.'

'Observers of the social scene, that's what we've been,' Georgie said, 'and to be honest I haven't regretted the lack of frivolity. I mean there's no pleasure in what's happening here, but I'm glad I've seen it.' She went to Jane and helped her to do up her dress. 'Or put it this way,' Georgie continued. 'I've seen what's happening and it frightens the life out of me. But at least I know it's there.'

At breakfast next morning Tim had very little to say. The thought of the bulls and horses was still tormenting him and he looked more than ever like a child in need of comfort. Well, she could give him that. She waited and watched as Don Ramòn and Doña Isabel's trunks, valises, cases, were loaded into their car and the elaborate ceremony of farewell wound its way at last to a conclusion, like a river reaching the sea, and they were gone. The marquis left almost immediately after, as if in fear that they might return. At last the marquesa and Georgie went, too. Jane picked up a newspaper and turned its pages. Georgie usually made at least two starts. True to form, the car returned in five minutes: Georgie had forgotten her purse. Jane took the newspaper into the garden. The servants would still be busy in the bedroom. It seemed a very Leftist paper for this household – *El Obrero Socialista* – which she suppose must mean 'The Socialist Worker'. It must belong to Tim. . . .

Child. The word came back yet again. When they did it he would be her child, and she would give instead of taking. He would always remember her, too. His first, who had been so good to him. So kind. . . . He came into the garden.

'I hope you feel OK after all that ritual slaughter?' he said.

She made no answer: she was looking at a photograph in the newspaper. It was of the young man in the Plaza Mayor. Of course. There had been three young men. Men seemed to congregate in threes. Wise men, kings, and young men, too. . . . Ollara, Tim, and this one who looked at her smiling, perhaps because he was wearing much better clothes than on the night of the riot, and her surprise amused him. She handed Tim the newspaper.

'Would you be kind and translate for me what it says about that young man?' she asked.

'Of course.' Tim took it and glanced at the headline. 'Did you know him?'

'Just interested.'

'He's been killed,' said Tim. She made no sound, and he continued. '"Riot Victim Identified." That's the headline. "The body of a young man found in an alleyway off the Plaza Mayor in Madrid has been identified as that of Juan Ybarra, a student of law at Madrid University.

'"Señor Ybarra was the son of Don Rafael Ybarra, a judge in the Province of Navarra. Unlike his father, the son held progressive, that is to say Left-Wing views, and when in Madrid lived and dressed as a member of the working class. He wrote and spoke frequently on behalf of Spanish Socialism, and will be sadly missed and deeply mourned. . . ."'

'That's enough,' said Jane. 'Thank you.'

He put down the newspaper. 'Sounds as if he was a good man,' said Tim, and then: 'Well – what shall we do this morning?' He smiled, tentatively, like a small boy wheedling for a treat. 'Care to risk another horse-ride with me?'

'I'm sorry,' said Jane. 'I'm afraid I can't. I've just realised something.'

'What's that?'

'I have to go home,' said Jane.